The Noise
UPSTAIRS

The Noise UPSTAIRS

LUCIEN STARK

Ivy House
Publishing Group
www.ivyhousebooks.com

PUBLISHED BY IVY HOUSE PUBLISHING GROUP
5122 Bur Oak Circle, Raleigh, NC 27612
United States of America
919-782-0281
www.ivyhousebooks.com

ISBN: 1-57197-460-1
Library of Congress Control Number: 2005909045

This is a work of fiction. Though the names of select businesses and landmarks reflect those actually existing in Wilson in the 1950s, all other names, characters, and incidents are either a product of the author's imagination or are used fictitiously. Any resemblance to actual events or persons, living or dead, is entirely coincidental.

Printed in the United States of America

I want to dedicate The Noise Upstairs
to the memory of my mother.

I want to thank Gayle Bradley Weiss, Rex Erikson, and my sister, Missy Brown, and all of my other friends and family who continually encouraged me to pursue my dream of writing this novel and publishing it.

I want to thank my daughter, Hannah Stark, for proofreading my novel and giving her candid advice and encouragement.

I, especially, want to thank Kelly Ohara, my colleague and special education teacher, for her consistent encouragement. Kelly believed in my novel's merit and in me as a writer. Without her, this novel would not have become a reality.

PROLOGUE
1957

THE SUMMERS THAT visited my hometown were always hot, but that summer seemed hotter than most. It was the summer of 1957 and dry, stinging heat came to our town and wouldn't leave, but I didn't care. This was to be the summer that would hold no boundaries for my friends and me—especially, for me. The five of us had reached sixteen, and I looked forward to the new freedoms that this age guaranteed me. Nothing happened the way I had planned during those few short summer months. I changed. We all changed and not necessarily for the better.

Something went terribly wrong. My summer of hope and promise turned schizophrenic. My day-to-day existence became a torture chamber. And the heat made it worse, intensifying everything. My life became a pressure cooker existence in which every emotion was tested.

I lost one of my best friends that summer, and the five close buddies became four. David Byrd was younger than I, turning sixteen the last week of May. I was surprised when his parents let that day go by without any kind of celebration with his friends. And I got mad when I heard there was not a family party. It did not surprise me that Byrd did not get the car he wanted. I knew he hurt inside. He was sensitive about most things but he could not hide his disappointment from his best friend.

Byrd had been under pressure at home. His house was a real-life drama and his parents were unreasonable. They wanted to ship him off to prep school his junior year. Byrd wanted to stay home and go to school with us. I had witnessed the arguments and shouting and cursing on those late summer afternoons. God knows what took place after I left. Mr. Byrd could be hard-nosed, and he was unsympathetic to his son's refusal. No reason Byrd gave for not wanting to go was good enough. Mr. Byrd asked me to talk some sense into his son's head and see if I could convince him to go. My mother told me to stay out of it. She said it was none of my business.

After it happened, I was asked if David Byrd had been unhappy. Yes, but he was not desperate. He had joked around that summer evening. That was the last time I saw Byrd alive. I was his best friend and the last of his friends to be with him. That fact separated me from my other buddies in ways that tested our friendship.

On Thursday night, the eighteenth of July, a cooler than normal July evening, the four of us returned to one of our favorite hangouts. It was our first time back without Byrd. His death was still fresh. It just wasn't the same without him. Even Jason said so, and he didn't always see eye to eye with Byrd. We practiced acting like everything was normal but each of us knew a part of us had been lost when David Byrd left us. The emptiness in my gut cried foul play and, like a hundred other times, we exited the small, brick corner restaurant after a quick, late night snack. Only this time I was apprehensive, almost fearful of the decision confronting me.

"Braxton, if you say a damn word to anyone else, your mother will get hurt again," said Matt, clenching his jaw as he spoke. My mother already knew. "Don't you know that by now?" The exasperation on Matt's face mirrored his determination to get me to agree with him.

"I can't just sit around and do nothing! I have to talk to someone." I turned from my friends, wiping the tears from my eyes. I was embarrassed for them to see me crying.

"Listen to him, Braxton," Thad said, pleading with me as he grabbed my shoulder. "Don't be stupid, for God's sake. The man's a whacko! You don't know what he'll do next—to you, or any of us."

"Let go of me, Thad. Your nails are digging into my shoulder." I turned and faced my friends. I knew they meant well with their objections, but I believed the decision had to be made by me and only me. I had the most to lose or, at least, I thought I did. I wondered what Byrd would tell me if he could have been with us tonight. "I . . . I'll think about it but I have to go home. It's getting late." I dropped my empty Coke bottle in the rusty container sitting by the front corner of the restaurant. I pulled my windbreaker collar up around my neck and started to walk across the parking lot. I could see the roofline of my house a block away.

"Wait!" called Jason.

"What?" I said, annoyed, turning to him.

"Who're you going to tell, Braxton? The police?" Jason still held the remains of his cigarette that had burned down to the filter. "You know no cop in this shit-hole-of-a-town will believe you. And if you go to anyone else, you'll involve all of us. And then my dad will really bust my ass."

"Why is it always *you,* Jason?"

In agitation, Jason kicked the beer bottle lying at his feet hard enough to bounce off the car parked across the narrow street. "Braxton, you prick, don't say a damn word to anyone else."

Later that same night, I decided my friends were right. I should remain silent and not risk bringing any more shame to our families, our town, and ourselves. And that is what I did. I told no one else. Like my friends, I pretended that everything was as it had always been and assumed that eventually, everything would be normal again. In our hearts we knew it never could be, and it never was. Time allowed the pretense to become a natural part of our behavior and some days, I honestly forgot it was all an act.

After high school graduation, we didn't see each other as often. And when we were together, we seldom discussed that summer or the events surrounding Byrd's death. But we knew we would always have one thing in common, no matter where we lived, and nothing could change this fact: we had allowed the events of that summer to make us liars and betrayers of the truth.

A long time has elapsed since that July 18th night in '57—thirty-five years to be exact—a long time to be imprisoned by the past. I now know I made a mistake. I should have told my story then, the summer it all happened—but I listened to my friends. Now it is time to let everyone know what really happened that summer—to Chad, to my mother, to Byrd, to me—to all of us.

This is not just my story. It is our story—a story of five frightened teenage boys, and the secrets we felt forced to keep in order to protect our community from the knowledge of the gruesome and sordid acts of some of its most respected citizens. There are only three of us now; and to this day I can attest with certainty that we never broke the pledge we made with each other on one of those many sultry summer evenings in 1957.

Chapter 1

GOING BACK

MOTHER AND I no longer talked about the events of that summer of '57. After she turned sixty, her memory became conveniently foggy regarding the details of those months. Maybe alcohol had something to do with her sudden forgetfulness. Anyway, she would tell me it was just a blur to her. And that would be the end of it.

I wished now I could ask her if she had pretended for my sake. That was the sort of thing she would do—attempt to carry the pain for me.

Now she is dead. My mother died unexpectedly five days ago—sometime during the predawn hours of February 2, 1992. The way she left seemed unfair. She gave us no warning, not even so much as a goodbye. Her dying reinforced what I had already learned about death—that it is never fair when it comes—not to its victim and not to the victim's friends and family.

It was ironic. My mother was the primary reason I was able to cope with the demons that haunted me during my last two years of high school and into my first year of college. In the five days since her death, my memory had repeatedly been pricked by what happened that summer of '57. It was a time of revelations—a time when my friends and I did not understand ourselves. When the five of us faced decisions that only an adult should be expected to make, we turned to my mother for direction. She did the best she could to help us understand how to cope with situations and things that we would not even discuss with our fathers. If there is such a thing as hell, that summer became our hell. My mother got us through it.

At the time, there were many stories about my mother. Mother was a complicated, determined woman and greatly misunderstood by many. Some said she was a decent woman with a big cross to bear. Some said she was no good at all, a disgrace to her family. I should know. She was *my* mother and before my seventeenth birthday, I had lived a lifetime under her roof. And I saw the good and the bad of Virginia Tomlinson Haywood.

Mother had grown up in a wealthy family, the youngest of five boys and two girls. Her father's holdings included farmland, racing horses, interest in banks, and a large mercantile business, the only one in his county. Virginia was born a rich kid and with her father's money, social status was a given and doors were automatically opened to her. When Virginia was thirteen, her father declared bankruptcy. Mr. Tomlinson grieved his losses to the extent that he died a premature death.

Virginia's mother, an enterprising and industrious woman, had Virginia to support and her husband's debts to pay. To survive, Mrs. Tomlinson opened a tearoom in her Victorian home, once a major hub of social activity. My mother, the apple of her father's eye, became her mother's live-in help, a role not unlike one of the several Negro servants that had attended the Tomlinson household. Mother worked hard at the tearoom but resented losing the social and educational opportunities her siblings had been afforded and over time, she began to nurture an inward jealousy toward her older sister, Josephine.

A love-hate relationship developed between these two sisters—mostly hate on my mother's part. By the time I was twelve, Mother had successfully convinced herself that Aunt Josephine saw our family as a charity case. She resented any of my aunt's kindness to our family, especially where money was involved. When my grandmother tried to intervene and help, Mother would turn against her. My sister and I were caught in the middle of this triangle. We always stood with Mother even when we thought she was wrong. We stayed loyal no matter how volatile her outbursts. This allegiance became an addiction that my sister never escaped. I began to break away that summer of '57.

It would have been easy to take sides and resent Mother—at times, even hate her. I knew this would be wrong, and I knew from listening to my aunts and uncles that this was not the family way. "Families stand together," they would say and I did not outwardly question this.

As children, my father would tell us to be patient with Mother and to love her at any cost. I did not comprehend the "at any cost" part until much later. It would have been difficult not to love Mother—she required our love, she demanded our love, and she expected our love, and despite everything and all the reasons I could think of to resent her, I gave her my love. When someone asked if I loved my mother, I always said yes. And I know now that I did love my mother.

When I was a child, my mother seemed moody and nervous and controlling. She continually vented her anger at someone or some thing. My sister and I never knew when it would come and the littlest thing could trigger it. We were often her scapegoats. On these days our bungalow seemed twice as small. I was afraid to ask her why she stayed mad. Inwardly, I think I knew the answer, but it was easier to blame myself for much of her misery.

The older I got, the more Mother began to change or maybe I had started seeing things that I refused to notice before. At twelve, I discovered Mother's intolerance with others; especially with neighbors she thought treated her like some provincial worrywart. Mother had developed a reputation: a stickler for details and a perfectionist about a lot of unimportant things. She did detest dust and she would not abide an unclean house. And she kept us busy with repeated, menial chores.

At thirteen, my family was declared financially poor but I do not think I realized it. We had a comfortable home and Mother had furnished it with antiques. I thought my home was as nice as the next person's or at least any home I had visited. We had a maid and there always seemed to be enough and sometimes, more than enough. Since both of my parents were the offspring of families with an accepted Confederate lineage, they were afforded, in our town, the respected title of a family of status.

The truth behind this facade I grew up believing about my family was kept from me until I entered high school. The revelation that bold me over was that the cost of my father's medicine alone was overwhelmingly high—that he was forced to cash in all of his insurance policies—that he had to sell the lot where Mother and he planned to build their dream home—that the company he had worked for kept him on salary by allowing him to sign payroll checks. Then there came that day when my father no longer received a monthly check and my parents fell heavier into debt. They kept all of this from me. There had been no sympathy for my ability to understand—no regard given to my ability to keep a secret. Hell! The whole damn town knew and they thought I was too young to handle it.

Truth be told, I lived in denial. When I concentrate, I can remember those nights I heard arguing voices coming through the walls of my father's room. Occasionally, Mother would break into sobs. I wanted to do something, I wanted to help but instead, I lay in bed hoping and praying that God would do something, anything to stop my mother and father's suffering.

I became conditioned to the scenes within our home. And I watched my mother deteriorate without fully realizing it. The pressures appeared insurmountable. These "molders of character" as she called them came daily. Her emotional strength that held our home together was attacked, shaken, and sorely tested. And to compensate, she drank. Two drinks before dinner became three and three became four and sometimes there was no stopping until she puked and then she passed out. The more she drank, the better she thought she could handle the pressure. And she put on a good act for the neighbors and for those few who took a genuine interest in my father's debilitating health.

I learned to feel sorry for my mother. She couldn't help what was happening to us anymore than she could stop her increased drinking. And at the same time in some bizarre way, I marveled at her. When Mother needed to be resourceful she could be. There were times when she and I would go out and collect bottles we found tossed alongside the heaviest-traveled roads. She would redeem them to have needed grocery money and, if there were any way possible, she would give me pocket change.

When I reached fifteen, Mother had isolated herself from all people other than family members, a few neighbors, and my sister and our friends. In a sense, she chose the lifestyle of a recluse, rarely going out. Our home, once her haven, became a prison of sorts for her. Mother's refusal to rarely leave the house or the premises of our yard tickled the local rumor mill. One group given to such amusement was the housewives of moderate to modest means who religiously kept their weekly appointment at Miss Mattie Sullivan's Beauty Shop located down the street from our house. My sister and I learned not to fall victim to the lies and half-truths of some of these women who entered the double screen doors of Miss Mattie's and in turn, predictably left with more than just a new hair style. Normally, it took less than thirty-six hours for these fabrications to make their way back to our home, attempting to undermine Mother's character. To say this did not hurt Mother would be to lie, but we could not protect her from the barrage of assaults that came, some by phone and some in person. Like Mother, we endured, but we did not forget.

And then came that chaotic summer of 1957. I depended on Mother more than I should have. I bombarded her with questions and despite my father's sickness and the other complications invading our lives, she took the time to listen and she tried to help me. She allowed herself no other choice. Some who knew my mother back then would still disagree with me but my mother was a strong person and she was a good mother, right until the very end. I find it difficult to believe that she went and died on us. There is an old Negro saying that goes something like "The dead stay dead. Once in the darkness, their spirit goes to rest. Once in the darkness, they never walk again." Yet, I sensed a part of her still here with me.

I SHOULD HAVE acted on my first impulse after I talked with Mother last Sunday—the day before she died. It was around mid-afternoon when I called her—the time I spoke with her each week. We didn't talk long, no more than three minutes.

I have replayed our conversation over and over within my head. Several times Mother moaned in despair. I had heard her moan before, but this time was different. This was a plea for help—a sound of fear. This was not something I had ever remembered hearing in her voice. My mother had such an indomitable spirit that one did not associate her with fear. I knew if she needed me, she would tell me. She had before.

I should have driven to see her—to see if I could do anything to help her feel better—to be there with her. She kept insisting that I did not need to come—that it was too far—that she would call my sister. And I listened to her and like so many other times, I did what she said. I did not go.

Mother and I never spoke again. The next morning around 7:00 A.M., I got a call from my sister. Mother had died during the night. Three days after her death, Mother was cremated. Her remains were placed in a tarnished burial urn borrowed from the crematorium for safekeeping until the day of her funeral. She had requested a grave-side service only. She wanted her ashes spread over my father's grave marker at the Haywood family plot in Wilson, an old tobacco town in eastern North Carolina.

Today is that day, the day of her funeral. It would be an early afternoon, informal service. I took the last swallow of coffee from my mug. My hand steadied and I unconsciously walked across the tiled floor to the stove and poured myself another cup. I didn't even want it. I picked up the paper towel lying on the counter and wiped the tears from my eyes. The pain of her death would not let go—it clung to me like a little child clinging to his mother's legs when he knew she was about to leave him for the first time.

When I was a teenager, Wilson was a quiet, sleepy kind of town—a town with old money and tired traditions—a town where people left their front doors unlocked when they went downtown. It was a town with little to do so people made it their business to know each other. People knew where I lived, who my parents were, the skeletons in our closet, and everyone I was kin to—living or dead. This was a practice passed down from generation to generation.

Over the years, I developed a habit of avoiding my hometown as much as possible. I did not totally dislike the place and I still don't. The town was beautiful then and still is. What I did not like were some of the people and what they represented—people like David Byrd and Jason Parker's parents—their superficiality and determination to prolong mindless traditions and force their children to do the same—their superiority and their system of blackballing anyone who didn't fit their rigid, social code—a mentality that hurt and choked and crippled some of my closest friends and kept them from seeing a world I had since come to know and love. There were too many bad memories and some of the worst, like silent anger, still chased me. And I still knew if I were not careful, they would try to capture my spirit and stifle me.

It is only natural to walk down memory lane on a day like today, regardless of the risks. And while I stood around awaiting my sister's arrival, memories of my youth bombarded my mind, resurfacing faster than I could keep up with them. And Mother was right in the center of most of them. Funny, I used to think my mother was too overprotective and sometimes, I wanted to scream just to get her off my case. She called it being a Mother. I called it interference and smothering. Another reminder that as a Mother, she did the best she could.

"*But it's still not fair, Mother!*" I slammed the mug down too hard on the solid pine surface of the kitchen table and coffee jumped from my cup, its dark stains landing on the morning paper. "Damn! It's not fair!" I blotted the coffee with the paper towel I still held in my hand. The thought occurred to me that maybe part of my grieving process involved returning to that time of my youth. Or, on the other hand, was it fated that I had to deal with this for a lifetime? At the moment, I didn't know the answer but I leaned toward the former.

I got up and walked into the living room and stood before the bay window overlooking our front yard—a yard filled with azaleas and dogwoods, tulips and camellias. Mother loved to sit here in the spring and stare at the colorful setting that mirrored a fairyland. She said it was a healing time for her. I needed that same kind of healing but I didn't know where to find it. All of us had suffered far too much. I walked back into the kitchen and filled my mug with the last of the coffee.

I sat down again, reflecting on the decision that I had made since Mother's death. I had to contact my friends and tell them that with her death, I thought it was time to make public the secrets we had been forced to keep—that it was time to break our pledge—to open old wounds—wounds that could only be healed if confronted. I believed a final closure would bring relief to everyone and I needed it. I hoped that with my telling, I could get back a semblance of the freedom that was so wrongfully stolen from me.

I did not know how many times the phone rang. A quick glance at my watch told me it was a little after eight-thirty. I wondered if it could be Anne. She should be here by ten o'clock. Had anything gone wrong with her car? I reached behind me and grabbed the receiver from the yellow phone mounted on the wall.

"Hello," I said, this time carefully putting my mug on the kitchen table.

"Braxton, is that you?" asked a strong male voice.

"Yes, this is Braxton," I said, not immediately recognizing the caller.

"This is Matt. Matt Beatty," the voice spoke quickly. "I was afraid you might be in Wilson but I thought I would take a chance on your being at home." Matt Beatty was one of my four closest friends in high school and a part of that '57 summer. We had seen very little of each other since our college days but we kept in touch. Still single, Dr. Beatty practiced obstetrics in Atlanta, Georgia.

"Matt, how are you, old buddy?" I asked. I was excited to hear his voice. "Where are you? I mean where are you calling from?"

"I'm at the hospital. I just delivered twins and I have another mother in labor so I can't talk long. Mother called last night and told me that your mom's funeral is today. Braxton, I'm so sorry. Are you okay?"

"Yes. At least, I think so. I guess I'm still a little numb. Mother's death came when I really wasn't expecting it. There had been a slight deterioration, physically and mentally, over the last year. But Matt, we were still caught off guard."

"Your mother was a great lady, Braxton. I'll never forget what she did for all of us. I don't think any of us would have made it without her . . . Damn! Braxton, they're paging me. I wanted you to know I'm thinking of y'all today. Give Anne my love and sympathy."

"I will, Matt. In fact, I'm waiting for her now." I could hear the hospital paging Dr. Beatty.

"Listen, Braxton, hang in there. I gotta hang up now."

"Wait just a second, Matt." I interrupted him. "Since you've mentioned it, I need your permission to go public now. I think it's time to tell our story."

"I agree." Without hesitation, he continued. "I've thought about it over and over and it's definitely the right time! Go for it!" he said. "I'm going now. I'll call you this weekend." Matt sounded so certain . . . so confident about my decision . . . so unaffected.

"Thanks for calling, Matt." He hung up before I finished. Matt had always been thoughtful, a true friend. He stood by me the whole time, refusing to let me carry any pain by myself.

I got up and walked to the back door and stood, watching two squirrels chase each other up and down the massive oak standing formidably in the center of our backyard. "Dear kind Matt, where have these years gone? If only we could just go back. If only we had not gone upstairs. If only we had gone straight to Jason's. Would we do it differently?" Damn—the game of "what if" had started again. I took a deep breath, screaming as loudly as I could, "*Damn it. Leave me alone! Leave me alone!*"

I paused, listening to the dancing echo of my words while, simultaneously, my stomach tightened. I went to our downstairs' den and took from the oak paneled bookcase one of my dusty high school yearbooks. An abstract cocoon was embossed in silver on the dark crimson cover and the yearbook name, *The Cocoon*, was written in white letters down the spine. I thought I would take a minute and see the way we looked in 1957. I can't explain why we became friends. We just were. We started school together, we were all in Mrs. Culpepper's first grade class, and we have remained friends despite our many differences.

When I opened my yearbook, a brown envelope fell out. I recognized it immediately and this was the last thing I wanted to be reminded of on this day. A pain of anguish rushed through my chest like the last breath of a drowning man. My hands shook when I pulled the black and white glossy picture of the five of us out of the soiled manila envelope. The photograph was just as clear as the day I had received it. There we were, the five good buddies, crowded around a rusty metal table like the kind a church might use at an outdoor picnic but without the white paper tablecloth. Above each of our heads, someone had written a number in red ink. From left to right, the numbers in sequence, read two to five and then a one, out of sequence. On the far left was Jason Parker, a muscular, good-looking, five-foot-eleven-inch brunette with high cheekbones and thin, wavy brown hair and brown eyes. Jason had a mouth like a sewer and was the jokester, the biggest goof-off among us. But behind this facade was a kind, brave yet insecure teenage boy who stood his ground with older bullies when they were ready to beat me to a pulp. Sitting next to him on his left was Matthew Beatty, a trim, six-foot-one-inch, scholarly type with reddish blonde hair and golden skin. Matt, a devotee of Ayn Rand, was the reader among us. He devoured books like the rest of us consumed french fries. In the middle sat Thaddeus Ruffin, a five-foot-eleven-inch boyish-looking athlete with curly, whitish-blonde hair. Of the group, Thad was the most popular, the most pleasant and least assertive. Next to Thad was David Byrd, a sandy blonde, quiet, and soft-spoken boy about five-feet-nine-inches in height. He was the runner and fast as quicksilver. And I was the solid, stocky, hazel-eyed brunette on the far right. At five-foot-ten-inches, I was the most serious and artistic. Written in the same red ink across the bottom of the photograph was that threatening message we had lived with all these years: "I will kill you. I will kill all of you. Don't screw up!"

My memory needed no prompting when it flashed back to that June day in 1957 when I first showed this picture to my mother. The scene had remained vivid like a photograph embedded in my mind: Mother sitting in the breakfast nook adjacent to the kitchen drinking a cup of coffee and smoking a filter king Kool . . . my hesitancy when I slid into the bench across from her . . . her reaction when she saw the photo . . . her facial muscles drawing tight and then becoming tense . . . her initial silence and then thoughtful yet deliberate response . . .

I could still see her shaking hands as she laid the picture on the envelope. Ashes fell from the cigarette in her hand, landing too close to the envelope. I recall being nervous but mostly I was thankful the ashes had not landed on the picture. I could still see her reddened face, her livid look—and the look of hurt—that same look I saw when she looked at my father laying comatose across his bed.

Her words to me were, "Braxton, the picture itself is not threatening; it is the sick mind behind this message we need to be concerned with."

I remember leaving the room, feeling worse. I had wanted an immediate answer. She needed time to think. I could be impatient. That day I wanted her to make it right and this time, she could not. She never did.

And after all these years, the aftermath of that threat still lived within me, even today. I kept staring at the five of us—five boys locked in a tight bond of friendship. The den was oddly silent as if listening to my innermost thoughts. I put the picture back into the envelope and returned it to the yearbook that had held it these many years. My hands were moist from sweat, signaling that old fears were on their way back. I received more of a memory than I had intended. My eyes filled with tears and I didn't even know why or for whom I was crying.

Chapter 2
A Cruel Hoax

THE HEAVY BLACK phone sitting on the table by the den sofa rang several times as I made my way back upstairs. I ignored it, not really caring at the moment, who might be calling. I was too fixated with the realization that the time many of us dreaded but ultimately had to face had arrived for me and I was not prepared. I was too young. My God! At the age of fifty, I was now robbed of both my parents.

As a child growing up in Wilson, I knew little about my parents. I never thought to ask. It didn't seem important. I was more acquainted with my mother's family than my father's and there were two reasons for this. First, I knew Granny, my mother's mother, would tell me what she wanted me to know if I asked. And secondly, from where our house stood, Mother's extended family smothered us. Within a block's walking distance of our front porch lived Mother's sister Josephine, and two great aunts, one an old maid and one widowed, and one great uncle and his wife. My mother was a Tomlinson from Wilson County. All the Tomlinsons were proud people.

My father's family, the Haywoods and Currins, moved to North Carolina from Virginia. I was named after my father, Louis Braxton Haywood, Senior. Granddaddy Haywood, my father's father, died before I was two and my father's mother died before I was born. My father had two brothers. Uncle John, the youngest, lived too close— five houses away but around the corner. He had married Jo Ellen Tindal, a beautiful woman with long, fine brown hair and slender fingers, the kind suited for a piano's keys. Jo Ellen was a party girl and with a questionable reputation that damned her in the eyes of many in our town, she was not considered suitable for Uncle John. My mother shared that opinion and despite the close proximity between our houses, my parents did not see them very much. Uncle Davis, the oldest of the Haywood brothers, and his wife, Sarah, drove from Greenville, North Carolina, every Sunday to see my mother and father for as long as my father lived. Originally from Scotland, the Haywood men, like their descendants, were good men, hard-working, stoical and sometimes feisty. Uncle John and my father were victims of a fiery temper but Uncle Davis was the opposite. He was mild mannered, patient, and quick-witted. And he listened when I talked to him. I never told my mother but I often wished Uncle Davis had been my father.

I am sure there were reasons why my parents never talked much about their pre-marital years or even how they met. Granny told me that they met at a dance—one of those larger than life Tobacco Festival events with a big name band held annually in one of the many downtown dry leaf tobacco warehouses in Wilson. After a whirlwind romance, they eloped to Dillon, South Carolina, and were married by a justice of the peace. That did not bode well with Mother's sister, Josephine. Although my grandmother was not pleased, she understood. Granny said my parents had little money between them and a big wedding and extended honeymoon were out of the question. In fact, after a one-night stay in Florence, South Carolina, they returned to Wilson and moved into a small apartment near downtown.

My father was only twenty-eight and two years older than my mother when they began their married life together. I was born a year and a half later, approximately the same time my father, unbeknownst to him, became infected with the early stages of cancer. Anne was born approximately four years later. When Anne was two, Mother left us for a much-needed rest, or that's what we were told by our granny. I know now that she was hospitalized for a nervous breakdown. It must have been serious because no one would ever talk about it.

Granny told Anne that Mother had taken a vacation and would be gone for an indefinite period of time. Anne was too young to recall any of this but I specifically remembered the night that she left. I remembered her screaming, and shouting, and falling. I remembered her pushing Aunt Josephine out of the way and saying bad things to my father. Two days later my father left for the opening of the burley belt tobacco market in Kentucky. Aunt Josephine took Anne and me to our grandmother's home. I didn't remember missing Mother or feeling her absence but I vividly remember being called the son of a crazy woman by the little girl who lived behind my grandmother. It was that same day that our grandmother gave us the first of what would become countless lectures on the importance of our heritage.

Whenever my grandmother wanted to impart something important to us, she would take our hands and walk us to the front hall foyer of her huge Victorian home. We quickly learned the protocol of these meetings. She always insisted that we sit on the first step of her somewhat dark, floral-carpeted staircase that wound upwards to the third floor. Once we were in place, Granny, without ever deviating from her ritual, would slowly back up to the foyer's marble fireplace and stand silently for a moment with her right forefinger beside her nose. And bending slightly forward, this gentle, wise lady peering over the rim of her wired spectacles, would look straight into our eyes and proceed to tell us not to ever forget what we were about to hear.

"Tomlinson and Haywood are good names, children," she would tell us, enunciating each name precisely. She could never bring herself to be openly critical and her tone was carefully chosen. "Nothing people say to you or about you can ever take your heritage away from you. Be proud of your names. They are strong and beautiful names. You come from a fine lineage and you have good blood in you. Despite what others might think and say, you have good parents. You are no better than anyone else but you are equally as good. Promise me that you will always remember this." And we would nod our heads affirmatively. "People are just themselves. Sometimes they try to be otherwise and sometimes, they speak without thinking." My grandmother had a lively intellect and it never occurred to either of us to question her wisdom and advice. She would then walk toward us and after we stood, she would pull us into her bosom, hugging us tightly, reassuring us of our safety with her. Even now, I remembered the comforting smell of Johnson's baby powder that she doused daily on her sagging breasts.

I heard this same lecture from Granny until I left for college. I knew her words by heart like I knew there were eighty-seven prisms on the chandelier that hung in the hall foyer of her home. I knew I would never forget what she had said, not only because I had heard her words with my ears, but, also, because I believed them to be true. Besides, my name would always be with me; it was not likely to go away. None of this mattered to me until an early summer afternoon at Byrd's Drugstore—that was when I drew upon Granny's message for strength each time Mr. Byrd savagely attacked my family and me.

It had to have been at least twenty years since Anne and I had taken a trip together to Wilson. And while I waited for her to arrive, my mind raced between then and now like couples at a marathon dance, exchanging partners and bumping into one another each time the music changed. This equated to too much idle time for someone waiting to bury his mother—too much time to let old mind games get in the way.

My energy level was up, far above its normal peak. I had to do something to occupy my mind. For me nothing was better than stepping outside and taking a brisk walk around the block. I liked being outside. Today was bright for early February and abnormally warm, liked a summer day unannounced. The weather chart in the morning paper predicted a high of seventy-five degrees, not a record for our area but close. This sudden temperature change was a good reminder that I had spent too much time worrying about what to wear.

"A dark suit is mandatory," Aunt Josephine reminded me when I started buying my own clothes. It was one of the few things Mother and she ever agreed upon. "You will need a suit for wed- dings, funerals, and special occasions, Braxton," she had said without leverage for debate. "Make sure you get the right color and get a good one." The only suit I owned that was respectable enough to wear to Mother's funeral was a three-piece banker-striped wool blend. Aunt Josephine was right—dark suites were expected attire and a social requirement for winter funerals. I knew I would be in for a bothersome afternoon—the sweat . . . the scratching . . . the itching . . . then more sweat—similar to the aggravations encountered on a tobacco-cropping afternoon under a hot North Carolina sun. I felt guilty even thinking about the discomfort considering all Mother underwent during her life for me: my near death at the age of six, the years following in recovery where I had to be constantly supervised, and her nurturing me because I didn't understand why I was not like other kids. This, in addition to my father's illness, systematically drained her both physically and emotionally. Faced with this combination, most women would have been driven to their wit's end. Not my mother. She possessed another strength.

Knowing Anne would want something to drink when she arrived, I set the switch for a new pot of coffee to brew. I grabbed my house keys off the hallstand, walked through the living room, opened the freshly painted front door and stepped outside. I stopped abruptly on the small front stoop, temporarily blinded by the sun's brightness as it shot through the remaining foliage loosely clinging to the limbs of the trees. I squinted and stretched and then continued down the steps to enjoy this unexpected gift of a warm early-February day.

I reached into the right front pocket of my pants reassuring myself that I still had the rabbit's foot I had taken from my faded ivory jewelry case last night. It was there. I squeezed it tightly and smiled, remembering that September night of fun and horseplay at the beginning of our sophomore year. Byrd and I were at the Wilson County Fair. We had circled the midway several times pretending to ignore invitations from hawkers drooling at the opportunity to make a fool of us and take our money. Finally we stopped and turned and faced the old, toothless carnie with skin as leathery as a lizard's. In his gnarled hand he held a baseball and he handed it to Byrd. Then it was my turn. Despite his continued barking and harassment, we surprised ourselves and knocked over all the leaded milk bottles sitting on his stool. In his anger, he hurled a rabbit's foot toward each of us. Byrd's was an ugly, putrid green and mine was faded blue.

We carried these charms everywhere we went pretending they were talismans given to us by a genie from a foreign land. Ours were not demonic; they had supernatural power: power to do well on tests, to get dates with girls who might otherwise say no, to win petty bets, to have the right answer when challenged. That is what we pretended and at times, I think we actually believed they brought us good luck.

It might seem bizarre that a grown man would take the time to find such a charm or even keep it for so long. I'm glad I did and I wanted mine with me today. I don't know why—for a remembrance—for good luck—it didn't really matter—it just made things seem right.

I walked rapidly up Yadkin Drive. Piles of raked leaves cluttered the grassy areas between the sidewalk and the street. Several speeding cars passed, disrupting the piles and blowing the leaves into little eddies. I turned the corner and continued, finishing my walk around the long block while allowing my mind to wander through the dark alleys of that summer with my friends. And when I thought of them, I thought of Mother. She seemed so present in my walk. I pictured her the way she was that summer: slim and neatly dressed, fine hair parted on the left side, thinly penciled eyebrows, and deep red lipstick that matched the red of her fingernails. I could not help but believe that her spirit was with me and in some uncanny way, waiting . . . waiting for me to set her free from the angry cloud of that summer that had hung over her and us these many years. I would do it. I had promised her that I would and Matt had given me the green light. I squeezed the rabbit's foot. It felt warm and I knew that if Byrd were here, he would have agreed with Matt. I needed a plan to make things right and I had little time to come up with one. I would have to make my move today.

My walk lasted less than thirty minutes. Opening the front door, I heard the phone ringing again. I ran to the kitchen and picked up the receiver.

"Hello," I said, panting and breathing hard.

"Will you be coming to the funeral today?" The voice was raspy, indistinct, and totally unfamiliar to me. It was difficult determining the sex but I believed it was a male.

"Who is this?" I asked.

The voice on the other end was silent. I could hear shallow breathing.

I took a deep breath and lowered my voice, "I want to know who you are?"

"That's not important!" A long pause and then, "What is important is that you remember that I will be there too."

"Who is this?" I hesitated, clasping my hand over the receiver wondering what to say next. Breathing deeply, I continued, "Is this some kind of sick joke?" There was no immediate response. I was tempted to hang up and should have, but I continued to listen.

"There is no glory in being a *fool!* Don't do anything foolish today." A click, then complete silence. Whoever called was gone.

When I put the receiver back on its base, I stood in the kitchen listening in silence to the noises of the house. The ceiling fan hummed as the blades made their circular turn. I felt clammy and my stomach churned giving credence to an unsettling feeling I had about the call. I began to sweat. My mind whirled with questions. Who was the caller? Was I in danger again? Anyone could know Mother's funeral was today. Her obituary was in the morning paper that served most of central and eastern North Carolina.

The paper had not left the kitchen table. I thumbed through the sports and comic sections until I came to the obituary section. There were two pages. The details of Mother's death were on the second page in the third column near the bottom. It was public notice for anyone to read—one paragraph in length and just as Mother had requested. It stated she would be buried February seventh, in Wilson, North Carolina, at two o'clock P.M. At first, I did not move but just stood there staring at the paper, feeling a sudden throbbing inside my head. When I regained my composure, I moved toward the counter, wanting to forget the crank caller.

I poured some fresh coffee into my mug and left the kitchen. I turned, walked up three steps, and down the hallway that led to our bedroom at the back of the house. On the table beside my easy chair in a silver frame was the only picture I had of my parents: a black and white, 4 by 6 taken shortly after their first year of marriage. I picked up the frame and brought the picture close. The man and woman holding hands and standing on an ice covered Lake Huron in Canada were my parents but not the couple I had known. I was looking at a man and woman who loved life; a couple who saw their life filled with expectations and promises and continued happiness. Their mutual love was evident in their facial expressions. I kissed the glass wishing that I could have known them as they were here—known them when my father was healthy—when they enjoyed laughing and having fun—when they were carefree and not burdened with the bad luck that had visited and never left, robbing them of their emotional, physical, and financial treasures.

In an instant I thought of what my granny had told Anne and me so many times when we were struggling to find ourselves. And my granny was right—Virginia and Louis Haywood were good people. They were good to each other and under the most difficult of circumstances, had been good parents—as good as they knew how to be. And "they comes from good stock" as our Negro maid, Lily, would have said.

My mother, Virginia, had the reputation of being a maverick. Being a woman of strong opinions, she liked to catch people off guard, especially kin. Unlike her siblings, she wanted to be cremated. After I accepted and got used to the idea, we would laugh about what some of Wilson's finest might say about being "burned." And to some in our town, the idea seemed ungodly. It was not sinful and besides, it was her wish, her death, and her funeral.

Mother's decision to be cremated was not to create controversy or to shock anyone. This time Mother tried to be financially prudent. She had wanted to be practical when my father died, but her sister, Josephine, thought he should have a traditional funeral. At that time, Mother was not in any kind of mental or physical condition to argue with her. The cost of my father's funeral left Mother burdened with unnecessary debt—one I had to eventually pay.

Today, we would honor Mother and follow her wishes. We would break the family tradition, and in some eyes, a Southern tradition. Mother had made us promise that we would fulfill her request for a simple funeral: brief, no fal-de-rah, no hysterics, no flowers, and above all, her ashes were to be scattered over my father's grave. In this request, she had planned the very opposite of my father's funeral. I chuckled. Had Mother, in her death, tried to have the last word with her deceased sister, Josephine?

A knock on the front door startled me. I jumped then walked back down the hall and into the living room. Peering through the peephole in the front door, I saw that my little sister had made it safely. Thank goodness. I would not be alone now.

"Come on in, Anne," I said, opening the front door. "I'm glad you're here." I gave her a strong brotherly hug not intending to ruffle her sweater. "What's in the box?" Anne held a tall box whose top had been taped shut.

"I'm glad to be here too," she said, walking into the living room. "I detest driving in Raleigh traffic. It makes me nervous." She took a deep breath. "Mother is in the box. I mean her remains are in here. I mean the urn is in here with Mother's ashes." I laughed. "You know what I'm trying to say, Braxton."

"Want something to drink? There's fresh coffee on the kitchen counter," I said, closing the front door. I paused and then hesitated. "May I . . . could I take . . . never mind." Did I want to look? No! I was not ready to see what was left of my mother.

"Just a half of a cup," she responded. "Where is Beth?" My wife and Anne had been casual friends in high school and had graduated together.

"She, Jonathan, and the girls drove down yesterday and spent the night with her mother. We'll catch up with them at Ingrid's."

We walked into the kitchen and I gave Anne the Metro section of the paper containing Mother's obituary. While she read, I poured her coffee. I wondered if I should untape the lid and look inside the box. No! I was still not ready. I joined my sister at the table. It was uncanny how much she looked like Mother. Both were beautiful women. The phone began ringing again. I hesitated.

"Aren't you going to answer it?" asked Anne.

"Of course," I said, uncertain I wanted to. "Hello." It sounded more like "Hel-low!"

"I have a collect call for a Mr. Braxton Haywood," spoke an articulate woman.

"I'm Braxton Haywood. Who's calling?"

"Sir, your name?" the operator asked the party on the other end of the line.

I heard his response. Chills grabbed me and I suddenly felt nauseated. Anne looked at me, her brow squinting in response. She began to rise.

"Mr. Haywood, the call is from a Mr. David Byrd. Will you accept the charge?"

"That's impossible! He's . . . He's . . . No! I will not accept the charge!" I slammed the receiver down on the cradle hard enough to crack it. For a moment I stood motionless . . . mortified . . . disbelieving the cruel act of the caller.

"Braxton, are you okay?" Anne asked, reaching for my right hand. "You're white as a sheet."

"I'll be okay," I said. "Just another crank call. Let's get the hell to Wilson!"

BACK IN 1957 the drive from Raleigh to the eastern North Carolina tobacco town of my birth took almost two hours. There was only a two-lane route that meandered through sleepy, little towns—the one traffic light, one filing station kind destined to go nowhere. It was a too heavily traveled black top dividing acres and acres of farmland—flat land that was an endless canvas of fertile, loamy soil—rich soil that was good for the tobacco, corn, beans and other crops that dotted the landscape.

This once pastoral setting had now given way to progress. Gone were the rows upon rows of tobacco plants that stretched as far as the eye could see. Gone were the occasional weathered, gray tobacco barns that stood proudly beneath the scraggly pines at the edge of passing fields. Gone were my hometown's bragging rights: The World's Greatest Bright Leaf Tobacco Market. Gone was the landscape I had known as a youth. I was certain the beauty was still there in some obscure form but it remained hidden from the driver's view.

Today, Anne and I would make the trip in forty minutes on a new four-lane highway that bypassed those once familiar areas. In 1957, I thought the drive was a nuisance—a barrier to progress—a tribute to the ineptness of those who had planned the roadways in our state. Today, I missed the longer drive and the lost beauty many people then found inconvenient.

The inside of my car was cool and comfortable, a protection from the outside humidity and unbearable heat. And yet, I felt very alone, afraid, and isolated. I was with my sister, but we were both numb and still in a state of shock. Why was being normal so hard at a time like this? I had other things to think about. I needed to finalize a plan—what I would do after the funeral—what act would I perform to bring to the surface the real truth about David Byrd and, in some way, finally free my mother.

I tightened my hands on the steering wheel and watched the white lines zip past us. I checked my speed and I was only five miles over the speed limit. I looked at my sister to make certain she was okay. Anne had dressed in one of Mother's black sweaters and skirts. She wore a strand of Mother's cultured pearls. Anne had become Mother's nurturer and comforter even before her unexpected series of strokes. Watching her hands caressing the box that carried the urn holding Mother's ashes, I knew Anne was still in her role as protector.

Both of us had been unnecessarily quiet. I knew Anne was experiencing a greater sense of loss than I. She had continually pulled nervously on the strand of pearls that rested on her breast. And the tears that had moistened her face were now streaks in her make-up.

"I wonder if a lot of people will come to the gravesite?" Anne said, finally making conversation.

"I don't know. Mother never had many close friends. Those who attend will come because they want to be there," I answered. I thought this would comfort Anne even though I was not certain I believed what I had said.

"I hope so, I truly hope so."

"Well, Sis. One thing is for sure; some of those damn vultures on the fringes of our neighborhood won't have Mother to prey on anymore. When I think of the way Jeanette Eicher treated Mother those years in Wilson, it burns me up!" I secretly hated the woman. She never accepted or recognized Mother's kindness. "But I don't really want to go down that road today." I had never told my sister of the happenings of that summer. I knew she didn't have a clue about what Mother went through for us. Mother had promised me she would never tell Anne. I didn't want Anne involved and at the time, she was too young to understand. My feeling was the less she knew, the better off we all were.

We were now entering the outskirts of Wilson and at the time of our youth, one of our town's most affluent residential areas. Called Millionaire's Row by us in high school, its official name was Raleigh Road. I always thought our nickname was befitting of its inhabitants: the "old money"—the doctors, lawyers, and owners of large family businesses. Today, the aftermath of a profound invasion was unfortunately evident—strip malls, convenience stores and the like had been allowed to become intrusive neighbors. The once beautiful entrance had transcended into an eyesore.

I saw David Byrd's home sitting as stately as ever on the large tree-lined lot. Time had not harmed it. Somewhere the mystery of what happened was hidden in those trees. My stomach felt queasy. The person of David Byrd was a memory I had never wanted to lose— not just because he was one of my closest and best friends in high school—but, also, because of what he stood for. While on earth, he had never been allowed to be himself much less fulfill his secret ambition and meet any of his goals.

Byrd's death was a tragedy that never should have happened. What a waste of a beautiful life. He was so young, so vulnerable, and so misunderstood. Truthfully, in seeing his home again under these circumstances, I knew for certain I had never made peace with what had been done to him and the same raw feelings of hostility, bitterness, and resentment were still there. I had not dealt with my anger; I had only buried it. Someone would pay, even after all these years.

"Braxton, can you believe it?" Anne said, excitedly. "We're here. We're back home!"

"I don't know if I'd go so far as to call it home, but we're back." For some reason "home" was not the word I would choose to describe Wilson.

"My Lord, Braxton, Lucy Thornhill's home is for sale." I looked to my right at the once beautiful two-story white home with its stately columns. The years had not been kind to the aging Thornhill house—no kinder than the residents of this town were to Lucy. "I wonder what ever happened to her."

"I thought she left after her baby was born," I said, uncertain of her fate. "Didn't a lot of her friends turn against her when she got pregnant in high school?" I didn't say anything for a moment. I wanted to give Anne a chance to remember. At one time, Lucy Thornhill had been one of her best friends. "Didn't some . . . uh?" Anne interrupted me before I could finish.

"I remember now," Anne said. "It was Graham's mother. What a cruel act instigated by the mother of one of our *supposed* friends! I think Mrs. Eagleston was more concerned about Graham's image than the welfare of Lucy . . . poor misguided girl."

"Image was important to a lot of people here," I interjected. "Probably still is. That's Wilson for you!"

"Lucy was so nice and pretty. She was so popular and then . . . I wonder if it happened today if people would be as cruel?"

"I hope not," I said. And from out of nowhere, it became suddenly obvious to me why I disliked this place at times—I never learned how to fit in with this town and its rigid social expectations. I was more like my mother than I realized. She, too, had felt thwarted and unable to be herself in this town—a twentieth century Hester Prynne. She never left and I did. I had found my freedom and I would do my damn best not to let this return visit trap me. I would leave with the freedom I came with and the truth that had been covered by a lie would finally be told. I took a deep breath and for a brief moment felt satisfied.

"Braxton, remember, we are to meet everyone at Ingrid's and Seth's. Ingrid said to take Forest Hill's Drive to her house," Anne politely directed me. It was good to have my little sister along to keep me focused.

My mind had begun to taunt and tease me again. I wondered if I could get through this day without being haunted by other old fears. Seeing Byrd's house made things all too real again and for a moment, I wanted to turn the car around and head back to Raleigh.

Chapter 3
AN UNEXPECTED REMINDER

DESPITE THE CHANGE of scenery along Raleigh Road, it seemed like only a blink since that summer in 1957. I saw us as we were then. When we got out of school in late May our mood was jubilant. Within a month, things had dramatically changed. Jubilation turned to sadness, fear, and apprehension. Most of the unhappy memories that I had successfully buried were all around me again. The five minutes we had been in Wilson was all it took for me to start refocusing on what happened that summer. This was not good for my sanity I reminded myself. Think of other things. Look around at what is different. Not working.

To my right I caught a glimpse of Ward Boulevard, the old by-pass around Wilson, and one of the best routes at that time to get us to the Creamery, the Wilson Country Club, and to Taps. Ward Boulevard would also take us to Five Points, home of Fleming Stadium where our high school football games were played and where, in an earlier time, the famous Wilson Tobs entertained the baseball fans of our hometown, my grandmother being one of the most ardent.

It was on the beginning stretch of this boulevard that crazy Lydia Hedley tried to kill herself while we were sophomores in high school. She got mad with her dad, a successful attorney, one spring afternoon when he wouldn't let her drive to Richmond to shop. In retaliation, she took his Cadillac and drove off the overhead bridge, landing tires down on the Norfolk Southern railroad tracks. Nothing but a broken wrist on her left hand but her dad's car was totaled.

I have no explanation as to why Lydia, shortly after her foiled attempt, started coming around to see my mother on an occasional Saturday afternoon. She and Mother would sit together on the back porch smoking cigarettes and drinking coffee. Sometimes, Lydia would drink beer pilfered from her mother's supply. It was a safe place to meet; no one could see them but Lily. Lily didn't approve of their meetings. I didn't either. Something about Lydia made me uneasy and I tried never to be at home if I knew ahead of time that she was coming.

"Miss Virginia don't mean no harm but she shouldn't encourage that Miss Lydia to talk that way. That girl needs to see a doctor. Yes, she does." Lily would speak in a whisper, thinking Mother couldn't hear her. Mother heard but ignored her Negro maid. In turn, Lily would stand in the middle of the kitchen, shaking her head, and voicing her disapproval at the antics and language of Lydia. However, when Lydia stopped coming, even Lily agreed that the feisty, freckled face tomboy's visits were, in some way, good for both of them. Mother enjoyed her company and I suspected Lydia's visits filled a void in my mother's life at that time—a desire to be needed by someone other than one's family—a link with the world outside 109 North Kincaid Avenue. And for Lydia whose Mother was a closet alcoholic, my mother became the ears she did not have at home.

"We just missed our turn," said Anne. "You need to turn around. I'm sorry."

"No sweat, Sis," I said, knowing I would have missed it anyway. I was just too distracted by the past. After I made a quick u-turn, I saw a green directional sign for Forest Hills Drive.

I turned my green Taurus right onto Forest Hills Drive and squinted as I looked up at the bright sun hovering against a clear blue sky. I wondered if my hometown, itself, had truly changed. It didn't make much sense that I would be the only ex-resident who thought, at age sixteen, this provincial tobacco hub was horrible and cruel: a town where many, regardless of their social standing, thrived on ridicule and harassment of those they deemed not worthy to be its citizens. The cosmetics of the town had definitely changed. Maybe the people had changed too.

Driving toward Ingrid's, I continued to be amazed at the disappearance of all that was once familiar. I had come back to my roots to bury my mother and already, I felt like an unwelcomed stranger. My response at reconnecting with this place was bizarre, something akin to being lost in a Jackson Pollock painting. I did not think I could ever call Wilson home again.

I accelerated, barely avoiding a pothole. We passed one street after another lined with expensive homes. I thought of the land my father had bought. It would be the site of my parent's dream home. "We had to sell it," Mother had explained to me. "We had to pay for your father's medical bills." I thought of her life here and the "black cloud" that continually followed her. "You have to take the hand life deals you, Braxton, and do the best you can. God allows things for a purpose and a hardship can make you stronger." While growing up, I heard that repeatedly from her. Well, it damned near killed Mother and it did kill my father.

Upon entering the block of Forest Hills Drive where Ingrid lived, lot after lot of more expensive homes greeted us. Elaborate facades stretching upward two and three stories, fancy brick walkways, and backyard pools lined each side of the road. Ingrid's two-story brick colonial home with its four white columns was set atop a well-manicured grassy knoll on our right. A paved driveway led up to a large two-car garage facing the front yard. Directly across the street was a man-made pond that had become the permanent home to a flock of Canadian geese. Our son fed breadcrumbs to his first ducks there.

Ingrid Watson, the oldest daughter of Josephine and Dr. Victor Thaxton's three children, was athletic, slim, and dark-haired. She had gone out of her way to be attentive to Mother during the last fifteen years despite the eighty-mile drive from Wilson to Sanford. Ingrid was one of the few people Mother respected. It was a profound respect.

"She is very intelligent," my mother said on more than one occasion. "When I dropped Ingrid on her head as a baby I was afraid she might have brain damage. Now I know the fall only made her smarter." Mother joked about that incident with Ingrid but she never told Josephine until Ingrid was in high school. I figured this explained why she was so paranoid about holding my children when they were babies.

Because of our age difference, I never knew Ingrid well until the summer of 1957. In between jobs, she stayed in Wilson that June and July and spent a lot of time at our house. That was when I learned that during high school, she had worked for Mr. Byrd at his downtown store. Ingrid was a private person and never spoke disparagingly of anyone, but she hinted that she thought there was something peculiar about Mr. Byrd. She never said what and I never asked, even though I wanted to.

About a half dozen cars were parked on both sides of the street in front of the Watson's home, including my wife Beth's blue Mercury. There was an empty space behind her car as if it had been left just for us and I pulled in and parked. I switched off the ignition and turned my face toward the house. A lone man stood on the front stoop smoking a cigarette. He waved, flipped his cigarette into the yard, turned, and went back inside. It was Seth, Ingrid's husband. Theirs had been a rocky marriage and I wondered why Ingrid had stayed with him so long. "It was the right thing to do with five children," Mother said. Seth had never liked any of Ingrid's family very much, including my mother. Mother tolerated Seth and his arrogance, and he, her. Seth had always treated me okay, distant but nice. It was his way and I was comfortable with that.

Before we exited the car, Anne carefully positioned the box she had been cradling on the floorboard. She did this in deference to Mother so none of the family members would feel as if they had to take a look prior to the service.

"Do you think Mother will be okay here?" Anne asked.

I chuckled, "Do you think she will complain if she isn't?"

"You know what I mean, Braxton. Is it safe to leave the box in the car?"

"Of course." I was certain Mother didn't care. "I'll lock the doors. If anyone does take it, they'll be in for a surprise when they look inside."

"Leave the windows cracked," said Anne.

"Consider it done."

Anne and I walked briskly up the pebbled walk to the front

door. The first person to greet us when we entered the foyer was Effie, Ingrid's Negro servant for more years than I could remember. Effie, slightly plumpish now, graying, and bespectacled and no longer wearing her stockings rolled below the knees, had babysat me when I was in grade school. More than anything, Effie had three lasting loves: gospel music, a need for a good laugh, and ghost stories.

She was a masterful storyteller and her ghost stories were chilling. As a child, I went to bed on many a Saturday night fearful of what might be under my bed. As I remember, I would always walk cautiously into my room and then take a running leap that would usually land me somewhere in the middle of my bed. I would never look under the bed until the next morning. When I told Effie this, she would laugh and laugh as if she knew something I didn't. And of course, she did. "Braxton, the only thing under that there bed is what you gots in that imagination of yours. Ifs it's dirty, it's gonna grab you, boy!" Effie was a morality play within herself without realizing it.

Effie and I hugged and hugged. Then she hugged Anne. When Effie hugged someone, she would rock you from side to side with her arms around your back and then she pulled you toward her and kissed you on the forehead. Today was no different. For a brief moment, I was ten again and knew I was safe and secure and I wanted to go back and be a child just one more time.

"Mista Braxton, you has grownup," said Effie winking, using the same deliberate and exaggerated Negro dialect she used when we were children to make us laugh. She never did this unless the situation at the time was heavy and comic relief was in order. "You're a fine lookin' man, too. And your children—well—you has three mighty fine children and so grown up. I knows Miss Virginia loved them. Welcome back, honey!"

"Effie, you look as young as ever and you're still wearing that sweet smelling perfume." (Effie prided herself on her five-and-dime perfume, "To a Wild Rose." The aroma was sickening sweet then and it still was today, but it was so much a part of her personage, I had long ago gotten used to the offensive smell.) Nevertheless, it bowled me over again today. "I have certainly missed you." I smiled, genuinely happy to see her after such a long absence. She had been a constant in my life when life seemed uncomplicated and others solved my problems for me.

"Mr. Braxton, you are stills a tease. Why, you never liked my perfume," she snorted, raising her voice. "You go on now and quit pullin' my leg." She laughed heartedly and turned, then turned back. "Mista Braxton, before I forgets, a letter came here for you yesterday. It's on the table there." She pointed to an antique lowboy. I'll go git it for you."

"Thank you, Effie," I said. I wondered who would write me at Ingrid's address.

"Here you is, Mr. Braxton," she continued. "Old Effie is glad she remembered. My mind just ain't what it was—like when you was a little boy."

Effie handed me a white standard business size envelope and returned to the kitchen. The letter was definitely addressed to me but in a shaky handwriting that was hard to read, and I didn't recognize it. It was postmarked February 5th from Wilson at 11:00 A.M. When I heard Ingrid calling, I put the envelope in my inside coat pocket.

Anne had walked toward the low murmur of conversation coming from the den at the back of the house. I smiled and nodded hello as I passed some of my relatives in the hall before joining my wife, my sixteen-year-old son, and two daughters, Mary Beth and Liza, ages nine and seven respectively, in the living room. I appreciated my wife's presence and support. Mother had not made Beth's life easy, especially in the earlier years of our marriage. Consequently, there was never a closeness between them; at least, not the kind I hungered for there to be.

I saw Ingrid enter the room. Almost able to pass as a double for Barbara Stanwyck, Ingrid looked radiant in her gray dress. Her hair, a brilliant brown, hung just above her shoulders. She walked toward me. With her head held high, her carriage exuded an air of confidence that made most people notice her immediately. Now in her late sixties, she was a striking woman with her athletic figure. She smiled and grabbed my hand. Her fingers interlocked with mine. Squeezing my fingers gently was her signal to let me know she was glad to see me again. I kissed her on the cheek. She dropped my hand and we backed away, looking at each other. She smiled again.

"Thank you, Ingrid, for having us in your home. It's kind of you. I know how much Mother loved you. And Mother lived for those times when you came to see her." I paused. "I think she recorded them in her mind so she could play them over and over until your next visit."

"Braxton, it's good to see you," said Ingrid, halfway laughing at my comment. Grabbing my right forearm with her left hand, she took one step forward and motioned with her other hand for me to follow her toward the back hall. "Virginia was a special lady and . . . yes . . . I . . .I'll miss her. I loved your mother's candor, honesty, and humor. Virginia believed in me when others did not, even when my own mother questioned my decisions. And she accepted me as I am and always did, even when I was a child. For this, I'll always be grateful."

Ingrid let go of my forearm long enough to grab my right hand—the way she would firmly grip the handle of a tennis racket. Her grasp was strong and as my father would have said, "She's a 'blue-blood', a person of worth." My father had a theory about handshakes. He explained it to me this way when teaching me how to avoid a fish handshake. "Give the other person a good grip, son. Don't try to break their hand. Just give them a firm handshake." He always maintained that the strength of a person's handshake was indicative of the strength of their character. And over time, I had come to believe that he was right.

"How are you, Braxton? I mean, honestly, how are you coping?" There was sadness in Ingrid's eyes.

"Right now I'm still sort of numb. It's hard to get used to. I'll be all right."

Letting go of my hand, we walked side by side down the hallway. "Look around, Braxton!"

In each room visible to me, I saw someone whose life had been directly impacted by my mother. With all of her many frailties, Mother was a dynamic personality and no one wanted to bury her memory. All of us had come today to celebrate the life of Virginia Eleanor Tomlinson Haywood and we wanted this day to be a true celebration, not a somber, morose, time of crying and reliving the bad times.

Effie reappeared in the kitchen doorway that opened onto the hall where we stood. "Mrs. Watson, everything's ready." The dialect she greeted me with was absent now.

We walked to the doorway that opened into their brightly colored den. It seemed crowded, filled with family members of all ages. A few close family friends of Ingrid and Aunt Josephine who had known Mother were sprinkled among them. "Everyone, let me have your attention," said Ingrid. "It's time to eat. Allen, will you give thanks?"

After the blessing, my family joined me and we followed Ingrid to the sunroom where the buffet luncheon was being served. Two long tables borrowed from the First United Methodist church were set up and decorated for the occasion. One table was laden with country ham, fried chicken, and turkey, deviled eggs and tomato aspic, sweet pickled peaches, watermelon rind pickles, and candied yams stuffed in hollowed-out oranges topped with melted marshmallows. The other table held casseroles, hot biscuits, raw vegetables with dip, and cakes, pies, and fudge brownies. Like her mother before her, Ingrid had spared no expense in planning. Her buffet would rival any Wednesday night family dinner at any Baptist or Methodist church. There was too much food—certainly more than was necessary to feed the thirty-four of us.

I leaned over to my wife and said, "Beth, you and Jonathan, serve yourselves first. Suddenly, I'm not very hungry." The sight of all the food overwhelmed me.

I took a glass of sweet iced tea from the buffet and visited with some of my relatives I had not seen for a while. Time passed too quickly. Glancing at my watch, it did not seem possible that it was already 1:10 P.M. Time to focus on leaving for the cemetery and the real reason we were here. I motioned to Ingrid and pointed to my watch. She announced to the others that it was time to depart.

Anne decided to ride with Ingrid and Seth to the cemetery. This would give them time to visit. I gave Anne my word that I would take care of Mother's remains.

Before I left, I made certain that I found Effie. I wanted to give her one last hug. I didn't know if I would ever see her again. Ingrid had told me that Effie only came to serve the luncheon because of her love for Mother.

"Effie, thank you for being here. You were always one of Mother's favorites in our family." I smiled, putting my hand on her arm. "Time passes too fast. It seems like only yesterday that Anne and I sat at Seth and Ingrid's kitchen table listening to you tell those scary, ghost stories." I pulled her toward me and gave her as big a hug as I could.

"Mr. Braxton, you've been a good son. Miss Virginia never had to worry over you. She told me dozens of times how fortunate she knows she was. I just has to agree," she said, taking the edge of her apron and wiping the beads of water from her forehead. If I didn't know better, I'd swear her eyes were filled with moisture but not the kind ones gets from cooking over a hot stove. I could remember only one other time that I had seen Effie cry and that was at the funeral of Ingrid and Seth's oldest child.

"Effie, you're so kind." I paused, uncertain what to say next. "Well, I have to say goodbye. Thank you again for being here today."

"Mr. Braxton, I did give you that letter, didn't I?"

"That's right, Effie. Thank you." I smiled and walked away.

I stepped into the downstairs powder room to straighten my tie. I reached inside my coat pocket and felt for the envelope that I'd forgotten was there. Slitting the seal of the envelope with my Swiss army knife, I pulled the contents out. There was one faded sheet of embossed stationary, the type that was once very expensive and probably no longer available. My hand shook as I read the short note written by the same shaky hand that had addressed the envelope. 'I have not forgotten and I am quite certain that neither have you. You have been very wise to exercise silence all these many years. I expect you to continue to say nothing. You are to relay this message to your remaining friends. If you choose not to remain silent, I cannot be responsible for what might happen to you.' I looked up from the letter and was startled at the face staring at me. It was pale, the nostrils were flaring, and the eyes appeared larger than usual, and then I realized I was looking at myself.

"My God, what's happening? Not again . . . Not today . . . Who is this insane person? I can't believe this! Shit!" I grabbed the edge of the porcelain sink to maintain my balance. "Oh shit! Shit . . . shit!"

"Braxton, are you okay?" said Beth, knocking on the door. "May I come in?"

"Just a minute," I said, throwing water on my face. I yanked open the door.

"What's wrong? You look like you've seen a ghost! Are you sure everything is all right?"

I stood in the doorway for a moment, not certain what I would say next. I found myself thinking about David Byrd and the day of his funeral. I thought of that night, wishing I had done something and maybe I could have prevented what happened.

"I . . . I'm fine. Everything just hit me at once. Let's go." I wished I could stay or go back to Raleigh. I walked with my family to the car. I thought about all those times I awoke in the middle of the night worried about what would happen next.

Chapter 4
A LAST GOODBYE

WITH APPREHENSION WEIGHING down my every step, I mentally forced myself to the car.

"What are you so nervous about?" Beth looked concerned and annoyed.

I shrugged. "I'll meet y'all at the car." I had stopped smoking at Beth's request but right now I wanted a cigarette in the worst way. If for no other reason, it would occupy my mind. It was not my nature to lie to Beth and introducing the letter's contents at this time would serve no purpose. Beth just stared at me, making it harder for me to concentrate on why I had come back.

The letter tucked inside my coat pocket had further opened the wounds that I had convinced myself were healed. At the moment I was certain of only one thing: whoever was behind our problems then is still alive and feels threatened by my return to bury my mother. Like that summer, my whereabouts were being tallied. I had a better than good hunch now just who the person might be behind all of this. Any hesitations or shadows of doubt about the identity of this person that I had lived with had all but disappeared. Today I would find out if I was right.

The ten minutes since Ingrid had called time to leave were unending. I dreaded the next hour and I feared it would pass just as slowly. The sun was bright, and even though it was still in the seventies, I was shivering. I didn't want to admit it but my real purpose for being here had begun to take a backseat to my desires to put an end to the horrors we had lived through.

Again, I felt myself becoming that man I had lived with for far too long—that man who had allowed himself to be shackled to the past, believing there was no chance of breaking the grip that unforgettable summer had held on him. My mind was a fast paced pingpong game and my thoughts moved back and forth from the past to the present. The past might win again. I kept repeating to myself I had come to pay honor to my mother. I had come to . . .

I need a plan, I kept thinking as I walked toward Anne, waiting at my car with Beth and our three children.

"Are you okay?" Anne moved toward me. "You look sick!"

"Of course," I said loudly, alarming myself.

"Are you sure . . . ?" Anne spoke, looking first at Beth and then me.

"Yes," I said, cutting her off. "We need to shake a leg." I unlocked the door. "Here, Anne, you take this." I gave Anne the box. "We'll see you at the cemetery." I knew I had been too abrupt with Anne as I watched her turn to join Ingrid and Seth. With each step, she carefully cradled the cardboard box. I turned to my family and said, "Ingrid gave us simple directions to the cemetery. Drive down West Nash Street and wind over to Vance and then over to Woodard and take a left onto Maplewood Avenue." Maplewood Avenue would take us directly to the cemetery entrance. The drive would be less than five miles.

Oh, Christ! Maplewood Avenue—another bad memory I had erased—another reminder of death—this time, it was the death of the Harrell boy. Dick Harrell was two months older than I and lived with his mother. A lanky boy with olive skin and freckles, he had a tuft of white hair that was always uncombed. No one knew where his father was or if Dick even knew his father. People didn't talk openly about such matters then. We just knew the father was not living in the home with his family.

We were in elementary school together where we shot marbles at recess. Dick was smart and was a nice enough guy, but he had very few friends at F. W. Woodard Elementary School. Most of the time, he came to school wearing old clothes. That was okay because I wore hand-me-downs too. Dick's clothes were always clean but his hands and nails were usually dirty and sometimes, in the hot spring months, he came barefooted. That never bothered me like it did some of the other kids in our sixth grade class. Sometimes he went days without bringing lunch and there was no free or reduced lunch program in those days. When I told my granny about this, she made arrangements with the woman in charge of the cafeteria at our school to give Dick a hot meal every day.

When Dick was not with me at recess, it was a sure bet that he would be walking and talking with Mr. Sam, the old colored janitor at our school. Dick loved and looked up to Mr. Sam. Everyone including Dick thought Mr. Sam bought his lunches because everyone knew Mr. Sam gave abundantly to "his chilluns" as he affectionately referred to us. He told Dick that the good Lord works in mysterious ways and He won't gonna let any of his chilluns starve cause He loves us too good. That answer was good enough for Dick.

When Dick's mother gave him a surprise party on his eleventh birthday at the Maplewood Avenue boarding house where they lived, Dick brought invitations to school. Everyone in our class was invited. I was one of the few who went. I liked Dick and I felt sorry for him. Some of my friends said their parents didn't want them going to that part of town to a party. It was too close to the railroad tracks. I remembered how Janet Hickman responded to her invitation, saying that Dick was dirt poor and no better than a nigger, and her mother didn't want her with the likes of that kind of boy. Funny, Mrs. Hickman was the head grade mother in the sixth grade. Janet's remarks angered me and I never liked her or her mother after that.

That was the way of many of our town's people. It didn't matter who got hurt. They happily passed this kind of an attitude to their children and in most cases, it was eagerly adopted. Even if I had wanted to, Mother refused to let me hurt Dick's feelings.

Dick dropped out of school the next year. By then we had moved to the only white junior high school located further down Kenan Street. Over two hundred of us from the four elementary feeder schools came together in the seventh grade. When we came we brought with us a combination of all that represented our community. At first we were not comfortable around each other. Some of the bigger town kids were unbelievably cruel to Dick. The farm boys would spit on him and call him "Albino boy" and many of the girls from Five Points laughed at him and teased him about his clothes and hair and said he smelled bad. Dick didn't come back to school after Christmas and I lost touch with him.

It was the summer after the rest of us completed our seventh grade year that the police cut down the rope that hung from the second floor outside balcony of the boarding house where he lived. This was my first introduction to "death not in God's will" as my granny called it. Rumor said he committed suicide. Immediately, a wave of disbelief passed through our town. There was no outrage, only shock because he was considered white trash, not much better than the coloreds. People who should have known better meant he was ignorant and dirt poor. Not many grieved his loss and only a few of us went to his funeral.

My lasting memory of Dick is of him kneeling there in the dirt behind Woodard School, marbles in hand, and ready to blast anyone who dared put his own agate in the circle he had drawn. And just like David Byrd, I will never forget Dick Harrell.

"Dad, are you ready to leave? Everyone is waiting." My sixteen-year-old son stood patiently waiting for my response.

"What? Of course," I said, regaining focus. "Definitely, let's go." I looked into Jonathan's beseeching eyes and knew he wanted to drive. I nodded affirmatively before he opened his mouth. He was full of energy and looked wide-awake and I was glad to have someone else drive. "Your mom and I will sit in the back with Liza. Mary Beth, ride up front with your brother. Just stay within the speed limit." I tossed him the keys. At that moment, I remembered how reluctant my own mother had been to let me drive with Anne in the car. With her, it was always, "Braxton, you need practice," mixed with a tone of authority.

Jonathan turned the key in the ignition. He waited for Ingrid and Seth to leave before pulling away from the curb, taking his place behind them. I sat in the back, directly behind my son. I leaned against the backseat and became suddenly attuned to how rotten I felt. My breathing was heavier than normal and I could feel the sweat collecting under my starched collar. Droplets of moisture ran down my chest and back. Little air circulated in the backseat. My head throbbed and before I could stop it, my mind raced back to that summer. The letter in my coat pocket verified that I was still a threat. Why? I had asked myself this question hundreds of times then. Now I had to ask it again. There had to be an answer; yet, none of mine satisfied me.

I just knew it had nothing to do with God, religion or Mother's funeral, and I knew it was not a punishment for some evil thing I had done. I just couldn't figure it out. Someone still had something to lose because of what we supposedly knew.

I was on my own now. With Mother's death there was absolutely no single person from our previous, familial generation to turn to for anything—no one to share these secrets with and no one to tell the stories of what had happened.

There was no one left who might challenge the exaggerated tales of our youth, no one to give a biased or un-biased view of my father, no one to give an authoritative word on the family's genealogy, which had not been important until now. My cousins knew no more than Anne and I. I had lost more than just my mother. All links to my heritage were disappearing and I had no way to retrieve or preserve them. Did my past have something to do with the answer I had been searching for so long? I should have thought to ask questions of my granny one of those times she sat us in her foyer reminding us of our namesake.

Jonathan had driven less than a mile when he was forced to stop and wait for a green light. It was one of those no-right-turn-on-red lights. To my left, a sprawling mini-mall now occupied the site where only a small family owned grocery store had once stood. I blinked and for a moment, I saw a scene from the year 1954: a crossroads where the city limits of Wilson ended—the site of a weary white wooden structure called Lamn's Grocery, a place offering a tired twelve year-old paper boy a respite from his five-mile delivery route. The chubby boy, sweating and breathing hard, sat on his black Columbia bike drinking a ten-cent Pepsi from a bottle he'd filled with a five-cent bag of salted peanuts. I was that boy and every Saturday morning I would stop around 11:00 A.M. to take a break from collecting the twenty-five cents a week subscription price my customers paid for their daily paper, *The Wilson Daily Times.* Despite the passing time, the scene was as familiar as yesterday. And I knew some of that little boy still lived in me. Would I want to go back? It was nothing more than a forgotten place, a vague memory brought into focus by the death of my mother.

I sat there mesmerized by the scene and waiting for the car to move. I stared at the crossroads, a modern day symbol indicating a span of time, like I had so many times before. It scared me to realize how much time had elapsed. It frightened me to think how some simple things became so complex. Somewhere in this time lapse, lay the answer to the question I had asked myself a hundred times. I could not go back to that night. I could not erase what we saw.

Without sufficient warning, the emptiness I had felt earlier was back. A pain of helplessness seized me, keeping time with the pounding of my heart and the throbbing in my temples. I had no idea what anyone had said, but I was acutely aware that my family was watching me. I tried to think of something pertinent to say but I couldn't find the right words. Then as quickly as this sensation began, it stopped.

The light turned green and I smiled admiringly at my son as he completed his turn onto West Nash Street. Following the Watson's car, we headed east.

"Are you okay, Daddy?" asked Liza. "You're so quiet."

"Daddy is lost in his thoughts again, sweetheart. I've been reliving some of my childhood days around here. I'll be okay." Liza patted my hand with the softness of her small palm and it was, indeed, comforting. I winked at Liza, allowing my mind to continue to wander between the present and the past.

"How am I doing, Dad?" Jonathan asked. I watched his confident smile grow larger as he looked at us through the rearview mirror. Beside me, Liza started to fidget.

"You're doing fine son, just fine. You're a terrific driver. By the way, did you forget your chauffeur's cap?" My one attempt at humor fell on deaf ears. I turned to Beth. She gave me a smile and a polite chuckle came from somewhere in the front seat.

Once on Nash Street, we entered the clearest drama of my youth: the two-hundred houses of my paper route, the two-acre watermelon patch behind the Crandall's home from where water balloons were thrown at passing cars on hot summer nights, the

McKenzie's two-story house with its white column pillars and pet monkey, Jasper, who attacked me on a Saturday morning when I tried to collect paper route money, and on our right, Aunt Josephine's handsome two-story brick Georgian-style home. On our left stood Dick's Hot Dog Stand, a famous landmark, and gathering place where my friends and I went for snacks, and where we went when there was nowhere else to go—a place where we were tolerated far too often. We passed Kincaid Avenue on our left, the street where my house stood, Jason Parker's large brick home on our right, the open field owned by the Thurstons on our left and the very same place Sonny Thurston targeted squirrels with his Whamo slingshot and many more scenes from my youth.

I was sad to see how West Nash Street had given way to spotty disrepair. I winced when I saw the numerous abandoned homes whose once aristocratic appearance stood proudly on this street. No longer maintained with respect and care and in some cases, empty, their dignity had been shamefully marred by peeling paint and boarded windows that faced the front of deteriorating broad, wraparound porches. Even some of the towering old oaks damaged by Hurricane Hazel in 1954 had made a feeble attempt to regain their rightful place along the edge of this once aristocratic thoroughfare where Negro maids in starched, pressed uniforms paraded in two's pushing their white babies in fancy strollers and carriages each sunny afternoon.

It was as if this once majestic street had almost been ignored and left behind in Wilson's pursuit of progress and prosperity. But even on this hot February day, Nash Street asserted some of its power. And I believe it was the beauty of its lasting order that impressed me: the many splendid, sturdy oaks that shadowed the pink and white dogwoods and a continuous rainbow of azaleas once spring made her debut. There was even power in the distinct absence of the many wealthy homeowners who once took immeasurable pride in being an inhabitant of this beautiful street. There was a lasting power in having witnessed this street in its majesty and being able to recall a well-defined portrait of its glory. And today, I realized how much a part of me identified with what this street represented and the effect this had had on my own life.

Suddenly and without any warning, the car in front of us turned left heading for Vance Street. We passed Matt's house on our left and I smiled. Good memories rested here. The modest New England style cottage hadn't changed much, maybe a recent coat of white paint to cover the wooden exterior. The shutters were now bluish gray and the white picket fence had been repaired. Continuing down Vance, we passed several side streets that led to Atlantic Christian Cottage and then Jonathan again turned left but not as abruptly this time. He now drove us through what was once a thriving neighborhood development of modest houses meant for a solid group of white, blue-collar families. None of this neighborhood with its shotgun houses had been preserved. Built mostly in the early twentieth century, these houses in their present condition stood as another pictorial reminder of what a lack of care and respect can do. What had happened to my hometown?

The small front yards of these bungalows joined in one continuous, overcrowded dirt parking lot filled with abandoned vehicles on cinder blocks, motorcycles, and outdated cars. Couches that were no longer fit for a living room, washing machines that had seen better days, and even a stove or two shamefully decorated the porches of many of these houses. Barefooted children of different races played in between the maze of whatever had been abandoned or dumped along the street's sidewalk. This area of humble heritage had become an ugly eyesore and yet, it remained as the primary entrance to our town's historical Maplewood Cemetery.

Jonathan followed Seth through the Maplewood Cemetery gates into the aging municipal cemetery, the one place in our town that ultimately revered the rich and poor, the Negro and the white, and the Jew and the Christian alike. Jonathan stopped momentarily to gaze at the gates flanked by towers and an arched pedestrian entrance and both girls seemed mesmerized by the same. The unique blond brick structure with its green tiled roof, similar to a Spanish mission, welcomed us . . . it was not at all forbidding or austere in any way. The inviting aura being projected was very comforting to me as were the words over the entrance: "In this garden of shrubs, flowers and grass lie the quiet ashes of our departed love ones in dreamless, protected, peaceful sleep."

"It looks like the entrance to a castle. Do people live in the towers?" Liza sounded excited.

"Almost seems like something Alice might find in the world of wonderland," said Mary Beth.

"I don't see Seth's car. Dad, help me look for the gravesite." Jonathan acted nervous, almost as if he had done something wrong. "I shouldn't have stopped."

"You're doing great, son. Just go around the circular Confederate Mound."

"What is that statue on top of that high hill?" Liza pointed, almost poking me in the eye.

"It's called a mound, Liza, and that's a Confederate sentinel standing with his rifle, guarding the gate and watching over the Confederate dead." I said.

"What's a sentinel?" Liza was at the right age to question everything.

"Liza, didn't you listen to Dad's answer. It's another name for a soldier standing guard." Jonathan's older brother response was typical. Had he forgotten that he used to ask the same kind of questions?

"Daddy, why didn't you just say soldier to begin with?" Liza turned and made a face at her brother that he didn't see.

"Too many questions, Liza." I looked over the top of my glasses at her to let her know not to push Jonathan too far. "A sentinel had a very important job as a guard, watching to make sure there would be no intrusion from the enemy. Look at his expression and the way he is standing. Looks as if he's ready for action."

"What's in the mound, Daddy?" Liza continued.

"Lots of dirt and rocks," said Mary Beth, proud of her answer.

"You're right. And supposedly, there are many confederate soldiers buried there. No one knows who they were or even if they came from Wilson County," I answered, remembering what my granny had told me about this part of the cemetery.

As Jonathan drove through the cemetery, familiar faces greeted us from every side. Different sized marble and granite headstones bearing the names Bell, Davis, Clark, Parker, Wilson, Smith, Woodard, Barnes, Byrd, Lucas, and Anderson beckoned us to drive past their alleys. All of these families had been solid citizens of Wilson and some of them had been a part of Mother's life and all had found their final resting place in the same older area of Maplewood Cemetery. This followed the southern tradition of keeping the families who grew up together in the same general proximity when they were buried. My granny used to say that 'Old Lizzie,' her colored nanny, said that this was the Lord's way of keeping friends together forever. I liked that idea although I'm certain many enemies ended up side by side.

"Son, ahead on your left is the Haywood family plot. Begin finding a place to park. If possible, pull behind Seth." I leaned over and patted him on the shoulder, acknowledging how well he had driven. The back of his ears moved, telling me he was pleased.

It was now less than twenty minutes before the start of the service. I was excited, amazed, and surprised to see that people had begun to gather. Here, on the east side of the cemetery, the sturdy pink crepe myrtle that had long stood as a landmark on our gravesite had been cut down to allow room for a wider road. Its absence left the corner plot without the characteristic beauty that we had so often come to enjoy and take for granted. Without this distinguishable tree and its outstretched arms, our plot was no different than any other, just stark and exposed and extremely difficult to locate.

As we got out of our car, there was a siren in the distance and I heard a dog barking. The wind blew gently as we walked the short distance to the gravesite to join the others. The two ministers, both nephews of Mother, shared what they had planned for a final tribute to Mother. They reminded us to stand with our own immediate family. As they talked, I watched Anne still holding the box close to her body. This was going to be difficult for her. We were assured the entire service would last no more than fifteen to twenty minutes. We were satisfied and knew Mother would be pleased.

I had been so preoccupied with the fundamentals of the service that I hadn't consciously taken note of how many people stood around the Haywood family plot. Ours was of good size but not large enough for the number gathering. People stood wherever they could plant their feet—along the roadside in the unmowed grass and in the graveled road that ran between neighboring plots. The sun had become a baking oven and annoying gnats were everywhere.

I recognized many of Mother's contemporaries from the neighborhood of our youth. Despite their aging, they looked beautiful and I saw them as they once were. I smiled to see some of our old hide-and-seek buddies as well as about a dozen of our high school friends. Friends of Josephine, a few parents of our closest friends, some ladies I did not know, and some of my father's business associates were present. My eyes moistened when I saw Matt and Thad's parents as well as Mrs. Parker, Jason's mom.

My heart warmed and for a moment, the joy I felt was enough to make me forget how much I disliked this town and so many of its inhabitants. Across the way stood Olivia Pugh, one dear lady and the aunt of David Byrd. Seeing her brought back tears from an earlier time when we had shared his tragic death together.

In deference to an elderly man sitting in the backseat of a black Cadillac, the crowd parted to allow him to visually participate. As I looked down this corridor of people, I knew I did not recognize the man or the male driver.

It was time to begin. Anne, Beth and I, and our children stood on the east side of the Haywood grave marker. A noble symbol, our family marker had stood in this exact spot for eighty-five years. With the exception of occasional traces of aged mildew, it did not belie its years. Positioning ourselves in this spot allowed us to look down upon a pair of flat marble headstones. I studied the name of my father etched in the marble surface of one and the name of my mother in the other, the one that looked too new.

There was no more whispering now. I could hear traffic in the distance and a distant voice coming from another area of Maplewood. Here where we waited, it was quiet, except for a few of those gnats' annoying refrain.

"Today, we have come to celebrate the life of Virginia Tomlinson Haywood who departed this world on February 1, 1992, in the year of our Lord. Virginia was a devoted wife to Louis Braxton Haywood, a caring mother to Anne and Braxton, and a good friend and neighbor. Those of you who have come to rejoice in her life can give testimony to this. Hers was not an easy life. From the time she was a little girl until now, her life has been beset by trouble, heartache, and turmoil . . ."

As my cousin spoke, my mind began to wander again. Reflections of earlier times passed before my eyes and I was instantly a viewer, watching a movie of my past. Everything was clear and vivid, even in the minutest detail. I recognized specific people, exact locations, and even seasons of the year. A smile from Mrs. Ernestine Adams standing across the way carried me back to the old neighborhood and there we were around her kitchen table, eating homemade chocolate chip cookies and drinking cold, plain milk out of mason jars on an afternoon after school. And I saw Jason, Thad, Byrd, and Matt sitting at our kitchen table eating some of Lily's chocolate meringue pie talking with Mother about college plans and laughing about sneaking into the Starlite Drive-In Theatre. A wink from a high school friend standing to my left took me to the state championship football game our senior year where he held the ball that scored the game tying field goal. Each face brought back a pleasant memory.

I don't know how long I did this. My preoccupation was not intended as disrespect to Mother. I wondered what the others thought as they stood listening to the two ministers. I grabbed Beth's hand and squeezed it. I could not mentally stop myself from this going back in time. She looked startled as if to say I had squeezed too hard. My mind became fixated on returning to that summer. Stop it! Refocus. My mind started prompting me—signaling me— attempting to get me to pay attention to what was happening at the moment.

Before I realized it, our time for participating in the service had come. "Virginia chose to be cremated and in keeping with her desire, we are honoring her request . . . please bow in prayer as her family now carries out her request. Father, God, your child, Virginia Tomlinson Haywood, is now at rest . . . "

During the ride to the cemetery, Anne had transferred Mother's ashes to a more suitable urn borrowed from Ingrid. I stepped back watching Anne's hands shake as she sprinkled the contents of the urn over the two markers. I was afraid Anne might faint. I stationed myself to catch her. Anne finished, turned and smiled at me, then passed the urn to Beth. She stood waiting; her left hand calmly playing with the pearl necklace—the same necklace my mother wore at our father's funeral. All eyes watched Beth as she methodically poured some of the contents of the urn into the hands of each of our children. Beth whispered something to our children and on her cue they began sprinkling the contents resting in their palms. Beth looked serene and it felt good to have her here beside me. Mentally I was ready; emotionally I was not prepared for my part in the ceremony. My eyes followed the hands of my children intently; they were being careful not to do anything that might be inappropriate.

I did not know what I was supposed to feel as I stood looking at Anne. Fearful that she still might break down, I made a supreme effort at self-control. My legs felt weak and my stomach again felt nauseous. I slowly turned to face Beth. This was not the time to lose my composure. After a few seconds, I nodded to Beth that I was ready. When she poured the ashes into my palms, my eyes bulged with surprise. This I wasn't prepared for. I never looked inside the original urn and Anne gave me no hint about what I now held. What I saw for the first time mixed in with the few remaining ashes was a significant number of grayish, white bone fragments, the size of a pinhead.

This was definitely not like the movies! There were not enough ashes to blow in the wind but there were enough tiny bone fragments—enough to lie on the ground for months and months to come. My hands trembled as I carefully bent to scatter the remaining contents of the urn over my father's head marker. When I finished, I stared at the bone fragments on the ground.

Startled—startled to think that these little chips were my mother or what remained of her. I knelt down, picking up some of the bone fragments. Is this what cremation does to the body? I shook my head in disbelief, momentarily forgetting the people who surrounded me. I laughed to myself. Ashes to ashes—balderdash! Mother wasn't going anywhere. She would still be around for a long time to come.

"Amen! Thank you for being here today to celebrate Virginia's life with her family," spoke Allen, my cousin, concluding the service.

The strong hand gripping my shoulder was unexpected and I jerked, turning and standing. Facing me was another of my very best friends in high school, Thaddeus Ruffin. Thad, as he preferred to be called, had maintained his boyish good looks. Still sporting a head of curly blonde hair but slightly graying at the temples, he stood as erect as ever. Thad had been with Matt, Byrd, Jason, and me on that upsetting summer night. Now a successful insurance agent, Thad lived with his wife and three sons in Farmville, North Carolina, about twenty miles east of Wilson.

"Thad, my God, I didn't expect to see you here," I said. I was overwhelmed with emotion again. Tears were forming in my eyes. I took off my glasses and wiped them with the back of my right hand.

"Braxton, it has been way too long, old buddy." He grabbed my shoulders and pulled me toward him and gave me a hug. Caught off guard by his massive arms around my shoulders, I began to fall. He steadied me by tightening his grip. This was the exact way he greeted his close friends when we were in high school. Again my eyes filled with tears, this time more quickly. I couldn't stop them. I didn't even try. There was never any pretension on Thad's part and there was none today. He offered me the security and comfort I needed and I took it. I missed my mother. I missed Byrd and I missed my friends. "Let it out, Braxton. I know you loved your mother. It's got to hurt." He was right.

Finally I pulled away. Taking my handkerchief from my back pocket, I wiped the tears that ran down my face. I blew my running nose in embarrassment. Looking at Thad, I put my hand on his shoulder. "Thank you, Thad, I needed that."

"Damn, Braxton, it's good to see you."

"It's been way too long, Thad . . . way too long!"

"You have that right!"

"God, Thad, there's no excuse in not getting together more often."

"I agree." Thad cleared his throat like he might change the subject then he stopped, took a breath, and continued. "Mother called me as soon as she heard about your mom. Did she go peacefully?"

"Totally." I thought talking about Mother would be easy. I pulled my handkerchief from my back pocket and wiped the moisture from my forehead.

"Are you okay?"

"I don't know." A damn cigarette is what I needed. I shrugged. "I think I'm okay."

"Is there anything I can do for you?" said Thad. "I mean it, Braxton."

"I'm still a little shaken. You've witnessed that." I cleared my throat. "And Thad, I'm a little numb . . . it's a strange feeling. Mother had been failing fast and the quality of her life was . . . you know . . . deteriorating more than I realized. It's just hard to believe she's gone."

"Braxton, I'm so sorry," Thad said. "I know I dread that day with my mother."

"Thad, you look fantastic," I said, changing the subject. "You're still as trim as ever. Playing a lot of golf?"

"That and coaching two town league baseball teams my boys are on."

"You're still the same, haven't changed a bit, have you?"

"Not much."

"Remember that time you coerced me into umpiring that little league baseball game?" We laughed.

"Braxton, you couldn't do anything right behind that plate."

"Me?" I stomped the ground with my right foot. "It was those annoying parents that got me riled. You know that!"

"I never could get you to do it again." Thad chuckled to himself. "Had to enlist Byrd to do the others." He squinted, shading his eyes with his left hand.

Thad and I looked at each other.

"Thad, this is not the best time but I really need to talk with you. I got another letter. It was sent to Ingrid's . . . arrived yesterday, I think. Will you be free sometime this week?"

"I can be."

"I've got to go public with this. It's choking me. I'm more determined than I've ever been about getting to the bottom of what happened!"

"Braxton, if you're looking for my okay, you've got it. I'll be in Raleigh on Wednesday. I'll call you and we'll meet for lunch."

"God! I've relived it so many times, Thad. It's bizarre, isn't it?" I paused, looking at the tears forming in the corners of his eyes. Thad

Ruffin's pain was as real and as fresh as mine. He, too, still suffered. I grabbed his hand, holding it steady. We did need to get together. "Oh, did you get another letter?"

"No. At least, not yet I haven't. I pray that I won't." He motioned to his mother that he would be coming.

"I'll look forward to your call." I gave him the firmest handshake I could without his muscular hand crushing mine. "One more thing, Thad. Did you know the elderly gentleman in the back of the Cadillac?"

"Oh, yes! That was David Byrd's father."

"You've . . . Damn!" I was shocked. My feet felt glued to the ground. I opened my mouth; nothing came out at first. "You . . . you've got to be kidding!"

"No, I'm not. That was Mr. Byrd, himself! Did he speak to you?"

"Absolutely not! Thad, can you believe he had the nerve to come here?"

"Yes, I can. I'm not surprised at anything anymore," said Thad with a reluctant smile.

"Who was the driver?"

"That was Charles. He's being considered for a possible judge-ship."

"Judge? Where does he live?"

"Still with his father in the same house. He's an attorney with a big law firm here in Wilson; in fact, he's with your great uncle. I thought you knew all of this, Braxton."

"I'll be damn," I said, shaking my head in disbelief. "I lost track of things here a long time ago. I guess I did it deliberately, thinking it would make things easier for me. Sounds selfish, doesn't it?"

"Not at all! If I had been in your shoes, I would've done the same thing," said Thad. His voice carried an empathetic tone.

"This is too much," I said, taking off my jacket. Sweat poured down my chest and back. "I best go. My family is waiting. Call me!"

"I will and soon. Braxton, thanks for being such a good friend. I miss our times together."

Thad turned and walked toward his mother. I joined my family and began walking. Only a few people remained. I was too upset to talk. Most were satisfied to simply focus on our children. I turned to my wife.

"Beth, honey, I want to stay here awhile. I may even spend the night at Ingrid's. I need to be with Mother alone. Then I want to ride by the old home place. I'll arrange a ride for you and the children to Ingrid and Seth's."

"That's fine. Take as much time as you need," she said. "If you want to stay the night, let me know. We'll ride back with Mother. The children and I will probably go on back to Raleigh. We'll take Anne."

"Can I stay, too, Daddy? Please! Please! I want to be with you," asked Liza, her big green eyes sparkling with excitement.

"Not this time, sweetheart. Not now. I need to be alone with Grandmother."

"I thought she was dead?" asked Liza.

"She is. Your mother will explain." I looked at Beth, nodding.

"Okay, Daddy." Liza smiled, grabbing my hand and squeezing it. I watched her skip back to the car with Beth and Mary Beth as Johnathan followed.

I looked at my watch again. It was three-twenty. Everyone had left. I took off my vest and tie and wiped the sweat from my brow. My handkerchief was soaked. I walked over to Mother's marker and stood looking down for a moment. I knelt to brush the bone fragments away from the marker bearing her name. I gave in, losing my composure. I cried unabashedly. After my crying stopped, I felt better—in some ways relieved. I wiped my eyes with my handkerchief and stood and spoke.

"Mother, many of your friends were here today. You would have been so happy to see how much you were loved and respected. I don't know whether you can hear me and I won't talk much. I know you don't like long speeches." I hesitated and then continued, "I loved you and still do. I'm sorry I didn't come last Sunday. I feel selfish because I wasn't there when you needed me. Please forgive me." I stopped and looked around. No one was near so I continued.

"You were always there for me, and I wanted to thank you—thank you for your kindness and your patience with me all these years. And thank you for teaching me to be strong and not give up."

I became self-conscious, believing my words sounded trite. Talking to the dead was awkward but I continued. "When Daddy died you said 'the spirit of love is stronger than the spirit of death.' I'm holding you to that."

I got down on my knees, bent over, and kissed her grave marker. "Mother, there is one last thing I need to say. Now that you are gone, I'm going to tell our story. No one can hurt you now. I don't care about myself. If I'm going to be any good to anyone, I've got to do this. After all we've been through together, I don't think anyone or anything can scare me now, not even Mr. Byrd."

Before leaving Maplewood cemetery, I rode over to David Byrd's gravesite. Once I found his family's site, I parked my car and sat for a brief moment. I hesitated and then swung my door open, got out, walked over to his marker, and knelt beside his headstone. Weeds and crabgrass had overgrown Byrd's stone marker, making it unreadable. I pulled the weeds away until I could see his name. Brushing the grit and dirt from his marker with my right hand, I pressed my fingers against what time and nature had left of the engraved letters of his name. The stone felt warm. I reached in my pocket and took out my rabbit's foot. "Damn it, Byrd. Why? Why? Why?" I stopped long enough to watch a car circle the area. "Byrd, I will never forget you or what you meant to me. You're among the best and I'm so sorry about what happened. God, if we could only do it over again. Remember this rabbit's foot?" I stopped and smiled. "I'm leaving it with you today. I don't need it anymore but it's the last thing I own that we shared together. I want it to be with you now." I dug a little hole beside his marker. I looked at the rabbit's foot one last time, kissed its worn material, put it inside the hole, and carefully covered it again.

I stood for a moment and in the distance I thought I saw the fair-haired boy running around the track again. Like always, he was out in front. With the wind blowing his hair back and his chest stuck out and breathing hard, he made the final turn, and then I blinked, turned, and went back to my car. I had to let go of the past. Byrd would want me too. I was satisfied with that now.

I got in my car and drove through the cemetery gates and made my way to the Cherry Hotel, an older brick structure that had outlived its usefulness and now looked out of place. I pulled up to the side entrance, got out, and walked slowly up to the building. The side door was locked as I expected. To my right side were the windows overlooking the once grand ballroom. Standing on tiptoes, I peered through one of the musty windows. With the exception of peeling paint that had faded over the years, it looked as regal as I remembered from the many dances I had attended here. Still standing proudly and overlooking East Nash Street, she was now a home for the homeless and the down and out and who knows what else. This was the last place my mother lived before moving away from Wilson.

I turned toward my car and saw across the street a tired Norfolk Southern Railway Depot. On the platform adjacent to the tracks an old green baggage cart stood by itself. Its long weathered handle rested against one of the many light posts that lined the platform. Not a soul was in sight. I got back into my car, pulled away from the curb, and turned right onto a deserted East Nash Street and headed west.

This is where our story should begin, and *we are now talking of summer days and evenings, the time of my youth, in Wilson, North Carolina*, in that year—the year 1957.

Chapter 5
KINCAID AVENUE

THE LAST WEEK of May, 1957 saw two very important but unrelated events. On Wednesday, May 29, the *Nautilus*, a U.S. atomic-powered submarine arrived in San Diego after setting an underwater distance record by traveling 3,049 miles from Panama. The other event, pale in comparison but more important to me, took place on Friday, May 31. I exited the hot, colorless halls of Charles L. Coon High School having successfully completed my sophomore year.

"An orderly exodus is expected from all of Coon's young scholars today. Have a pleasant summer," was the final decree given over the intercom on that Friday afternoon by our fiery Dean of Students, Mr. Merton Andrew Pincher. My friends and I thought he got his last name from his perverted habit of pinching many of the male students on the shoulder or on the back of the neck. Just getting away from 'The Pincher,' himself, was a treat but exiting Coon for the summer was cause for celebration.

While many of Coon's juniors threw three ring binders and poorly written essays out of the massive windows of their third floor English classrooms, I chose to walk down the three flights of circular cement stairs dressed like the Mad Hatter. It was a tight fit on my one hundred and eighty-five pound stocky frame. I borrowed the authentic costume without asking from the drama department. I won no kudos from prissy Mr. Stanley who stubbed out his cigarette butt on the second floor landing and ran after me shouting, "Louis, you're late . . . wait . . . too late. School is out . . . you're late." I thought that in his exasperation he had forgotten the lines to his best production in his tenure at Coon. I would not have considered doing this if my good buddies, Matt Beatty and David Byrd, had not been too chicken to do it themselves. Besides, they promised to get me a date with David's first cousin, Molly Cannon, one knockout cheerleader for the Charles L. Coon Cyclones. Since it was preplanned, I received thunderous applause from those in the tenth grade class who were assembled in the courtyard awaiting my appearance. This was totally out of character for me until I dressed up like Mr. Spaceman for a performance in Stunt Night near the end of my senior year.

The next morning I ate breakfast alone on our screened-in back porch. Lily had fixed my favorites: blueberry pancakes with scrambled eggs and sausage links. I lived at 109 North Kincaid Avenue with my nervous mother, my dying father, and my twelve-year-old sister in a small but comfortable bungalow.

On this morning, the first day of June, my mother had left the house to pick up my sister from a slumber party at one of her best friend's. My father was in his room, probably smoking and listening to CBS news blasting from the television. A few of my friends had packed and were already at Atlantic Beach for the weekend to celebrate the end of another school year. Warren, our Negro yardman and the spitting image of Gregory Peck, was edging Mother's flowerbed in the backyard.

I celebrated my first day out of school and my first time on the A honor roll by helping Warren in the yard and running errands for my mother. I finished my day by joining my mother and father in his smoked filled bedroom to silently watch *Gunsmoke* at 10:00 on CBS. I spent that first hot uneventful night of June on our back porch fantasizing and dreaming about what it must be like to be a grownup.

On Sunday, June 2, CBS aired a *Face the Nation* TV broadcast in which Soviet C.P. First Secretary Nikita Khruschev predicted, "America's grandchildren would live under Socialism." Secretary Krushchev was not aware American correspondents were taping him but he certainly must have been aware of the backlash this would cause among American parents. At this same time, I was totally unaware of the events that would radically change my life over the next three months, precluding any more pranks or nonsense at least for a while.

Before America decided to get so serious about the perceived Soviet Russia's threat to our nation's independence, I had already started taking steps toward my own independence. On April 18, I celebrated my sixteenth birthday with a party at my Aunt Josephine's home. It was on this occasion that I stood on the landing at the top of the stairwell and announced to my friends, "As of this minute and hour, I want you to call me Braxton, my middle name. I am dropping the name of Louis." This was my first step toward my desired independence and had nothing to do with being called "Lucius" in Latin I and II over the last two years. However, that, in itself, would have been sufficient reason for my decision. I did not confer with my parents and I didn't stop to think that it might hurt my father since I was named for him. At the time, I didn't care and besides, I liked the sound of my middle name.

My second step toward independence was an authentic driver's license with my name on it. It took me two attempts before I satisfied the plump DMV officer who told too many jokes while I tried to concentrate. The first time I touched the rubber cone with my rear bumper while attempting to parallel park. "That's it, sonny," he said. I wanted to tell him that was not my name. "No more crashes today, sonny. Better luck next time." He walked away laughing and I sat behind the steering wheel humiliated, banging the dashboard while tears filled my eyes. I had tried and come so close but I failed. No one ever fails, but I did.

The next time, a week later on the 25th, I proved capable enough to be awarded my own driver's license. The first thing I did was exactly what my father told me not to do—and that was drive through downtown Wilson at peak traffic hour. I thought he must be kidding. Being seen driving for the first time in downtown Wilson was like telling your salvation story at a Southern Baptist baptismal service.

When I turned sixteen, my mind became alive with new thoughts. Something inside of my head that I could not understand itched me with an anxiousness I could not identify. I had convinced myself I had no life outside my home. To be completely honest, I decided I was miserable—miserable from not having moved up at least one rung on the ladder of adolescence. I only knew I was tired—tired of being treated like a child. Plain and simple, I wanted freedom—freedom from the confinement of my home and my neighborhood and my church activities.

It was about this same time, the first week of June, 1957, I decided I needed more responsibility: the kind that would make people take me more serious so I decided to get a summer job. Now that I had my driver's license, I couldn't wait to take my father's newly renovated '48 Buick Sedan, tagged the "Tank" by my friends, and experience all the newfound freedom it was going to bring me—like having the flexibility to go and come without depending on someone else—like dating without a chaperone escorting us or without having to walk everywhere—like being able to take a girl to the Starlite Drive-in Theatre. I would still have to live at home but I would be, in my mind, one step higher on the ladder of entering the world of adulthood. This would be the beginning of my newfound lust for freedom.

Since my sixteenth birthday, I thought I couldn't wait to be mature—however that word could be defined. As it stood, I couldn't do any of what I perceived to be grownup things because if I did them, it would be illegal. I couldn't buy cigarettes yet my dad worked for a tobacco manufacturer; I couldn't buy beer but our refrigerator was full at times, and I couldn't buy some of the magazines behind the counter at any of David Byrd's daddy's pharmacies.

I believed my life was a tad below okay at best and definitely not in the lane of excitement—there were no flashing lights and no neon signs blinking on and off telling me to slow down, that there was danger ahead. I was a nice, middleclass, overweight kid, maybe too nice in the eyes of some of my peers, trying too hard to find the grownup world. Several of my closest friends had begun to find their niche and I was trying hard to compete and getting nowhere. Matt had already renounced Christianity and declared himself an atheist. Jason swore he had already had sex with an older woman but I didn't believe him. Thad knew where he wanted to go to college and was definite about his career tract. David Byrd was allowed no choice. And I—I did what was expected. I lived by the mores of my family and mimicked the lifestyle of most good American teenage boys—I went to Sunday school and church—I watched TV—I listened to rock-n-roll and I went to the Creamery and the teenage club when given a chance. Whenever possible, I sneaked a look at *Playboy* which wasn't very often. My lack of independence allowed me to stay out of serious trouble.

I needed this summer of 1957. I was sixteen and restless and determined my life would radically change. In answer to whatever it was ringing inside of my head begging for freedom, I declared that this would be the summer I would mature. Unfortunately, it waited for me.

There was one thing that made my life different from most of my classmates: the internal turmoil that had rapidly intensified within our family. Mother seemed more on edge and my father's condition had worsened. Most nights I fell asleep listening to the sad sounds echoing throughout my house—my father writhing and moaning in pain and, in turn, my mother's uncontrollable sobbing in the hallway. In my dictionary of life at that point, I would define mine as the pits. I wanted to escape.

I was sandwiched between two bookends: the atmosphere inside my home and the atmosphere on the outside—the neighborhood in which we lived. This was the arena where I wrestled with the thoughts I did not understand as they bounced around inside my head. And this was the arena where the emotions I did not understand ran through me like a riptide.

The atmosphere of my neighborhood was one of open friendliness but dark secrets hid behind many doors of the homes that faced our street and other streets in our town. Ours was a white Anglo-Saxon middle class neighborhood of hardworking, honest, God-fearing men. Most of these Kincaid Avenue men were of middle age, predominantly bald, and successful in their chosen careers whether it was representing Exeter Tobacco Company as a buyer like my dad or managing the only TV appliance store on West Nash Street like Mr. Thurston. There were no doctors, no lawyers, no one of any significant social standing residing on our block but there was pride residing in the homes that lined our street—pride that traced its roots to the Daughters and Sons of the American Revolution. And in the eyes of some, this was the best prestige—the best badge of honor—the kind that allowed one entrance into any door regardless of one's monetary status.

Most of the houses on Kincaid Avenue were one-story bunga-lows, each with a different facade. A wooden floored porch with inviting splinters stretched across the front of our house. It had long offered itself, sometimes without Mother's approval, as a gathering place for the twelve kids who lived on our block and each of our names were etched more than once in the white wooden railing that stretched its way the length of the porch. This was where the sum-mer activities began in a ritual commencing around 7:00 P.M. while it was still light enough to be recognized and ended around 10:00 P.M. with one last game of hide-and-seek among the six younger off-spring who were their parent's hope for a more successful future.

Many of the Kincaid men could be found sitting on their porch-es on humid summer nights smoking, clad in seersucker trousers and thin white or gray cotton shirts that stuck to the drops of sweat run-ning down their chests. This was a treasured respite from their day of labor—a time not to do a damn thing but sit back and carry on their desultory conversations—everything from the threat of the U.S.S.R. to Ike's golf game to the recent death of Senator Joseph McCarthy to the negative effect of rock-n-roll on their children. My father, once a regular participant, had been forced to retire from this ritual by the insidious cancer that had now enveloped his entire body—like the tentacles of an octopus choking the life out of an unsus-pecting victim.

The Kincaid wives still wearing their aprons—a symbol of their rightful place in the family—would routinely serve sweet iced tea or their husband's preferred drink and wait dutifully for their dismissal. My mother sat with my father during this time. Her nightly ritual began at 7:00 P.M. and unofficially ended whenever my father fell asleep. Most nights he didn't sleep; he just moaned and groaned. If he slept, it was intermittently. This would explain why Mother looked tired and haggard in the mornings.

I could see my father dying. His deteriorating condition neces-sitated hiring a nurse and three nights a week on Tuesday, Thursday, and Friday, Mrs. Crawford, a private duty RSN, would arrive around

9:00 P.M. to stay with my father. Aunt Josephine arranged for Mrs. Crawford to sit with Daddy. Mrs. Crawford had been Dr. Thaxton's nurse, Aunt Josephine's husband, when he was in practice. After he retired, Mrs. Crawford left the clinic and now she chose her patients.

Having an evening nurse was supposed to give Mother a needed respite—one she did not know how to value. Mother was so devoted to my father that she couldn't bear being away from him for any extended period of time. This presented problems for Crawford (the name she went by) but she tolerated Mother's interference until Mother, herself, decided to get out of the way and go to bed.

Outside of 109 North Kincaid Avenue, everyone seemed to be at leisure with himself; and, indeed, happiness might be mistaken as a theme for our street. Most Kincaid men and occasionally their sons dutifully kept their lawns mowed and neatly trimmed where each edged the curbing. There were no sidewalks to sweep. Each of the wives proudly oversaw her own backyard flower garden, which consisted at different times of the year of multiple varieties such as petunias, zinnias, peonies, pansies, jonquils, tulips, daffodils, sweet peas, roses, snap dragons, and gladiolas.

Mr. Sam Ross, the only widower on our block, lived across the street from us. His yard and gardens were the showplace on Kincaid Avenue. He had a choice lot, larger than all the others on our street, and he helped design and build his house. His backyard, over one-half of an acre, was meticulously divided into different sections. In each section, there was something different planted. Quite often, I heard one of my aunts say that his backyard was an open invitation for a page in any reputable home and garden magazine.

Mrs. Ross loved flowers and every year, her husband set aside four rows where he planted her favorite flowers. Shortly after their only child, a son, was born, Mrs. Ross died. Mr. Ross continued to plant and cultivate these beds just as if his wife were alive.

This was a time in our town when women enjoyed the bragging rights that accompanied their flowers being chosen by the altar guild to decorate the front of church sanctuaries. And it was not unusual to see Sam Ross's flowers decorating the altars of the First Baptist and First Methodist churches. The fact that he might be available kept the level of jealousy far below its boiling point and if there were protests among the women, they were silent.

According to neighborhood rumor, it was Mrs. Ross's death that caused Mr. Ross to start spending a good amount of his afternoons and early evenings working in his backyard, tending his chickens or his vegetables or his grape arbor or his fruit trees. Sometimes he let me work with him. And after a while, I surmised the neighbors were right; his backyard ritual was to fill the loneliness that was so evident in his blue eyes.

Mr. Ross was a fair man and highly respected in our town. On North Kincaid Avenue he was my mentor, always considerate and willing to listen to my questions.

Most June summer nights in Wilson were hot and sultry. Sweat was a given and in the warm evening air, it just stuck to our bodies like flies sticking to sweet syrup. This nightly perspiration was not something we fought but just accepted, and we knew there would be hell to pay in July and August.

There were no escapes. Being inside a house was more unbearable than being on the outside. Very rarely was there a breeze on these stubborn June evenings and there were no towering oaks on our street to provide any immunity from the choking humidity that accompanied the advent of tobacco season. Even if the wind did make an appearance, it would only agitate the muggy presence of an already hot summer evening. Most of us were not yet privileged to oscillating fans or air conditioners, only handheld fans—the tulip shaped or square kind normally found in the rack of a church pew or in a funeral parlor—the kind that advertised Yelverton's funeral home on the back side and pictured Jesus in the Garden of Gethsemane on the front side. But who took the energy to use them—maybe Mrs. Landruff—who swung them at detested flies?

On these nights one could always depend on Skippy, the feeble, black cocker spaniel, to take his rightful place in the street in front of the Thurston's home at 108 North Kincaid Avenue. The paved street was cool enough after Johnny, one of the three Thurston boys, watered it down to provide Skippy with a sanctuary and only neighboring cars knew to drive around him. Our street was Skippy's street and Skippy, after rolling around in the dirt under the Thurston's hammock, would slowly walk to his spot, plop down, and assume his role as guardian of Kincaid Avenue.

I didn't understand how someone could be happy on a hot, sticky June night on Kincaid Avenue when we all knew there was a good chance that Mr. Landruff might run out shortly after the neighborhood ritual began, yelling and swinging at his only son, Daniel. No one ever protested—maybe the sweat from his muscular chest pushing through his short sleeve white shirt and the beet redness of his face told us how unbalanced he really was. His wife, Loretta, mousy and small of frame, would stand on those hot nights behind the soft white curtains at their front window watching the scenario on her front lawn but never saying a word.

But the echoes of Daniel screaming, "Daddy, stop! Please stop!" on that first June Sabbath evening clung to my inner soul just like the sticky sweat that danced over the foreheads of the neighborhood. The few men and women sitting on their porch that night refused to move from their position and no one looked toward the frightening pleas; no one thought it was their place to interfere. After all, that was their problem and the men nodded in agreement that a father had a right to discipline his son. It was not the women's place to comment openly but many displeasing comments were exchanged from backyard to backyard the next morning when the bruises on Daniel's body became known.

The next morning I asked Mr. Ross for his opinion on the subject. Mr. Ross thought for a moment and then said, "Mr. Landruff is given to too much drink and a drinking man will do crazy things." Mr. Landruff's eyes always had a glazed look so I just assumed he was sort of crazy. I had already seen what too much drink could do to somebody and I didn't have to leave my bedroom for additional understanding. Sometimes it was just hard to breathe on this street.

The beating of Daniel came to an abrupt stop the third week of June. We all heard his screaming and his daddy's cursing and still no one got up. What we didn't see was the fist that knocked Daniel against the side of the garage and what we didn't hear was the thud Daniel made upon impact. Without help, Daniel managed to crawl out of sight. His mother found him later curled in a fetal position in a flowerbed behind the garage. Only her screams brought Mr.

Adams, her next-door neighbor, running to her aid. Daniel was taken to the hospital suffering from a concussion and a broken left arm. The entire neighborhood emerged when we heard the howling ambulance leave shortly before ten o'clock. Mr. Landruff was hospitalized for a month and then Loretta let him come back home. He never took another drink and the neighborhood didn't learn a lesson.

A large vacant lot sat on the south end of our block paralleled to West Nash Street. On the northwest corner of this lot, four tall oaks and two spindly pines stood as sentries observing the unrehearsed ceremonies that took place daily. On the northeast end of the lot, an old majestic magnolia patiently rested on the mossy surface that surrounded it. Skippy found his daytime security beneath the low hanging limbs of this hearty evergreen. This was our neighborhood football field in the fall and our softball field in the spring. On some nights when we could get out unnoticed after 9.00 P.M., it served as a meeting place for the five good teenage friends: Matt, David, Thad, Jason, and me. This was where at night we told our secrets, shared our desires, and made our plans for the next adventure we would take together. And this was the same place we expressed our fears and consoled each other in the darkness after the terror that awaited us emerged.

Kincaid Avenue became the rallying point for us during the summer of 1957. We returned time after time to either 109 North or the lot across the street or to Mr. Ross' backyard to refocus, get our bearings, and make some sense of the craziness that was pervading our lives. Four of us lived within a two-block radius from what became our point of stability and it was convenient to all of us. Even though David Byrd lived two miles away in an affluent upper middle class neighborhood, the two-mile distance did not separate the five of us until . . . his premature death tested our resolve.

Chapter 6
CHESTERFIELDS AND OVER-SEXTEEN

TO MANY ADULTS in our town, every summer was a season of headaches. They equated our being out of school for three months with time moving too slowly. The older these same adults got the worse the summer became for them. On many hot summer afternoons, white teenagers looking for a cool place to hang out bombarded the downtown business section. A favorite target was Belk-Tyler Department Store with its newly installed central air-conditioning system. Mr. Tyler, the store manager, hated to see any teenagers in excessive high spirits come into his store on a Friday and Saturday afternoon. Since Belk's was the only store in town with an escalator, Mr. Tyler knew too much of his time would be spent chasing teenagers off the moveable stairs, a new novelty to all of us. An often-repeated refrain among some of his workers was, "This younger generation gets bored after a week out of school and what is left for them to do? Trouble . . . they get into trouble and then more trouble." To me, these same twenty-four hour days went by too fast. And I knew before you could shake two raccoons at a rattlesnake, I would be saying, "Drat it, I have to go back to school tomorrow."

The people in our town who got downright excited about the summer were the families who were wealthy enough to take a vacation, the farmers on the outskirts of town who would bring their tobacco crop to market and those of us who were out of school and didn't have to work in the tobacco fields.

On Monday, June 3rd, our first official day out of school and away from the repetitive grinds of Charles L. Coon High School, I knew I was more than ready to take on the summer and all that it would offer. My feet hit the hardwood floor of my bedroom at 6 a.m. and I was excited, almost too anxious to get started. The sun was up, it was already hot, and the window box fans in our house were turned on. This first Monday of the month promised to be a true scorcher. Mother was in the kitchen brewing her morning Maxwell House coffee and waiting for Lily to arrive. My sister had spent the night with friends, and Daddy's daytime Negro male sitter, Jackson Nichols, would arrive by seven. Jackson was on loan to us, so to speak, from Aunt Josephine. Daddy's nursing expenses had skyrocketed and this was my aunt's way of again helping her sister. Mother accepted this assistance because she had no other choice; but, inwardly, I knew she resented having to rely on Aunt Josephine again—Mother perceived herself as a charity case and this gesture did prick her pride.

I had exactly two weeks before I would begin my summer job at Byrd's West Nash Street Drug Store. I would work four days a week making minimum wage, around one dollar an hour. According to my calculations, this would give me gas and dating money and some left over for school clothes. I bought most of my clothes from Parker's Haberdashery because Jason's dad allowed me an employee discount. Mr. Parker was good to Jason's closest friends and sometimes he didn't even charge me for the clothes I got at his store. I felt unusually good this June morning and I believed this summer would rank as my best summer ever.

Jason Parker, David Byrd, and I planned to meet around ten o'clock at one of our gathering places. Until recently, the three of us were inseparable and had been since second grade. Jason, bright and articulate, had to repeat the seventh grade putting him a year behind the rest of us—a fact that had stuck in his craw, making him impossible at times. That was the same year Jason had gone through one of his "episodes" as he called them and his psychiatrist convinced his parents to send him away for a while. In some ways, I think this was almost as hard on us as it was on him. When Jason returned from his stay in Maryland, he had a foul mouth, smoked cigarettes, and knew more dirty jokes than all of my other friends and I put together. He acted more hyper after he came back, was more argumentative, and was far more willing to take foolish risks. To make matters worse, he was determined to proselytize us so that we could enjoy participating in his coming of age as he called it. None of us wanted to be converted; at least, we didn't at that time—we were too young and didn't trust ourselves. Why should we trust Jason now? This didn't stop Jason from introducing the four of us to the seamier side of life he had proudly found in Baltimore. Unlike before his Maryland trip, he constantly acted as if he needed to prove something to each of us. Unfortunately, this behavioral pattern kept escalating and each year Jason had gotten a little worse. I knew it bothered Jason that he was a grade behind us, but he didn't want to talk about it and we honored his request.

Nothing had been quite the same between Jason and Byrd for the last year. Their friendship, if it could be called that, had weakened from constant testing, sometimes over the smallest of things. The subtle friction that existed between them had become like two pieces of coarse sandpaper rubbing against each other.

The five of us were at Jason's house on the last Saturday afternoon of April when it happened, but we didn't do one thing to stop it. We were paralyzed with fear. Jason tried to "pull" the rest of us in when Byrd and he started sparring with each other but none of us wanted to be a referee. I knew I didn't and I refused to take sides. At the end of that afternoon I knew, in my heart, I valued Byrd's friendship more than I did Jason's but I could never let Jason know this; it would kill him if he knew I felt this way.

Jason had always been there for me: he fought Tommy Eicher, the neighborhood bully, when he tried to push me in front of an oncoming car, he gave me money when I didn't have enough to buy lunch at school, and he entrusted me with a key to the backdoor of his house. Thrusting the key in my hand, he said, "Take it, Braxton, you might need a place to stay some time. Hell! If there's one thing we've got here, it's extra beds!" I used this key on Friday nights when things got really bad at our house. Sadly, my friendship with Jason had to be on his terms now and sometimes that made being with him almost unbearable. It was obvious to me that Byrd found it difficult to like this new Jason.

As I made up my bed, I relived that April 27th day at Jason's. Everything that happened that afternoon had vividly pressed itself in my memory. I knew I would never forget it. The five of us had spent a lazy afternoon not doing anything of importance; we just hung around. Mr. and Mrs. Sam Parker were at Morehead airing-out their apartment at the Bogue Sound Club for the summer season. Jason's sister, Millie, short for Mildred, was away at school in Richmond, Virginia, finishing her junior year in high school. Artis, the Parker's Negro manservant, was left in charge.

For most of the afternoon, we stationed ourselves on the worn, bulky furniture in Jason's third floor den, overlooking the Parker's backyard. The entire third floor of the Parker home had been renovated to meet the needs of the Parker's two children. Both Millie and Jason had their own bedroom with their own adjoining den. Each had a bathroom with a walk-in enclosed tile shower and off each bathroom, stood a large walk-in closet. (Jason's closet was bigger than our breakfast room.) One thing I will give Jason credit for is that he never seemed overly impressed with any of this. To Matt, Thad, and me, it was a luxury and one we never thought we would have. We believed Jason had everything any teenager could ever want.

On the south end of the third floor was another spacious room that Mr. Parker, himself, converted into a game room complete with jukebox, pool table, and two pinball machines. We named this room "The Webb." When we were in the fifth and six grades, Jason hosted several cool parties in The Webb. Many of us got our first kiss in that room while dancing to some silly, romantic song being played on the jukebox. Now shrouded in mystery, The Webb was no longer a hotbed of activity. When Jason came back from his recuperation period in the psych ward at the Maryland hospital during his initial seventh grade year, he no longer desired to go into The Webb. And he didn't want us in there. He gave no explanation. It was final. The Webb became off limits to us.

The afternoon began, mirroring the same routine as any other Saturday afternoon at Jason's. We started by listening to some of Mr. Parker's dirty Redd Foxx records. Jason and, surprisingly, Matt were the only two who seemed to appreciate Redd Foxx's humor. Thad, Byrd, and I checked out Mr. Parker's hidden sex material. From earlier visits, I knew Mr. Parker stashed his raunchy books and magazines in the back of his liquor cabinet. Under the magazines, we found three books that were familiar to me: *Sexteen, Over Sexteen* and *More Over Sexteen*. My dad had these same books and on occasions, I secretly borrowed a copy to learn about the facts of life. I thought the jokes were funny. Sometimes, the pictures disturbed me. Honestly, in thinking back, some of the sexual content was bizarre, and I can't say that at age sixteen I understood a lot of the kinky stuff. About an hour into the afternoon, Jason insisted on entertaining us by blowing smoke rings with his newly acquired taste in Chesterfield cigarettes.

Artis allowed "Master" Jason, as he called him on occasions, to do almost anything he wanted to when the Parkers left town. I had never seen Artis get angry with Jason but I had seen him discipline Jason. It had worked easily when Jason was younger but as Jason got older, there was more of a power struggle between the two of them and the bull-headed Jason usually won. Jason was not afraid of Artis and Artis was more reluctant to manhandle Jason, even with Mr. Parker's permission. "Beat the shit out of the boy if you have to," Mr. Parker often said when Mrs. Parker and he pulled away from their driveway and headed east to the coastal waterway.

The Parker's frequent trips to the beach were an opportunity for the tall, hefty, former Army corporal to escape the rigidity of Mrs. Parker. Artis was vehement when he said that Missus Parker could rival any Army sergeant. He would say, "That woman! She's just as damn mean as any Army sergeant, but she's twice as ugly." When Artis could get by with it, he became lazy and he knew that Mrs. Regina Parker continually looked for an opportunity to catch him slacking off. He also knew that he had a "good thing" going at the Parkers and he didn't want to mess it up. Artis was a good friend to us. I could count the number of colored men I actually knew on four fingers and he was the darkest and funniest of the four.

The afternoon quickly became old. Around four o'clock, Artis came upstairs to check on us. Just when I was about to say that I thought we should leave, Jason did something that frightened all of us, even Artis. It devastated David Byrd. Without any hint or warning, Jason's behavior radically changed. He got up from the water stained brown leather couch, walked barefooted across the imitation Oriental rug and into The Webb, leaving all of us puzzled.

"When did he start going back in there?" said Matt, unbelievably.

"Damn, if I know," responded Artis, shrugging. "Lately, he's been unpredictable as hell."

Jason returned shortly with his arms over his head. In one hand was a BB rifle and in the other, a pump rifle. He held both rifles high, waving them wildly. On his head was an old Daniel Boone coon cap. I knew Jason could be a practical jokester but this was different. He looked insane, his face was ashen and his eyes, wild looking, had taken on a hunted look. His facial muscles twitched nervously as he gnashed his teeth like a rabid dog. He had ripped open the front of his shirt and as if we were not present, he walked to the back of the room and stood behind the sofa. No one said anything. I looked at Artis and then, Jason.

"What in the hell are you planning, Jason?" Artis was alarmed, getting up from the pale green easy chair. "You know your Mama forbade you to touch that pump rifle!"

"My mother isn't here! What you gonna do about it?" Jason turned and moved toward the three windows overlooking the backyard. He pushed the center window open and placed both rifles on the sill. He picked up the pump rife and put it to his shoulder. He took aim. All eyes were on Jason's trigger finger. I held my breath.

"Don't do something stupid," warned Thad who normally tried to avoid confrontations. He and Matt had positioned themselves a few feet away from the sofa and faced Jason's back.

I stood to the right of the sofa trying to decide what to do. David Byrd sat on the other side of the room. I could tell he was as scared as I. I motioned for him to join me. He shook his head no. I looked at the others. Their mouths were agape as if wanting to protest. No one moved. I could hear Artis take a deep breath. At last he broke the silence.

"Put that damn rifle down now!" said Artis, pleading. "Put it down, Master Jason!" Artis moved toward Jason, his voice growing louder. Beads of perspiration formed on his forehead. His face took on a look of panic. Jason spun on his heel and stared at Artis with that same wild look in his eyes. He took one step toward Artis making me uneasy. He lifted the pump rifle high and swung it around several times. None of us moved.

"Shut-up, you shit-faced nigger!" Jason's voice was loud and savage-like. "Shut up! Shut up!" His words attacked, piercing the silence that shackled us. No one spoke for what seemed like an hour. Only the echo of Jason's vulgar, demeaning words shattered the stillness that surrounded us. I could not stand it any longer.

"Artis, he didn't mean that. Tell him you didn't mean that, Jason. Tell him!" I said. I could feel my face burning. I was scared. I didn't know what Jason would do. He kept turning, aiming the rifle at different objects in the room. I looked at David. He was out of his chair and near the door that exited to the stairway. His eyes reflected panic and he shook his head from side to side. I knew he was about to leave.

"You shut up too, Braxton, you nigger-lover!" he screamed, his voice taking on a viciousness that was foreign even to Jason. "Get the hell out of my house. All of *you!* I mean it—Get the *hell out—now."*

Jason turned away for a minute. When he turned back his face was contorted, he breathed heavily, and his eyes had rolled back in his head. His mouth drooled and his lips moved but no words came out.

"Damn it, Jason, give me the rifle," said the black corporal in a commanding voice that scared the hell out of all of us, but not Jason. Without flinching, he lifted the rifle, aiming at Artis.

"*No, Jason! What's wrong with you?*" I screamed, realizing I should have kept my mouth shut. "Artis, please, he's not himself. Look at him." I stepped closer. "Do something, Artis!"

"Be quiet, Braxton," said Artis.

"Yeah, Braxton, do what the nigger says!"

"Jason, I am telling you this one last time. Give me the rifle!" Artis moved another step closer to Jason.

"Don't butt in, Artis. Remember you're hired help. Niggers are plentiful in this town so you better do what I tell you," said Jason. The tone of his voice was unfamiliar, almost demonic. He spoke in a deeper, guttural voice that solicited fear. He raised the rifle again and pointed toward the mirror hanging against the game room wall.

Jason's head shook and drool continued to collect around his mouth. I had seen Jason pull some dumb stunts but I had never seen him behave like this.

"Let's go. All of us! Now! You, too, Artis," ordered another voice, but this time the speaker stood in the hall. It was David Byrd. I thought he had hightailed it downstairs.

Jason stood transfixed. His eyes frightened me. Taking a deep breath, Jason moved to the windows again. He appeared to be staring into the backyard. It was as if he was there bodily but mentally he was somewhere else. I knew something was powerfully wrong with him but I didn't know what. This scene had not been rehearsed and it was fifteen minutes too long in production.

"Jason, please stop! You're scaring the shit out of me." I knew I had to do something. "Please put the rifle down!" Without hesitation, I moved directly in front of him, blocking his view of the outside. Continuing, I looked straight into his eyes, pleading. The expression in his eyes told me he could not see me. I could feel the flesh on my face tightening and there was a sudden rush of energy moving upward from within my chest to the top of my head giving me a sudden, dizzy feeling. I didn't know this person. I moved away sensing something awful was about to happen. A chill overtook my body and I started sweating profusely. The realization that I was alone with Jason heightened my fear; everyone else had slipped outside, including Artis. They had moved to the carport on the eastside of the three story brick Tudor home. Jason dropped the rifle. I grabbed it when it hit the floor.

"You see those two birds, Braxton? Which should I shoot?" Jason, picking up his BB rifle, directed me to the backyard. He pointed the rifle toward the fountain area adjacent to the swimming pool. I moved closer to the window, again nudging my way in front of him. I could feel his hot breath on my chin and neck.

"What birds?" I was afraid he would shoot David. "What in God's name are you talking about?" I took one step sideways, getting out of his aim, hoping I could think of a way to detain him. "I don't know what you're talking about! Where? Show me!"

He hesitated and grinned. "Your good friend, David Byrd, and the red bird sitting on the birdbath, you dumb ass! Get out of my way!" He pushed me aside with his right shoulder.

"*Jason!*" Before I could finish, Jason aimed the rifle and shot through the screen at his target. "*My God! What have you done?*" I gasped not wanting to look. Then Jason let out a chilling scream and fell to the floor. His heels kicked hard against the wooden floor and his head banged against the floor, keeping rhythm with his feet. I didn't know what to do.

I grabbed a pillow off the sofa and put it under Jason's head. And then turning toward the screen, I yelled for Artis as loudly as I could. There was no response. Fearing what I might find outside, I ran down the three flights of red-carpeted stairs. Taking two and three steps at a time, I banged up against the wall knocking several pictures off their hangers. Pushing the back screened door open, I dashed outside, tripping over a cement flower urn.

My visibly shaken friends stood behind the fountain area looking down on a wounded cardinal. A small spot of blood covered its wing. I looked at David Byrd. He had been winged too, but in the heart.

"Artis, Jason has fallen on the floor," I said, excitedly. "He's acting funny. He's having some kind of a fit."

"*Oh blessed Jesus!*" Artis took off running back toward the house. "Jason! Jason! Jason!" Running back into the house, his screams pierced the stillness of the moment bringing us back to reality.

I turned toward David Byrd. His sandy blonde hair had fallen in his face. It was stuck to the top of his forehead, having been matted by sweat. He stood quietly, just looking at the cardinal, breathing heavily, and moaning. This young boy loved by girls for his easy manner had taken on the pain of the fallen bird. Byrd, the fastest runner I knew, had a compassion for animals that I was envious of. This was evident—he was the only one among us who seemed both hurt and sad when Jason winged that cardinal with his BB gun.

Matt told me later that when the cardinal fell from the birdbath, Byrd ran to it without hesitation and turned it on its side. The cardinal lived in Byrd's garage for over three weeks while he doctored it. He fed it chicken broth and put iodine on the wound. His medicinal supplies came from his father's pharmaceutical bag comprised of salesmen freebies. I was there the day he set the cardinal free and we watched together as it flew away.

"No question about it," I said. "You are the bird man, David." He laughed and I knew I loved him and wanted him to be my friend for life. This was the day I unconsciously nicknamed him "Bird." He preferred it be spelled like his last name, Byrd.

A calmer Jason called me several days later. His parents wasted no time in returning that same night after receiving a frantic call from Artis. Jason spent the next day and a half in the hospital undergoing neurological tests. I didn't know what that meant at that time and out of respect, I didn't ask him then. Jason did tell me that he had something he needed to show me. I thought whatever it was might explain his bizarre behavior. He said he would have to wait until the timing was right. Once again, it had to be on his terms.

Jason never apologized to any of us for his actions. In his typical cavalier manner, he just pretended the whole thing never happened and assumed we would go on being friends as usual. He only gave me an explanation. It was just as well because I'm not certain that even he fully understood what actually happened that April afternoon. None of us understood the medical implications; at least, we didn't at the time. Matt, Thad, and I continued to be good friends with Jason and we put the traumatic events of that afternoon behind us. This was not true for David Byrd; he became more reticent in Jason's presence. It was almost as if Byrd was afraid of Jason. Maybe he was. He had reason to be.

"Braxton, what are you doing in that room?" Lily's soft, firm voice penetrated the screen of my bedroom window that overlooked the back porch.

"Making up my bed. Why?"

"Your breakfast is gonna get cold," she said. "Ain't never taken you that long to make up that bed."

"I'm almost through," I said. "Just a minute, please."

"Come on out here," said Lily. "*Right now!*"

Chapter 7
CAPONS AND REGINA ALEXANDER

LILY GRIFFIN HAD worked for us since I had been in elementary school. Lily came when my mother, still somewhat uncertain of herself, returned from the hospital after a four-month recuperation period for nervous exhaustion. I loved Lily like a second mother and I knew I was one of her favorites. She always took up for me, especially when she thought my mother unjustly criticized me. "You just gonna sit out there on that back porch and not help me?" Lily stood in the kitchen doorway with both hands on her hips looking at me over the top of her red-rimmed glasses. She was wearing a starched one-piece gray uniform with a white apron accented by large red earbobs about the size of a silver dollar and several reddish colored bracelets that matched the frame of her glasses. "Did you hear me, young man?" She stepped matter-of-factly onto the back porch swinging her right hand in my direction.

"What?" I pushed the week old newspaper aside. "What did you say?"

"What's wrong with you this morning, Braxton?" said Lily. "You was like this yesterday morning too. Are you sick?"

"No, just human, like you."

"Humans don't go acting that way, least not where I come from. You act like you're in another place on this here planet."

In the early '40s, Lily and Nathan Griffin moved to the United States from Canada. They had been married one year and came south looking for good jobs and to be near relatives. Their search brought them to North Carolina and, eventually, to Wilson. Her husband landed a respectable job for a Negro as an assistant foreman at one of Wilson's largest tobacco warehouses. Lily chose domestic help.

"I'm sorry, Lily." I said. "I really am."

"Don't hand me that sorry routine again, Braxton." She raised her eyebrows and her glasses moved up her nose. "If you're not gonna help me, just please move. I need to have that table to polish Miss Virginia's silver." Lily walked out to the porch where I sat and swatted me playfully on the back of the head with her hand. She picked up my plate and silverware and walked back into the kitchen. I turned to see her standing over the sink, washing the remaining breakfast dishes.

As I watched Lily maneuver around the kitchen straightening the canisters and wiping off the large white G.E. stove, I thought about Jason Parker, David Byrd and myself, and what we shared in common. Each of us had at least one sister. Byrd had twin sisters, two years older than he, and like Jason's sister, they attended boarding school in another state. We believed our dads were incapable of understanding us and at best, were too autocratic in their demands. They never showed us any overt affection, and their desires for our futures were self-serving. In the father-son relationship, I thought my situation had become the most tolerable because of my father's waning condition. This was about to change.

When we were in elementary and junior high school, it was our mothers who had been more willing to accept us as we were; at least that was the image they portrayed. They were relaxed in our presence and showed a genuine interest in our friends. Once in high school, Mrs. Parker and Mrs. Byrd seemed to have less time for their sons and their son's friends. My mother continued to welcome us when possible and thus became a surrogate mother to Byrd and Jason.

On the outside, our home lives appeared to be normal and perhaps the envy of some of our peers who lived in similar situations as we without realizing they shared this commonality. On the inside of our homes, there was turmoil of different dimensions, sometimes explosive and dangerous. Each of our mothers coped with these differing pressures in their own home in a similar way. They chose to imbibe at the end of each day. Rarely was there ever an exception to this ritual. Each had her own preferred friend whether it was Jack Daniels, Chevis Regal or a Tom Collins. Sometimes, they satisfied themselves with too many "old fashions" followed by nightly medications. It was a miracle the combination did not kill them.

Only David Byrd had a younger brother, Chad, short for Charles. Chad was twelve years old and a rising eighth grader at Charles L. Coon Junior High School. Jason and I would return to Coon High School in the fall but Byrd's father told him that he would attend his alma mater, a private preparatory school in Virginia, for his final two years of high school. Family tradition would win this battle. Mr. Byrd's preparatory alma mater, without question, would be David's and if Oscar Byrd had his way and he usually did, it would be Chad's.

My thoughts drifted to the other members of our group, Matt Beatty and Thad Ruffin. Both lived in comfortable homes and their fathers took as active a role in parenting as their mothers. From David's, Jason's, and my perspective, their lives seemed unscathed by those disturbances plaguing our lives and homes. Sometimes I envied Matt and Thad and the closeness they seemingly enjoyed with both of their parents. And because Matt and Thad were close to their parents, they were teased and called yo-yo or square. This happened to Matt more than Thad.

When Warren Bridgers told Matt that his mother sucked camel toes, he was reminded that none of my friends were yo-yos or squares.

I helped Lily carry the silver out to the back porch table then completed my early morning chores. Already it was as hot as blue blazes inside our house so I could only imagine how unbearable it would be outside. Shortly before 10:00 A.M. on Wednesday, June 5th, our third day out of school, I walked onto the back porch and waved goodbye to Lily who stood under the towering walnut tree in our backyard taking a cigarette break. She smiled and waved back. I found Mother in Anne's room and told her that I would be with Byrd and Jason and I promised to be back within an hour and a half.

Our living quarters were more cramped now since Mother had turned our dining room into a makeshift bedroom for my father. His door was closed when I walked by. That was not unusual because it was always closed. Last night there had been too much noise and movement in his room. I was curious to know what had happened but I was too smart to ask yet. I understood that there might never be a right time to ask. I opened the screened door and before I remembered, I let it go; it slammed hard against the doorframe. This always disturbed Mother and she told me repeatedly not to slam any door because it bothered my father. I was glad to be outside if only for a little while.

Sometimes when Jason and I wanted to sneak a few smokes together, we would meet behind the chicken coops that Mr. Ross had erected in the far end of his backyard. In 1957 in Wilson, there was no city ordinance against having fowls on one's property. I looked across the street. Mr. Ross' Lincoln was gone. Even though he had retired, he still liked to go back to his nursery business and watch over the plants and flowers he had nurtured for years. Crossing the street, I waved to Mrs. Thurston. She stopped sweeping her walkway long enough to ask about Mother and Daddy. Skippy laid in a dirt pit he had dug under their rope hammock, the one Mr. Thurston proudly said came from Pauley's Island, South Carolina. Mr. Thurston had carefully tied what had become our weather beaten swinging bed to the only magnolia tree on our block. Over the years, all of us, in our neighborhood, took turns laying on our backs against the frayed roping, holding onto the sides with our strongest grip as our friends turned the hammock over and over as fast as their arms would let them. We prided ourselves on which one of us stayed in the hammock the longest. No longer able to serve as our swing, it stood as a memorial, a memory of shared good times on Kincaid Avenue when as children, trouble did not exist in our minds.

I walked up the neatly trimmed driveway that Mr. Ross carefully tended, stopping once to look at my watch. It was 9:55 A.M. I was five minutes early. I strolled up to the chicken coops. No one was there save the capons and a few Rhode Island Reds and one rooster. I sat on the hard dirt and watched a colony of ants as they moved about their morning routine, performing their duties with a restlessness that equaled the restless pacing of my mind. My thoughts returned to my father and the different noises I had heard coming from his room. I recognized the screams but I was uncertain of the other male voice. I realized my father's pains must have increased for him to yell as much as he did. There had been an unfamiliar knocking sound coming from his room and I heard what I thought was a chair falling on the floor. The extent of his suffering was never discussed with me. It was as if Mother tried to shield me from the horrible realities taking place across the hall from where I slept.

A little after ten, Jason rounded the side of the coop on my backside in hopes of scaring me but I saw his reflection on the large, outside mirror attached to the side of the chicken coop that faced me. Mr. Ross had a theory about mirrors. He believed that various reflections in addition to the sun bouncing off the mirror would frighten any squirrels or birds of prey. His theory worked.

"Sorry I'm late," Jason greeted me. "I had to clean my room before I could leave." Since the April debacle, Jason's father held him more accountable to completing household chores. I thought this was good for Jason because he'd been ruthlessly lazy when it came to holding up his end in his home. The rest of us had our duties. Now Jason had to fall in line with us rather than standing on the sideline bragging about how he "was of the manor born" and Artis was paid to do his chores. There would never be another like Jason Parker. Despite all of his unlikable outside qualities, I knew there was some good in his heart. We just had to look closer now to find the goodness.

Jason alluded to that incident in April only once with me. The only thing he told me was that his doctor had put him on a stronger kind of medicine—a kind that might help his temperament level out. He offered no other specifics and he never volunteered any other forms of discipline or punishment that his parents might have given him. I never asked for further explanation.

"That's okay. I was watching these ants," I said, pointing to their attempts at carrying the loose grains of corn and breadcrumbs. "I wonder if these ants ever get tired of their routine. They never stop. Makes me tired looking at them." I had lost some of my early morning exuberance and had become uncomfortable sitting in the bright sun. Sweat was encircling my neck, dripping down my chest, and settling in my little roll of extra stomach.

"I've never thought about it." Jason flicked one of the ants with his forefinger and I watched the small grain of yellow corn fly against the coop. The ant was unhurt and his movement continued as if nothing had happened. Jason pulled his Chesterfield pack from his shirt pocket; then taking one out, he packed it against the top of his left hand and lit it. In my eyes, Jason Parker had become a pro at the smoking routine. He took a long drag on his cigarette while squinting through the sunlight hitting his face. "Want a smoke?"

"I brought my own. Thanks anyway." I reached in my shirt pocket and pulled one of three filter king Kools that I had pilfered from Mother's pack, hoping the missing cigarettes would go undetected. My mother smoked so much I doubted she would miss any. About the only time I smoked was when I was alone with Jason. I had almost learned to inhale and I actually enjoyed the cool, smooth menthol taste as the smoke traveled down my throat and back out my nose.

"Here's a light," Jason popped the top of his silver Zippo lighter and the flame nearly singed my nose. "Watch out, Braxton! Don't clutch! You're still new at this."

"Hold your hand still," I inhaled, coughing slightly. I decided to ignore his comment, letting him think he was my mentor when it came to giving advice on how to smoke. I inhaled again and this time I muffled my cough by swallowing some of the smoke. It was foul tasting and I opened my mouth, instantly releasing the remaining smoke. I gagged and Jason laughed. I laughed too, watching him mimic me. The cigarette in my hand continued to burn. I tried again. I knew I would eventually get the hang of it if I practiced. And I didn't want to be the continued brunt of Jason's teasing. I refused to give him that satisfaction.

I sat there a long time with Jason. Neither of us said anything. We were content to just smoke. I could hear the chickens cackling behind me, trying to break our silence. Occasionally, they would stick their beaks through the chicken wire attempting to peck my arm. Several attempted to fly, hitting the wire and stirring a thick layer of dust and molten feathers lying on the floor. Jason's only comments were several deep sighs.

The rays of the morning sun fell on the ground around us making me more aware of the heat so common this time of year. It was a headache kind of heat—the kind that could affect a person's breathing, making it shallow. The smell of the chickens combined with the odor of manure emanating from Mr. Ross' compost pile was not helping either of our breathing any more than the smoke we inhaled. I was afraid I might puke at any minute.

On this particular morning, Jason, himself, smelled like week-old molded bread. Jason was normally neat in his attire but, today, he even looked like he had slept in his clothes. Something was wrong and he was deliberately not telling me.

"What are you pissed off about this morning?" I asked bluntly. Jason didn't answer. He looked annoyed and distracted. I noticed that both his eyes were red like he had been crying. Jason cry—not Jason—he never cried—too macho—too much like his idol, John Wayne.

I stared at Jason and the cigarette casually dangling out of his mouth, envious of his good looks. Despite the fact that his face was covered in sweat, Jason, especially when he smoked, looked like he could handle anything. He looked cool, and calm, and in control—just like those studs in the cigarette ads in magazines. I wanted to hold a cigarette and look rugged and cool. It wouldn't work with me. Hell, I couldn't even inhale one without choking.

Hidden under the beads of sweat on Jason's chin, there were stubby hairs poking out. I was taken aback and for the first time, I realized Jason shaved. I didn't think Matt and Byrd shaved but I wasn't certain about Thad. Being able to shave was important to me—it was a right of passage into the grown-up world that I desperately wanted to enter. Several of my classmates began the ritual last year but I had never even considered that one of my close buddies might have started. Unfortunately, I was without facial hair. Inwardly, I envied Jason even more.

As a little boy, I had always wanted to imitate my father when he shaved. I watched in awe when he began his morning routine, wanting to participate in some way. First, he would take his position at our old porcelain lavatory and meticulously mix the cream in his wooden shaving bowl. Next, he would take out his Gillette safety razor and with the hand of an artist, clear his skin without a single cut. I thought my father was a master and he made shaving something I hungered to do in order to be like him. I even thought about the times we might shave together. This would never happen now. Shaving himself was no longer an option for my father. Simple things like standing for a short interval of more than one minute pained him. In addition, his face had thinned terribly allowing the veins of his cheek and neck to take residence too close to the surface. Now he went days without shaving and when someone did shave him, it was too horrible to watch.

Jason took another drag on his cigarette and blew smoke at me. He waited for a moment. Then he spoke, "Damn, Braxton, when in hell is this humidity going to leave us? I'm about to die out here."

"Huh?" I stared at Jason but I was still thinking about my dad.

"I hate this heat. When will it ever let up?"

"It's still early June. You know it's going to get worse. It's not even prime tobacco season yet and the humidity will get a far sight worse then," quoting what I had heard my father say many times before. "And it's not just the humidity. Take a deep breath," I said, swatting the flies off my arm. "These flies like hot weather and where there is fertilizer there will be flies."

"Especially around a damn chicken coop," Jason laughed half-heartedly. "Feathers, chicken shit, humidity, and heat—what a damn combination." He laughed again. Jason defined being cool and in control. A smoker wasn't supposed to let anything rattle him but something bugged Jason. I wanted to know what.

"I can't stay long, Jason. I think we should get the five of us together this Saturday night at Dick's. What do you think? Can you be there?" I smiled. I was glad to hear him laugh again. It had been a long time and today, I thought in some ways despite the way he looked, he seemed more like his old self. I did not want to be wrong.

"If I can get out of the house, I'll be there." Jason punctuated his answer by obliterating an ant with the hot end of his cigarette.

"For crying out loud, Jason! What did you do that for?" I grimaced, realizing the burning ash had consumed the ant.

"Just felt like it," Jason responded, rubbing what remained of his cigarette against the ground with the palm of his right hand. No longer the smoker, he had lost his coolness. "Where is Byrd? Isn't he coming this morning or is he still bent out of shape with me?" Jason's tone took on a sudden anxiousness that had been clearly absent until he brought Byrd into our conversation. "He used to be 'with it!' Screw him!"

At first I didn't answer, wondering what was happening with him. Is this another mood change? They were becoming all too frequent with him. Okay, give him a chance, Braxton. What did Jason want to tell me? Jason's demeanor was changing again. His voice got deeper and his new expression matched the tone of his voice. Jason had gotten so he would change his voice when he wanted to be serious and taken seriously. "I thought he would be here. That's what he told me last night," I said. This was the closest Jason had come to referring to that unforgettable spring afternoon at his house. I took out another Kool.

"You shouldn't smoke, Braxton."

"Why not? You do."

"It doesn't suit you." Jason said. "You look spastic; besides, it'll stunt your growth."

"Then I won't inhale." I hated it when he took cheap shots at me. "Just light it, Jason!"

"Oh, you'll inhale all right. You'll do anything until you get it right."

I didn't know whether Jason intended his comment as a joke or whether he had insulted me. Either way, I didn't like it.

"Jason, just light the damn cigarette!"

"You shouldn't curse either."

"Don't lecture me on morals! You, of all people."

"Anybody that goes to church as much as . . . " He stopped, changing the subject abruptly. "Get your cigarette ready."

"Don't get too close this time." After lighting it, he pulled out another Chesterfield.

"Well, at least, you're getting the habit, Braxton. Your dad would be proud of you. You're helping put food on your table." Jason laughed again—this time it was forced.

"You seem to be in a better mood again," I said. Since his mood kept changing, I decided to probe a little to see if I could get any kind of a response.

"Well, I'm not—not really. You want to know why?"

Yes, I want to know. I want to know now but to him, I said nothing. I waited. Why do we have to play games with each other?

"You remember that day back in April when I told you that I wanted to show you something—something that might explain some of my behavior." I wondered if this was another one of his excuses—a refusal to accept responsibility.

"Yes. I think so," I said, anxious but hesitant, not wanting to say the wrong thing. Jason's expression changed. He lifted his eyebrows causing his forehead to furrow. There was a deep frown on his face and suddenly he looked too serious for Jason Parker. His earlier sophistication was gone.

"Well, at first, I changed my mind. That's why I haven't said anything more about it to you. I wanted to figure out the best way to tell you this plus I had to figure it out for myself." Jason looked at me. There was a pronounced sadness in his eyes. Then he carefully took an envelope out of his back pocket, ran his hand across its face to smooth the wrinkles and handed it to me. "Can you keep a secret?"

"If I have to, I can."

"You have to. I want you to read what's inside." Jason hesitated. I was afraid he might change his mind. I tried to contain myself.

"Okay. Give it to me! You make it sound so mysterious." When I saw the face of the envelope, I immediately stopped talking. My eyes widened. On the outside I saw in a woman's handwriting "Children's Home-Adoption only." I looked at Jason. "Ah! What does this mean?"

"I'm not trying to make an excuse or nothing about my behavior that day, but this might help you understand me a little. I found this that morning while I rummaged around in Mother's closet for some 45-rpm records she'd taken from me. I saw this shoebox tucked way back in the back corner so I pulled it out. It was marked personal—to be given to Jason only when he is ready. You know me. I'm not going to turn down an invitation like that." He stopped again almost like he had lost his train of thought. "Go on, Braxton, open it and read it."

I pulled the worn paper out and saw a birth certificate. The child's name was Robert Jason Alexander. The mother's name was Miss Regina Rosetta Alexander and the word miss was underlined. The daddy's name was . . . there was none. The certificate stated that the father was not known. The place of birth was Danville, Virginia, at Danville Community Hospital. The date of birth was May 20, 1941. I looked at Jason and saw fear in his eyes. It was his first name and his birth date.

"Are you saying this is you?" I said. Before he could answer, I blurted, "Maybe it's another boy?"

"No, Braxton. It's *me!* And my mother was *not married!*" Jason looked depressed now. I wondered what I could say to make things better. "I don't even know who *my real father is!* That's a crock of shit for you." His Chesterfied froze between his lips.

"Wait, Jason. Hang loose! Not so fast." I stammered. Jason looked crestfallen. He sat motionless.

"This better be good, Braxton." Jason lifted his drooped head. His face had lost all of its animation. He had a lost look, almost desperate.

"Maybe your mother worked there. She was a nurse, wasn't she?" I knew this answer was going to get us nowhere.

"Yeah . . . Right! She was a nurse. You don't know what you're talking about, Braxton."

"Hold on!" I said. "It could've happened that way."

"And shit comes from churned butter."

"Get serious, Jason!"

"Okay, Braxton . . . what are you saying?" He gave me a weird look like he was disgusted. "You think that's how she got me? She had contacts or something?" Jason cleared his throat. "Brilliant Braxton . . . real clever."

"I don't know . . . I thought maybe she might have adopted you." For some reason, "adoption" carried an ugly connotation. "I'm sorry, Jason. It was just a thought." I shouldn't have said anything. I should keep my big mouth shut.

"*Think about this*—maybe my old lady got knocked up by some doctor who was already married. What do you think of that?" Jason had a point. "Well, what do you think, Einstein?"

"Well, I . . . I . . . I don't know what to say, Jason. I . . . I'm sorry." I paused and took a deep breath. It was too hot and the heat was interfering with my capacity to think clearly. "Have you talked to your mother yet?"

"Are you shitting me? Do you think I'm going to bring this up now after all that's happened?" Jason angrily threw the butt of his cigarette into the chicken coop I was leaning against.

"For Christ's sake, Jason. You asked me. I didn't mean to upset you."

"Braxton, you didn't upset me. I'm already upset. Don't you know what this means? Don't you?" he said, trying hard to restrain his anger.

"What are you talking about Jason? I mean, what's the big deal?"

"*The big deal?* Do you have a loose screw, Braxton? *The big deal?*" Jason gazed at the chickens running around inside the coop. "Braxton, what it means is . . . that . . ." He stopped, took a deep breath, and screamed, "*I'm a bastard!*" One look at Jason was enough of a reminder that he wasn't accustomed to being humiliated.

I looked down at the letter again, reread the name on the birth certificate, and I stood, looking at Jason. "I don't care. I'm still your friend. I don't care if you are a bastard. Besides, lots of kids get adopted."

"Braxton, *I'm a bastard!*" He looked away and then turned back. His eyes met mine. "Do you know what a *bastard* is, Braxton? Do you?" he stood, grabbing me. Tears ran down his cheeks. "My God, I'm *illegitimate*. I'm one of those bastard children every one makes fun of."

"Your parents still love you, Jason," I assured him. Jason heaved and fought back the tears. I wanted to hold him and tell him to cry but I didn't know how. He heaved again and again and finally turned away from me, putting his hands to his face, letting it out, and sobbing loudly in jerks. His body arched forward each time he sobbed. I wanted to reach out to him but I just stood behind him until he stopped. Finally, I mustered the nerve to speak, "What are you going to do?"

"I don't know. I'm so confused. The mother and father I thought I did have . . . one or both are not my real parents. They get on me all the time for lying and they're bigger liars than I am. Those S.O.B.'s! How can I ever trust them again?" He lit another cigarette. "Fuck, I can't trust them. I might as well . . ." He didn't finish. Instead, he took a step backwards, stood rigid, and stared at me, picking at the mole on the side of his neck.

For the first time in my life, I felt uncomfortable with Jason. I knew he wanted me to respond but I did not have an answer for him. Finally I spoke, uncertain of what I would say. "Give it some time, Jason. I know things will work out." The expression on his haggard face told me I was being of no help but I already knew this. Hell, I had no basis for what I was saying and I had no reason to believe anything would work out for anyone. This summer vacation was going to hell in a hand basket and fast.

"Anyway, do you want to hear what else the old man who calls himself my father is going to do with me? He's sending me away to military school next year. I guess they don't want a bastard son living under the same roof with them, especially a crazy one. *What the fuck, Braxton? What the fuck . . . what am I to do?*" He turned toward the other chicken coop. Beads of sweat stood on the back of his neck and his shirt, wet with perspiration from the midday sun, clung to his back.

"Jason, give me some time to think," I said. "I need time to think." I watched him shake his head. He turned and faced me again. Tears dripped from his eyes and brown dirt was unevenly smeared across his face from the many times he had unknowingly wiped it with his fingers, the same fingers that had drawn circles on the dusty ground where we had sat.

I looked at my watch and it was 11:25. "Oh, crap! Jason, I told Mother I would be back at 11:00. She'll give me more chores if I don't get home. I'm sorry, I really am. I'll call you later, I promise." I felt like a heel having to leave.

"Promise me that you won't tell the others?"

"I promise. That's your call." I forced a smile and grabbed his hand attempting to shake it. He was pathetic—like a little boy needing comfort from a daddy who has spurned him.

We walked out to Kincaid Avenue. Jason turned left and walked toward Nash Street. I walked across the street to my house. Lily stood in the kitchen waiting. She had fixed tomato sandwiches, sweet iced tea, and some of her key lime pie. The thought of losing two of my best friends to prep schools took away my appetite. I didn't have a good feeling about the way this summer vacation had begun.

Jason and I stayed friends. We identified with each other's infirmities. At times, ours was a less than positive bond. Our differences had started forging a wedge in our friendship. I'm not even certain how much we really liked each other. But we continued to go to each other's houses, do things together, and support each other like we were good friends.

At lunch my mother was preoccupied and did not seem to notice that I was upset. Her comment without any correction, "I guess you boys had a good time this morning since you were so late," was unlike her because she was usually more perceptive. Lily took notice but I shook my head, signaling not now. I passed the afternoon doing various chores for my mother. After two hours of pulling weeds in Mother's flowerbeds, I still didn't have an answer for Jason. I was determined to think of something that would make him feel better about being adopted.

Chapter 8
A China Doll

SHORTLY BEFORE FIVE o'clock, Mother asked me to walk down to Rita Stallings and borrow a cup of sugar. Rita and Harry, nicknamed Bo-Bo, lived several houses down from us on the same side of the street. The Stallings were a young, progressive couple with four boys, all under the age of eight. Mr. Stallings, like my father, was a tobacconist with Exeter Tobacco Company. Three things were murmured in the shadows of Kincaid Avenue about this unique pair: they were nudists, they liked to party, and they enjoyed sex.

I could smell the scotch before Rita Stallings opened the screened door all the way to let me in her house. Dressed in dark blue, her outfit was a stark contrast to her China doll complexion and rose-colored cheeks. She smiled, lifting her hands, one holding her glass and the other a cigarette, to give me a hug. My eyes moistened reacting to the sweet smell of her perfume. For a moment, I thought my allergies had kicked in. As she leaned forward, I blinked and then I did a double take when I saw her large boobs bouncing inside her loosely fitted housecoat. Her nipples were hard and they glistened. Her long brown hair fell across my shoulders as she leaned into me and kissed me on the cheek. I could feel a sweet stiffening inside my pants. I knew immediately I wanted to stay next to her as long as possible.

"Let the boy have some air," called a short, obese figure standing only in his underpants in the dining area. Mr. Stallings came forward and greeted me with a firm handshake. He was no taller than five-feet-eight inches, weighed at least two hundred and twenty pounds, and his hairy stomach was his most prominent feature. He was fairly good-looking and muscular and as solid a man as I had ever seen.

"Come with me, Braxton, honey, and I'll get you that cup of sugar," Rita's sexy voice commanded as she grabbed and squeezed my hand, leading me to the kitchen. "Your mother called to save you the embarrassment of asking. My, my, you're getting to be a cutie. I bet all the girls are chasing you." I caught another whiff of scotch as she spoke. Standing back, she rested her arms on the crest of her breasts and looked at me and smiled. I was noticeably uncomfortable. Then she winked. She was beautiful—her slender fingers, her deep red lips matching the color of her long nails, and her mountainous breasts jumping around like water balloons inside her housecoat. To me, Rita Stallings was a goddess. Jason Parker would be so jealous.

"Not quite," I said. "At least not the ones I wish would chase me." I attempted a smile, thinking she must have a thing for stocky men. "Oh . . . here's the cup Mother sent for the sugar."

"Sometimes girls are fickle, Braxton. They'll come to their senses," she said, taking the cup and carefully filling it with sugar. When she had finished, she wet her right forefinger and gently stuck it inside the sugar bag. Methodically removing it again from the bag, she ran her tongue down her finger in a slow, deliberate manner licking off the sugar. I didn't know the proper response to her tongue motion. I was confused. *Why was she teasing me?* As she handed the cup back to me, she leaned into me and pressed her body against mine and whispered in my ear, "Braxton, honey, if you ever get lonely, call me and I'll make you feel better."

"Yes ma'am," I stammered. *Had I heard her correctly?* My mouth felt dry, like it had been stuffed with cotton balls. "Thank you for the sugar," I said, taking the cup from her hand. Mrs. Stallings picked up her drink glass from the counter and followed me back into the living room. I wondered if her husband had watched us and if so, did what he saw bother him?

"Braxton, how is your dad? Is he doing any better?" asked Mr. Stallings, standing again at the bar in the dining room.

"No, Sir," I said, watching him pour dark liquid into his glass with one hand. With his other hand, he rubbed a cube of ice across his sweaty chest. "I need to get back home. Thank you for asking, Mr. Stallings."

"Tell him the tobacco market misses him," said Mr. Stallings.

"Yes, Sir, I will. Thank you for the sugar, Mrs. Stallings," I said, opening the front screened door. I didn't want to leave.

"You can call me Rita," she said rolling the "r" and we both stepped onto the front stoop. "And remember to call me when you need me. I mean that, Braxton. I really do." She leaned into me again, deliberately letting me see her breasts. *Take a good look, Braxton. My God! They were gorgeous. Oh no!* My mouth was suddenly dry again. My tongue moved restlessly inside trying to find a comfort zone. I wanted to lick her breasts.

"Yes, ma'am," I said, sheepishly. "Thank you." I walked away in a daze thinking about three things: Why was this beautiful woman coming on to me, and why didn't her husband squash her when he was on top, and when could I see Rita again?

At ten o'clock, I went to bed. I was tired and perplexed and I could not get either Jason or Rita out of my thoughts. I had given Jason's situation little attention and my visit with Rita Stallings had begun to have a strange, tantalizing affect on me. I fell asleep wondering if I would ever take Rita up on her offer. It was a pleasant thought for a sixteen-year-old whose serious kissing experience had been with only one girl.

Shortly before midnight, I awoke to noises coming from my father's bedroom. Not wanting to be detected, I left my room quietly and walked across the hall. A light came from under my father's closed door and he had shouted something. Mother pleaded with him to stop his ranting. Pressing the wall with both palms to keep my balance, I slid to my knees. Using my right eye to see through the keyhole, my gaze fell immediately upon my father. He was in his normal position in his rocking chair, his back supported by pillows. Mother stood beside him. I held my breath as he spoke again, "Damn it, Virginia, I've already told you I do *not* want Don Carlton as one of my pallbearers. He's the son of a bitch who stole countless money from the company. The only reason he still has a job is because he's the brother-in-law of Dick Thornton, a vice president in Richmond."

"You don't have to be talking about your funeral arrangements tonight, Louis," said my mother. "Please stop and try to rest."

"Rest? Did you say rest? You know damn well I'm at death's door. How can I rest?" He threw his coffee cup across the room hitting the door I was leaning against. Startled, I fell backwards. At the same time I heard pieces of the cup hit the floor. Mother started crying.

"Don't do this to me, Louis!" she begged. "I can't take it much longer." Putting my eye back against the keyhole, I saw her lean over my dad and wipe his forehead.

"Virginia, this is not living. I'm ready to die," he said, choking. "Please get me some water."

I knelt there not able to move, hoping that I had misheard my father, hoping that his words were part of a bad dream. My father continued to cough. I wanted to get the water myself and take it to him. Then he would know I had heard. I couldn't risk that—that would allow him to twist my intentions into something that they were not. I walked back to my room and closed the door. I got back in bed and cried myself to sleep.

Chapter 9
JASON AND JAMES DEAN TO THE RESCUE

I GLANCED AT the clock on my bedside table. It was 5:00 A.M. and I was tired. An early morning sun had begun to sneak under the shades that covered the two windows that sat on the driveway side of my bedroom. Not a sound could be heard in the house. It was too early to consider getting up so I decided to stay in bed a little longer. I lay there thinking about the dispute I overheard between my parents. My room was suddenly alive with their voices and I recounted again what I had heard my father say about dying. I knew things were serious.

The next time I saw the hands on my clock it was 6:20 A.M. My concern for my parents had been lost in an early morning dream of Rita Stallings. I felt a sense of contentment that was evidenced by the sticky moisture that clung to my pajama pants. As much as I wanted to linger in this rapture, the situation needed my immediate attention. I slid out of bed like a snake and began to investigate my bed sheets. Only a small amount of moisture appeared on the bottom sheet and fortunately, none had penetrated the mattress. I slid quietly across the hardwood floor of my bedroom. At the hall door I glanced around and saw Mother was not where she was supposed to be. I tiptoed into the bathroom, grabbed my bath cloth off the tub's side, wet it, and returned to my room. First, I wet the sheet to remove any stain and next, I wiped the groin area of my pajamas. My salvation was in my memory: this was laundry day and my sheets and nightclothes would be a part of the wash. I stripped my bed of its covers, stopping only to fantasize about the possibility of being next to Rita in bed with our bodies rubbing against each other.

After I dressed, I walked through the hall and into the kitchen. I tiptoed into the breakfast room and gently pushed the swinging door that led into my father's room. Mother lay on her side on the twin bed my father no longer used. Her back was towards me and only her snoring told me she was asleep. Of course, she would deny this when she awoke. My father sat in his rocking chair facing the black and white Motorola television set that had become his closest friend. I watched the snow dance across the fifteen-inch screen. The national anthem was playing above the static, telling me that the station was delayed in welcoming a new day. A lit cigarette burned in the ashtray beside him. He did not move. The room smelled musky and stale.

I let the door close gently. I was determined to have an early morning cigarette on the back porch and wait for Lily. I knew where she kept some extra Kools. I just hoped the container hidden on the top shelf in the pantry wouldn't be empty.

I tiptoed back through the kitchen and into the pantry. Standing on the pantry stool, I managed to get the metal canister down without dropping it. Inside were eight filter king Kools and a book of matches with a Texaco emblem on the front. I took one out, slid the matches into my side pocket, and returned the stash of cigarettes to its rightful place on the top shelf. Everyone I knew had something hidden in a secret place somewhere.

I went to the back porch and pulled one of the wooden chairs away from the table and sat down. Tearing a match from the book and striking it against the cover, I lit my first cigarette of the day. I took a drag and squinted out at the backyard. I could hear the pigeons on the roof. My father hated the constant noises they made. Only last year he requested the police to come and get rid of them. The very day of his request, they shot every pigeon that roosted on our roof. This spring another group had come to await their execution.

I took another drag on my cigarette. I trusted that my mother was still asleep because she definitely would not approve of my smoking. A sudden realization hit me—either I was daring or just plain stupid.

I saw Lily turn the corner of our backyard tossing the remains of her cigarette into the brown grass. I put mine out just as quickly in the glass ashtray on the table.

"Aren't you afraid you'll start a fire?" I said.

"Sweet Lord Jesus, Braxton. You do gives me a fright at times," said Lily, taking a handkerchief from her uniform pocket and wiping her brow. "And just what do you mean by me starting a fire?"

"The grass is dry, Lily," I said, remembering how last summer a tossed cigarette caught Mrs. Barbee's entire front yard on fire. The local fire department was called to put it out.

"I'll have you know I'm a very responsible person, 'Mr. Haywood'," said Lily. "What's you doing up so early?"

"Couldn't sleep," I said. "Too much on my mind." I knew I couldn't fool Lily. "I think Daddy had a rough night again. He and Mother were arguing about how long he had to live." I got up and walked into the kitchen. Lily followed me.

"When my pappy died," Lily said, her soft voice dropping an octave, "I thoughts I would never get over it." She hung her purse on the pantry doorknob, reached around and took her apron off the hook on the back of the door and tied it around her waist. "Braxton, I never has quite gotten over my pappy dying." She walked over to the stove and turned back towards me. "I justs stopped expecting him to come home at the end of the day."

I walked over and hugged her. "Thank you, Lily." I sighed. "I'm just tired of waiting on death to come. Sometimes, I just wish it would happen. Daddy would be better off and so would Mother. That's what I think."

"That's the good Lord's decision," said Lily. "He knows the right time. He just don't tell us when he comes a calling."

"I wish I could believe that mumbo-jumbo," I said.

"Hush your mouth, Braxton," said Lily. "Don'ts you go runnin' on like that this early in the day." Lily put a pot of coffee on the back eye of the stove to brew.

"I'm sorry," I muttered. "I just don't understand all that God stuff."

"I knows it's confusin'," said Lily. "Would you like a glass of orange juice?"

"Good morning, Lily." Mother looked kindly at Lily. "Is the coffee ready?" One glance at Mother told me she was tired and without makeup, she aged another ten years.

"No ma'ams. Not yet," said Lily. "I'll have you a cup in one minute." Lily turned the gas eye up to high. She knew Mother was inoperative without her first cup.

"Good morning, Braxton," Mother said. "You're up early today."

"Yes ma'am," I said. I wasn't about to tell her about my dream with Rita or what I heard her and my father talking about.

"Braxton, would you get me my Kools off the hall table?" said Mother.

"Yes ma'am," I said. It took me no time to find her weeds and return them to her. I took the opportunity to take a few for myself counting on her not noticing their absence first thing in the morning. I was right and unfortunately, stealing Kools had become too easy for me. I didn't realize it at the time but I was in the early stages of an addiction to smoking.

After I finished a quick breakfast and my morning chores, I called Jason. I still didn't have an answer or even a suggestion for him about his dilemma. I wanted him to go swimming with me in the public pool at Recreation Park. My parents couldn't afford membership in the Wilson Country Club and that was cool with me. A pool was a pool and water was water. Not true, bragged some of my classmates whose parents were club members, saying the club's water was cleaner than the public pool because coloreds and Jews weren't permitted to swim at the club. I never heard Jason say that but he did brag off and on about taking a piss in the club's pool when he didn't want to take the time to go inside. I figured if he took a leak in the pool so did a lot of others. I knew lots of swimmers did at the public pool.

I laughed to myself. Since when did the club member's urine start purifying the water? All that hog wash started when Wilson had a polio outbreak in the forties and public facilities were under quarantine. The country club pool never shut down. Even Uncle Vic told Mother it was okay for me to swim at the club. I don't think I ever did. Besides, the club's pool was too small to do much swimming.

I told Jason I would be at his house around one-thirty. Mother insisted that I had to rest an hour after lunch. She said this was sufficient time for my lunch to settle. I didn't want her to know it but I liked laying on the daybed on the screened back porch during the summer. There was a constant breeze on the north side of our house and I was shielded from the pesky flies that clung to the outside of the screen. When I wasn't reading one of my many comics I would play war with the flies. They were the Nazis and the force of my index finger thumping against the screen would send them sailing out into the yard like a cripple having his crutches knocked out from under him.

When I got to Jason's house, he told me George Whitley called right after I did and he wanted us to stop and pick him up at his house. Since I was restricted as to when I could use the Tank and Mother considered going to the pool a frivolous outing, I counted on Jason and his limo to get us there. Today Jason didn't have access to any wheels so we had to walk. It would take us about twenty-five minutes to get there on foot. Fortunately, George's house was on the way.

George and Jason started getting friendly near the end of the school year. Since George was still fifteen and Jason was one of the few freshmen who could drive, he conned Jason into double dating to the final dance of the school year. George was a tall boy with a strong upper body and the beginnings of facial acne, and he was fanatical about James Dean. He greased his hair like James Dean, combed it back like James Dean, wore his collars turned up in the back like James Dean, and wore pegged pants and boots to school. He even imitated James Dean when he walked and he worked hard at getting his speech to match the popular movie star. Rumor at school said he sat through three entire Saturday showings of *The Giant* starring Dean, Elizabeth Taylor, and Rock Hudson. I had to admit that George was darn good at imitating James Dean and most of the kids at school thought he was pretty cool. I agree.

Jason and I walked down South Kincaid Avenue to Branch Avenue where George joined us. The three of us worked our way over to Kenan Street. As we walked, the afternoon heat greeted us rising from the pavement. There was no doubt; it was summertime—

June bugs were out in force, horse flies had invaded the city limits and the air smelled thick.

We picked up our stride and moved briskly down Kenan in the direction of the park, anticipating an afternoon of fun in the pool. When we got to Sunset Road, we turned right. Listening to Jason and George exchange digs took my mind off the oppressive heat and the sweat that had taken up residence inside my shirt and on my neck and face.

When we were within a block of Recreation Park, we saw more teenagers walking with rolled towels tucked under their arms and talking with excitement. We passed several small children eating popsicles and being escorted by their mothers and older siblings. For many of us, this would be our first swim of the summer season.

When we reached the front of the First Presbyterian Church, we could look down the street and see that the parking lot was half full, meaning that the pool population would be heavy. An occasional bicyclist would zip into the parking lot giving no thought save that of wanting to be the next person to dive in the water. I just wanted to jump in the water and sit and relax.

As we neared the parking lot, a solid black '54 Ford scanning the scene eased its way around the other parked cars. Two studs in their early twenties occupied the front seat. When they saw us, the driver slowed his car and pulled along side us. The man sitting shotgun was a greasy blond with a flat top.

"Hello boys," he said, stepping out of the car. "Where are you turkeys going?" He appeared to be around six feet tall and his muscular chest carried a picture of a red heart with some sort of inscription tattooed on the left side.

"Swimming," said Jason. "Come on. Let's go." He motioned for the two of us to pick up our stride.

"Hold up!" said the driver, a peroxide-blond with a crew cut sliding out from behind the steering wheel. "We have a proposition for you boys." He was equally as tall as his buddy but more muscular and hairy and without a visible tattoo. Both looked like they wanted trouble.

"We're not interested," I said. "Jason, George, let's get inside."

They both laughed. The driver took a pack of Camels out of his swimsuit pocket and lit one.

He made his way toward me. I stared, backing up.

"What's your name, fatso," he said, taking a drag on his cigarette and blowing his smoke my way. "You could stand to lose ten ugly pounds!"

"None of your damn business," I said. Damm redneck had insulted me. I was mad as hellfire.

"What did you say, shithead?" He grabbed me by the shoulder. I pulled back. He stood there staring at me, casually smoking his Camel. Occasionally, he would knock the ashes off.

"Why don't you guys leave him alone and go find something worthwhile to do," George said in his James Dean accent.

"Well, what do you know? A James Dean look-alike," said the blond with the tattoo. "You think you're pretty smooth, don't you?" George kept still, not saying a word. He showed no signs of fear and no desire to take him on. "What about it?" he said, throwing his head back demonstrating his cockiness. "You think you're tough shit, don't you?"

Jason remained cool and stepped forward. "Look! I don't know who you guys are or where you came from but this is public property and I suggest you take a hike! We're going swimming."

"Not so fast, prick face," said the driver. "Who put you in charge of this sorry crew?"

"We need to go, Jason," I said. "We better go." I didn't know how much longer I could draw my strength from Jason and George.

"Fuck off, fat boy," said the driver who had now taken charge. His face had a small scar below his left eye.

"Leave him alone. What's he done to you?" said Jason. "Go pick on someone your own size."

"What was that, prick face?" the driver said. His face had reddened and both his hands were drawn into a tight fist.

It happened so quickly that I might as well not have been there. The bleached blond driver took a swing at Jason; but before he could complete it with any force, Jason pounded him in the face with his right fist. The sound was the sound of an icicle snapped from the gutter of a house by the cold wind of winter. The driver fell to the ground, grabbing his face. Blood flowed down his chin and into the hair on his chest. Before the other man could complete his move, George hit him in the stomach with the force of a fast-pitched softball. He went down and folded into himself. He didn't get up. George grabbed him again. He began to sob asking for mercy.

"Let's go swimming," Jason said. George moved forward but I just stood there looking down in astonishment at the two men on the ground.

"Braxton, are you coming or not?" asked George. "We're going in."

I still couldn't believe what had just happened. The realization that it could have been me on the ground if it hadn't been for Jason fighting my battle began to take root in my brain. The two men on the ground were in pain. The driver's nose looked like it had been repositioned on his face and the other man still moaned in the gravel.

I ran to the pool gate, paid my money, and found Jason and George in the men's locker room.

Jason was at one of the sinks letting cold water run over the cuts in his knuckles. I stood beside him, watching his blood join the water flowing into the sink. I patted him on the shoulder to let him know how much I was indebted for what he had just done for me.

George came up behind me and slapped me on the back. "You owe me, Braxton. Don't forget it." I watched him dance out the door and into the pool area.

I looked around the room until my eyes found what I had been searching—a Red Cross first aid kit. I walked across the wet concrete floor, grabbed the box, and went over to where Jason still stood. "Sit down, Jason. It's my turn now."

Jason turned and inched out a grin. "I wouldn't do that for just anybody, you know."

I knew and I would never forget it. I owed Jason a debt I could never repay. If I had been the one hit in the head, I would be dead. I doubt Jason thought of that when he intervened. I knew he had acted out of impulse. I wanted to believe that he cared and maybe we were better friends than I thought.

Chapter 10
Bananas and a Pair of Melons

I ROLLED OVER and squinted, looking for the time. I could barely see my alarm clock on the bedside table. If I squinted just the right way, I could see the face of the clock. Ugh! It looked like 6:50 A.M. I needed no convincing; it was too early to get up. Then I heard the enemy. Reluctantly, I sat up, leaned over and peeked beneath the shade. They were there, a flock of them. Damn pigeons had recently returned to our roofline and now, in unison, as if auditioning for a chorus, they had started cooing. *Won't they ever stop?* I jumped back into bed and pulled both pillows over my head, hoping to drown out their cacophony. It was no use; they desired to torment me. The noise grew louder. Forget this—off came the pillows. I wiggled out from under the covers, threw my feet on the floor, and in one stride moved to the windows. I lifted the shade, clasped my hands together, and clapped loudly numerous times. They took my hint. I could hear them flapping, ready for take-off. As they flew away, I heard them making the same obnoxious, unintelligible sound. A rooster in the distance crowed, a car door slammed, and Skippy barked, telling us that he was not happy with the beginning of his day.

The civilized world was awake. What was the time? Only 7:00 A.M. and much too early to get out of bed. Our house was quiet and as still as the outside atmosphere. I got up again and cut on the window box fan then fell backwards across my bed. Wednesday, June 3rd. Oh shit! Today I had to do my once a year chore: clean out the garage.

As I lay there, my thoughts rushed back to those punks at the swimming pool and Jason and George's willingness to stand up to them. I didn't know George well but I did know Jason Parker. Jason was the type of person that was either liked or disliked. Many of our acquaintances at school didn't like Jason. He was always one of the last chosen for anything. It is apparent to me why Jason has enemies—he is brash, lacks tact, and shows an unwillingness to admit when he is wrong. I saw another Jason: a person who does have a good heart, and does care, and can be kind. I don't disagree that he is loud and uncouth on occasions and what he did to Byrd was wrong. Even though I wrestle over the value of my friendship with him, I do care for him and what he is going through and I will miss him if he is shipped off to school.

No one got in Jason Parker's face and got away with it. He had that certain rawness that I wished I had and he never allowed himself to be intimidated by anyone. I was a formula for disaster, but none of my friends thought so. My problem: I wanted to be liked by everyone, to be part of the in-crowd, to be the person others wanted me to be. I didn't have the confidence to be the real me. I lived in conflict with myself: I wasn't willing to be the bad dude to be liked but I would eagerly be an onlooker when trouble started brewing. Jason was always Jason and his personality was an invitation for some people to criticize him. Inwardly, I couldn't handle rejection. And most of all, unconstructive criticism—and some constructive—inflicted me emotionally and sometimes, it took a long time to put this pain to bed. I just didn't let my friends see this part of me. However, when I was with Jason, I felt empowered and safe like nothing or no one could harm me. If Jason's mouth did get us into trouble, I knew he would get us out with or without my help.

Jason looked athletic. He had an athlete's physique: a strong upper body, wide shoulders, and small waist. The only real exercise he did was lifting his barbells on an irregular basis. His biceps had grown and any time we would let him, he would show us with a measuring tape just how much. The two buttholes at the pool had muscular bodies too. I was short, chunky, and solid with no visible, upper body strength. Many times I had heard Lily say to my mother, "Miss Virginia, leave that boy alone! He'll lose that weight when he gets older." I hoped she was right.

I reluctantly pulled myself out of bed and dragged myself to the bathroom. I grabbed my bath cloth from the side of the tub and cut on the cold water in the lavatory sink. After three washings, I felt awake enough to return to my bedroom and get dressed. Since I had to spend the morning with soot and dirt, I grabbed a tee shirt out of the top drawer of my chest and a pair of old Bermudas lying in the back of my closet. After I put on old socks and my Wilson tennis shoes, I stumbled into the kitchen. Mother was in the breakfast nook drinking coffee and smoking. Lily stood at the sink washing what looked like vegetables and humming "Swing Low, Sweet Chariot."

"Good morning, Mother," I said. "Hello, Lily." Neither of them responded. "What's for breakfast?" No one said anything. Lily turned and put her finger over her mouth and motioned me to the back porch. She followed me.

"Your mother is upset," she said. "Your father had himself a rough night."

"So what else is new?" I said. I bowed my head. I didn't mean to sound sarcastic. "Sorry. That didn't come out right." I looked at Lily. Even she seemed to be in low spirits.

"Do you minds fixing yourself some cereal this morning?" Lily said. "It would help me out a lot."

"No, I can do that." I followed her back into the kitchen, poured some Kellogg's corn flakes into a bowl. "Do we have any peaches left?" Lily didn't act like she heard me. "Thank you for your kind attention."

"Braxton, don'ts you go and get an attitude with me, you hears me boy!" said Lily. "I ain't in any kind of mood for that mouth of yours this morning."

"Well excuse me for getting out of bed." Lily's eyebrows arched over her glasses. Her eyes just glared at me and her hands were on her hips. "Okay! I admit it. I've overstepped my bounds. I'll hush." I walked to the refrigerator. After a casual rearrangement of the contents on the second shelf, I found a small bowl of peaches covered with Saran Wrap. I grabbed the Sealtest milk bottle, balanced the bowl of peaches on top, and gingerly made my way to the stove where I finished doctoring my cereal. I went out to the back porch to eat in silence. What a great day this was going to be.

"Braxton, before you begins your chores, your mother wants you to carry Rita Stallings the sugar back that we borrowed," said Lily.

"The best news I've heard today!" I said.

"I thought you would like that," said Lily.

"Isn't it too early?" Not that I minded.

"I don't thinks so," said Lily. "She's got them young 'uns to feed."

"Okay." I tried to sound nonchalant.

"You aren't supposed to stay," said Lily clearing her throat. "You hears me?"

"Yes, I hear you." I hadn't had time to enjoy even a mild flirtatious thought without Lily spoiling it.

I gulped my cereal down, ran to the bathroom to comb my hair and brush my teeth. Seeing my father's Old Spice aftershave lotion was too tempting—I pulled the top off, shook some on my left hand, and patted it against my neck. I repeated the exercise again but this time I rubbed it across my chest. Lady Rita, your knight cometh.

I returned to the kitchen to get the sugar. "Where is the parcel to be delivered, Lily?"

"The *sugar* is on the stove in that plastic container." Lily was not amused.

"My God! This is a lot more than Mother borrowed, Lily," I said. "You want me to put some back?"

"Carry what is in that container, Braxton," came Mother's voice from the breakfast nook. "And please don't argue."

"I'm not arguing," I said. "I was just putting the math I've learned at Coon into practice."

I was the only one to laugh.

"You is in one fine mood, today," said Lily. Grabbing my elbow, she pulled me to the back porch. "You knows how your mother is when it comes to repaying borrowed items. If I hadn't spoken up, she was gonna send Miss Rita the entire bag of sugar."

"What?" I said. "I momentarily forgot how she felt about being indebted to someone."

"Just go and get back," said Lily. "I'll handle things here."

"Thanks, Lily," I said, closing the screened door. I ran down the back steps, took a deep breath, almost choking on the stale heat of the morning, and walked confidently to Rita Stalling's house.

I rang the bell. There was no response and I heard no activity in the house. I checked my watch; it was about 8:15. I rang the bell two more times before Richard, her oldest son, opened the back door. As soon as I saw him, I knew I had come too early. His hair was not awake yet and his Lone Ranger pajama bottoms hung below his belly button. I chuckled to myself. He didn't say anything but just stood there barefooted, wiggling his toes on the kitchen linoleum. The sandman had paid him a visit during the night. His eyes widened and he opened his mouth and then yawned. The expression on his face voiced surprise as if asking me what I was doing there.

"Hi, Rich," I said. "Is your mother up?"

Rich turned his head back toward the kitchen, searching for his mother. Then, without saying anything to me, he ran toward the door that led into the hallway. A large horse fly joined me as I stepped inside the kitchen. A strange feeling came over me as I stood alone in an empty kitchen hoping to see a woman I had fantasized about. I could just leave the sugar on the table. On second thought, I could leave a clever note. I searched the room for a pencil and paper.

"Who's there?" said Rita, whispering. She sounded close by and then I saw her hand appear on the frame of the hall door.

"Rita, it's Braxton," I said. "I didn't . . . "

"Braxton, honey," she said, cutting me off. "I'll be right there."

"I didn't mean to wake y'all up," I said, finishing my previous thought. "I brought your sugar back."

Rita stepped into the kitchen. She had just bathed. Her head was wrapped in a light blue and white towel like a turban. Several strands of wet hair resembling eels dangled from under the towel along her neck. She had wrapped a matching light blue towel tightly around her body. Her round, melon-sized breasts pushed hard and upward against the towel. Beads of water glistened like diamonds on her slightly exposed upper breasts. The sight of her took my breath away. I thought I might faint.

"Good morning, Braxton," said Rita with a smile. "I didn't expect to see you first thing today."

"No m'am," I said. "I guess not." I wanted to pull that towel off her body so badly.

"Now what did you say I could do for you?" she said.

"Mother wanted me to return the sugar that she borrowed," I said, repeating myself. *If you really want to know what you can do for me, drop the towel and come close.*

"My goodness! She didn't have to do that and so much, too!" said Rita, moving toward the table where I stood. *Could she read my thoughts?*

"Well, I guess I better get out of here before I get into trouble." Again, I spoke without thinking. I was getting too good at fumbling, especially around Rita.

"Braxton, whatever do you mean by that," said Rita. "Are you being a naughty boy?" She took another step closer to me.

"Ah! No! No ma'am," I said. I could feel my face getting flushed and I was embarrassed. "I meant that if I didn't get back home quick, Mother would pile on more chores."

"Now wait just a minute, young man," Rita said. "Want you have a glass of juice or a cup of coffee with me?" She came closer, resting her hand on my shoulder.

"Rita, I really need to get back home," I said. Water from her hand penetrated the hole in the shoulder of my tee shirt. I could stand the temptation no longer. "Maybe I could come back another morning?" I knew that must be a line from some movie I had seen. I backed away, knocking the kitchen table too hard, sending several bananas to the floor. Klutz . . .klutz. . . klutz.

Rita joined me as I bent over to pick up the bananas. When her knees touched the floor, the top of her towel suddenly loosened, exposing her supple, ripe melons. *My God! They were beautiful with each nipple perfectly formed and pink and hard. Don't grab the melons—pick up the bananas. No, dope, grab the melons and forget the bananas. Be quiet, klutz! Just get out of the house.* "Rita, I'll pick up the melons while you get the towel back on." Shit! What had I said? Rita chuckled at first and then began to laugh until tears ran down her face. I just stood there with three bananas in my hands. I could barely smile. My face felt flushed. I was a fool and knew I looked the part.

"You are so cute and sweet, Braxton," said Rita, still kneeling and looking up at me. "I just love your sense of humor. You are too clever with your words." She repositioned the towel to cover her exposed breasts.

"Thank you, Rita." I said. "I wish my English teacher saw the humor in my writing."

Dropping the bananas on the floor, I grabbed both her hands helping her up. They were silky soft and a bolt of electricity shot through my body. I held on longer than I should. Then letting go, I let my fingers slide over hers. What a woman! She was beautiful and now the goddess of my dreams.

"One last thing, Braxton," said Rita. "Could you possibly baby-sit for us tonight? Our regular sitter canceled last night."

"I can't tonight, Rita," I said, remembering we had made plans to go see *Fear Strikes Out,* the story about Boston Red Sox star Jimmy Piersall. "I wish I could."

"So do I, Braxton," said Rita. "I can make it worth your while if you say yes."

"I really can't tonight," I said. You can make it worth my while now. "Give me another chance sometime, will you?"

"You bet," said Rita. I made my move for the back door. "Wait a sec, hon'." Rita walked toward me. "Thank you for being such a gentleman this morning." She kissed me on the cheek.

"Any time," I said. "See you later." I ran down the back steps and headed toward my house. I wanted to turn around and see if maybe she was still standing at the door but I was afraid to. I wanted to stay but I had that damn garage to clean. Before I reached my yard, I thought I heard Rita call my name, telling me to come back soon.

When I stepped onto the back porch, I met Lily face to face. She didn't smile but had that inquisitive look on her face. "I'm home and ready for work."

"I just bet you is," said Lily, standing with that "sinner, you're going to hell" expression on her face. "I just bet you is, Mr. Braxton Haywood. Well, don't just stand there! You got all that energy. Gets to it, boy!" It would take me at least two hours to complete this chore to Mother's liking.

Our white wooden frame garage had a weathered look and sat at the back of our driveway, a combination of grass and gravel worn heavily over time by the Tank's tires. Our garage did not serve its intended purpose but was used as storage for an assortment of lawn and garden tools plus two bikes, two sleds, and some rarely used household equipment. Added to the west side of our garage was a lean-to filled with wooden slats and assorted sizes of kindling. Unfortunately, it had become a hiding place for neighborhood rats and snakes. My job was to rearrange the kindling that lay behind the door so that when it was opened, nothing would fall out. I never knew what I might encounter when I stuck my hand into that lean-to. Beside the lean-to was an open coal bin. The coal had to be arranged neatly since Mother thought it could be partially seen from Kincaid Avenue. "Your mother says none of that coal is to be on that grass when you finish," said Lily as I departed the back porch. I didn't see what difference it made. A large yellow forsythia bush, taller than the garage, sat in front of the coal bin. No one walking by our house that had good eyesight could possibly see any coal on the grass.

I always started the cleanup inside the garage. The floor was solid black dirt and passing time had made it as hard as stone. A nail would sometimes bend when driven through the dirt surface; but ironically, blades of grass could make their way through it. It was a paradox to me how this happened. Mother couldn't appreciate this natural wonder and she had to have each blade of grass pulled, picked, or boiled out of that dirt. I wore down more than one fingernail getting those weeds out but I always managed to do it. Hot water and ammonia were my best aids.

If someone were to ask me, "Name one thing from your pre-teen years that you most identify with your father, what would it be?" Without hesitation, I would say, "Our garage." At that time, my father was healthy enough to work and function effectively in his role as husband and father. Our garage did not serve as a facility for housing a car but rather for other sundry activities. It was here that my father did three completely unrelated things that left an indelible impression on me. The first was when he built me a soapbox cart to ride in our town's annual derby race. It was a classic and I won second place in the Clyde Avenue Soap Box Derby the year he made if for me. I think my winning was one of the few things I ever did that made him proud of me.

The second was when my father instructed me to go out to the garage one brisk fall afternoon and retrieve the box that had been delivered from the Texaco station that he co-owned with a friend. Inside the box, I found a beautiful German shepherd and collie mixed puppy that I named Jojo. I had begged and begged my father to get me a dog even though I never thought he would. Three years later I stood in our gravel driveway watching the whole thing. I was afraid and Jojo was afraid. Our town's dogcatcher and one of our police officers had my rabid dog cornered trying to put a wire loop around his neck. Jojo barked and growled and wailed. He was confused and hurt and sick. Jojo was taken to the vet where he was put to sleep. Later we learned that Mr. Harmon Taylor had poisoned my dog for pooping in his yard.

And in this garage at the age of eleven I got my one and only "real" whipping from my father. I won't ever forget his making me drop my pants while he took off his leather belt. That day he wore my fanny out for leaving dog poop in a paper bag on Mrs. Barrow's front porch. "Daddy, it was only a prank. I didn't mean anything by it," I pleaded. "Don't whip me. I won't do it again."

"You're damn right you won't do it again," my father shouted. "Louis, haven't you learned anything? Decent white boys don't put dog shit on anyone's porch, much less a lady. Do you understand that, Louis?" These were my father's last words on this subject. I never pulled that prank again.

I finished my cleanup by noon. The garage floor had been weeded and swept with a broom. The hoses, ax, hoe, rakes, and ladder were hung in their designated spot on the back wall. Everything else had been neatly arranged around the interior walls, and the wood and coal were in their rightful place. My fingers burned and a large blister formed on my right hand. I was proud of my work. Our garage stood ready for my mother's inspection. I was ready to take a few minutes to relax. I walked around to the back of the garage and stood facing the large hedge at the back of our property. I allowed my legs to bend until I sat and taking one of the Kools I had pilfered from Lily's stash, I rewarded myself. The rest of that day I hung around the house doing odd jobs and daydreaming of Rita.

The movie *Fear Strikes Out,* starring Anthony Perkins as Boston Red Sox star Jimmy Piersall and Karl Malden as his father, came to the Wilson Theatre, one of only two all-white movie theaters in our town. Jason, Byrd, Matt, Thad, and I arrived for the 7:00 P.M. showing about twenty minutes early. After Jason parked his father's limo in the lot behind the theater, we walked through the theater alley to purchase our tickets at the box office booth located on West Nash Street. I always got excited walking up the enclosed breezeway leading to the theater lobby. Lining the walls on either side were colorful framed posters, each giving a preview of up-and-coming attractions and the dates they would be shown at this grandiose theater. We entered through the velvet curtained brass doors, gave our tickets to the usher, and my buddies made their way to the concession stand to buy popcorn, candy, and drinks. I walked over and waited at the door on the left that led to the downstairs seating sections. Byrd, Matt, and Thad joined me. We were ready to go inside and make our way down the aisle and find our seats.

"Come on, Jason," I said. Jason hung back socializing with some younger girls at the candy counter. A "Tom and Jerry" cartoon had started and I didn't want to miss any more of it. I told Byrd, Matt, and Thad to go ahead. Along with other moviegoers on both sides of the lobby, they passed through the brass doors and into the theater where everything became deathly quiet.

"Keep your pants on, Braxton," said Jason. "I'm coming." The girls at the counter laughed.

Walking down the dark aisle trying to find the others was like navigating with our eyes closed. The single lights at the bottom of every ten seats were spaced too far apart, thus serving no practical purpose. It was not cool to ask an usher for assistance.

"Hey guys, where are y'all?" I said, muffling my voice and hoping not to be recognized.

"Braxton, over here," called Byrd who was seated in the middle section about ten rows back from the screen. *Gee, thanks so much for trying to enter incognito.*

"Hey Jason! Hey Braxton! Come sit with us!" called some ninth-grade girls seated about half way down.

I waved, mumbling to Jason not to stop. By the time we joined our buddies, the cartoon was over and the newsreel had started. "Shit," I said under my breath. "We missed the best part." I could care less about world events and I generally spent the newsreel time looking around to see who else was in the theater. Hot damn! I couldn't believe my eyes. Seated three rows back to my right were Rita and Harry Stallings with another couple I didn't know. Harry had his right arm around his wife and his left hand fed both of them popcorn. Feeding Rita popcorn could be a right sexy undertaking, especially if it was from my tongue to hers. Oh crap! She must know by now I'm here. I hope she doesn't know where I'm sitting. When the previews for coming attractions started, I eased down in my seat hoping Rita couldn't find me.

Paramount Pictures had produced a heavy, intense psychological drama lacking the kind of baseball action we had hoped for. I was not a fan of Karl Malden and I liked him even less as Jimmy's overzealous father. The combination of the pressure placed on Piersall by his father and the pressures of driving him to excel in America's favorite sport pushed Jimmy to a breakdown. With the exception of Jason, the rest of us were engrossed with the story and the tragedy that occurred. At some point during the movie, Jason moved several aisles down to sit with three rising sophomore girls from Wilson's Five Point's area, a hub of hardworking, blue-collar families. Jason slid into the seat next to Peggy Harper, a buxom, tanned brunette. The next time I looked, Jason had his arm resting around Peggy's shoulder and then later, her head rested on his shoulder. I knew Jason would deliver a forthcoming tale after the movie.

We exited the side door when the feature was over and walked sullenly back to the limo. With the exception of Jason, we agreed that our first movie of the summer had been a downer. I had managed to avoid eye contact with Rita and I just hoped she was not parked in the same lot as we. As soon as we were back in the limo getting ready to head home, I turned to Jason, "Well, let's hear it."

"Hear what?" said Jason, pulling out of the parking lot onto Pine Street spinning a wheel.

"How was it?" I asked.

"The movie?" he said. "It was okay. I didn't get into it much. I had other things on my mind."

"Duh. That's for sure," said Matt. "I think you meant fingers. Right, Braxton?"

"I'm without words, guys," said Jason. "But I will tell you one thing. They were real!"

"What are y'all talking about," said Thad.

"Her boobs," said Byrd. "Her boobs are the real thing!" The rest of us sighed as Jason turned left onto Nash Street.

"Where are you headed?" said Thad. "I need to get back home."

"Okay, but let's cruise Goldsboro Street first," said Jason.

"Why?" I asked.

"Where is your sense of romance, Braxton?" Jason asked. "Let's just see what whores are out tonight."

"Oh for heaven's sake," said Matt. "Can't you have a decent thought that doesn't involve your pecker?"

"When was the last time you found yours, Matt?" Jason said, turning right onto Goldsboro Street. None of us said anything hoping there would be no prostitutes out on a Wednesday night. Jason drove a couple of blocks and there they were on our right, standing in front of a tobacco warehouse. Jason took his foot off the accelerator, slowing down and then he blinked his lights a couple of times. One of the prostitutes dressed in a tight white sleeveless sweater and a black skirt that rode-up her hips stepped out into the street. Her face was heavily made up and she looked well ridden for a young woman.

"Move on, Jason. I don't have time for any of your crap tonight," said Matt.

"Don't be a sissy, Matt," said Jason. "This won't take long."

"Let's hope not," I said. Jason rolled the shotgun window down and the prostitute stuck her head in. Her breath reeked with the odor of stale cigarettes.

"What's up, boys?" she said. "Do your mamas know you boys are riding the town tonight?"

"Well, let's put it this way, sweetheart," said Jason. "What they don't know won't hurt them!"

"Cute!" she responded. "I'll be direct. Which of you boys want to fuck?"

"The driver does but he can't find his weenie," said Matt. We all laughed and Jason got livid.

"Look, asshole," said Jason, turning to Matt. "Just because you can't find yours doesn't mean the rest of us are lacking in the tool department."

"While you boys argue with each other, I'm just going to stand here and wait for a real man," the prostitute said.

"Good idea," I said. "I'm sure you can find one dick in Wilson tonight."

"Well said, Braxton," said Matt. "Jason, let's go. Some of us boys have to work tomorrow."

Without his usual finesse, Jason took a cigarette out of his pack and lit it. A wave of smoke made its way through the car. Jason cracked a fart and started his engine at the same time.

"What did you do that for?" asked Thad. "The cigarette smells bad enough."

"Sorry," said Jason. "Hold onto your hats, boys!" Jason gripped the steering wheel with both hands, sat up straight in his seat, kicked the accelerator and we were off, leaving the prostitute standing in the street. Jason's limo began to soar down Goldsboro Street hitting a speed of sixty miles per hour, forty miles over the speed limit. The rest of us threw our backs against the seat while Jason took advantage of the empty street swerving from one side to another. He drove like he was crazed and despite a chorus of repeated 'slow down' from the back seat, he increased his speed another five miles an hour. I sat next to Jason scared shitless.

"Stop this damn car and let me out now!" said Matt, leaning over into the front seat. "Braxton, do something!"

Before I could say anything, Jason said, "Don't tell me how to drive!" He increased his speed another five miles per hour. Suddenly, a dark figure darted out into the middle of Goldsboro Street.

"Jason, watch out!" I said. "My God, don't hit the guy! He's drunk." I grabbed the steering wheel and pulled it to the right. The limo began to rock from side to side and the tires screamed as we turned, narrowly missing the colored man who had fallen on his butt. Jason took his foot off the accelerator and patted the break until the car slowly came to a stop against the curb, several blocks from Ward Boulevard.

Jason turned to the backseat and said, "Don't any of you ever embarrass me again!" Jason got out of the car, came around to my side, and opened my door. "Braxton, drive us home." My heart pounded and I felt nauseated. As I got out of the limo, I looked at Jason. Sweat covered his now ashen face. What I saw in his eyes was the fear of a young boy who had suddenly acted maniacal. Of the four us, I was the only one who had some clue about the pressure driving Jason to sudden fits of insanity. To Matt, Thad, and Byrd, his behavior was without just cause.

None of us found any humor in his behavior but we knew something had happened to him and we were concerned. I was nominated by my friends to find out what but I already knew one thing. I could not reveal what Jason had already told me but I promised Matt, Thad, and Byrd we would keep Jason's chauffeuring to a minimum.

I was too worried to sleep that night. Jason's behavior did concern me. This was the second time in two months that he had acted erratic without any warning. What other pressures could be driving him to act this way? What if he had a relapse and had to go back to the psycho ward? Thinking of Rita didn't even help. Everything was going the wrong way. Why was all of this happening now? Was this part of growing up?

I closed my eyes and saw the Jimmy Piersall of tonight's movie. Why did pressure have to ruin his life? Why didn't they leave him alone and let him enjoy his sport? Is that what's going to happen to us? Will we be able to handle the pressures life throws at us? Jason can't!

My God! Would Jason self-destruct? Would I? Would Matt or Byrd or Thad? I didn't like this road and I wanted to get off.

I leaned over and turned on the radio. Elvis Presley singing "All Shook Up" played. I smiled, thinking how appropriate. I rolled over on my back and stared at the ceiling. The house was quiet. I was not scared but I felt alone. I did not want to go through this summer feeling alone. I had plans—big plans. I closed my eyes and fell asleep thinking of them.

Chapter 11
HOT DOGS WITH GRECIAN CHILI

AN UNEXPECTED VISITOR came to our town in 1919 and two years later took up residence one block northwest of Kincaid Avenue. The industrious gentleman from Samos, Greece, brought his secret chili recipe from the old country and opened Dick's Hot Dog Stand, one of the best known and loved eating establishments in eastern North Carolina. Mr. Socrates "Dick" Gliarmis opened his little brick diner on the corner of West Nash and Pearson Streets before the construction of many of the fancier homes that eventually surrounded him became his neighbors. Dick's Hot Dog, as it was initially called, quickly became a hotbed of activity for its all-white clientele. Later the restaurant became known as Dick's and even later, black people were allowed to order carryout.

The elderly Mr. Gliarmis was loved and revered by most of the people in our town. Only a few cantankerous citizens protested the idea of his establishment sitting across the street from their neighborhood. In time, some of these hypocritical souls couldn't resist the taste of his hotdogs and they joined a long list of patrons and Mr. G.'s business thrived and his restaurant became as much a part of our neighborhood as the house next door.

Of the five of us, Jason Parker and I lived closest to Dick's. Both of our homes were within earshot of the small restaurant. This gave us immediate access to Mr. G.'s hospitality more often than he needed to extend it. During the summer of '57, the five of us made Dick's one of our regular hangouts, sometimes meeting there up to two and three times a week. There was something about the little restaurant that made us feel safe. In some ways, Dick's became our home away from home and we enjoyed the ten-cent hot dogs with its secret chili and the five-cent Pepsis and Cokes with too much ice.

In the summer months, Jason, having a lot more spending money than the rest of us, visited Dick's several times a week to eat lunch. There was a catch to this privilege given to Jason. Julius could get out of fixing lunch for him and still tell Mrs. Parker that Jason had had a filling meal. And by promising Jason that his mother would not find out, Julius could get what he wanted—three hotdogs all the way and a large Dr. Pepper. What Jason would bring to me was a tale about something funny that happened while he was there, usually involving Lee and his father. To be quite truthful, I didn't always share the humor in his stories.

Among Jason's many questionable qualities, he was a prankster and he enjoyed this role. I have to admit it. Jason could be funny and when he was, he would leave me in stitches. I would get to laughing so hard that tears would run down my cheeks. This didn't happen to me often but when it did, there was no feeling quite like it. It was like a catharsis—leaving me feeling rejuvenated and alive—like being given a shot of extra energy that penetrates the soul.

For no apparent reason, Jason, at times, would have a sudden impulse to target Lee and on rare occasions, Mr. G. This was Jason's way, he said, of getting his jollies off. Every time he got this particular urge, I would tell him that it was one thing to mess around with Lee but it was a totally different matter when it came to screwing around with his father.

I think Jason's desire to test the good nature of the elderly gentleman could be characterized as a flaw in his complicated psyche. There had to be a place and time to draw the line—a time when any of us could say directly to Jason "you've gone too far." Matt and I both told him this several times when he overstepped his bounds but Jason would just ignore us. I didn't like Jason when he felt the need to harass Mr. G.

Jason was less likely to tease Mr. G. if Lee was on the premises. He would joke with Mr. G. but he would not cross over into the arena of harassment. Lee, not always as good-natured as his father, was given to a fiery temper when anyone teased his father. Jason recognized this but still there were days when he liked to see how far he could push Lee's limits. As anyone could tell, Jason could be a real bastard at times. When this happened, we were ushered out the door.

Protective of his father, Lee practiced the mores of the old country when it came to respecting the elderly. I had no problem with this, but Jason did. Once, when kidding around with Mr. G., Jason let out a couple of vulgar words and Lee practically jumped across the counter to get in Jason's face, making it clear that cursing was strictly prohibited. In shock, Jason fell backwards off his counter stool landing squarely on his butt. Embarrassed and beet red in the face, Jason pulled himself up off the floor, apologized to Lee and Mr. G., and without any coaxing, promptly left the restaurant. He never cursed in front of the gentleman from Samos again.

Over time, we learned not to be embarrassed by Jason's on-again off-again maniacal behavior. We just accepted that this was Jason being Jason. Without question, he was the dominant personality among us, especially in public places.

It had been close to four weeks since I'd offered my idea of a fairly harmless way to trick Mr. G. The idea sounded novel the spring night I presented it to my buddies. It was closing night of Mr. Stanley's production of "Alice in Wonderland." The curtain had fallen for the last time. Standing in the wings, the cast could hear the thunderous applause. After our second curtain call, Mr. Stanley said no more. We all knew the play had been a rocking success and we were overwhelmed with excitement. That was when I turned to Jason who had helped out backstage and presented my idea to him. Jason took to it like flies on molasses. In typical Jason style, he took the idea, dressed it up a bit, and presented it as his own to Thad, Matt, and Byrd. They, too, thinking the prank was innocuous, jumped on the idea.

I had begun to have second thoughts about the whole thing. I don't know why I came up with the lame idea. I honestly suggested it without thinking; it was not even in my nature to want to hurt or tease the old man. I could just imagine my mother's reaction if she found out about it, "Now Braxton, I thought I'd taught you better than that. How could you do this to Lee and his sweet father? They've been so good to us." She would continue on and on until she had made her point. And being sensitive, it didn't take much chastising to make me remorseful.

Mother always expected her children to behave close to perfection. She received a lot of compliments from adults in our town on how well mannered we were and what a nice gentleman I was. Our town focused on things like lineage and dress and manners and Mother relished in this praise. I guess this was one of the few bright things she could count on that qualified her as a good parent by others. For me, it was like being on stage all the time playing a character I didn't always want to be. I did it for her. I did it to please Mother.

This time Mother would not be pleased. She was right—Mr. G. had always been more than kind to me. In fact, it was Mr. G. who last summer about this same time allowed me to bring Lily's nephew, Walter, from New York, inside his restaurant to buy a hot dog despite the "whites only" sign hanging on the front door. Walter was as dark as any colored boy I'd ever seen and with my fair skin we turned heads wherever we were seen together. He had no reservations about going inside Dick's. I actually think he enjoyed the attention.

"Walter, I don't think we should go in," I said resolutely. "Blacks just don't go in Dick's."

"You white folks sure are backward down here in North Ca'lina," he said unabashedly. "Up in New York, I go in restaurants all the time where you white people eats."

"Yeah? Well, maybe you do and that's great. But down here, things are different." I was ashamed of my cowardice. If Walter could spend the night with me and eat at the same table with me at my house, what was wrong with him going into Dick's with me? "I really want to, Walter, but I just don't think it's a good idea. Not today at least." I had seen how cruel some ignorant white people could be to colored people and I didn't want Walter to be humiliated. And truthfully, I wasn't certain I could handle that kind of scene. "I don't make the rules, Walter."

Mr. G. saw us walking around outside and must have guessed our dilemma. He opened the door and called to me, "Braxton, would you and your friend like to get something to eat?" I saw the

surprise register on Walter's face and the next thing I knew, we started running toward Mr. G.

"Mr. G., this is my friend Walter Davis from New York. He's staying with me today." I was glad and proud for Walter to meet him. I
had never had the chance to introduce Walter to anyone. I was certain they had things in common, especially being victims of racial
hatred.

"How are you, Walter?" Mr. G. spoke gently, extending his hand.
"I'm happy to meet you." Walter smiled and shook Mr. G.'s hand.
"How do you like this warm weather down here in the South?"

"I don't like it at all—least not without any air conditioners,"
Walter shot back gleaming as if he had known Mr. G. all of his life.
"It's mighty hot here, but you know what they say about us coloreds
down here in all this heat, don't you?"

"I'm not certain I do," said Mr. G. with a quizzical look on his
face. "Anyway, you two boys come in and sit up here at the counter
and I'll take your order."

"Thank you, Mr. G.," I said, butting in. Whispering, I leaned over
to Walter, "Not now, you dummy, please don't tell him that joke. It's
not really funny."

"Okay, I guess you're right," he whispered back. Raising his
voice an octave, "Mr. G., I'll have two of your famous hot dogs I hear
Braxton talking about all the time, please."

"Me, too, and make 'em all the way," I responded. "And let us
both have a large Pepsi, please." I turned to Walter who seemed quite
taken with the negative attention he was receiving. The atmosphere
was charged. I could sense the unhappiness of the patrons who were
forced to eat with a Negro. I could feel the eyes of hostility bearing
down on us and the low buzz of murmurs around the restaurant carried an unfriendly intonation. "Walter, as soon as we get our food,
we're heading outside to eat."

"You can go, Braxton, but I'm keeping my ass on this here stool."
Walter smiled, bearing his teeth. I could tell he intended to enjoy
every minute of this lunch break. Well, I was not a bit comfortable
with the stares of the patrons. My mind heard all kinds of ugly racial
comments and I was embarrassed that I lived in the same town as
these people. I sat there speechless and I knew I was a big chicken.

I couldn't help it. Walter was every bit his normal self and he and Mr. G. got along just fine.

We drew more than a few raised eyebrows among the patrons that day. Lily didn't take to the idea when she heard what we had done. In fact, she was furious. I found out later that she had specifically instructed Walter to stay outside if we ever went to Dick's. I took the rap, not wanting to get Walter in any more trouble. Lily didn't buy my reasoning for going in at Mr. G.'s invitation. In the time that she had lived here, she had bought into the old South's thinking on segregation. Of course, she didn't really have any choice and I'm not sure she would understand anyway.

The next day I was called "nigger-lover" by several of the older white boys who resided on the south side of Nash Street. It surprised me that their taunts didn't bother me. I lived a lesson in intolerance that day and learned to appreciate Walter even more for standing up for what he believed was right. Each summer he continued to come to Lily's, and with each visit, he would spend at least one night with me. That eighth summer cemented our friendship and color never was a factor with us.

When I made my suggestion to my four friends that night after the play ended, I had forgotten about how kind Mr. G. had been to Walter and me. I had hoped Jason would just forget about the whole thing. Knowing Jason, that was unlikely. Then yesterday on the way to the movies, I had to go and suggest that the five of us should get together at Dick's. That kicked Jason's memory and my idea surfaced again. He thought the five of us should meet this Friday and finalize our plans and put it to the test this Saturday. Jason said there was no problem graciously extending the Mad Hatter's madness into the month of June and the 8th of June would be perfect. He called it a kick-off to what we hoped would be one hell of a summer. It had definitely started that way.

Friday evening, June 7th, the neighborhood was winding down. It was close to nine o'clock when Matt, Thad, Jason, and I arrived at our usual meeting place on the corner of Nash and Kincaid across the street from my house. A cape of darkness had spread overhead when Byrd with his head down meandered across Nash Street to join the four of us.

"Let's get started. We can still call it March Madness," Jason proudly proclaimed, kicking one of the pinecones resting at his feet.

"This is June," said Matt. "Besides, why give it a name? And if you're going to name it, you need to be more original." Matt could be intolerant if he wanted to be, especially of Jason's pranks. Matt made a guttural noise noting his disapproval.

"So what, fuckhead? Let me remind you—the Mad Hatter was late for the Tea Party with Alice. It'll just be delayed," Jason said. He pretended to be unaffected by Matt's comment.

"I don't think it's a good idea," Byrd said nervously. For some reason, this protest by Byrd irritated Jason. He didn't give a reason why. One look at Jason's flushed face highlighted by the nearby streetlamp was enough to let us know he was pissed.

"Fine, Byrd, so bow out!" Jason countered, giving him the middle finger. Jason reached in his front shirt pocket and took a cigarette from his pack, lit it, and sucked on it hard before he let any smoke out—a sure sign of how royally pissed he was.

"Jason, I think Byrd is right on," said Thad, the most conservative among us and the self-appointed advisor of the five of us on most occasions when we were together. Thad was one of the few who could get Jason's attention and keep it long enough to make his point. This time Jason chose to be bullheaded and it had an opposite effect.

"Damn it, Thaddeus, no one asked you. Take your unwelcome advice and butt the hell out!" Jason took another drag on his cigarette, speaking with self-appointed authority. He obviously thought we were ganging up on him.

"Jason, why don't we drop the whole idea," I said. "Mr. G.'s never done anything but be nice to us." Thinking about Walter again, I felt a pang of conscience. I hoped he might respect my suggestion. I hated myself for coming up with this lame idea. None of us wanted to participate in the prank but we had previously committed and Jason would hold us to our promise. Generally, when the five of us agreed to do something regardless of how foolish, we had an unspoken agreement not to back out unless someone could give a justifiable reason. Tonight, Jason was not going to allow this to happen.

I sensed that Jason's tight friendship with Matt, Byrd, and Thad

had started to deteriorate. The caring camaraderie and laughter that was the glue of their friendship was crumbling. Taking its place was a negative bond, a hostility that ignited whenever they sparred with Jason. Jason wanted his way and they simply let him have it, giving him, at times, too much control. I was in the middle, being pulled in two directions but not wanting to take sides. We were all concerned about Jason, especially his mood swings. We were reluctant, almost fearful, not to go along. It was a thin line and we didn't know where the middle ground was. If we didn't let him have his way, he might go off again and do something really stupid.

"You, too? I thought you were with me, Braxton." He flipped his cigarette toward me; the fire from his cigarette briefly danced with a lightening bug before it landed in some pine needles. "Are you going to be a turncoat like the rest of your friends?" I watched the tiny fire burn itself to oblivion.

"What's that supposed to mean?" Speaking in a professorial manner, Matt stepped forward. He used this tone when he wanted to sound like the wisest among us.

"All right, Jason!" I sighed. "I'm with you. Leave the others out. It's okay. Friendship has nothing to do with this." I grabbed a lightening bug and held it in my fist and let it go. Smiling, I thought this gesture was symbolic of the way Jason had begun to hold us captive always wanting his way.

"The hell you say! What about it, Matt? What about *you?*" Jason loved to needle Matt whenever he had the opportunity, which was not often. Matt was too quick witted for Jason.

"I think your idea is totally sophomoric!" Matt laughed, knowing Jason didn't understand him.

"Screw you, too, Matt. Go back to your dictionary!" said Jason angrily. He looked at Matt in disgust, picked up a pinecone, and threw it against the nearest tree. Jason Parker did not like to be the brunt of anyone's teasing. He could dish it out but he couldn't take it.

"Thesaurus!" said Matt in a scholarly voice. "It is called a thesaurus."

"Sit on it!" Jason, losing his composure, started pounding his left palm with his right fist. "I'm tired of you, assholes, backing out on me at the last minute." He lit another cigarette and threw the match in the pine straw. Thad immediately stepped on it. The light from the streetlamp allowed us to get a good look at Jason's face. He stood for a long time without speaking, becoming quiet and sullen. Watching him exhale an endless stream of smoke through his nostrils, he looked like an enraged bull ready to charge. He was intent on something but on what, none of us knew. This was our cue to back off and let him have his way again.

A part of me wanted to jerk a knot in Jason; but instead, I entertained myself by watching the fireflies dance around the streetlamp. "Okay, Jason, count us in," I spoke, breaking the silence. I stepped forward, slapping Jason across the back in a friendly gesture.

"Yeah, okay, we'll go along with you on this," said Thad. "After all, we did promise." It was settled. Jason looked up and smiled in the face of the light shining across him. He had scored another victory. A bat flew wildly around the street lamp, even hitting it a couple of times. And just as manically, it changed course and came our way. It was like he had one of us in mind as a target. We ducked, covering our heads and with relief, watched it retreat back to the lamp and then fly away. Granny always said bats liked to nest in a human's hair and if it ever got in, there would be little hair left when it got out.

The plan we concocted was to fill as many of the sugar containers used by Dick's Hot Dog with salt as we could in a reasonable amount of time. Jason took my proposal and finalized it. Our plan was innocent enough and the best part was that no one would be harmed. It only required removal of sugar from eight containers, one from each of the eight booths and then adding salt. We decided to leave the four containers sitting on the counter facing the entrance alone. Attempting these would be too risky. Jason had two empty sugar containers at home, similar to those used by Mr. G. He had also temporarily borrowed one from Mr. G. yesterday. This would give us three legs up. Jason estimated that we could complete the exchange between 10:00 A.M. and 11:00 A.M. on Saturday. If we worked fast, we could be out of the restaurant before the big lunch crowd arrived.

Matt and Thad would supply the salt. Byrd would bring a container to put the sugar in. I would help Matt empty and then refill the containers from the outside. Thad and Byrd would carry two containers already filled with salt into the restaurant. They would eat and run interference, if necessary, while Jason did the switching and passing of the remaining containers from the inside to us. We had to hope there wouldn't be an early rush for lunch.

After finalizing our plans, we walked up the street to Dick's. A June moon pushed its way through the clouds that had been holding it prisoner. A stray dog walking on the other side of the street kept eyeing us, giving the impression he had knowledge of our little secret. Jason was the first to enter Dick's followed by Thad, Matt, Byrd and me.

As Byrd pushed against the heavy glass door, he turned and whispered, "Braxton, I need to talk with you after we leave here."

"Okay," I said, wondering what was so important.

Five silly junior high girls had taken the booth we called ours. We forced ourselves into one of the smaller booths. We were more than cramped, but our stay would be short. After a round of Cokes and some fries, we said our goodbyes to Lee and exited laughing and energized, knowing that in less than twenty hours we would be back.

We stepped out of the restaurant and the same stray dog that had followed us sat in the parking lot. His piercing eyes met mine and I felt no better about our plot than I did when I entered. Byrd grabbed me by the arm breaking my pace with the others.

"Hold back so we can talk," he said, lowering his voice.

"Jason, ya'll go ahead," I said. "I'm going to see if anyone inside knows this dog." A lie—but the only thing I could think of at the moment.

After Jason, Thad, and Matt crossed the street, I turned to Byrd, "What's so important?"

"I need you to spend the night with me tonight." There was a panic tone to his voice.

"I can't tonight," I said. "What's going on?"

"It's my Mother," said Byrd. "She's been chewing me out every night at bedtime for no reason."

"That doesn't sound like her," I said.

"You don't know the real Helen Copeland Byrd."

"There's got to be a reason, Byrd," I said. "Think!"

"You've got to keep this to yourself," said Byrd. "I can't let the others know, not now at least."

"I'm not going to tell anyone," I said. "You know that."

"Braxton, I'm afraid she might kill herself and us, too." Byrd's voice was barely audible.

"What do you mean?"

"My mother . . . she . . . she's back to drinking and . . . "

"I thought she'd quit for good."

"Well, not exactly. She tried because it hurt her liver but now she drinks off and on during the day," added Byrd. "Last night I went downstairs and found her on the den floor. She'd passed out and her cigarette had burned a hole in her prized rug."

"What about your father?" I said. "What did he say?"

"He's out of town for the week—a business trip. Mother doesn't believe him." He stopped, spit, rubbed his head, and then continued, "And yesterday morning I had to clean her shit out of her bed when she got up." Byrd's face took on a momentary look of shame. He dropped his head.

"Why didn't you let the maid clean it up?"

"Mother fired her Monday morning. Mother accused her of stealing her silver and threatened to call the police if she didn't leave immediately. Braxton, I don't know what to do and I don't want to face her again tonight." He lifted his head. "Help me!"

"What about Julian? Why can't he help you?" I didn't understand why Byrd hadn't thought to get him to intervene? He had been with their family a long time. "He's right there!"

"He's on vacation this week," Byrd said. "I don't even know where he is?" Byrd sounded nervous.

I put my hand on his shoulder. "Come home with me." I hoped tonight would be quiet at my house.

"I can't leave Charles by himself," Byrd sighed. "He doesn't know how to handle her."

"What about calling your Aunt Olivia?" I took my hand off his shoulder. "She's bound to be able to help you."

"Yeah, I'd thought of that, too," said Byrd "I don't want to make trouble."

"Trouble? You've got trouble as it is!" I stopped. "Listen to me, call her tonight as soon as you get home!"

"You really think I should?" said Byrd, looking like a helpless puppy.

"Damn right!" I said. "Subject closed!" I ran my hand over his head mussing up his hair. I wanted him to know I was there for him.

"See you tomorrow," Byrd said, sticking his hands in his pockets and dropping his head.

The stray dog followed him across Nash Street. As I watched Byrd and the dog walk up the street, I crossed my fingers. I trusted a phone call to his Aunt Olivia would help and not keep him from participating in our prank tomorrow. I wanted him to be with us.

Chapter 12
A Dirty Deed

SATURDAY, JUNE EIGHTH, came and we made eight switches before 11:00 A.M. It was then that Thad told Jason that it was best to get out while we were ahead. Remarkably, Jason agreed. Once outside, the five of us stopped at the edge of the parking lot and in unison, burst out laughing, knowing we had scored a winning touchdown. Now we waited on the outcome—it would be the most aggravating part of our plan—but that was what we had to do—wait nine hours—then come back in the evening after the supper rush and see if we had succeeded. Our plan was to meet at Jason's no later than eight o'clock and return to enjoy our spoils.

The heat seemed to turn up a few degrees on this fine Saturday afternoon. By late afternoon, the sun bowed to heavy clouds forming and collecting together and gaining control of the summer sky. A person given to superstition might have said that the clouds colliding together combined with the blustery wind could be an omen that something bad was to come. Shortly before eight o'clock, I left for Jason's. As I walked up Kincaid Avenue toward Nash Street, I couldn't help but think how eerie it felt outside.

"I nearly pissed in my pants, I got so excited," Jason told me when I arrived at his house.

"That exciting, was it?" I said, not sharing his amusement. I walked over to the large globe setting atop the waist high stand in the parlor corner. I turned it around and around, first slowly and then rapidly. "Jason, why was it that much of a thrill for you?"

"The thrill was in the prospect of getting caught, but we did it. We did it!" Jason was ecstatic. If I hadn't known better, I would have sworn he'd robbed the place. "Braxton, you can be such a square sometimes. Don't tell me you didn't get a charge out of screwing Lee and his old man.

I stopped spinning the globe and turned toward Jason. "You want the truth, Jason? No! Not a damn bit. I think Mr. G.'s nice and he puts up with a lot of crap from us, especially you."

"Who's full of crap?" asked Byrd as Matt, Thad, and he entered into the downstairs' parlor without being detected by either of us.

"Nothing! Braxton was just telling me how we're all going to hell for what we did today," said Jason, laughing. "Come on, let's boogie on over to Dick's and see what's cooking!"

Shortly after eight o'clock, the four of us followed Jason out of his house for our one block walk. The earlier breeze of the evening had mounted in unexpected intensity and now blew hard, making a mocking sound as it passed through the neighborhood oaks and pines. Without introduction, the heavens opened, spitting sheets of raindrops that bounced off the sidewalk like ping pong balls when they hit a hard surface. We picked up our pace and jumped over puddles, hoping not to get soaked by the unexpected shower.

Matt pushed the heavy, singular glass door open and held it while the rest of us barreled inside the nearly empty restaurant. The Pabst clock mounted on the light beige wall read eight-fifteen. It was time to see if our plan had succeeded. I looked around and my eyes locked with the aging, slightly stooped Mr. G. standing at the cash register behind the counter. He bowed in a gentlemanly manner and his usual friendly smile greeted me.

"Hello, Braxton. How are you boys tonight?" He nodded to each of us as we entered.

"Everything's cool," said Jason, speaking in a loud, boisterous voice, announcing our arrival to the few diners in the small restaurant.

"We're okay, Mr. G.," I said, ashamed of my earlier participation in the charade. "How are you tonight?" I paused and swallowed hard. "Have you had a busy day?"

"Never better, Braxton." He looked at each of us. Business has been very good today," answered Mr. G. "What can I get you fellows tonight?"

"Nothing," Byrd and Matt said in unison.

"We ducked in here to get out of the rain," said Matt. "Hope you don't mind. Can we stay until the storm passes over?" Matt's quick response surprised me.

Heavy sheets of raindrops pounded the roof and the first roll of thunder rumbled, shaking the glass windows that surrounded two sides of the restaurant. A scream came from an elderly lady on the other side of the restaurant. Lee went over to comfort her.

"I'm glad you came in. Now, let me treat you boys to a round of Cokes," said Mr. G. He always showed a slight favoritism toward his teenage patrons living in the immediate area. This was good business because we brought our parents back. "You should be safe here. It's not good to be out in an approaching storm, especially an angry one."

None of us said anything. Matt and I stood rigid, exchanging looks. I turned my head toward Thad. He attempted a smile and continued patting his foot against the tile floor. Byrd stood leaning against the counter in front of the cash register. Where was Jason?

The first bolt of lightning sounded like a sudden clash of symbols and a bright flash lit up the outside. Another crackling bolt of lightning followed, again shaking the glass windows giving all of us a scare and reason to pause. An elderly man sitting at one of the smaller tables near us bellowed a four-letter obscenity, his right hand covering his lips. We all stared at him. Mr. G. patiently awaited our response. We stood mute. Thunder pierced the sudden silence that had overtaken the restaurant. We could hear tree limbs snapping and falling resoundingly to the ground. I felt like we were being judged . . . and the heavenly gods had pronounced their sentence. The expression on Matt's face told me that fear had gripped him. I was uneasy myself. Another snap from outside made me jump.

"Well now, like I said I think a round of Cokes is in order," announced Mr. G., raising his voice to be heard over the outside noise.

"That would be great, Mr. G.," said Thad. Matt and I both laughed nervously. Thad never passed up a chance to put something in his stomach. "How about it, guys?"

"Thank you, Mr. G.," Matt said, patting his stomach in jest.

"Here boys, sit over here. I'll be right back with your drinks."

Mr. G. gave us the best seat in the restaurant. It was the booth we claimed as ours: the one circular table in the restaurant with maroon cushioned bench backs and hard wooden seats. It sided the largest glass window overlooking Nash Street, a perfect movie screen for viewing all outside activity. Tonight, I hesitated sitting there. Thad took the window seat on one side of the booth and I slid along the surface of the bench seat, taking the window seat on the other side.

I peered out the window. A ghostly wind whipped through the tall oaks lining the street and their heavy limbs, made brittle by the force of the sudden storm, swayed back and forth in a continuous, mocking manner. The intruding thunder popped harder and lightning pierced the evening sky quicker than a photographer using his flash. All five of us stared at the outside stage, watching with intensity the mounting storm as it bathed all of the props in continued zigzags of bluish white light. The debris blowing through the outside parking lot took on a bewitching character. And the loudest clash of thunder yet shook the massive plate glass window next to our table. The tone of the evening became an early Fourth of July celebration. The atmosphere inside the restaurant was intense, leaving the other patrons nervous without any desire to finish their evening meal.

There was no doubt about it. The outside activity had grabbed everyone's attention and silence visited each table. Our focus became the sugar containers, interrupted spasmodically by the flickering of the inside lights. The containers all appeared to be intact and close to where Jason had left them. The overhead lights flickered a few more times and then settled for the duration of our stay. The tone of the evening had turned suddenly creepy and I felt like an extra in the opening scene of an Alfred Hitchcock movie.

"Taste it, Braxton!" Jason murmured his command, hitting me on my right arm. "Go on, taste it!"

"Okay, just muffle it!" I took the container and poured a small amount of its contents into the palm of my hand and licked it. "Tastes like sugar to me. I think we might be in trouble."

"Let me see! Give it to me!" said Jason. His voice grew louder. "Damn it! Give it to me." Jason grabbed the container out of my hand. He poured some of its contents on his palm and licked. "Shit. It's sugar. Let's go." He attempted to stand.

"No, we *will* stay." I was surprised at myself when I answered him.

"You can stay but I'm not." Jason attempted to move Byrd by pushing him with his left hip.

"Oh, yes! You will stay!" I moved closer to Jason and motioned to Byrd to do the same. Jason found himself sandwiched between the two of us. He wasn't going anywhere. "Take your poison like a man, Jason."

"Here comes Mr. G.," said Thad. "Try to act normal."

"Here we are boys—a round of Cokes and enough French fries for everyone. My compliments." He placed two large baskets of steaming, hot fries in the center of the table and passed a fountain Coke to each of us.

I noticed there was an extra drink on the table. Before I could say anything, Mr. G. pulled up a chair from another table and joined us. He had a smile on his wrinkled, sunburned face. His eyes sparkled like a young boy visiting the Ringling Brothers and Barnum and Bailey circus for the first time.

"What got you boys out of your homes on such a nasty night like tonight?" Mr. G. passed one of the baskets of fries to his left. No one said anything. "Eat up. You boys need to put meat on your young bones." He laughed, eyeing us one by one.

"Boredom got us out and we were headed home when the rain started. So we decided to duck in here and stay dry," said Thad. There was some truth to what Thad said but we all knew why we were here and I was beginning to think Mr. G. might know too. "I'm always hungry, Mr. G., regardless of the time. I don't know about these guys, but you have tempted me," continued Thad. "Pass the ketchup, Matt." Thad didn't hesitate to dig in, dousing his fries with the dark red contents of the Heinz bottle. I honestly believed he had momentarily forgotten why we had come back.

"I'm glad you stopped by. We had an interesting thing happen here today." Mr. G.'s serious expression showed no signs of anger as his eyes met each of ours. Without any prompting, each of us sat up, pressing our backs tightly against the back of the booth.

My stomach began to flutter. *Here it comes,* I thought. Let's get it over with as soon as possible. I began to feel sick. As Mr. G. continued, I sat rigid, ashamed.

"When my young college gal over there . . . " He interrupted himself, pointing toward the grill area. "When she filled the sugar containers today, she made a mistake and put salt in just about every one. Imagine that—a college girl. Can you believe an educated girl would do such a foolish thing?"

"Salt and sugar do look alike, Mr. G.," said Jason, trying to be uncommonly agreeable. It didn't suit him. His sugary attitude made me want to puke.

"Yes, they do, don't they?" Mr. G. nodded, studying and eyeing us one at a time. The gentle expression never left his face. Another pang of guilt pierced my chest.

"Anyone can make a mistake Mr. G.," Byrd said.

But we didn't make a mistake, I thought to myself. I felt more and more uneasy with every minute that passed. If my dad finds out about this, he will have my butt in a sling.

"Do you think so? Well, I guess that's possible. I told her I would have to take all the returned drinks out of her wages. We had two hundred drinks returned at five cents a drink. That was ten dollars— almost ten hours' wages. I hated to take it from her since she is so young and working to help pay college expenses. But she needs to learn." *This could be me,* I thought. In a couple of years, I'll be working my way through college and I'd hate to think some asshole would do this to me. The now warm tingling on the tips of my ears reinforced the guilt feeling I had carried all day. My ears always turned red when I felt guilty of something or when I was mad. I was both, mad at myself for participating and guilty of hurting this girl. I looked at Mr. G. and wondered if he knew what we had done. He was definitely no dummy and his expression never changed. I kind of figured he knew, but I think he also wanted us to squirm a little.

"Mr. G., why don't you let us . . . I mean me, pay for those drinks," said Byrd.

"Why would you want to do that, David?" asked Mr. G.

"I don't know. It just seems right," said Byrd, speaking with authority and looking at Jason. Jason wasn't amused.

"Are you sure you want to do this?" asked Mr. G. "It is not your responsibility." Mr. G. spoke slowly and deliberately and precisely. Jason and Mr. G. locked eyes with an intensity that made Jason Parker squirm.

"Yes," we answered, again in unison. We each chipped in fifty cents, which was two weeks allowance for three of us. Jason and Byrd paid the difference and still had money left.

"That is very kind, boys. Lillian, come here," called Mr. G.

A slender blonde with braces and hair pulled back in a ponytail came to our table. She smiled at Mr. G. Her massive braces looked like iron bars. Mr. G. explained to her that we would pay for the losses. Her eyes filled with tears.

"Thank you, fellows. That is s-o-o sweet of you," Lillian said, smiling.

"That's cool," said Jason. He had a big grin on his face. The jerk now thought he was doing something noble. That was typical Jason, believing he would exit as the hero of the young damsel in distress.

"Well, let's go. I need to get home," I said. I needed air and couldn't wait to get the hell out of the place before I said something to Jason I knew I'd regret. "Thanks Mr. G. for all of your generosity."

"But you have not finished your fries," reminded Mr. G.

"I'll carry them with me," said Thad. "I don't want them to go to waste." He took the napkin holding the fries out of the basket and wrapped another napkin around it and stuffed it in his windbreaker pocket.

"Let's go," I said as another reminder to my friends. "Thanks again, Mr. G."

"Come back, fellows, any time! Be careful going home." Mr. G. walked us to the door.

Once outside, we all gave a big sigh of relief and Jason hollered as loud as he could. I looked back and saw a smiling Mr. G. still standing at the front entrance. We stopped in the parking lot and stood among the puddles of water left by our first storm of the summer. Only a few drops of rain fell now and the air smelled of freshly mowed grass and around us, a few lightening bugs chased each other. The neighborhood was basked in silence and summer vacation was underway and Mr. G. had been gracious enough to allow us to save face in the first among many summer adventures we would have together.

Standing here with my friends, I knew I was not at all happy with my participation in this harmless prank. Tonight we visited the school of life and our teacher taught us two valuable lessons: one of generosity and the other, an emphatic lesson in humility. I never bothered Mr. G. again despite Jason's continued desire to test the kindness of the gentleman from Samos. Jason continued to play his little pranks but the rest of us never actively participated. We, I am ashamed to admit, would continue to serve as onlookers to Jason's foolishness and this would be all the encouragement he needed to continue.

"I'm glad that's over," said Thad. "I felt down right guilty in there."

"You could've fooled me the way you were stuffing those damn fries down," said Jason.

"Well! I did . . . despite what you think, Jason." Thad growled, kicking his foot at the nearest puddle, accidentally sending a spray of water toward Matt.

"You should have too, Jason. All of us should've," Matt said. "It was a dumb thing to do—a damn stupid stunt. I can't believe I even took part in it."

"Why? I don't feel guilty and you can go fuck yourself, Matt. Go fuck all the stupid shit out of yourself. Besides, we paid for the damn drinks, didn't we?" Jason shrugged, kicking his left heel against the sidewalk. "What else do you want?"

Byrd took a few steps toward Pearson Street, stopped, and turned around, facing Jason. "Think that makes what we did right?"

"Oh shit! Get off your fucking soapbox, you turkey." Jason grabbed Byrd by the neck, putting him in a tight bear hug. Then he started running his knuckles across the top of Byrd's head. While Byrd struggled against Jason's hold, Jason tightened his grip around Byrd's neck.

"Let go of me, Jason. I can't breathe. I've had enough of you and your crap today!" Jason let go. At the same time Byrd pulled away, falling down. We all laughed.

"Let's go home," said Matt. "I would like to wipe this night out of my memory."

"Ain't that the truth!" said Thad.

"Go fuck yourselves," said Jason. His victory party had been spoiled but knowing Jason, I was certain he would find some way to celebrate.

Calling a halt to the day's activities was the one thing we all agreed on. It was after ten o'clock and the next day in ecumenical terms was the Sabbath. That meant Sunday school and church for all of us, but Jason. Our parents believed it was their duty to make us go. It was expected of them to do so—to do the right thing. After all, isn't that what good parents do? And our parents genuinely wanted to be good parents. It was not that we would refuse to go or did not want to go, but on some occasions, we might like to do something else—say for example, stay home and sleep.

Jason's parents gave up on him going to Sunday school and church. For a long time, they hadn't cared whether he went or not. Giving in to Jason was easier than putting up with his mouth and all his excuses for not wanting to go. Sometimes he would go with me if he thought Patsy Wentworth would be there; but mostly, he said that he didn't have time for that sissy Sunday school stuff.

Jason didn't even know what denomination he belonged to. When he first told me that, I decided to find out. I had a hunch his parents were Methodists. On some Saturday mornings I would help the secretary at our church run the Sunday bulletins off on the old steno machine. She did confirm that his family was a member of our church but considered inactive. Jason's response to this news was, "That's a lot of crap. They don't even step foot in a church whether it's Methodist, Baptist, Presbyterian, or whatever. I guess my father thinks membership is good for business. Anyway, thanks for telling me. I might need that info some day."

Chapter 13
BLUE CHEESE AFTER TEN O'CLOCK

THE RAIN HAD stopped. The air smelled fresh. Lightening bugs danced through the fog from the rain's aftermath. Street gutters were a torrent of rainwater. All of us needed to get home but we took our time ambling up West Nash Street. Jason called a halt to our procession in the middle of the 1400 block. His addiction had kicked in again and he needed one last smoke before he left us. Behind us was an empty field that could just as easily serve as the future site for two homes. Marking the back end of this field and serving as a fence bordering two thirds of our backyard was a thick eight-foot tall hedge. I could see most of my house easily now and lights were on in every room that ran parallel to the empty field that fronted Nash Street. This included my father's and I felt more of an urgency to get home but I really wanted to stay with my friends a little longer.

For me there was nothing better than stepping outside after a summer's rain—the feeling of freedom it gave me—the sound of crickets and the smell of tobacco dust dangling in the air. I loved being surrounded my by my four best buddies. For a brief moment, I could anticipate the limo rides on the airport runway, girls in short shorts at the Creamery, loading the trunk of the Tank with my buddies and sneaking into the Starlite Drive-in Theater. The thought of this summer and the excitement awaiting us made me smile. For a moment, I forgot what had already happened.

I had lived for this stage in my life. For the first time, I did not have to sneak behind the garage to risk a smoke. My thinking was more independent. I had begun to question some of the tired traditions passed down as wisdom. I was growing up.

We all jumped at the sight of another flashing light that suddenly appeared from the opposite direction. This time the light was blue and it flashed on and off in quick succession. We knew who it was and relaxed, knowing it would soon pass. When the police cruiser got within a half of a block of where we lingered, the siren began to scream, blasting the stillness of the moment.

"Here's the fuzz," said Thad. "He's out for some cheese tonight!" We laughed. We all knew our police department was notorious for its "on scene" behavior. Rumors snaked through our town about some of their tactics. I had heard some of the men in our neighborhood tell my father wild stories about the police's clandestine involvement in bootlegging, gambling, racketeering, and prostitution.

"Wonder who the cheese is tonight?" asked Matt, picking a weed from the field and sticking it between his teeth.

"I hope it's not us," answered Byrd. "I mean we haven't done anything!" It was unlike Byrd to verbally reassure himself.

Before Matt had a chance to respond, the cruiser screeched to a sudden halt and stopped beside where we stood. Two policemen in full dress uniform got out. Neither appeared too friendly and my first instinct was to run. There was no time for that. We all froze.

"Where have you boys been?" asked an overweight, mustached sergeant with a pouchy face pulling out his billy club. He began hitting his left palm in repetition with the wooden club. The other officer stood aside and watched.

"We just left Dick's," said Jason. "About five minutes ago."

"Oh yeah? I just bet you did." The sergeant grinned, taking on the look of a Cheshire cat. He moved first to the left where Thad stood and then to the right where Matt stood, sneering and mocking each of us with facial expressions that resembled those made by cartoon characters on a Saturday matinee. At first, it was hard to keep a straight face. I giggled and so did Byrd.

"Shut up, fatty. What in the hell's so funny?" For the second time this week someone had called me fat. This baboon really ticked me off. I could handle being called solid and chunky but not fat.

"Yes, sir," I said. "You've got a lot of room to talk," I whispered under my breath.

"*What did you say,* you little *punk?*" He moved closer and as he did, his breathing became heavier.

"Nothing . . . I said nothing." I looked at Byrd. The grin on his face had departed. Taking its place was a panicky look.

"Whether you want to believe us or not, we did just leave Dick's," said Byrd. I was thankful for his intervention but not thankful as I watched Jason move forward, attempting to get between the sergeant and Byrd.

"Sure, you did, Goldilocks. And who's this coming?" The sergeant looked at Jason and spit in disdain, hitting the ground in front of Jason's feet. Jason took another step forward. His eyes met the sergeant's. The sergeant stared back all the while slapping his club against his thigh. This cop personified the rumors that ricocheted from backyard to backyard in our town: uneducated, uncivil, mindless, and looking for trouble.

The last thing I wanted to see was Jason do anything stupid. Just as I was about to speak, the sergeant turned, stopped for a moment, and then walked around us. He continued hitting his billy club against his thigh and spitting tobacco at our feet. He wanted to intimidate us. Hell, as far as I was concerned, he had already succeeded. He took a cigarette from his pocket and lit it.

"Why don't you go ask Mr. Gliarmis? He'll tell you we . . . we were just there." Jason stammered. He was irritated and I was afraid he would get us in more trouble if he didn't stop.

"Shut up, kid! I'm not talking to you." The sergeant took a drag on his cigarette and let the smoke out in short spits. "And when you speak to me, you address me as Sergeant Rankin. Now, all of you get up against the car and spread eagle. Powell, don't just stand there. Help me out." The other policeman walked forward and stood beside the obstinate Sergeant Rankin. Smoke encircled my face as I moved toward the police cruiser.

"What do you think we've done, Sergeant Rankin?" With an uncle as a criminal lawyer and an aunt as acting clerk of municipal court, I had heard enough about the injustices of civil rights to know ours were being violated.

"We know what you've done. We don't have to think," he said, fumbling over his words. "We've had reports of teenage boys breaking out street lamps in this area within the last hour. And you're the only damn teenage boys we've seen out on the streets in a five block radius of the person who called in the complaint," continued the fat, beady-eyed police sergeant, pushing me up against the car with his stomach. "Spread your legs, chubby." He slapped my left leg with his club. "Now, all of you spread."

I was flat up against the cruiser with him leaning over me. First, he blew smoke in my face and then he took his club and ran it up and down the back of my rigid torso. "Powell, start at the other end." The officer named Powell did not move. He didn't appear to be enjoying this scene anymore than we were. This was harassment and we were powerless to do a damn thing about it.

Perspiration trickled down my back and chest. My mouth tasted like cotton and I was about to wet my pants. Through the tears forming in my eyes, I saw a dark shape sitting in the back seat of the cruiser on the driver's side, observing and smoking. Cigarette smoke clung like a misty vapor around the shape, making it too difficult to see any expression. The shape turned toward me. I could not tell if watching Rankin jerk us around amused him. After a moment, the shape lit a match and nodded to me and leaned toward me and I knew instantly who he was. I was eyeball to eyeball with Captain Bertram Mays better known as "Bully Bert." I had been his paper-boy when I was twelve and I went to school with his daughter, Mary Anne. The captain had the reputation of being unfair and unneces-sarily cruel in handing out punishment, especially to Negroes and teenagers of any race.

"Captain Mays," I tapped on the window and motioned for him to come out.

"What in the hell do you think you are doing, fatso? I told you I'm in charge here!" the clone of Captain Mays said. Rankin was pissed off. I had broken protocol and his partner had given him no support.

"Sergeant Rankin, I know Captain Mays," I said, trying to find enough saliva to moisten my mouth. I hated the way he kept repeat-ing "fatso" like it was the refrain to some poorly written poem. I was piping mad and a rush of adrenalin swelled within me. The tips of my ears felt hot and I knew at any minute I would erupt. My father warned me that one day my mouth would get me into trouble. Maybe this was the day.

"So what? Lots of people in Wilson know him?" the repulsive sergeant said, leaning into me and pushing me further forward with his watermelon-sized stomach. I grabbed the roof of the cruiser to keep from falling and for the first time, I got a good whiff of his breath. He had been drinking. "You're really getting on my nerves, punk." He pushed against me again.

Captain Mays opened the back door of the cruiser on the street side and got out. He walked around the front of the car and threw his cigarette on the pavement and smeared it out with the toe of his boot. He strode over to where I still leaned against the car and spoke to all of us in a calm, deep bass voice.

"Turn around boys." His stern eyes met mine. "Do I know you?"

"Yes, sir . . . I mean . . . I think so. I'm Braxton Haywood. I used to be your paperboy and I go to school with Mary Anne."

"Don't you live around here, Braxton?" The captain put his massive hand on my right shoulder.

"Yes, sir. I live right over there." I pointed to the top of my roof that could be seen over the hedge at the back of the field where we still stood. "I was on my way home."

"I know your father, Braxton. He's a good man. He's been sick a long time. Is he any better?" He pulled a cigarette from his shirt pocket and lit it. He seemed genuine and I took this as a good sign. His hand still resting on my shoulder gripped my shoulder bone and I began to relax. He squeezed it several time in a friendly, manly way before letting go. I lost whatever fear I had.

"No, sir. If anything, he's getting worse, but thank you for asking."

"I'm sorry to hear that, Braxton." He smiled, lifting his head and blowing a circle of smoke toward the clearing night sky. "By the way, you were the best damn paperboy we've ever had."

"Thank you, Captain Mays." The captain before us was a tall, strongly built hulk of a man but he showed he could be nice. This was a contradiction to what I had been told by some of the older boys at school who frequently had skirmishes with the law.

"Sergeant Rankin, I think we've detained these boys as long as we need to. We know where Braxton, here, lives. I believe Mr. Gliarmis will verify their story. If not, we know where to find Braxton and he will take us to the rest." The captain reached out and shook my hand.

"Thank you, Captain Mays." I could tell Sergeant Rankin was not pleased with his captain's decision. It did not bother Powell. I looked at Rankin and he had fire in his eyes and I knew he hated me, especially after the reprieve we had received from his captain. Rankin now had to find some other cheese to mess with to fulfill his nightly jollies.

Captain Mays seemed certain I would rat on my friends but I believe he knew we told him the truth. This was my first encounter with the police and little did I know it would not be my last this summer.

I told my friends good night. Byrd nodded to let me know he was okay. I had not even asked about his mother. I walked the rest of the way home by myself. I decided I would not mention any of today's activities to my parents. Once in the house, I quietly told my mother good night and went into my bedroom. A train whistle blew signaling the eleven o'clock hour as it made its nightly run on the rickety tracks of the Norfolk-Southern Railroad that divided "colored town" from the white area of Wilson

Silence fell across the night and for a brief time, I felt secure. I slept like a possum until I was awakened the next morning.

Chapter 14
AUNT EVA ON SUNDAY MORNING

SUNDAY MORNING WAS my day to get up before anyone else in our house. It used to be my father who got up but now it had fallen upon me. Every Sunday I repeated the same ritual: fix cereal with bananas for my sister and myself, and for Mother, prepare her breakfast. It had to be exact—one piece of dry toast cut diagonally and one cup of Maxwell House coffee with one teaspoon of sugar and slightly less than a teaspoon's portion of milk, already stirred. On Sunday mornings I was not to disturb my father unless he called for me. This he seldom did unless it was to bring him another pack of Lucky Strikes or a cup of black coffee. His attendant, Jackson, was off on Sundays.

Sundays were Lily's days to be with her husband, go to church, and do whatever else she couldn't get done the other five and one half days of the week. Sunday was the one day of the week that our house seemed cold and empty, and I felt tense and alone. There was no real laughter when Lily and Jackson were gone. I hated it when they had their day off. I missed Lily terribly.

It didn't matter to me that Lily was colored or that she wasn't a Southerner or that she liked cats better than dogs. She was infectious—someone you wanted to be around regardless of the reason. Just the sound of her voice gave me a sense of security. And knowing she would set me straight if I got out of line was reason enough to show her my respect. She cared about us and that was what mattered.

Anne could be difficult on Sunday mornings. It fell on me to help her get ready for Sunday school and church. Even if she'd wanted me to help her choose the right clothes to wear, I was not the one to give this kind of advice. Anyhow, she was too old. And furthermore, I was far too incapable of tying bows and ribbons for her hair. I just left her alone and that suited Anne fine.

On Sundays, Anne moved at a snail's pace. If I pushed her to move faster, she became moody. When we did argue on these mornings and we usually did, we yelled at each other in a whisper so as not to bother our father. In turn, this irritated me. Most weeks, Sunday was like trying to start a car with a dead battery. These were inconsistent days and on these mornings, I knew I needed assistance. I needed Lily and with her came her patience, her advice, and her wisdom.

Wilson was not what I thought defined a religious town. If it was, we had our share of hypocrites filling pews every Sunday morning. Wilson did have its share of Protestant churches with the Baptist having the most. There was one Jewish Synagogue and one Catholic Church. With the exception of the non-protestant denominations, men attended the church where their fathers had gone and wives went where their husbands went. In the South, attending church with one's family was a tradition that many families practiced faithfully. It was a duty and it was expected and many families like robots mechanically fell into line and went. People equated religious with goodness. To hear someone say, "They're a good family. They go to church every Sunday" was something parents hungered to hear. My parents were not what some church-going people in our town called religious people.

If you put any faith in what my great Aunt Eva, my granny's younger sister, said, then the Baptist were the most religious in our town. "They think they are," she would say. "And, you know, they claim to be authorities on scripture as well as who will and will not get into heaven." I don't know why, but I think she was a tad jealous. My Aunt Josephine was a member of the First Baptist Church but she wasn't at all like the Baptists Aunt Eva described.

To my recollection, my mother never went to church with me but I do remember sitting on occasions in the center balcony of the First United Methodist Church with my father. My father would never sit downstairs and I retained his habit of sitting in the balcony when he could no longer go with me. I missed our church time together, especially that sense of comfort I got as a young boy leaning against his shoulder. A father can sometimes shed light on those tougher-than-nails theological questions a young kid can't figure out—like what is the Virgin birth or what does resurrection mean?

My father was not an educated man; in fact, he only had a high school diploma—eleventh grade was graduation in his time. He never taught a Bible class and he rarely even read the Bible but I was still proud of my father. When it came to his knowledge of theology, he knew how to respond to most of my questions without making me feel stupid. That was before the cancer grabbed him, making him so sick. His sickness stopped him—stopped him completely—from going to church with me, from answering my questions, and from being interested in me.

After coming home from church one Sunday, I asked him a question about The Second Coming. It was mentioned in the sermon and my eight-year-old ears had never heard this term. I shared my confusion with him and waited for an answer. There was a brief period of silence and I repeated that I wished he would explain to me what it meant. He responded by getting mad and telling me that if I had any common sense, I'd know the answer. Lily told me, "don't you go and get angry with your daddy, Braxton. That there's his sickness talking. He don't mean nothing by it." Lily knew how sensitive I could be.

From that time on, I promised myself that I would never forget his hurtful words and the way he said them to me. I decided if he could hurt me, I could hurt him. I became determined never to ask him anything else about religion or any other subject. Who needed him? I certainly didn't.

It was near the end of my third grade year at Woodard School when my uncle, Dr. Victor Thaxton, and two other Wilson doctors went with my father to New York City to have him examined by cancer specialists. The doctors in New York City opened up my father and saw that his cancer had spread like a raging fire. There was nothing they could do but sew him back up and send him home. That's what they did. Cancer was everywhere and like acid, eating him alive. That was how Mother explained it to us. The cancer got to my father in a bad way and reduced him to a living skeleton. The New York doctors gave him six to twelve months, at most, to live. My father beat those odds, living almost another seven and one-half years.

After his diagnosis, my father slowed down a lot. He began to distance himself from everything and most everybody. His will to live had not been totally squelched but his death sentence changed him dramatically. He lost interest in me and my schoolwork and my outside activities and everything about me. We drifted apart and over time, I decided that in addition to not having any common sense, he was disappointed in me as a son. I tried to convince myself that it wasn't my fault—that it was the cancer's doing. This was hard to practice because he still found time for Anne and openly loved her. They grew closer after his return from New York. He would even go to the movies with her when I knew the cancer screamed inside of him. Oh, he would ask me to come along, but I didn't. Lily and my mother said I was being too sensitive. Hell! It was obvious. He didn't have much to say to me before he left and he had even less to say after his return. He all but ignored me.

Even after my father could no longer attend church, Mother insisted that Anne and I go to Sunday school and church every Sunday. Mother made no effort to go with us but to her credit, sometimes when she felt well, she would get us there in time for Sunday school, leaving it up to me to find us a way home. I hated this arrangement. Most often, the people we might ask for a ride either attended church with their family and there was not enough room in their car for two more or they were going out to lunch immediately after church.

On this Sunday, the ninth of June, my great aunt, Eva Lucas Ruffin Young, volunteered to take us to Sunday school. "This will give you another jewel in your crown," my great Aunt Grace said, teasing her. Aunt Grace, Granny and Eva's other living sister, was an atheist and thought her sister was too deeds-oriented. This was another term used with religion I did not understand. All I knew was that Aunt Grace was against organized religion and never went to church.

Aunt Eva was very active in the First United Methodist Church. At the age of sixty-eight, she taught the Ladies Bible Class and she was the secretary/treasurer of the Women's Missionary Society. And she had an opinion on everything that took place in the church. Her zeal for being involved in the life of the church carried over to her insistence on being prompt and carrying her Bible every Sunday. Aunt Eva was faithful that way.

I received a New Testament Bible when I was baptized at age twelve. I didn't know where it was and if I did, I doubted I would carry it with me. No Sunday school teacher ever asked us to bring one was what I told Aunt Eva when she chided me that I needed one. "Everyone should carry a Bible to church," said Aunt Eva. "Don't y'all have another Bible in the house?" We did but it was too big to take to church.

My father and mother kept the large, tattered Haywood family Bible in the top drawer of the desk in the living room. I had never unlocked the drawer but I knew the book was there. I saw my father put it back in that same drawer after he had last read to me the comments his own father, a self-taught biblical scholar, had written in the front. I do not remember my grandfather's comments but I do remember the beautiful colored pictures in the old Bible and my fascination with the picture depicting Sampson pushing over the temple pillars.

Today was promotion Sunday at church and this was one time I didn't want to be late for Sunday school. Finally, I would move up to the eleventh and twelfth grade boy's class, the class envied by every fifth through tenth grade boy in our church. I had wanted to be in this class for a long time, primarily because of who was teaching it. I had heard many stories about my new Sunday school teacher, Charles Anderson. Everyone in Wilson called him Chuck, regardless of his age. Chuck was Wilson's war hero and every boy knew his story and how our town gave him a true hero's welcome on his return from World War II.

I didn't know how much I would learn about the Bible in his class but I expected to be entertained by his war stories. Chuck had the reputation of being a vivid storyteller who could hold his teenage class captive with his war stories and I understood that he had hundreds to tell. I wanted to hear first hand about his capture by the Nazi's and how he escaped. This was the first time since I started junior high school that I actually looked forward to going to Sunday school.

At most churches in our town, Sunday school started at 9:40 A.M. and at exactly 9:10 A.M., Aunt Eva was outside our house, blowing the horn of her 1952 light blue Chevrolet. Like always, she was early. Mother said Aunt Eva wanted to get there before the other old ladies so she could flirt with the older men who could still breathe and walk. I understood Mother's kidding and anyway, that was okay with me. Aunt Eva had married again after her first husband died. She outlived that husband too. I figured she deserved to have a little fun, even at church.

Thinking we had not heard her blow the horn, she laid a loud honk on again and held it there for a few moments. This annoyed Mother because she thought it bothered my father. I rushed to the door, opened it, and waved.

"We're coming, Aunt Eva." I turned, grabbed my sister's hand and pulled her out the front door with me. With my sister still trailing, we ran down the steps, over the stepping-stones that served as a walkway and over to the car.

Already a steamy morning, the streets shimmered under the morning sun. Aunt Eva's body moved from side to side behind the steering wheel of her beloved Clara, the name she had given to her Chevy. She appeared to be singing but the car windows were up and I couldn't be certain. My aunt looked joyful but then, she did most of the time. As she rolled down her window to speak, I thought I saw tiny beads of perspiration on her plump cheeks.

"Get in the back, children. I have flowers up here with me." She always carried flowers or cake or something to church. "Don't roll down the windows, please. I wouldn't want to mess up my new hairdo." She cleared her throat, hinting for a compliment. Silence. We did not respond. "You children look handsome in your Sunday clothes."

"Thank you. You look pretty, too," said Anne, smiling. "Aunt Eva, that's a fancy hat you have on."

"Then you like it?" Aunt Eva said, fishing for another compliment. "I bought it just this week at Miss Bessie's Hat Shop. I just couldn't decide about this veil." She blew lightly with her pursed lips against the mesh hanging on the bridge of her nose revealing too much powder on her forehead. The veil moved outward and fell back in place.

"Oh! Yes ma'am. It looks real nice on you." Anne said. "I particularly like that flower. What kind is it?"

"It's supposed to be a peony. I didn't know if it was too red. Maybe I should have gotten a pink peony instead. What do you think, Braxton?"

"I agree. It's nice." I couldn't hurt her feelings but I wanted to tell her the flower was too big for the hat. Aunt Eva had a Lucas head just like her two brothers and her hat was too small for such a large head. Besides, it definitely clashed with the dye in her silver-blue hair. The whole thing looked silly but how do you tell someone that without insulting them.

"You smell good, too," said Anne. I put my finger over my nose, kicking Anne's shoe with my right foot.

"I saw that, Braxton," Aunt Eva said. "Thank you, Anne. It's Chanel # 5 and very expensive. My perfume is one of the little ways I treat myself." My aunt had overly blessed herself today with this fragrance. Maybe she did have a new beau.

The inside of her car with the four windows up was too warm and my nostrils began to close. My palms were wet and I could feel the sweat gathering inside my collar, clinging to my neck. "It's hot in here, Aunt Eva." She didn't answer. "Aunt Eva, roll the window down a little bit, please." She caught my eyes in the rear view mirror but ignored my request. "Today is promotion Sunday at church. I will be going into Chuck Anderson's class."

This time I got an immediate response. "Umph! I don't know whether I agree that Charles Wesley Anderson should be teaching you boys."

"But he's taught a long time," I said.

"Some people in the church think he has taught too long and that he's a bad influence on young boys." She glared at me through the rear view mirror. There was nothing wrong with her hearing. Like my granny said, Eva selectively listens.

"That's crazy," I said without thinking. "Why would people think that?"

"Well, let's just say that his version of teaching and the church's version are different."

"What do you think, Aunt Eva? You teach Sunday school," I asked, knowing that my great aunt was a reader of the Bible and would have an opinion.

I was surprised at her response. "What I think doesn't really matter, but I do believe every Sunday school teacher should teach from the Bible and that includes Charles Anderson."

"Well, maybe he does. Maybe he just has his own way of teaching it," I said.

"That's not what I hear." I could see her face in the rearview mirror. She had pursed her lips smearing her lipstick. Ever since Aunt Eva had cut back on her smoking, she did this whenever she got a little flustered. "He should follow the version approved by the church." Agitated, my aunt cracked her window letting in the first breath of hot air since we had stepped into the car. It was of little help.

"I hear he's a good teacher and tells good stories," I said, not knowing what my aunt meant by the church's version. I wiped the sweat from my brow with the back of my right hand.

"I'm certain he does tell good stories, just the wrong kind. You'll see, Braxton. You'll see. You'll see that I'm right," she said, making me wish I had kept my mouth shut. It was now hot enough to fry an egg in her car. The overpowering smell of the Chanel she had liberally doused herself with forced me to roll down my window about an inch. Remarkably, my aunt did not even notice.

"Okay, okay." I wondered why older people always thought they knew what was best for us young people. Had they forgotten what it was like to be young and have different opinions? Next time I would avoid this subject with her. I did not want to get Chuck in trouble with our church.

Aunt Eva got her usual place in the parking lot on the north side of the church. Her name was not on the space but it might as well have been because she would have had a "hissy" if someone had beaten her to it. She always claimed the same parking place just like some people claim a pew in the church. I think it had something to do with what she perceived as an earned right. I wanted to say something but I bit my lip and said nothing.

"The Lord blessed me again today by saving this parking place for me," she said. I smiled.

"Yes ma'am," Anne said. I waited for an "amen," but it never came.

"You children come straight to this car as soon as the service is over. I don't want to have to sit around and wait for you. Make sure both of you are prompt," my aunt said in her best Sunday elocution.

Anne and I got out of the car just in time to watch the very plump figure of our aunt slide from behind the steering wheel and maneuver her feet onto the pavement of the parking lot. Once standing, she reached back into the front seat and grabbed her bouquet of flowers. The back of her dress went up and her black slip hung slightly above the back of her knees. Pulling herself out, she bumped her head on the sill of the door knocking her hat forward. Trying not to show any impatience, she put the flowers on the roof of the car and straightened her hat. "Does it look okay, Anne?"

"Yes ma'am."

"Thank you, Anne." It was all I could do not to laugh. I could feel myself beginning to grin. "None of that young man. Don't you disrespect me in the Lord's parking lot!"

"No ma'am. I'm sorry," I said. It was just kind of funny to watch her come apart after such careful precaution to be prim and proper.

"Damn!"

"Pardon, Aunt Eva?" I asked.

"Nothing, Braxton . . . Absolutely nothing." Aunt Eva straightened her blouse. "You didn't hear me say anything!"

"Yes ma'am." I looked away, muffling a laugh.

Aunt Eva took her hands, put one on each hip and pulled on her dress to realign her corset. She reached behind with her right hand and grabbed her dress in the fanny area. She gave one hard pull, her dress came down, and the black slip disappeared under the hem. Taking her flowers from the roof, she huffed off in anger, leaving us standing at the car. I wondered how long she would make us wait for her once the service let out. If she talked to everyone she knew we would have to wait at least forty-five minutes to an hour.

"Come on, Anne, let's walk uptown and I'll buy you a cherry Coke," I said. Some Wilsonians thought the Soda Shop's cherry and vanilla Cokes over crushed ice were the best in all of downtown. They were good but at the moment I didn't care. All I could think about was getting something cold in my mouth. My throat was dry from being cooped up in Aunt Eva's car and I figured Anne's was too.

The Soda Shop was a little alley shop next to Singer Sewing Machine Company on West Nash Street. A popular location on Sundays, it was only one long block's walking distance from our church. It was too early to go to class and this would be a practical way to kill time.

Most every Sunday the same crowd of older kids walked to the soda shop during the church service and then returned, sneaking back into the sanctuary during the singing of the last hymn. It was an old trick and their parents usually thought their children had been in church the whole time. Most of them got away with it most of the time.

Anne got over the shock of my invitation by the time I placed the Coke in her hand.

"Thank you, Braxton. What gives?"

"Nothing. Can't I treat my little sis to a drink?"

"Yes. I just know there'll be a payback some time."

"Probably, but just enjoy it, okay?" I loved my sister and felt sorry for her. She was having a difficult time with Daddy's sickness and Mother was on her back too much, nagging, picking and correcting her over silly things like twisting the rug when she walked across it. I just didn't want her to think she was by herself in this. I knew things might get worse.

Chapter 15
CAPTAIN CHUCK AND THE PAPER AIRPLANE

ANNE SAT ON the only wooden bench, now painted another coat of dark green, outside the Soda Shop sipping her cherry Coke through a straw. Above her head hung a weather beaten green awning with white stripes that momentarily shielded her upper torso from the penetrating rays of a hostile morning sun. I sat beside her. Her legs swung back and forth and I watched her little feet clothed in white socks and black patent leather shoes dance in and out of the sunlight to whatever music played inside her head. We stared at nothing in particular. A middle-aged white male dressed in overalls and a white shirt stood on a tall wooden stepladder meticulously changing the letters on the marquis of the Center Theater, formerly the Oasis Theatre. The new feature titled *Blue Gardenia* starred Anne Bancroft and featured Nat King Cole singing the theme song. Anne and I were not allowed to go to a movie on Sunday, the Lord's Day. Our parents, like some of my church-going friend's parents, were conservative, almost fundamental, in their thinking and practices on the Sabbath. Going to the movies, playing cards, and dancing were considered dishonoring to God. I never got any satisfactory reasons as to the why of these practices.

Teenagers came and went out of the Soda Shop. A couple of older boys walked across the street and stood under the awning of Moss' Shoe Store. They turned their backs to the street in order to catch a secret smoke before Sunday school started. Their goofy antics and laughter gave the impression they were much younger.

"Do you know any of those boys in front of the shoe store, Braxton?" Anne asked.

"I know their names but I don't really know them. Why?"

"Well. They didn't speak to you before they crossed the street."

"They're seniors in high school now and it's not always cool to speak to underclassmen."

"That's not right," a disgruntled Anne remarked. "Braxton, can I ask you something?"

"Sure, you can," I said. "I don't know whether I'll answer you or not."

"Do you smoke?" Anne asked, matter-of-factly.

"Heck, *no!*" I said, crossing my finger behind my back. "What made you ask that?"

"Just wondered," Ann smiled in a funny way. "Have you ever tried?"

"Yep, a couple of times." I didn't think telling the truth this time would hurt me.

"Did you like it?"

"Yeah . . . I guess," I said. "Yes, I was surprised I did." Anne's eyebrows did a double take, moving up and down several times before returning to their normal position.

"I'm never going to smoke, Braxton. I don't want to get sick like Daddy." After a deep sigh, Anne continued, "Braxton, will you promise me something?"

"I don't know," I said. "What is it?"

"Please don't smoke," Anne grabbed my hand and squeezed.

"I'll think about it," I said. "I'll probably never get addicted."

"And Braxton, thank you."

"For what?"

"Being so nice to me today," Anne said, releasing her grip on my hand. "I love you even if you are my big brother."

"Okay, let's not get too mushy here," I said, feeling my cheeks getting warm. "And I think you're real cool, too . . . I mean . . . for a little sister."

By the time we got back to the church, it was time to go to class. Anne's age group had already been promoted. All rising seventh graders started their new class in early May. It had something to do with junior high and starting Methodist Youth Fellowship. She was excited too, but not as excited as I.

I left Anne at the door of her first floor classroom and walked up the seventy-five-year-old, wooden stairs to the second floor. Chuck's room number was 210. I immediately recognized the handsome, controversial war hero standing in the doorway, greeting the boys as they entered. I ducked into the boy's bathroom to see if my short brown hair had a part in it. The mirror told me that the part was where I had left it and my cowlick was down for a change. My tie was tied the best I could get it. It was a self-taught knot but I wanted to learn to tie a Windsor.

I turned and grabbed a towel from the rack, wiping the perspiration off my forehead. I walked a few steps toward the door, wadded the towel into a ball, turned, and aimed for the canister. Two points! My armpits were sticky wet and I felt sweat on the lower part of my back. Despite these slight annoyances and the worn hand-me-down burgundy sports jacket, I thought I was ready for inspection. Turning around, I checked myself again. The mirror did not lie. There was room for improvement but my jacket more than made up for any imperfections. I liked this jacket; the stud Johnny Thurston had worn it first. The fact that his coat was passed on to me and I could fit into it gave me more confidence. I pulled in my stomach as far as I could and left the boy's bathroom. My five-foot-nine-inch frame walked up to the tall brunette standing outside room 210. He greeted me with a firm handshake.

"Good grip, son," said my new Sunday school teacher. With his neatly combed hair, closely trimmed mustache, and strong looking physique, I was certain there was no way he could be intimidated by what other people said and thought of him. I knew for a fact that many women, single and married, thought he was one of the best looking men in our town—medium skin complexion that tanned easily, chiseled features, thick, wavy brown hair with some graying at the temples, dark eyebrows, penetrating hazel eyes, and a dimple on his right cheek when he smiled. Above his left eyebrow was a small scar left by a German sword. Without a doubt, Chuck Anderson mirrored the adult version of a real stud.

"Thank you, sir," I said, standing erect with my stomach pulled in tightly. I looked him straight in the eyes.

"Dispense with the sir, private," he laughed, slapping me on the back. I swallowed a cough.

"My name is Braxton Haywood," I said with the greatest pride.

"My name is Charles Wesley Anderson. Call me Chuck, Braxton. Glad to have you on our team this year." His baritone voice caught the attention of other teens milling around in the hallway. They stopped and turned in our direction and then continued with their conversations.

"Thank you, Chuck," I said. I walked with renewed confidence into the already crowded classroom. Matt and Thad sat on the other side of the room facing the door. They had saved a seat for me.

"Hey guys. Y'all got here early." I took my seat beside Matt.

"Right on time!" said Matt. "You're running a little late. That's unusual for you."

Before I could answer, the bell rang. Chuck strolled into the room, the taps on the heel of his polished black boots clicking in rhythm each time they struck the wooden floor. There was a sudden hush—an awed silence. After shutting the door, he walked toward the left side of the room, each step followed by a click of the taps, echoing in perfect cadence as if he had practiced it hundreds of times. He stopped behind the teacher's desk and stood still, surveying his audience. Then he pulled out a chair and promptly put his right foot on the seat. Taking a cigarette from the pack inside his jacket pocket and packing it against his watch, then flipping his lighter with controlled ease, our teacher lit his Camel. He inhaled deeply and with little effort, let the smoke exit his nostrils with great finesse. He was calm, in control and better than any TV commercial. I looked at my friends and then those who sat directly across from me. Some showed surprise; the older boys took it in stride.

Chuck Anderson's attire confirmed my earlier impression that he was one heck of a stud man. Removing his dark blue sports coat, he folded it and laid it over the back of his chair. I was amazed at the massive size of his chest. His pectoral muscles pushed hard against his thickly starched white shirt with monogrammed gold cufflinks in each cuff. His pleated trousers had been carefully pressed and his blue and gold striped tie was knotted in a perfect Windsor. I knew I would like this man and his class. Then he dropped a bombshell.

"Boys, welcome to my class. I'm glad you all came today and I hope you will continue to come back. Some of you might think I'm a bit unorthodox but remember I'm a military man through and through and because of this, I don't expect any crap from any of you. If you give me any shit, you'll leave this room. Any questions so far?" He had a natural, good-natured delivery that enunciated each word and challenged anyone to find fault with his comments.

All the new boys, rising eleventh graders, sat scattered around the room in silence, afraid to look at each other. I wanted to scan the room, to see their reaction, but I wanted to be a part of this group. I wanted to blend in and give our teacher the reaction he wanted to see.

Inside my mind, I was confused. Was I in boot camp or Sunday school? I didn't know what unorthodox meant and I had never heard a holy man curse, much less in church.

"Are there any questions, I said?" repeated the stud man.

"No sir," chimed the rising twelfth grade boys in unison

"Let's get some preliminary introductions out of the way." He paused and looked around the room. All eyes were on stud man, waiting for him to continue. "First, I want you to call me Chuck. No one need call me Mr. Anderson. Second, I was a captain in the infantry and I fought in the Great War, the War of Wars, and if you don't know what war I'm talking about, you haven't been listening in school. Who knows the war I am alluding to?"

"World War II was the great war, sir," answered Walter Dixon, a rising senior and fullback on the football team.

"Thank you, Walter," Chuck said. "You sound like a damn apple polisher."

"Yes, sir!" responded Walter before realizing what he had said.

"You know better than to say sir." Chuck gave Walter a stare that made him squirm uncomfortably in his chair. "Just drop the sir crap, Walter. In fact, that goes for all of you! Understand?"

"Yes, sir," We said together.

"My God, what's wrong with you kids? Don't you *listen* to any-thing? I said do *not* refer to the Captain as sir. Do *you* understand?" For the first time, the stud man seemed rifled.

"*Yes!*" The choral answer reverberated off the faded beige walls of the large room with its nine-foot ceilings. I began to see our teacher in a new way. The stud man who had mesmerized me with his good looks and reputation had taken on a new dimension. He was now in the role of our captain. I wondered if the captain was into mind games and if so, was this a test for the new boys. He did seem to be watching us more keenly as we reacted to his style.

"Good! Now men, you will hear me talk about a half of a man named Adolf Hitler. The first thing you need to know about this maniac is that . . ." The captain stopped abruptly, looked around the room demanding attention from each of us. "Make no mistake about it; Adolf Hitler was an S.O.B. Yes! You heard me correctly and each of you already knows what that stands for." He paused. No one giggled; in fact, no one made a sound. "He was a real bastard and I'll tell you enough about him that will make all of you hate his damn guts, too!"

Chuck paused again, this time wiping his mouth with the back of his hand. I didn't think this sudden break in his delivery was due to some uncertainty or hesitation. His eyes had taken on a quickened look, telling me that he was lost in thought, perhaps a painful memory from the war. Chuck Anderson was believable in his role as our captain. And wherever the captain was in thought, he stayed less than a minute. He dropped his cigarette butt in the Styrofoam cup sitting on the table, cleared his throat, took out another cigarette, and with the same ease, completed his former ritual. This time it didn't have the same macho ring to it. I turned my head slightly, hoping to get Matt and Thad's attention. Neither looked my way. The captain began speaking again.

"Now, men! Make no mistake about what I am getting ready to tell you." He rammed one tightened fist into the other, making a popping noise. *Ouch! The force of that punch would hurt any man,* I thought. I corrected my posture, pulling in my stomach and sitting more erect in my chair despite the hard wooden seat. "Clear your heads and make no mistake about whose side God was on in WWII." The captain paused. "There is no debate. There is no question. There is no doubt about it! God was on our side. We would not have won that damn war if God had not been on our side. Men, make no mistake! God was our leader and guide and as I like to think, God was our general." The captain inhaled and blew smoke rings across the table. I watched each ring drift upward and disappear and I wished Jason could have been here to see the cool way Chuck smoked—the finesse he used that was natural. The manner in which he held a cigarette, took it to his lips, and then followed the ritual through to completion was neither forced nor contrived. It was a display of perfection. "Does anybody have a question for me?"

"I do," said Dwight Cummings, a pale, slender boy with a slight case of acne. Dwight and his family had recently moved to Wilson. His father, an attorney, had joined one of Wilson's oldest and most profitable firms.

"Speak up, kid!" ordered the captain.

Dwight was fast to get up from his wooden chair. He uncrossed his arms, letting them fall to his sides. He exercised his fingers, allowing them to move slowly until they found their way into the pockets of his trousers. Hesitating at first, he looked directly into the face of our captain and asked, "Is the cursing really necessary?"

"You have a problem with the way I talk, son?" asked Chuck, turning slightly red in the face. I wondered if this was the first time he had been challenged by a student. Was Dwight crazy?

"Yes and no. I just don't think it's necessary to curse in a Sunday school class," said Dwight. There was a movement of chairs scraping the floor, letting the outsider know he stood alone in this confrontation. "You . . . you're not setting a very good example as a teacher." The class, again, became deathly quiet. I was afraid to breathe. This time I looked at the others: there was shock and disbelief in the eyes of the seniors directly across the room from me. The fact that a student had challenged Chuck Anderson, our captain and Wilson's wartime hero, was unthinkable, especially a skinny newcomer to our town.

"I tell you what kid. If you have a problem with the way I teach, I suggest you meet with the ladies next week. Maybe that's more your cup of tea. This class is for young men!" said Chuck. Despite the low blow delivered by the captain, there was a loud burst of applause from the other side of the room and stomping of feet against the floor. The captain said nothing. Instead, he glared at the seniors, not in disapproval, but to give a signal that it was time to stop the noise. The room became quiet again.

Dwight stood there in front of his chair, looking lost and abandoned. He never took his gaze off our teacher. I stared at Dwight in disbelief. I thought he was a nitwit and yet, he had to have had balls of steel to challenge Chuck Anderson. I wondered if any other teenager had ever challenged the war hero on his own turf. One thing I could be sure of and that was Dwight didn't know how to choose his battles wisely. Knowingly or unknowingly, Dwight Cummings had made a mark for himself that would never be forgotten by any of us in this room. I couldn't help but admire this new kid in town and I wanted to get to know him better. One look at our teacher told me that he was peeved. At exactly what, I was uncertain.

Chuck motioned for Dwight to take his seat. He had another cigarette lit and his wristwatch dangled from his right hand. A slight grin fell across his lips.

"Well men, we are going to stop here today. I will see you next Sunday. Have a good week and remember who the great general in the sky is. You may go."

The class got up to leave. At first, everyone remained quiet and each boy took his own time leaving the room. A few seniors stopped to say goodbye to our teacher; others mumbled among themselves but most of us said nothing. I now knew what the word unorthodox meant. I was pleased that I had learned a new vocabulary word. I was not pleased that my first class with Chuck Anderson ended abruptly. I was proud of Dwight for exercising his free speech. This class would not only be a challenge for the teacher, but it would be an exciting twist from the previous year with Miss Laura Claxton who cried and ran out of the classroom whenever she could not control us.

"Hey kid, come here a minute," Chuck said, motioning to Dwight.

Walking out the door, I glanced back and saw Dwight standing before Chuck listening to whatever was being said to him. I wondered if Dwight was getting his "you know what" chewed out royally. I wanted to find out, and I would later.

Matt and Thad waited for me in the musty, dimly lit hall. We exchanged comments between ourselves about our first introduction to Captain Chuck Anderson's class.

"I wasn't impressed," said Matt. "I got tired of all his military verbiage. I think he's full of B. S. I wanted to ask him where were we to sign up."

"We need to give him a chance," said Thad. Thad always gave everyone the benefit of the doubt the first time around. "I think he had a few mind games he wanted to try out on us."

"He is unorthodox," I said, borrowing the word I had learned from Chuck. "He does have a different style of teaching."

"Aren't we throwing the words around this morning? Who have you been listening to?" said Matt. "I know that comment didn't give birth in your brain."

"Come on Matt, can't I have an original thought, too?" I said. "But you're right; I did hear someone say something like that not more than thirty minutes ago." I smiled. "Weren't you listening in class? It came right out of the captain's mouth." I slapped Matt on the back in jest.

Matt shook his head. He really didn't know it had been used in class. I winced. Obviously, the captain was unable to keep his attention and knowing Matt, he probably turned the captain off. Matt was smarter than he let on. He was more serious than the rest of us when it came to things like religion, politics, war, morality and adhering to the system. He operated on a deeper thinking plain than the rest of us. He had recently begun questioning whether going to Sunday school served any purpose. He only went to pacify his parents. His regular attendance was a smoke screen until he could gather the nerve to tell his parents of his existing doubts about God.

I blame Ayn Rand's anti-God philosophy for influencing Matt. He had read one of her books and was on his second. It was almost as if her words and ideas had hypnotized him, turning him completely against everything his parents and the church had taught him about God. Matt recognized his need to be individualistic and for him, that meant God had no place in his life.

Right now I didn't know what I believed. In fact, I wasn't sure I knew who God was or is.

We lived at a time of imperfection—a time when all of our souls were restless and some of us didn't even know it. It was a time when we either did right or we didn't. When I finally did get around to asking about this God I'd heard so much about, my mother, my grandmother, and Aunt Eva said there was a God and questioning the existence of God was not right. Aunt Eva said church-going people in the South felt this way; therefore, the subject was closed.

"We need to move into the sanctuary," said Thad. "Try to get the front row."

Our Sunday school building was old and dingy looking. Flakes of peeling paint were more than noticeable on the walls of the hall-way that led to the sanctuary. Thad opened the heavy, solid pine door and the three of us entered the upper right hand side balcony. The sanctuary was an oven, the stately old church not having air-conditioning. The movement of hand fans kept time with the organ music. There were six smaller than normal sized pews in this section to choose from. We took our place in one of the two first row pews. A total of fifty boys could pretend to worship here if we all squeezed together tightly. By eleven o'clock or shortly thereafter, we were packed in these solid pine seats like sardines.

Each of us grabbed a bulletin before we sat down and hurriedly looked to see how long the service would last. Today's text was "Honor Thy Father." It appeared to be a typical Sunday service beginning with the usual choral opening sung by the choir, an opening prayer, three hymns, a communal reading where the minister read and the congregation responded, then the sermon, ending with the Lord's Prayer, and a doxology—a typical United Methodist liturgical service—very predictable, controlled, and unexciting—totally different from the class we had just attended.

I knew nothing about being a good Methodist. The only reason I attended a Methodist Church was because my mother switched her membership from the First Baptist Church sometime before my fifth birthday. Aunt Eva said Mother's decision to move her membership was the honorable thing to do—to attend her husband's church.

My father's parents were United Methodist as were their parents before them. I figured since my father grew up in this church, he wanted us to follow him. I was baptized here when I was twelve. Big deal! I didn't feel any different then and whatever the feeling was supposed to be, still hadn't kicked in. Aunt Eva and Granny said baptism should make me feel purer. Well, it hadn't.

I hadn't learned anything about being a good Methodist in the last four years. I wasn't even certain I knew what a good Methodist was supposed to be or believe in. I'd never had a class on it (Methodism) and it wasn't taught in the Sunday school program here. I had heard the name John Wesley bantered about and according to Matt he had something to do with it all. I had a coping strategy: I'd take it all in stride, going through the motions without ever thinking about them. I thought this was the way everyone did until Matt told me that my reasoning was scary.

It was a good thing that the Methodist Church did not see the need to give admittance tests. If they did, I would have flunked and so would all my friends, but maybe not Matt. At least, he'd read a book about Wesley. He would pass.

Methodist ministers, on the average, didn't stay much longer than four years at one church. Our minister, Robert W. Bradshaw, was an exception to the Methodist Conference rule on appointments. No one was anxious to see him leave and this sentiment extended far beyond the threshold of our church. As a minister, he was loved and revered and to some in our town, he was almost saintly. As a man, he was honest, a gentleman, and a friend to all he knew.

Robert W. Bradshaw, a good looking, middle-aged man with three teenage sons, opened the door to the sanctuary. The sun attempting to burst through the stain glass window of Paul cast a reddish, purple hue on his slightly graying hair. His confident manner reinforced his distinctive appearance. Whenever Mr. Bradshaw entered on a Sunday morning wearing his long flowing black robe as he did today, he assumed a powerful presence like a judge ready to pronounce a pardon on a convicted criminal. He would directly proceed to the chancel and kneel in prayer by the big chair that we used for the king's throne in our annual Christmas pageant. This Sunday was no different.

I liked Uncle Bob, as he preferred to be called. This is what I called him unless I was at church. Then I addressed him as Mr.

Bradshaw. I couldn't bring myself to say Reverend Bradshaw. It sounded too formal.

Uncle Bob visited our home fairly regular now, primarily because my father's sickness had worsened. He didn't come to see Daddy so much as a minister but more as a friend and he was good to my father. Uncle Bob prayed with my daddy during these visits and I suspected my father talked about death with him. On occasions, if I were at home, Uncle Bob would come into my bedroom and take time to talk with me about whatever was of interest to the both of us at the time. On one visit, a copy of *Over-Sexteen* lay on top of my comforter. When he saw it he just smiled, saying something like, "I'm certain with three sons, that book has been passed around our home, too." He was nonjudgmental—a rare quality in my hometown.

Uncle Bob's visits were good for Mother, too. Recognizing his genuineness, Mother would openly share her problems with him and sometimes, Uncle Bob would smoke a cigarette with her and that really delighted my mother. Uncle Bob used to tell Mother that she was one of only two people in Wilson with whom he smoked. To some people in our church smoking was taboo, akin to sinfulness and smoking with my mother would not be understood, especially by those who already thought of her as the worst kind of sinner.

Uncle Bob knew he could trust Mother to keep their little secret. I never believed he was the type of man who would deliberately deceive anyone much less try to hide anything. He was too genuine. That was the way preachers were supposed to be and the way many were in our town.

Mr. Bradshaw got up from his knees, moved to the pulpit, and greeted the congregation with his big smile that made any visitor sitting before him feel welcome. The organist kicked the pedal of the pipe organ switching to a hymn with a slightly upbeat tempo. This was our warning to settle down and get ready to listen.

On occasions, in my opinion, Mr. Bradshaw preached too long. Aunt Eva would later tell me that these sermons were the ones we all needed to hear. The length of these longer sermons almost put me off to coming to church. My survival strategy was to find a way to entertain myself. I did this by counting—counting the number of bulbs in the chandeliers or the number of women with hats versus the women without or the number of tiles in the ceiling or the number of men versus the number of women—I don't think there was a single thing in this sanctuary that I hadn't counted. I was a master at counting but no good at keeping my mind focused on thirty-minute sermons even if I did need to hear what was being preached.

Just as Mr. Bradshaw opened his mouth to speak, a paper airplane formed from one of the creamy colored church bulletins took off from our side of the balcony. First, the little plane dipped, taking a long glide over the center section of the downstairs. Then, unexplainably, it picked up momentum and sailed to the back of the church.

Everyone in our church followed the flight of that little plane, even those who had to strain noticeably in their pews to keep up with it. Those of us who sat with the unknown pilot began to squirm. We didn't know how to respond. A few coughed nervously. We did everything possible not to laugh out loud. Some grabbed their sides, some bit their lower lips, others looked down at the floor, and some stuffed handkerchiefs in their mouth. Then Dewey Sutton did what we all wanted to do.

"Hahahahaha . . . haaaaahaaaa haaaah." Unable to stop, Dewey's chubby cheeks rose to meet his twinkling blue eyes. "Oh, My Lord," he murmured like a deacon echoing in the back at a tent revival.

The entire right side balcony joined Dewey. All of us erupted in laughter at the same time. I laughed so hard my insides hurt. This was the perfect release from the previous hour with Captain Chuck. Just as quick as the laughter started, it was over. Mr. Bradshaw had his right arm outstretched and his entire focus was on our section of the balcony.

"Thank you, boys, for your wonderful welcome. I knew you would be glad when school was out but I had no idea that it had been that bad of a year," our minister said, looking up at us. That started our laughing again but when Uncle Bob lifted his arm again, we stopped. There were no reprimands but the ushers never left bulletins in our pews again.

"The beautiful thing about what we just witnessed is that every young man sitting in that balcony is a child of God and each one has an earthly father, too." Mr. Bradshaw said. "And it is to you, young people, I am speaking today. The Bible in the book of Genesis talks about fathers and says that children are to love and respect their fathers. In fact, this is one of the Ten Commandments—honor thy father and mother. Now children, what can you do to honor your father and why is it important to honor them?" he asked.

Mr. Bradshaw preached for a good thirty minutes but this time he kept my attention. He talked about honoring our Heavenly Father and our earthly father. The one thing he said that sucked me into his sermon was that we were on loan to our earthly fathers and mothers, and the way we treated them showed how we valued our relationship with our Heavenly Father. This thought scared me and bothered me since I hadn't had the best thoughts about my father recently. The best way I could describe my reaction would be to picture a crab with its claws around my heart wanting to pinch it until it burst. I would have to think a long time about what Mr. Bradshaw said. Little did I know that that very night my love for my father would be tested.

Aunt Eva was late, just as I thought she would be. She was a little more than upset about the airplane flying through the sanctuary and had stopped to talk to the Chairman of the Council on Ministries. We had barely pulled out of the church parking lot when she turned to me while driving and said, "Braxton Haywood, I know you know who threw that airplane and I want you to tell me who it was." She turned back, maneuvering her car towards Nash Street.

"Aunt Eva, I'm not sure who threw it and it wouldn't be right to name someone who might not have really thrown it." I swallowed hard, expecting her to grill me further.

"I knew it! I knew you knew who it was," she said. "Why are you trying to protect someone?" she paused and turned back toward me and gave me one of her courtroom looks that made me realize that she had no intentions of giving up until she got an answer. "Why, someone could have lost an eye!" Her Chevrolet hit a pothole and I heard her utter another damn under her breath. I said nothing. Anne turned toward me and smiled nervously.

"Lose an eye? Why do you think someone could lose an eye?" I said, trying to divert her thinking about who had thrown it. "Aunt Eva, please turn around and look at the road!"

"You are certainly no one to be telling me how to drive, Braxton Haywood," she said, slowing her car as she took a right turn onto Nash Street. "I've been driving a lot longer than I care to admit and I've never had a wreck." Then, unexpectedly, she pulled over in front of the Center Theatre.

Turning toward me again and this time, with her right index finger pointing and waving at my face, she raised her voice, and shouted, "The point of that paper could have hurt someone. Besides, that's getting away from what I want to know. Now tell me who threw that plane!" Her eyes glared at me through her powder-tinted glasses. "Tell me now so I can take you children home."

"Aunt Eva, I really don't know the guy. Besides, I was sitting on the other side of the balcony from where it took off," I said, knowing that I had not really told a lie but only stretched the truth. I couldn't tell her that Gray Barnes had been the culprit. His grandmother was one of Aunt Eva's closest friends.

"What airplane?" Anne asked. Anne had helped in the two-year old nursery and missed the service.

"I'll tell you later," I said.

"Braxton, are you going to tell me who threw that airplane off that balcony?" Aunt Eva glared at me. I sat still wishing I was at home.

"I've already told you I don't know," I said. "What is it going to take to convince you?" My tone of disrespect further angered my aunt.

"The truth, Braxton Haywood," she shot back. "*The truth!*" Aunt Eva turned around and grabbed the steering wheel with both hands. I could see her tense up when she accidentally peeled rubber pulling away the curb. The car swayed momentarily before she gained total control. She was pissed off with me and I didn't blame her.

A few blocks down Nash Street my aunt spoke again, "Since you aren't going to help me, Braxton, I'll find out another way." Lowering her voice, she continued, "Now tell me, how did you like your Sunday school class today? Was I right?" Aunt Eva appeared calmer and I saw no reason to give her just cause to become emotional again.

"I haven't made up my mind yet. Chuck Anderson does have a different way of teaching," I said, wanting to keep him out of trouble and make my aunt think I was agreeing with her too.

"I told you," she said. "Your old Aunt Eva is not as dumb as you think I am."

Wisely, I chose not to respond. Anne and I sat quietly for the remainder of the ride home. I hoped that she would just let everything die and not revisit this subject. All I wanted to do was exit her car without answering any more questions or being dragged into another argument. Slowing down, she turned right onto Kincaid Avenue.

"Tell your mother hello for me and that I will call her this afternoon," Aunt Eva said as she pulled her Clara in front of our house.

"Thanks for the ride," I said. Anne echoed my thank you. We got out of her car and walked slowly to the front door. Anne's legs stretched to make each stepping-stone. I understood Aunt Eva a little better now and I knew that if she had her way, trouble was not far behind.

Chapter 16
HONOR THY FATHER

ANNE AND I walked up the four cracked concrete steps onto the wide, freshly washed porch of our small bungalow. Uncharacteristically, on this Sunday, Mother opened the screen door and stepped out to meet us. She was dressed in a casual, flowered house-dress that was too large on her thin figure. Tied neatly around her waist was the same torn white apron she wore most days. Despite the pained expression on her face, our mother was still a beautiful woman. She had a strikingly manicured appearance with fine wavy, white hair neatly parted on the left side and a slender figure, just as when I was in the fifth grade—a time when my classmates wanted to know if she was my grandmother.

Mother had a cup of coffee in her left hand and a cigarette in her right. One thing I knew for certain when my eyes met hers—I had no explanation for the strange look on her face or why she had been crying. Her look told me she was eager to reveal something. I expected her to speak, say anything or, at least, issue a warning, but she didn't. This was not the right time to quiz her about what had happened while we were gone.

In a period of a few days, Lily had become more concerned about my mother's behavior. Lily said it was much too predictable. "Braxton, your mother ain'ts her usual self." Like Effie, Lily would slip into her colored folk's talk and get carried away trying to make her point. Over time, I had learned that her deliberate use of ain't was for emphasis only. I nodded. "You know that, do you? Braxton, your mother's too young to be actin' this way. I almost knows what she's gonna do before she does it. That woman has taken to drink-

ing too much lately and she's hiding this from your daddy, and you
children, and she thinks she's hiding it from me. She can't fools me
though, not any day on this good earth. I knows how many bottles
are on that pantry shelf." I hadn't observed anything close to what
Lily said. Maybe I didn't want to see it.

But today Mother having done everything but put on her
Sunday dress and then coming onto the porch to greet us threw me.
There was nothing wrong with it; in fact, it was kind of nice. It's that
. . . I . . . I just . . . I don't ever remember her doing this. Mother would
never make this effort on a Sunday unless she knew my aunt and
uncle from Greenville were coming. Something was up and I wanted to know what it was.

"How was Sunday school?" she asked, pretending that nothing
was wrong. She swallowed before taking a long draw on her cigarette, blowing the heavy gray smoke over her left shoulder.

"It was fun. Not a whole lot different but more fun," said Anne,
seeming as surprised as I at her question. Anne stood still, waiting for
Mother's command to go in the house.

"Braxton, how did you enjoy your new class?" Mother looked at
me with a forced smile and then flipped her cigarette into the front
yard. Her words, carefully phrased, were delivered calmly. I was certain something had happened while we were at Sunday school and
church. Mother's face was unreadable as she reached into her pocket for another cigarette. That would be one more butt in the yard I
would have to pick up.

"It was good. I really liked it," I said. Her hand trembled as she
lit her cigarette. Her hand shaking was nothing new but lighting up
one cigarette after another was not her usual habit. Maybe Lily was
right.

Seeing my mother standing there made me feel sorry for her. I
felt sorry for her because she had been chosen by many in our town
to scrutinize and she could never win in that game. Mother wanted
approval as a parent, a wife, and a good manager of her house. She
could never meet the standards of those ghostly few. She knew it,
Lily knew it, and I had started to understand it. She simply tried too
hard.

I asked Lily why people made it their business to choose one person in a neighborhood to pick on. Lily surprised me when she asked if I had heard of the Salem Witch Trials. We had just studied about them in American history. Lily said just like in the days of the witch trials, it was that chosen person's behavior, actions, and lack of actions that made people suspicious and they would go to any means to prove their suspicions right.

Mother's witch hunters faulted her for her impeccable house-keeping. They said she was compulsive. Lily said she acted out of nervousness. "Miss Virginia, we don't need to spring clean every week. We aren't going to eat off these floors, are we? The good Lord knows you got a clean heart. I declare, you done gone and tested my gospel again, Miss Virginia." Lily's refrain was echoed at least once a month but no one other than my aunts, my sister and me heard it.

Aunt Josephine explained Mother's obsession with cleanliness this way, "Braxton, it is Virginia's way of coping with stress. You need to be patient with your mother and help her as much as possible." I hated all the chores that fell upon me to do and resented every minute of doing them. And to make matters worse, if they weren't done right, I did them again. The only benefit I saw was that Mother had one less thing to fret over once they were to her satisfaction. This equated to peace within our house and everyone enjoyed those times.

I knew Aunt Josephine was right about my being patient with Mother. And since she was a doctor's wife as well as Mother's sister and seemed to understand my mother, I figured that her analysis of Mother's condition was correct. I guess Aunt Josephine and Lily meant the same thing but just had different ways of explaining it.

Her critics claimed she neglected her children and this forced Aunt Josephine to be our mother at times. I know this hurt my mother more than I could imagine. Lily told Mother to let Aunt Josephine help her. "Miss Virginia, your sister's trying to help you. Why don't you let her? Her children are gone and she's got that big house . . . " Unfortunately, these words fell on deaf ears. This accusa-tion was one of the biggest influences in her decision to get us involved in church. Mother said she trusted the church to give us the stability that my father and she were not always able to provide. How much she allowed the comments from her critics sitting in the pews each Sunday to torment her, I'm not sure. What mattered to me was my not allowing my behavior to give anyone an opportunity to throw a stone of criticism at her.

Mother's witch hunters gave her some slack when it came to Daddy. Maybe they felt sorry for her and my father. I don't know. Maybe they understood my parents never realized what could have been. I thought of the nights I knew my parents never slept and all of the days my mother never left the house and the turmoil slowly building within our home because of my father's failing health. I wanted my mother to be happy about something.

"Braxton, did you hear me?" said Mother. "I want you to know that I'm excited for both of you," she said with a forced smile.

"Ma'am?" I watched her suck on the end of her cigarette and blow the smoke through her nose. It stood still for a moment and then drifted toward the green ceiling of our front porch. It seemed so natural to see her with a cigarette. She enjoyed smoking but the habit contradicted my image of beauty. And to me, my mother was beautiful. "I mean, you are?" I had no idea why she was excited.

It was obvious to me Mother loved and adored my father and I believed she would do anything to give him a moment of happiness. Sadly, the sicker my father became, the more of a hostage Mother became to him and his predicament. This is why Mother seldom left the house. I could not confirm Lily's assertion that her drinking had increased but I knew her headaches had returned. They always returned when her nervousness came back. She tried hard to cover it up but the fact that Lily said her smoking had jumped to almost two packs a day was a dead give away. On top of this, Lily said her daily coffee intake had reached the level of nine or ten cups. We both knew these were habits she would never forfeit. This routine would keep most people down but not my mother. It was not that she thrived on her addictions; but rather, these addictions propelled her. She had truly convinced herself she needed them and she couldn't get through a day without them. This was that compulsive nature in action and by adopting these habits, they were, as she said, "justifiably hers."

Unlike her critics, when I watched Mother, I saw a strong, courageous woman struggling in her determination to keep her family intact, at least while our father was alive. It was a game of survival with unknown limits heading for disaster. I feared for Mother's emotional health and what else would be expected of me. I felt guilty for thinking about myself but I couldn't help it. I had to be honest with myself.

"Come in, children. I have your lunch ready," she opened the door for us. I looked at Anne and she looked at me. Why the formality? "And remember to wash your hands. Your daddy is resting so try to be quiet," she continued, still maintaining her earlier enthusiasm. "And don't twist the rugs." Anne and I looked at each other, nodded, and smiled. We were used to this command.

"Yes, ma'am," we chimed together as we entered the rose colored living room of our home.

"Oh! Braxton, before I forget, you received two phone calls. David Byrd called and wants you to call him and Mrs. Stallings called. She wants you to baby-sit. You may want to wait and make both calls after lunch."

My mind raced back to the last time I saw Rita. Did she want me to stay with her children or did she have something else in mind? I was both excited and fearful at the prospect of going back to her house. I felt a slight tightening inside my pants. The excitement of Rita calling pushed my concern for Byrd aside momentarily. His life had become a jigsaw puzzle with some of the pieces missing.

After washing my hands, I walked to the back porch for lunch. We always ate Sunday lunch on our screened back porch when the weather allowed. Today was a beautiful early summer Sunday. The sky was cloudless and the sun's rays baked the dying, brown grass. A slight breeze traveled through the two-screened sides, temporarily releasing the porch from the claws of this scorching heat. The airflow was still warm and I needed no persuasion in taking off my coat and tie.

Our porch was as comfortable as any room in our house and more so than most. Mother had a creative and daring side and enjoyed experimenting. She was ahead of her time with her talented ideas and color schemes. In much the same manner as a plantation owner overseeing the picking of cotton, Mother made her presence known to the two workers as they painted each room in our house in a different, bold color. Like an interior decorator, she took pride in her selections and for a long time, I believe the reaction of those who entered our home was one of the few happy moments in her life.

Mother's fastidiousness in decorating extended to our back porch located off the kitchen. On the kitchen end sat a large white wooden drop leaf table covered with a blue and off-white checkered plastic tablecloth surrounded by four white spindle chairs. On the other end of the porch separated by a tall, brown wooden screen with carved designs was a daybed. Beside the bed was a small side table topped with a lamp and a Philco radio. Sometimes when the heat of the night became oppressive, I used this as an alternate bedroom. It was a haven for me—a safety net to escape from the havoc that attempted to strangle me. It was here I became familiar with the voices of the night.

In the center of the porch was a woven brown, blue, green, and orange oval rug. A long, white wooden shelf mounted against the exterior of the house ran the length of the porch. Mother used this for a place to display her baskets and houseplants. I would soon learn that it was on this shelf that she hid things she didn't want us to find—like her near empty bottles of whiskey and pills.

Anne and I sat down, ready to eat our Sunday lunch of warmed-over pot roast, mashed potatoes, and green garden peas. This used to be one of my father's favorite meals when he could still digest his food. My father favored piling his green peas on top of his potatoes. This would cause my mother to grimace and when he stirred them with his fork, Mother grew annoyed. I copied him not to aggravate Mother but the taste was better this way. If this had not been one of my father's habits, Mother probably would not have allowed me to do it. In some small ways, I did imitate him. In time, I did not like to think that I did.

"Anne, would you say grace?" Mother asked, putting her cigarette out in the cut glass ashtray that acted as the table's centerpiece.

"Yes ma'am," said Anne, bowing her head and putting her hands together. She gave the Moravian blessing that had become a standard in our house since Aunt Josephine's youngest daughter, Kate, had married a Moravian minister. "Come Lord Jesus, our guest to be, and bless these gifts bestowed by thee. Amen." Anne lifted her head and looked at Mother, waiting for permission to pick up her fork and eat.

"Anne, Linda's mother called. Linda wants you to come over this afternoon and play and if you want to, spend the night with her. Would you like that?"

"Oh, yes ma'am," Anne dropped her napkin on the floor. "Sorry, Mother."

"I knew you would be excited but do slow down. Call her after lunch and tell her you would like to come. Your brother will drive you." Mother looked at me with a reluctant grin.

"What?" I asked, nearly dropping my fork in my plate.

"While you were at Sunday school I decided that it was time to let you drive short trips with your sister in the car. But I expect you to be careful. I mean that, Braxton! Do you mind taking her?"

"No ma'am," I answered excitedly. "I mean I don't mind taking her and I will be careful. Thank you, mother." I jumped up and hugged her around the neck.

"You're welcome. Just don't speed like the last time," she reminded me. I did speed down Nash Street one Saturday afternoon because I was late. I didn't realize Aunt Eva was behind me and for the life of me I don't know why, but she didn't waste any time calling Mother to give her a report. I was mad—mad with myself because I lost my driving privileges for a week—mad with Aunt Eva because I had to cancel my date for that night. It would have been my first car date—the first car date of my life. My date understood and we spent the evening at her house. Aunt Eva was totally unsympathetic.

Linda Hinkle lived with her parents and younger sister about five blocks away from us on Anderson Street, in an upper middle-class neighborhood. The Hinkles were one of a small number of Jewish

families who had lived in Wilson for any length of time. Mr. Levi
Hinkle owned several men's clothing stores in eastern North
Carolina, one located in our downtown. Wilson's civic and social
community showed no interest in the Hinkles. Mean is a better way
of putting it; Wilson was downright mean to the Hinkles, especially
Mr. Hinkle. Not only were they blackballed from membership in the
Wilson Country Club because they were Jewish, Mr. Hinkle was
denied membership in several men's clubs in Wilson for the same
reason. Some of Linda's friend's parents belonged to the country club
and they invited her to spend the night in their home with their
daughters. And some of these same girl's fathers belonged to the
Lion's Club and the Kiwanis Club yet Mr. Hinkle was never invited
as a guest. The whole anti-Jewish thinking made no sense to me and
shouldn't have made sense to anyone else.

By the age of fifteen, I had decided I disliked all the Jewish haters
I frequently came in contact with. They were bigots and they ran-
kled me. Curiously, most of them were educated people and some
had college degrees. Wilson had a fair share of these people. And
many of these skeptics boycotted Jewish-owned stores and publicly
ostracized specific Jewish families.

The Hinkles were nice, genuine, law-abiding people and Mrs.
Hinkle and Mother enjoyed each other's company. In time, they
became friends. Mother was one of the few women in Wilson to
reach out to Alma Hinkle during those times and Mrs. Hinkle
responded. They were able to empathize with each other—both
women had sick husbands and both had to daily confront their own
crippling phobia and nervousness. Both women had a strong com-
mitment to their sick husbands and both became victims of the cruel
gossip train that traveled through our town.

The one contradiction I saw in this relationship between the
Hinkles and my family was that I was not allowed to date a certain
Jewish girl. I wanted to take out Helen Bernstein, a cute cheerleader,
one year younger than I. Helen was beautiful with long blonde hair
and deep blue eyes. I begged and begged. The answer was always the
same—no.

Mother's attempts at giving me a sufficient explanation fell short
of what is reasonable and right. She just kept saying this particular

girl's family was not nice and upstanding protestant boys did not date some Jewish girls. Mother talked like Mr. Bernstein was a disgrace to Wilson. She said he was not honest. I knew Mr. Bernstein owned and operated a small general store across the railroad tracks on East Nash Street because I had been there. Most of his customers were Negroes. There was no disgrace in that.

I kept asking Mother; she just repeated the same answer. I didn't buy into her rationale and I don't even think my mother believed what she said. It was not a good reason and it was hypocritical. I stopped pursuing the subject when I lost interest in Helen.

"Braxton, would you give me all of your attention!" said Mother.

"What?" I said. "Oh, yes. Go ahead."

"Thank you. Now, while you're out, Braxton, I want you to stop by your grandmother's and pick up a few items she has gathered for me." Mother tried hard not to acknowledge that she had to rely on her mother for anything.

My grandmother continually did things for us and anytime Mother had an argument with my grandmother, which was at least once or twice a month, Mother would verbally attack her. I hated it when Mother, in anger, assassinated my grandmother. Another side of my mother would appear. I didn't like this Virginia—the Virginia who would say things like, "Mother, I know damn well you don't believe me when I say I will pay you back. But I will. I will some-day. I'm sorry I can't be another Josephine and do for you and make over you. I know you begrudge having to do for my family and me. If Anne and Braxton really knew how you felt, they wouldn't love you so much." During these confrontations, my granny never said a word. If she was tempted to lash back, she never did. She just let Mother vehemently attack her. When the anger left Mother's system, she would call my grandmother on the telephone and apologize. Overtime, Anne and I became the innocent victims of this same rage that lay dormant inside my mother.

I had heard my mother say on more than one occasion that she hated her mother. I didn't know whether to believe Mother when she said this or not. My father once said there was bad blood between them and that their history went back a long way. I didn't know what he meant and he never would tell me. As far as I could tell, my father liked and respected my grandmother. She was a wonderful help to Mother and him when I almost died at the age of six.

"Anything else you want me to do while I'm out?" I asked.

"No. Just don't drive around Wilson. I need you to do what I've asked you to do and then come right back. I need you here for awhile," she said, almost pleading.

"Okay," I said. Damn! I had been taught that Sunday was a day of rest. I translated this to mean a day of freedom—a day I could do anything I wanted to do. Wrong. No movies on the Sabbath like some of my other friends, no swimming on God's day and God forbid if we danced at home. Mother had started letting me play cards if for no other reason than to keep me from nagging her. She was still a victim of her Southern Baptist upbringing, which influenced and dictated what we could and could not do on this day.

As soon as lunch was over, Anne hurried to the phone in the hall to call Linda. Mother wasted no time in telling me why I needed to be back so quickly.

"Braxton, I need to talk with you about your father's condition," she said gravely. "I arranged with Linda's mother for Anne to go there this afternoon."

"What's wrong?" I asked. I didn't think he could get much worse.

"Not now," Mother said. "I'll explain when you get back from your grandmother's. After we finish, you can do what you want to do."

"Mother, is it real bad?" I asked, remembering the noises I had heard a few night's earlier.

"Please just wait until you get back," she said. Moisture gathering in her eyes told me the news would not be good. Unknowingly, she began to play with Anne's iced teaspoon.

Anne returned to the porch, her face beaming with happiness. I almost envied her being twelve years old, a time that allowed her to be naïve without apology and embarrassment. Anne seemed unaware of the deeper problems facing our family.

"Mother, Linda said I could come now if you'd let me," Anne said, fidgeting with the hem of her dress. "She wants me to spend the night. May I? Please!"

"Yes, you may. Go pack your bag and be sure to put some shorts on," said Mother.

"Braxton, help me clear the table, please."

"Yes, ma'am." I looked down at my plate realizing I had hardly touched any of the food on it. That was surprising since I used to be a member in good standing of the I-Keep-My-Plate-Clean-Club. The club had been Aunt Eva's idea. Enrolling me had gotten my aunt a subscription to some magazine at a reduced price. First, she had to convince Mother and Mother did just about anything Aunt Eva asked her to do.

My mother loved Aunt Eva the way she should have loved her own mother. My grandmother sensed this and internalized the pain. The thought of my grandmother being hurt by anyone bothered me. Like my grandmother, Aunt Eva was a good person, too; but when she started her snooping, Aunt Eva could be a real pain in the butt. Mother looked weary. The twinkle that had been the personality of her brown eyes for years and years was gone. Mother carried a serious look now and people who didn't know her mistook her expression for anger. I hated to see my mother when she looked worried. She did what she could to hide her internal worries and stress—everything from painting her nails and plucking her eyebrows to dressing up after her early afternoon bath, as if she was expecting someone to come and visit or take her out.

I admired my mother for trying to keep our household together. I didn't know how much pressure she could endure. And I didn't know how long this proud woman could last if my father was as sick as she had made me suspect he was. I did know one thing—the continued decline of my father's health would force Mother to make a decision she did not want to make, leaving her more vulnerable to her sister and mother.

It took Anne less than fifteen minutes to get ready to go to Linda's. I waited on the front porch for her. Outside the world looked wonderful. The color of the sky had changed to mostly blue and the bright, early afternoon sun shot its hot rays with all its force to our part of the state. On the south side of our porch a spider wove an elaborate web from the corner column to the rose trestle abutting the end of the porch. At the moment I was a fly caught in that spider's web. I wanted breathing room and lots of it. I wanted a time away from the web of our home and the entanglements that kept surfacing. For the first time, I began to fear what might happen next at our house and what might happen to my mother.

Anne grabbed my hand. "Let's go, Braxton. I don't want to be late."

Anne pulled me to the driveway. I jumped into the Tank, allowing Anne time to do the same from her side. I turned on the ignition, revved the engine for effect, and shifted the gear from park to reverse. My left foot gently reached for the clutch. With as careful precision as possible, I accelerated and slowly backed the Tank out of the driveway. I shifted the gear down to the forward position and drove up to West Nash and stopped. After looking both ways, I crossed onto South Kincaid Avenue. A shirtless Jason pushed his dad's mower across the front lawn. I honked the horn two short times and without looking, Jason shot me the bird. He knew the sound of the Tank and he knew my signal just like I knew his. We all had our horn signals for greeting each other.

"That wasn't very nice of Jason," said Anne.

"No, it's not," I said. "But that's Jason Parker."

"What does it mean exactly?" Anne said. "I don't think I've ever been told."

"Trust me, little sis, you don't need to know what it means. It's very vulgar."

"Braxton, why does a good-looking boy like Jason do that?"

"He thinks it makes him cool." I turned left onto Anderson Street.

Driving Anne to Linda Hinkle's home was another step toward giving me independent status. I drove with both hands on the steering wheel and with both eyes straight ahead. I was careful to use hand signals and stay within the posted speed limit. Linda lived on the same street as my grandmother but several blocks west. I waited until Mrs. Hinkle greeted Anne at the front door before I continued my drive to my granny's home.

My grandmother was not at home when I arrived but she had what Mother needed neatly packaged on the front porch. There was a brief note taped to the box saying where she had gone and two crisp one-dollar bills for me in case I needed any gas or spending money.

Chapter 17
FEARFUL OF A SHOT

I ENJOYED EVERY minute I sat behind the steering wheel of the Tank. The sense of power I received from driving that old Buick overwhelmed me. After leaving my grandmother's house, I decided to backtrack two blocks on Kenan Street and detour over to Branch Street and drive by the Bernstein's home. Since it was a lazy Sunday afternoon, I thought I might stop by and say hello to Helen. When I saw Helen and several of her girl friends sunbathing in her side yard, sweat began to gather at all the wrong places on my body. I gave the Tank's horn two short honks and sped up just enough for them to see the rear end of my car if they chose to look. It was my understanding that girls liked that kind of attention. I was back home in less than twenty minutes.

The house was a spooky quiet. I took my shoes off, leaving them just inside the living room and next to the front door. I tiptoed past the bathroom where Mother was taking a bath and into the kitchen where I deposited the box on the table. Since Mother planned to talk to me about my father, I decided to check on him. I tiptoed through the breakfast room and carefully pushed against the swinging door. It squeaked once before I got it open enough to peer in. The room was dark. My father, a toothpick frame of a man, sat silently in his rocking chair, now his bed for twenty-four hours a day. No one outside our family would recognize him. He was too thin and too emaciated, looking more like a corpse than a human being. Next to his rocker was a cherry ashtray stand. I stepped inside his room. Bracing the swinging door with my right hand, I guided it back until it was closed. Moving closer to my father, I saw a lone cigarette smoldering among the half a dozen or so butts left in the glass container. "I don't need to stop smoking," he had told us. "I already have cancer." The room smelled of Lysol, old cigarettes, and death.

Most of the time my father was so doped up on morphine and Dilaudid that he didn't feel the full brunt of his pain. His fragile body slumped downward and he appeared more like a wooden puppet that had been weather beaten beyond repair than the vibrant man who had once been heir to the position of President of Exeter Tobacco Company. His eyes were closed. I just stood there, staring at him. He didn't even know I was beside him. How could this happen? Thinking I heard him snoring, I left the room and walked to the back porch.

I wanted no part of this kind of living. I kept asking myself, why does any man deserve to suffer the way my father suffers. It is unfair and it is cruel. What does a man have to do to deserve such a hopeless sentence? And what kind of God would cause this? Mr. Ross told me that God sometimes allows bad things to happen—something about God's permissive will. I didn't get it anymore than I understood God. All I knew for certain was what I saw—an almost lifeless body barely holding on to a fragile life. Nothing made any sense to me. I didn't understand and as a matter of fact, I didn't want to understand. I wanted to blame somebody and I blamed God.

Mother came to the door. She had changed into a blue and white patterned dress. The soft text of the material resembled silk. She wore her new blue opened-toed sandals that she had gotten for a steal, as she would say, from F.W. Woolworth's Five and Dime. Deep red lipstick accentuated her full lips and her penciled dark eyebrows looked almost unnatural. Standing in the doorway on that early Sunday afternoon, she looked more like a model or a movie star than my mother. Uncle Jeff, my Granny's son, seconded the people in Wilson who said that my mother and Josephine, in their younger years, were two of the most beautiful girls in town; but, in the same breath, he agreed with them that Mother was prettier. I believed him.

"How long have you been waiting? I stood, recognizing my mother's presence.

"I've been back about thirty minutes. I put the package from Granny on the kitchen table."

"Did she say anything to you?"

"No ma'am. She wasn't there." I knew instantly from Mother's expression I had said the wrong thing.

"That is so typical of her. She never stays at home. Where was she?" Mother's demeanor changed. She took a cigarette from the pack still resting on the porch table and handed me the matchbook. "Light this for me, Braxton. My hand is shaking badly right now."

"I don't know where she was," I lied, pulling a match from the flap. I struck it against the cover and held the flame over the table for Mother to light her cigarette. I didn't dare tell her that Granny left a note saying that Aunt Josephine had invited her for Sunday lunch.

"I bet she's at Josephine's house eating steak or lamb," Mother said.

"What did you want to talk to me about?" I said, hoping to dissuade Mother from getting on one of her tangents about Josephine and how her mother favored Josephine over her.

"I called Dr. Wright and he came this morning while you and Anne were at Sunday school and church. He told me your daddy's condition has worsened. In fact, it has become critical. He wants to increase your daddy's dosage of medicine, hoping he might sleep more at night." Mother stopped abruptly and looked into my eyes. "Your daddy is in bad shape, Braxton, real bad shape." Tears filled the corners of her eyes. "Until recently, the medication was the only thing keeping your daddy alive. And suddenly, his current dosage no longer helps him. Your daddy's temperature has been rising higher and there have been a few nights in the last week that his body temperature has been so hot that he could barely stand it."

"I heard scary noises coming from his room the other night and I didn't know what to think," I said. "What happened in there?"

She paused, took a deep breath, and continued, "That was the night your daddy said he felt like he was on fire." Mother stopped again, this time to wipe the tears from her eyes with a silk handkerchief my father had given her.

"What can I do to help?" I said. I didn't know if there was anything I could do.

"I want you to learn how to administer his morphine and Dilaudid," Mother said. "I will teach you how to boil his needles, how to fill them, and how to give him his shots." She hesitated then grabbed my hand. "The hardest part is finding a vein. I think I can handle the IV by myself. That's what we depend upon during his sleeping hours."

"Mother, I want to help but I don't think I can give Daddy a shot," I said. "I've never done anything like that. What if I make a mistake?" I felt an inside ache and sweat started popping out everywhere—on my brow, under my arms, and even my hands were wet. I had no confidence for this sort of thing. "Mother, I can't. I'm afraid . . . I might hurt him. Then what?"

"Braxton, you've got to help me. My hand shakes so bad now that I can't hold the needle still long enough to get it into a vein. I need your help. Please!" Mother squeezed my hand until it stung.

"Okay! Okay! I'll try," I said, pulling my hand away from her grip. I stepped back and at the same time, I pulled in my stomach and wiped my moist hands against my pants. "When do we have to begin?"

"At five o'clock, today!" said Mother. "That will give you time enough to go to M.Y.F. if you want to and be back in time for his nine o'clock shot."

"Mother, is Daddy going to die soon?" I tried to act manly and not cry.

"He has already lived way beyond the time the doctors gave him," said Mother, touching the top of my hand with hers.

"Are you saying yes?" This time I grabbed her hand and holding it in mine, I tried to offer comfort that I needed myself.

"I'm saying I don't know, but I don't think your daddy wants to live. If he gives up his will to live, it won't be long before he leaves us."

"It's not fair! It not fair, damn it!" Without hesitation, I opened the screen door, ran down the back steps, and into the backyard. I stopped near the flower garden long enough to pick up a small stone. I threw it hard against the rock barbecue pit screaming at God about the sentence of injustice that my father had been given. "*Damn it, God! How could you do this? How am I supposed to honor my father if you are going to let him die?"*

Mother followed me into the yard. She put her arm around my right shoulder and pulled me to her. This was as scared as I had ever been and I was glad she was there.

"I tell you what's not fair, Braxton. Life is not fair. It is like everyone is dealt a poker hand and you play the hand you are given," Mother said. "Don't blame God for this, Braxton. You are too young now to understand."

"*Understand?* What's there to understand? I hardly know my father," I said. "I have never had a chance to get to know him! I understand that!"

"I know son," Mother said, leaning over and kissing me on the cheek. "Come on back in the house now. I'll pour you a glass of tea and give you a piece of chocolate cake."

"Cake? I don't want any cake," I said, kicking the ground with the toe of my shoe.

"Braxton, please don't get mad!" said Mother. "Please come back to the house." She turned and with her head down, slowly walked toward the back porch. The Mother I thought beautiful a short time ago suddenly looked old and pathetic.

"Wait, Mother!" I moved toward the shadow cast by the back of the house. "I didn't mean to be ugly . . . please forgive me."

"Braxton, you have no reason to apologize," she said, turning toward me. "I know you love your daddy and that it hurts you very much."

Mother didn't know my real feelings about my father. And if she did, she would have been horrified to know that at times, I hated him and resented him and wanted him to die. His illness prevented me from being able to have any friends over or do anything in the house that made the slightest noise. At other times, I loved him realizing he couldn't help that he was so sick. I knew in my heart I wanted to hate him and use him as an excuse for all the bad shit that had begun.

As Mother and I walked back, I realized that if we were to make it, we had to pull together. I had a sudden pang of conscience or maybe it was a hunch—but I knew that the best way I could honor my father was by being strong for my mother. Maybe if I acted more like an adult, Mother could depend on me more and this would lessen the strain on everybody.

By mid-afternoon I had worked up enough courage to call Rita Stallings. I dialed her number slowly, hoping that she was not at home but secretly wishing she would be.

"Hello." She was out of breath.

"Mrs. Stallings, this is Braxton," I said. "I'm returning your call."

"Hi Braxton," she said, clearing her throat. "I was expecting you to call. I need you to baby-sit for me tomorrow afternoon about 3:00 o'clock." There was brief silence. "Can you help me out at that time, honey?"

"Well . . . ah . . . maybe . . . I mean I think so." I wavered sounding like a ninny. "I mean it's possible. For how long?"

"How long?" she repeated. "Let's see." She mumbled something to herself.

"Yes ma'am. How long do you need me to baby-sit?" Surely she had thought of this.

"I just need you to be here while the boys sleep in case they wake up and need someone to play with." She didn't hesitate. This told me she had given thought to how long she needed me.

"Yes, ma'am," I said with confidence. "I can help." I wanted to help her and I wanted to see her again.

"Braxton, let's say, be here around two-thirty. The boys will be asleep and this will give me time to show you where some of their things are."

"Okay," I said. "I'll be there at two-thirty." I would go now if she asked me. No one knew how I felt inside at this very moment. I had to be careful not to be so obvious with my true feelings. "Anything else, Mrs. Stallings?"

"No hon,' nothing else," she said. "Oh yes, there is one more thing. Braxton, if you and I are going to be friends, you must quit calling me Mrs. Stallings."

"Yes, ma'am." I smiled, knowing I was right. She did want me to do more than baby-sit or at least that's what I hoped. "I have to go now, Rita."

"See you tomorrow, handsome," she said. Looking down, I saw a familiar bulge in my pants near the bottom of my zipper. For a brief moment I was happy, having completely forgotten the earlier scene with my mother.

On the fourth ring, Byrd picked up his phone. "Hello, Byrd's residence. This is David speaking."

"Byrd, what's up? Mother said you'd called."

"I can't talk too long." His voice became suddenly serious, losing all of its enthusiasm.

"What's going on? I can barely hear you?" I said. "Stop whispering."

"Mother didn't come home last night. I still don't know where she is."

"What did your Aunt Olivia say to do?"

"I haven't told her anything."

"What? I thought you were . . ." I stopped and then hesitated. "What about Julian?"

"He's not back from his vacation yet?"

"How about your dad?" I hated to even mention this to Byrd as an alternative.

"Still on his trip!"

"What can I do?"

"Nothing now, but can you spend the night with me tonight?"

"Damn, Byrd! Not tonight," I said. "Mother wants me to start giving Daddy his shots tonight."

"Are you sure?"

"Yes. I've got to be here but I can call you after nine. Will that help?"

"Yeah, ugh, I guess."

"I'm sorry but I just can't leave Mother alone tonight. I'll call you later." I put the heavy black receiver back on its cradle and walked into the backyard. I pulled a bent cigarette from my shirt pocket, kneeled and lit it, and walked behind the garage for a quick smoke.

There was little movement in the backyard. A weak summer wind pushed the tops of the three Catawba trees that stood like sentries inside the hedge. A wasp tried to attack me from behind as I flipped my ashes on the sun-scorched grass. I leaned my head against the back of the garage and blew my last puff of smoke into the air. I wished I knew what to do.

Chapter 18
NOT IN GOD'S ARMY

WHETHER MY MOTHER really was fearful of giving my father his medicine by herself, or whether she wanted me with her because she knew he didn't have long to live—I don't know. It was clear that this task had become too consuming for just one person. It was also clear that she had no inkling of the breakdown in my relationship with my father.

"Mother, I'll be back," I said. I had forty-five minutes before I had to meet her.

"Where are you going?" she said, turning from the kitchen sink.

"Outside. I'll be back in plenty of time."

"Braxton, make sure you are," she said. "I need you this afternoon. I really do."

"Okay," I said. "I promise." I took the screen porch exit.

What a crock, I thought to myself. What a bunch of shit! I didn't have the right to complain. It wouldn't be fair to Mother. The smart thing for me to do would be to keep my mouth shut. This was hard for me to do sometimes. But it wasn't fair. So what if my father was dying? So what if my mother was falling apart? So what if my summer vacation was going to the dogs? I just can't say a word about anything. Everything was happening too fast. I had to get out of the house. I needed some breathing room, some time alone. I needed to think. What I really needed was a silent talk with God.

I needed to pound the pavement. I did my best thinking when I walked. I would walk around the small, almost rectangular block that our house sat on. Since there were no sidewalks on Kincaid Avenue and the town had finally gotten around to repaving our street on

Friday, I had no other choice but to walk through everyone's grass. It was either this or walk on tar that was still not dry in places and risk getting tar on the bottom of my shoes.

Outside, it was sticky hot and what little breeze we had was gone, making the afternoon more unbearable. The lingering smell of tobacco from the downtown factories, operating at near capacity, had traveled as far out as our neighborhood, permeating the air like dust particles being shook from a winter's hibernation. This clashed with the smell of the freshly laid asphalt.

Steam danced off our poorly paved street. Sweat was everywhere on my body and uninvited gnats seemed to find comfort in this. Whether I walked fast or slow, it made no difference. Large amounts of moisture kept rolling off my forehead, cheeks, and upper lip. I took some on my tongue to test the taste; it was salty and warm. Walking with the sun's rays beating down on me was unbearable, but it was June's way of introducing itself, reminding me that it would only get worse. I knew not to question whether being inside my house would be better. It made no difference if I was inside or outside, I still wouldn't be able to escape this unwelcome, early June heat and humidity.

Several neighborhood fathers in tee shirts and shorts washed their cars. Children shouted, begging their dads to wet them with the garden hose. I was tempted to ask for a soaking myself. I missed having these moments with my own father; but, then, I don't ever remember him washing our car in the driveway. It was usually washed at his Texaco Station on East Nash Street, about a block and one-half from Mr. Bernstein's store.

It was hard to think and speak to everyone at the same time. My first decision was not to go to M.Y.F., Methodist Youth Fellowship. My rationale was that Mother might like for me to stay close to home. She may need me. Next, I came to the conclusion that I knew absolutely nothing about God. I didn't want to accept this. What else could it be? I had trouble praying at night. Aunt Eva said God listens and answers. She added that we might not like His answer but He answers. No answers I wanted had come my way. I wanted to believe there was a God but I wasn't sure I even knew what this meant. My grandmother called it faith.

I thought of what Chuck had said in Sunday school about God being on our side in the war. If that was true, how could He desert my father? My father didn't even fight in WWII because he was sick. How could he be a part of God's army? Surely God wouldn't hold that against him. Would He? I wasn't one hundred percent clear on this.

I wished I had the faith my grandmother had in God or the connection my minister, Mr. Bradshaw, had with God. Then I could ask God, "Why did you do this to my father?" Maybe if I got really brave I could just say, "How could you let this thing get my father?" and "Why don't you make him well, damn it, if you're so powerful?" I would probably leave the damn it off. I wanted to believe there was a God. I'd been told there was enough times. People like my grandmother and Aunt Eva who said they knew God talked like He was here in person. I just didn't get it! There had to be a connection and I had to learn how to make it. I had no idea how to begin.

The first thing I did when I got back home was wash my face and change my shirt. I called Matt and Thad to tell them I was not going to go to M.Y.F. I didn't give a reason. I called Byrd but there was no answer. I thought I would walk over to Jason's house later. I wanted to know if he had ever talked with his mother about the contents of the shoebox and find out how she'd reacted.

I was probably the only one of the four of us who genuinely felt sorry for Jason. The others continued to think he was a pain in the butt most of the time. And he was. But in fairness, he was misunderstood by just about everyone, even his parents. I remained the only person he ever confided in. I didn't know exactly why he'd chosen me to share his inner secrets with but he did. I knew he trusted me. That's why he'd let me see a side of him that he didn't reveal to anyone else. No one but I knew that he kept rubbers inside his tennis racket cover. He bought Trojans at the truck stop on Highway 301 near Elm City and was proud of it. Jason bragged about the number of prostitutes he saw hanging around the Black and White Checkered Truck Stop—like he was buddy-buddy with some of them. He said if a man wasn't getting it at home, he went there to find some on the side. Jason had been my source of sexual information for as long as I could remember. He was my teacher and he knew the facts.

Jason told me of other lewd activities that went on at the truck stop. He claimed that it was a good place to go for a sexual release. He was explicit in his details; but, at that time, I didn't believe him. I thought he was just full of bull. Later, I found out differently. He did invite me to go along with him a couple of times but I was too chicken. I confessed that this was a world I wasn't ready to enter. Jason never gave me any grief about this but just accepted my reasons because he knew I was being honest. I respected him for not riding me.

I was the only one who knew which girl he was banging and that she was twenty-six, ten years older than he. I thought Jason was nuts. She was a woman and the mildly retarded daughter of one of Wilson' respected doctors who just happened to be a golfing buddy of Mr. Parker. She had an illegitimate child, a little girl, who was three years old. The crazy thing about this affair was that she and Jason did it in her parent's home, sometimes with them elsewhere in the house. That was Jason's story and knowing him, it could be true and probably was.

I had urged Jason to be careful. Wilson County had a high percentage of people with venereal diseases. "Braxton," Jason would say, "You don't know shit about sex or diseases. You've never gone 'south of the border' with a girl. What do you know?" He might be right about the girl thing but I knew Uncle Vic was right on the other. He was a doctor and I told Jason the source of my information. "Don't worry, Braxton," he would say. "I know what I'm doing. That's why I carry my rubbers with me." Carrying them was one thing and using them was another. I doubted Jason Parker ever used one. Jason thought he was immune to catching anything. And what was even more stupid, he believed he was the only one this woman was giving it to. But according to Wilson rumor mill, Jason wasn't the only one this blue-eyed blonde was having sex with. Eventually, Jason and I had it out on this subject. He told me I nagged him just like his mother. I gave up on trying to persuade him to be safe. I turned the focus on myself because I found myself potentially in Jason's shoes. Probably not, but it was an arousing thought.

The one thing I wanted to say to Jason I never did—I wondered if Jason being a bastard child, himself, would make any difference to him now when he had the urge to screw Sadie Brock. A bastard having a bastard—I wondered what Jason would say about that? He probably would say nothing and I never had the nerve to bring it up.

I entered this summer wanting to grow up but now I wasn't so sure. Why had life become more complicated since I had turned sixteen? It was like I had been in a cocoon all of my life and suddenly, I'd been pushed out into a sordid world that I didn't even know existed.

We had been out of school less than two weeks and already I was bombarded with all kinds of damn grown-up situations that I was supposed to respond to. Things I once took for granted suddenly seemed more complicated. Things we used to laugh at were now no longer funny. I kept asking myself if this was what maturing was all about. I had looked forward to this time in my life like a little boy standing outside of a confectionery shop with his face pressed against the window, seeing aisle after aisle of candy. I thought all I had to do was go inside, pick the piece I wanted, pay for it, and walk out. The choices were still there but getting in would be far more complicated, if not, impossible.

My mind was filled with all kinds of unrelated thoughts all banging into each other, vying for my attention. I knew what I wanted to know but had no clue as to where to go and get the answers. To me, it was analogous to my driving on a large metropolitan freeway with six lanes going in the same direction. Driving seventy plus miles per hour, I frantically looked for the right turnoff; the only clue given to me was the exit number—the only thing—I didn't know which lane to stay in and I didn't know when my exit was coming up. It was maddening.

It was almost 4:30 P.M. when I turned off of Nash Street and back onto Kincaid Avenue. I could take this tour in my sleep I had done it so much. I didn't settle any problems but the walk helped me to clear my mind and focus on those things I had to address. The real question was, would I do anything? Would I move beyond the thinking stage?

Walking up the front steps of our home, I took a deep breath, hesitating when both my feet were solidly on the front porch. I could feel sweat gathering on the back of my neck and under my arms. I could not stand the idea of what I was expected to do but there was no option. I opened the front screened-door and quickly closed it behind me. The clock on the mantle chimed the four-thirty hour. Time to practice with the hypodermic needle. If I had to do this, I wanted to do it right and concentration would be the key. First, I had to wash my face and hands.

I joined Mother in the kitchen for lesson number one. On the counter, she had two medium sized oranges, a 16-ounce bottle of rubbing alcohol, and several cotton balls. There was also a small wooden tray holding two needles, tongs, and a syringe.

"Mother, I'm here and on time . . . and I hope . . . I mean I think I'm ready to practice."

"You'll do fine, Braxton. Actually, it is fairly simple," she said, moving toward the counter. "I've already boiled the tongs, needles and the syringe. They should be cool enough to touch." Using the tongs to pick up the needle, Mother demonstrated how to attach the needle to the syringe. I watched her hand shake making the simple procedure more difficult.

I tried next. Once I got use to maneuvering the tongs, I was able to copy her with little difficulty. Some of my apprehension about giving my father a shot began to leave me. "You're right, Mother. It's not so difficult."

"Watch carefully," said Mother, picking up the syringe. "Watch how I take water into the needle by letting out slowly on the syringe." She did this several times. Each time she pressed the syringe with her thumb, the shaking of her hand forced the release of too much water. I saw her grimace each time it happened. Neither of us said anything. Then I practiced.

"Suppose I get too much morphine in the syringe?"

"Gently release it back into the bottle." Mother said. "It will take you a while to get comfortable with doing it. Sometimes I still put too much in the syringe."

"What are the oranges for?" I asked. Both of the dark oranges on the counter were bruised and not fit to eat.

"The oranges will act as your daddy's arm and you can practice releasing the liquid in them. Just don't do it too fast. Take it slow and easy," Mother said, demonstrating. Her hand continued to tremble, and even more now, like a nervous and anxious gambler shaking his dice before releasing them. I had never seen her hand tremble like this. I backed away for a moment wondering if there were other warning signs I may have missed—signs telling me of other things gone wrong within our family. We did this activity for about ten minutes. The routine became boring and I got tired of using the same mushy oranges, repeatedly washing my hands and cleaning the syringe. The juice seeping from the oranges was the biggest nuisance: it was heavy and sticky and another reminder of the outside heat and humidity. I was somewhat confident now, having lost most of my earlier reluctance. I thought I was ready. "This should be a piece of cake," I murmured to myself. And I wanted to go ahead and try it on my father but it wasn't time.

"Did you say something?"

"I was talking to myself," I said.

"Remember, your daddy gets his next shot at five o'clock," Mother said. "I will supervise the first couple of times and then you can do it by yourself."

"I'll be in my room if you need me sooner," I said.

"Thank you, son."

I had less than twenty minutes. I walked over to my bedside table and reached for the novel, *The Catcher in the Rye*. J. D. Salinger's controversial novel had not been allowed on our high school library shelf because our local school board didn't think it was appropriate reading material—it didn't even meet the school board's standards for educational material. That was all Mandy Brown, head librarian of our public library, needed. Being a progressive thinker and champion of reader's rights, she took on the school board and ordered the novel. I immediately put my name on the waiting list. Mandy's only stipulation was that the reader had to be sixteen to be on the list but since she knew Mother well, she put my name at the top of the list. That was early February and two months shy of my sixteenth birthday, but it was close enough. I had one week to read it. The waiting

198 • The Noise Upstairs

list was unbelievably long. I couldn't wait to get on the inside of this best-selling novel.

My real reason for wanting to read it was because Mrs. Brenda Frye, my sophomore English teacher, talked about Holden Caulfield like he was her brother. She was fascinated with him. She told us about some of his adventures and called them escapades. This was a new word for me and I liked the way it sounded. She read the definition to the class several times pointing out that to get this book on our school shelf someone would have to take action and go against the grain of some of our local thinking. We knew exactly whom she meant. The dividing line in our adult community was clear—clear enough that we all knew who was behind her losing her job because she talked about this book to us. And despite what some adults said, Mrs. Frye never encouraged us to go on escapades.

After a week of articles and letters to the paper surrounding this book and Mrs. Frye, I decided to memorize the definition of escapade. The word was powerful, it created controversy, and it, alone, made me want to read the book. One thing I did know was that I'd never been on one of Holden Caulfield's escapades or, at least, not yet.

Mrs. Frye said that some of her male students reminded her of Holden. The first chapter was short and after reading it, I knew I wasn't a candidate but Jason Parker definitely was. In fact, he and Holden Caulfield should have been twins. They both horsed around a lot and cursing was their primary choice of communication. I would soon learn that they had other things in common.

I laughed. I bet Holden Caulfield could not boil hypodermic needles. After five pages, I decided this Holden Caulfield was a cool guy. He might even know something about morphine. He and I might even have some family concerns in common. Without realizing it, I began to identify with him. A few minutes before five o'clock, I put the book down and joined Mother in the kitchen.

At five o'clock we walked into the dark makeshift bedroom where my father lived twenty-four hours a day. The shades were pulled to keep the room cool and there was a sickening sweet odor that kicked us in the face. A white light grew and lessened in intensity accompanying the character's voices on the show playing from our black and white RCA television. The CBS News's affiliate out of Richmond, Virginia, was broadcasting the events of the weekend. The screen was somewhat snowy and the newsman was barely visible but the sound was perfect.

My father sat where he always sat and the way he usually sat, slumped in his rocking chair.

Mother said he couldn't sit up straight because of the pain in his spine. I couldn't imagine what it must be like and I didn't want to. Saliva was drooling from the badly wrinkled lips that helped form his mouth. He was awfully thin. The fine, wavy gray hair he once had had fallen out. There was one small splotch left at the top of his forehead and Mother had given up on trying to comb it.

His face was pale, a yellowish white in color. Thin red and blue veins ran through his cheeks or what remained of them. His cheekbones looked like two raw, protruding elbows that were ready to pop out at any time and each cheek had a harsh scab or blister, the result of his constant scratching and rubbing. His skin was pulled tight against the bony structure of his face. He needed a shave. The black and white stubby hairs forming the beginning of a beard were the most alive things about him. And his breath was foul. This was the closest I had been to my father in months. Anne and I usually sat about ten to fifteen feet away. Mother said he could see us better because his vision was getting poorer. This shell of a man was only forty-five years old. If he lived, he would be forty-six in October.

"Hello sweetheart," Daddy said, opening his bluish, gray eyes as if he sensed the time and Mother's presence in the otherwise ghostly dark room.

"Louis, it's time for your shot," Mother said. "I'm teaching Louis Jr., to help me." There were two times when Mother addressed me as Louis, Jr. One was when she was uncontrollably mad at me and the other was when Daddy and I were together.

"Fine," he said, without any expression. He didn't speak to me.

"Hey, Daddy," I said as his expressionless eyes met mine. "I'll be careful."

"It won't make any difference," he answered. "I won't feel anything."

Mother had everything we needed sitting on a nearby television table. She picked up my father's arm and moved it toward me.

"My God!" I said, stepping back in shock at the bony arm she held, almost knocking the TV table over. Daddy's arm was bruised, purple, and there was a noticeable presence of sores on the yellow-ish-orange looking skin. The long feint blue vein in his arm looked like a tiny blue eel ready to burst through the water's surface.

"Louis Jr.," Mother's tone quickly corrected me for my poorly timed reaction.

"I'm sorry . . . I . . . I just . . . " I stopped talking and stared at the pathetic figure in front of me. My stomach was now in my chest. I broke out in a clammy, cold sweat. It came fast. I grabbed my throat, put my hand over my mouth, turned, and walked as fast as I could out of the room. I barely made it to the bathroom. I hung my head over the commode, heaving. As soon as the sweat broke, I saw my breakfast and lunch floating in the water before me. I flushed the commode, rinsed my mouth out and rinsed it out again. I washed my hands thoroughly with Ivory soap, threw cold water on my face, and returned.

"Are you okay?" asked Mother. Her face had a concerned look.

"Yes ma'am," I said. "I'm ready." I saw the sadness in my daddy's expression. He knew I'd reacted to the deathly presence that hung over him. I bowed my head. I was ashamed at the way I had responded and I didn't want to make eye contact with him.

With Mother's help, I did find a vein we could use. Giving the actual shot was not difficult. I did exactly as I'd practiced. I got through it by pretending my father's arm was a porous piece of drift-wood that another shift in the tide could not damage any further. The damage was already done to his arm. My father was right—one more shot could not help him or hurt his arm any further. After giving my first shot, I gave up any notion I may have ever had of wanting to be a doctor. We left my father still slumped and still drooling in his chair.

Mother could no longer afford around the clock nurses; she could barely afford to keep Crawford. Money was tight and private duty nurses were expensive. Daddy's insurance was quickly being depleted and this was only further stress with which Mother had to cope. Crawford's time with my father had been reduced to twice a week. But I heard her tell Mother she was available any time my father needed her. I looked back at the man in the rocking chair before I closed the door—a figure of a man I hardly recognized and knew—a man who was still my father.

In crowds and among his peers, my father, in healthier times, was usually quiet, stoical, and said little unless asked. He was more of a listener but when someone sought his opinion, he would give a candid response. Like his father before him, my father and his two brothers were buyers for Exeter Tobacco Company. It was expected of them—to carry the tradition. The Haywood men were well known in the tobacco industry. Tobacconists from Canada to Florida lauded my father for his intuitive ability to grade tobacco and predict a fair market price for each grade. The farmers revered him for his fairness and honesty. Our pantry was a shrine to their generosity as was his liquor closet. The bright leaf tobacco farmers throughout the tobacco belt knew two things when Louis Braxton Haywood walked the warehouse floor during a tobacco sale. He could not be bought and he would never turn a grade. He had too much integrity.

I was one of the third generation of Haywood sons in Wilson and I assumed at the early age of eight after my father took me to my first bright leaf tobacco auction that I would follow him. I would become a tobacconist. I was proud of his reputation as a tobacco buyer and I wanted to carry on the tradition and be as good as he. I was shocked at the advice he gave me after my first time on the tobacco market floor with him. I remember it went something like this . . .

"Louis," he said. "Promise me one thing."

"What Daddy," I answered, knowing that I would do anything he asked me to do.

"You are not to pursue tobacco as a career!" he said.

"Why? I want to be like you and your father. Tobacco has been good to you," I said, challenging him. At least, that's what I had heard the Haywood brothers say on those occasions when they were all together. They lived comfortably and they seemed happy. That's what I thought. I was wrong—they weren't as happy as they made us think. Alcohol was the proof.

"Son, tobacco holds no future for you. There will be a time when association with the tobacco industry will prove to be morally unpopular in some circles. Tobacco quotas will change and tobacco farming will change in your lifetime. You can do better with your life. Get an education. Remember, there is no future for you in tobacco." He seemed so certain that I knew not to argue. "Now, you must give me your word as a Haywood and, as my son, you will do what I ask."

"I will Daddy. I promise." That was the last time I went on a sale with him and that was the last time we talked about tobacco together. I'll never forget that day—it felt like he had shut me out of a part of his life. Some of the closeness between us died that day.

In retrospect, my father was right about two things. He was correct about his tobacco predictions and he was right about man walking on the moon. The first was more believable at the time than the second. I just figured he had read too many Buck Rogers comic strips.

On Monday morning I got up and mowed the grass before the heat could attack me. I called Byrd and for the third time, he did not answer his phone. Jason promised to come over later since we missed getting together Sunday night.

Last night had bothered me more than I realized. I just didn't want to do much or go anywhere today. A week from today I would begin my part-time job at Byrd's Drug Store #1, the store located closest to downtown on West Nash Street. I was anxious to begin a real job. It would give me something to do and I needed the money. I hadn't had a date since early May and since I'd been told not to see Helen Bernstein, I didn't want to lose contact with Sarah Hadley over the summer. Most importantly, I had to save for school clothes and supplies.

Friday, June 14th, would be Matt's sixteenth birthday. His mother had invited a small group of Matt's friends over for dinner. Later that evening, Matt, Byrd, Thad and I were invited to Jason's for a sleepover and the real party. This would be the first time we'd been back to Jason's as a group. I made Jason promise me there would be no funny stuff and that he would behave.

Jason's parents would be entertaining friends at Morehead like they did almost every weekend and Artis would be our chaperone again. Jason promised us beer and a long-awaited cruise in his daddy's limo through the red light district on Goldsboro Street. I looked forward to something a little tamer but I knew Jason did not bluff when it came to his promises, especially on initiation nights. And Jason was fired-up. It was Matt's turn to be initiated. I knew Matt wasn't going to like what Jason had cooked up. He wasn't the type. Jason needed to be careful with his exuberance and not get carried away. Until that time, I planned to stick close to the house and help Mother, read more about Holden Caulfield, clean my room, and baby-sit for Rita when she needed me.

Chapter 19
AN AFTERNOON TO REMEMBER

WE HAD ONE phone in our house. It was a heavy black rotary and it sat on the walnut telephone table outside my father's room. Not the best location for us but like most homes with a single phone, the only outlet was in the hallway. It had a short, harsh sound that could be depended upon to ring in the early evenings during the school year and in the summer, chaotically from nine o'clock in the morning until ten-thirty at night. We were one of the lucky families; we were exempt from a party line because of my father's illness. Thad and Matt were on party lines and had the irksome task of reminding their line sharers when it was time to get off and free the sound waves. Families with money and social status like Jason and Byrd's didn't have to concern themselves with this bothersome interference. Upon request, they were given a private line.

Our phone rang early on Monday afternoon. I caught it on the third ring. "Hello."

"Braxton!" Jason shouted.

"What?" I jumped, pulling the receiver away from my right ear. The wax inside my ear, jolted from the sudden blast of Jason's voice, tickled. I stuck my little finger inside to make it stop.

"I'm on my way over. Just wanted to let you know." Music played loudly in the background.

"Not yet!" I said. "Wait until around four o'clock."

"Four o'clock? What in the hell for?" Jason's voice rose to a level of irritation.

"Because I won't be home from babysitting until then," I said.

"That's over two hours from now, for Christ's sake!" Jason said, an excitement added to his voice.

"Look Jason, lay off, okay?" I said. "I need the money."

"Fair enough," he said but the tone of his voice spoke otherwise.

"And Jason, when you come, meet me on the back porch," I said.

"So, it's take the servant's entrance now?" A hint of sarcasm had crept into his voice.

"That's right!" I drew my response out in a whispering sound. "If you must have an explanation, this way we won't disturb Daddy."

"That's cool!" Jason said, abruptly hanging up.

I went back to my bedroom and read my novel until about two-fifteen. I stopped after Holden finished telling about his brother, Allie, and what a great kid he was. He died when Holden was thirteen and Holden spent that night in the garage. That was the same night Holden broke all the garage windows with his fist just for the hell of it. Holden said they were going to have him psychoanalyzed and all that but they didn't. The more I read about Holden Caulfield, the more I believed my answer for Jason Parker was hidden in Salinger's novel.

Before exiting from the back porch, I stopped to look at my mother. She laid on her side on a borrowed daybed in the back hall. A cigarette burned in the ashtray. A glass of liquid set on the table. Her eyes were closed and her breathing, heavy with distorted snorts. Her housecoat was unbuttoned at the top. She looked peaceful. I wished she could awake and find all of her troubles gone—that it all had been a terrible dream. I slipped out quietly into the back yard. Lily stood under the walnut tree smoking and humming one of her spirituals. I told her I would be at the Stallings and to watch for Jason and to expect me back before four o'clock.

I walked down Kincaid Avenue, being careful to stay in the grass as well as close to the curb. The scent of freshly cut grass, the sound of a dog barking, and the hint of a light breeze blowing through the crepe myrtles proudly trumpeted the beginning of another summer afternoon. I wondered about the scene I was close to entering and what script Rita might have chosen for our time together. To me, she was my leading lady, the prettiest young mother in Wilson, and I wanted to be close to her—close enough to touch her soft, creamy skin—close enough to kiss her fiery lips. The mere thought of her was to want to touch her in some way.

In less than two minutes I was standing on the stoop outside Rita's side screened porch, the porch leading into the living room. I took a deep breath, pulled my stomach in, and knocked lightly not wanting to awake the children. I waited. No one came. Rita's burgundy '55 Chevrolet was parked in its usual place, in the gravel driveway in front of their garage. The French doors leading into the living room were open. I turned the knob of the screened door and stepped onto the porch calling Rita softly. Still no answer. I walked to the doors and knocked on one of the glass panes. When Rita didn't answer again, I stepped into the dark living room. Her white curtains on the other side of the room moved in response to the oscillating fan sitting on the hearth. I stood for a moment wondering if I should proceed. I heard what sounded like two pots banging together coming from the kitchen. I walked toward the noise and saw Rita standing on a ladder attempting to move things around in a cabinet she could barely reach. Her back was to me and she was standing on her toes. Her heels rose off the steps forcing her shorts to pull tightly against her buttocks. Her multi-colored blouse ridding up her back gave me a glimpse of a dark birthmark at the lower part of her tanned back.

"Rita." I announced myself.

"Jesus!" she gasped and turned around. "You about scared me to death."

"I knocked several times but you didn't answer." I swallowed hard. The sight of her took my breath. Everything about Rita Stallings was beautiful.

"That's perfectly okay, Braxton," she smiled, stepping down from the small, white kitchen ladder. Her freshly washed brown hair hung loosely over her shoulders. The top two buttons of her blouse were undone exposing the upper part of her magnificent, round breasts. Her nipples pushed hard against her blouse, leaving two clearly defined impressions, one behind each of the pockets of her blouse. Each appeared to be standing at attention, giving a sensation of urgency to her appearance. The shadowy rays of sun bursting through the three kitchen windows fell on her, creating a white, halo effect around the upper part of her body. She looked perfect. Her legs, a light tan, appeared strong and were firmly shaped. For a second, I thought I was standing before a pin-up of Lana Turner except Rita was real and alive and before me in the flesh.

Rita stepped down from the ladder, walked toward me and stopped. Our eyes met. Neither of us moved. She smiled and her breathing became heavy. I thought I wanted to take her and hold her and kiss her. I wanted to touch her tits. In my fantasies I would have with no hesitation. Here, before her, I hesitated. I wanted to . . . no woman had ever affected me this way. I had a light dizzy sensation in my head and I knew my sexual desires had told me it was okay— I had never felt this way toward another female.

"Where are your boys?" I finally said. Why did I have to interrupt the mood? *Braxton, you're a dope,* I said to myself. You probably won't get that chance again.

"Follow me," she said, taking my hand. I almost pissed in my pants when my skin touched hers. We walked into the dim hallway, turned a corner, and moved to the other side of the house. In turning, her tits brushed my shoulder and she squeezed my hand. We stopped in front of a closed door. Rita quietly opened the door and motioned for me to look inside. As I moved in front of her to look, I could smell the scent of her afternoon perfume. All four boys were asleep like unsuspecting cherubs—totally innocent of their mother's flirtations with a sixteen-year-old boy who had never kissed over three girls in his entire life.

"What would you like for me to do until they get up?" My mouth spoke before my brain assessed the situation. *Braxton, that was brilliant—you idiot.*

"Come with me," she said, putting her right arm inside of my left, asking me to escort her back through the hallway. And then she pushed the side of her body hard against mine, knocking me lightly against the wall. We stopped, allowing me to catch my balance. She giggled and pushed again. I liked the play Rita had chosen for us.

"Lead the way, my lady."

"Would you like some tea, my lord?" Rita said, playing along with me. We both giggled as we walked back to the kitchen.

"Yes, my love . . . I mean my lady." *Braxton, damn . . . give yourself the idiot award.*

"Sit down, my lord," Rita said. "How doth thou desirest it—sweet or unsweetened?"

"Sweet, my lady." If only she knew how I wanted it then she wouldn't have to ask. I watched her closely as she poured the tea from the pitcher over the cubes of ice inside the rose-tinted plastic glasses. Her gestures were inviting and her body moved gracefully.

"Lemon?"

"No, thank you," I said, my voice cracking. That hadn't happened in a long time. Why here of all places on this particular afternoon? Rita giggled and I wanted to reach out and touch her hair and pull her close. As I picked up my glass, she spoke again.

"Let's go into the den where we will be more comfortable," she said, winking. "We can talk there." Rita took a cigarette from her pack of Kent's, put it between her lips, and picked up her silver lighter. "Braxton, light this for me please." She tossed me her lighter. I caught it with my left hand as she moved forward. We met and Rita leaned over, again exposing her breasts. She deliberately pushed herself toward me, as if waiting for me to make a move, and I, uncertain of myself, did nothing but stand there, looking stupid.

"My pleasure," I said, flicking the lighter. The flame shimmered before I lit Rita's cigarette. She inhaled once, threw her head back, and blew the smoke toward the ceiling. Her brown hair fell behind her shoulders and her blouse pulled tight against her breasts. She inhaled again, repeated herself, and then undid the next button on her blouse. She stuck her right index finger in the glass of iced tea I still held. After making a stirring motion with her finger, she carefully removed it, and then gently rubbed her finger between the upper parts of breasts. I licked my lips, swallowed hard and sighed. Smiling, she took this same finger and rubbed it against my lips in a deliberate motion like one would make the infinity sign. The after taste of sugar remained on my lips as she removed her finger. My body wanted to push against her in the worst kind of way. Rita rubbed her finger against my chest, making the same kind of swirling motion. I felt the intensity grab my chest muscles. For a moment, I thought I couldn't breathe.

"Relax, Braxton," said Rita, tilting her head. "Come, let's move toward the den."

I smiled not knowing what else to do. *God, she was beautiful!* My stomach began to knot.

"You're a nice boy, Braxton," she said as we walked. "I hope you know that."

"I know. Too nice!" I said. "All my friend's mothers like me."

"You can never be too nice, Braxton, especially to a lady." She inhaled, again blowing her smoke toward the ceiling but without the other motions that followed. Her every move was classic—she was Susan Haywood in *I'll Cry Tomorrow.* "I like you, Braxton."

"You do?" I jerked. "I mean, you do!"

"Yes, very much," she said, motioning for me to sit beside her on the worn couch. I've watched you with your friends. You're different."

"Rita, may I say something?" I said, clearing my throat and sinking further into the cushion at the same time. Before I could speak, she reached over and grabbed my hand, lacing her fingers between mine. The softness of her skin against my hand made my heart beat faster.

"Yes," she said, throwing me an innocent smile.

I cleared my throat a second time and a third and I hesitated and then quickly blurted, "*You're beautiful.* I mean you are beautiful to me."

"You really think so, Braxton?" She turned her body toward me and leaned over, making certain her chest was close to mine. I was on fire with evil, lustful thoughts I knew I couldn't act upon.

"Absolutely!" I was never more serious.

Rita's body backed away from mine. She hesitated for a minute and then, she stood. Looking at me, she took a last draw on her cigarette and then put it in the ashtray on the coffee table, allowing it to burn itself out. She reached for my hands, grabbed them and pulled me up until I stood before her. My heart pounded in my chest like a chef pounding his dough before baking.

"Braxton, would you like for me to kiss you?" Rita's eyes told me I would be foolish if I said no. My heart pounded as I stood waiting to answer.

"You are so beautiful," I repeated. "My God, you're beautiful!" What was wrong with me?

"Shush," she said, taking my chin in her hands and gently moving my face toward hers. "I want you to be in complete control the next time you kiss one of your girlfriends. And I'm not doing this just for you. I'm doing it for myself too." I didn't care. I just wanted her to get started. She tilted her head to one side, throwing her hair behind her. Leaning forward, she put her lips against mine and began pressing ever so slightly. Her lips were soft and I could feel another tingling sensation overtaking my body. Her lips parted allowing her tongue to find its way into my mouth. It was wet and warm and I gave in to this new experience. My tongue found hers and as we became acquainted in a new way, Rita pushed hard with her breasts against my chest. My hands found her waist and I let them fall on her ass. I pushed my body hard against hers, moving my fingers slowly around and around, rubbing her while we continued to kiss. I pulled her as close to me as I could without smothering her. I lost total control and before I could stop it, I had let go in my pants. I pushed harder, knowing I never wanted to forget this.

"We have to stop, Braxton," she said, but she made no move to stop.

"Why?" I knew the answer. "I don't want to stop . . . not yet, at least."

"Braxton, we have to stop. I'm being a bad influence," said Rita, pulling back. My hands dropped by her side. Placing them on her waist, I held her before me.

"No, you're not!" I said. "I've wanted to kiss you. Don't stop."

"Braxton, I don't know." She stopped then started again, "Are you sure?"

"Oh, yes!" I pulled her against me again and we kissed. Her hot breath entered my mouth again. Out tongues touched. I moved my right hand inside her blouse. A last chance and I was too eager. I grabbed her right nipple. It felt as hard as it looked. My single thought was I wanted it in my mouth. A car door slammed making us both jumped. Rita pulled back quickly and ran to the window. "Well?" She turned and I saw that I had wet her shorts, too. I should have been embarrassed but I wasn't.

"Across the street," she said. "Braxton, I have enjoyed our time together but I think you need to leave."

"What about the boys?"

"They won't be up for another thirty to forty minutes," she said. "It's three-thirty now and if you stay, I fear I'll continue to take advantage of you. It's just that it has been so long since I've touched someone so sweet and nice and young."

"Please don't make me leave," I said.

"You must, Braxton," she said. "Later, you'll think I'm terrible."

"No!" I felt the dampness in my underwear. I got excited all over again. "I won't ever think that, Rita." My heart raced, my mind wouldn't think clearly and physically, I felt drained. "Can we get together again?"

"Maybe, but not right away," she said. Rita had a sad look in her eyes and I was afraid that she had begun to regret what happened between us.

"Rita, this is our secret and it's safe," I said. "I promise I won't tell."

"I'm not worried about that," she said. "Braxton, do you still think I'm beautiful?"

"More than ever!" Smiling, Rita walked with me onto the screened porch. We did not hold hands this time. We stood looking at each other. I knew not to say anything stupid. I reached for the handle of the screened door and as I opened it, I turned back to her. "Good bye, Rita. Call me again when you need a babysitter."

"I may," she said. "I probably will." She turned and walked back into the living room, closing the French doors behind her.

"Rita, thank you for today." She smiled. I thought I saw a tear in her right eye.

I walked around two extra blocks before I went home. I had to think, to sort things out, to understand more about what had happened between the two of us. My conclusion: I had taken another step toward growing up. It would be Rita's and my secret, but oh, how I wished I could tell Jason about this afternoon. He would crap in his pants if he had seen the two of us. He and Sadie had nothing on me. I could be anything Jason was and maybe, be better.

I was back home in my bedroom waiting for Jason by three fifty-five. No one asked questions, not even Lily. I kicked off my shoes, removed my socks, and sat on my bed in front of the window fan seeking relief from the humidity and the heat that had swallowed our house. My heart raced, beating just as rapidly as it did during my hour and a half with Rita. I had no regrets. I had been with a woman, a beautiful woman, and I had a smile on my face. She had treated me like a man.

Chapter 20
NO WAY TO JOKE AROUND

SEEING JASON COMING up the driveway, I waited until he was by my window and then I gave him a wolf whistle. He shot me the middle finger.

"What's up Jason?" I asked, stepping out on the porch in my bare feet to greet him.

"Not much, prick," he said with that shit-eating grin on his face which usually meant he was up to no good.

"How was your weekend?"

"Dullsville, unless you call getting a piece of ass exciting," Jason said, throwing his head back, trying not to sound too much like a bragger.

"Come on, Jason!" I said, cocking my head as if I was confused. "You know what I mean. Quit shooting the B.S."

Jason cleared his throat, dropped his voice, and grabbed his crotch with his right hand making a pumping gesture. "I'm not shooting any bullshit, Braxton, and why don't you just say *bullshit*. You're not going to hell if you curse, you know! That church is really doing a number on you. You need to relax, man!"

"Okay, whatever you say, Jason. But can't you be serious for a minute?" I shook my head.

"I am being serious. I fucked Sadie Brock Saturday night on her bedroom floor," he said. And I didn't use a rubber either." Jason threw his chest out like he was the only teenage boy who had a corner on sex.

"Where were her parents?" I thought I could nab him.

"Her mother had taken the little girl to the club swimming. Her old man was passed out on the downstairs den sofa. What a stupid fuckhead he is! He's about as dumb as my old man."

"You watch your mouth young man!" Lily said, stopping at the doorway of the porch.

"Sorry, Lily," said Jason. He turned toward me grinning like he had won some kind of a prize for being gross.

"I just bet you is!" Lily said emphatically. She gave me a harsh look as she turned back toward the kitchen.

"Way to go, Jason. Do you have to talk so loud?" I said, hitting his shoulder. "Mother is going to hear you next!" I looked toward the hall door and then the kitchen door. Lily was standing over the kitchen table, hands on her hips. She was not happy.

"Sorry, I forgot where I am. How's your dad?"

"Worse," I said. "I'm helping Mother give him his shots now. He looks like he's ready for an early grave."

"Damn, Braxton, that's a pile of shit. Your dad deserves better," he said. "I mean that, and you deserve better too." Jason turned toward the backyard.

"Thanks Jason, it's beginning to get to me," I said, thinking that was the nicest comment he had made to me in a long time. It was a good reminder that Jason had a human side.

"All right Braxton, don't go get shit faced on me." He turned around to see if Lily had heard him. She was preoccupied, playing with the knob of the radio that sat on the windowsill above the stove. Jason began to finger the pack of cigarettes in his shirt pocket. He always needed a smoke when the subject between us got heavy. And this was serious stuff.

"Jason, quit dictating my feelings," I said. "How's your mother doing?"

"Okay, I guess. She's been hitting the bottle a lot lately. Evelyn Kern, Melissa Ann's mother, is having problems again with Melissa's dad. It's got so Evelyn drops by our house every afternoon around five and she and my old lady comfort each other while downing their vodka tonics."

"Yeah, I know what you mean," I said, looking toward the door that leads into the hall. I motioned for Jason to move to the backyard where there would be some privacy. "Mother's been drinking more lately too. I hope she doesn't start all of that again. I don't think I can handle that on top of everything else that's happening in this house." I closed the screen door quietly and jumped onto the concrete slab at the foot of the five steps.

"No shit, Sherlock," Jason laughed. "We're really fucked up! What else is news?"

"Jason," I paused. "I'll get right to the point. Did you talk with your mother about the contents of the box you found?"

"Are you fucking crazy? No way!" he said. "At least, not yet." Jason moved toward the swings at the back of the yard.

"But I thought you were all ready to go have it out with her," I said, following him. "I thought you wanted to get it out in the open." He continued to walk.

Suddenly, he turned and leaned toward me. "I was ready and I did want to, but then after I'd calmed down, I remembered you said something that made a lot of sense to me."

"Refresh my memory?"

"Not now," he said. "It did get my attention."

"Well, I'm glad I could help," I said. "And I'm glad you didn't go ape shit with your mother."

"Yeah, me too," Jason said, taking on a more serious tone. "I love my mother, Braxton. It's my old man I'd like to shit on. He's a real turd. Did you know that? A real fucking turd."

"Has he said anything else about military school?" I asked, trying to cover as many touchy subjects as I could.

"Are you fucking me? He talks about it every day . . . every damn day. Braxton, that's a given. I'm being shipped off in a trunk come August."

"*Damn!*" I said. I looked into Jason's eyes. He was lost. "Maybe it won't be so bad. Things could be worse."

"Is that the best you can do—just say damn and things could get worse? You can be a real crock sometimes, Braxton, a real crock." Jason stood. "I need a cigarette."

"Wait!" I said. "What am I supposed to say, Jason? I don't know what to say and besides, nothing I say will make you feel any better." He stepped inside Anne's playhouse, turning his head to the side, acting like he was half listening to what I said. "You know that as well as I do. Give me a break, will you?"

"Shit! At least, I'll be out from under his mouth. That's worth something," Jason said, attempting to nab the fly playing with a breadcrumb at the edge of the card table sitting in the corner.

"I don't like it, Jason. First you're leaving, and now, Byrd. I feel like I'm losing all my best friends at once." A cramp grabbed the pit of my stomach. And I didn't even know where Byrd was.

"You'll get over it, dick face. Besides, you won't have me irritating you with my foul mouth, as you call it. Your life will be boring then," Jason said, laughing half-heartedly. He walked to the door of the playhouse. "I've got to have a weed, Braxton."

"Seriously, I'll miss you and Byrd," I said. And I knew I would probably miss Jason's cursing. The more he cursed, the less I wanted to.

"Hello, Jason." Mother said, calling from the back porch. She carried a tray of iced tea and cookies. "You, boys, come back in. I thought you might like some nourishment."

"Thanks, Mrs. Haywood," Jason said, returning to the porch. He quickly stuffed the cigarette into one of the back pockets of his tan trousers. "Hello, Mrs. Haywood. Braxton just told me his dad's getting worse. I'm sorry, Mrs. Haywood. I'm really sorry Mr. Haywood isn't any better." At times, Jason's attempt at making just the right impression could be sickening.

"Thank you. That's kind of you to say," Mother said, passing Jason the cookies. "By the way, how is your mother? I don't see her as much as I used to. Of course, I don't get out very much any more."

"Mother is . . . well, you know Mother. Nothing changes. I guess she's okay," Jason said, hesitating as if trying to hide something. Jason's eyes went blank like he was in another world far away from the pain of his present one.

"I guess. You sound a bit frustrated, Jason," Mother said with concern. My mother loved to play the armchair psychologist and she was good at it.

"Huh? I mean ma'am?" Jason stared blankly at the cookies and then spoke again. "Things aren't too cool for me these days, especially between my parents and me." Jason's answer was an invitation for Mother to pursue the conversation further.

"I'm very sorry to hear that, Jason," Mother said. "If I can help you in any way, please let me know." Mother cleared her throat. "Sometimes, Jason, I feel like I helped raise you." And that was true. At one time, Jason had a standing invitation to eat with me three nights a week, Friday, Saturday, and Monday. And he slept over almost every Saturday night he was in town. This stopped after those New York doctors diagnosed my father with incurable cancer. Mother explained the situation to Mrs. Parker and she understood. Jason did too.

"Yes ma'am," Jason said. "Thank you."

"I mean that Jason. I don't want to interfere, but I'm here if you need me." Mother had been a listening ear to a lot of teenagers in Wilson. My friends didn't hesitate talking about most things with her and what she said back seemed to help them. There were times I resented this—not because she wanted to help them but I was jealous of the attention they got and the way she gave it to them. She was calm, intuitive, and unbelievably understanding. Mother acted genuinely interested in their problems. I guess she was and over time, I came to understand that helping them gave her own life more meaning.

"Thank you, Mrs. Haywood," said Jason. "I might just surprise you."

"You come anytime you need to, Jason." Mother looked away from Jason for a minute. When she looked back, she continued, "I mean that, Jason Parker. I'll leave you boys alone now." Mother returned to the kitchen. Mother knew more about Jason's life than she let on at the moment. I learned later that Lily had kept Mother informed of the bus gossip that filtered through the minds and then out of the mouths of the maids who rode in and out of our neighborhood each day. Negro servants were very protective of the people for whom they worked. They didn't mind the truth being told but they wouldn't stand for any lies being said.

"Mother?" I hesitated. "May I borrow the keys to the car?"

"Now?" she asked. "Where do you boys intend going at this hour?"

"We thought we might ride out to the Creamery and see who's there," I said, not thinking that she would let me.

"All right. But don't be gone more than one hour."

The Creamery was a popular hangout for area teenagers. A drive-in restaurant with a two-row half-moon parking lot, it occupied one entire corner of Ward Boulevard and Goldsboro Street. Teenagers from around the county gathered there to meet friends, pick up dates, and be seen by anybody and everybody. The country kids had their days and we had ours. Everyone had their night and their favorite parking area. Back row center was the best parking space on the lot, especially on cruising nights. Old pickups with loud exhausts, customized Impalas with chrome wheel covers, and souped-up Ford Fairlane convertibles would enter the parking lot from Goldsboro Street and take their rightful place in the caravan that circled the lot, exited, and returned again. Squealing, pumping and riding breaks, the drivers of these cars were on show and they knew it. It was both a time to showboat and to ignore the jeers and taunts of those who didn't appreciate your style.

The Creamery was a watering hole for all of us . . . a place where romances were made and hearts were broken . . . a place where rival social groups glared at each other and pretended it didn't matter whether they were liked or not . . . a place where angry teens temporarily running away from their parents could get the solace they wanted but didn't necessarily need . . . a place where it was okay to be confused, lonely, and misunderstood. The Creamery was ours: the social misfits, the outcasts, the cool and the not-so-cool. At least, that's what we thought and felt and we took ownership of this.

The Creamery gave us live drama through its carhops. Namely colored boys whose sole job was to take drink and sandwich orders, they were good at maneuvering their trays as they weaved in and out and in between cars jiving to the music. These colored boys had all the right moves and they were keenly aware of the thin line that separated black from white. They knew their place on these nights and it was to carry cheeseburgers, Jew burgers, French fries, Cokes and Pepsi Colas until eleven or twelve o'clock depending on the day of the week. Watching these carhops hustle trying to outdo each other for the biggest tips was the real show. If a carhop was really fast, he could pocket a fifteen-cent tip from every car that gave him a quarter to play their favorite 50's song. This was his second job—to run inside, deposit ten cents in the jukebox and run back to the next car, thus keeping the music blasting through the outside speakers until the last song played, bringing an end to the evening and forcing us back to reality.

On this Monday we rode through twice and didn't see anyone we particularly wanted to visit.

As we headed back home, Jason asked a peculiar question. "Braxton, would you stand by me if I did something really stupid?"

"Of course I would," I said. "At least, I think I would."

"Not so fast. I mean if I did something that might get me in real trouble. Would you still stand by me?"

"Yes, I would," I said. "You know I would."

"How can you be so sure? You don't even know what I'm talking about," Jason sighed to himself.

"Jason, we're friends. We are damn good friends. Friends stand by each other," I said, not knowing what he might do or be planning.

"Okay, then," Jason said, taking a deep breath.

"What did you do?" Silence . . . "Tell me what you did, Jason!"

"Nothing yet!" Jason said, grinning.

"What do you mean *nothing yet?*" I asked, feeling the tips of my ears getting hot.

"I mean I haven't done anything yet, you dumb prick," said Jason. "Braxton, you are so fucking serious."

"What is that supposed to mean?"

"It means just what I said."

"I could knock the shit out of you," I said, pulling the car over. "How am I supposed to feel when you ask me a question like that? I don't think it's very funny, Jason, and I don't think you're being fair."

"Lighten up for Christ's sake. Maybe I was just messing around with you—just having fun," said Jason. "What's wrong with that?"

"That's a hell of a way to have fun," I said, pulling back on the road. "Let's go home."

"Look! You're mad," Jason said. "Can't you take a fucking joke?"

"Not today," I said. "Not today, you insensitive prick!" I'd begun to sound like Jason. I didn't want that either. Silence ruled the rest of our ride. I turned into Jason's driveway, pulled into his carport, and cut off the engine.

"Time to relax, Braxton." Jason slapped my knee as if that would make everything okay.

"Time to get out, Mr. Comedian," I said. I wanted to get rid of him—like thirty minutes ago.

"You pissed off?"

"Not really!" I said. "I just get tired of your silly ass playing around all the time. I can't tell anymore when you're really serious."

"Gotcha," Jason said, getting out of the car and running up the steps.

As I pulled out of the carport, I heard Jason calling me. I backed up again and stopped.

Jason walked down the porch steps and over to my side of the car.

"What?" I asked.

"Goodbye," Jason said, laughing. He turned, ran around the back of the car, and up the steps.

"Shit!" I said, whispering to myself. This time he didn't call out goodbye or even glance back in my direction. "You deserve military school, Jason, and it deserves you!" I put the Tank in first gear, drove off, and took some gravel with me.

Chapter 21

HOLDEN CAUFIELD AND THE GARDEN HOSE

EARLY TUESDAY MORNING as I got dressed to go out and pull weeds, a deafening crack of thunder came from nowhere shaking the house and sending both Mother and Lily screaming onto the back porch. Daddy was in his room with his attendant and Anne ran into my room and grabbed my hand. We stood at my bedroom windows overlooking the driveway and watched our first hailstorm of the season. Before the storm ceased, icy golf balls had blistered the ground, leaving lumps, at least a fourth of an inch in size standing in our yard. A soft rain followed the angry intruder and it was one o'clock in the afternoon before we saw the first rays of sun.

A quick phone call let me know Byrd was at the beach and would not be back until midweek. He said he would explain. Matt worked at his Aunt Ethel's bookstore on Tuesday and Thursdays and nothing could lure him from the fascination he had with the piles and piles of books he catalogued, dusted, and put on shelves. Thad's mother had drafted him into helping her with Vacation Bible School for the next two weeks. I wanted to call Rita but knew I shouldn't. I had no desire to call Jason.

With some extra time on my hands, I decided to read more of *The Catcher in the Rye*. I was into chapter six and Holden was on one of his cursing rampages with his roommate, Ward Stradlater, who also had a sewer mouth. Both attended Pencey Prep in Hagerstown, Pennsylvania. Stradlater had come back from a date and blew his stack (not the way he worded it) with Holden for not writing a descriptive composition for him on one of the assigned subjects.

Holden wrote about a baseball glove, but Stradlater had told him to write about a room or a house or something.

" . . . You always do everything back asswards. No wonder you're flunking the hell out of here," Stradlater said. "You don't do one damn thing the way you're supposed to. I mean it. Not one damn thing."

Holden's response was the way Jason would've responded. Holden got up, pulled the composition out of Ward Stradlater's hand, and tore it up, leaving Stradlater dumbfounded. Holden went back to his bed, laid down, and lit a cigarette—exactly like Jason's reaction to similar situations. Their likeness was uncanny. Maybe I should consider being more like Ward Stradlater without the cursing. At least, he stood up to Holden. I put the book down to consider this alternative.

Every day Jason became more difficult to understand and to be around. His behavior was consistently inconsistent and his mood swings were back. His thirst for being the grossest among us was appalling and his bullying me was getting old. I liked Jason and I wanted to be his friend and I wanted him to like me. I thought I needed him more than he needed me and I let him push me around. His set of values was foreign to mine. I knew I had to stop giving in to him time after time. Heck, it was only the beginning of summer and Jason could do as he damn well pleased, but I didn't have to be his scapegoat. I picked up my book and continued to read. I only read a couple of pages when there was a knock at my door.

"Who's there?" I asked.

"Braxton, come here," said Lily. "I needs you right now."

I left my book on my bed and opened the door. Lily's dark skin looked ashen and I heard Mother talking with somebody in the front of the house. "What's up?"

"It's your father," Lily said, grabbing my hand. "Comes with me to the kitchen."

"What's wrong with Daddy?" I pulled away and started toward the front of the house.

"You can't go up there yet," said Lily. "Now comes back here with me and I'll tell you."

I followed her back and sat down at the kitchen table facing her. "Okay, give it to me straight!"

"Your daddy's had a turn for the worse," she said. "His medication's not working right. Dr. Wright's up there now in the living room talking to Miss Virginia."

"Daddy's always taking that turn," I said. "What happened this time?"

"His IV is in okay but his medication's not taking likes it shoulds." Lily had a tense, bewildered look. "Now go on up there and sees what Dr. Wright wants you to do."

"Thanks Lily," I said. I walked hurriedly to the front where Mother and Dr. Wright stood talking.

"Hello, Braxton," Dr. Wright said. He extended his hand to mine.

"Dr. Wright, how's my father?" I said, shaking his hand.

"We've upped his medication and I need you to drive to Byrd's drugstore and get it and bring it back so I can administer the dosage with your mother. It's ready now."

"Yes, sir," I said. "Mother, where are the keys?"

"Braxton, you must drive carefully," Mother said, handing me the keys. "Don't speed, please."

"Yes ma'am, I won't." I was out the door, in the car, and on Nash Street driving east within three minutes. I was back home in twenty minutes and I did not speed. I stood with Mother watching Dr. Wright administer the highest dosage of morphine my father had ever received. I don't even know if Daddy knew we were in the room. His eyes looked weak and he stared straight ahead, void of any expression. He gave a slight grunt when the needles were changed and once the IV started again, his head turned toward the French doors leading to the living room. His body was motionless—he was just there—almost a lifeless form in the shell of a dying man. Within minutes, he was out and remained that away for the rest of the day.

The next night, a copy cat of a previous sultry June evening, I fell asleep before the eleven o'clock Norfolk Southern train announced its arrival through our town. I awoke to an unfamiliar sound of something rumbling outside my window in the driveway. I dismissed the noise thinking it was the rattling of the old yellow window box fan sitting on my windowsill that blew hot air across my sweating legs and chest. I was tired and I turned back over and fell asleep. Must have been my imagination.

I had not been asleep long when I heard it again. My bedside clock read 11:30 P.M. I looked out my window into the driveway but I couldn't see much and what I could see looked the same. I heard the noise again; it definitely came from our driveway.

Barefoot and in my summer pajamas, I tiptoed from my bedroom, past the hallway where Mother slept, through the living room, and onto the front porch, then down the front steps and into the front yard. A choking humidity greeted me as I walked toward the driveway. My already pounding heart began to pick up rhythm pulsating against my chest.

The noise I heard came from our Buick. A frail figure sat slumped behind the steering wheel. Unaware of what was about to take place, I unconsciously but instinctively ran to the car, hoping that my suspicions would be unfounded. A green garden hose stretched from the back of the exhaust around the driver's side and up through the top of the closed window. The strong smell of carbon monoxide took my breath away. I gulped and coughed several times reaching for the car door.

The man behind the wheel was my father. He was asleep or unconscious or something.

I yanked the hose from the partially lowered window and threw it in the driveway behind the car. I stumbled as I opened the driver's door. Moving as fast as I could, I reached over my father's legs and switched off the ignition.

"*Oh, no! My God, Daddy! Daddy, Daddy, what have you done?*" I said, puking all over myself. I wiped the tears streaming down my face with the top of my left arm. Mustering all of the energy I could, I gently put my wet, sticky arms around his shoulders and lifted him out of the car. Just as I stepped back from the car, his emaciated body turned and slid down into my arms. I struggled to hold him. I couldn't let him fall.

Daddy began to wet himself uncontrollably and his urine ran over me. The sweat from my face and chest ran onto his head and down his face and neck. I cradled his body against my stomach and walked as rapidly as I could back to the house, and up the cement steps, and into the living room. My heart pounded keeping rhythm with itself. I continued to perspire profusely and it ran off my body leaving little wet marks on the wooden floor.

Still crying, I walked through the living room and through the opened French doors that led into in his makeshift bedroom. I laid Daddy on his bed and ran to Mother who slept soundly in her bed in the cordoned off section of the hallway (adjacent to my daddy's room).

"Mother, wake up," I said, nudging her shoulder with my hand. She didn't move. On the table beside her bed was a glass full of what appeared to be water. I was thirsty. I picked it up and hurriedly took a swallow. The water burned my chest as it went down. It burned enough for me to know immediately that I had drunk some brand of alcohol that Mother had used to induce sleep.

"Mother, *get up,*" I said, pushing her harder this time. She didn't respond. I ran back to Daddy's bed to see if he had moved—to see if he was all right. He just lay there. I couldn't find a pulse and he didn't look like he was breathing. Mother still hadn't moved. I didn't know how much she had drunk but whatever the amount, it knocked her out. I ran back to her bed.

"*Get out of the damn bed, you drunk!*" On impulse, I picked up the glass and threw the remains of the alcohol in Mother's face. She stirred.

"Braxton, what . . . what are you do . . . doing standing here?" she said, not cognizant of what I had done.

"Mother, Daddy tried to kill himself. I don't know whether he is alive or not! Get up! Please get up!" I yanked her arms and lifted her to the floor.

"What are you talking about? Your daddy is in his rocking chair. I just checked on him," Mother said, believing that she had just fallen asleep.

"*Mother, Daddy tried to kill himself!*" I yelled, pulling her into Daddy's room. "Look in the bed. That's Daddy, over there!"

"*Louis, Louis, my Louis! Oh Louis, what have you done? What have you tried to do?*" Mother screamed, running to his bed. She flung herself over the body of my father catching herself with her hands pressed tightly against his mattress. She touched his face and lips, threw back her head, and screamed his name again.

"*Call an ambulance now!*" Mother shouted, crying uncontrollably. She wouldn't stop.

"*Mother, stop it! Stop it!*" She continued screaming and shouting. Daddy just lay there.

"Do something, Braxton," she said, begging me. Then she lost it . . . went completely out of control . . . screamed at me . . . her fists beating my chest.

"*Stop it! Mother, stop it!* Forgive me for this," I said, slapping her across the face with my right hand. I felt a slight tingling sensation in my hand and fingers. I had never hit my mother before. I felt immediate shame and shock, a combination that left me questioning from where this sudden impulse came. I froze, stepped back, and stared at her.

She stopped immediately, fell to her knees, and looked up at me in disbelief. Her swollen eyes were red and wet. I extended my hand reaching for hers. She grabbed mine and I pulled her back to her feet. Mother kept looking at me with those penetrating brown eyes that gave you the feeling that she could read your every thought. She turned and looked behind her.

Anne stood in the room now with Mrs. Thurston and Mr. Ross. I didn't know how long they had been standing there and what or if they had witnessed anything I had done. At the moment, I didn't care. Mother had said to do something and I did. I wasn't going to put myself on a guilt trip that I was so famous for doing. It was the right thing to do at the time.

"Braxton, why don't you go change first. Then come in here and sit down," Mr. Ross said. "Mrs. Thurston and I will take care of things now."

"Yes, sir," I said, glad to have a chance to let someone older take over. I hurried to my room.

Mrs. Thurston brought a crying Anne into the living room and sat her on the sofa. After I had cleaned up and dressed, I joined Anne. Sitting down next to her, I put my arm around her and pulled her close to me. I touched her cheek with my left hand, rubbing it gently, and then pulled her closer to me. This was not something she needed to witness, but she had. It was time to move on.

"Your Aunt Josephine is on her way to get both of you," Mrs. Thurston said. "She'll take you home with her."

Three men in white suits entered the room with a stretcher. Two lifted Daddy and put him on it; the other put an oxygen mask over Daddy's nose and mouth. Mother stood in the hall just watching. She was in shock. She had a cigarette in one hand and the empty glass in the other.

No one said anything until the siren rang out piercing the darkness of the night.

I walked out into the yard. Porch lights appeared up and down the street as rising neighbors came out seeking an answer to what had interrupted the stillness of this late summer night. I just stood there crying and afraid, afraid that my daddy was dead.

Chapter 22
AN UNEXPECTED REACTION

IT WAS AFTER midnight when Aunt Josephine cut on her Cadillac to take us to her house at 1501 West Nash Street. It was an oven-hot June night and so airless, I had trouble breathing. When my aunt pulled away from the curb, I rolled down the back window hoping I could get some relief from the gagging mugginess. Heat lightning danced like skeletons in the eastern sky. Aunt Josie had called my grandmother and we had to drive to her house first. I sat silently in the back seat with my eyes closed letting the warm air slap me in the face. Anne sat motionless in the front with Aunt Josephine. Only my aunt mumbled to herself as she sped through the dark streets to my grandmother's home.

I figured my grandmother was recruited in case Anne or I needed her. It was about one in the morning when we sat down in my aunt's den to bring some closure to my dad's suicide attempt. Nothing either one of them said comforted me. In fact, their talk angered me. I already knew my daddy was a sick man. I knew that I was not responsible for what had happened. What they didn't say was that my daddy was a desperate man. Anyone has to be if they consider suicide and then act on it. They didn't say he was cowardly or irresponsible. They didn't say he was going to hell. They just said that he was tired of being sick and this was his solution.

"Solution? Is that what you call it?" I asked my aunt not wanting to believe that my daddy's suicide attempt could be justified so easily.

"Braxton, your daddy has been sick for a long, long time," Aunt Josephine said. Her eyes carried a saddened look. "His illness cost him every penny he has saved and every dream he had for you, Anne, and your mother."

"But why now and why tonight? There must be a better way." I knew a new day had started but we were still living on Thursday's, the thirteenth of June, time.

"I'm not saying he did the right thing," said my aunt, looking toward my grandmother for assistance in answering my question. "I don't know the answer to your question of why tonight?"

"You must trust in God," said my grandmother. I was in no mood to hear about religion.

"*Please, don't bring God into this! What has He got to do with it?*"

"God knows all things, Braxton," my grandmother said. "God is all powerful and, in situations like this, we must trust Him." She never hesitated when she spoke of God.

"*Why? Why do I have to trust God? What kind of God would let my daddy suffer like he has? I don't want to know this God!*"

"Braxton, you mustn't say things like that," said my grandmother, lovingly correcting me.

"He's tired and upset, Mother. Let's wait until tomorrow morning," my aunt said, motioning to my grandmother that it was time to quit her sermonizing. Aunt Josie rose, pointing her finger toward the hallway, hinting that it was time for me to go to bed.

I left them in the downstairs den and walked through the spacious entry hall past the marble bust of Madame Bovary sitting aristocratically atop the cherry hallstand. And I walked up the nineteen stairs past the grandfather clock on the landing and up the remaining seven stairs I had climbed so many times before.

My aunt had four large bedrooms upstairs. Each opened onto a small hall that fed into the upstairs sitting area. Anne was already asleep in Kate's room, the room across from Aunt Josephine's. My grandmother usually slept in Ingrid's room on the other side of the hall. I was assigned the daybed in the alcove off the sitting area. It was a small area but comfortable, and it overlooked my aunt's front yard and Nash Street. In there, I felt secure.

Mine was a restless night filled with tormenting thoughts, wild dreams when I was able to drift into slumber, and intermittent crying. I wanted to talk with God again but I didn't know how. I wanted to know why I was supposed to honor a father who wanted to kill himself. I really wanted to challenge God again and shift the blame to Him.

Why did everyone keep bringing God into everything? And why was knowing God so necessary? Why was the whole process so complicated? Was God trying to get my attention through my dad's sickness? Was this God telling me that I needed to be more attentive to my father? Was God punishing me? Was this God thing to be an integral part of my growing up? If yes, why did it have to be so painful?

As I lay there reflecting on the events of the night, it became obvious to me that my idea of what it took to grow up was immature, almost childlike. I had had my whole summer planned before school was out and every event was going to be fun-filled with little or no complications. I had not factored God into my plans at all. I had been out of school less than two weeks and already, I was being forced to look at the madness of life—ugly things I thought happened only to other people. I began thinking that maybe this God everyone kept talking about was trying to get my attention.

I wondered what Captain Chuck's answer would be to my questions. I felt fairly confident that Holden Caulfield would tell me that I was dumb to bring God into all of this. I could hear him playing with me.

"Braxton, what does Jason being a bastard and your dad trying to commit suicide have to do with God anyhow? Who knows what God thinks of man's stupid decisions? And what makes you think God really cares?" Holden would probably say in his cocky undertone.

"Holden, it must have a lot to do with God." I would say almost convincing myself.

"Why? Braxton, you need to think for yourself and quit overreacting so fucking much," he would say.

"Holden, you're really messed up. Didn't you learn anything on your escapades?" I would respond walking off.

LATER IN THE morning Aunt Josephine told us that Daddy had spent the night in the hospital for observation. Apparently, his suicide attempt had had no adverse affect on his already weakened condition. The doctors were amazed that Daddy had found enough strength to walk to the garage, get the garden hose, and then drag it out to the car parked at the other end of the drive. Apparently, they were more baffled by the strength he exerted cutting the garden hose in half and positioning it the way he did. Daddy would return home in the afternoon by ambulance.

Mother had stayed with Daddy at the hospital but returned home earlier this morning. Mr. Ross had driven to the hospital to sit in the room with my daddy, saving the expense of a private duty nurse who would have to be brought in from outside. Mrs. Thurston stayed at our house until Aunt Eva could get there to stay the night. That bothered me because even though she meant well, Aunt Eva was a gossip. And if Aunt Eva was not careful, the events of last night would circulate around Wilson by nightfall like rushing water from an overflowing sewer.

I told Aunt Josie I wanted to return home to be with Mother. She and my grandmother thought this was a good idea. They also thought that Anne should stay with my grandmother a couple of days. I agreed but I was concerned about how last night's activity might have affected Anne. She had neither asked me any questions about what Daddy had done nor had she said anything about what she had witnessed. I didn't know whether she was afraid to ask or if this was her way of mimicking the stoical response of our father she had often witnessed.

The two-block walk from Aunt Josephine's house to our house was the loneliest walk I ever remembered taking by myself. Suddenly, I felt completely cut-off from the security my own little world had been providing me. Now there was no distinct attachment to anything or anybody. I wasn't afraid, I wasn't dreading going home, and I wasn't trying to deny what had happened. I was completely confused and more confused than I had ever been. Only ten days before, my world seemed almost perfect. I thought I was in control of myself and my world and the summer looked bright and promising. I had everything figured out. Today I knew I wasn't in control of anything much less myself but I better damn well be in control of my actions. I felt as if I had aged ten years since yesterday.

Would I ever look at things the same way again? My friends had already accused me of being too serious and too good. I couldn't let this event or any other take the joy and fun out of life.

Mother, Aunt Eva, Mrs. Thurston, Mr. Bradshaw, and Mr. Ross were sitting in our peach colored living room when I entered the front door. Mother and Mr. Bradshaw sat on the sofa facing the front door. Everyone looked relaxed and if I hadn't known differently, I would have guessed this was just another morning coffee time among friends.

Mother gave the appearance of being calm and the redness in her eyes was gone. Her hand was free of a cigarette and she was dressed in a navy blue summer outfit but not the kind that would indicate a formal invitation to anything. In my mind, I hastily assumed she had reconciled herself to the events of the past evening. She seemed in control of herself and the situation at hand and was acting the part of a successful hostess. Mother had that ability to immediately swing back from a tragedy and continue as if nothing had happened. This she had done many times and this she would have to do again.

"Good morning son," Mother said, getting up and meeting me in the center of the room.

"Hello Mother," I said, kissing her on the cheek and hugging her tightly. She responded, reaffirming that everything between us was okay.

"Hello Braxton," Mr. Bradshaw said, standing and extending his hand. His handshake was firm, nothing like a limp fish. (Daddy said that a man without a firm grip was not much of a man.) I liked our minister and the strength of his handshake reaffirmed my respect for him.

"Good morning, Uncle Bob." Mother said we could call him that when we weren't on church grounds. "Thank you for being here."

"Hello," the others said in unison.

"Where is Anne?" Mother asked, seeming surprised she was not with me.

"She'll be here later," I said, not wanting to upset Mother by telling her the truth. I knew she'd want to have a part in the decision of where Anne would stay.

"Have you had anything to eat?" Mother asked. "Lily is in the kitchen."

"Yes ma'am," I said. "But I'll go check things out. Excuse me, everybody." I was glad to have a reason to leave the room. Normally, when we had guests I enjoyed visiting with them. It made me feel grown when they included me in their conversation. But today, I didn't feel like being talkative with this many people this early, especially since I hadn't even had a chance to speak with Mother.

I walked through the French doors leading into Daddy's makeshift bedroom. The room had been straightened and cleaned. Nothing was out of place and Daddy's bed had fresh linen on it. The smell of Lysol permeated the air giving it a hospital odor. I crossed the room pushing the swinging door open that led into the breakfast nook. Food was everywhere. There were cakes on the counter, plates of sandwiches, trays of deviled eggs, and tins of biscuits on the table. More food was on the bench seats and even on the floor under the table. Whenever there was a tragedy in our town, people were quick to respond. Some brought food out of genuine love and others, out of old-fashioned curiosity.

I walked in the kitchen where I saw Lily smoking a Kool cigarette and writing in a tablet. As soon as she heard me, she put the cigarette out in the big yellow clay ashtray that I had made years earlier at summer camp. She acted as if she had been caught doing something she shouldn't have been doing.

"Braxton, you startled me," she said, grinning.

"Lily, I'm glad you're here," I said, pulling out a chair and sitting down at the table with her.

Lily Griffin had all but raised Anne and me. There was nothing she did not know about us. She had seen some ugly things happen in our family but she had been able to enjoy some of the good times too. Lily knew in situations like this she would be considered family by many visitors, but Lily also knew when not to cross that thin line that reminded her and all the others that she was black and that pushing too far into the white man's world was a big mistake.

Lily was a member of our family. At least that's how I thought of her. I've seen her hold my daddy and weep with him when he was in too much pain. I've seen her when she stayed way past her normal working hours and put my mother to bed when she'd been drinking too much. Once, when I was in the fourth grade, she came to my school on parent's day when my mother was in the hospital. It was hard not to love Lily almost as much as I did my own mother. I didn't care what color she was and I really didn't understand why everyone made such a big fuss over it anyway.

"Honey, do you wants something to eat?" Lily asked.

"Oh, I don't know. I'm not really hungry," I said.

"Well, there's plenty of food in that room," Lily said. "Let me go gits you a piece of chocolate cake and a glass of milk."

"Lily, did Mother tell you what happened?"

"Your Aunt Eva did. You knows she can't keep nothing inside very long. She's a dear sweets woman of the Lord. But she do like to talk." Lily chuckled to herself.

"I believe that," I said, laughing at Lily's imitation of my aunt.

"I'm sorry that it happens the way it did, Braxton," she said, "Are you all right this morning."

"Yep! I guess as good as I can be." I picked up the fork and bit into the big slice of cake Lily handed me. She knew I liked the end piece and that is what she gave me.

"You eat all of that now. You hears me?"

"I hears ya," I said, mimicking her as I sometimes did. "Pure ambrosia—food of the gods. This is a sin, but it is so good." I bit into the cake and slurped just to get a reaction from Lily. She smiled letting me get by without a social reprimand.

"Where is Miss Anne?" Lily asked. I knew Lily felt responsible for her if she was in the house.

"She's going to stay with Granny for a couple of days. I guess Aunt Josephine will tell Mother," I said. "I don't want to be the one to tell her."

"I will if I haves to," Lily said. She knew she could approach Mother when no one else was able to reason with her. Sometimes I think she can read my mother's mind before Mother has even had the thought.

"Lily, don't B.S. me when I ask you this. Okay?" I said.

"How long you known me, Braxton?" she said, her eyebrows rose.

"Tell me honestly. How is Mother taking all of this?"

"That's a strong woman, Braxton, you has as a mother." Lily stroked her chin. "She was back and on her feet when I come here this morning and she had your daddy's room practically clean." Lily leaned forward and looked straight into my eyes, "Braxton, honey, your mother—she'll be all rights." Leaning further, Lily put her arms around my neck and pulled me close to her bosom and held me tight. "Yes sir, that woman's got grit. Any woman with grit can handle most anything."

"I hope you're right," I said. "I hope you're right, Lily."

"Don't you go to worrying, Braxton," Lily said, patting me on the shoulder. "She gonna needs you. You gonna have to be strong, Braxton."

"A lot of people have been here already," I said, looking toward the breakfast nook.

"These are the peoples who've come so far," Lily said, handing me the tablet where she had been keeping a list of all the names.

"Why is the phone off the hook, Lily?" I asked.

"It's done rung too much, too early," said Lily. "Miss Thurston took it off the hook. Your Aunt Eva done flung a fit when she done it. Just too many peoples being nosey."

"I think it's time to put the receiver back on the cradle."

"You is right. I'll do that now."

"I'll do it," I said, pushing the empty plate away. "That was delicious."

"Braxton, there's something you needs to know. That Miss Eicher—that woman who lives over across the street—she calls late last night after you left. Miss Eva answers the phone. Miss Eicher—she wents to accusing your dear sweets mother of trying to kills your daddy. I swears under heaven I don't know why that woman's so mean."

"That bitch," I said under my breath. "What did Aunt Eva do?"

"I don't rightly knows," Lily said. "She talk with Mr. Ross this morning about it." Lily bit her lower lip. She always did this when she knew more than she was pretending to know. And this was most of the time. I knew she was doing this out of love for me so I didn't push her for any more information.

"Did I get any calls?"

"I know Mista Thad and Mista Matt calls. Jason was here about an hour ago."

"What about Byrd? Has he called?"

"I don't knows about him. Least I haven't heard he called," Lily said. "You sit there and keep me company but I got lots more work to do."

"Did anyone else call?" I asked, hoping that Rita might have called.

"Just whose else you expecting to call, Braxton?"

"No one in particular," I said. "Lily, thanks for everything. I'm going to go to my room for a while. I walked across the hall and into my bedroom where chocolate colored walls and an off-white ceiling matching the trim around the two doors, three windows, and fireplace, greeted me. These colors chosen by Mother were rich and inviting, reminding me of a better time. I loved this room and felt a sense of pleasure whenever I entered it.

In my bedroom, there were two oval throw rugs that had some of the same chocolate color of the walls. My bed was an antique—a mahogany four-poster bed—complimented by a matching chest, dresser, and desk. My room had a high ten-foot ceiling with dental molding. My room was functional, comfortable, and in décor, the most handsome of all of my friend's.

I picked up *Catcher in the Rye* with the intention of starting the next chapter. I took my shoes off and stretched across my bed. I didn't know when Daddy was returning home from the hospital and I didn't know how long Aunt Eva, Mr. Ross, and Mrs. Thurston were planning to stay. The clock beside my bed indicated it was after ten in the morning. They would certainly go home for lunch unless Mother decided to share some of our bounty with them. I just wanted to be alone for a while.

"Braxton, wake up. Your daddy is back," Mother said, nudging me.

"Huh? What time is it? I must've fallen asleep," I said.

"It's ten after three. Get up and get ready to visit with your father. He's been asking for you," said Mother, smiling.

"How is he?" I asked, thinking that it was unusual for him to want to see me. I couldn't remember the last time he wanted me to visit with him.

"He's awake and he looks better than he did last night. He's still a very sick man and he's in a lot of pain," Mother said carefully. "You shouldn't stay long. He needs to rest."

I got up from my bed and walked over to my dresser looking at myself in the mirror. I straightened my hair with some spit and ran my brush through it. My door was already opened and I walked into the hall and around the oil stove and went to Daddy's room.

"Daddy, may I come in?" I asked, knocking lightly on his door.

"Come in, Braxton," he said in a deliberate tone, almost too businesslike. I didn't feel comfortable with his invitation. It didn't sound like my dad. It sounded cold.

"You wanted to see me?" I walked over to where he was sitting in his rocking chair. A bed pillow had been positioned behind his back. He sat erect but rigid. His ashen face was without any expression of warmth.

"Yes, thank you for coming." He hesitated, licking his lips. "I wanted to talk with you about last night," he said matter-of-factly. "I need to tell you . . . "

"I don't know what made me wake up. I'm just glad I did," I said, interrupting him.

"I'm not!" he said with a painful, stern look.

"Huh? You're not? Why?"

"*No!* You should leave well enough alone." He coughed, then took a deep breath.

"I did what I thought I was supposed to do . . . what I thought was right," I said respectfully.

"If you really loved me, you wouldn't have interfered," Daddy said in a harsh voice that made me feel isolated and alienated from him—especially as his son.

"But?"

"And don't you have enough common sense to know that by now I'm ready to die?"

"Daddy, don't talk like that—I don't want you to die—I think—we need you."

"You what?" He coughed. "Look at me. What kind of father am I to you and Anne? And what kind of husband am I to your mother?" He hesitated again. "You would all be better off without me!"

"That's not true. We love you. I did what I thought you wanted me to do."

"Braxton, that's your trouble." He took a deep breath to finish formulating his words. "It's always 'I' with you. When are you going to stop thinking about yourself all the time?" His tone was mean spirited. He coughed again.

"You're being unfair," I said, looking uncomfortably at my father. I couldn't believe he was talking to me this way. This was not the way I had hoped our time together would go. I could feel my cheeks and ears getting warm—my signal that I had started getting angry.

"Unfair? What do you know about unfairness?" He stopped, took a shallow breath, and began again. "Do you think this state I'm in is fair? Well, it's not!"

"Well, no . . . and I do know some things about being fair," I said.

"Listen to me. If you honored me as your father, you would have let me die in that car last night."

"Now, that's unfair," I protested. I felt my breathing picking up and my palms were becoming sweaty. I felt flushed and my head pounded. I feared I would lose control and say something I would regret.

"Get out, Braxton! Just get out." Daddy looked suddenly strange. His eyes rolled back into his head and saliva was pouring out of his mouth. He was beginning to cough uncontrollably.

"Daddy, what can I do?" I said. "I love you."

"Don't talk to me about love," He said spewing white liquid down his chest. "Go get your mother!" He tried to push himself up but he was too weak. He started coughing again.

I ran from his room into the kitchen looking for Mother. She was in the backyard with Lily. I opened the screened door of the porch and jumped into the backyard startling both Lily and Mother who were weeding Mother's flowerbed.

"Mother, go quick. Daddy is acting funny," I said. "I'll get him some water."

Mother dropped her cigarette and walked as fast as she could to the backdoor. She moved and looked like a race walker in her first meet—anxiousness and uncertain about what she would encounter once on the track.

"Come, Lily and help me," I said, pulling her by the hand. We both ran to the house and up the few steps onto the back porch and into the kitchen. Mother was pouring Jack Daniels into a shot glass. I started protesting, "Mother, please, not now . . . "

"This is for your daddy," she looked at me displeasingly. "He is visibly upset but won't say why. This will calm him momentarily." Mother started toward his room and turned, looking at me. "Bring some warm water, Braxton,"

"What can I do, Miss Virginia?" Lily asked.

"Get some towels and wet a bath cloth with cold water, and bring them to me," Mother said.

We did as she requested and then I left. I wasn't needed and I didn't want to be in there anyhow. I felt responsible again. I walked back to my room and slumped down in my old, dark brown wing chair. It welcomed me with its many sags denoting the years and times it had been occupied. Inwardly, I thought I hated my daddy for what he had said to me. I didn't understand at the time why he wanted to hurt me. Could his sickness cause him to take his pain out on me? On this hot afternoon, I didn't know the answer to that question. But I did know I would never feel the same way about my father again. It took me thirty years to forgive him and understand that the poison of cancer had been my persecutor. It only used my dad as its vehicle.

It took my mother and Lily over an hour to calm Daddy so that they felt comfortable enough to leave him alone. I never told my mother or my sister about the exchange I had with my father. Lily knew because she heard everything from the breakfast nook where she had been shelling beans. I didn't know at the time that she was there. I thought she must have been in the backyard with Mother. What I found out was that she had gone out to get Mother to intervene. Something stopped her. She would not tell me what. This is what she did tell me.

"Braxton, your daddy, he loves you. Don't you forget that—ever! You hears me, boy?"

"Yes. I hear," I said.

"I means it—you hears with your heart and not just with those ears of yours," she said demandingly.

"I'll try." I didn't want to try and I didn't want to believe Lily.

"Promise me you is going to try," said Lily as if she had read my mind.

"Okay!" I said. "I really will try, Lily." My heart was not in it and I knew instinctively Lily knew it, too. She could read me all too well.

"Only the good Lord knows what's going on in this here house. Lord knows I don't understand it. But I do know you is loved by that sick man in that room."

I LOST A part of Daddy that Thursday afternoon, the thirteenth of June. I also quit loving him that day. I still respected him because he was my father. I had been taught to do this. But our relationship was never the same. Maybe it was my fault. I didn't want to visit him anymore but I did because I wanted things to appear normal to my sister and Mother. I didn't want to hurt him but I couldn't disguise my feelings. He could tell how I felt because he knew me. And I saw the pain of anguish in his eyes whenever he looked directly at me.

Inwardly, I bore a new pain—the pain of rejection. I didn't wear it at all well. It changed me and made me angry at the inconvenience of the sickness that had overstayed its visit in our house. I wanted it to leave. I never regretted what I did to help my father but I did, at certain times, wish he would die. This was another pain I had to carry—the pain of guilt for falling out of love with the man I called my father. I began to believe I was a bad person at heart.

The topic of guilt was to become a part of my many conversations with God that summer. The answer to how I could resolve this feeling would not come until I had children of my own. As a result of that afternoon with my father, I became a little more serious and a little less jovial around my friends, especially as more weighty matters began to confront us.

Ironically, this put me more in a leadership role in the eyes of my friends and peers. I didn't choose this role. It chose me.

Chapter 23
A MEMORY OF VIOLETS

FOR ME THAT second Thursday in June would be one of the longest days of my life. It's amazing what can happen in a twenty-four hour period and it's even more whimsical to sort through all the thoughts a person can have after a traumatic event occurs. I had loved my father in some way as long as I could remember knowing him. It's hard to describe the feeling a son has for his father. It's a love that involves admiration, awe, pride, and loyalty. I thought my father was one of the most intelligent men I knew. He always seemed to have an answer or advice for any question I had whether it was helping me with a word problem in math, giving me advice on how to invite a girl out on a date or explaining how to get along with my first cousin, Riley. He knew what to tell me and he was usually right. For an uneducated man, he was acutely aware of himself as well as what was going on around him. Regardless of the complexities that entered our lives, he unceasingly maintained a beautiful balance for all of us. *That is until* the last twelve months. He remained stoical about his illness but the balance was no longer there. And after yesterday, I convinced myself that I was, without question, the chosen scapegoat for his pain.

Initially, his impatience with me manifested itself in little ways. I tried not to be too available but I still gave him his shots. Things that had never bothered him until that night in the driveway became his primary source of conversation when I was with him. Things he used to never comment on became little irritants to him. He would make snide comments about my weight because I was on the stocky side. He would comment unfavorably about the way I combed my

hair up in the front rather than down, allowing a scar from an earlier operation to show. He didn't like the fact that my shoes were not
polished. And he would say that I needed to watch my anger. I
learned to respond with a simple "Yes, sir." The fact that I would not
disagree with him irritated him too. He told me I was weak. He had
lost all concept of what it was like to be a father to a teenage boy.
This side of my dad's personality I had never witnessed. I didn't like
it and it made me dislike him, almost to the point of hating him.
Inside, I felt guilty because I wanted to love my daddy, but I just
couldn't.

After the driveway incident, my feelings of hostility towards my
father became acutely intense. He hurt me and a pain emerged and
burned within my soul and became my motivation to ignore him.
Somewhere in my mind, I convinced myself that I could identify
with his suffering through my own suffering that I chose to believe
was inflicted by him. It was easy to convince myself of this and it
made me feel good. In my heart, I knew this wasn't right. I tried
prayer. After my immature attempt at conversing with God, I even
managed to convince myself that this was the way God saw it too
and that He approved of my reasoning. Therefore, I concluded, God
must approve of my feelings about my daddy.

The afternoon was full of sun as well as a lingering, offensive
smell from last evening's spraying of the chemical DDT to rid our
town of a sizeable mosquito population. It was four-thirty when I
stepped outside and smoked one of Mother's cigarettes behind the
garage. The tall hedge around the back of our yard protected me
from being discovered. Every time I inhaled, something stirred within me and it felt warm, giving me a sense of exhilaration—a
momentary sense of being older. My thoughts turned to my buddies, to what they were doing and what they were buying Matt for
his birthday gift. I wished I knew if Byrd was still at the beach and
why he hadn't contacted me. I wondered about Rita and knew I
needed to see her–needed her comfort—needed to touch her. I felt
the sweat forming on my forehead, under my shirt and on the back
of my neck. A signal for me to move on. I inhaled one last time and
threw the remains of my cigarette on the ground, grinding it into
the dirt with the toe of my shoe.

I had an hour or so to buy Matt's gift and I needed out of this house. I checked my wallet and found three dollars. I hurried back into the house. Mother was in Daddy's room. This was a good time not to answer questions. I walked quietly to the living room and picked up the car keys from the marble-top table. I stepped onto the porch closing the screened door gently behind me. I walked to the porch edge, took a leap, landing solidly on the grass, and ran to the car, waving to Lily as I left. Backing out of the drive, I changed my direction and rode down Kincaid Avenue to Rita's house. I was surprised to see her. She was taking towels off the clothesline. She didn't see me so I deliberately revved the engine to get her attention. I crossed Vance Street, drove about a half of a block, turned around, and dropped my speed considerably as I rode by her house again. This time she saw me. She waved, blew me a kiss, and motioned with her hand to the right, indicating that now was not the time to talk. I read her lips as she said, "I'll call you later" and I headed the car toward Nash Street. The light was green at the corner of Kincaid and Nash and I turned left heading for downtown.

My next turn took me right onto Tarboro Street and luckily I found a parking place in front of Robbins's Jewelry and Music Company. Robbins had the largest collection of music and musical instruments in our area. Mrs. Beatty had told us that she and Mr. Beatty were giving Matt a new hi-fidelity system for his birthday that played both 45- and 78-rpm's. Matt didn't particularly dig Elvis Presley like the rest of us but he did like Nat King Cole, Pat Boone, Sarah Vaughan, Ray Conniff, and Harry Belafonte. Once inside, I made my way toward these labels passing several racks of 78-rpm recordings of Broadway musicals. Mrs. Robbins found me fumbling over which 45-rpm record to buy and suggested I give him a gift certificate. Two dollars was not quite enough to get an album but he could definitely get two 45s and the newest releases would be coming out the following Tuesday. If Matt hadn't been such a good friend, I wouldn't have spent more than a dollar because there were several singles I wanted to buy. I suspected Byrd would give records too. I wished I had thought of the certificate idea. That way Byrd and I could have gone in together on a gift. Once the thought came to me that Byrd would probably spend more than one dollar, I felt satisfied with the gift I had purchased.

By the time I returned home, Mother had had two cocktails and I found her in a jovial mood. She used the excuse that she had been waiting for me and needed something to occupy her time and give her peace of mind. Anne had returned from Grannies but had been invited by the Lancasters to spend the weekend at their beach cottage. I think this unexpected invite added to Mother's merriment. The less Mother had to do at night, the easier it was for her the next morning. She rose early, sometimes around five o'clock, and worked continuously until noon. Work was an efficient scapegoat for Mother, giving her the needed release for her mounting nervous energy. Mother had become a prisoner to her emotional state of mind and helpless to its grip that presently held her under its control.

"Braxton, you and I are going to eat on the back porch tonight," said Mother.

"What?" I mean, "What time?" I couldn't believe Mother would tackle this after all she had gone through. I liked to eat on the screened porch and this would be our first evening meal of the summer there. Our first summer meal on the porch used to be a family ritual. Since we couldn't afford to go out to eat a lot, Mother and Daddy tried to kick off each summer with a special evening on the Kincaid veranda as they called it. I would have scrubbed the whole porch down for the occasion, Anne would have set the table with Mother's best china, and Mother would have lit candles, and Daddy would have brought her a bouquet of violets. There would've been soft music playing from the Philco radio beside the daybed. On those summer occasions, Mother always prepared a special dinner. Sometimes, after dinner, my parents would hold each other and dance to a slow song. Anne and I would laugh but secretly I liked to see them dance together. It gave me a warm, secure feeling, as if to say everything was all right and would be for a long time to come. I missed those times. We were a family then and there was harmony in our home.

"Around six o'clock," she said, responding to my question. "I'm letting Lily leave at five-thirty so I will need your help cleaning up."

"That's fine with me," I said, trying hard to be agreeable. I looked at my watch; it was now ten after five. I could hear rumbles of thunder in the distance and I wondered if another summer storm had decided to visit us. I liked eating on the screened porch but if it did rain and the wind blew in from the right direction, we would be forced back into the breakfast nook. I had taken a dislike to eating in there. It was too stuffy and too close to my father's room.

There was just enough time left to run across the street to Mrs. Thurston's and pick some violets out of her empty lot. She and Mother shared the same passion for these small flowers and at this time of year, there was an abundance of the deep purple and light blue varieties growing wildly and waiting for someone's hands to take them. If Mrs. Thurston was agreeable, I would pick Mother a cluster.

I knocked on Martha Thurston's front door but no one answered. Mrs. Thurston was known to hold-up in her bedroom at the back of her house and many times, she just refused to answer the knocks even if she heard someone at her front door. Skippy was in his usual position under the hammock. I left her front door stoop, spoke to Skippy who ignored me, and walked over to where the violets grew. Knowing there would be no objection and seeing there were enough for the entire neighborhood, I knelt down and started pulling them out of the hard dirt. My only thought was to make Mother happier than the alcohol could make her. By the time I stopped, I had two large handfuls of violets. I ran back in time for Lily to put them in a small vase for me. She promised to set them on the back porch table on her way out. As I excused myself and walked to the bathroom to wash my hands, I heard Lily say, "Braxton, you watch yourself tonight and don'ts you go gits in any trouble!"

By six o'clock, a light mist had settled in giving the evening an uncomfortable, sticky feeling.

Mother was slightly tipsy when she sat down for dinner. At first, she didn't see the violets because she was checking to see if Lily had set the table properly and warmed the foods that she had chosen from those that had been brought by friends.

"It feels good to sit down," Mother said, almost missing her chair.

"Watch out, Mother," I said. It had been a long time since I had actually seen Mother in the early stage of being unbalanced from too much to drink. I was uncomfortably amused at how this woman of such perfection could allow herself to be the least bit out of control.

"Don't laugh at me, Braxton. If you'd been a gentleman like I've taught you to be, you would have held the chair for me," she said, lighting the filtered end of her cigarette.

"I'm sorry, Mother," I said. "I'll try to control myself." I stifled another laugh as Mother realized what she had done to her cigarette.

"I didn't think I'd had that much to drink," Mother said, putting the cigarette in the glass ashtray and taking out another and lighting it. "Did I get it right this time?"

"Yes ma'am," I said. The realization hit me unexpectedly—just how unfunny the situation really was—it was too serious to laugh about. I picked up my fork and began to eat. I didn't wait for her to ask me to say grace. She must have forgotten.

"What are your plans this weekend?" Mother asked, taking a long draw on her filter king Kool and releasing the smoke slowly through her nose. The smoke traveled across the table and forced itself into my face. I hated it when she did that.

"Tomorrow night is Matt's birthday dinner at his house and then we are spending the night at Jason's." Either she had forgotten that we had discussed this earlier in the week or the alcohol had completely clouded her memory.

"That should be fun. Matt is a nice boy. I'm glad he is one of your close friends," Mother said, blowing more smoke my way. I was afraid the violets would wilt before dinner was over if Mother continued to send what looked like mini smoke signals my way.

"I can be back early Saturday if you need me," I said, hoping she would say no.

"Will Jason's parents be at home?"

"I don't believe so," I said, wishing she hadn't asked that question. I took a deep breath waiting for her next comment.

"Braxton, I don't like for you to stay at Jason's house when his parents aren't at home."

"Mother, Artis will be there. We'll be fine."

"Artis is less responsible than Jason," Mother said, laughing. "I never have understood why the Parkers think that Negro is so irreplaceable. He appears lazy to me."

"He's nice and he won't let Jason get by with too much. He knows when to draw the line," I said, thinking of the afternoon when Jason acted so bizarre.

"Well, okay. You can stay but I don't like it. If they didn't live so close, I might not let you go." We had also discussed this earlier in the week. Surely the alcohol didn't erase Mother's memory.

"Yes ma'am," I said, hoping she wouldn't change her mind.

"Are his parents at Morehead again?" She finished the last of her drink. I hoped she wouldn't fix another one.

"Yes ma'am. They took some new furnishings for their apartment. They'll be back on Sunday," I said. "Byrd's mother and sisters are supposed to be at their cottage at Atlantic Beach too." It dawned on me that Byrd had not planned to stay all week at the beach but if he wasn't there, where was he? Had he disappeared for a reason and not gone to the beach. I had no clue. "I think I remember Byrd saying that his mother and sisters would be there for the entire month of June."

"What about David's father and younger brother? Are they there, too?" Mother spoke with heightened interest. She had yet to eat anything on her plate. Now on her fourth cigarette, her unsteady hand had left a trail of ashes from her plate to the ashtray. The odor coming from the ashtray was offensive, robbing me of any further desire to eat. Mother was loose and enjoying herself but I knew further drinks could make her violent. I wanted to keep her talking.

"Not this weekend. Mr. Byrd will probably take Byrd and Charles down next weekend."

"That Oscar Byrd was a mess in high school. Did I ever tell you that I dated him a couple of times?" Mother said amusingly.

"You're kidding!" I said. Somehow I could not picture my mother and Byrd's father together. Mother was beautiful and Mr. Byrd was a short, squatty man with the early stages of a beer belly.

"He was quite a dancer in our day. And he wasn't bad looking either. He had beautiful blonde hair much like David's. It was wavy and all the girls liked to run their fingers through it."

"Mother, please! You didn't run *your fingers* through it, did you?" Mr. Byrd was almost bald now and to think that my mother ran her fingers through his hair somehow sounded unnatural to me.

"I may have," she said, laughing. I couldn't imagine Mother with her fingers in Mr. Byrd's hair.

"Well, I hope you didn't," I said. "And if you really did, don't ever tell me please."

"Braxton, thank you for the violets. That was a sweet idea and I do appreciate it. They are beautiful," Mother said, picking the little glass container up and bringing them closer to her nose to smell them. For a brief moment, I chose to believe she had been touched with a happy memory as evidenced by an almost smile and traces of moisture in her eyes.

"You're welcome." I didn't know what Mother was thinking but I did know the violets made her happy.

I helped Mother clear the table. When we were through with the dishes I went to my room to spend the rest of the evening. The television was in Daddy's room so watching TV was out. The telephone sat outside his door; therefore, talking on the phone was prohibited. With nothing else to do, I decided to catch up on the activities of Holden Caulfield. Tonight Holden and Stradlater had come to blows, fighting over Stradlater supposedly "doing it" to Jane. Pissed, Holden grabbed a couple of things and headed off in the snow, walking to the train station. Holden's destination was New York. Once in the train car, he unfortunately found himself sitting with Mrs. Morrow, the mother of one his classmates, Ernest Morrow. Her son was the biggest bastard that went to Pencey, in the whole crumby history of the school according to Holden who'd assumed the name of Rudolf Schmidt, the janitor's name in Holden's dorm. Holden convinced Mrs. Morrow that he needed to have a tumor removed from his brain and that was why he was leaving school a few days early on Christmas break. I left Holden at the Edmont Hotel and called Jason to finalize our plans for Matt's birthday. The similarity between Holden and Jason—well, they were like two peas in a pod.

At ten o'clock each night I flipped the switch of my radio to the on position and settled in bed to listen to WPTF out of Raleigh and my favorite program, *Our Best To You*. Hosted by one of the best DJ's in the state, Jimmy Capps, the popular musical show took song requests and dedications for teenagers, college students, and anyone else who cared to send a postcard. It was fun to hear the same names aired over and over night after night. Once in a blue moon, I would recognize the names of two lovers from my own high school who asked that a certain song be played to commemorate their time together. Other names from other towns became permanently embedded in my memory and I would follow a couple's romantic relationship by the type of song that they requested for each other. These people became my mythical friends. I got to know them through the words they wrote on their dedications to each other and in my imagination, I created how they looked and acted. I often assumed a romance had died when suddenly one night I never heard of them again. Sensing the death of a relationship was maddening because there was never a way to find out what had happened to the couple. The thought occurred to me that I could send in a request for Rita. I could hear Jimmy Capps now saying, "This song is for Rita from Braxton who wants her to know he misses her and looks forward to their next time together. He hopes it will be soon." Wait! *Put on the breaks, Braxton!* Bad idea and a dangerous one at that—what in hell are you thinking about? I'm not, dumbo.

Like most nights, I fell asleep listening to music of the fifties. And like many nights when Mother was still awake, she came in and cut my radio off before she went to bed.

Chapter 24
A Birthday Surprise

I WOKE UP later than I usually do on a Friday morning. It was June 14th and today was Matt's sixteenth birthday. Mother let me sleep longer because, as she said later, she knew the sleepover tonight would keep us up late. For most of Friday, the day was routine—I cleaned my room, did my regular chores, and ran errands for Mother. The day was like a long sigh. Only the anticipation of celebrating Matt's birthday with my friends kept me from going stir crazy.

It was about a quarter to six when I cast a quick glance out the living room window and saw Jason pull up in front of my house driving his daddy's 1957 Cadillac limousine. Similar in style to a funeral hearse, Mr. Parker's limo was long and black and sleek and sported three rows of seats. A regular buyer of expensive cars, Mr. Parker could afford to be particular about his cars but if he knew everything that went on inside his car and some of the things Jason did while it was in his care, I doubted seriously if Jason would ever sit behind the steering wheel again. As a father, Mr. Parker was overly generous in letting Jason drive it. Maybe this was his way of coming to grips with his own guilt for lying to Jason about his birth.

"Mother, I'm leaving now," I said quietly as I poked my head into Anne's bedroom where she was changing the sheets.

"Have fun," she answered. "And try to get back early."

"We will." I took a deep breath, hoping I would make it. "I should be able to be back first thing tomorrow morning."

"No later than ten, please," Mother said, continuing to make up Anne's bed. "Braxton, be careful!"

Before I exited the living room, I walked over to the French doors leading into Daddy's room. They were slightly ajar giving me a chance to peer into his room. The shades were pulled. The only light came from the flickering movements on the television screen as they bounced off the surrounding darkness of the room. Daddy was slumped over in his chair and his eyes appeared to be closed. He could have been asleep. It was hard to tell in the dark. I told him goodbye simply out of respect. He didn't answer. He was probably glad to see me go. Strange. The last two times I'd given him his shot he hadn't said a thing to me; in fact, he refused to respond to any of my attempts at conversation. Even Mother had begun to notice the strain between us. She just hadn't said anything to me about it.

I turned and was surprised to see Mother standing in the doorway that led from Anne's room into the living room. I didn't know how long she had watched me, and it didn't really matter. She smiled but said nothing. I made a weak attempt at returning a smile. I walked over to the marble-top table sitting outside Anne's room, picked up Matt's gift certificate, kissed Mother on the cheek and exited the house. Once outside, I felt a new sense of freedom and I ran down the steps to Jason's limo. "You're right on time, chauffeur," I said, opening the back door and hopping into the second row of seats.

"Yesa, Mr. Haywood. I'sa aims to please," Jason said in his best Artis dialect.

"Well, James, on to Mr. Matt Beatty's home, if you please." I said, playing along with Jason's charade.

"All right, Braxton, get into the front seat." Jason turned, threw his right arm over the back of the seat, and motioned for me to get out. "You don't seriously think I'm going to chauffeur your ass to Matt's house."

"Why not?" I asked. "It would be a lot of fun."

"Yeah, right!" Jason said, pointing to the door. "Get your fat ass up here. Besides, we need to talk about initiating Matt after dinner tonight."

"Well, I don't know about that one," I said, opening the car door and getting into the front seat. "It might not be such a good idea."

"Why in the hell not? It's time for him to lose his cherry!" said Jason with a demanding look, pulling away from the curb and screeching his tires.

"He might not be ready for it," I protested. "He wasn't with us the last time, remember?"

"Who in the fuck cares if he's ready? He's sweet sixteen today, isn't he?" Jason took his right hand and slapped me on the knee.

"You know why, Jason! Matt hardly knows anything about women." I said.

"And you're suddenly an expert?" Jason laughed.

"What's wrong with you anyhow?" I said, ignoring his mockery. "Why is it so important that it's tonight?"

"Look, Braxton, first of all there's nothing the fuck wrong with me." Jason's impatience surfaced whenever anyone interfered with his plans. "Second, I get tired of Matt's namby-pamby ways."

"You didn't answer my second question." I shot back.

"*It's his birthday, stupid!*"

"We've got all summer!" Jason was hell bent on having his way and he refused to accept the fact that Matt wasn't totally comfortable with girls yet. How was he going to deal with a woman?

"*Bullshit!*"

"I don't want to ruin his birthday. That's all I meant. And quite honestly, the whole idea makes me nervous."

"We initiated you, didn't we?" said Jason, smugly letting out a loud fart. "You survived. Didn't you enjoy it?"

"I was scared shitless at the time," I said. "I just didn't say anything to you and the others."

"I don't get Dad's limo all the time either. Braxton, tonight's perfect. Trust me."

"It has nothing to do with trust but I'd like to check with the others and see how they feel about it." I was certain Jason would balk at this suggestion.

"Okay," Jason said, pulling up in front of Matt's modest white home. I nearly fell out of the car. It had only been a three-block ride but arguing with Jason made the drive seem longer. I knew that he had a wild hair up his ass and there was no telling what he would pull tonight.

Jason and I, both dressed in short-sleeve Madras shirts and khaki pants, walked briskly up the winding walk to the Beatty's front porch. Mrs. Ruffin was bringing Thad and Byrd.

A big grin stretched across Matt's face as he opened the door to greet us, "Welcome to my humble abode. Come in, *gent teel men,* and join the others." Because Matt read books constantly, I wondered from which of his novels he'd borrowed his greeting.

We followed Matt through the small entry hall into the Beatty's living room. Mrs. Doris Beatty, Matt's mother, had decorated the room with a combination of multicolored streamers, blue and gold party balloons, and she had hung a "Happy Sixteenth Birthday" banner over the entrance into the dining room. Jim Rusnick, Matt's cousin and one year our junior, was already seated. Coming in behind us were Charles Davidson and Zack Weatherspoon, mutual friends of all of us, but closer friends with Matt. They both lived in Matt's neighborhood and he grew up playing with them. The total number in the party was eight and Mrs. Beatty had fixed her specialty—spaghetti and meatballs with her special sauce.

"Patsy Wentworth is having a slumber party tonight," said Zack, breaking the silence of the group, and completely ignoring Matt. "She's having twelve girls over for the night. Can you imagine, *twelve girls?*"

"Why aren't you there?" Jason blurted out before any of the rest of us could respond. "You'd fit right in."

"I was invited for later," said Zack, giving Jason a bolted look. "You mean to tell *us,* Jason, that you—the Wonder Boy—*you* weren't included?"

"I wasn't invited either," I said, realizing this discourse was heading in the wrong direction. I looked at Matt and from his downcast expression I could tell he wasn't happy with the present discussion. "Hey! What the . . . this has nothing to do with why we are here!"

"She called me too," said Charles, smiling at Jason and not letting the conversation go. Charles Davidson had been the president of our sophomore class and was one of the most popular guys in the tenth grade. He was blessed with good looks and being athletic, played three sports. Charles was just the kind of guy Jason would try to upstage. I knew Jason was jealous of Charles and after Jason's comment, I think Charles suspected it too. "Jason, I can't believe a stud like you wasn't included. Have you fallen off *the* list?"

"*Me?* Hell *no!*" Jason said, flashing a "screw you" look at Charles. "Besides, I'm not going to any silly girl's sleepover. Why would I want to anyway?"

I looked over at Matt but saw that he had retreated to the dining room.

"Maybe because all the other guys will be there!" Charles said, beginning to banter. "Or maybe because you think you're such a cool stud!"

"Okay, that's enough!" I said. "What in the heck are y'all thinking about? Have you gone completely apes? We're here to party with Matt so let's get on with the party here."

"Right, you are!" said Zack. "Oh, one more thing about Patsy Wentworth, Braxton. She tried to reach you about tonight but you weren't there when she called. She wanted me to relay the message to all of you. Anyone that wants to come over later and dance is invited."

"Sounds good," said Matt, coming back into the room. A smart move on his part. Matt didn't even like to dance but he was usually a good sport about most things.

"What sounds good?" Byrd asked as he and Thad entered the room. The shock of seeing him left me speechless. Thad had worn his short sleeve Madras shirt and khaki pants like we had planned. Not being clued in on the dress for this evening, Byrd wore a long sleeved pink shirt and black pants. I thought it odd that he chose to weather the heat in long sleeves. I would find out later what he wanted to hide.

"Going to Patsy Wentworth's house later to dance. She's having a bunch of her friends over tonight. Peggy will be there, Thad," Charles answered.

"I'm in," said Thad, blushing.

"Me, too," said Byrd. "I'm in a dancing mood tonight." He glanced my way and winked.

"Fine with me," said Matt, trying to gain control of the conversation that had monopolized his birthday evening ever since we had arrived. "Everybody in?"

We all nodded in agreement. Even Jason, beginning to sulk, nodded. I was glad and relieved that our dialogue had ended on a positive note. This would also eliminate Jason's opportunity to initiate Matt. Mrs. Beatty entered the living room again. She was a plain looking woman who tried very hard to make all of Matt's friends feel at home whenever we were over. Like my mother, she loved antiques and had been successful in acquiring some as witnessed by her living and dining room furniture. It didn't hurt that her brother was a successful antique dealer. He had two stores in Wilson, the largest located on Highway 301.

"Are you boys ready to eat?" she asked.

"Yes ma'am," said Thad.

"Come in our dining room and have a seat," Mrs. Beatty said. "Look for your name and you will find where you are to sit."

We all followed Matt into the dining room. It was a tight fit, not because the room was small but because the cherry dining room table was large—too large for the Beatty's room. Fully extended, the table would seat sixteen. Matt had told me the dimensions at an earlier time after they had hosted a family reunion. Tonight there were eight of us seated at the table. I knew that Matt had helped his mother in the seating arrangement because the personalities had been evenly balanced. Jason was at one end of the table and Charles was at the other end. It was no secret to anyone present that they had a love-hate friendship. Jim sat on one side of Charles and I sat on the other. Thad and Zack sat on either side of Jason leaving Byrd and Matt in the middle. I was glad Byrd sat to my right because I had nothing in common with Jim. Nice and timid and not good in a social setting was Jim Rusnick for sure. The opportunity to pick Byrd's brain and find out where he had been never presented itself. Strange as it may seem, Byrd said little to me. When he wasn't drinking iced tea and chatting with Matt, he stared aimlessly at the ceiling. There were so many other things I wanted to find out about—how his mother was, what caused the slight bruise on his left cheek, why the limp when he walked, what caused the scratches on his left arm he tried to hide by his shirt sleeve, and why hadn't he called me.

After several helpings of spaghetti, French bread, and salad, we moved back into the living room for the opening of Matt's presents. The dinner had gone smoothly with most of the talk being about sports on Charles' end and about girls on Jason's. I thought the conversation rivaled any of Edna Kline's most boring English lectures and that was pretty bad. For once, I sat and just listened. I learned a lot about my friends that night by watching them, their facial expressions, their antics, and the way they responded to each other. We were a neat bunch of guys just trying to succeed and measure up to what the world and our parents expected of us. Jason tried hard to act civil while we were at Matt's house. I think he did this strictly for Matt and not because he was afraid of being challenged by Charles.

Matt received gift certificates to Robbins's Music Company from seven of us. At least Byrd and Thad were creative in their wrapping by putting their gift certificates in larger boxes, momentarily relieving the boredom of knowing what the next gift would be. I kept thinking poor Matt but like the classy guy that he was, he showed genuine excitement after opening each gift. The monotony was finally broken when Matt's last gift was a carrying case for his 45 records given by his cousin. His parents must have sunk big bucks in their present—a new RCA Victor Hi-Fi with two built in speakers and four detached. It was the neatest phonograph player I'd ever seen.

After homemade ice cream made the old fashioned way topped with chocolate syrup and a large piece of birthday cake, it was decision time for the rest of the evening—the time before we landed at Jason's house for the night. Charles called Patsy Wentworth confirming with her that the invitation was still open. A few more guys would be coming but she didn't identify them. Seven of us would be going. Only Jim Rusnick opted out even though Patsy's invitation included him.

Once outside, the warm, balmy night greeted us with a light wind from the northeast. The moon was shining brightly and as I looked up, I saw a caravan of clouds moving rapidly across its face. There was something about the night that bothered me, but I couldn't put my finger on it.

We agreed to take two cars and meet at Patsy Wentworth's house on Raleigh Road. Zack would ride with Charles and the rest of us would go with Jason in his limo. Thad called shotgun first and got in the front with Jason. The rest of us scrambled into the limo and plopped down in the second row of seats. I sat directly behind Jason, Matt sat in the middle, and Byrd sat next to the other passenger door. The seating arrangement wasn't planned this way but it would definitely take on significance as the evening passed. I hoped Jason would go directly to Patsy's house and not pull any of his funny stuff. I trusted that he had forgotten the idea of the initiation but as he turned on the ignition, he announced that we would be taking a brief detour.

"Why?" Thad asked. "We're invited to a chick's party and I'm ready to dance."

"I have another present for my friend, Matt," said Jason, pulling away from the curb and heading toward downtown.

"What?" said Matt in a surprised voice. "You've already given me one. I don't expect another."

"That's okay. What are friends for?" said Jason. He was determined to go through with this. "You'll like this one even better! It's what every average, full-blooded American boy craves on his sixteenth birthday." Jason could hardly contain his enthusiasm. My eyes watched him in the rearview mirror as he ran his tongue around the outside of his dry lips, licking them. He never once made eye contact with Matt or me. I continued to follow his expression.

"Jason, don't you think we should go to Patsy's home first," I said, hoping to get the others to second my suggestion. Silence.

"Not on your life, asshole," said Jason with a grin. It's time to party and Matt, *this is your night*—a night you'll never forget."

"Jason, I don't know . . . maybe you should . . . just take me back home!" Matt said nervously. "I don't like the sound of this."

"No way, buddy," said Jason coldly. "You're staying with us. We've all planned this for you."

"Braxton, did you know about this?" Matt turned toward me, his voice quivering. I could feel his breath. His heart was beginning to palpitate rapidly. I knew he was scared.

"Well, sort of, but we never finalized anything." I hesitated. "Oh! Shit yes! I was a part of it." I confessed. "Jason, let's call it off now and go onto Patsy's party."

"I'll do it with you or without you, Braxton! It's your call," said Jason, gripping the steering wheel of the car with impatient anger and slowing down.

"*Please tell me what's going on!*" Matt begged, beginning to shake. I knew we shouldn't have started this but I felt hopeless. I didn't know how to make Jason quit.

"Jason, *stop it! I mean it,*" I said as forcefully as I could. Jason muttered something and shook his head from side to side. "*I'm not playing your stupid game any longer! Now, stop, damn it!*" In a way I thought Jason would understand. More silence. He didn't flinch and just kept driving. I waited for his response.

"Come on, Braxton. Don't chicken out! You didn't complain the night of your sixteenth birthday," Jason said, slamming the gas pedal to the floor throwing all of us back against our seats. "That's enough talk!"

"What are you talking about?" Matt asked, reaching for the front seat and pulling himself forward. Matt wasn't able to attend my birthday party and the other initiations had been mild in comparison to mine. "What are you doing?" Jason gunned the gas pedal again. "Jason, *slow down!*" We sat stunned and the mood within the car was suddenly a quiet dawn before an unexpected eruption.

"We won't let him hurt you," said Thad, turning for the first time to look at Matt. "I'm with you, Matt."

"Me too," Byrd said.

"You guys sound like a bunch of pussies. *This is 'break the cherry' night,*" Jason said with laughing vigor hidden in his voice.

"*Hell no, it's not!*" Matt's face was flushed. Sweat had broken out and danced on his face. "*Take me home now, Jason Parker! I mean it, you fuckhead, take me home!*" A crescendo of passion erupted in Matt's voice.

Matt reached across me for the door handle but couldn't maneuver it to get it open. I pushed his hand back, fearing he would jump out of the car. I had never heard him use foul language. Signs of panic had taken hold of him. He beat the back of the front seats with his fists and his face had turned red revealing an anger that rarely surfaced. I wondered what he would do next.

"*Quit hitting the seat!*" Jason was equally angry and the red in his face was an even match with Matt's. The whole damn situation was out of hand. This was totally foreign territory to Matt and he had every reason to fear the unknown, especially with Jason as pilot.

"*Fuck you, Jason Parker. I wished I had never . . .*" Matt suddenly stopped.

"Don't do something stupid, you prick," Jason said, looking at Matt for the first time in the rear view mirror. "Now, shut up and sit back! It's time for you to grow up!"

Matt's blonde hair had fallen onto his forehead and his expression as he spoke was one of total disgust, "Jason, I don't need you of all people to give me advice about growing up. You know you're a real horse's ass—and you don't know when to quit! This little game of yours has gone far enough . . . " I'd never seen Matt this determined.

We had just passed Oscar Byrd's downtown drug store and pharmacy and the Wilson County Public Library on West Nash Street when Jason pulled his limo over and stopped abruptly. He turned around and looked squarely at me, then Byrd, and then Matt.

"*Look, you crybaby.* This is *your night* to meet *Arlene.* I don't *give a shit* whether you *want to or not; you're going to!*" Jason slammed his fist on the back of his seat. "Braxton, me, and Byrd have been initiated. When Thad hits sixteen he will be too. *Tonight, fucker, is your night.*"

"*Tonight is not my night I don't want to meet Ilene or whoever she is,*" said Matt with his jaw locked while gripping the edge of his seat

"*Her name is Arlene. And if you don't stop your bitching, I'll knock the shit out of you and no one—I mean no one in this car will stop me! Now damn it, shut up!*" said Jason, grimacing at Matt in the loud voice he uses when he wants total control.

"Jason, this has gone too far. *Turn around!*" I ordered in disgust.

"*Shut the shit up, Braxton. I mean it now!*" said Jason, bursting into a scream. I watched the veins pop out on his neck and just as quickly, disappear.

Within a split second there was complete silence in the car—almost a silence of death. Only our breathing and the unseasonably high temperature of the evening penetrated the deafening silence. No one was in sight of the car and the continued breeze from the northeast made a rushing sound through the tall oaks surrounding us. Jason accelerated and we sat in continued silence until he entered the downtown area.

"Where will we find her?" Thad moved and squirmed restlessly. Was he getting excited?

"She'll either be walking on South Tarboro Street or South Goldsboro Street," Jason said.

"Try South Tarboro Street first," suggested Byrd with a spirit of cooperation.

Jason passed Pine Street and drove to Tarboro Street and turned right. It was a little after nine o'clock on the busiest shopping day of the week. Only a pre-holiday sale day would be bigger. Most of the downtown merchants had hung their closed sign on their door or in their window. Door shades had been pulled. We passed Sam Parker's clothing store. It had closed but inside lights were on indicating that workers were still on the premises. This gave me a secure feeling. If things did go too far, we could, at least get some help. We had driven about three blocks when Jason began to slow down.

"There she is, boys," said Jason pointing to a woman dressed in a white blouse, tight black slacks, and wearing stacked heels, the typical attire of a Wilson prostitute. As he drove closer, the dark haired woman stopped, turned toward us, and flipped the cigarette she was holding into the gutter. Jason pulled over, stopping under a streetlight mounted atop a telephone pole. "Roll down your window, Thad," said Jason.

"I don't like this, Braxton," murmured Matt. "Please get him to take me home! *Please!*"

"You'll be okay, Matt," I said. "I promise you that." Tears of fear filled his eyes.

The ugly, wrinkle-faced woman around fifty years of age walked without hesitation to the car window, then stopped and leaned forward. Her coarse black hair with a texture like steel wool had obviously been dyed. Having been blown wildly by the evening breeze, it stood out from her head like the quills of a porcupine. She wore a see through cheap white blouse of the Woolworth or McClellan variety and her large boobs were overflowing her tight red bra. Her body wasn't bad for an older woman but she was no Rita Stallings.

"Hello doll," Jason said, leaning across Thad. He lit his first ciga-rette of the evening and blew the smoke toward the woman's face. Thad coughed, eliciting a smile from the ugly whore.

"What can I do for you young men?" She had a wide smile that showed too many of her teeth. I couldn't help but notice she was missing an upper tooth on the right side and with the light of the streetlamp shining on her face, her front teeth looked yellowish brown like the color of nicotine.

"We have someone who wants to meet you, Arlene." This was not the way I had pictured this woman with the name of Arlene. I thought she would be almost angelic in appearance. The one Arlene I knew was a really nice and quiet Catholic girl who wanted to be a nun. No, this woman was in no way an Arlene. "Have you got time?" Jason and Arlene grinned at each other.

"I've always got time for you, Mr. Parker," Arlene said casually. We all just about flipped. She knew Jason by name.

"Get in doll," Jason said. "Byrd get up here with us. Let the lady have your seat."

When Byrd opened the limo's door to make the transfer, Matt's torso became rigid and he pressed hard against the back of the seat. I fully expected him to make a run for it. Instead, he froze, becom-ing completely silent. If fear could make a person numb, it had turned Matt into a breathing statue. Arlene got in and sat then slid over next to Matt. Her cheap perfume permeated the humidity that had already taken up residence inside the car. If I had not known better I would have thought a dead skunk had joined the party.

"Mr. Parker, what's the occasion?" she asked before undoing the top four buttons of her blouse.

"Tonight we're celebrating Matthew's sixteenth birthday. And he needs to come into manhood if you know what I mean." Jason paused.

"Yes," said Arlene. "I know exactly what you mean. Please go on."

"Do you think you can help him?"

"I certainly do. Which of you lucky boys is Matthew?" she asked. I watched her breasts tighten as she took a deep breath. As she exhaled, her breasts pushed against her blouse accentuating her hard nipples.

None of us said anything for a moment then Arlene spoke again, "I know that two of you in the front seat are not the birthday boy. There is Mr. Parker and I believe Byrd was the name Mr. Parker called you," she said, looking directly into the widening eyes of David Byrd.

"I'm Thad," Thad said, sticking out his hand. "I'm not the birthday boy but it's nice to meet you."

"Nice to meet you too, darling," Arlene said, shaking Thad's hand. "My you have a firm grip."

"Thank you, ma'am," Thad said. I almost laughed at Thad for the politeness he showed this town whore. He acted like Arlene was someone of dignity rather than the slut she really was. But that was Thad—nice and considerate to all people regardless of race and station in life. I almost felt ashamed of myself for not following him in introducing myself.

"Too bad you're not the birthday boy," Arlene said. "You're a real cutie and so muscular for a young lad. I love a muscular man's hand on my body." Thad coughed again, this time in response to Arlene's comment.

"Speak up, Birthday Boy," Jason said. The inside temperature of the limo felt like it had shot up a good ten degrees. I suspected it was due to our hormones getting activated. I had started a good sweat and Matt had sweat on his forehead and cheeks.

"It's me. I'm Matt. It's my birthday today and *I don't want any part of this,*" Matt said, looking at Jason and then turning to Arlene. He appeared petrified.

"Why not?" she asked. "What could you possibly be afraid of?" Arlene reached out and touched Matt's hand.

"I'm not afraid of you . . . I . . . ah . . . I just don't want to," Matt said sheepishly.

"Don't want to what?" Arlene asked in a motherly sort of way.

"I dunno," answered Matt, unable to communicate.

"I won't hurt you honey." Arlene patted Matt's leg. "What's your last name?"

"Beatty," Matt said, seeming to relax a little. I didn't think Matt needed to give her that information.

"Unhook my bra, Matthew Beatty," Arlene said as she took off her blouse. "I want to show you something." She handed me her blouse. It reeked of her perfume and I sneezed as soon as I touched it. Wanting to get rid of it, I tossed it over my head trusting that it had landed on the third row of seats.

"Huh?" Matthew responded dumbfounded.

"Give me your hand, sweetie," Arlene said, taking Matt's hand and guiding it to the back of her bra. "Now unhook it. It won't bite."

"Holy shit," Thad said, looking excitedly at the enormous boobs that suddenly broke loose from their restraint.

"Now, how do you like these, Matthew?" Arlene said, clasping her supple breasts and forcing them into Matt's face. She jiggled them around several seconds rubbing them against his cheeks, and then after teasing his lips with her protruding nipples, she pulled back. "There's plenty for all of you. But Matthew gets it free."

"I . . . uh . . . I'm . . . I am not . . . uh . . . I . . . ," Matt stuttered, not knowing how to respond to the sexual teasing that he had just experienced.

"Come here, sweetie," said Arlene, running her tongue around the outside of her lips tempting him to partake. Again, she took Matt's chin in her hand and pulled his face close to her breast. "Open your mouth." Arlene carefully slipped her right nipple into Matt's mouth. "Suck it, sweetie. Suck it."

Surprisingly, Matt lost his earlier inhibition and he grabbed her nipple with his mouth holding both boobs with his hands. Like a hungry baby nursing for the first time, Matt first sucked the hell out of one tit and then started on the other. Back and forth, back and forth, and each time with more intensity. This must have gone on for two to three minutes. Arlene seemed to be enjoying it as much as Matt. She gave no indication that he was hurting her but as he began to bite her nipples, I could see her wincing; yet, she moaned in delight.

The rest of us sat waiting our turn. We were jealous that Matt was getting all of the attention and at the same time, we were silently observant, making certain we could imitate what came so naturally to him.

"Okay Matthew," said Arlene warmly. "Don't be too greedy."

"*Yes ma'am,*" Matt said, reluctantly dropping his hands and letting go of Arlene's right nipple. "Damn! They were some kind of good. Shit! I don't believe it."

"If the rest of you boys want to suck, it will cost you," Arlene said, becoming more businesslike in her tone of presentation.

"How much?" Thad asked, taking a deep breath. He ripped his wallet out of his back pocket.

"Five bucks a tit," she said, throwing her buxom chest back. Both nipples were hard and red from Matt's aggressive sucking.

"Five bucks? I don't have five bucks," said Thad in disappointment.

"I'll tell you what I'll do. For ten bucks total, I'll give each of you one long drink from my left breast—only because it needs lots of attention." Arlene smiled, ruining the mood of the moment. "But first I have something for Matthew."

"What do you want to give me?" Matt moved forward without any hesitation.

"A taste of heaven," Arlene responded. "Would you like to taste a part of another world?"

"Yes ma'am," Matt said, letting his tongue roll around his lips imitating Arlene's earlier tongue action.

"Are you absolutely certain?" Arlene leaned against the back seat waiting for Matt to respond.

"Yes, ma'am. I'm quite certain," Matt answered. His misty eyes widened revealing an expression of stupor.

With that Arlene reached over and unzipped Matt's pants. She reached inside and pulled his pecker out. Matt began to wriggle in excitement and almost laughed as she moved her hand around playing with it. Matt's expression took on an intoxicated look and small amounts of saliva drooled from his mouth onto his lips and ran down his chin.

"That tickles sort of," he said. "But it feels so good. Please don't stop!"

"Not bad for a little man," she said, massaging Matt's pecker while pulling it out of his pants. "Watch it grow boys."

Arlene rubbed Matt's little headstone with a repetitive forward motion and we watched it get larger and larger. I looked at Matt. He had kept the stupid grin on his face but now his eyes were rolling back and he was grunting and moaning.

"Ah-oh yes-ah," he uttered. Then he lost it. He shot off right in her hands.

"A nice load you carry Matthew." She took the white liquid in her hands and rubbed it gently all over her breasts and around the tips of her nipples. Her tits glistened like diamonds under the light that fell into the car from the streetlamp. First, she pulled Matt into her breasts. "Take a good lick, Matthew."

He took a big lick with his tongue rubbing up and around, up and around. Then Matt fell back against the car seat moaning and panting. This was the first time I had ever seen someone get off with a woman. It was both exciting and mysterious and I felt a rush inside of me.

"Damn! Damn! *Damn!* That was fucking wonderful!" Matt said.

"Come and get it boys. Put your money in my palm."

Jason took a ten from his pocket and thrust it into Arlene's hand. He went first, then Thad, then Byrd, then me. By the time it was my turn, her tits were completely dry and sticky. I felt robbed, but any sense of loss was replaced by the softness and beauty of her breasts. The sheer thought of touching them with my lips was ecstasy enough.

"It's time for you boys to go home and go to bed," Arlene said. "Y'all have been naughty tonight," she continued teasingly. "Next time I'll take you to bush country."

"Huh?" asked Matt.

"Bush country. Don't you know where that is, Matthew?" She asked in a gentle voice.

"Africa?" responded Matt.

"You are a sweetie, Matthew. But you have a lot to learn," Arlene said, pulling her slacks down to her knees revealing her vagina. There was an abundance of gray and black hair encircling the area. "Welcome to 'bush country' Matthew." She took Matt's hand and pressed it against her vagina area.

"It'll cost you five times five to touch and five times ten to enter. But I have to go boys," she said, pulling Matt's hand away. She then leaned over and kissed him on the forehead. "Help me get dressed, Matthew."

After she had herself put back together with Matt's help, she got out of the limo. As she was exiting, she turned and said, "Happy sweet sixteen, Matthew. I hope you will always remember your first time was with me, an older woman."

"*I will!* I most definitely will," Matt said, grinning. "Thanks, Arlene. Thanks a lot."

"Good bye boys," Arlene said. "I'll tell you a little secret. I had a good time but I have to entertain our town's big Chief at eleven o'clock." She turned and walked back toward the main part of downtown. She never looked back. She stopped once to straighten her blouse in the back and light a cigarette. We watched her until she was only a dot several blocks away.

"Holy shit!" exclaimed Jason. "What a woman!"

"You can say that again," echoed Matt.

"Let's forget Patsy Wentworth tonight and head on back to my house," Jason said out of the blue as he turned on the ignition and pulled away from the cherry launch.

"Let's go for it," Thad said, speaking for all of us.

Matt came of age that Friday night in June. The shy, timid, hesitant boy around girls took to Wilson's most famous prostitute like bees take to honey. He came of age that night maybe not the way society and his parents or even God would approve of but the way many teenage boys in this small tobacco town came to taste sex around their sixteenth birthday.

Chapter 25
SHOCK AT TAPS

THE FIVE OF us shared an equal addiction in wanting more of Arlene. As Jason drove the limo down South Tarboro Street in no particular hurry, her body was all we talked about, what her tits felt like, and how Matt took to her like a flea on a dog's back. We had salivated over plenty of naked women in *Playboy* magazine while playing with ourselves and sharing our fantasies seeing which of us could get aroused first. But if the truth were known, Jason was the only one of us up until this night who had regularly played with real breasts. We yearned for our next time with Arlene; but we also knew there would probably never be another time with her.

Like most teenage boys in the throes of adolescence, we were both innocent and ignorant at the same time. Innocent because we acted out of lust and it continued to control us. Ignorant in that it never occurred to us to consider the health questions and even though we didn't know it, we hadn't done anything to put ourselves at risk. The important lesson is that we didn't think, and that is **both** scary and dangerous. Tonight was the real McCoy: our previous fantasies brought to life by the pictures of naked women paled in comparison to our first group experience with a real woman.

"We're within a block of the Creamery," Jason said, bringing us back to reality. "You farts want to ride through?"

"Why not?" Let's see who's there!" said Thad in an attempt at being more enthusiastic after coming off an erotic high with Arlene.

"Go for it, but it's going to be packed on Friday night," said Matt.

"Wow! Would you look at the cars out here tonight!" exclaimed Thad as Jason turned the wheel and drove into the asphalt parking lot. "There's a full house tonight," continued Thad with more excitement in his voice. "I didn't expect this!"

"It's redneck night," Matt said. "Look at the trucks."

Jason followed the traditional ritual of entry into the Creamery. First, he dropped it into low gear and drove slowly around the oval parking lot riding his break at different intervals just like the farm boys did. The first drive through was to look and be seen. We received the customary honks, waves, and occasional middle finger.

"See anyone we know?" I shifted in my seat.

"It's hard to tell. At least no one I care to see," said Jason. "What about y'all?"

We agreed and Jason completed the circle. "Rock around the Clock" by Bill Haley and the Comets blasted from the outside speakers signaling to passing older drivers to keep on moving. And in the parking lot, many of the customized trucks and cars rocked from side to side as their teenage passengers moved with the music. Jason began the expected second drive through. The purpose this time was to mark our parking space by taking it before someone else could.

"I don't believe it! There's not a damn place to park." Jason's head kept turning, looking everywhere for any possible spot.

"There's one over there!" Thad exclaimed, pointing toward the middle of the second row.

"No, I don't think so. The limo's too long. We'll be sticking out on Ward Blvd," said Jason, slamming his fist against the steering wheel. "I don't want one of those fucking tobacco trucks to hit me. No offense, Braxton."

"Relax, we can always park in the gravel parking lot until some-one moves," I said.

"Let's just take it to Jason's house," said Thad. "We're wasting our time here. And besides, it's after ten o'clock."

Byrd had stayed preoccupied most of the evening. He had not opened his mouth since we'd left Arlene. This deliberate attempt at silence was unlike him. I knew he was thinking something over just like I knew there was something terribly wrong.

Jason paused for a minute, trying not to get angry. Then he took a deep breath and continued, "Okay! What's it going to be?" We agreed with Thad's idea. Pulling away from the Creamery, Jason surprised us again. "I need to make a side trip first."

"Oh for Christ's sake, Jason. What is it this time?" Matt pushed his glasses up and gave Jason the finger.

"I need to make a quick run to Taps to get some supplies. We're almost there anyhow." Jason was determined to make another detour a necessary part of our evening.

"I thought Artis was taking care of all that," I said.

"He was supposed to but the damn nigger forgot," said Jason. "That's just like him. If it isn't for him, he doesn't seem to give a shit."

"Is Patsy's party definitely out?" Byrd spoke the first time. I knew Byrd was anxious about not being with his girl.

"Byrd, put it on hold, will you? I'll get you there eventually," said Jason.

"Jason, Taps is at least two to three miles in the wrong direction," said Byrd.

"Tough shit!" said Jason, turning and looking at Byrd. "I'm the driver and I say we're going to Taps." Byrd threw himself against the back of his seat and closed his eyes and clenched his fists. Was not being able to see his girl the reason he had been so quiet?

"I've had about all the crap I'm going to take from that bastard." Byrd whispered to me but everyone heard him.

"Are you talking to me, Byrd?" Jason shook his head kicking the accelerator.

"Just drive, would you," said Byrd. "Just go get your lousy beer."

"I'll remember that when you want to pop one," said Jason, kicking the accelerator again.

Taps was a seedy two-gas-tank filing station that sold a little bit of everything plus wine and beer. Located outside the city limits a few miles passed the Wilson Country Club, it was owned and operated by Korean War veteran Richard "Taps" Morgan. Taps catered primarily to blue-collar workers, motorcyclists, college students, and under-aged teenagers seeking to buy beer, wine, and cigarettes. I knew Taps through my first cousin, Charles Staton, nicknamed Chuck. They had served together in Korea.

Jason drove the two miles on Highway 301. It was dark, the heat was bad, and most of the motels that dotted the highway had turned off their office lights. Only a few had turned on their no vacancy lights. We were on the main drag from New York to Florida and cars passed us at what seemed like reckless speeds. Jason crossed the Toisnot Swamp Bridge, slowly rounded a winding curve, and drove an additional mile to where he turned off onto a bumpy dirt road and into a barely noticeable, poorly graveled parking lot. He slowed, shifted into neutral, and coasted into the nearest available parking space. Sitting about seventy-five yards back under a stand of pine trees was a one-story dirty white building with a neon Pabst Blue Ribbon beer sign hanging in one of the two windows covered with bars. Changing his mind, Jason backed up about fifteen yards and pulled his limo along side the gas tanks, switched off his engine, and opened his door leaving it ajar.

Jason turned and rested his right arm on the top of the front seat. For once, he looked like a young boy, not quite sure where he should be. He hesitated and then said, "Thad, how about getting out and pumping two bucks of high test. I'll pay inside."

"You bet!"

"Braxton, come with me. You know this guy. Matt, you and Byrd stay put. We'll be back in a minute." We stepped out of the limo and the warm air encircled us like a sudden rush from a clothes dryer. For once, Jason was not in total control. Not knowing Taps Morgan gave him a sense of uneasiness. Having lost an edge of his confidence, his nervousness was apparent to me. I enjoyed watching Jason when he was not as cocky. For once, he would have to rely on me.

The wind blowing from the northeast had picked up in intensity. The evening sky had become mostly clouds and the earlier moon was barely visible now. Rolls of thunder could be heard in the distance signifying the possibility of an approaching storm. It was a typical June night in early summer.

Jason brushed his tousled hair off of his forehead, straightened his pants, and the two of us walked up the paved walk to the screened door entrance. Jason stopped and looked back as if he was going to change his mind. And just as quickly, he stepped on the concrete pad, put his hand on the screened door handle, and stopped again. "Do you think this guy will sell to me?"

"I don't know. The only thing he can say is no," I said confidently, watching the nervous twitch of Jason's eye. Whenever Jason was unsure of himself, his left eye would twitch.

"I know that, Braxton. I mean do you think he will rat on us?"

"Heck no! You'll be fine; trust me," I said, opening the screened door and letting Jason enter first. The room was presently filled with strangers. The floor was white tile and looked like it hadn't been cleaned in at least a week. Cigarette butts, plastic wrappings, peanut shells, and bottle tops littered the floor. The room was dimly lit and most of the light came from the neon beer signs hanging on the naked, faded white walls that were suffering from years of neglect. Taps would definitely not win any award for his interior design. The room had a distinct smell—extremely pungent and almost offensive.

Men of different ages and sizes dressed mainly in blue jeans and white tee shirts were milling around, talking to each other, drinking beer, smoking, and waiting for one of the two pool tables to clear in the small back room. We were definitely out of place with our "Joe College" looks. Again, Jason hesitated. He stopped to survey the small room as if to ask what are we doing here. I cleared my throat and motioned for him to move forward.

Directly in front of us was a long counter with a glass display bottom. On top of the counter were two glass containers of assorted nabs, a large jar of pickled eggs floating in some kind of liquid, an assortment of nickel and dime items carelessly arranged in little boxes, and a cash register. On the wall behind the counter hung two black and white army photographs in inexpensive frames. Both featured Taps before his accident.

Standing behind the counter were two men. I knew the taller of the two but I didn't know the short brunette with the wild looking beard. They were talking to two customers about the shortest route to Atlantic Beach. Both men behind the counter seemed equally relaxed at the moment and both appeared to be in a jovial mood.

Taps was easy to recognize with his black eye patch and missing right forearm and muscular upper body. Chuck told me a live grenade went off in his right hand during an army drill and Taps had lost his right eye and right arm from the elbow down. Above his elbow on his right forearm was a colorful tattoo of an intricately drawn Chinese dragon. Taps' jet-black hair was beginning to show noticeable signs of thinning in the front and one of his front teeth was capped in gold. His piercing brown eyes carried an expression of pain from suffering he had endured during his childhood in Wilson County as well as the war. I thought it was interesting that he and my cousin had struck up a friendship. Their interests were totally different and they came from two totally different backgrounds. Chuck had befriended him during the war and stuck by him ever since. Taps looked over to where we were standing and his eyes met mine.

"Braxton, what brings you out here? Is your sorry cousin, Chuck, with you?" he asked with a cackle.

"You know I've got better things to do than to waste my Friday nights hanging around with him," I said teasingly. "But I did bring a friend. Taps, meet Jason Parker."

"Nice to meet you," said Jason moving to the counter and extending his right hand to Taps before he thought. A sudden flush of Jason's face told me he was embarrassed.

"That's okay. People do it all the time," Taps said in his slow paced Wilson County accent, giving Jason his left hand to shake. "What you guys up to tonight?"

Jason looked at me and then turned back, saying, "Just been cruising around the big town tonight. We need two six packs of Bud, one pack of Chesterfields, and one pack of filter king Kools."

"You get right down to business," said Taps. "Well, I don't know if I can oblige you, Jason. You look mighty young to me!" Taps looked Jason directly in the eye then turned and winked at me? Taps was testing Jason and having a little fun at the same time.

"What?" Jason turned and looked at me. "What in the hell is he talking about, Braxton? You said there wouldn't be a problem." Jason was becoming noticeably flustered.

"I don't think there is a problem, Jason. Tell the man you're legit."

"Are you legit?" Taps smiled and looked at me.

"What do you mean legit?" asked a red-faced Jason, who was now more irritated with the scenario taking place. Jason didn't like to be jerked around. He just couldn't take teasing very well.

"You know what I mean, Jason!" exclaimed Taps. "Are you old enough to . . .?"

"Hell, no. You know that and so does Braxton. Damn you Braxton! You said we wouldn't have any problems here!" The room had become suddenly quiet and everyone was watching Jason as he began to make an ass of himself. Regulars here knew that Taps loved to tease first time underage buyers. It was a litmus test to determine the trustworthiness of the buyer. If the buyer was too smooth or calm, Taps knew he couldn't trust him and he wouldn't sell to him. Jason had passed and didn't even know what had taken place.

"Why don't you let the man finish his sentence?" I interjected. "Give him a chance."

"Fuck it. I'm ready to go."

"Not so fast, Jason. What I was going to ask was, are you legit? In other words, can you be trusted?" interrupted Taps. "In my business, you have to be very careful. I know now you're okay."

"Huh? What? Okay, I-ah-I understand," Jason replied, his voice calmer now. A smile returned to Jason's face. "Glad I passed. Thank you, I guess." I couldn't believe Jason was showing gratitude. It was very unlike him but the evening had tested his ego and his confidence level had been badly shaken.

"Zeke," Taps turned to the man beside him who had done nothing but observe the little scene since we had entered and said, "Get these boys what they need."

"Mums the word, Jason. Remember that," Taps said. "He rang the three items up on the cash register and the total was three dollars and fifty-five cents. "Anything else?"

"Yeah, I got two dollars worth of gas," Jason said, giving Taps a five and a one.

"Your change is forty-five cents," said Taps, handing the money over the counter to Jason. "Hope you'll come back again, Jason."

Jason was about to reply when the screen door flew open, and two colored men boldly entered despite the "whites only" sign on the outside. Each held a gun in his right hand. They were nervous, angry looking, and sweaty. Both were dressed in jeans, tennis shoes and dark colored shirts, and looked to be in their early twenties. Both men sported a mustache and closely cropped hair. Only one spoke and when he did, it was hard to understand him. He spoke fast and he was loud.

"*Freeeze! I tells ya. Alls you white fuckers betta freeze now!*" he said approaching the counter area in a cocky manner—his head turning in a funny manner—first to the left and then to the right as if he was watching a tennis match. His beady eyes shifted from side to side and his upper lip was curled like a snarling dog. He was drunk. I could smell the odor of cheap whiskey from where I stood.

"Don't do anything heroic!" I said to Jason in a whisper.

"Shit no," Jason answered quietly.

"*Shuts up, white boy!*" the darker one said looking at me. No one in Taps moved.

The speaker moved to the door leading into the back room. There were five white men in the room. "*Hey you white fuckers, gets out here! Now!*" He lost his footing, staggered a few feet, caught himself and turned, surveying the whole room.

The men exited quietly from the smoke filled back room leaving beer bottles and cue sticks on the pool tables. Their boisterous behavior had become instantly subdued. Deadly silence penetrated the room. Everyone stood motionless waiting for the next directive from the angry colored men.

I stood as still as I could, wishing they would get what they wanted and get out. I looked at Jason. He stood there expressionless showing no apparent signs of fear. I was scared shitless and I could feel my knees shaking, my stomach quivering, and the sweat accumulating under my arms.

"What can I get for you fellows?" asked Taps in a calm voice that shouldn't alarm them anymore than they already were.

"Looks like he's already be shot once," the speaker said to the darker one. I looked at Taps, then Zeke, and then Taps again. Taps remained calm with his one good eye firmly set on the speaker. I could tell by Zeke's clenched jaw that he didn't appreciate the comment.

"You're very observant," said Taps. "Happened during the war."

"I don't gives a shit, bossman. I wants your cash and all of it. Don't you trys to play games with me, white man," the speaker demanded. *"I'll shoots your other fucking eye out!"*

"I don't have a lot cash tonight. It's still early. I went to the bank this afternoon and made a deposit," said Taps, still maintaining his cool and continuing to look directly into the black man's eyes.

"Fuck ya! You lying sack of shit, white man. The clock on that wall seys it'sa close to eleven-thirty. I tolds you not to play games with me." He raised his pistol and pointed at Taps.

"Now there's no need for that gun. Put it down and I'll give you what I have. Open the till, Zeke, and give the man what he came for."

"Yes, sir, boss," Zeke said, touching the cash drawer key on the register with his right forefinger. At the same time, he reached with his left hand under the counter. Pulling out a gun, he brought it up slowly to the edge of the counter top, allowing the tip of the muzzle to be seen.

Seeing the tip of the gun, the darker colored man pointed his pistol at Zeke and fired. Zeke fell to the floor behind the counter screaming, "My God, I've been shot! My God, the *nigger* shot me! Oh, my God . . . " and then he started moaning and moaning and then he was quiet.

"You dumb shit," the speaker said to the darker man. *"Let's git out of here! Runs now! Runs! You hear!"* They both turned and hightailed it out the door. No one tried to stop them. All of us stood in place too scared and dazed to move.

"Braxton, you and Jason get the shit out of here," Taps said with urgency in his voice. "I've got to call the police. I'll get in touch with you later. Now, go!"

"Come on Jason, let's get out of here," I grabbed his hand and turned to run.

"Wait!" Jason said, picking up the bag with our supplies sitting on the counter. "Okay, let's get the shit away from this place." We both ran, knocking the flimsy screened door off its hinges and didn't stop until we reached the limo that had been moved during our stay inside. Jason jumped into the front seat and I ran around the back and got in behind the driver.

"Take off!" Jason commanded Thad who sat behind the driver's wheel. "Move it fast, fuckhead." Pandemonium had broken out inside Taps. Men were running out the door, getting in their trucks and on their Harleys and taking off. Two trucks sideswiped each other and both kept on moving. One motorcyclist lost control and turned into a growth of azalea bushes. It was wild and everyone had panicked. We needed to get away and get away fast.

Thad was doing close to eighty in a fifty-five mile speed zone. After he had driven about three miles at breaking speeds down Highway 301, he pulled the limo over, turned around, and asked, "What in the hell happened back there?"

"Was anyone killed?" Matt asked. "We heard a shot!"

"Y'all weren't hurt, were you?" asked Byrd excitedly.

"No, tell 'em, Braxton," said Jason, trying to catch his breath.

"A man was shot," I said, trying to catch my breath. "Don't know if he's dead. One of those damn colored men shot him. He drew a gun on the two coloreds. They were going to rob the place."

"Slow down, slow down, will ya?" asked Thad. "Who was shot?"

"Zeke, Taps' assistant," I said. "Taps told us to get out."

"I hope we don't get into any trouble over this," Matt said.

"Trouble? Why in the fuck would we get into any trouble?" asked Jason not thinking.

"We were at the scene of a shooting, do-do bird," said Matt. "You and Braxton were inside and are key witnesses to a shooting!"

"I don't think Taps will involve us," I said. "If there's an investigation, he can't incriminate himself for selling to minors."

"True," said Thad.

"I don't like it," said Byrd. "You and your side trips, Jason."

"Fuck you, Byrd. Fuck you!" said Jason.

"That's *it!* Come on, big man. Come and get it. I'm no green cherry," Byrd shot back. This was the most animated I had seen Byrd since school had let out.

"You've got it, Byrd," Jason shouted coming over the back of his seat with his right fist.

"*Stop it!*" Wait just a damn minute! The last thing we need is for you two to start fighting," I said, pushing Jason back into the front seat. "It's no one's fault. We just happened to be in the wrong place at the right time. That's all. Now calm down, both of you."

"Braxton is right," said Matt, beginning to cough. "Just cool it!"

"Let's go to Jason's house and think this thing through," I suggested after several minutes of silence among us.

"Good idea," Byrd said approvingly.

"Yeah, good idea," Thad said, turning on the ignition, pulling back onto Highway 301, and heading for downtown Wilson. It was just about midnight according to the clock on the dashboard.

"One more request," said Byrd, panting. "I need to stop by my house and get my bag."

"No, you don't," Jason responded. "I've got extras of everything. You can use mine."

"Are you okay, Byrd?" I asked. "You don't look so good and you're breathing funny."

"I need my medication. My asthma is acting up. We have to go by my house first. It won't take long," said Byrd in a pleading voice.

"Oh, that's just great! Another stop means another adventure to celebrate my birthday. I wonder what awaits us this time," said Matt, trying to inject some badly needed humor.

"Shut up, Matt!" said Jason, totally missing Matt's point. "Didn't you hear him? He's having trouble breathing!"

"Yes, I heard him," answered Matt. "And since when did you become so sympathetic?"

"All right, you two," I said. "Knock it off!"

We rode most of the way to Byrd's home in silence. For at least three of the five miles no one said anything. The only noise we heard was the wind rustling through the trees and the continuous thunder in the distance. We were exhausted, scared, and anxious about what had happened at Taps. We made our first pact of that summer en route to Byrd's.

"I don't think we should tell anyone about tonight," I said. "We need to keep everything that happened to us tonight among the five of us."

"I agree," said Thad.

"Me too!" responded Matt.

"I go along with that," Byrd said. "I can't afford not too," Jason said. "My old man will kill me if he finds out where we've been tonight and what we've done. Man, I'll be in a whole sack of shitting trouble."

My mother never found out about the shooting at Taps until I told her many, many years later. I was already a college graduate and settled in my first teaching position in Virginia when I related the story to her. She wasn't the least bit surprised or shocked. I guess she reacted this way because what happened at Taps was mild compared to the other events that happened in June of 1957.

I never told her about Arlene nor have I ever told anyone else until now. I think it would have killed my mother's faith in me if I had hinted at what had occurred in Jason Parker's limousine. It went against the very moral fiber that she had tried to instill in me. She might remind me that her own brother had been disowned by their father for marrying a woman from Wilson with a questionable reputation.

Besides, how does a teenage boy explain to his mother the hardness he feels below his belt when he touches the breasts of a woman? You don't. There are some things that are better left untold.

Chapter 26
THE NOISE UPSTAIRS

TRAFFIC MOVED STEADILY on Highway 301 North until we reached our left turn onto East Nash Street. We stayed on this route through the colored business district still alive with sidewalk activity. Dodging a few whistles and an occasional beer bottle, Jason eventually crossed the railroad tracks and connected with West Nash Street. Traffic had diminished considerably inside the white district of Wilson. Once in a while we met a car. Jason, ignoring Byrd's asthmatic condition, took one last drag on his cigarette and flipped it out the window. Turning left onto Raleigh Road, he drove the six long blocks to David Byrd's home. The earlier fun of the evening seemed like a week ago. We were tired and upset and hungry, and the desire to go to Patsy Wentworth's party had faded like a fierce wind after a summer storm.

I felt older and less protected after being with Arlene and Taps. I wasn't scared but I had been affected. I didn't feel dirty or tainted but, in some way, I knew I was different. I felt it inside, but I couldn't define it in words. I, along with my friends, had crossed over to the other side tonight—a side where guns are real and not bought at Woolworth's Five and Ten Cents Store, a side where women who market their bodies are real in the flesh and not some centerfold on a page of a magazine, a side where "don't enter" signs for underage teens mean just that, and a side that gives credibility to all our parents and teachers have tried to caution us to avoid.

Jason drove his limo up the lengthy, paved driveway to Byrd's three-story home and around to the back of his house. Following Byrd's directions, Jason parked next to the butler's entrance then stopped, turned off the lights, and shut off the ignition. None of us moved or made an effort to talk. The only sounds inside the limo were Byrd's repetitive wheeze and cough. These served as a distinct contrast to the outside noises of the night: a continued rumbling of distant thunder and the singing of crickets.

"Okay, it's time for me to boogie. I won't be long," Byrd said, anxious to get out of the car. "It looks like Julian's asleep."

"Byrd, I need to take a leak really bad," said Jason. "Can I use your head?"

"Sure but be quiet. I don't want to wake up my dad and Charles."

"I've got a better idea. I'll piss in those bushes over there." Jason pointed to a line of azaleas that grew along side the Byrd's brick three-car garage. The backyard light attached to the top of a very tall pole shined over the azaleas casting their shadows against the garage giving them a presence of mammoth proportions. Above these shadows were two equally dark opened windows indicating that no one was awake in the small apartment over the garage that served as the home of Mr. Parker's live-in manservant, Julian.

"No! You'll wake up Julian! Just come with me."

"Byrd, I know you don't want a party but I need to go too," I said.

"Okay, but please be quiet."

"Me too!" said Matt. "We might as well make it a threesome." He laughed but none of us joined him. Matt's attempt at comic relief was ill timed.

"Damn! We passed several all-night gas stations where any of you could have taken a piss. Why didn't you ask to stop then?"

"I just want to use your john. Is that a crime?" Jason grabbed his crotch, letting Byrd know that he had reached the emergency stage.

"I can't afford to wake up my dad. He and I are not on the best of terms these days. He'll really be teed off if he gets disturbed and not just with me."

"We'll be quiet and careful," I said, pulling him aside. "I'll handle it. I promise." Turning to the others, "All of us need to listen to Byrd and do what he says!"

"Come on. We'll go in the back door," said Byrd, seeming satisfied. "Julian always leaves a key under the outside mat."

"Don't slam the door to the limo!" I said as a reminder of Byrd's request that we be as quiet as possible. (David Byrd and I spent a lot of time together. We had been good friends ever since grade school and we enjoyed each other's company. I guess we were about as close as two male friends could be. There were times when I thought we could read each other's minds. He stood by me and I by him. I knew every room in his house and I knew his mother and daddy, their good points and their bad. What I hadn't seen personally, Byrd told me about. I understood when David said he didn't want to wake up his dad, that's exactly what he meant. Mr. Byrd was a nice enough guy but he also had a hell of a temper and I had seen him slug both David and Charles on more than one occasion, especially when he'd had too much to drink.)

The clock in Jason's limo read twelve-twenty-something when we got out. The pitch- black darkness of the night was reminiscent of an eerie setting in a horror movie and gave an uncomfortable feeling to the stillness surrounding us. The wind was still blowing and the thunder and sheet lightning were closer now. The four of us followed quietly behind Byrd to the back door. He reached down under the mat for the key but it wasn't there.

"Oh, great! The key is gone!" said Byrd. "I don't believe this. It's always been here."

"What do we do now?" Thad turned to Byrd, waiting for an answer.

"I'll check the side doors to the den. Sometimes Mother leaves an extra key under one of those mats." The part Byrd left out was that his mother left the key there so that she could get in without Mr. Byrd's knowledge after one of her evening sessions with their Episcopal priest, Jim Gordon.

The five of us walked around to the other side of the house and onto the side porch outside their den. The white wicker furniture decorating the porch had been carefully arranged leaving a narrow walkway to the French doors leading into the den. Almost in unison, each of us took a seat while Byrd looked for the key. First, he looked under both mats with no luck. He then searched over both doorsills and came up with nothing. Frustrated and embarrassed, Byrd turned, looked at me throwing his hands in the air, and then fell onto the chaise lounge heaving.

"Are you okay?" I was worried that he might start having chest spasms again.

"I can't breathe. I can't . . . breathe. We've got to get in to get my medicine."

"Well, rest a minute while we decide what to do," I said, pointing to the chaise lounge.

"I'll have to. Just give me a minute. I'm sorry, guys."

"Hey, quit your worrying! Thad and I'll go look under the front door mat." Thad joined me and we guided each other through the maze of English boxwoods back to the front of the house and up the steps to the circular front porch. Neither of us could find a key. As we were leaving, for no apparent reason I looked up and saw a light flickering in one of the second floor bedroom windows. I thought it was his younger brother's room. "Thad, isn't that Charles' room?"

"I think so but I'm not sure. It looks like a flashlight is on in there," Thad remarked. "Doesn't it to you?"

"Something is on," I said. "Wonder if he's awake? Maybe we could get his attention."

"Let's ask Byrd first. I don't want to irritate his father." Thad had a good point.

"I'm almost certain it's Charles' room but I guess you're right. Come on; let's go back." I tripped over a flower box as we exited the porch. We carried back the news of no key. Byrd didn't think getting Charles involved was a good idea. Byrd's breathing was no better and as he lay there, we could see his chest muscles beginning to constrict under his shirt.

"Wait a minute! Doesn't Julian always leave the bathroom window next to the butler's entrance unlocked?" I said, wondering why it had taken me so long to remember this.

"You're right, Braxton. I completely forgot about that," said an excited Byrd. "Braxton, you're a genius. Let's go!"

Adjacent to the side porch where we had been sitting was a large, open field with some scattered pines and oaks. Stepping off the porch, I saw a sudden movement that made me jump. It was Jason running and he didn't stop until he'd reached the closest pine tree. We all knew what he was up to and quickly joined him. Once we had all relieved ourselves, we walked to the back of the house and crept to the window we hoped would be unlocked. The window was too high for any of us to reach. Thad and I hoisted Matt up to get a look.

"It's unlocked," Matt whispered. "Give me a second and I'll have it up."

"Push hard," encouraged Byrd. "Sometimes the sash gets caught."

"Umph! I can't budge it any further than I've already got it," answered Matt.

"Let me try, Matt. We'll have to trade places," said Thad. Thad was the strongest among us and he was confident that be could open it all the way with no problem.

Thad and I lowered Matt. This time we hoisted Thad who had the window up within seconds to a level where Matt, the smallest among us, could crawl through. Once inside the house, Matt opened the butler's door and the five of us entered the darkness of the house and walked into the spacious kitchen.

"Y'all stay in here and just stay still!" said Byrd in a whisper.

Byrd gently pushed the swinging door that led into the dining room and disappeared into the darkness of the next room. Almost at the same time of his exit, we heard a muffled noise from upstairs, and then another, and then another; each time the noise grew louder and louder. The four of us froze. Someone tapped me on the shoulder and I jumped.

"What do we do next?" It was Thad wanting me to give some direction.

"Come on," I said. "Let's go see what going on." We walked silently one behind the other into the darkened dining room feeling our way on the furniture until we were in the foyer.

"Shush!" whispered Byrd. "What are ya'll doing out here?"

"We heard noises," I said. "For one thing, we wanted to make sure you were okay. What in the heck is going on?"

"That's what I'm getting ready to find out," Byrd said. "Now go on back. I'll check upstairs."

"Not by yourself you aren't!" I said, correcting him.

"For crying out loud, Braxton, I live here," Byrd said in agitation. "Now y'all leave!"

I looked at the others. Thad shook his head from side to side. Matt joined him and I knew Jason wanted to find out what was going on. Byrd saw their reaction and gave in.

"Okay. Come on, but be quiet." In single file, the four of us followed Byrd up the circular stairs attempting to be as quiet as possible. As Byrd put his right foot on the first landing, a loud crash came from the west side of the second floor bedroom area. Byrd picked up his stride and so did we. On the second landing we abruptly stopped when we heard Byrd's younger brother, Charles, scream. Taking two steps at a time, Byrd ran up the remaining stairs to the second floor and stopped momentarily in the sitting area. We followed running until we joined him outside Charles' bedroom door.

"Daddy, no! Please stop!" pleaded a hysterical voice.

"Relax, son, and enjoy it!" Mr. Byrd's response was calm but firm. "It feels so good. Give it a chance."

There was no mistake—it was Charles pleading. I looked at Byrd with a quizzical look and he turned away from me. He began to shake. His breathing became heavier and without hesitation, he took his right foot and kicked in Charles' door. The door swung against the inside wall and Byrd boldly entered the room as if he knew what hideous scene was awaiting us.

None of us were prepared for what we saw after the door was opened. We caught him in the act. I saw it before Byrd attacked. It chilled me and at the same time, it sickened me. A naked Charles was lying prone, faced down on the bed. One bedside table was overturned and a lamp lay shattered on the floor. Several books were scattered across the rug. Mr. Byrd was naked from the waist down and sat striding Charles' buttocks. He held a whip in his right hand. When I looked closer, an unfamiliar terror seized me. My stomach began to cramp and I could feel my body suddenly chilled. I broke out in a cold sweat. I thought I would throw up.

Mr. Byrd's penis was inside of his son. I couldn't stand it any longer. I ran to the corner of the room, picked up the wastebasket, and deposited everything I had eaten for dinner. I took my handkerchief out of my back pocket and wiped my mouth and face with a hurried motion. I turned and looked at my friends. They were just as horrified and stunned as I. The unspeakable act of Mr. Byrd was mirrored in their facial expressions. Thad was the first to back out of the room. Matt stood paralyzed. His eyes filled with tears and he started weeping. Jason stepped forward and threw his arm around Matt's shoulder and together they backed slowly out of the room.

Mr. Byrd turned and his eyes met mine. His expression was foreign to me. There was something about his eyes. They were glazed and relaxed looking, almost closed like they would be during a drunken stupor. Saliva ran from his mouth and I could hear the echo of his last moan. Charles lay there crying, his sobs muffled by the sheet his face was pressed against. I watched in horror at Byrd jumping on the bed, grabbing his daddy by the shoulders and violently throwing him to the floor.

"You drunk son of a bitch," Byrd screamed. "What in the hell do you think you're doing?"

"Get out of here, David," his dad said, slurring his words. "You get your fucking ass and your friends out of this room immediately!"

"*No! You get out!* I'm not leaving Charles alone this time."

"*Don't you disobey me, boy! Do you hear me?*"

"*Do you think I care what you think? You're drunk!*" Byrd screamed, falling face down on the bed beside his brother. He reached over and touched his brother's head, and began to cry uncontrollably.

"*Don't touch him! Do you hear me?*" Mr. Byrd shouted while he tried to get up off the floor. He was three sheets to the wind and kept losing his balance.

I was still standing in the doorway when Mr. Byrd screamed at me and called me names I'll never forget. A new anxiousness seized me that led me to turn and tell Thad to go and get Julian up here immediately. When I turned back toward the bed, I saw Mr. Byrd standing over Byrd and Charles with the whip in his right hand. Before I could warn Byrd, the whip came down across his back—the heavy force of the lash ripped his shirt open. Trickles of blood oozed from the open skin where the lash struck tearing Byrd's flesh.

I screamed and ran back into the room knocking Mr. Byrd to the floor.

"Get off of him! Get off! What in the hell is wrong with you?" I pushed him again as he tried to get up causing him to fall against the wall.

"Get out of my house, you bastard!" he shouted, slurring his words again and falling back to the floor.

"I'm not leaving until you . . . " I could feel a strong hand on my shoulder. It was Julian.

"You boys need to go on home now. Don't breathe a word of this to nobody. You hears, Mr. Braxton?"

"Thank God, you're here." Julian grabbed my arm helping me up.

"Did you hear?"

"Yes, Julian. I promise," I said. I turned back to the hall leaving my best friend bleeding and holding his brother in an attempt to comfort him. Mr. Byrd lay passed out on the floor and Julian walked from the adjoining bathroom carrying a towel in his hand ready to assist Byrd.

"Come on, Jason. Let's get out of here," I said.

"Are you sure we should leave?" Jason asked.

"I'm sure." The four of us walked down those winding stairs in muted rhythm. We were all exhausted and Matt's birthday night had turned helter-skelter. Once outside, we heard the wind as it gently stirred in the hot air. I knew what I was hearing and it was the echo of what we had witnessed whispering to itself.

My head ached and I felt pale and dirty and betrayed and scared. Once inside Jason's car, I laid my head back against the seat feeling safe for the first time since we had left Matt's house. I let my breath out slowly, turned to Jason, and asked him to drive us home.

Chapter 27
SODOMY BRINGS CONFUSION

IF THERE IS one thing I can't understand, it's how this summer has gotten all screwed up. This summer was supposed to be swell and different. It was to be my first "real" summer not being a kid—I had my driver's license to take me where I wanted to go. I would start my first real job giving me some financial independence. And I was now an upperclassman in high school. My first real summer: a summer of fun, a time to explore my teenage years with my friends, a time to assume greater responsibility, a time to explore my sexuality, and a time to find out more about myself. I had my June, July, and August calendar planned and I was not afraid of any interference. The first two weeks of June had been anything but swell, but they had been different, though not what I had planned and expected.

The earlier wind and thunder of this sultry evening were gone. The black night sky had lightened and there were a few faded twinkling stars pushing through the thin clouds. Raleigh Road was empty, silent, almost as if it was acknowledging its shame.

I turned and looked at Jason as he drove toward West Nash Street. His face was white and his brow was wrinkled. Both of his hands gripped the steering wheel tightly and his cold eyes looked straight ahead with abnormal concentration. I imagined he was as filled with fear as I. Here was my friend that had rightfully been given the nickname of "motor mouth" as silent as the rest of us. I could feel my own face tightening and hardening. My mind raced through the events of the evening leaving me with unanswered questions. I closed my eyes trying not to concentrate, hoping to momentarily forget all that puzzled me.

None of us talked on that drive back to Jason's house. No one knew what to say or even dared to be the first to address the issue. I believe it was out of respect for Byrd. We had been shocked beyond our most extreme sexual fantasy. What we had just witnessed didn't fit in to any sexual picture I'd ever remembered seeing.

All of us knew where to find Jason's dad's sex magazines and books. If the magazines were not behind Mr. Parker's liquor bottles in the back of the bar, they were between the two mattresses in the downstairs' guest bedroom. The books could usually be found under some towels in the downstairs' linen closet. And we knew what pages had the dirty pictures on them. Jason had invented a code for finding them quickly. The code was too complicated for the four of us. We found it easier to just turn the pages until we found a naked woman. Some of the pictures and jokes were gross and gave me an uncomfortable feeling—like the picture of a nude woman having sex with a donkey. The quality of these pictures was always blurry but still clear enough to understand what was taking place. This type of sexual content was not only disturbing to me but also to Byrd, Matt, and Thad. Jason liked these or so he pretended.

The other pictures were titillating—close ups of women's breasts and vaginas blurred by pubic hair, men and women simulating the sex act with a big blur across the place of entry but none of this compared to what we had seen tonight. There had been an occasional picture of an overweight woman bent over with an overweight man "sticking it" to her but nothing involving a father and son. I didn't know that fathers even did this to their children and I certainly didn't know what it was called. I'm not certain I even wanted to know a name for it.

I suppose I should be thankful for these first two weeks of the summer—I couldn't erase them, I couldn't change them, and I certainly could not have known they were a preparation for the rest of our summer vacation. I did know one thing as I sat in the front seat of Jason's limo and that was I didn't want to grow up any more. I wanted the five of us to be able to go back to being kids without a lot of responsibilities. I wanted us to be kids together for the rest of our lives without disturbances—the prostitutes, the robbers and their guns, and the sexual abusers. Even my minister had told us as we

grow older, to be childlike in our faith. I wanted to stay a child forever.

I drank my first beer tonight. Actually, it was at one-thirty on
Saturday morning sitting in Jason's carport. The five of us took turns
passing the opener and ceremoniously waited until we could take a
good sip of our Pabst at the same time. From the first swallow, I hated
it. I didn't like the warm taste going down my throat or the bitter
aftertaste when I had finished. I drank the whole damn thing hoping somehow it would let me forget the night. It didn't—it just
made matters worse because I ended up with the most indescribable
headache I've ever had.

A tapping on my side window aroused me. At first I was disoriented. I didn't know where I was and why I was here. Then I realized that I was still in Jason's limo and that the light of the morning
sun was working its way into the open carport. The others, also in
the limo, were still asleep. The tapping came from a long, meaty, black
finger. It belonged to Artis. I rolled down the window.

"What's in God's name is you boys doing sleeping out here in
dis here carport?" asked Artis bending in an authoritative way and
peering into the limo. His hands were on his hips.

"Wait a minute, Artis," I said. I leaned over and tapped Jason on
the shoulder until he was awake.

"What the . . . ? What the hell is going on?" Jason sat up so fast
that he hit his head against the ceiling.

"Good morning," I answered. "Someone's here to greet you."

He looked at me, then over his shoulder and said, "Oh shit, you
mean we all slept out here last night?"

"That's right," I said. Jason was the type who liked to take his
time getting up.

"What time is it?" asked Jason wiping the sand from his eyes and
stretching at the same time.

"It's seven o'clock," Artis answered, smiling. "If you boys don't
look a mess, I ain't no handsome black man." Artis laughed from his
stomach showing his pearly, white teeth.

"*Thad, Matt, wake up!*" Jason said, stretching his vocal cords.

"Huh? What in the heck are you yelling for?" Thad looked confused. He sat up from his makeshift bed in the second row of seats.

"Because it's time to get up," Jason said. "What happened to Matt?"

"I'm here," said Matt, rising from the third row of seats and showing his face. You know you don't have to yell!"

"Excuuuuse me, your Royal Highshit," said Jason. "Just get up."

"You boys get out now and quits your arguing. I'm gonna fix you some breakfast," Artis said, turning and walking briskly up the stone steps and across the tile porch. He stopped and turned around. He looked at us, shook his head laughing, and then turned again and entered the house. I wished I could enjoy his humor but there wasn't anything funny. I thought about Byrd and the pressure he was under from his father to attend private school. I wondered if Mr. Byrd wanted him to leave because Byrd knew too much about his father's sick behavior. The last time we had talked about his leaving for private school, Byrd said that he'd do just about anything not to go.

"Come on, let's get out of this damn limo so we can figure out what we're going to do next," Jason said, sluggishly forcing himself out of the limo.

"Hold on! Not so fast, Jason," I said. "Remember what Julius asked us. We can't discuss this in front of Artis. We'll have to wait until after breakfast."

"No problem," said Jason. "Let's go get cleaned up." He walked around the front of the limo and up the steps to the porch.

The three of us simultaneously pulled ourselves off the warm, sticky leather seats that had been our sleeping quarters for approximately the last five hours. We followed Jason into the house and up the stairs to his living quarters. He handed out towels and gave us a choice of bathrooms, his or his sister Millie's. Thad and I opted for Millie's because we thought it would be less hectic. Her pink and blue flowered wallpaper with matching trim stood in stark contrast to the stained, faded, putrid green color of Jason's. His was never clean and Millie's looked like it had never been used.

We doused our faces with cold water several times, and scrubbed and cleaned our faces with Ivory soap like we were trying to wash off the sins of the past evening. I borrowed Thad's comb that had been dipped in Vitalis at least one hundred times. I cringed when I saw it but I needed to get my cowlick to stay down. A dark green fungi-looking substance clung to the comb's teeth like hot spaghetti noodles to a fork. I ran the small, black comb under the hot water one time and pulled it as fast as I could through the front of my hair. It did the trick. Thad gave me his Old Spice and I splashed some on my face imitating him.

I stood there in front of the mirror looking at myself while Thad put his shirt back on. Unconsciously, I started rubbing my chin; and again, my thoughts returned to my good friend, David Anderson Byrd. I was sorry he had to walk in on his father and Charles, especially with us there. I know it must have sickened him like it did us as well as embarrassed the hell out of him. I wanted to talk with him to see if he and Charles were okay and to find out about his father's behavior after we left. I hoped that Byrd would not be a continued victim of his father's anger. Victimizing was not a new word to some of us. It was a term that Jason brought back from his hospital stay in Maryland. Several of us identified with being the victim of our fathers. I wondered what today would bring my friend. "Damn you, Mr. Byrd. What kind of father are you?"

"Are you talking to yourself, Braxton?"

"Huh? Sorry, Thad. I was thinking about Byrd," I said.

"Yeah. I'm having a tough time with it, too."

"I can't believe his dad would do that! Can you?"

"Heck no!" said Thad. "Any man who does that to his child has got to be either sick or screwed up."

"What do you think we should do next, Thad?"

"Dunno! Maybe get with Byrd," said Thad.

"I hope he calls today."

"If he calls, he'll call you first," Thad said, acknowledging the closeness of our friendship.

Jason stuck his head in and said, "Thought maybe you two had fallen in the head. Come on. Let's eat."

"We're right behind you," said Thad. "How do you think Jason is taking this?"

"It's hard to tell," I said. "He'll hide his true feelings as long as he can. My guess is that he's as uptight about it as we are."

When we entered the kitchen, Artis was standing over the stove scrambling eggs. Like many black people when they cook, he sweated heavily. The undershirt covering his massive chest was soaked from the perspiration fighting to get out. He stopped long enough to wipe his watery brow with his apron. He directed us to take a seat.

In the corner, stood the familiar rectangular table. The table was solid pine and had been hand-made by Mr. Ross's son, Danny. Danny had won first place in the arts and craft's division at the North Caroline State Fair with this table when he was a senior at Coon. Mr. Parker's wife saw it and wanted it and Mr. Parker bought it for her. I wished I had a quarter for all the afternoons that we had done homework sitting around this table. If a person looked hard enough, he would find our names carved somewhere on its top. Mrs. Parker said it was okay but not to practice this habit on her other furniture. Mrs. Parker was good about things like that.

There were six captain chairs around the table. They didn't match the wood of the table but that didn't matter to Mrs. Parker. She went for what was comfortable. Each of us sat in the one we called our own. I liked these chairs: I always felt important when I sat in one, mainly because I was elevated enough to make eye contact with everyone. They were so different from the seats of our booth and the circular arms of these chairs gave me plenty of room to rest my lower arms and elbows.

"You boys must had one fine evening last night," said Artis. "Is I right?"

No one said anything, waiting for Jason to speak. Jason looked at me and I gave him the same look back. His eyes wandered over to Thad and Matt and then back to Artis. I nodded picking up the pitcher of orange juice.

"It was different," said Jason.

"How's that?" Artis turned his attention to the pancakes on the griddle.

"Artis, can we talk about this later?" Jason said. "We're starving." He took the pitcher of orange juice, poured a glass full, and then gulped the contents down in one long, noisy swallow. He then belched as loudly as he could. "Do you want me to bring it up again for a vote?" Jason took great pride on his ability to belch on command.

"Hell, no! We heard you," I said, pointing my right thumb downward.

"Everything gonna be ready in a minute," said Artis, continuing to wipe and sweat, wipe and sweat. I wondered how much of his liquid run-off had made it into the food. I caught myself—that is exactly what my mother would be thinking. It really wasn't important.

The horror of last night still haunted me and I suspected, the others sitting around this table. It was still hard to look in each other's eyes. Thad thumped his fingers against the table. Matt, cleared his throat saying, "We appreciate you fixing this breakfast, Artis. I think I could eat a horse."

"You is welcome, Mr. Matt," Artis said, setting two platters on the table. One held pancakes and link sausage. The other contained southern scrambled eggs, not hard and lumpy. When he had finished serving, there was, in addition to the platters, a side dish of grits swimming in butter, one plate of buttered toast with homemade strawberry jam on the side, a bowl of warm maple syrup, and a plate of unbuttered blueberry muffins. All of us were given a large glass of cold, plain Sealtest milk.

Twenty minutes later, there was nothing left on any of the platters or plates. We devoured this manly breakfast like two hundred pound farmers getting ready to go out in the fields and crop tobacco. I ate until I had to loosen my belt one notch. We had successfully managed to steer clear of any of the events of last evening and when Artis asked where Byrd was, we just told him that he had gotten sick. This really wasn't a lie, just an exaggeration. When Artis commented on our being less talkative than usual, we just told him that we were overly tired. This wasn't a lie either because we were. But when he asked why we stayed in the car, Jason didn't have a good answer. He just used the old excuse of not having his key but Artis reminded him that the back door was unlocked. Jason faked ignorance but didn't fool Artis for a minute. Artis knew we were hiding something but he didn't push for details.

When it came time to leave Jason's house, the three of us decided to walk home. None of us lived that far away and we agreed that each of us needed some time alone to refocus and sort things out. I just lived across West Nash Street and down a half a block. I got my bag out of Jason's limo, said good-bye to Matt and Thad, and started across Jason's manicured front lawn.

This Saturday morning was bright and it was already piping hot outside. From all that I could see, the transition from weekday time to weekend time had been made successfully. It was still too early for the neighborhood kids to be out. Looking up and down West Nash Street I saw that the early morning ritual of sweeping the walkways had been completed. Since Saturday was still a workday for most of the neighborhood men, they had left. The lack of outside activity supported my theory that another ritual had begun—the migration of the housewives to one of their two favorite gathering places—the beauty parlor or the local supermarket. Those women who chose not to phone in their food orders to one of the small, more costly, privately owned groceries could be found either at the Piggily Wiggily or the Winn-Dixie. Shopping at one of the bigger market chains not only offered more variety of foods, it was also a fast way to catch up on the week's gossip that would then be carried to church on Sunday morning and mistranslated from pew to pew. A person's reputation could be badly tarnished between the produce aisle and the bread counter. In our town, this happened on a weekly basis. Our fathers would sometimes throw a dollar in a hat and bet on which grocery store offered the meatiest tidbits of gossip.

My mother bought her groceries from Mr. David Charter. He spoiled Mother by giving her what she referred to as "hands-on" service. According to my mother, Mr. Charter got her coffee and sugar during the Depression when these items were hard to find. He also let Mother pay him on a monthly basis and I'm certain there were months when she couldn't pay his bill. If he hadn't been a good friend with my grandmother, I don't think he would have been as lenient with my mother's payments.

A brown bird with a yellow breast kept making a coarse sound, almost like "witchety-witchety-witch," as it followed me flying from one tall white oak tree to another. Byrd would have known the kind. For some reason, this nagging bird reminded me of the event that had occurred at Byrd's house. Oddly, it was this bird that helped me make an important decision. After crossing Nash Street, I stopped and looked up. The same bird had followed me and was now perched in a small dogwood tree in Mr. Brendle's side yard. It continued to make that awful sound. If he was trying to attract a mate, he was surely going to fail. If he wanted to get my attention, he had succeeded. His annoying behavior complimented the chaotic confusion I found myself facing. And it was then that I decided that the only way to get to the bottom of this matter with Mr. Byrd and get it off my mind was to tell my mother. She knew him and I thought the situation was crucial enough for me to get some advice.

I was back home by nine-thirty like I promised I would be. I found Mother polishing her brass, Daddy watching television, and Lily in the kitchen. When I asked Lily, she told me that no one had called. She also reminded me that this was the day I had promised to wax the floors in the hall, living room, and both bedrooms. I immediately got out the Johnson's wax and the heavily stained Charles L. Coon High School athletic sock that I used every two weeks when faced with this same chore. Waxing the floors the way my mother wanted them waxed would take a couple of hours. This was hard work but I didn't mind. It would give me time to think. Every time I finished waxing our floors, I had a strong belief that our house had the cleanest floors in Wilson. I often told my mother that they were clean enough to eat off of. She never found this funny.

Cleaning house continued to be an obsession with my mother. Lily reminded me again that cleaning along with drinking was Mother's way of coping with her increasing inability to control her nerves. Lily never meant any disrespect to Mother by repeatedly sharing this concern with me. She was more afraid now that Mother would wake up one day and just lose it. Even though Lily had told me this many times, it always scared me when she talked this way. All I could think about was what would I do then. "With your daddy's illness and your mother's drinking like she do, she just ain't gonna be able to continue," Lily said over and over.

"Braxton, how was Matthew's party and the sleepover?" Mother asked.

"Hi, Mother. I didn't hear you coming," I said, looking into her weary face.

"These old slippers don't make much noise any more," she said. "You didn't answer my question?"

"Oh? The party. The party was fun and the sleepover was, you know, the typical sleepover."

"Did ya'll behave yourselves? Did you stay out of trouble?" Mother cleared her throat.

"Why do you ask that?" I wondered if she had heard anything about last night.

"I'm your mother and I wanted to know that you were acting responsibly."

"Of course, we were. And Julius made us behave," I said, trying to anticipate her next question. I hated to lie to her but I couldn't tell her now everything that had happened.

"I'm glad you had fun. I see Lily has already reminded you of your chores."

"Lily? Is she here?" I paused. "Yes, Mother, she did."

"Carry forth, young McDuff," she said. I didn't know what that expression meant but she said it so much that I had decided it meant "get to it" or something like that.

"Mother, can we talk later?"

"Certainly, Braxton."

The rest of the day went smoothly until four o'clock. Without fail, Daddy's medicine was usually delivered by three o'clock on Saturdays. Today, the merchant's delivery truck didn't come. Mother called Byrd's West Nash Street Pharmacy and spoke to Mr. Jerningan, the druggist. He said the prescription had been filled and he thought the deliveryman had picked it up. He called later and told Mother that Mr. Byrd had held it out for some reason and that he wanted to know if maybe I could come down and pick it up. Mr. Jernigan suggested to my mother that I should pick it up by four-thirty. When Mother told me this, panic set in. I knew something was desperately wrong. I hadn't heard a word from Byrd. And I didn't want to see his dad before I talked to Byrd. Hell! I hadn't even talked with my own Mother about it.

I left my house shortly before four o'clock to go and get my father's medicine. As soon as I walked out of the house, I was hit in the face with the ninety-seven degree temperature. This Saturday afternoon heat was suffocating as it rose shimmering from the street in front of our house. The humidity was thick and the air smelled like processed tobacco. I just hoped I could endure it while driving the Tank. To keep from getting overheated, I rolled all the windows down and opened the side front windows. This would allow the hot air to travel freely through the car and hopefully, provide some relief. It was definitely summer—a real June barnburner as the tobacco farmer would say.

Driving the half block to West Nash Street where I would make a left hand turn, I felt a rush of blood go through my face. Once on West Nash Street, I felt my flushed face getting hotter, and the tips of my ears began to burn. I had become angry and nervous and I dreaded a possible confrontation with Oscar Byrd, something that I wanted to avoid. Since the drive to the pharmacy was less than two miles, I decided to ride by David Byrd's home first. It was out of the way but I had to see him and talk with him before I faced Mr. Byrd. I could still make it to the pharmacy by four-thirty.

When I got to Byrd's house I saw two unfamiliar cars. There was no activity outside the house and it was dark inside. I drove through the driveway and around the back to the garage hoping to see Julian. I didn't see anyone so I parked the car and rang the back doorbell. A woman about Mother's age with grayish brown hair whom I had never seen before came to the door.

"May I help you, young man?" she said, showing her irritation over my presence.

"Yes ma'am. I am a good friend of Byrd's," I said, looking into a very unpleasant face with a wrinkled forehead. "May I see him?"

"No one by that name lives here," she said and turned away.

"Wait! That's his nickname. I am looking for David Byrd."

"David is not here," she said in a firm manner making it clear that I had annoyed her.

"When will he be back?" I was getting an uneasy feeling about this woman. This only added to her impatience with me and my confusion over the absence of Byrd. She acted as if she didn't even know who I was talking about. I wanted to get inside the house to find out what was going on but I knew I didn't have a lot of time left to get to the pharmacy.

"He is at the beach with his mother and sisters."

"That's odd. He told me to come over today," I said, crossing my finger behind my back.

"They left yesterday afternoon. I believe they will be back tomorrow afternoon," she said, staring directly into my hazel eyes as if to say I dare you to ask another question.

"Yesterday? Is Julius here? Maybe he can help me."

"Julius went with them," she said. "You certainly are a persistent young man. Whom did you say you were the son of?"

"I didn't. Thanks for your help," I said. "I need to get back home now." I turned and walked quickly to my car and got in. She closed the back door and drew the thin linen curtains. I had a strange feeling about this. The house was completely dark on the inside and I had a suspicion that she didn't belong there.

Whoever the woman was she was a stranger to me. I knew a lot of Mrs. Byrd's friends and Wilson was not a large town. Everyone was either kin to each other or they knew each other or they knew about each other. I was positive that I had never seen this woman before.

Back in my car, I turned the ignition and looked at my watch. It was four-thirty. I had overshot my time and I knew I had to get to the pharmacy as quickly as this old Buick would carry me. Mr. Byrd's store didn't close until six o'clock and the medicine would be waiting when I arrived. For one fleeting moment I hoped that my being late might allow me to miss seeing Mr. Byrd.

While pulling away from the house, I looked back and saw a figure standing behind the kitchen curtains watching me leave. I supposed it was the mysterious woman but in truth, it could have been anybody.

My mouth was a cotton ball—parched and dry. I wanted a drink of cool water. The sweat on my face dropped on my shirt making little circles when it hit. I could feel the moisture running down my back and finding its way into the crevice of my buttocks. My head was pounding keeping time with the beating of my heart. I was as uncomfortable as any teenager could possible be and scared to death of what was about to take place.

Chapter 28
THE WRATH OF MR. HYDE

OSCAR ANDERSON BYRD II, like his father before him, was a pillar of our small town and one of our most prominent citizens. Mr. Byrd, a father of four children, had been married to his wife for over twenty years. Being one of only two white pharmacists in our town gave him an entrée into the lives of many of our town's people. He knew as much if not more about what took place behind the doors of the homes in Wilson as anyone. His was in a position of trust and as of yet, he hadn't broken it.

Mr. Byrd was an elected member of the Wilson County School Board, a member in good standing of the Wilson Country Club, and an active member of the Shriners. He was an appointed trustee of Branch Banking and Trust Company, a member of the Lions Club, and a member in good faith of the Episcopal Church. To the people of our community, Oscar Anderson Byrd II was the ideal husband and father, the picture of a successful businessman, and a valued contributor to society. And *now,* I could add to this list that he had sex with his youngest son. *No one* would ever believe me even if I chose to tell.

It was four fifty-seven when I pulled into the litter strewn parking lot of the small shopping center on West Nash Street located only one block west of the downtown business district.

Byrd's Drug and Pharmacy was nestled between the newly renovated Winn-Dixie Supermarket and Wilson's only One-Hour Cleaners. There were less than twenty cars in the block-long parking lot allowing me to grab a choice space and be at the pharmacy's door at exactly 5:00. Before I pushed open the heavy glass door that had been repeatedly smeared by the dozens of greasy and lotion hands that had touched it during the day, I stopped and took a deep breath. I was not looking forward to this visit and I shivered at the thought of what Mr. Byrd might say to me. I kept telling myself to go in, get my father's medicine, and get out.

"Hello, Mr. Jernigan," I said as I entered the cluttered pharmacy. Unpacked boxes of recently purchased summer supplies, stacked one on top of another, sat in front of aisles waiting to be stocked. I guessed that would be my job when I started on Monday.

"Hi, Braxton. How's your vacation been so far?" asked Mr. Jernigan, resident pharmacist and manager of this location, and the primary reason so many people did repeat business with this store.

"It's been wild so far," I said. "I hope it doesn't go too fast."

"It will though," he said. "Want a Coke? It's on me."

"Yes, thank you," I said. "I came to get my father's medicine."

"Yes, I know. Mr. Byrd has it in his office. I'll tell him you are here," he said, picking up the receiver of the heavy black phone and dialing to the back of the store. "Mr. Byrd, Braxton Haywood is here to pick up his father's medication."

The soda jerk had left for the day and that was okay. No one could make shakes and fountain drinks like Sam Jernigan. During his summer vacations from high school and college, Sammy Jernigan had worked at this very same store for Mr. Byrd's father. His first job was behind the fountain area and this was where he trained himself to be the best soda jerk in Wilson. Mr. Jerningan could tie one hand behind his back and keep his eyes closed, and no one this side of Raleigh could beat him when it came to pulling those hand polished chrome handles on the fountain and turning out sodas.

"Here you are, Braxton. Enjoy it," Sam Jernigan handed me a cherry Coke. He had no idea how thirsty I was. The phone by the cash register rang catching me off-guard, making me jump. "A little edgy, Braxton?" *If only he knew,* I thought.

"Byrd's Drug and Pharmacy. How may I help you?" he said in his usual inviting and friendly way. Suddenly, the smile that had been present on his face turned into a scowl. He hung up the receiver and said, "Braxton, Mr. Byrd wants to see you now."

"Thanks for the Coke, Mr. Jernigan." Putting the cup to my mouth, I tipped it and swallowed hard. "This really hits the spot," I said, turning and eyeing the back of the store. I took one last gulp and set my cup back on the counter. "Here goes. See you later."

"Braxton, you be careful back there," he whispered. "I'm right up here if you need me."

I stood there for a minute and then started walking down the aisle that led directly to Mr. Byrd's office. I looked from side to side as I braced myself for my meeting with Oscar Byrd and whatever he had planned for me. On my left were the hair products, dental needs, and ladies facials. To my right were toilet articles, Kleenexes, and baby needs. I wished I was a baby and that none of this had ever happened. I stopped and shook my head. I was standing in front of Mr. Byrd's office door. Before I knocked on the solid pine door, I took a deep breath pulling in my stomach and then I let the air out quickly. This didn't calm me and without further hesitation, I knocked firmly three times hoping to disguise my fear.

"Come in," said the muffled voice on the other side of the door.

I turned the knob, opening the massive door leading into the paneled room, and waited. Mr. Byrd, sitting at his father's antique mahogany desk, turned in the leather swivel chair toward me. He tapped the end of his cigar on the brass spittoon sitting beside his desk, took a deep draw, and blew the foul smelling smoke toward me. He smiled but made no attempt to get up. A gentleman would stand and greet me and ask me in, but I knew the man sitting before me was no gentleman.

"Come in," he said lacking warmth and sincerity. His stained green tie was untied and hanging loosely against his badly wrinkled white shirt. His stomach was pushing against one of the buttons of his shirt showing white skin that was badly in need of a tan.

"Mr. Jernigan said that you had my father's medicine. I've come to get it." I stood in the doorway waiting for him to make the next move.

"Braxton, don't be bashful. Come in and have a seat." Mr. Byrd still made no attempt to rise but instead pointed to one of the two brown leather chairs sitting in front of his desk. "Mr. Jernigan is right. I do have your father's medicine," he said, pointing to a bag sitting on top of his desk. "*But,* we need to talk first."

I walked over and stood in front of the chair closest to the door. Before I sat, I spoke, "I don't have much time, Mr. Byrd. Daddy is already an hour late getting this medicine into his system."

"Sit down! One hour, two hours or three hours—it won't make much difference to a dying man when he gets it." Mr. Byrd took several quick puffs on his cigar and again blew the smoke my way. I tried not to cough.

"The medicine please!" I said, standing and extending my hand toward the bag on his desk. The veins in my neck tightened and I felt a flush of anger take hold of me. My face was hot and my ears burned again. His comment about my father hit me hard and I wanted to strike back but I knew that would make matters worse. He had the advantage here in his office. I kept telling myself to "cool it" and try to stay calm.

"*Not so fast,* young man. *Sit down! Now!*" He paused and then with his voice dropping several octaves, he said, "Whether your father gets this medicine or not is immaterial to me. You know it's really not going to help him—maybe prolong his life for a few more days or weeks but it won't help him. *But what you do and say about last night is very important to me.*" He put his cigar back in his mouth and inhaled deeply—so deeply that he turned red in the face. When he could hold the smoke no longer, he exhaled and deliberately blew it across the table and into my face again. I squinted and said nothing.

The only thought I had was how my mother could have dated this man. Without thinking, I said, "Where is Byrd?" I stood and reached for the bag of medicine.

"Braxton, shut up! Listen and listen well," he said, knocking my hand away. He sat erect in his chair and looked at me with crazed eyes that seemed to get larger when he spoke. "*Sit your ass down, damn it. You best listen and listen well!*" He took one last drag on his cigar, blew the smoke toward the ceiling, and dropped the cigar into the spittoon. "The way I see it, you don't have much choice here. Your daddy needs that medicine and I'm the pharmacist. Your daddy owes me for last month's medicine in the amount of fifty-six dollars and now you want to pick up some more. Who in the hell do you *think I am? I'm not some Santa Claus you're going to dick around with— do you hear me?*"

"Yes, sir," I answered politely not wanting to.

"*You fuck around with me one time and your father will never—I repeat, never get his medicine from this store again—or from any other store in this town.*" His rage mounted.

"That's *not fair,* Mr. Byrd." I stood, protesting.

"*Shut up and sit down,*" he said, leaning toward me propping both of his elbows on top of his desk. He positioned his face as close to mine as he could. I drew back. His steel blue eyes mirrored his boiling anger and hatred. His behavior frightened me and his words took on a sound of revenge. The room was getting hotter and the odor of the used cigar was rank and nauseating.

"May I please just get the medicine and go?" I wanted to escape but I did not move.

"You'll go when I say you can go and not one minute sooner," he said, standing up. My eyes followed him as he walked around the desk stopping beside me. I did not take my eyes off of him, fearing he would hit me. He said nothing but stood there staring at me. His nostrils flared and his mouth grew moist but he remained silent. I felt a sudden chill run up and down my spine followed by several quick twists in my stomach. I didn't know what he was getting ready to do. He spoke again, "You're a *loser,* Braxton. Why my son would want a loser for a friend is beyond me. Everyone in this town knows that you're the son of an alcoholic mother and a pathetic, dying man who can't take a piss without help."

"*Shut up!*" I shouted. "*You just stop it!*" I leaned over the desk and grabbed the medicine bag. "*You don't know my parents!*"

Mr. Byrd took a step towards me and grabbed the back of my shoulders and pushed me back into the chair, digging all of his fingers into my shoulder blades. I could feel the pain shoot down my spine and I knew he had broken the skin. I immediately jumped up, dropping the bag of medicine to the floor. I remained rigid. An undefined strength began to calm me. I reached down and picked up the bag. Mr. Bird took the bag out of my hand and continued to stare at me but the look on his face was obscene.

"You're one stubborn boy. I like that," he said, moving behind me and running his hand down my back and then across my crotch.

"*Don't touch me!*" I recoiled. "Let me out of here—*now!*" I said, attempting to break loose. He pushed me back into the chair again.

"You say one thing about last night to anyone—*anyone*—and I will make your life and the life of your mother and father a *living hell. And if you don't think I can do it—you test me one time. One time and you'll regret it the rest of your life.* Do you understand me?"

I sat mute. Water filled my eyes. I was helpless. My heart was pounding faster than I'd ever remembered it . . . my breathing was jerky and my knees kept knocking together . . . I felt a surge of cold air like the unexpected arrival of a chill creep up and down my body. I felt his warm breath as it hit the back of my neck. I was frightened—more frightened than I'd ever been in my life and I was deathly afraid of the man standing behind me—the father of one of my best friends. One minute he was a Dr. Jekyll and the next minute he had transformed himself into a Mr. Hyde.

"I understand," I said in response to his question.

The phone on his desk rang twice. He made no attempt to answer it. It rang two more times before he moved to answer it. "What do you want, Sam? . . . Yes . . . No . . . I'm certain, just a little emotional release. I will . . . thank you." The call meant that Mr. Jernigan was aware that something abnormal was happening in here. I just wished he'd come back here and not called.

And another thing—*you are not to ever see or call* my son again. I mean not today—*not* tomorrow—*not* next week—*I mean never. Your friendship is over!* I don't want him having a *loser* the likes of you as a friend."

"What does Byrd have to say about this?" I asked, gripping the arms of the chair as tightly as I could. This crazy man had done everything he could to hurt me and I didn't want to do something I would regret the rest of my life.

Mr. Byrd gripped the front arms of my chair and turned me around so I would be facing him. He leaned over and put his face in mind and shouted, "*I don't give a rat's shit what David would or will say. He will do whatever I damn well tell him to do. And I will tell him that you are not good enough to be his friend. If he wants to make friends with shit, let him go to Five Points or Greenhill.*" He laughed wildly and his face got crimson red. He returned to his chair and set the medicine bag on the top of the desk. Reaching with his left hand, he took another cigar out of the box sitting behind his polished brass nameplate, bit the tip off, and lit it. Acting as if everything was normal, he leaned back inhaling the smoke and gently blew it toward the ceiling. He became quiet and his facial expression changed. For a moment, he had that same look that he had when we caught him last night.

My ears burned from the loudness of his words. My heart burned from the hurt of his words. My mind went blank. I shook my head. I didn't want to believe what I had just heard. I spoke without hesitating, "Mr. Byrd, you're being unfair to Byrd and me! Byrd should make this decision and not you!"

"Unfair? *Unfair?* Life can be unfair, Braxton," Mr. Byrd said in a preachy tone of voice while he knocked the ashes from his cigar. "So what else is new? Besides, don't you presume to tell me what is fair and unfair when it comes to raising my children!"

"May I have the medicine now?" I asked, wanting to leave.

"Yes," he said, handing me the bag. He drew a deep puff from his cigar blowing a little cloud of smoke into the already foul air and then put the cigar to rest in the oversized ashtray on his desk.

"Thank you." I reached for the bag. He handed it to me but in doing so grabbed my hand with his chunky fingers refusing to let go. He turned his fingers so that his palm was facing mine and then he squeezed my hand hard. I couldn't believe that a man as small as he could have this much strength in his arms and hands. His fingers danced against my palm.

"One last thing! Aren't you supposed to start work here on Monday?"

"Yes, sir," I said, taking a deep breath wondering what was going to happen next.

"You really need this job?" he asked with a sudden change of tone, becoming polite and almost decent.

"Yes, sir, I'm depending on it to make money for school supplies and clothes."

"Any other job offers?"

"No, sir. I didn't apply for any more after you gave me this job."

"I see," Mr. Byrd said in a businesslike manner. "Well, Braxton, your normal starting time would ordinarily be at eight o'clock. But in your case, I'm making an exception."

"Yes?"

"Your starting time will be *never. You think I want a fucking loser like you working here?*" he said, leaning back in his chair laughing. His mood and behavior seemed to change in the middle of a sentence. I immediately became defensive again.

"Mr. Byrd, please don't do this to me! I was counting on this job," I said, standing and leaning across his desk. I looked in those steel blue eyes that had successfully raped me for the last thirty minutes. I saw no regret, only pleasure and a desire to tease and humiliate me. I took a deep breath and said with as much authority as I could, "*You're crazy. Do you know that? You are crazy, Mr. Byrd. I feel sorry for David, and Charles, and your two daughters, and your wife. You're a crazy man!*" I backed off and looked at him.

He immediately stood and with his right hand extended, he put his forefinger in my face and with volcanic anger let out the last of the stored poison, "*You stupid son of a bitch! Get out of my office now before I knock the shit out of you!*" He came around to where I stood and bumped me with his chest and stomach. "*Remember what I told you. I will make your life a living hell if you fuck with me and my family. Now get out! I don't ever want to see the sight of you again.*"

I backed away from him until my hand felt his office door. Still looking at him, I grabbed the knob with my left hand and turned it until the door started opening. Mr. Byrd immediately reached over my shoulder with his right hand and closed the door. He put his face within a breath of mine. I could feel his hot, smelly breath against my face. I stood as straight as I could trying to put some distance between us. My eyes glared back into his blue eyes until I could no longer focus. He stood in front of me breathing and grinning, breathing and grinning, and then he backed off, still grinning. He stopped between his desk and me, placed the smoky forefinger of his right hand beside his nose, and said, "Remember, Braxton, *there are Jews, dogs, niggers, and then there is the likes of you.*" He moved toward me again stopping about a foot away. "*Don't fuck with me, Braxton!*" he said, spitting tobacco on my right loafer.

He turned, walking back to his desk. Sitting, he picked up some of his papers and moved them from one side of his desk to the other. He selected another cigar from his box and cut the tip off and dropped it into the spittoon. I watched him light it and blow the first curl of smoke into the air. Then opening his office door, I walked out and down the same two aisles to the front of the store. I did all I could do to withhold my tears until I passed Mr. Jernigan.

"Is everything okay?" Mr. Jernigan asked, knowing by looking at me that it wasn't.

"I'll be fine. Please call my mother and tell her I'm on my way home."

I pushed the heavy glass door open and ran to my car. Once I was behind the steering wheel of the car, my emotions rang out. I began sobbing uncontrollably. I don't remember exactly how long I sat there crying but Mr. Sam Jernigan knocking on the hood jerked me back into reality. I looked up and nodded.

Coming around to my window, he asked, "Do you want me to drive you home?"

"No, thank you anyway."

"You need to go on home, Braxton. I called your mother over thirty minutes ago to tell her that you were on your way. It's now 6:20," he said, looking at his watch. "I know she must be worried."

"Thank you, Mr. Jernigan," I answered. "You're right. I'm leaving now."

"Braxton," said Mr. Jernigan, leaning into the car. "I'm sorry for whatever happened in there. He told me you wouldn't be working here. If I can do anything to help you, please call me."

"Thanks again, Mr. Jernigan. I might just do that."

"Any time. Good luck." Mr. Jernigan turned and walked toward his car.

I turned the ignition, pulled forward, drove to the parking lot exit and turned left onto West Nash Street and headed home. The usual tall oaks and maples that lined both sides of this beautiful street seemed more towering and larger around their girths tonight. Their strong roots laying exposed along the curbing was a reminder of how easy it is to break through what we think of as being safe and solid. In their case, it was the ground. In my case, it was the desire to respect and trust authority. Their canopies, even on this hottest of June nights that had not seen rain in days, entwined in a glorious tangle overhead. Only the earliest of stars could find a way to break through this attempt to blot out the sky.

As I drove through this familiar green tunnel, I felt safe again. I contemplated a life without my good friend, David Byrd. It was too unnatural to even consider. Mr. Byrd could take my job away but I knew I would not let him break up my friendship with his son. I would find a way to preserve it.

Chapter 29
FEAR BREAKS OUT

WHEN I PULLED the Tank into the driveway, I saw Mother already positioned at the front door, waiting for me. I checked my watch. It read 6:35 P.M. Approximately an hour and a half had passed since I'd left to get my father's medicine. It seemed more like two days to me. I was not in the mood to be yelled at and I hoped she would understand. That would depend on how many drinks she had had. If she started at five o'clock, she could be on her third or fourth. I didn't know whether Mother was being more open with her drinking in front of me or if I had just begun to notice what had been there all along. Obviously, others had taken note and had labeled her as one of Wilson's untouchables—a female drunk and a town alcoholic.

Mother's drinking was not being excused like some of the mothers of my friends and acquaintances. These women did not share the handicap of my mother: a lack of social position and money to get by with an abusive habit gracefully—especially, in a town that thrived on gossip—talking about the wounded, the infirmed, the outcast, the dejected, and those with mental illnesses. In Mother's case, fondness for alcohol placed her in the latter category.

Mother even had her own cheerleader by the name of Jeannette Eicher. Mrs. Eicher, an alcoholic herself and a fairly well-to-do widow, lived in our general neighborhood and took a general dislike to my mother. Anytime she could spread ill will about Mother, she wouldn't hesitate leading the cheer. It didn't help Mother's case that Mrs. Eicher and the Byrds were social friends. I figured that this is where Mr. Byrd got his misinformation.

Such is life in a small southern town where old money rules, despite the immoral character of its leaders. They make the rules and if a person wants to belong—then they play by the rules. Since my mother's father had lost all of his money when she was a young girl, my mother had no choice but to forfeit her position among the town's elite. She continued to have many acquaintances among Wilson's finest but she had no close friends. Unlike her sister, I don't believe my mother would have found lasting happiness in the country club circle. She was too fond of being a "rabble-rouser," a nonconformist among people who had a desperate need to conform. My mother held a strong opinion about certain things and often she felt the need to express herself—especially toward the Wilson "do-gooder," her name for the socially, self-righteous, imperfect Christian—the self-appointed anointed who were quick to look over their own shoulder and criticize the imperfections of another. A person lacking an acceptable "pedigree" didn't stand a chance of pardon when the local do-gooders set their eyes on their prey. Given a chance, they would pick the flesh off the bones of their carcass. Mother would immediately jump to the defense of the unwanted and become the devil's advocate. Mother might say, "Well, look at Mrs. So-n-So. She came from what you call "white trash" and she's accepted. Now give me one good reason why she can't be included?" Mother despised two-faced people and made little attempt to tolerate them.

Most of the neighborhood wives loved my mother and respected her for her frankness. She never used it against anyone to inflict hurt or pain; but she would use it in a heartbeat to make someone face hypocrisy (or to put someone in their rightful place). Mother was one of those women whom people knew they could trust and she had a good listening ear. I was surprised that with all of her own troubles, she was willing to listen to other's pain and council them. She had saved more than one teenager from running away from home and had kept several marriages together. My mother wanted no applause and she didn't seek praise. It is unfortunate that more people knew her bad habits and majored on them rather than becoming her advocate, pointing out the good things that she had done and continued to do.

"Braxton, how long are you going to sit in that car before you come in?" Mother called.

"Coming. I'm coming now," I said, getting out of the car. I was lost in a sea of thoughts and I guess I didn't realize I was back in my own driveway. I walked to the porch and joined my Mother. Tonight she was dressed in a casual linen smock shaded in light summer colors that complimented her facial makeup and the dark red lipstick she wore so often. It was classic Mother: holding death in both hands—a drink in one hand and a lit cigarette in the other.

"Braxton, I have really been worried about you. Where on earth have you been?" she said, without any hint of anger in her voice. "It has been over forty minutes since Mr. Jernigan called me saying you were on your way. Are you all right?"

"In truth, no. I had a very bad experience with Mr. Byrd. At first, he wouldn't give me Daddy's medicine and then he finished by telling me I didn't have a job."

"What? Come in the house and we'll talk about it," said Mother, opening the door and following me into the living room. "Did you say anything to make him mad?"

"Probably. But that's not why he doesn't want me to work for him."

"What then? Something must have happened. That doesn't sound like Oscar."

"You don't know Oscar Byrd. At least, not the one I know," I said. "Can we go to the back porch to finish this? I'm suffocating in this room." Mother's attempt to keep the house cool for Daddy by closing the front windows and lowering the shades had had an adverse effect; instead, the humidity from outside had taken up residence inside from the constant opening and closing of the doors. Now everything in the room had a sticky feeling. It was just too damn hot!

"Of course, son," Mother said, coming over and patting me on the back. "Wash up and I'll bring you some supper. Lily fixed you a cold plate before she left."

"Mother, I'm really not in the mood to eat, but I would like a glass of iced tea," I said, handing her the medicine and walking to the bathroom. The scent of fresh shampoo greeted me when I entered our long, narrow bathroom. The only window was open, allowing the outside humidity to mix with the remaining humidity from Mother's bath, creating a muggy presence that took my breath away. The fact that there was no evening breeze encouraged the smell of Jergen's lotion to hang around. Before I could exit, I thought I would gag.

I stopped in my bedroom and took my yellow box fan out of its window position and carried it with me. Once on the back porch, I plugged it in on the far end next to the driveway and cut on the switch. An artificial breeze, I decided, was sometimes better than none at all. Byrd and Jason had attic fans that helped to keep their homes cool. Matt had enough trees surrounding his house to maintain a coolness and Thad was like me, grab a fan and hope for the best.

I had gone all day with no word from Byrd and apparently, none of the others had called me. I couldn't help but wonder what in the hell was going on? I walked into the kitchen where Mother had taken the plate Lily had fixed for me from the refrigerator. I fixed myself a glass of sweet iced tea, grabbed a fork and napkin, and walked back onto the porch and sat at the table waiting.

Mother set the plate on my placemat. Lily had fixed it just the way she knew I liked it. There was chicken salad, wafers, tomato aspic on lettuce topped with mayonnaise, and congealed fruit salad. Too bad I wasn't all that hungry but I would make an effort. Lily would be offended if I didn't put some kind of a dent in it and I didn't want to hurt her feelings. Lily did pride herself on being a good cook (although this meal was taken from the remaining gifts of food) and among the Negro servants in our area she had the reputation of being the best. And besides, she was too good to my family and me. Mother came out and sat across from me.

"Try to eat, Braxton," she said. "Now what is all this with Oscar Byrd and losing your job?"

"Wait," I whispered. "What about Daddy's medicine? Don't you need to give it to him?"

"It has been taken care of."

"What about Anne? Where is she?"

"She's spending the night with your grandmother," Mother said, picking up her drink glass from its plastic coaster and wiping the moisture from the cork surface. "Anymore questions?"

"Yes, one. Has anyone called me since I left?" I leaned back, anticipating a "yes" response.

"Only Patsy Wentworth. She's having another party and wants you to call her back."

"No one else called?" I answered with disappointment.

"No one else called! Now please tell me what happened." Mother leaned forward ready to hear what I could possibly have to say about Oscar Byrd.

"Okay, but please don't interrupt me until I have finished. I promise to answer most any question you might ask but only when I'm through telling you what has happened. Mother, do you promise?"

"Yes, Braxton, I promise," she said, lighting one of her filter king Kools. She took one long draw and blew the smoke to her left. I watched the smoke pass through the screen and disappear into the early summer night.

I began my story with us trying to get into David's house. That brought forth a few chuckles from my mother but the rest of my story solicited only a concerned silence. I told her about finding Mr. Byrd and Charles in bed, what pursued afterwards between David and his father, my participation, and the filthy comments spewing from the mouth of Mr. Byrd. I concluded with Julius coming into the room and the last mental picture I had of David and Charles. During this entire narration, my mother never showed any shock or disgust or anger. She listened quietly as I spoke. I was grateful for that.

"Mother, do you want me to continue with what happened today?"

"Please, go ahead" she said, lighting another cigarette even though she had never smoked the first one she lit. It lay with the other butts in the glass ashtray having burned itself out.

I told Mother about going by David's house and what the strange woman told me, how that had delayed me getting to the drugstore, and that Mr. Byrd was waiting for me in his office. I recalled every detail I could remember about my meeting with Mr.

Byrd, even down to his spitting on my shoe. I left two things out: his attempt at fondling me and his comments about my mother. The first I left out because I was too embarrassed to tell her. His comments about my mother being an alcoholic would have been too hurtful and Mother didn't need any more hurt. I did share the hurtful comments he blasted toward me and I kind of toned down what he said about my father. From the look in Mother's eyes when she heard his remarks about Daddy, I knew I had made a big mistake. It wasn't my intent to be insensitive and cause her more pain. I finished my scenario by sharing Mr. Byrd's threats and his refusal to let me see David again.

When I finished my story, I waited for Mother to say something. I hoped she would because I was about to start crying. Mother said nothing but sat quietly looking out into the backyard that had turned a golden hue from the setting sun. I wanted her to respond but I knew to respect her silence. I got up and went into the kitchen and poured both of us a glass of tea. I set hers down on the tablemat in front of her and I returned to my seat and began to drink mine. I pressed the cold glass against my forehead, enjoying the immediate relief from the heat that it gave me. The coldness of the glass absorbed the sweat standing on my forehead. It felt good.

"Braxton," she said finally. "I wasn't prepared for what you have told me. I know that's obvious to you just like I know you want me to give you some kind of answer. But I have to think about all of this first." Mother sat back and looked at me.

"What I need is some guidance, Mother," I said. "The sooner, the better."

"You will have to give me time to reflect on this. This is not what I expected," she said, reaching across and patting my hand. "I wish your daddy could help me advise you."

"Please don't bring him into this," I pleaded.

"Of course, I won't. He's far too sick to be listening to this. Interesting though, he never has liked Oscar Byrd for some reason and that's unusual. Your daddy rarely says a bad word about anyone. But I do remember him saying one time that he didn't trust Oscar Byrd," she said getting up from the table. "Is there anything else you want to tell me?"

"No. But I do have a question. Is there a term for what Mr. Byrd was doing to Charles?"

She hesitated. "I believe the correct term is *sodomy,*" Mother said. She closed her eyes for a moment, then stood and spoke again, "I have to go check on your dad. We'll talk again later."

"Mother, thank you," I said, suppressing a desire to cry. "And, Mother, I love you. I just wanted you to know that."

"Thank you, Braxton," she said. Before she disappeared into the hallway, I noticed her eyes had filled with tears.

I sat alone on the back porch recounting the events of this summer, or at least what I could remember in detail, back to the last day of school. Outside it was beautiful. The setting sun had cast the backyard in orange, a fitting color for the heat that prevailed. And in the quietness of this early evening, the only movement was from an occasional rabbit hopping through the yard or the lightening bugs flittering here and there as if they were performing some mystical dance. We had been out of school a little over two weeks and all ready ten summer's worth of events had taken place. I couldn't help but wonder what other surprises this summer had in store for my friends and me.

Here I was alone on an early Saturday night slumped over the back porch table playing with my fork and spoon. I didn't want to feel sorry for myself but I was getting close to having one big-time pity party. It's not supposed to be this way I kept telling myself. I should be at the park with my friends dancing to the latest rock-n-roll music from the outside jukebox or up on the hill, swimming in the public pool. I could even be at the movies with Rhonda Morgan. We dated once, the first of May, and I'd told myself not to wait too long before I asked her out again.

These first weeks of vacation had been a hell of another kind for all of us. Matt and Thad didn't seem to have it so bad but Jason, Byrd, and I had a lot of sticky stuff going on in our personal lives. And now the five of us had been infinitely linked by an act of sodomy. I questioned how far Mr. Byrd would carry his threats or to what lengths he would go to make certain his nasty behavior was kept secret. I kept wondering how afraid were we to be of him. One thing I was certain of: I was afraid not to take him seriously because I didn't want him to hurt my parents.

Another question kept nagging at me and I knew I didn't have the answer and probably wouldn't come up with an answer on my own. And that was where is God in all of this? Isn't He in control of all things? At least, that's what my grandmother keeps telling me. "If it's God's will, it will happen," is what she always says. "Braxton, remember that God controls the heavens and the earth and all things happen in His time," is another of her favorite reminders.

I stopped. I had little practice with what I was getting ready to do but this was as good a time as any to begin talking with God. "Okay God, where are *You* now? And God, if *You're* in charge, why don't *You* do something and do it quick? And what would *You* have me do regarding Byrd? You will take care of him, won't *You?*" Somehow, this talking out loud to God didn't feel real to me. It felt awkward trying to talk to someone I couldn't see. I needed to know that God was listening but how was I supposed to figure that out? I needed someone that had the inside scoop on this and that would be my grandmother.

I trusted my grandmother and I knew she loved God and I knew she read her Bible. I used to think she used God for an excuse whenever it was convenient for her or she didn't want me to do something. But this God was real to her and when she talked about God, He started becoming real to me. I'd just about decided her faith in God wasn't phony and it wasn't something she'd picked up by sitting on the fifth pew from the front every Sunday at the First Baptist Church on West Nash Street. Although, the last time I went with her to that church, I left feeling a little guilty. Pastor Peterson kept looking at me wagging that finger of his saying if you're gonna try to hide from God and do bad things, then you don't love Him and you're a sinner or something like that. And how does a person hide from God? He didn't explain that one. About this loving God—well, I can't love God yet because I don't know Him yet.

"Okay God," I began again. "We've got to start somewhere together. Here it is, I am a sinner, whatever that means, and I guess being with Arlene makes it so. Now You know it from me but You probably already knew. But where are You tonight and where were

You last night and where were You this afternoon? And God, I can't help but wonder why a God as important as so many say You are would let a man like Oscar Byrd father four children? God, Byrd deserves better. He never hurt anyone and You let this happen to his brother, Charles. I just don't get it, God."

This conversation with God was going nowhere. My mind would not stay focused and I was being bombarded with wonderings and questions. I wondered why God didn't stop the evil in the world. I wondered why fathers don't honor their sons. I just didn't understand all this God stuff. It was too complicated and just when I thought I was beginning to have some idea of where to begin, all this shit starts happening. It just didn't make a damn bit of sense!

I looked around; no one was nearby. The orange of an earlier hour had turned itself into a grayish black. I got up and walked from the back porch to the hall. I needed to make a phone call. I picked up the heavy black receiver off its base that sat practically glued to the solid cherry telephone table outside my daddy's room. This was the telephone's permanent resting place. Whoever decided to put the jack here made a terrible mistake because there was never any privacy and I could only use it when it wouldn't bother my father, which was most of the time. Tonight, I didn't ask. I carefully dialed David Byrd's number. I held my breath through the sixth ring but there was no response. I was disappointed but kind of relieved, too. I don't know what I would have done or said if a voice had answered. I guess I'd hang up unless Byrd answered it. Knowing Mr. Byrd, he's probably taken Byrd's phone privileges away. Not knowing about Byrd was eating away at any peace of mind that I might pretend to have had.

Then out of nowhere, it occurred to me exactly how to find out where Byrd was. Where this idea came from was a mystery to me. I couldn't believe I hadn't thought of it before. Putting the heavy phone receiver on my shoulder, I took the directory from the phone table and turned to the section marking customers with the last name beginning with P. I scanned the pages until I came to the name Pugh. Olivia Byrd Pugh was listed as O. B. Pugh. It remained an enigma to me that Byrd had not told his aunt anything about what was going on, especially since she was his favorite relative. Equally puzzling was the fact that Olivia could be Mr. Byrd's sister. Olivia Pugh, wealthy in her own right, had married a successful farmer and landowner. Unlike her brother, her position in our community had not given her an air of self-importance and she made no attempt to laud her background over anyone. In fact, Mrs. Pugh was one of the nicest women I knew in our town. Not only was she always willing to help someone, she loved to make people laugh and she was a master at it.

I knew Olivia well enough to call her by her first name despite my mother's initial objections. Olivia was what she preferred to be called and her request was granted by all of her close family friends, regardless of their age. I dialed the number 4265 and sat on the floor waiting for an answer.

"Hello. Pugh's residence," answered a raspy Southern female voice.

"May I speak with Olivia please?"

"This is Olivia Pugh," she said, unaware of who I was.

"Olivia, this is Braxton Haywood." I hesitated. "Please forgive me for calling you so late."

"Late? It's only eight o'clock," she guffawed. "Honey, this old lady plans to stay awake at least another three hours. What brings you my way tonight? Nothing is wrong, I hope?"

"No, ma'am," I said. "I'm trying to get in touch with Byrd and he doesn't seem to be at home. I went by his house and a stranger, a lady unfamiliar with David's nickname, answered the door. I wondered if he might be staying with you or you might know where he is."

"Braxton, I haven't seen my nephew in several weeks but I do know that Helen and the girls are at Morehead this weekend and will probably stay the rest of June. I can't be certain on this but I think Charles and David are planning to go back and forth on weekends with their dad."

"I see. Byrd and I were together last night and it's important that I touch base with him. I went to his house late this afternoon and this strange lady answered the door."

Olivia laughed. "Was she about your mother's height with grayish hair and very serious looking?"

"Yes, ma'am. That describes her to a T."

"That's Helen's sister, Greta, from Nash County. She comes over every so often to mooch off of Helen and Oscar," she said, laughing again. "Braxton, I'm just kidding but Helen did say Greta might come over this weekend to watch the house and keep Oscar's setters company. I bet that's who it was."

"It makes sense. I just didn't know Byrd was headed for the beach." This baffled me.

"Do you want me to call over and find out when David is coming back?"

"No ma'am. Please don't do that. I mean, I can call," I said, beginning to fall over my words.

"There's nothing wrong, is there?" she asked, raising her voice indicating concern.

"No ma'am, not in the least," I said, not being totally honest. "It can wait until David gets back."

"Well, okay. I really don't mind, you know," she said.

"Yes, ma'am. Thank you very much," I said, trying to discourage her from calling.

"Okay then, but you know I don't mind." Olivia could be too insistent, but she would do anything if she thought it would make a situation better.

"Yes ma'am, I know," I said. "Thank you but that isn't necessary." It was time to move on.

"Braxton, before I hang up, how's your daddy? Is he any better?"

"No, ma'am," I said. "Well, maybe about the same, I suppose. Maybe even worse."

"That's what Josephine told me yesterday at our bridge luncheon," Olivia said, sighing. "I'm so sorry to hear that. Your daddy has suffered far too long, poor man."

"Yes, ma'am," I said. "Thanks again for your time."

"Braxton, you call anytime you want and please give your dear sweet mama my love, you hear?"

"Yes, ma'am, I will," I said. "Good-bye and thank you."

"Good-bye." Olivia hung up and I sat wondering if I had made a further mess of things.

Well, well. If what Olivia told me is true then Mr. Byrd took his boys to the beach to be with their mother. If he wasn't the clever one, no one would suspect anything. I wondered how long he had been doing this thing called sodomy. Could he have done it to David? I didn't even want to consider the possibility. No wonder he's afraid of someone finding out. Why did adults think they are the only ones who ever had any problems?

I called Patsy Wentworth and she made me promise I'd be at her swimming party on Friday night, June 21st. I lied when she asked me if I knew where David Byrd was. I told her yes when she asked me if she should invite Jason to her party. And I said I didn't believe her when she told me that Claire Barnes wanted to go out with me. She dared me to call her and see.

I stepped onto the front porch before calling an end to the day. In another thirty minutes, it would be dark. Some of the smaller kids were playing tag at the other end of our block. Mr. and Mrs. Griffin were sitting on their porch. He was smoking his pipe and reading; she was stroking her poodle and mentally taking notes of the neighborhood. Mr. Ross was in his backyard, probably tending his garden. Skippy was napping in the middle of the street and fireflies were hovering around the light hanging from the pole across the street. From where I stood, everything seemed calm and in order. I stepped into the yard and walked across the street to visit with Mr. Ross, hoping that a chat with him would put some order back into my topsy-turvy life.

Chapter 30
AN UNEXPECTED WARNING

MR. WILLIAM ROSS, an unassuming man, was a short balding gentleman with a Roman nose, small ears, heavy eyebrows, and eyes that had lost their original smile. Now in his late sixties, he carried a small, trim frame but his arms were muscular and he had large, hairy hands that were covered with calluses. In our neighborhood, Mr. Ross's attire was usually bib-overalls. He loved to be in his garden and work with his hands and watch things grow. People said he had a gift and could bring almost any dying vegetation back to life. The widows in our neighborhood spoiled him and everyone was distressed when his only child, Danny, ran away from home after his first year in college. That was seventeen years ago and as far as I know, Danny has never contacted his father. I could count on one hand the number of times Mr. Ross has mentioned his son in front of me. Mother said his love for nature is the only thing that saved him. She and daddy befriended him during his early years of loss and Mr. Ross, in his own way, watches over my parents.

Mr. Ross was not an outgoing man but he was a wonderful communicator one on one. For as long as I can remember, Mr. Ross would let me work with him in his garden. I would hoe or pull weeds and wild onions or remove tiny rocks, and together we would talk about life—the kind of things that I couldn't talk about with my own dad. In some peculiar way, I became the son he had lost and he became my second father. We never acknowledged this in words to each other but we were both aware of our feelings toward each other.

On those afternoons or evenings we worked together, Mr. Ross would lead the way through his garden and I would follow listening, trying to learn whatever I could from this wise mentor I had secretly adopted as my second dad. From him I learned that life was much like a garden, and if my life was going to bear any fruit, I had to endure hardship and inconvenience without complaining.

I strolled up Mr. Ross' driveway, surveying his backyard, looking for him. I spotted him on his knees at the edge of the area he had marked off for his vegetable garden. There were two medium-sized, silver-coated buckets beside him. I knew this routine well: he was picking vegetables and placing them in his containers.

There was a rhythmic beauty about the arrangement of his plantings. Everything was planted with the utmost care and everything was artistically arranged in rows. Nothing seemed out of place. Even the colors of the flowers seem to compliment each other. Like players on a stage, none were positioned so as to upstage the other. This was precision in gardening at its best and the master gardener orchestrated all that was in his care. I stood there for a moment at the edge of his yard admiring the motion of his hands. Mr. Ross hummed, carefully picking each tomato and just as carefully, he laid them in one of the two buckets.

In order not to startle him, I called from where I was standing, "Hello, Mr. Ross. May I join you?"

Without turning around or even breaking his movement he called back, "Please do, Braxton. I would enjoy your company."

When I was with Mr. Ross, I felt good about myself. Things fell into place and just his presence gave me a confidence that was absent when I wasn't with him. I walked toward him then dropped to my knees imitating his position.

"You're just in time to take some tomatoes to your mother."

"Thank you, but I didn't come over to get freebie tomatoes."

"I know you didn't," he said, patting me on my back. "I know your mother and daddy love tomatoes and I have more than enough for myself. Just look inside my buckets and please help yourself."

Mr. Ross had taught me when a tomato was ready to be picked and I knew he wanted me to choose tomatoes that were ready to be placed in a salad or a sandwich. I reached in the bucket closest to me and he looked me dead in the eyes. "Not table ready," I said. Mr. Ross smiled.

I leaned over and from his other bucket, I took four red tomatoes that were ready to be eaten. They were neither too hard nor too soft and had few dark spots. If eaten within the next few days, they would have a near perfect taste.

Mr. Ross handed me another tomato and a paper towel. "Eat up," he said, taking a bite out of his, wiping his mouth with the back of his hand.

"Now? Here in the garden?" I said, not meaning to be ungracious. "Do I need to wash it first?" I'd never eaten a tomato straight from the garden.

"You *are* like your mother, Braxton," Mr. Ross said, laughing and slapping his knee. "Eating a tomato fresh from the garden will *not* kill you. Just eat up."

He was right. My response was typical of my mother. Mother washed everything that needed to be cleaned before it found its way onto our plates or in our mouths. I didn't want him to think I was namby-pamby. I laughed, too, and then taking the paper towel, I wiped off some of the dirt and took a big bite. Red juice ran from my mouth down my chin onto my pants. As usual, Mr. Ross was right. The tomato was sweet, juicy, and delicious.

"What brings you over this Saturday evening? I would think a young man like yourself would be courting some lucky girl tonight."

"I wish that was the case. Boy, do I ever wish that was true," I said. "Actually, I saw you out here and I kind of wanted to talk if you have the time?"

"Braxton, you don't have to have a special reason to come over to see me. You know that you're always welcomed here."

"Yes, sir, but Mother has told me repeatedly not to bother you. She thinks I'll wear out my welcome."

"That's a mother's job. I know your mother means well but I'll tell you something that I don't think I've ever told you. I look forward to your visits. You keep me in contact with the world of youth, a world that has fast passed me by."

"I don't know about that. You seem to be up on most everything," I said, beginning to feel confident again. "But, I do need your insight on something that's bugging me."

"Okay, help me pick those cucumbers over there and we can talk while we move down the row," he said. "I believe I've got as many tomatoes in this bucket as I can carry."

I followed Mr. Ross to the rows of cucumbers. He never stood but maneuvered on his knees and I followed knowing Mother would make some comment about the reddish dirt stains on my pants.

"Just watch me and pick the cucumbers the way I pick mine," he said, pulling the first one from the vine. It looked about six inches long and was primarily a darkish green in color. "We won't be eating any of these tonight."

"That doesn't look too hard," I said, pulling a thick one and putting it in the bucket that rested between us. "Mr. Ross, I want you to shoot straight with me. It's important that I get an honest answer."

"I'll do my best," he said, moving on his knees down the row, continuing to pull the green fruit. "I don't want to be responsible for misleading you."

"How long have you known my parents?"

"I've known your mother since she was a teenager and I knew your father's father."

"Wow! That's a long time! How long have you known them since they've been married?"

"My guess is that your parents have been in their home for about twelve years, so I guess I really got to know them well when we became neighbors. They've been very kind to me."

"Okay, so what is your impression of them?" I asked. "What kind of people are they?"

"You get right to the point don't you, Braxton?" Mr. Ross said, stopping in the middle of the row and letting out a breath I didn't know he had been holding. He had a concerned look in his eyes when he asked, "Where is this line of questions leading us?"

"I don't know!" I said, looking at the rich soil packed around the rows of plants. "I guess I want to know if they're good people. I know what I think but I need to hear what you think."

Mr. Ross pushed himself from his kneeling position and stood. He looked at me then extended his hand and pulled me to a standing position. There was a period of silence before he spoke, "Are you asking me if I think they're good people or if others think they're good people?"

"Both."

"Come over here with me," he said, walking to his back steps. He sat and patted the steps, indicating I was to sit beside him. "I don't know why you're asking me this but I can only answer for myself. I won't pretend to answer for anyone else. Can you live with that?"

"Yes, sir." I braced myself for the worse if it came.

"Your parents are good people, Braxton. Your dad, prior to his illness, was a hard-working man. He's never been anything other than who he is. I found him to be direct, honest, and, like myself, a man of few words. Now if you wanted his opinion on something, you better be darn sure you wanted the truth because that's what you'd get. There is no hypocrisy in your father."

"What about bad habits?" I asked, hoping not to hear a confirmation of Mr. Byrd.

"You would know that better than I," Mr. Ross said with a quizzical look. "No man is perfect, no matter who he is. He smokes and some people think that's bad. Personally, I don't."

"And my mother?" I asked, wishing he would be a little more specific.

"Your mother has had a hard life beginning when her dad lost everything. She's tough and has never let any obstacle take her down. Most women would've given up long ago," he said, stopping to remove his hat and scratching the top of his bald head. "Virginia has more or less lived in the shadow of her sister, Josephine, and I know that's impacted her life. But she's been a good wife to your daddy and she's been faithful to him during his long period of sickness."

Mr. Ross stopped and turned to look at me. He continued, putting his left arm around my shoulder, "Braxton, your mother is beautiful, and smart, and talented, and loves you and Anne very much. I think she has been a good mother to y'all. She is extremely lucky to have you as her son. I hope you realize this. You are a good boy, Braxton. Everyone knows that."

"Mr. Ross, somebody told me my mother was a drunk and everyone knew it? Is that true?"

I caught Mr. Ross totally off guard. He looked at me with a res-olute expression in his eyes. His pink face told me that I had pricked something within him; I just didn't know what. I waited and he said nothing. There was a period of awkward silence between us broken only by the distant barking of a dog and the passing of cars. Finally, he cleared his throat and spoke again, "Yes and No!" he said. "Some people think your mother drinks too much and I have seen an increased amount of drinking in the last year. One reason is because she gets together with my brother, Jack, and he encourages her to drink. Jack does nothing but drink these days. That does concern me and I've talked to Jack about this many times."

"Would you say my mother is an alcoholic?"

"No, I wouldn't. Your mother is under an enormous amount of stress and most anyone in her situation is going to find an outlet and maybe drinking is hers."

"I see," I said, thankful to hear what Mr. Ross thought.

"Braxton," he squeezed my shoulder with his massive hand, con-tinuing in a determined voice, "I want you to remember what I'm getting ready to say to you. It is always easy to kick someone when they're down. Some people thrive on this and they're the ones who are pathetic and in need of help. You and Anne have as good a her-itage as anyone in this town or in this state as far as that matters. Your mother and father are not prosperous people but they are good peo-ple and they come from good people. You have a solid background and you can be very proud of your lineage. Don't forget who you are because you have no reason to feel less than anyone."

"Thank you, Mr. Ross," I said, smiling. "I won't forget; I promise you that."

"Now give our conversation some thought. Come back tomor-row if you have any more questions about this foolishness that some-one has been feeding you. I need to finish picking these cucumbers."

"I'll see you tomorrow," I said, shaking his hand. I walked back home with tears forming in my eyes. I respected Mr. Ross and I would remember what he said but it didn't dispel the accusations of Mr. Byrd.

I went to bed before 10:00 and like so many other nights, I lay there listening to *Our Best To You*. Mr. Ross had comforted me in a way no other man but my father could have and he gave me the reassurance that a young boy needs to hear from someone other than his mother. I was almost asleep when Mother came to my bedroom door and told me that David Byrd was on the phone. Holy Mackerel!!! I jumped out of bed, slipped on the oval throw rug, hit my elbow on the edge of my door, and knocked a picture frame off the hall wall on my way to the telephone table. I grabbed the receiver off the top of the table. "Hello, Byrd," I said, taking quick breaths. "Is that really you?"

"Braxton, it's me," Byrd murmured.

"Where are you, Byrd?"

"I can't talk long," he said, faster than he usually talked. "Listen, I'm in a pay phone not far from our cottage. What is going on back there between you and my father?"

"News travels fast. How did you find out about that?"

"My Aunt Greta called my mother. I picked up the upstairs phone and I heard Mother talking to her. All I got were bits and pieces." He continued to talk in a fast pace like someone was after him. "Something about you not working for him and that we're not to see each other. Is that true?"

"Damn right," I whispered, not wanting to upset Mother again. "Your dad scared the hell out of me today. I swear, I thought he'd lost it or had gone crazy. I've never seen anything like it."

"Braxton, listen to me." I heard him take a deep breath and then he continued, "I don't know when I'm coming back home. My father's putting a lot of pressure on me and Mother is joining his side. She doesn't normally pay any attention to him but this time she's listening. Now they're talking about sending me to summer camp in addition to shipping me off to prep school. I don't know what the fuck is going on, Braxton." He let out a deep sigh, "But the reason I called was to tell you to be careful, real careful." He paused.

"I didn't like the tone of my Aunt Greta's voice. She thinks my dad is perfect and she kept telling Mother that Oscar said, 'she'd better damn well do what he said.' Braxton, promise me you won't try to screw around with my dad." I could hear a siren bleating from Byrd's end and noises like a lot of people talking.

"Why not?" I answered. "Give me one good reason. You don't know what he did and said to me in his office."

"First, I've got a good idea and secondly, I don't want you to get hurt." Byrd's voice had an air of excitement. "My dad can be dangerous when he's upset. Remember that. He can be very *dangerous*."

"Can I call you there?"

"*No!* Not yet, at least. Let me figure things out here first."

"Are you okay?" I said in anger. "Did he hurt you?"

"Not really. Not yet anyway," Byrd continued. "Listen, I've got to go. I'll call tomorrow night if I can get out." After Byrd hung up, I stood in the hall thankful that he was okay and wondering what my next plan of action should be. No solution came immediately and I returned to bed. *At least he's okay,* I thought; maybe God is in control.

Sunday morning after breakfast I told Mother about my talk with David Byrd. She told me that she had given serious thought to the conversation we'd had yesterday afternoon and that she wanted to talk with Jason, Matt, Thad, and me between three and four o'clock this afternoon if it was convenient with everyone. In light of Byrd's call to me last evening, she thought the sooner we all talked, the better things would be for all of us. Mother didn't believe Oscar Byrd was through and she didn't want us to be caught off guard or hurt in any way. I called Jason immediately and told him when to be at my house and not to be a second late. He promised without fail to be here by 3:00. I planned to talk with Thad and Matt at Sunday school.

Anne had stayed another night with my grandmother and was not going to Sunday school and church with me. No one could keep me away from Sunday school today. I had two important reasons for going: to hear Captain Chuck again and to tell Thad and Matt about Mother's request to meet with us. It didn't bother me at the time that neither of these were justifiable reasons for my attending. I left home a little after nine o'clock and much too early. I had a lot of time to kill so I decided to stop and get a Coke and look through the Sunday *News and Observer,* the state newspaper from Raleigh, to see if there was anything about a foiled robbery and shooting at Taps. I used my offering money to buy the paper. The thought that God would forgive me for my misuse of money ran across my mind and lessened any guilt I might have. I really didn't feel guilty.

I sat in the church parking lot for at least thirty minutes drinking my Coke and skimming the paper, trying to find an article about the activity at Taps. There was nothing in the opening section and nothing in the metro section. I turned to the obituary page but found no mention of any white male in Wilson dying from a gun-related accident. I took that as good news but I hoped the two black men who had caused all the problems would be caught.

I was the first person in the classroom. I sat looking at the bare walls and more peeling paint. The room was in pretty bad shape but the church was getting ready to build a new Sunday school building so I figured no money would be spent painting and fixing-up these old rooms. That was what I heard my Aunt Eva tell my mother and Aunt Josephine. She ought to know since she was on one of the main committees. As I sat there, I wondered what Captain Chuck would say to us today. I supposed he would do less cursing since Dwight Cummings had challenged him. The next person to arrive was Robert Cornwall, a rising senior and athlete who was overly impressed with himself. One on one he wasn't so bad but with his buddies, he could be obnoxious. Normally, he didn't speak to us non-athletic juniors, but today he didn't have a choice.

"Hey Braxton, looking cool today, my man," he said in his typical jock style.

"Hello Robert," I said, trying to be as friendly as possible without overdoing it. "What have you been up to since school ended?"

"Screwing the new cheerleaders," he said, laughing. He hesitated. "It's a joke, Braxton."

"Ha, ha, ha," I forced myself to laugh. "How many are there?" Before he could answer, another member of our class entered. "It's a joke, Robert."

"What's so funny?" asked Thad, walking into the room.

"Thad, how in the heck are you?" greeted Robert. "Come and sit by me and let's talk about August football practice." Since Robert was partial to jocks, Thad fitted right in with Robert's little elite circle of those deemed by him to be good enough to be asked to sit with him. Then I remembered what Mr. Ross had told me and I smiled.

"Thanks Rob, but I need to talk to my buddy, Braxton, here. No offense intended," said Thad. Robert blushed and his shoulders fell forward as if to say 'I can't believe you turned down my offer to sit next to me, you inferior little junior.' "Braxton, what's going down?"

"We need to be at my house today at three o'clock," I said. "Mother needs to talk to the four of us."

"Are things worse?"

"Sort of. I'll explain, but not in here."

"Why don't we go outside?" Thad asked, obviously anxious to know what brought about the need for a meeting.

"Not yet. Wait until Matt gets here," I said. "Oh! Byrd called me last night!"

"*What?* From where?" Thad moved to the edge of his seat.

"Hey guys, let's don't be so secretive. Let your buddy, Robert, in on the news."

"Butt out, Robert!" I said, surprising myself. "This is private stuff."

"Come on, guys," begged Robert. "You know you can trust me. I promise."

"No way! This is *real* personal," said Thad.

"Hey Thad, we need to stick together here," said Robert, getting excited. "We're on the same team."

"Robert!" I said, speaking with surprised confidence. "This involves me, too, and I'm not on your team. In fact, you hardly even speak to me when I see you at school and I don't really know you. Can't you take a hint?" (Surprisingly, Robert and I were fraternity brothers in college and I introduced him to his future wife.)

"Okay, okay," said Robert, backing off. "I get the picture, Braxton."

By this time, other boys had come in and taken their seat. Each seemed to be listening intently to the conversation between the two of us. There was still no Matt. At 9:50 A.M., ten minutes after Sunday school was supposed to start, our assistant minister, Mr. Dawson, stuck his head in to tell us that Captain Chuck would not be teaching us today.

"What?" we said in unison, obviously disappointed.

"I'm sorry, boys," said Mr. Dawson. "Due to circumstances beyond his control, Chuck cannot be with you today. Miss Cathy Spearman will be in to teach you." As soon as Mr. Dawson disappeared, all of us rose together and walked out. Listening to Captain Chuck was one thing, but listening to Cathy whine while she tried to maintain discipline was another. I felt sorry for her but I just wasn't in the mood today to see a grown woman cry because a junior in high school refused to quit leaning in his chair against the wall.

Walking down the stairs, Thad and I ran into Matt taking two steps at a time, trying not to be too late. When he saw us, he just kept going. As soon as he realized who we were, he turned and said, "Where are you two going?"

"No Sunday school today. Captain Chuck isn't here," said Thad.

"Let's go to my car and talk," I said. "Oh, by the way, all of us are meeting with my mother at three o'clock today. You need to be there on time. Mother wants to talk to all of us about what's been happening with Mr. Byrd."

"You told her about everything that happened that night?" Matt asked as if he had been caught with his pants down.

"Only about the things that happened at Byrd's house," I said. "I had to tell her because I needed some advice. A lot more has happened since Friday night. When we get to my car, I'll fill both of you in on all the details."

The three of us walked at a fast pace to the church parking lot and got into my car. We decided to leave the church parking lot. That way we could talk without having to explain why we weren't in Sunday school and church. We rode to the Creamery. Since it was closed on Sunday morning, we had the whole parking lot to ourselves. I parked in my favorite spot and cut off the engine. I entertained Thad and Matt for the next hour by carefully telling them everything that had happened from the time I met the strange woman at Byrd's house to my visit with Mr. Byrd in his office. When

I had finished, neither Thad nor Matt said anything. Both were silent for a long time. Finally, after what seemed like an eternity, Thad said, "Holy Jesus! I can't believe Byrd's dad! He sounds like he's gone off his rocker."

Matt sighed and was silent a moment longer and then spoke, "I don't care about that asshole, Mr. Byrd, but I am concerned about Byrd. Did he say when he was coming home?"

"No," I said. "He just said he might try to call me tonight."

"Let's hear what Mrs. Haywood has to say to us before we do anything else," said Thad.

"I agree," responded Matt. "None of this sounds good."

"Okay, be at my house at 3:00 today," I said, turning the ignition and driving back to the church parking lot. The church service was just ending when I pulled in the lot behind the sanctuary. "This was good timing," I said. "And about the first thing that's worked for me this week."

Thad and Matt got out of the car. I waved and pulled out of the lot and drove home. Mother was in Daddy's room when I walked into the house. She called to me when I passed his open door saying, "Braxton, come in. Your dad wants to speak to you."

"Oh, great!" I whispered under my breath. "I wonder what he wants." I walked into his room and to my surprise he was sitting up in his chair smoking a cigarette. "Hello, Daddy. Do you want me to do something for you?"

"No," he said, looking at me with a smile.

"Mother said you wanted to see me," I said, avoiding eye contact.

"How was church today?" he asked, attempting to lean forward and stay upright.

"Oh, about the same—a lot of singing and a good sermon."

"I miss being able to attend Sunday services with you and Anne," he said. "I want you to always go to church, Braxton. That's a good foundation for your future."

"Yes, sir," I responded, still wondering why he wanted to see me. He had not taken the time to talk with me in weeks and I was confused by his sudden niceness. Mother stood behind him smiling.

"Virginia, leave Braxton and me alone for a minute," my father requested.

"I'll be in the kitchen preparing lunch if you should need me," Mother said.

"Braxton, your mother said Mr. Byrd was reluctant to give you my medicine yesterday. Is that true?"

"Yes, sir," I answered politely. "I asked Mother not to tell you that."

"She told me because I asked her why the medicine had been delayed."

"Mr. Byrd did eventually give it to me."

"He won't mess with you again. I called him this morning and told him if there was a problem with my payment, to call me, and not bother you with it."

"Daddy, that's okay." I couldn't believe Mother had told him after I asked her not to.

"The hell it is! You have enough on you without some S.O.B. hounding you for something that's not your responsibility." The veins in his neck became pronounced and his face became flushed, turning a purplish red. I think he was embarrassed. "I'm sorry he did that to you, Braxton. It's not your fault."

"Yes, sir," I hesitated. "Daddy, where was Mr. Byrd when you talked with him?"

"He said that I was lucky to get him because he had just returned from Morehead."

"Did he say if Byrd returned with him?"

"No, but he did tell me what a fine son I have and that he was glad that you and David were such good friends."

"Did he say anything else?"

"Yes. He said that he was sorry that you'd decided not to work for him this summer. Why did you decide to stop before you even got started?"

"He did?" I hesitated. "Well, I thought I could make more money working somewhere else."

I didn't think my daddy would buy that one but I didn't have an answer and that was the only thing I could think of.

"I'm glad that you, at least, had something to fall back on," my daddy said smiling. "Your mother said that you were going to talk to Mr. James Tolson about a job at Exeter Tobacco Company."

"She did?" I said, coughing. "Mother is full of surprises today."

"Braxton, if you need me to talk with James, I'll be happy to," said Daddy. "However, I don't think you really need me. You can get a job there on your own."

"Thank you," I said. "I'll let you know if I need your help." He was ahead of me on this one and I realized Mother had run interference for me so I wouldn't get in trouble with my father.

"I'm getting very tired now," he said, resting his head against the back of the rocker. "I've enjoyed our visit, Braxton." He closed his eyes for a moment and then opened them again.

"I have too, Daddy," I said, turning and walking toward the door.

"Braxton, one more thing."

"Yes, sir?"

"I'm very proud of you. You're a lot like my own dad and that's a good thing."

"Thank you," I answered, smiling proudly. Mr. Ross did tell me I had a fine heritage. The conversation I had with my dad boosted my confidence, at least for the moment. It had been a long, long time since he had said anything kind to me. I didn't know it then, but it would also be one of the last times.

Chapter 31
BLOOD BROTHERS

IT WAS A lazy Sunday afternoon, the sixteenth of June, and beautiful. There wasn't a cloud in the azure sky. Like the preceding fifteen days, today was dry and steamy and hot—a muggy, North Carolina hot where temperatures hovered between ninety-five and one hundred degrees, and the foliage in our town fought hard to keep from wilting, and even the heartiest of birds sought refuge under lawn sprinklers and in the shallow water of birdbaths when they could be found. It was the kind of day where sweat came and stayed like an unwanted visitor and the host had no other choice but to be tolerant. It was the kind of a day when the only ice delivery truck in our town had to make multiple trips to the ice plant across the railroad tracks to keep up with the demand for the big ice blocks it pedaled. It had already taken one unaccustomed run down our street before one o'clock with the promise of a second return by six o'clock.

Wilson needed rain and needed rain badly. There was none forecast for the immediate future according to Joe Hayes, our local weatherman, operating from his backyard. Some lawns on Kincaid Avenue, including our own, had already turned brown and the sun much like an unattended hot iron left too long on a shirt had scorched a few too many. There was talk of a possible water shortage and that meant water rationing and some of the locals had begun to brag of ways to beat the system.

When our grandfather clock chimed three, Thad, Matt, Jason, and I were sitting around the table on our back porch shooting the breeze and waiting for Mother to join us. Only Byrd was absent. On

342 • The Noise Upstairs

the table was one plate of homemade chocolate chip cookies accompanied by a pitcher of homemade lemonade and a pitcher of sweet iced tea. Crushed ice floated in each pitcher, cooling the contents, and moisture clung to the outside of both. My yellow window box fan sat in the corner kicking out a semblance of a breeze, entertaining us with a knocking rhythm all of its own.

"You need to oil that, Braxton, if you want it to stay alive," said Thad, jabbing me in the side to make me laugh.

"I know," I said. "Like other things around here, I just haven't gotten 'round to it. I kind of like the noise it makes. It helps me fall asleep at night. And on these nights, I need all the help I can get." I poured myself a glass of tea making certain some of the crushed ice got into the glass. This took practice and I hadn't quite mastered it. It was a good feeling whenever I could be with my friends, but the circumstances of late, like the shackles on a prisoner, prevented me from being able to relax and enjoy anything, not even my closest buddies.

"I make my own noise," said Jason. "It only takes two hands and it's a guaranteed satisfaction every night. I mean every *single* night."

"Okay, Jason," I said. "Please remember your voice travels further than you think." Jason prided himself on his smooth, sexy baritone voice without the nasal twang so prevalent in eastern North Carolina. He could easily have a future in radio if he would clean up his act.

"Lighten up, Braxton," said Jason. "You're too damn uptight." He was right and I thought he was too laid back, considering the circumstance we had been through during the last week.

"How is your dad?" Matt changed the subject quickly, almost like he was trying to prevent a verbal war from beginning. "You haven't said much about him lately." Before I answered, I watched Matt wedge a lemon slice between his gum and upper lip and then press against it to enjoy the flavor. He, too, seemed relaxed and almost carefree. All of them did, but not me.

"Actually, he's having a good day today," I said. I appreciated Matt thinking of him. "I don't know what this sudden upswing means because he's been going down hill fast up until today."

"That's a bummer, but I'm glad he's having at least one decent day," said Matt, putting his now shriveled lemon wedge on his plate. The used lemon looked the way I felt—all chewed up and spit out to dry. I knew I was too uptight but I didn't know how to relax.

"Me, too," said Thad, putting a stick of Juicy Fruit gum in his mouth.

"Got any more?" asked Jason.

"Sorry, that's my last piece." Thad grinned and poured himself another glass of tea.

"Damn, Thad, you go through that stuff like Sherman went through Atlanta," said Jason. "Give me one little piece, just one little piece."

"You'll have to go somewhere else for that!" said Thad. We laughed.

"Chalk one up for you, Thaddeus," said Jason. "You are indeed sharp today." He gave Thad the middle finger.

"I'll pretend I didn't see that, Jason," Thad said good-naturedly. "By the way, are any of you going to M.Y.F. tonight? I heard we're having a watermelon party at Mary Lu Duncan's afterwards."

"I may," said Matt. "Depends on whether my dad needs me to help him get ready for tomorrow. His work load has picked up." I envied the relationship that Matt had with his father. They'd always been close and done a lot of things together. They shared an unspoken respect for each other. Unlike the rest of our fathers, I don't ever recall Mr. Beatty speaking harshly to Matt in my presence. Of course, he was a no nonsense kind of man and Matt did what his dad told him to do. I thought Matt was lucky to have a dad who loved him that much.

Mr. Beatty owned and operated one of the most successful florists in Wilson. And having recently added gardening supplies as well as a large section of indoor/outdoor plants, his business volume had increased another ten percent. Matt willingly helped his dad on weekends with some of the grunt work—stacking, cleaning, and unloading supplies. Matt swore that the exercise he got from lifting bags of fertilizer and bales of straw was as good as lifting barbells. He vowed that this regimen kept him in shape. Just by accident, I was one of only a few who knew he measured his biceps with a tape measure at least once a week. At any rate, his upper arm muscles were a lot larger than mine, and the girls loved to feel them when he would relax enough to let them. And that wasn't very often. Too bad he was terribly shy around girls.

"I might go. It depends on how this meeting with Mother goes and whether she has anything she wants me to do. I know I'll have to pick Anne up at my grandmother's."

"I think I'll go with or without you guys," Thad said. "Jason, want to join me?" Thad knew Jason's answer before he sent out the invitation. He knew Jason was not into church but that was Thad making certain Jason didn't get left out. Jason had begun to pull away from us when it came to our doing things with anyone outside the five of us. He hadn't always been this way. I didn't know whether finding the letter in his mother's closet had any bearing on his behavior or not. The "fun-loving" Jason had begun to drift. He was definitely more withdrawn than he had been before finding out that he was born illegitimately. Finding out that he was a *bastard* had done a real number on him. I feared for him in the sense that I thought he might do something really stupid.

"Go to Mary Lou's? Hell, Thad, she's a pig. No thanks, old buddy," Jason said, looking at his watch. "Besides, I've got a hot date tonight and better things to eat than watermelon."

"I just bet you do," I wanted to tease him but not make him mad. "Want to tell us who Prince Charming's Cinderella is tonight or is it one of the stepsisters?"

"Braxton, you know and no, I don't!" Jason said. He wasn't amused at my attempt at humor. No one seemed to be. "When's your mom going to show up?"

"Here I come, Jason," Mother said, stepping onto the back porch. "Hello boys. I'm sorry you had to wait but I had to take care of some other things first." Mother was dressed in one of her three Sunday afternoon outfits—a one-piece cotton dress that was dark blue in color with white embroidery around the collar and two pockets. She wore some of her favorite costume jewelry, a strand of red pearls and matching triangular shaped, red earbobs. She had darkened her eyebrows with a black eyebrow pencil and she wore her dark red lipstick that accentuated her thin lips. She looked stunning, resonating beauty. For a brief moment, I was reminded once again of the obvious—where my sister, Anne, got her good looks.

"Hey, Mrs. Haywood," Jason said. Slightly embarrassed and with blushing cheeks, he stood immediately. "I didn't mean for you to hear that!" My mother smiled. She knew Jason well.

"Hello Mrs. Haywood," said Matt and Thad in unison, and we all stood as a sign of respect when Mother moved toward the table where we now sat.

"Please sit down." Mother emphasized her request by a slight movement of her left hand. "Braxton, would you get me a chair from the kitchen?"

"I'll get it for you." Thad jumped up and moved quickly toward the door. "I'm closer than he is."

"Thank you, Thad," said Mother. "You are so polite, and I do like that in a young man."

"Please sit in my seat," said Jason. He pulled his chair out for Mother not wanting to be outdone by Thad. "I insist, Mrs. Haywood." Mother sat. She patted the beads of sweat on her forehead with a piece of Kleenex, trying not to wipe off the cold cream that she had applied.

"My goodness, you boys have your best foot forward today," said Mother with a light laugh. "Thank you, Jason."

"Braxton told us that Mr. Haywood was feeling better today," Thad said, returning with the kitchen chair and scooting in between Matt and me. "That's good news!"

"It certainly is." Mother reached into her pocket and pulled out her book of matches with Piggily Wiggily stamped on the front and a newly opened pack of filter king Kools. She placed both on the table, then picked up the pack and took one cigarette out. "It's good to see you boys. I just wish it could be under better circumstances." Mother put the cigarette in her mouth and reached for the matchbook.

"Allow me." Jason reached for the book and pulled a match out.

"Why, thank you, Jason. You're a dear," said Mother, leaning forward as Jason lit her cigarette. She threw her head back as she drew her first puff, and then blew the smoke into the air. "It certainly does feel good to sit down for a minute even if it does feel like we're sitting in a steam bath."

"May I have one?" asked Jason. He caught the rest of us off guard with his request but not Mother. I looked at Thad whose mouth had dropped open and then Matt who had one of his "I can't believe you asked that" kind of grins on his face. It didn't surprise me. At times, Jason was predictable and then, at other times, he was totally unpredictable. This was one of those times.

"Normally I would say no, but I guess it's all right," my mother said. "Do your parents allow you to smoke, Jason?"

"No, ma'am, but I do all the time anyway. Mother knows, but pretends she doesn't," said Jason. He took one Kool and packed it on the back of his left hand. "I don't think my dad cares one way or the other. We don't talk about much of anything these days."

"You don't have to pack filtered cigarettes," I said, deliberately trying to get a rise from him. I smiled and took another sip of iced tea. I wanted to make him laugh but I think he thought I was taking a dig at him. In a way I felt sorry for Jason and I wished he could accept being adopted.

"I know that," said Jason. He lit his Kool and blew several smoke rings my way. "Won't you have one, Braxton?" My mother looked at Jason, then me, then back at Jason, and then the others. Everyone had set his glass on the table and all eyes were on Jason.

"Yes, Braxton, won't you have one?" asked my mother. I knew she was going along with Jason but the look on her face showed some concern that I might have taken up the habit so prevalent among teens in our town, the world's largest bright leaf tobacco market.

"You and Jason both know I don't smoke," I said and then I kicked him under the table, forcing him to inhale too much smoke. He immediately gasped and blew the smoke out. Then he began to cough, losing the macho image he was trying so hard to portray. We laughed again.

"Since when, Braxton?" asked Jason. He grinned at me with his "I'll get you for that" expression then he shot me the bird. Thank goodness, Mother didn't see him.

"Jason, you know Braxton doesn't smoke!" said Matt, again coming to my rescue even if was a white lie. "Quit ribbing him."

"I know you boys don't have all afternoon to sit around here and tease each other," Mother said. "Thank you for coming on such short notice. I'll get right to the point. I asked Braxton to invite you over because it appears y'all have backed yourselves into a hornet's nest. I understand the "King Hornet" is unreasonably mad and wants to sting you."

"That's a great metaphor, Mrs. Haywood," said Jason. Jason was actually very smart but didn't want other people to think he was. His understanding of the metaphor used by Mother escaped Thad and me.

"Thank you, Jason. Before I begin, do any of you have any pressing concerns regarding what has happened since you walked in on Mr. Byrd and Charles?"

"Mrs. Haywood, it has been very scary and mind boggling to me," said Matt. "I've had a hard time dealing with this whole thing, especially when I'm in bed at night. Just thinking about it makes it difficult to sleep some nights. And I dream about it—I mean crazy dreams."

"I agree with the scary part," said Thad. "I'm concerned about Mr. Byrd's threatening us and if he will really go through with it. If he is, then when is he? The waiting is tough."

"I really worry about Byrd and what his father might do to him," I said.

"I don't think any of us know what to do," said Matt. "Or do we do anything? I was glad when Braxton said you wanted to talk with us."

"What about it, Jason?" asked Mother. "Do you have any concerns?" Mother knew Jason and she knew he had a hard time opening up in a frank discussion without some encouragement.

"I honestly don't know what to think, Mrs. Haywood," Jason said. "Actually, I've tried not to think about it. I figured since Mr. Byrd and my father are social friends that maybe Mr. Byrd is only bluffing me."

"Maybe, but I kind of doubt it. I've known Oscar Byrd since high school and to you boys that equates to a long time." Mother reached for another cigarette and Jason obliged by lighting it for her. He, too, took another but this time without asking. Smoke hovered over the table.

"What should we do?" asked Matt. "Can you give us any direction?"

"Yes. I think we all need some. I know I do!" said Thad. "But we need to stick together on this."

"Very wise, Thad. All right. Now listen carefully to what I'm getting ready to say to you. This is not a lecture but some guidance from Braxton's mother who loves each of you."

We became quiet and leaned toward my mother, anticipating what she was going to say. Jason put his cigarette in the ashtray stubbing out the tip with his thumb. Mother continued to smoke. Matt and Thad rested their chins on the palms of their hands while their elbows pushed hard against the table. I sat erect, repeatedly watching my mother and then my friends like I was observing an intense badminton game. We forgot how miserable the heat had made us feel. We were totally captivated by the thought of what my mother was about to say to us.

"I think it's important for you to have the opportunity to air your concerns to an adult if you want to. I don't know whether you have confided in your parents or not. Braxton doesn't think so and since I'm fairly familiar with the situation and all of you are like my own sons, I'll be your listening ear and give you guidance since you have indicated that's what you want."

"I agree with that. Yes, please continue, Mrs. Haywood," said Jason. His response surprised me. He tried so hard sometimes to make us think he had it all together. Now he wasn't. "My life is screwed up enough as it is and I certainly need someone to help me through this. It sure as hell won't be my dad." There was silence and I grimaced. "Sorry, I didn't mean to curse."

"Well, first of all, I don't want any of you to think I'm trying to take the place of your mother and father. That's not fair to them. If you want to, we can get all of us together and talk about it."

"No, I don't want to do that," said Thad. "I don't think I could talk to my parents about this; it's too heavy. I don't think they could deal with it."

"I could talk to my dad, but not Mother," said Matt. "I would just as soon leave them out at this time." I knew I couldn't talk to my dad and even if he weren't sick, I couldn't talk with him.

"Okay," said Mother. "Secondly, I plan to meet with Oscar Byrd on Tuesday night." She paused and then continued. "Braxton doesn't know anything about this and I know he won't approve." Mother stopped and looked at me, waiting for my response.

"You got that right, Mother. I don't approve. I think it will only make matters worse!" I tried to hide my anger from my friends but I thought my mother had lost her mind. "I think you're playing right into his hands. He's already told each of us not to talk about this to anyone."

"He did threaten us, Mrs. Haywood," said Matt.

"Each of you will have to trust me if you want me to help you," said my mother. "My reason for visiting him relates only to your visit in his office, Braxton. I plan to concentrate solely on your daddy's medicine and the fact that he fired you before he even gave you a chance. Any good mother or father would do this. And remember, I've known Oscar, I mean Mr. Byrd for a long time."

"Your mother's right," said Thad. "It sounds like a good idea to me."

"What do we do in the meantime?" said Jason. "We're kind of just sitting here in limbo."

"Yes, you are," Mother said. "And that's an uncomfortable feeling, but that's where you'll be for awhile."

"Great!" I said. "Just great!" I had a bad habit of showing my impatience. It was kicking in again.

"Cool it, Braxton," said Jason. "Listen and don't *react* so damn much!" He was right again.

"You boys walked in on something that you were never intended to see. Mr. Byrd could get into a lot of trouble. He could lose his family, he could go to jail, and his reputation would be destroyed. He knows this and he is *scared*. And he should be!" said Mother. "Right now he doesn't know what any of you are going to do. His threatening you is his way of trying to frighten you so that you will not do anything—that's the only self-protection he has."

"He's doing a good job," said Thad.

"Damn right!" said Jason. Then he apologized to my mother for having "foot in mouth" disease.

"Are you going to the police?" I asked.

"Not now! I may later."

"Why?" I asked.

"Because we are all protecting a criminal and a very sick, pathetic, little man," my mother said. "Mr. Byrd's reaction to you is typical and it's a sign of weakness. You are all so young, but what he has done is unspeakable and it is immoral, and whether he is punished or not is in your hands."

"Holy Shit!" exclaimed Jason. "Oh, sorry, Mrs. Haywood. We're in deep, guys. We're in real deep."

"Yes, you are," Mother answered. "That's why, for the moment, you don't *do* anything and you don't *say* anything to anyone. Is that clear?"

"Yes ma'am," we said at the same time. Just saying "yes" to my mother was a relief in itself. I just hoped my mother was right. She was now our Captain and we were no longer floundering out here by ourselves. Knowing that she was at the helm directing our course of action gave comfort to all of us.

"Don't go near his store and don't call his house looking for Byrd. That means you, too, Braxton," said Mother. "The best thing is for all of you to put distance between yourselves and him." We looked at each other and nodded in agreement.

"Will he hurt Byrd?" asked Matt. "I'm really concerned about him."

"I don't know the answer to your question," said Mother. "Right now, Oscar will use Byrd as leverage to get you to do what he wants. I, too, feel sorry for Byrd. He is his daddy's pawn and until I look him in the face, I don't know how far Oscar Byrd is going to carry this. One thing is for certain though," Mother hesitated then emphasized her next point, "I will not let him hurt any of you!"

"But Byrd is one of us; he's number five. It's not the same when he's not around," said Thad, his face etched in desperation.

"Exactly, and the fact that you are so close to Byrd is a problem for his father," Mother said. "If Mr. Byrd allows you to see his son then the problem stays current. Byrd is caught in the middle. You *must* not push Mr. Byrd too far. If you do, then he will definitely overreact."

Mother sat quietly, her eyes haunted by an inner pain that I had never seen before. "And now, if there are no more questions, I'll leave you boys." Mother stood. She smiled but her face carried a sad look. I knew then that she had taken our pain upon herself. That was so unfair to her but I believed she was doing what any good mother would do to protect her children.

We all stood and thanked Mother for her willingness to help us. I was so proud of my mother. The fact that my friends sought her advice was a compliment to her. She exited and for a moment, the four of us just looked at each other. Our fear had been heightened and we realized that we were the holders of a powerful secret. We had the power to destroy another human being and with him, his entire family and reputation. We were, also, very aware that the entire town of Wilson would be affected if we chose to share our secret.

We had agreed before to stand united in our decisions. Today would be no different. Standing together on my porch on that muggy, late Sunday afternoon in June, Jason Parker took his Swiss Army knife out of his Bermuda short's pocket, opened it up, and made a hair line cut at the head of his palm. My heart pounded hard and I felt a momentary nauseousness as I watched him cut himself and then extend the invitation to us. Like a scene from a buccaneer movie, each of us let him cut our palms in the exact same place and then we each pressed our palm against Jason's, our blood mixing with his. In turn, we pressed against Matt's palm, and then, Thad's palm, and then mine until we were certain that we had sealed this secret as blood brothers. No matter what Mother decided, we decided that afternoon it would be best not to tell. We did not do this to preserve ourselves; we did it in hopes of saving Byrd.

No one went to M.Y.F. that night. Jason did go on his hot date with Sadie Brock. As far as I knew, he was still banging her and still unworried about fathering a child or catching a venereal disease. He told me Sadie had a friend for me and I told him, maybe later. I waited for Byrd's phone call but it never came. He did say he would try to call me and that was the best anyone could ask for. I knew Byrd well enough to know if he could call, he would. What I didn't know at the time was that his father had found out about his Saturday night call to me and had beaten him badly with his belt and fists for disobeying him. I learned much later that beating David had become almost a daily ritual that Mr. Byrd enjoyed as much as having sex with his youngest son, Charles.

Chapter 32
AN ANONYMOUS PHONE CALL

I LAY STILL for a moment. It was six-thirty on another hot June morning. Today was Monday, the seventeenth, and my first visitor was the bright sun shining its brilliant rays through my bedroom windows. This was the day I was supposed to start my job with Mr. Byrd. I had looked forward to working at his West Nash Street Pharmacy and getting to know Mr. Jerningan better. I had looked forward to seeing a lot of the high school crowd when they came in to get their shakes and Cokes. I had accepted the fact that I would not be working at the drugstore, but I definitely resented having to lose a month's salary.

At breakfast, I slouched at the table on the back porch picking at my Kellogg's cornflakes. Lily was already in the kitchen preparing for her daily routine. I looked outside and cursed the heat that had already taken hold of the day. It was too bright to be this early and too hot to be going into the third week of the summer. I took my unfinished breakfast into the kitchen and tried to get rid of it before I was spotted. I was caught.

"You didn't finish your cornflakes," Lily said. "Aren't you at all hungry or do you wants Lily to fix you a real breakfast."

"I'm just not hungry," I said. "Thank you anyway."

"Is you sick?" said Lily. She wanted to pry and then she reached over and felt the back of my neck. "You don't have no fever. You're worried, aren't you?"

"You have *that* right," I said. "I'm worried about a lot of things plus I'm broke and thanks to Oscar Byrd, I have no prospect of making any money—at least, not yet."

"I has some money saved up." Lily hugged me around the neck. "You can have some of mine."

"Thank you, Lily. I have a little saved." I lied, but I wasn't going to take her money when I knew she needed it worse than I. Lily was the sole provider for herself, her husband, and on occasions, she sent money to her mother. Her husband could not work presently, having sprained his back at the factory. A forklift carrying a hogshead backed into him, knocking him up against a stack of hogsheads and pinned him there.

There were not many women like Lily in the domestic workforce in our town. Lily was smart, a hard worker, and proud. She had an unbelievable spirit and rarely complained. Mother and Daddy were darn lucky to have Lily. Just how much longer my parents could afford to help pay her wages was another question. Before I left the kitchen, I promised I would take Lily to the Piggily Wiggily and the open-air market to buy some fresh fruit and vegetables.

In early afternoon I decided to would walk down to Rita's house to see if she needed help with the boys. I needed some of Rita's attention. I was disappointed to find no one at home. Her shades were pulled and her car was gone. Just my luck. The rest of the day was fairly uneventful. I kicked around the house, trying to look busy. I thought Bryd would call but I didn't hear from him. I wondered if he'd call again. Just another disappointment racked up.

Tuesday began much like Monday, hot and humid and no rain. I called Mr. Tolson, President of Exeter Tobacco Company and my daddy's boss, about the possibility of a summer job. According to his secretary, he had left on vacation for the remainder of the month. She, also, said they would not be hiring temporary help until July first. I didn't tell her I was the son of one of Exeter's tobacco buyers and that Mr. Tolson was one of my daddy's best friends. I didn't tell her that he came by the house at least twice a week and had done so ever since I was a little boy. If I was going to get this job, I wanted-ed to at least set up the interview on my own. I knew if Mr. Tolson had anywhere he could use me, he would. I knew if he didn't have a job for me, he would create one. I'd just have to be patient a little longer before I started a job. There were still two months available for work and maybe I'd make more money an hour at Exeter's tobacco processing plant.

Shortly after lunch on Tuesday, Aunt Eva dropped by to visit Mother and offer any help she might need for the afternoon. Lily and I had a wager with each other—would Aunt Eva find her way into our kitchen and would she sample anything she could get her fingers on. Yes, she did find her way, but today Aunt Eva was out of luck. There was no food out and available. Aunt Eva's habit of picking at food allowed us to keep our family expression for anyone who went into the kitchen after a meal with the sole purpose of pinching the leftovers. We would simply say, "All right, Aunt Eva!" This became an inside family joke, never used in front of her but used to tease others with a little sarcasm mixed in. No explanation was necessary.

Aunt Eva loved to tell Mother what was going on in Wilson, or in the family, or at church, or at the Salvation Army, or at the courthouse where she'd worked until her retirement. Actually, Aunt Eva had an important job. She was the clerk of court for the district court. Today, I overheard her tell Mother something that burned me up. She reported that Captain Chuck had been asked by the Administrative Board of the First United Methodist Church to step down as a Sunday school teacher. She told Mother that a Mrs. Elliot Cummings complained to the board about Chuck's cursing in Sunday school. That had to be Dwight Cumming's mother. That little piece of shit—a new boy in town and he'd already had one of the best things going for religion at our church removed. This was another gross unfairness. *What in the hell was going on around here? Why this summer of all times does the shit have to hit the fan?* I didn't let Aunt Eva know I heard her tell Mother about Captain Chuck. I didn't want to give her the satisfaction of saying to me, "I told you!" The rest of Tuesday was normal and uneventful *until* . . .

That same evening my sister, Anne; my cousin, Ingrid Thaxton; and I were on the front porch listening to the beginnings of a summer storm. The northern sky was darkening. A flickering light could be seen ripping the low hanging curtain of cumulus clouds followed by a low, rumbling sound like that of a big cannon being shot off in the distance. Tonight was a miracle night: not only was there the prospect of a long awaited rain, it was the first time in over a year that my daddy felt like leaving his bedroom. Daddy liked nothing better than to sit on the front porch during a fierce summer storm, especially the electrical kind. I can remember, as a little boy, my mother begging Daddy to come inside when the lightning popped like Fourth of July firecrackers around our house.

Tonight, Jackson Nichols, former manservant of my uncle, the now deceased Dr. Thaxton, carried Daddy to the chaise lounge on the north end of our porch. Jackson was a tall, dark skinned, educated Negro, as strong as a bull and as humble as a little boy standing in line waiting to get his baseball mitt autographed by the superstar, Peewee Reese. Having served as a medic in Korea, Jackson had had multiple experiences assisting and carrying men who weighed far more than my ninety-eight pound Daddy on and off the battlefield. Aunt Josephine made arrangements with him to take some time away from his volunteer work at Mercy Hospital, the only Negro medical facility in Wilson, to sit with my daddy. He loved my daddy and looked forward to being with him every Friday, Sunday, and Tuesday night, giving Mother a chance to get away if she wanted.

Even though the front door was open, none of us heard the phone when it started ringing. The noise of the children playing in the neighborhood coupled with the beginnings of thunder was enough of a distraction to override the sounds of the phone.

"The phone is ringing," said Ingrid. "Braxton, run and answer that. If it's your mother, tell her I'll come and get her." I looked at my watch. It was about nine-fifteen and not quite three hours had passed since Ingrid and Jackson had taken Mother for her meeting with Mr. Byrd. I ran inside the house and picked up the black receiver.

"Hello," I said. "Haywood's residence."

"Your mother is lying on the sidewalk in the 1200 block of West Nash Street," whispered a muffled female voice. "If your mother can't hold her liquor any better than she has tonight, I think I'd lock her in the house."

"Who is this?" I asked, my voice beginning to shake. "Please tell me who this is and how do you know it's my mother?"

"Just say I'm your savior tonight and I know Virginia Haywood.

She's a disgrace to motherhood." I didn't have a clue as to who was on the other end of the phone but I could tell that she was an adult female with a grating voice. "*You best come and get her now. She's passed out.* Goodbye." She hung up the phone as I yelled.

"*Wait!* Don't hang up!" My voice croaked. "*Ingrid, come here quick!*"

"For God's sake, why are you shouting?" Ingrid asked, running to where I stood.

"Mother's hurt!"

"Is she all right?"

"I don't know! On the phone . . . just now," I stammered. "A woman said Mother was laying drunk on Nash Street."

"Where on Nash?" asked Ingrid. I could see the normal calmness so characteristic of Ingrid turning to fear. Her face had turned white and her eyes had widened in alarm.

"Uh? The 1100 block or the 1200 block? One of those—I don't remember." I felt a sickening wave of terror welling up from my stomach.

"Who called you?" asked Ingrid, speaking faster. "Do you think it was a joke?"

"I don't know who it was," I said. My facial muscles began to twitch. I was about to lose total control of my emotions. "She wouldn't give her name. Ingrid, I'm scared! *We need to go and get Mother now.*"

"Okay, but get a grip! Quit yelling!" she said. "We have to walk out that front door as if nothing has happened." She turned toward the living room.

"All right. Let's do it!"

"Do you think you can, Braxton?"

"Yes, but we need to go *now!*" I took a deep breath and said, "Okay, I'm ready."

Ingrid and I walked through the house onto the porch and down the steps. She turned to Jackson and said, "We're going to get Virginia. I think you better take Louis back to his room now."

"Yes ma'am, Miss Ingrid," said Jackson, turning to Daddy. Just as he was getting ready to lift my daddy, a loud crack of thunder shattered the calmness being enjoyed by these three porch sitters. Anne screamed and ran into the house. Just as quickly, the unexpected, long awaited rain began to plummet from the sky bringing shouts of joy from up and down the street.

The wind pushed the rain hard, creating a sweeping motion as we ran to Ingrid's car. Between the thunder and the lightning and the wind, we paid little attention to how drenched we were when we got in the car. Ingrid seemed unaffected that her brand new '57 Buick might have just received its first water baptism from the rain dripping off our arms, legs, faces, and clothes.

With the mission of a mystery writer, Ingrid turned on the ignition, the headlights, and wipers, and screeched away from the curb taking the one-half block to West Nash faster than most people can find their pulse. As she turned left onto West Nash, I couldn't help but jump at the intensity of the lightning and the boldness of the thunder that followed. We passed the first two houses of the 1300 block when the tall oak on the right side of the street was struck by lightning sending several larges branches thundering to the ground. The fact that my mother was laying somewhere on this street in the midst of this storm sent a twinge of fear up and down my spine.

"With it raining as hard as it is, finding Virginia is going to be difficult," said Ingrid. She quickly slowed the car and turned on the bright lights. There were no other cars on the street, making it easier for her to deliberately sway from one side of West Nash to the other.

"I know, but I'll get out and walk the block if I have to!" I said, determined to find my mother.

"You might just have to. Do you know what side of the street she is on?"

"No, but my guess would be our left," I said. My breathing became heavy. "*Stop!* We're in the 1100 block! *Let me out!*"

"Okay, but be careful!" she said. "As soon as you find her, yell!"

"*I will!*" I shouted, jumping out of the car before Ingrid came to a complete stop. I hit the pavement running and then slipped in the current of water washing across the street. I got up and crossed to the side I thought Mother might be on. The rain was pounding and the velocity of the wind was breathtaking. The massive arms of the tall oaks that intertwined among themselves overhead had broken loose and now swayed back and forth as if trying to prevent the storm from voicing its fury.

I jogged slowly down the sidewalk in front of the handsome, two-story homes that fronted the eleven hundred block of this stately street. There were only four homes on this block. Attempting to find my mother, I stopped at anything that could be the size of a person: a fallen limb, a pile of leaves that had been raked and left for pickup, an overturned trashcan. There was no human body lying on this street. I looked for any possible hint of where she might be: a lit porch light, a lighted lamp post, someone standing at a window, anything that might say stop, but there was nothing to give me direction. I hollered her name out in the night and again, yelled for my mother. There wasn't any answer.

I was mad and I sobbed. I screamed out at God at yet another injustice and I feared what I actually might see when I found my mother. I was rain-soaked from my waterlogged tennis shoes to the rain cap I took from Ingrid's car. My shirt clung to me, having been beaten by a combination of wind and rain. I could identify with the savage I remember seeing in Jason the afternoon he shot the cardinal. Crazy thoughts shot through my mind like marbles being rapidly fired from a Wham-o sling shot at a squirrel running for its life. I wondered if this was what it's like to lose touch with reality? I wondered if I was capable of murder? I wondered if all of us had a point where we could be taken and not returned? I wondered if screaming would help? And I screamed a howl much like that of a coyote—one that I had practiced in fun so many times in my backyard when I was trying to learn to imitate as many animal sounds as I possibly could. My chest lunged first out and then back, exhausting the little wind I had to give. I even scared myself and Ingrid slammed on her breaks, thinking I had found Mother. Howling had felt good and the noise had brought me back to the reason I was out here.

"*She's not on this block,*" I yelled to Ingrid while moving to the 1200 block, a block that had twice as many homes and twice as much shrubbery lining the frontage of the broad lots. The search would take longer and I only saw one lit porch light as I jogged over the curb. I passed three homes and still didn't see my mother. I was using the same method as before, trying to be very careful not to overlook anything. As I passed the fifth house, I stopped and looked back. I thought I'd heard a mumbling sound. Maybe it was the wind howling. It was damn hard to hear anything out here. I heard the noise again—a low guttural sound like someone was puking or throwing up. *But,* there was nobody visible on the grass or the sidewalk. I heard it again and I walked backward, trying to detect where the sound was coming from. I crouched, trying to see and hear anything. Another faint grunt came from behind me. I turned. About twenty feet from the sidewalk were four or five very large azalea bushes that had grown together, I saw a woman's shoe. I immediately recognized it as belonging to my mother.

"*Mother? It's Braxton. Answer me! Where are you?*"

The noise sounded again and I moved toward the bushes. Mother lay on her side in the mud, entangled in the low-lying limbs of these beautiful bushes.

"*Mother! My God! What's happened to you?*" I screamed in horror at what I had found. "*Who did this to you?*" I turned and yelled to Ingrid that I had found Mother. Ingrid immediately did a u-turn in the middle of the street and pulled her car parallel with 1202 West Nash Street, the home of Mr. and Mrs. John Ellerson Beamer. She ran to where I stood.

"Help me get her out from under here and up on her feet!" I said, kneeling and receiving a mouthful of rain at the same time. The weather was just as mean and cruel as the person or persons who had done this to my mother.

"Let's turn her over first," said Ingrid. She gasped when she saw the blood running from Mother's nose and mouth. "My God, Virginia, how could this have happened?"

After we got Mother turned, we saw that her dress was torn down the front. In the dark it was hard to see how bad she'd been hurt but the smell of alcohol was overwhelmingly evident. She reeked with it and there was no doubt about her being drunk. I had never seen anyone in this state of drunkenness, much less my own mother. As we began to lift her so we could get her to the car, she shocked us as she spoke, slurring her words, "Get your damn hands off of me."

"We'll have to use force, Braxton," said Ingrid, grabbing Mother around the waist and lifting her to a standing position. Mother immediately fell sideways and would have hit the ground if I hadn't caught her. "Use force, Braxton. Help me get her to the car." Together we lifted her and started dragging her to Ingrid's car.

"Leave me alone, damn it! Leave me alone! Stop! You're hurting me," Mother said, slurring every syllable that came out of her mouth. "Shit, who in the hell are you?" The realization that Mother didn't know us cut through me like the stinging sensation when something acidic gets into a deep paper cut.

"Be quiet, *Virginia,*" Ingrid said. "We're going to put you in my car!"

"I don't want to get in your *damn* car, I tell you," Mother said, kicking and screaming. "Shit! I don't know you! *Leave me alone!* " She continued to resist. "*Ow! You're hurting me. Don't touch me! Please don't touch me.*"

"*Mother, please,* just let us get you in the car." My spirit became as intoxicated with hurt as she was with liquor.

"Hell, *no!*" Mother answered. She swung at my face and missed. She began to cry. It was obvious that she didn't know us or where she was. The rain gave us no mercy and it pounded harder now. All three of us were soaked, and we were dirty, and we smelled awful. The wind was no ally—it haunted us with its ruthless chanting, dropping tiny limbs on the car, sidewalk, and street. The weather appeared hungry in its pursuit to let us know who was in charge of this night.

We struggled to get her to the car and with me on one side pulling her and Ingrid on the other side pushing as hard as she could, we managed to get her into the back seat. Mother lay on her back and from the inside car light, we saw that her face, arms, and legs were badly bruised. The arm bruises explained why she screamed whenever we touched her. Her slip had been ripped. Mother was a mess and a picture of abuse.

Ingrid and I hurriedly got back into the front seat. Ingrid turned the ignition and pulled away from the curb. Mother's right arm dangled off the seat. She cried uncontrollably, and cursed obscenely, and uttered nonsensical noises. I didn't know my mother knew some of the words she used. In fact, I didn't know the woman on the back seat. She was not my mother, yet, she was. I saw the flashing light from the police car coming up behind us. It stopped in front of the same house where we'd found Mother. Two officers got out and walked over to the bushes. I wondered who called them. Someone wants to make more trouble! I breathed a sigh of relief as Ingrid drove toward home.

"I'm taking Virginia to Mother's," said Ingrid. "Then I'll take you home." The drive to Josephine's would be a short one.

Once inside Aunt Josephine's home, Ingrid and her mother took Mother's clothes off, cleaned her, and put her to bed in Ingrid's former bedroom. I waited in the kitchen adjacent to the den, wondering what would happen next. Ingrid came back downstairs to tell me that she and her mother had decided that Jackson would spend the night with Daddy. Ingrid would stay with Anne and me. We would address what was best for Mother the next morning. Ingrid never asked me about this night again. Her concern was with Mother and her recuperation. I never volunteered anything about this night to Ingrid. She knew Oscar Byrd better than I and I'm certain she had her own idea of why this had taken place.

The next morning Ingrid and I went back to her mother's. We found Mother and Aunt Josephine seated at the dining room table. The rich smell of brewed Maxwell House coffee and the foul smell of cigarette smoke combated each other for control of the air space in Josephine Thaxton's exquisite dining room. Surrounded by antiques and sterling silver, the two sisters sat in silence. My Aunt Josephine wore an expression of disbelief and disgust. My mother looked defeated, and helpless, and alone, and pathetic—not at all like the Virginia Haywood who sat with four frightened teenage boys on our back porch two days earlier.

Mother looked like hell—like death warmed over. I couldn't find enough adjectives to describe her. The first thing I noticed was the swelling around her right eye and then the several cuts on her face. Her right arm was in a makeshift sling.

"I'd like to be alone with Mother if I may," I said. Aunt Josephine and Ingrid respected my request and went upstairs. "Mother, who did this to you?"

"Braxton, you were right," Mother said, her left hand trembling and knocking ashes onto the white, linen tablecloth. "I thought I was doing the right thing."

"Did Mr. Byrd do this to you?" I wanted a confirmation for what I already suspected.

"Yes," Mother said, crying. She put the butt of her cigarette in the circular, sterling silver ashtray. Her hand shook as she pulled another Kool from her pack. "Light this for me, Braxton."

I took the cigarette from her hand and put it in my mouth. I picked up the silver lighter from the table and ran my thumb across the switch. The flame rose, I lit the cigarette, and inhaled slightly, blowing the smoke to my left, and then I gently put the Kool between my mother's lips.

"Braxton, he is mean. He is like a man possessed," she said. Mother inhaled slowly and deeply, then let the smoke return through her nose. "When I first got there, we went to his den and he fixed me an 'old fashion' and we talked about old times. He offered me another drink, but I refused. He kept insisting and I kept refusing. I reminded him the reason that I came to see him was to talk about his dismissing you from your job before you had a chance to start." Mother stopped.

I watched Mother's hand shake as she attempted to sip her coffee. She took another drag from her cigarette, blowing her smoke into the air. I watched the smoke encircle the arms of the crystal chandelier and then disappear. She continued, "He suddenly changed demeanors and became angry and hostile. He called me a bitch and threw me to the floor, saying that I was no good and that I wasn't going to dictate to him. He had been drinking Jack Daniels straight and he took his bottle of bourbon from the coffee table and tried to pour it in my mouth. I refused and he slapped me. He held me down by putting his knees on my arms and he spit in my face and said terrible things about me. He opened by mouth against my will and poured the remains of that bottle down my throat and over my clothes. He got up and stood over me laughing. When I tried to get up, he would knock me down. I couldn't resist him. I don't know how long this went on. I don't remember anything after that." Mother put her good arm on the table and then rested her head there and cried and cried. I reached over and patted her on the head. I felt helpless because I didn't know how to comfort her.

"That son of a bitch," I said, murmuring to myself. "You *will* pay for this."

Mother looked up. "Braxton, you must believe me. What I have told you is the truth. I have no idea how I got to Nash Street. Josephine is livid with me."

"The important thing is for you to feel better and then come back home and . . . " She interrupted me.

"Braxton, I only told Josephine that I met Oscar because he fired you. Believe me when I say I haven't told her anything."

"I believe you, Mother." I said. "Did you tell Mr. Byrd you knew about him and Charles?"

"No, I did *not!*" Mother said, continuing to shake. She put the remains of her cigarette out. "He assumed I knew. I acted like I didn't know what he was talking about."

"He knew." I hit my right fist against my left palm. "He knew."

Ingrid and Josephine returned to the dining room. They had decided that Mother would stay one more night with my aunt. Ingrid would coordinate things at our house and Jackson would continue to stay with Daddy as long as Daddy needed him. Anne would go back to my grandmothers for a few days. Mother protested. As usual in disagreements with her sister, she lost. I would return with Ingrid and pretend everything was normal in hopes that Daddy would not catch wind of what had occurred. Ingrid would handle the "whys" of Mother's being away from home with my dad.

It seemed unreal that one person could come into our lives the way Oscar Byrd had entered ours and completely rearrange our normal routine. I was consumed with him—what he had done to me already and what he might do again today or tomorrow or the next day. He was dictating to us the way we would live or would not live and we had done nothing wrong. He had no right to do this to my family or me. I didn't know how to stop him; at least, not yet. I would not break the blood pledge I made with Jason, Matt, and Thad, but I was going to disobey my Mother and do one thing she had told us not to do. As soon as I got home, I would make a very important phone call.

Chapter 33
A Sneak Attack

IT WAS EARLY Wednesday morning and no longer raining when Ingrid and I returned to my house. I went to my bedroom and sat dispiritedly by my windows, watching the empty driveway that ran between our house and Mrs. Barbee's home. I watched nothing in particular, just the gravel that lay on both sides of the grassy center that stretched from Kincaid Avenue back to our old, wooden garage. One lone robin perched itself on the gravel near the large forsythia bush standing outside our bathroom window—the bush from which we had to pick our switches when we were whipped by our mother when she had the need to punish us too severely. I called this Mother's Judas tree.

This bush with its yellow bell-shaped flowers in the spring was massive and tall enough to overshadow our only bathroom window, giving us protection from outside observers. This was the same bush from which Byrd, Thad, Jason, Matt, and I cut our long switches. We would then strip them of their foliage, turning them into makeshift whips in order to imitate Lash LaRue after watching him perform in person at the Carolina Theater down on Goldsboro Street. We were proud of ourselves and our ability to mimic one of our cowboy heroes, but we knew if we used them, permanent scars could be inflicted. And it was from underneath the low hanging limbs of this bush that birds came to dig for worms to take back and feed their young.

It was from this bush that I made my little sister a garland of yellow flowers for her to wear in the May Day celebration at her school. And it was under this bush that I became acquainted with the hurt a little boy can receive when he tries to catch a hornet with his bare hands. The stinger was buried in my palm until I found Lily. She pulled it out and put a compost of tobacco and water on it to take away the pain. This was the day I learned I was allergic to stings and I could expect cold chills and fevers to follow along with a fair amount of swelling.

Now I faced another hornet. Only this time, the hornet is more dangerous and the sting is more powerful and more painful, inflicting hurt on everyone who means anything to me. This time, I can't depend on Lily to rescue me or the forsythia branch to protect me. This time I have to let the hornet pursue me but not sting me.

Lily came in and spoke, "I know I can't takes your pain away. But I do luv' you and I wants to help you if you will let me."

"Thanks, Lily," I said. "I'll be all right. It'll just take some time."

"If you need me, I'm in the kitchen."

"Okay. Right now I think I need to be alone." Lily smiled and returned to the kitchen.

I heard the phone ringing, reminding me of the call I had planned to make. I heard Lily answer and I heard her call to me but I didn't respond at first. I didn't have a good reason; I just didn't want to get up—it was too easy to stay where I was. "Coming."

"Hello. This is Braxton."

"How does it feel to have a drunk for a mother?" the male voice asked. I immediately hung up. The phone rang again. Foolishly, I picked it up and put the receiver next to my ear. I didn't say anything at first. Then I spoke, "Yes?"

"Don't *you* ever hang up on me again, you *son* of a *drunken bitch*." Then the caller hung up. I stood there, stunned. It was only ten-thirty in the morning and, already, news of Mother's behavior from last night was hitting the airwaves.

"Who was it, Braxton?" It was never in Lily's nature to ask who had called me.

"A wrong number."

In every small town, there are some people who make it their business to know everything that goes on in their community. They see what they want to see and hear what they want to hear. I called them vultures and like many Southern towns, Wilson had its fair share. They were experts, these purveyors of their own brand of truth. As inconceivable as it might sound, they prided themselves on knowing every little, bad thing that happens and something about all the big scandals that rocked our little community. They were the experts of another's misfortune and they were close observers of the fallen: the alcoholics, the pregnant teen, the wife beaters, the unfaithful (both wives and husbands), the men who pursue other men, the dishonest businessmen, the immoral teachers, ministers, doctors . . . their victims were made known to all who would listen. These were the ones who would rather stay awake at night to do their homework, hoping to hear something bad rather than getting a good night's sleep.

Like birds of prey, they were never satisfied with facts or what they knew to be true. Instead, they often chose to exaggerate their stories in order to make their tales more believable. And once they had formulated their own brand of truth, they never hesitated publishing their findings. Add my mother's latest scenario to their case study and the answer was undeniably clear as to why our phone had rung so many times before noon today. Granted that some called with genuine concern for Mother but others called to fill in their missing blanks or to get their story straight. And then there were those whose mission was to inflict more pain like the first man who called. We took the phone off the hook for two hours so Daddy could get some rest. When we returned the receiver to its base, the calls started again. At four o'clock, I knew it was time for me to make my call.

Jackson was with my daddy watching some afternoon soap opera, Lily was fixing dinner in the kitchen, and Ingrid was sitting around the wading pool reading. I walked to the telephone table in the hallway and sat down. I dialed the number 3152 carefully and on the third ring a male voice that I recognized, answered, "Byrd's Pharmacy."

"Mr. Jernigan, is that you?"

"Yes, whom am I speaking with?"

"Mr. Jernigan, this is Braxton Haywood. Can you talk?"

"I believe so," he said. There was an edge of doubt to his voice.

"I mean are you alone in the store?" I said, trying to stay calm and control my excitement. "I mean is Mr. Byrd there?"

"No, he is not here at the moment, but there are customers in the store," he said in his best businesslike manner. Did he now find it awkward to talk with me? Was I getting him in some kind of trouble? Something just didn't sound right.

"Braxton, tell me, how is Virginia?" he asked. "Is she okay? Is she hurt badly?"

"What?" His question caught me off guard. How did he know about Mother? "What do you mean?"

"Braxton, don't play coy with me. How is your mother after last night?" he asked again. "Is she okay?"

"Mother was beaten, bruised, and dumped out of a car on West Nash Street and I hold Oscar Byrd accountable!" I said, my heart hammering. Control yourself, Braxton. "How did you know? Did he tell you what he did?"

"Slow down, Braxton," Mr. Jernigan said. "I haven't seen Oscar Byrd today but Mrs. Eicher was in and she told me that your mother drank too much last night and jumped out of Mr. Byrd's car when he tried to carry her home."

"How did she know?" I asked, my face growing hot.

"She said that she was with your mother and Mr. Byrd last night."

"What?" I yelled into the phone. "Where?"

"She came into today to get some gauze because she had scratches on her arms and neck. She said your mother did this to her. Then she told me what happened."

"Mr. Jernigan, that woman is lying to you," I said. I was rip roaring mad—so mad that I had dug my fingers into my palms hard enough to draw blood without realizing it. "Did you believe her?"

"Not completely," he said. "I don't know what to believe around here anymore."

"What my mother told me is not at all what you heard," I said. "And if anything happened, the truth is that Mr. Byrd and his friend, Mrs. Eicher, dumped Mother on West Nash Street! Did you hear? They *dumped* her out of his car."

"Oh, my God!" he responded. "I'm so sorry. Can I do anything for you or your mother?"

"Yes," I said without hesitation. "I need you to get in touch with David Byrd for me. I need you to do it this afternoon. And as soon as possible."

"I don't know if I can do that, Braxton. David is getting ready to go to Camp Seagull for the rest of the summer."

"What?" This was news. "Since when?" I didn't want to hear this.

"Mr. Byrd decided it would be best if he didn't come back to Wilson and he has made all of the necessary arrangements with the YMCA office in Raleigh."

"Mr. Jernigan, Byrd is too old to be a camper at Seagull!" I said, not wanting to believe the measure this man would go to keep his son away from us.

"He is going to be a counselor-in-training or something like that," Mr. Jernigan said. "He's leaving tomorrow for camp."

"I've got to talk to Byrd today, Mr. Jernigan," I said. "Please help me this one time. Call the cottage and ask to speak to him or get someone in the store to call for you!"

"Braxton, do you know what time it is now?"

"Yes sir, that's why I need for you to hurry," I said. I was now on my knees by our telephone table begging a man who couldn't even see me.

"All right. I'll do it for you," he said. "I don't like what is going on around here and if this will help bring some sanity back into this situation, I'll call. Hang up."

"Thank you, Mr. Jernigan," I said. "You're a real friend."

"If I don't call you back, Braxton, then you'll know I've made contact with David." He hung up.

I was excited, scared, and confused at the same time. Then I realized that Byrd might not be able to reach me if our phone continued to ring like it'd done all day. As I stood there with the receiver in my hand, I shot an arrow prayer to God. I asked God to intervene in this mess, making it possible for me to talk with David. The humming noise coming from my hand reminded me to put the phone receiver back on its base.

Our phone rang repeatedly until around six o'clock. The callers were mostly family friends and genuinely concerned about Mother and desirous of helping. Ingrid took these calls. People loved to bring food at times like this and we were thankful. Ingrid coordinated the food orders with Lily to prevent duplications in what people brought. The good news was that Mr. Jernigan was not among the callers. I now had hope that I would be talking with my friend soon.

When Ingrid suggested we go back and visit Mother after taking Lily home, I told her to tell Mother that I had reason to believe Byrd would call tonight. She might not like that bit of news but I knew she would understand. After Ingrid and Lily left, I grabbed the book I had been reading, *The Catcher in the Rye,* and positioned myself in the corner of my bedroom closest to the hall to wait for Byrd's call. This way I would have no problem getting to the phone after one ring. I started reading on page fifty-nine. The first thing Holden did when he got off at Penn Station was go to a phone booth. *How ironic,* I thought. It was easy to get caught up in the adventures of Holden Caulfield. Despite all his hang-ups, I couldn't help but like him and when I read about him, I lost track of time.

I looked at my watch. It was eight-forty. I was tired of sitting in the same position and my bottom was sore from sitting on the hard, wooden floor. I was also getting impatient and irritable. I walked into the kitchen, opened the refrigerator, took out the iced tea, and poured myself a glass. I grabbed a handful of crushed ice and ever so slowly, plopped it in the dark crimson liquid that had now risen to the top of my glass. I took it with me onto the back porch.

It was clear tonight and a tad cooler, thanks to last night's horrific storm. It was that time of day when the summer light was just before yielding to the approaching darkness. The moon was in its position and an occasional star had appeared. It was peaceful. I enjoyed being still and watching the lightening bugs flicker around the backyard. The voices of the summer night were already at work—first Mrs. Lange calling her children, and Mrs. Barfield chanting "kitty, kitty, here kitty," looking for Maggie, her cat, and then Mr. Sampson, who lives behind us, pulling in on his Harley-Davidson from his second-shift job at the body works manufacturing plant. And the usual backup chorus of crickets, barking dogs, passing cars from nearby streets, and children yelling were already in place. This was a true sign that all was the way it should be. It was a ritual on which I could depend. I liked order because it allowed me to feel good and safe inside, and I needed that. I didn't know Jackson was standing in the doorway behind me until he spoke.

"Excuse me, Braxton," he said. "You have a phone call."

"I do?" I said, turning and looking at him. I knew he thought I was in a daze. "Gosh! I didn't even hear the phone ring. I've been so lost in my thoughts."

"I understand," said Jackson. "Do you want to take the call or do you want to call him back?"

"*No!* I'm coming now," I said. "Thanks Jackson, I don't know what's wrong with me."

Jackson moved aside so I could step into the hall and maneuver my way through my bedroom and back into the hall where the receiver was dangling off the table, held in position by its cord. I reached for the receiver with my right hand. With my left hand behind my back and my fingers crossed, I said to myself, "Please, God, let it be David Byrd."

"Hello," I said. I held my breath.

"Braxton, this is Tweety Bird," Byrd said with a light chuckle. "How in the heck have you been?" Byrd's upbeat mood was a surprise and a puzzle to me.

"Okay, but things are so crazy. When are you coming home?" I exhaled in relief.

"I'm still at the beach but will, hopefully, be home on Friday."

"That's *good news!* So much has happened since we last talked," I said. "Are you all right?"

"Yes and no!" He said and then paused. "I've got to see you when I get home, maybe late Friday night, even if I have to sneak out of the house. My father is sending me to Seagull on Sunday and prep school is a definite. Braxton, he won't yield on anything."

"That's a rip! Hey, I thought you were going to Seagull tomorrow?"

"That was his original intent but it didn't work out. Sunday is the date now."

"Listen, Byrd, I can't believe your dad doesn't want you to see any of us! How long does he think he can play this game of his?"

"He plays to win, Braxton. I think he believes if he can get me away for the rest of the summer and next year, then none of you will want to see me again."

"We all want to see you and we all miss you. No one will tell us anything. That's why I called Mr. Jernigan. Byrd, did you hear about Mother?"

"I'm sorry about that, Braxton. I only know what I heard my mother and Aunt Greta say after talking with him on the phone. That was last night and Mother told Greta that he'd had too much to drink." Byrd paused and then asked, "Is your mother okay?"

"Not really. He did a pretty good number on her. She was bruised pretty badly."

"Damn, I hate that! I can't believe he's my father or I'm his son. We are so different."

"You're different! There's no question about that!" I said. "He's being a real son of a gun and has done everything he can to make my life miserable."

"Yours and mine, Braxton," said Byrd. "I wish I could come and live with you."

"That would be neat but not the answer," I said. "Can you go to Patsy Wentworth's party?"

"Hell no! The old buzzard opened the invitation she sent me and he nearly flipped. I can't do anything in Wilson. If he keeps this up, I don't know how much more I can take."

"Call your Aunt Olivia. Let her help you. I know she'd want to."

"Believe me, I've thought about it." Byrd stopped then continued. "I can't talk much longer."

"Okay. Call me about Friday. I definitely want to get with you Friday night. I can pick you up somewhere near your house after the party. Why don't you meet me on Raleigh Road somewhere? How about across from the park behind the Dairy Bar between eleven-thirty and midnight?"

That may be too early. Right now, leave it as it is," Byrd said. "Wait for me because I will be there one way or the other."

"Byrd, be careful."

"I will." Byrd hesitated then said, "Okay, Braxton, goodbye."

"Goodbye, Byrd," I said, placing the receiver back on the base. Goodbye, good friend. I hope you make it Friday night.

I walked out on the back porch again, thinking about my conversation with Byrd. When he comes home, we've got to figure a way to stop his father's madness. I thought Byrd sounded good considering the pressure he's under. The most difficult part of this whole scenario was Mr. Byrd. Ever since that night in Charles's bedroom, it's been me he's targeted, not any of the others. Somehow I've become his scapegoat. I can't talk with him and my mother had no success talking with him. There must be someone who can stop him. The only person I could think of was his sister, Olivia. I wished my uncle, Dr. Thaxton, was still alive. He could put an end to this immediately. I heard Ingrid come in the front door and I met her in the kitchen.

"How's Mother?" I asked.

"Better, but she wants to see you," Ingrid said. "She's concerned about you right now. I assured her you were doing fine."

"Thank you," I said, comforted by her statement. "How did Mother react when you told her why I wasn't coming?"

"She took it well. She made no comment, just smiled."

"Good. I thought she would understand," I said, taking my tea glass and putting it in the sink. "Is she coming home tomorrow?"

"No. Mother wants her to stay there through Friday. If she is better by then, she'll come home."

"Will you be staying here with us?"

"Yes, as long as y'all need me but I have some social commitments coming up this weekend."

"Me, too!" I said. "Patsy Wentworth is having her big pool party at the club on Friday night."

"That will be fun," Ingrid said. And with a smile, she continued, "Oh yes! I remember those days. Enjoy them because they are some of the best years of your life."

"You're kidding, of course!" I thought they've got to be better than what I've been through since school let out.

"No, I'm not, and college is even better. You wait, you'll see that I'm right."

"I think I'll call it a night, Ingrid. I've had just about all the excitement I can take for one day. Good night." I turned and walked into my bedroom and closed the door. In two nights I would be able to see David Byrd again and for the first time since all of this began, I felt a sense of relief when I crawled into bed. When the Norfolk Southern rambled through, blowing its piercing whistle, I just smiled in my contentment and rolled over and went back to sleep.

THE NEXT MORNING, as I waited for Ingrid to finish getting dressed, I hoped that this day would be better for our family. As much as I hated to admit it, I was ready to turn the clock back four or five years and return to being a preteen. I didn't like those years because I thought I was being treated like a baby. But after the last nineteen days, I was ready to make a change—being sixteen and growing up, having your feet knocked out from under you almost daily is not my idea of slipping into maturity gracefully. What a foolish notion I must have had when I said I wanted to be treated like an adult. Someone told me to be careful what I wished for and now I agree. I definitely had been given the opportunity to make adult decisions or maybe a better way of stating it would be, I had been forced into making adult decisions. And it's hard—too darn hard, and it's *no fun, absolutely no damn fun.*

Ingrid and I went to my grandmother's first to check in on Anne and see if she needed anything other than those clothes that Ingrid had taken from her dresser. Mrs. Alexander, who lived across the street from my grandmother, had invited Anne to spend the afternoon and night with her daughter, Janet. I was happy for Anne that she could be with her friends during this unsettled week.

Our next stop was at our Aunt Eva's home to pick up some vegetables that she had taken from her garden. Getting away from her was like trying to *help* feeble Dr. Ruffin, now in his late seventies and still practicing his dentistry, *pull* my wisdom teeth. Aunt Eva's intentions were good but she had to know every detail about everything that had happened. I was thankful Ingrid was there to help me get away from her.

We stopped at Aunt Josephine's house to visit with my mother. Today, Mother looked better. She was neatly dressed and had put her makeup on as if she was waiting for someone. Some of the swelling on her face had gone away. Her arm was no longer in the makeshift sling and her attitude was remarkable. She wasn't bitter but, rather, determined not to let this one incident defeat her. I told her about Byrd's call and that we planned to get together on Friday. Her only comment was her standard "please be careful."

While we were there, Mr. Bradshaw, our minister, did come calling. He had telephoned my aunt before he came but I'm not certain Mother knew he was coming. Uncle Bob had the wisdom not to believe everything that passed through the gossip channels of our town. He had heard something about Mother's debacle but he knew Mother and dismissed the gossip for what it was. Of course, a man in his position shouldn't presume anything but one man of the cloth did and helped feed the chain of falsehood that surrounded Mother.

And on this Thursday morning, before sitting down with Mother, he did an unusual thing. At least I thought it was unusual. He asked me if he could visit with me alone. We went out to Aunt Josephine's foyer that was the size of two small rooms in most homes. We stationed ourselves beside Madame Bovary, the marble bust of a French Countess, sitting atop a cherry stand, and still wearing a loosely fitted, lacey top that exposed her left breast and nipple. This is the only female nipple I had ever kissed until Rita and I kissed. Believe me, there's a big difference! I smiled at the place he chose to stand.

"Yes, sir?"

"Braxton, how are you personally holding up with all this going on in your household?" asked Mr. Bradshaw. His expression wore the genuine concern that I knew he had for my family and me.

"I'm sort of okay," I said. Boy, if he only knew the half of it but I wasn't at liberty to tell him.

"Now if there is anything I can do for you and Anne, I want you to call me. Will you promise me that you will do that?" He leaned forward and looked right into my eyes when he asked. He was a good listener and no problem was too small for him to address. There was definitely no "bull hockey" about him.

"Yes, sir," I said. I would call if I could, too, because I liked and trusted Mr. Bradshaw. I wished I could talk to him today because I really needed to talk with someone but I couldn't break my pledge.

"One more thing, Braxton," he said. "What did you think of Chuck Anderson as a Sunday school teacher?" He observed me carefully as I gave his question some thought.

"Well, I was only with him one Sunday and I guess he is a little unorthodox," I said. I knew this was a safe answer, truthful and not too critical. (*Give Aunt Eva two points.*) I couldn't believe my minister was asking me my opinion on such an important matter. I certainly didn't plan to side step my opportunity. "Uncle Bob, I learned a lot the one Sunday I was in his class and I'm very disappointed that he won't be back." I stopped here, waiting to see how my minister would respond.

"I understand he was an excellent teacher but maybe chose the wrong words at times," he said.

"Yes, sir," I said. But in all fairness, he's a military man and he talks like John Wayne and Burt Lancaster do in their army movies. He's more salty, using more descriptive language."

"Did this descriptive language offend you?" my minister asked. He was watching me again to see my reaction.

"I don't know if I would say that, but it surprised me," I said. "Can't Captain Chuck be given another chance?"

"You obviously think he deserves one," Uncle Bob said, nodding and rubbing his chin. "I'm giving it serious thought." He didn't have to make his decision today nor would he—he's much too prudent.

"Maybe he could tone down the words a little," I said. "He's the first male Sunday school teacher I've ever had and I'll be in the eleventh grade next year. Don't get rid of him, please. And you know what? I need to be around as many men as possible just to hear their views on things." I thought I had made a darn good plea for his return. I could tell by Mr. Bradshaw's reaction to my last statement that he did too. He nodded and patted me on the shoulder.

"You're very convincing, Braxton," he said, smiling. "I'm going to give your comments a lot of thought."

"May I say one more thing?"

"Yes, you certainly may."

"I don't mean this to be disrespectful, but you told my mother you didn't smoke with many people yet you will smoke with her. I hope you wouldn't take that pleasure away from her if one of the members of your church protested."

"Et tú, Brute!" he said, this time patting me on the back.

I returned to the living room and told Aunt Josephine and my mother goodbye. I leaned over and kissed Mother and whispered in her ear. I reminded her that I loved her. She smiled and patted my hand.

The mail had arrived when we returned home. The usual bills, advertisements, flyers, and occasional letters were in the black mailbox hanging on the front porch to the left of the front door. One envelope stood out. It was an eight and a half by eleven-inch brown manila envelope addressed in cursive writing to me.

I excused myself and went to my bedroom. I undid the clasp and took the monogrammed sterling silver letter opener given to me on my sixteenth birthday by my Aunt Mildred and slid it through the upper back of the envelope, prying loose the remaining tape used to close it. I reached in and pulled out what appeared to be an eight by ten glossy print. I turned the picture over and my eyes fell upon a black and white glossy photograph of the five of us. I stood rigid and my mouth fell open when I saw what some "sicko" had done to the photograph. I was flabbergasted and a rush of heat overtook my face. My right hand shook and I stared in fascinated horror.

Whoever sent this had gotten hold of a copy of a picture, a picture taken of us before an early, fall football game. We were sitting around a table at the teenage club, drinking a Coke and eating chips and having fun the way teenagers do when they are carefree and excited. We sat left to right as follows: Jason, Matt, Thad, Byrd, and me. The sender had taken a red pen and had carefully printed a number over each of our heads. There was a two over Jason's, a three over Matt's, a four over Thad's, a five over Byrd's, and a one over my head. Printed in red ink across the bottom of the photograph was a warning. It read, "*I will kill you. I will kill all of you. Don't screw up!*"

This threat scared the hell out of me and I dropped the picture on the bed. My head screamed with a burning pain of helplessness that wanted to escape. The pulsating pressure mounting against my temples was unbearable. I went to the inside wall of my room and beat my head up against it, hoping to release the grip that fear had on me. This only intensified the throbbing. I ran to the bathroom and threw cold water on my face. I felt angry and hurt and I wanted to strike out and inflict pain—the kind of pain that will cripple another and never go away—on whomever had sent this. I didn't recognize the expression of the freckled, round-faced, sixteen-year-old brunette staring back at me. The pain of fear that was haunting me was visible in his eyes. They had taken on an almost maddened look, similar to the look I saw in Jason's face that afternoon in his den. Why did this image keep reoccurring? It must have something to do with death. The thought that the number *one* was above my head might mean that I would be the first to die turned me around. I fell upon my knees, vomiting in the commode. When I stood again and looked at myself, I saw the same face, but this time I looked into the eyes of a pale-faced boy with a stricken expression. I had no one I could turn to at the moment—no father, no mother, no one, but myself.

Matt was the first to call me. He, too, had received the picture. Matt was scared, too, and cried over the phone. Jason called cursing, ready to go to Byrd's house and have it out with Mr. Byrd. I convinced him that Mr. Byrd may not be the sender and the wisest thing for us, at the moment, would be to sleep on the threat. I reminded him that we had to be united in whatever we did and we needed to calm down first. He seemed okay with this. Thad was the last to call and his calmness was not natural. Thad is normally self confident, but his tone sounded too forced. He admitted he was afraid but he, also, acknowledged he didn't know what to do. He asked my advice. I repeated my refrain. By their calling me and not each other, they had made me their leader. If there was one thing I had learned from Mr. Ross, it was calmness in the face of adversity is the best weapon a man can carry. I tried to be calm when I talked to my friends, and I was calm when I suggested we wait a few days before we responded. I didn't have an answer and I'm sure they knew that—but hell, they needed direction and by damn, somehow, I was going to give it to them. I wasn't going to let them down. If it took this for me to grow up then by damn it, I was going to make it—someway, somehow.

That afternoon I wandered around the block thinking about the picture and talking to myself about how I would approach Mother with our latest threat. I wondered who the sender was and could we be certain it was Mr. Byrd. I walked by Rita's house and again, it looked deserted. The blinds were pulled but I decided I would see if anyone was at home. I walked up to the front stoop, rang the doorbell, and waited. No one answered but I could have sworn I saw someone peep from behind one of the living room curtains. Thinking that someone was at home, I walked around to the screened-in porch. The screened door was unlocked and without any hesitancy, I walked inside and over to the French doors and knocked. I waited a couple of minutes but no one answered. I would try one more door and as I walked around to the back of the house, I again thought I saw someone peer out from behind a curtain. This time it was from Rita's bedroom window. No one answered when I knocked on the back door. Strange. Rita didn't tell me they were going out of town, but why else would all the blinds be down and the curtains pulled? Maybe she and the boys went to the beach. I knew her husband was traveling on the tobacco circuit and was probably in Tennessee. I returned home and fiddled around the house. Lily had a well-deserved afternoon off and Jackson was sitting with my father.

We got to Aunt Josephine's house around six o'clock, in plenty of time for dinner. I helped my grandmother out of the front seat and walked with her to the back door entrance. Ingrid was ahead of us carrying some of the food that had been delivered to our house. Once, in the house, my grandmother joined my aunt and Mother in the den adjacent to the dining room. I stopped in the kitchen to chat with Lulu, my aunt's Negro servant. Lulu was light skinned. She had very few Negroid features and her hair was as fine as mine. Lulu could easily pass for a white person. This had been an advantage for her further north but hadn't served her as well in the South. She'd told me that some of the black people in her neighborhood thought she was uppity. I'd told her they were jealous. She and her husband, Roscoe, had moved to North Carolina from Washington, D.C. some fifteen years ago. Lulu had worked for my aunt about twelve of those years.

Lulu was an educated, kind-hearted person who tried to be the best she could be in everything she attempted. She credited her great grandmother, the daughter of slaves, with her work ethic. She was an excellent cook and her area of expertise was making pies, especially chocolate and lemon meringue.

"Well, Braxton, I haven't seen much of you this summer," Lulu said, and went to the cabinet holding the dinner plates and took five down.

"I just haven't had much of a chance to get over here," I said, reaching over and undoing her apron, thinking she didn't know I had done it.

"Braxton, I don't have time for any of your foolishness tonight!" She put the plates on the counter.

"What are you talking about, Lulu?" I tried to stifle a laugh as her apron fell to her feet.

"This kind!" she said, reaching down and pulling it up and retying it around her waist.

"You left these," I said, handing her a pack of cigarettes. Like Mother, she smoked filter king Kools. Sometimes, she would let me smoke one with her in the kitchen if my aunt was busy elsewhere in the house.

"Thank you. Now is there anything else you want from me now?'

"I guess not. You're no fun tonight!"

"Braxton, I told you that I don't have time tonight. I try to do my job the best I can and tonight, I have too much to do to play."

"Okay, what time are you aiming for?" Her no nonsense attitude tipped me off and I knew she wanted to leave early.

"You think you're smart, don't you?"

"Yep," I said. I had a big grin on my face.

"Well, I have to admit that you are most of the time. Now go on and get out of here."

"See you in the dining room. Make certain you move fast when I step on the butler's buzzer." The butler's buzzer was located under the rug area where the head of the household's feet rested. I used to love to sit at the head of the table and push down on the buzzer with my right foot and call for service. That's when I was younger and

Lulu would play along with me, making me feel grown-up and in charge. Those days were over and it's silly to even think a person should feel powerful by putting another under their control. Now, I did it because it's a fun way to tease her. My aunt doesn't use it anymore either. She calls from the dining room now or uses a little hand bell that sits permanently on her dining room table.

After dinner, we retired to the living room. I hadn't mentioned the manila envelope or its contents during dinner and I didn't plan to tonight. I would show it to Mother when she came back home. The only bombshell dropped was by Josephine. She told me that she had talked with her good friend, Olivia, about what Mr. Byrd had done to Mother. Olivia was incensed and planned to visit with him on his return from Morehead. In the conversation, Olivia mentioned my calling her about Byrd and that led to their discussing the "why" behind Mr. Byrd's not letting Byrd see me. Neither had a clue. Mother had told her sister, Josephine, the basic facts and I guess it was good that much was out. Maybe Olivia could do something to make Byrd's life more pleasant and if so, then he might not have to go away for the summer. I suggested that it would be nice if Byrd could spend the summer with his Aunt Olivia. We left the conversation at that juncture.

The rest of the evening I listened half-heartedly as they talked about family things and argued over their differences. I have always believed if a person was going to argue with another, it should be over something important and not whether, for example, Ava Gardner, who was at the moment visiting her sister in the Wilson area, should marry again. My family loved to argue. The larger the family gathering, the more heated the arguments. I could always count on my mother having an opinion about whatever was being discussed and tonight was no different.

I said my goodnights to everyone under the guise of having to do some reading from my required reading list for junior English. All English students at Coon were given summer reading lists. It was pathetic to see how few students actually read from this list or read at all. My friends and I tried to read and stay current so we could have a respectable showing in class. We all wanted to go to college and this is the sort of thing we couldn't shirk anymore.

I walked the two blocks back to my house. I fought off the mosquitoes as I cut through the empty field facing West Nash and backing up to our side yard. Stars lit the sky and I saw one star shooting towards its unknown destination. I made a wish concerning Byrd and felt content again as I entered my backyard. I jumped when I put my foot on the first step leading up to our screened back porch. A menacing figure barely visible in the dark was standing behind the screened door with a cigarette in one hand and a paper fanning himself in the other.

"Boo!" he said. A laugh followed.

"Jackson, you just scared the *hell* out of me!"

"Sorry. I thought you saw me."

"That's almost impossible, you know!"

"Yeah, I guess you're right. I blends in well, don't I?"

"Tonight you do. For crying out loud, you don't even have a light on in the back of the house."

"I didn't want to wake your daddy. He's had a rough day today. He only went to sleep about thirty minutes ago and if he sleeps an hour, he'll be doing good."

"Is my daddy going down hill again?"

"I'm afraid so. I sure am."

"Jackson, can I have one of your cigarettes?"

He reached into his pocket and pulled out a pack of Marlboros. I pulled a cigarette from his pack and put it in my mouth. Jackson reached into his baggy pant's pocket and took out his silver lighter and lit it for me. I took a draw, inhaling more than I'd planned and blew it out, coughing. He didn't laugh but put his massive hand on my right shoulder and said, "You hang in there, boy. One day, all of this will be over."

"I sure hope so, Jackson. I sure hope so." I shook his hand. He opened the back-screened door and flipped his cigarette butt into the backyard. He turned without saying another word and sauntered back toward my daddy's room. I stepped outside and sat on the back steps and when I'd finished my cigarette, I tossed the filter into the dirt packing around the foundation of the house. I continued to sit, looking at the starry night and wondering how many other sixteen-year-old boys in the bright leaf area of North Carolina were lonely and confused like me and just wanted to get on with life—just skip the remaining teen years and get on with their lives. Maybe that is what I should have wished for when I saw the shooting star.

Chapter 34
DECEIT AND LIES

WHEN I WAS little, I was taught never to lie. I don't remember why my parents told me I shouldn't, but I do remember they said never ever tell a lie. When I entered parochial school in the second grade, the subject of not lying was a big deal with the nuns. Sister Mary Frances was emphatic about not lying and Sister Helen Agnes, the Mother Superior, used her ruler on our knuckles if she ever caught one of us in the act of lying. When I joined the Boy Scouts, honesty was stressed and that meant no lying. I reentered public school in the fifth grade and by then, I understood that I had wasted a lot of time and energy worrying about my nose growing longer every time I lied. By the time I was in the sixth grade, I understood that lying was unethical.

My father had a stellar reputation in Wilson. He was known as a man of his word and in his time, a man's word and his handshake were as good as a signed contract. Repeatedly, my father had instilled in me that I was only as good as my word. "Braxton," he would say, "your word is your bond; it's like money in the bank. When you speak to someone, look them in the eye and tell them the *damn* truth. Your word should always be good; be truthful." I believed him and I tried; I honestly tried to live up to his expectation of me when it came to telling the truth.

Peer pressure can make a child do a lot of foolish things. We are all tested sooner or later, and sometimes, what our parents have repeatedly imparted to us is not good enough. It should be, but on those rare occasions, it's just not good enough. My biggest test came my first year of junior high school and I learned the consequences of lying the hard way.

I was in Miss Alice Calhoun's seventh grade English class when my integrity was challenged. Miss Calhoun, whom I admired and respected, caught Sally Castles, the daughter of one of our state senators, cheating on our final exam. I sat next to Sally and saw her cheating. Sally had done it all year but had never gotten caught. When Miss Calhoun found the cheat sheet on the floor beside Sally's desk and recognized the handwriting, she approached Sally first. Of course Sally said she hadn't been cheating and told our teacher that if she didn't believe her to ask her friend, Braxton.

Miss Calhoun was a gorgeous woman and a good teacher and it was hard not to be truthful with her. The next day, she did ask me to verify Sallie's cheating and instead of telling the truth, I said no. I looked Miss Calhoun square in those beautiful blue eyes of hers and told her that I'd never seen Sallie Castles cheat, not then, never. Sallie gave an approving smile when she learned of what I had said to our teacher. The last day of school Miss Calhoun called me to her desk. First, she told me how much she had enjoyed having me in class and secondly, she said she knew I would continue to be an excellent English student. The last thing she said to me burned my soul when she spoke. In her usual quiet voice, she said, "Braxton, I want you to always be true to yourself. Remember a good friend will never ask you to misrepresent the truth to another." She took my hand, shook it, and said goodbye. I knew then Miss Calhoun had known all along that I had lied to protect Sally. I felt lower than cow shit and I was genuinely sorry I had lied to Miss Calhoun. More than even that, I was sorry that I had betrayed her trust in me and had let her down. The icing on the cake came at the end of August when Sally Castles mailed out invitations to her big end of the summer party. I didn't get an invitation, confirming she didn't value me as a friend. Miss Calhoun was right about friendship. And it was Miss Calhoun who demonstrated friendship to me, although I wasn't wise enough to know it at the time.

Today, Friday, June 21st, I've been a party to another big lie. It involves people I care about. This lie could be classified as a white lie or it could be called stretching the truth. Whatever name or label I give to it, it is still a lie, a lie to protect my father. Why? Because in his condition, he couldn't handle the truth. When he asked where Mother was, Ingrid told him that she had taken a nasty spill. This was true. When he asked her what happened, Ingrid told him that she had fallen on West Nash Street and had bruised herself badly. This was, also, true. When he asked if Mother had been drinking, Ingrid said Mother might have had one drink. This was also true but not the complete truth. When he asked if Mother had been alone, Ingrid said that when she went to get her, she was alone. This, too, was true but evaded his question.

I stood beside Ingrid when she told my father this and after each of Ingrid's answers, my father looked directly at me for confirmation. I never said a word, giving him the impression that what he had been told was true. Standing there, looking in the hollow cavities that held my father's eyes, I felt like I was spitting what he had taught me back in his face. Ingrid assured my father that Mother needed a few days of rest to recuperate from her bruises and that's why she was staying with Josephine. Seeing the pain and anguish in his face convicted Ingrid to offer him more comfort. "Louis," Ingrid said, "Virginia will be fine and there is no reason for you to worry. Please believe me." Like Mother, my father respected and trusted Ingrid and he chose to believe what he had been told.

I understand the logic behind what Ingrid did. I understand the difference between complete and half-truth. I also know that the truth can do more harm sometimes than what Ingrid did. This didn't fit the rulebook I had been given as a boy, but maybe little boys need only the black and white rules because that's all they can deal with. No one can explain at what age the rules change and when the rulebook given to the little child has to be tossed aside. It does happen. The rules change when the lies get bigger and the game becomes more complex and the players are no longer children. This game of deceit and lies keeps its own agenda and we're not always given advanced warning. It's happening again, this summer, to my family and me. I feel as if I'm swimming in a sea of lies, both little and big, and have been since school let out. I can deal with it now and not forfeit my friendships.

Today was the perfect day to do nothing. By nine o'clock, it was hot, steamy, sticky, and the humidity was already unbearable. But there was work to be done because Mother would be coming home later this morning. Lily with some small assistance from me had the house cleaned the way Mother likes it. The floors had been waxed, the main rooms dusted, the front windows washed with vinegar and water, the bathroom cleaned and sprayed with Lysol, the kitchen floor mopped, and the kitchen stove scrubbed. Mother should be pleased and she can continue her rest here.

Anne was lucky and got out of this army inspection. Lillian Hayes and her family invited Anne to spend a week at Morehead with them. They left this morning. Jackson agreed to stay with Daddy this weekend and into next week before he takes a little time off. And tonight is Patsy Wentworth's party. I get to drive because Jason's dad said no to his using the limo. My plans are to start picking everyone up at six o'clock. The party starts at seven. And then, I get to meet with David Byrd later in the evening.

I was ready for lunch when Lily put it on the back porch table. She had one place set. On the mat she had put a plate, a fork, and a coaster. That was it. I couldn't bear the thought of eating another meal alone.

"Lily? Come here please."

"Yes, Braxton?"

"Join me for lunch."

"I can't do that!"

"You most certainly can," I said. "I'm asking you. Come on. I'll set another place."

"I reckons it's okay." I had eaten in the kitchen many times while she cooked at the stove or did other work in the kitchen. We had never set down together and shared a meal. Lily knew this all too well and she wanted to be careful not to cross that fine line that exists between blacks and whites. It wasn't any big deal to me. I saw no difference between sitting down and eating together and my eating and sitting while she stood and worked. Eating is eating.

"It's perfectly okay." I set a place for Lily and she brought out pimento cheese sandwiches and cucumber sandwiches with mayonnaise, one of my favorites. There was a dish of potato chips and a small bowl of dill pickles. And each of us had a mason jar of sweet iced tea.

"Take what you wants of the sandwiches so I can puts them back in the refrigerator. I don't knows when Jackson will get to eat. And the good Lord knows, your daddy do eat like a bird." I took one of each and she took one pimento cheese sandwich. We both grabbed a handful of potato chips and left the pickles in the bowl. After she returned the food to the kitchen, she sat down.

"Lily, you look tired." Her face was thinner now and her eyes were red.

"I am tired. I sure is." She had worked doubly hard since Mother had been at Aunt Josephine's. She came earlier and left one to two hours later.

"Lily, do you like working here?" I asked, trying to be subtle. "Be honest."

"Well, I do likes your mother but she's a hard woman to work for. She's demanding but I can lives with that. I likes your daddy, too. I just don't likes being around sickness all the time." Lily looked toward the inside of the house when she said that.

"And?"

"And?" she responded with a grin. "What you asking for?"

"You said 'well' and I'm waiting for you to finish."

"All right, I don't believes your daddy's gonna lives much longer and I can't imagines what your mothers going to do when the good Lord takes him home," she said, looking down at the table. "And I worries about you and Miss Anne. You kids done seen too much hardship and trouble. You needs a rest. No child should go through all you two has."

"Thank you, Lily," I said. "I guess I don't think of it that way. Since I'm not used to anything else, I think this is normal."

"It's anything but normal," Lily said. She patted the back of my right hand. "Your daddy's a good man, Braxton, but no man should have to suffer the ways that man do."

"Lily, do you really like my daddy or are you just saying that?"

"Yes, I certainly do," she said. "But, I knows you have a hard times liking him."

"Huh? What did you say?"

"You hears me, Braxton Haywood. I've known you since you was a little boy. You and your daddy's never been what you calls close but that's not his fault. He's been sick ever since you been born. You needs to look for good in your daddy. He can't help that he's so sick."

"You're a damn smart woman, Lily," I said. "Damn smart!"

"Thank you, Braxton," she said. Lily stood grabbing the plates and glasses. "Braxton, can I says something to you?"

"You know you can, Lily. You're practically my second mother."

"You needs to laughs more. You is too serious sometimes, Braxton," Lily said. "I loves you, Braxton, and I can tells you that the good Lord will take you out of this boiling pot one day. You remember that old Lily told you that. Trys to learn to enjoy the situation the good Lord has puts you in and lets Him help you. He wills, you know."

"Thank you, Lily," I said. After we finished clearing the table and cleaning the dishes, I told Lily to sit down and take her shoes off. Her feet were large and flat. She had numerous calluses on the bottom from walking barefooted. I wanted to do something for her that I had seen her do for my mother so many times. I went to the bathroom and took Mother's foot pan from the linen closet. I poured in some Epsom salt and filled it with warm water. I brought it back to the porch and told Lily to rest her feet. She laughed. When she finished, I gave her one of Effie's hugs.

I had already been to Wild Bill's Texaco Station downtown on East Nash Street and filled the tank with low octane gas. There were stations closer to our house but since Bill Hudson had bought the station from Daddy and Billy Farmer, another tobacco buyer with Exeter Tobacco Company, when Daddy's health got so bad, I thought we should still give him our business. Bill knows the situation with my daddy and always gives us a special discount on everything, even gasoline. I think he appreciates the effort I make to get the car down to him whenever I can. He has always taken a lot of time with me and made over me. He taught me to change a tire and when Mother was too nervous to teach me to drive, she called on

Wild Bill. I learned to master the art of keeping the car in the same lane in one afternoon. He is one of the few men here in Wilson who has ever told me he saw a lot of my dad in me. That means a lot to me.

"MOTHER, WELCOME HOME," I said, walking toward her when she entered the house early that afternoon. "It's good to have you back." I gave her a big welcome home hug.

"Thank you, Braxton," she said. "It's good to be home."

"Miss Virginia, it's good to have you homes again," Lily said as she walked in from the hallway after putting the folded, air dried sheets in the linen closet. "I hope you will finds everything to your satisfaction."

"I'm certain I will, Lily," Mother said. "Thank you for taking care of everything while I was gone. Everything looks so fresh." Mother knew just what to say to please Lily and bring a smile to her face.

"I couldn't of done it without Mister Braxton," Lily said. "He done worked mighty hard."

"Thank you both," Mother said. "Now if you will excuse me, I want to see your daddy."

Mother opened the French doors that led from the living room into Daddy's room and disappeared behind the white curtains that hung tightly on the other side of the French doors. Lily and I looked at each other and I gave the thumbs up sign. Lily followed with an "amen" and retired to the kitchen. I went to my bedroom to find a bathing suit that would still fit me. I knew the jock strap would. That area had seen little growth over the last year much to my disappointment. I found a madras suit that I'd worn once. Putting the jock strap inside my bathing suit, I neatly rolled my towel around the suit. I was ready for the party.

The afternoon dragged toward a long awaited-for night. Everyone was going to Patsy Wentworth's swim party at the country club. Excited was an understatement to describe the feeling I was experiencing. The first big party of the summer and it couldn't come at a better time for me. At last I could get out of the house and release some of the tension that had been building up inside me over the last few days. Being with my friends should take my mind off these unpleasantries.

There was no reason to catch up on Holden's adventures because I wouldn't be able to concentrate even if I tried. I had already called Rita's number twice and no one answered. She had to be on vacation but I didn't know how to confirm this. She would certainly be on my side if I dared telling her some of what had happened. (*Bad idea, Braxton!*) In spite of my effort to take a nap, I was too wound up and stayed wide awake. Not calling Byrd tried my patience and for once, there was nothing to do around the house. I felt like a wound up top with no place to spin. I had a two-hour wait. I walked into the kitchen and poured myself a glass of sweet iced tea. I walked out onto the porch, cut on the radio with the intent of finding some rock-and-roll music. I lit a cigarette and for a few minutes, I lost myself in another world.

Chapter 35
OTHER HEINOUS THINGS

AT SIX O'CLOCK I grabbed my towel, picked up the car keys from the marble top table in the living room, walked out the front door, said goodbye to Mrs. Thurston and Mother who sat in the rocking chairs on the porch visiting, got into the car, and drove toward Jason Parker's home up the street. For a change, Jason was ready when I pulled into his carport. He seemed in a down mood when he jumped into the front seat. He sat perfectly quiet.

"What's wrong with you tonight?" I asked, tossing my rolled towel into the back seat.

"It's been decided for sure," Jason said. His mouth turned down with a marked sadness.

"What are you talking about Jason?" I asked, cranking the motor, pulling out from the carport, and heading toward Matt Beatty's house.

"Going to Fork Union Military Academy!" said Jason. "I'll be leaving the third week of August for a three-year career in the military."

"That's nothing new," I said. "You saw that coming."

"I had hoped that my old man would want to keep the bastard around. But no! He's decided to kick me out!" He shrugged his shoulders.

"Come on, Jason," I said frowning. "Don't start that mess tonight!"

"It's just some no account academy in Virginia. I have to go up there the first of July for what they call a formal visit."

"Who knows, you may enjoy going to school there! I've heard good things about FUMA."

"Yeah, right!" he said. "Just like I enjoy taking a fucking enema."

"Okay, you've made your point." I laughed. "Do me a favor and have some fun tonight? Oh, where's your bathing suit and towel?"

"My suit's under my bermudas and I'll get a towel out of my locker at the club."

When I pulled in front of Matt's house, he was standing in the doorway waiting. He walked briskly to the car and got in the back seat. His suit, obviously wrapped in a towel, was tucked under his left arm. "I'm ready for this night!" Matt said, leaning over the front seat. "By the way, Braxton, have you heard from Byrd yet?"

"Yes," I said. "He called last night."

"What?" Matt's face mirrored shock.

"That's right," I said. "He hopes to be in tonight but he won't be at the party because his daddy doesn't want him hanging around with any of us."

"*Fuck* Mr. Byrd!" said Jason. "He's worse than my old man. Two pieces of horse shit right out of the same bowel movement."

"Look! Maybe we can make some sense out of all this soon. I hope to talk with him tonight, but that's just between the three of us. His dad's putting a lot of pressure on him."

"I'm afraid for Byrd," said Matt. "I don't believe he can take this pressure much longer."

It took two honks of the horn for Thad to bound out of his front door and run the short distance to the car. He was dressed in his swim trunks. His towel swung from his neck, resting on his muscular upper chest. His shirt was in his right hand. He definitely had the body girls would kill for. "Greetings! Are you gentleman ready for some fun in the water with some of Coon's finest?" Thad slid into the backseat, bumping Matt over to the other side. He laughed.

"If you mean me, just forget it!" said Jason in his old, devilish manner.

"All right, let's go for it!" I said. "Our next stop is the Wilson Country Club, home of those born of the manor of which some of us are not, but should have been."

"Amen! Amen! And amen!" said Thad.

"I hate to break your mood party up, but I need to stop by Taps first," said Jason.

"Oh, no!" said Matt. "You know what happened last time."

"Count me out too," said Thad, throwing his hands up in disgust.

"Is it absolutely necessary?" I asked.

"Yes," said Jason. "Why in the fuck do you think I asked you to go there first?"

"Absolutely no, Braxton!" said Thad. "We need to get to the party before it ends."

"I take you guys everywhere you want to go," said Jason. "But let me ask one thing, and no, you won't hear of it. Well, you won't have me around much longer to be your chauffeur."

"And what does that mean?" asked Matt. He sighed, possibly from Jason's antics.

"Never mind, Matt," I said. "I'll drop you and Thad off first and then drive to Taps. It's not but about a mile from the club."

"That's cool with me," said Thad, sounding relieved.

"Fine," said Jason. "I just want to come prepared and not be mooching off Teddy Sanders and Joe Lockamy and their crowd." Jason was referring to the football team and cheerleaders. Jason had succeeded in temporarily putting a damper on the evening's festivities, and for the rest of the ride, we were fairly quiet.

There was a cavalcade of cars turning left off of Highway 301 into the club's entrance. The short drive up the rocky knoll to the front entrance was bumper to bumper. We followed in single line formation with the other guests. Some were in Cadillacs, Lincolns, and Chryslers; others, in Mercurys, Chevrolets, and Pontiacs. The drive took longer than usual because every car was coming to a standstill to view the light blue '57 Chevrolet Impala convertible with a big red ribbon tied around it, sitting in front of the club's main building. One policeman dressed in full uniform was standing beside the car to protect it from any potential damage. "Holy shit, will you look at that!" said Jason. "Who does that belong to?"

"Duh!" said Matt. "Who do you think, birdbrain? It's a birthday present for Patsy."

"I didn't know it's her birthday!" said Jason. "You think you're so damn smart, Matt."

"Stop it, Jason," I said. "This isn't a birthday party where you have to bring presents. You're on edge and taking it out on everyone. If you keep it up, I'll take your ass home." Jason looked dumbfounded and he leaned against the seat with his eyes shut and his mouth closed.

"We'll hop out here, Braxton," said Thad. "Thanks. We'll see you guys when you get back." Thad and Matt got out and joined some of our classmates who were giggling and pushing each other like regular teenagers do when they're carefree and their life is uncomplicated. I drove Jason the one mile to Taps. I didn't ask him what he needed that was so important but I figured it was beer and cigarettes.

The gravel crunched raucously under the tires as I pulled the Tank into one of the vacant parking spaces outside Taps. Jason and I got out and walked to the entrance of the familiar white building with the neon Pabst sign that still hung against the bars. It had been one week ago tonight since the shooting and still no word on the whereabouts of the two black men. Unlike last week, tonight was splendid, a clear and luminous North Carolina evening.

I held the screened door for Jason and with confidence he walked into the small, smoked-filled, dimly lit main room of Taps' Tavern. I followed Jason into the room tripping on the doorsill. Four or five beer bellied, blue-collar workers standing around the room drinking beer and smoking cigarettes stopped to glare at us. We walked to the counter and stood. I saw Taps out of the corner of my eye coming out of the room that served as his billiard's room. Tonight Taps wore a blue patch over his right eye and his Myrtle Beach tee shirt accentuated his muscular upper torso.

"Can we have some service in here?" I said, poking Jason in the side and pounding my fist on the scarred, wooden counter.

"What the hell are you trying to do?" whispered Jason. "Do you want to get us kicked out of here?"

"Well, well," said Richard 'Taps' Morgan. "Look what the garbage truck brought in!" Taps came over and slapped me on the back and then we shook hands.

"Good to see you, Taps," I said. "And before you ask, I haven't seen that no-account cousin of mine." I laughed.

"Played golf with him yesterday," Taps said. "He told me to kick your ass out of here the next time you came. He told me to tell you that you're too young to frequent this sort of place without him holding your hands." Taps laughed boisterously and then turned toward Jason.

"Hello, Taps," said Jason. Jason remained calm and extended his hand.

"The man with the attitude is back again," said Taps. "Whoo-eee, to what do I owe the privilege of your company on this glorious night?" Taps gripped Jason's hand and squeezed it hard. Jason grimaced and his eyes squinted until Taps let go.

"The same as last week," Jason said. "I want to buy a six pack of Bud and a pack of Chesterfields. Are you open for business tonight?"

"I don't know Jason, you cost me plenty last week. Do you think I should sell this young fart anything, Braxton?" He smiled, knowing he was pulling Jason's chain. I watched to see how my friend would fire back at Taps.

"My money is as good as the next man's," said Jason, looking at Taps without any hesitation.

"A six-pack of Bud and a pack of Chesters is what you'll get," said Taps, obviously impressed with Jason's response. Taps liked you if you gave him shit for shit. If you backed down or acted offended, he would ride you until you either broke or came around.

"Say, how's Zeke doing? I haven't seen anything in the papers about the incident last week."

"Jason, that's a dollar twenty-nine coming my way. Braxton, Zeke is doing quite well, thank you. The shot he took turned out to be more of a flesh wound. He spent one night in the hospital and the doc told him to take four days to recoup. I gave him an extra week to get back in gear."

"That's good of you," I said. "Please tell Zeke we're rooting for him."

"Where's your other buddies tonight?" Taps asked. "They too scared to come back?"

"That's not it at all," I said. "I dropped them off at the club. Patsy Wentworth is having her annual, summer swim party."

"Oh-oh! Them little virgins better watch their little cherries tonight, hey Jason?"

"You're right," said Jason, putting his money on the counter. "They're in for a treat tonight! They just don't know it yet."

"Taps, it's good to see you again," I said. "Come on, Jason, we need to get going."

"Behave yourself tonight, Braxton. I don't want to have to give your cuz a bad report at next Thursday's tee time."

"Never!" I said, opening the screen door and walking into the parking lot. Jason followed, drinking the first of his six "Buddies" for the evening. He had his first beer downed by the time he got back in the car and closed the door. I had a sneaking suspicion that he was going to get in trouble tonight.

"What did you mean back there, Jason?" I turned the ignition and backed out of the space where I had parked. Jason didn't answer. "Did you hear me?"

"Just wait! You'll be the first to know," Jason said, lighting a cigarette and chuckling to himself. He threw his empty beer can out the window and popped another. Before he took a sip, he let out one of his thunderous belches. "Now I'm ready for number two!"

"Hey! You need to slow down, Jason, and just cool it. Don't do something stupid tonight!" I said, turning left onto Highway 301 for the short drive back to the club.

"You drive and let me enjoy my 'Buddies.' I paid for these charmers and I plan to enjoy them, one-by-one," said Jason. "Braxton, be a good boy and don't nag." He leaned his head back and took a long guzzle then followed with another belch equally as loud.

"Jason, this is when you irritate the living shit out of me. What you're doing makes no sense."

"Makes a lot of sense to me and that's what counts."

"I didn't drive you out here tonight to be your babysitter. I came out here to relax and have some fun. God knows I deserve it!"

"No one's asking you to baby-sit! For Christ's sake, Braxton, *let it go. Enjoy* yourself and let me *enjoy* myself. I can take care of myself, thank you."

"*Yeah, right! Like shit you can!*" I said, determined to put an immediate halt to his stupid quest. "*Give me the rest of the beer.*" I reached over for the remainder of the six-pack sitting between his legs.

"Get your *fucking hands away from me!* I don't want to *hurt you! Get this through your head—you're not my father. I repeat, you're not my father.*" Jason's face was beet red, either from yelling or drinking too much too fast. He drank the remainder of the can with the fury of a mad man and then threw it out the window.

From my side view mirror, I saw the can bouncing down the highway as I turned right into the entrance to the club.

"You're not leaving the beer in this car!" I said, slowing my speed to a crawl. Cars had started pulling over and parking along the shoulder of the drive that led up to the main building. I took this to mean that the main parking lot was full and I joined the line by pulling in behind a '55 Ford. I cut off the ignition, turned toward Jason, and waited for him to say something.

"What the hell? Why are you parking here?" he asked. "Christ, we're a fourth of a mile from the pool."

"Get out and walk! That's what I intend to do," I said, annoyed with his asinine behavior. "Be back here at eleven or you'll be left!"

Jason didn't respond. Rather, he got out of the car, slammed the door in anger, and stopped. He looked at me with killing eyes and popped another beer. I left him beside the car drinking his third beer and smoking another Chester. Jason was a pathetic picture of a misunderstood sixteen-year-old trying to be cool. At least that's what I thought at the moment. I was wrong.

"Screw him!" I muttered to myself as I walked up the knoll and around the circle in front of the main building with its large columns and small balcony. I stopped to admire Patsy Wentworth's new car, thinking every jock at Coon will pursue her just to drive this American beauty. "God, it's gorgeous," I murmured. I ran my hands across the matching light blue leather interior, across the back and over the tail fins. It was a classic! The cop smiled and nodded in agreement.

"Hello, Braxton, are you by yourself tonight?" came a high-pitched female voice. I turned around and found my good friend, Cassie Sutton, standing before me in her pink two-piece bathing suit that accentuated her beautiful figure. Cassie was a scholarly brunette with freckles and curly brown hair that fell off the shoulders of her slender five-foot-four-inch frame. Without her glasses, she was actually pretty. Her dark brown eyes were one of her best features but she was blind as a bat without the blue-speckled frames that dangled from the silver chain hanging from her neck and resting on her buxom chest.

"Yes and no," I said. "I brought Matt, Thad, and Jason."

"Thad is poolside with Peggy Lassiter. I haven't seen Matt yet."

"What are you doing out here in the parking lot alone, without Eddie?"

"I wanted to get away from him and smoke a cigarette." She exhaled a long stream of smoke and dropped her cigarette on the pavement. "Come on, I'll walk you in. Get prepared because Rhonda is with Dave Shepherd tonight. I thought you two had a thing going?"

"Only in my head," I said in disappointment. "I haven't even called her this summer."

"Why not?" Cassie and I had been good friends since the seventh grade. We shared most everything together. She was the first girl I kissed and that was practice for her first date. Her mother always said that she wanted us to get married because we were right for each other, whatever that meant.

"Let's go through the entrance between the holly hedges so you can appreciate the beauty of all the fabulous decorations." I had been chairman of the decorating committee for the sophomore prom and Cassie knew I liked anything done with an artistic flair.

"The beauty will be ruined by that sickening, racist sign they have hanging on the gate," I said. "If I was a member of this WASP, elitist club, I'd argue to have it removed. Damn! I hate that thing!"

"It depicts ignorance and stupidity," said Cassie. "They just don't realize it, but one day soon they will and it'll be sooner than any of us realize." She spoke like a prophet.

When we got to the gate's entrance where the tall holly hedges that surrounded the entire pool area and offered privacy met, the sign that hung by a chain over the gate was missing. The sign that read, "No Coloreds, No Dogs, No Jews Allowed" had been removed.

"I bet Dr. Wentworth took it down for tonight or he had someone take it down," I said. "Good for him." The sign's absence gave me a minute of joy and hope for a future unclouded with ignorance.

"Isn't it beautiful, Braxton? Look at the different lighted, colored lanterns," Cassie said, grabbing my hand and pulling me onto the cement deck that surrounded the pool. A disc jockey was in charge of the music and "Little Darlin'" by The Diamonds broke the stillness of the star-lit night. The newly installed outdoor phonic system added a richer tone to the music and gave a more festive air to the party. Patsy's party was infested with what some of our parents called "the lost generation," teens caught in the claws of the pioneers of rock-n-roll. A number of couples danced on the wooden deck, one ground level above the pool. Colored balloons surrounded the entire pool, hanging from fishing wire, giving the illusion that they were dangling, keeping time with the music. The white, interior pool lights had been replaced by fluorescent green, giving a mystical effect. Blue, white, and gold crepe paper streamers intertwined together formed an arch over the pool area where below some forty of our classmates were enjoying the cool water. And on the balcony of the main building hung a large "Happy Birthday Patsy! Soon to be Sweet Sixteen!" banner.

Suddenly, there was no music. Stillness took over the entire pool area like an unwanted visitor and there was no movement. Everything and everyone stopped. There followed a hushed roar and every person inside the pool swam to the poolside closest to them. The people on both decks remained as rigid as matchbox figures. An eerie quietness enveloped the celebration. Even the night bowed in stunned silence. And all yielded to the figure on the diving board.

Jason had taken center stage. Standing at the back of the diving board, wrapped only in a white towel that hung loosely around his waste, his tanned, well-formed body staggered, offering the only movement before his appalled peers. All eyes fixated on him as his voice exploded in agony, "*I wanted to say farewell to all of you tonight!*"

I stood, not only frozen in fear, but also afraid of what he might do. He walked unsteady toward the edge of the diving board carrying a can of beer in his left hand. Around his neck hung the offensive sign that we missed from the gate when we entered. Jason had added a fourth line to those not welcomed. In black marking he had printed in bold letters, "NO BASTARDS." He took another unbalanced step forward and again shouted, "*My good buddy, Braxton, told me not to do something stupid tonight. Are you here, Braxton?*" His words slurred badly when he screamed and his balance was becoming less steady. Cassie grabbed my hand, squeezing it.

"I'm here, Jason," I yelled, stepping toward the edge of the pool. Cassie, still holding my hand, stepped with me. We were a pool's length from the diving board. "Get down and tell me what you want to, but let everyone else enjoy the party."

"*Still giving orders, aren't you, Braxton?*" He took a long swig from his beer and continued, "*Braxton, over there, knows something the rest of you don't!*"

"He's drunk as hell!" Cassie said, squeezing my hand tighter this time. "Braxton, do something *now!*"

Looking across the pool area, I saw Dr. George Wentworth, Patsy's father, running from the main building. The policeman who had been standing guard out front rushed through the hedge opening and onto the pool deck. I ran quickly around the side of the pool, slipping once but catching myself, and then I stopped. Jason looked down at me and I stared up at him.

"*Many of you assholes here think you're better than I am and you are! You know why? Read my sign!*" Jason put the beer can to his mouth, threw his head back and took another swallow, and threw the can into the pool. No one said anything. Everyone stood looking and waiting. His face was a snarl of agony and his eyes carried a wounded look. Looking directly down into the pool area, Jason unpredictably pulled his towel from his waist and stood stark naked in front of forty percent of the rising junior class. The tone of his voice changed, becoming calm and deliberate as he spoke, "Take a good look girls! See what you've denied yourself. And you football studs, I don't think many of you can match this. Jason reached down and held his large dick between the fingers of his right hand. "Eat your heart out! Any of you girls want to bust your cherry tonight? Meet me on the ninth green." Jason staggered, turned, and with his back to the pool area, he began jumping up and down on the diving board. "*Watch me!*" he shouted.

"My God, he's going to try a back flip," I said to Cassie. "He prides himself on this."

I saw Jason go into the air and begin his turn. When he completed his arch, something bizarre happened. It was as if a hand appeared and snatched the air space out from under him. I watched his body make a flopping motion on his way down and then I saw his head hit the diving board. I think everyone heard the loud cracking sound when his head hit the wood—a rumble of moans followed from the crowd of witnesses. I watched, horrified, as Jason's lifeless body disappeared under the water. I don't know how many seconds passed but Jason didn't come back up.

"Oh, my God! Jason!" I screamed and dove in the water, going under to find him. Thad, Matt, and Dave, Patsy's older brother, joined me. It was Thad who got to Jason first, pulling him to the side of the pool. Matt and I helped Thad get him out and up on the cement deck. We laid Jason on his back. Kneeling over his body, Matt gave a startled gasp and my heart leaped when we saw the blood running from his forehead, nose, and out of his mouth. Our friends crowded around us and I could hear their reactions of shock and surprise.

"Out of the way, everyone," said Dr. Wentworth. "Dave, go call an ambulance *now!*" Jason just lay there. His eyes were closed, his face was ashen white with the exception of the blood streaming down his face and he didn't move. I reached for a pulse and felt a slight one.

"Is he alive?" Patsy Wentworth was beside herself. "Can you find a pulse?"

"Barely," I said. I put my ear against his heart trying to hear something. A hand pushed me aside. I looked up and saw Patsy's father.

Dr. Wentworth bent down, wiped the blood off Jason's lips and chin, and proceeded to give Jason mouth-to-mouth resuscitation. Within a minute, water came rushing from Jason's mouth. He gagged and spit. More water ran from his nose and his mouth. He coughed and his legs began to squirm but there was no real movement yet.

"Braxton, who did Jason come with?" Dr. Wentworth asked.

"With me, sir," I said.

"He's going to the hospital. Go call his parents and tell them to meet us at the Woodard-Herring Hospital. Patsy, go get my medical bag out of the front floorboard of my car."

"Is he going to be okay?" asked Thad, speaking for all of us.

"I think this boy may be hemorrhaging. We need to get him to a hospital quick. Is that damn ambulance here yet?" said Dr. Wentworth, showing his agitation. "Thad, go and tell the disc jockey to start the music. You kids go back and get this party restarted."

Most everyone dispersed into little groups discussing what had just happened. Jason was not that well liked among our classmates so I didn't expect him to get a fair shake when the rumors started bouncing off the wall. No one, better than I, knew the pressure that he was under and even I, practically his best friend, took him for granted.

I called Jason's parents and Artis answered the phone. The Parkers were at a party and Artis wasn't told where the party was being held, but he assured me Jason knew. I told Artis briefly what had happened and that Jason was in no condition to give me a phone number. I didn't want to alarm Artis but I insisted that as soon as the Parkers walked in the house, they were to turn around and go directly to the Woodard-Herring Hospital.

Jason was still lying on the pool deck when the ambulance finally arrived, some fifteen to twenty minutes after it was called. Dr. Wentworth had stopped as much of the bleeding as he could. Only a small amount continued to ooze from his nose. A bandage covering half of Jason's head was in place. Dr. Wentworth advised there would be a fair amount of stitches taken but he didn't want to make an educated guess. Jason was still lifeless but he was breathing, although taking shallow breaths. I didn't know how bad Jason's condition was and I feared asking Dr. Wentworth. It seemed inappropriate and rather stupid.

Jason was placed on a stretcher and carried to the ambulance parked in the center circle. Dr. Wentworth and Thad got in the ambulance with Jason. Matt and I ran to my car, and Dave Wentworth took his father's keys. We were to follow. Everyone else stayed at the club. When we left the pool area, "Chances Are" sung by Johnny Mathis was coming over the sound system and I thought what an appropriate song for a send off. I glanced over my shoulder as I shot through the hedge opening. With the exception of a few guests standing behind the ambulance, everyone went back to what they were doing before the untimely interruption. I turned to Cassie and said, "We are a fickle crowd, aren't we?"

The ambulance took Highway 301 like a roadrunner being chased by a coyote. It was hard for me to keep up with the ambulance pushing speeds of eighty-five to ninety miles an hour. Dave ripped past me easily in his daddy's Cadillac. I was afraid to push my old Buick past seventy-five mph for fear of blowing an engine. Even at seventy-five miles an hour, the car was jumping and hissing. I pushed the Tank to the max and rolling down my window, I yelled out in the dark, empty air.

"Feeling any better?" asked Matt.

"Damn right!" I said, following an adrenalin rush. "For a while back there, I thought Jason was a goner."

"Why does he do these crazy things for attention, Braxton?"

"I'm not so sure that was the reason this time . . . but you may be right."

"If you don't stay with them, then we have to go the speed limit. They're our meal ticket in case the 'Highway Fuzz' stops us," said Matt.

"I realize that, but I'd rather get there in one piece than be the next ambulance rider."

"Quite true," Matt said. "Just keep it in the road and do your best."

I was very familiar with the Woodard-Herring Clinic since my daddy had practically been a permanent boarder there at one time. Upon arriving, I parked in the doctor's parking lot. Matt and I jumped from the car and wasting no time, we rounded the tall brick structure until we came to the emergency entrance. Pushing the heavy steel doors open, Matt and I stepped through the frame and ran the distance to the waiting room. It was so quiet in the narrow hallway that I could hear the echo from our shoes attacking the green tiled floor and bouncing off the wall. "Please, God, let Jason live," I said as we ran. Arriving out of breath at the waiting room, we practically plowed into Thad, Dave, and Artis, who were already there.

"They just took him in, Braxton," Thad said. "Dr. Wentworth will let us know something as soon as possible."

"Did he show signs of improvement in the ambulance?" I asked.

"He opened his eyes a couple of times but other than that, nothing," said Thad. "He's got a nasty cut in his head and one on his chin. And his nose may be broken. He's going to have a hell of a hangover when he comes to."

"Artis, where are the Parkers?" I looked around the waiting room for them.

"They's here," Artis said. "They came in right after we hung up. They's with some doctors around the corner."

"What an evening this turned out to be!" said Matt.

"Yes, but it could've been worse," I said.

"What time is it, Braxton?" asked Artis.

"My God, it's ten-fifteen," I said, remembering my appointment with Byrd at eleven-thirty.

The doors of the emergency room finally opened. Dr. Wentworth and another doctor came out. Dr. Wentworth began walking to where we were sitting. He had a solemn expression on his face and he was taking his time walking. The other doctor turned and went around the corner.

"Okay, fellows, this is all I can tell you now," Dr. Wentworth began. "Jason had fifteen stitches taken in his forehead and five stitches in his chin. The cuts on his forehead area are deep and he has lost a lot of blood in that area and it appears that the frontal skull is badly bruised. He had one petite seizure on the table but that doesn't mean he will continue to have them." I looked at Artis and he returned my gaze. "One more thing—Jason's nose has been dislodged and it may be broken. The bleeding has been stopped and Jason is resting." He paused and looked at Thad, then Matt, and then me.

"Is there more, Dr. Wentworth?" asked Thad.

"Yes. Jason had a lot to drink tonight and his blood alcohol was very high. His breathing is very shallow and he is currently hooked up to a respirator. I need to ask a question and I need a straight answer." He paused and then began again. "Does Jason drink a lot?"

Matt and Thad looked at me and I looked toward Artis. No one made an attempt to say anything and then Thad said, "Tell him, Braxton. If any of us knows, you'll know."

"For someone our age, I think Jason drinks a whole lot. Tonight, he may have had six beers. I know he drinks several times a week but I don't know about the quantity." I turned away from Dr. Wentworth, feeling like a heel. I had ratted on Jason and I knew I had to, but good friends don't betray one another.

"Thank you for your honesty, Braxton," said Dr. Wentworth. "Jason is fortunate to have all of you boys as friends. You may have just saved his life." I turned back toward the group, shaking my head in disbelief.

The three of us looked at each other. We were confused and baffled at what Dr. Wentworth had said. His comments contradicted our understanding of friendship. Jason's drinking was more than just teenage boozing; he had a real problem. "May we see him?" I asked.

"Not yet. Tomorrow would be better. His parents are with him now," said Dr. Wentworth.

"Will he be going home tonight?" asked Matt.

"No. Jason will be kept here for observation until at least Monday and then his regular doctors will determine what course of action to take," said Dr. Wentworth. "Fellows, you have a very sick friend in that room. That's why I said he's lucky to have you as friends."

"Come on Matt and Thad, let's go home," I said. Tonight I had learned a new meaning of friendship. Yet, in my heart, I still felt as if I had let Jason down. Knowing myself, it was going to be hard for me to balance my feelings of sadness and betrayal with the fact that my honesty had actually helped Jason.

"That's a good idea," said Dr. Wentworth. "Dave, let's go back to the club and help wind the party down."

We all walked to the parking lot together. None of us said anything until we got to our cars. We told Dr. Wentworth and Dave goodbye and again expressed our thanks to both of them for all they'd done. Matt, again, apologized for the disruption of Patsy's party. I didn't know it at the time, but the evening's excitement had just begun.

The night was still calm and the sky was decorated with hundreds of thousands of celestial lights. I didn't know when I had last seen so many stars. They seemed close enough to touch and yet, they were so far away. Tonight, I felt we had rubbed elbows with some of the cold, darkness that lay between the stars and us.

The murky Milky Way stretched across the sky. If I could've had one wish tonight, I would've wanted to take a running jump and leaped into its midst and lose myself in its entire splendor. I knew this would never happen and I would have to stay here and deal with all the crap that life was throwing at us.

"What now?" asked Matt.

"I need to take you and Thad home. I'm supposed to meet Byrd at eleven-thirty," I said, looking at my watch. "Crap, it's almost eleven o'clock now."

"Do you think he'll show?" asked Thad.

"I'm counting on it," I said. "But you know, I believe he'll be there. Yes, he'll be there." I smiled for a moment, thinking how good it would be too see Byrd again.

"Poor Jason," said Thad. "I feel bad for him. I gave him a hard time tonight when I should've been there for him."

"Yeah, me too," said Matt. "I really do like him. It's just that he can be a pain in the ass!"

"No more guilt trips tonight, please," I said, turning on the ignition and pulling out of Dr. Mark Thorne's parking place. We drove the rest of the way in silence, our windows open to the warm, dusty, tobacco-leaf smell of our town.

Chapter 36
A WARNING WITH TEETH

A HALF OF a mile down hill from David Byrd's home was a small strip mall designed to replicate what a tourist might see in the commercial district of historical Wilson. Our miniature setting housed only six shops. The most popular was the Dairy Bar, serving homemade ice cream to a fourth of Wilson each week. Opening an ice cream bar across from the town's recreational park was a smart business investment, especially since the largest public swimming pool in Wilson was less than five thousand yards away. It was not the ice cream I came for tonight, but rather, to rendezvous with my good friend, David Byrd.

It was a little after 11:30 P.M. when I drove into the narrow, empty back parking lot that was as dark as night itself. I had to be careful not to drive into Ripley's Creek that abutted the edge of the entire parking lot. There was no barrier and no warning. One moment there was asphalt and the next moment there was water. And the last thing I wanted to do tonight was to end up in murky water. I backed the Tank up slowly until I was beside the rusty, brown trash bin and cut off the motor. I turned the radio knob on and moved the dial to WPTF to listen to Jimmy Capps and his musical wrap up. "The Great Pretender" by the Platters was playing. I rested my left arm on the window molding, leaned my head back against the seat, and closed my eyes. My intent was to relax until David came. The hot night air combined with the putrid odor lifting itself from the creek smelled like a dead possum that had been overheated by a noonday sun. Add in crickets, a few croaking frogs, and noises from bugs I didn't have a name for, and the result was a strange combination of two worlds competing for my attention.

"*Holy Mary, mother of Jesus!*" My voice rose an octave when I felt something grab my arm. I opened my eyes, turned, and saw what I thought was another hand wrapped around my forearm. It gripped me tight. A laugh followed and then the owner of the arm stood.

"Gotch you!"

"Byrd, you scared the *hell* out of me," I said, getting out of the car and grabbing his hand.

"I wish you could've seen your expression. It's worth the price of admission."

"It worked. In fact, I'm still shaking," I said, grabbing him in a big bear hug. "Damn, it's good to see you. You've been away too long!"

"It's good to see you, too, Braxton." David responded by hugging me equally as hard. "I don't have much time. I think I got out without anyone noticing."

"Let's get into the back seat of the car and talk. That way if a cop comes by we can hit the floorboard." I opened the back door on the driver's side and jumped in.

"Good idea," said Byrd, following me into the back seat. "Catch me up to date on what's going on."

"Okay, but first, tell me about you and your dad. What's going on?"

"It's crazy. He's making my life a living hell. One day I get up and everything's fine. The next day everything smells like shit. And it's all got to do with my friends and the weird ideas my father has gotten into his head. I swear the old man has flipped. He's determined that I never see y'all again, especially you. I don't know where he came up with all this crap. I resisted him at first, Braxton. But I can't take his beating me anymore. You should see my back and upper arms and the sick thing about it, I think he enjoys hitting me."

"May I ask you something?"

"Shoot. We're best buddies, aren't we?"

"Doggone right and always will be! Has he ever done to you what he did to Charles?"

"Well (silence) . . . don't ever repeat this, Braxton. Hell, he's done it lots of times, but not as much now since he's started on Charles." David lost his composure, grabbed the back of the front seat, and cried quietly. "I hate him, Braxton, and sometimes . . . sometimes, I want to kill him . . . *my own father, and I want to kill him!*"

"I know that feeling of hate, but I know you really don't mean it."

"I'm not so sure about that. I've thought a lot about it the last few days. Either that or run away."

"What about living with your Aunt Olivia?"

"Hell, he nixed that the first time it was brought up . . . said Aunt Olivia and I were ganging up on him and he'd be damned if he'd let me get away with that one."

"And your mother? What about her?"

"She drinks and pretends everything's okay. He's threatened her so much that she doesn't say anything anymore. I've seen him knock her all the way across the room when he's drunk."

"Why doesn't your mother leave him?"

"Damn good question! All I can figure is he's got the *money!* She doesn't want to lose the sweet life that she has—not even to protect her own son. How fucked up is that?" It was not Byrd's nature to curse like this. He could almost rival Jason. Byrd was changing.

"Byrd, we've got to figure something out and quick."

"Do you have any suggestions? I'm desperate!" He gripped my arm tightly.

"I still think that you should go to your Aunt Olivia's home and tell her what your father's doing to you, Charles, and your mother. She's not stupid and she's got a lot of powerful friends here and in the state. Forgive me, but your father is sick and needs treatment."

"*You think so, you stupid little shit. Didn't I tell you to stay away from my son?*" said Mr. Byrd, leaning his head into the car and startling us. Neither of us heard him come up or knew that he was outside the car. He must have followed Byrd.

"Daddy, how long have you been standing there?"

"*Long enough! Long enough to hear what this asshole has been advising you. Now get out of the car or do I have to knock a hole in the window?*"

We got out on the opposite side of where Mr. Byrd stood. David got out first and then I followed. Mr. Byrd had a stick in his hand and I didn't want to get hit. We tried not to get too near his father.

It was obvious that he had been drinking and was over his limit. We hung together on the front seat passenger side of the car. Mr. Byrd walked around the back of the car and stood about a foot from us. His breath reeked of alcohol. He stepped forward and poked me in the stomach with his stick, using enough force to knock me against the car. I stumbled backwards, catching myself before I hit the door. "What are you doing? What was that for?"

"Don't hit Braxton, Daddy! I'm the one you came for."

"*I didn't hit him. He fell against the car.*" Mr. Byrd lifted his stick toward David like he was going to hit him and then pulled it back. David ducked like a cowering dog that knows his master is going to beat him.

"*Listen to me, Braxton! I told you not to contact my son and so help me God, if you ever do again, you will sure as hell live to regret it!*" He screamed like I was deaf, spitting saliva out of his mouth at the same time. Some of his spit hit me in the face. I moved toward the center of the car.

"I'm not afraid of you anymore, Mr. Byrd," I said, wiping my face with the back of my hand. "You're drunk!" Mr. Byrd blinked and backed up. "I want to ask you something. Why are you threatening me again? I can make your life as miserable as you're making mine." I didn't take my eyes off his face. I wanted him to know I wasn't afraid of him tonight.

"*You think so? Well, little man, you just try it if you think you're so smart!*" He grinned and drools of saliva rolled from his mouth and down his chin. I began to realize a lot of his bravery was induced by alcohol.

"What are you going to do? Beat me and dump me out of a car like you did my mother? Huh? You're pathetic. Do you hear me? *You're pathetic.*" I stood my ground and watched him stagger in disbelief at what I was saying to him. I had never talked to an adult like this. It surprised me that I would.

Then Mr. Byrd drew back on his stick and I stepped backward. He came forward with such force that I knew he would crack my skull if he hit me. I ducked and he came down on top of the front windshield of the car, cracking the window as well as his stick. He recoiled and turned to David and said, "I followed you here to see what in the hell you were going to do. I told you not to see this one ever again. What's it going to take, David, to make you do what I say? *Answer me by damn it! Answer me, you little asshole!"*

David backed around the front of the car until he was on the driver's side again. His father followed him. I stayed where I was. My eyes widened at what I began to witness. Mr. Byrd grabbed David by the collar with his left hand and with the back of his right hand he slapped him across the mouth. David fell, his legs buckling out from under him, obviously in pain. I ran around to where he was kneeling. Blood was coming out of his mouth. Mr. Byrd grabbed him again and pulled him up. The crazed look on Mr. Byrd's face frightened me. His face turned red and the veins in his neck stuck out like sticks holding up a teepee. He pulled back with his right hand and I thought he was about to hit David again. David just stood there—stood unflinching before his father waiting for whatever he was going to deliver. I lunged forward and grabbed Mr. Byrd's arm, pulling him to the ground.

"Don't you ever hit your son again! Do you hear me?" I let him go. *"Do you hear me, Mr. Byrd?"* He didn't answer me. Instead, he just stared at me. I looked into his eyes and saw what I thought was the pain of a defeated man. I couldn't be certain, but it was almost as if his fall had sobered him completely. The previous anger that had been so prevalent had disappeared. I had no pity for him. He just wouldn't answer. He just kept staring at me with his stone cold eyes. I hated this man for all that he had done.

"It's over Daddy. I won't disobey you again," said David, helping his father off the ground. I looked at David and he wore resignation in his eyes. Did he see in his father what I saw?

"You better go on home, Braxton. I'll get him home."

"But?" I didn't want to go. There was so much we hadn't talked about.

"Please go. If you stay, it will only make matters worse." David had anchored his father. "Where are you parked, Daddy?" Mr. Byrd didn't say anything. He just stared at the creek.

"Okay, I don't want you to get into any more trouble because of me." I looked at Mr. Byrd but he showed no overt interest in what I was saying. "Byrd, I'll go, but only because you've asked me." We didn't say goodbye. I hoped I would be able to get with him tomorrow and together, we could find a way to get him out of the hellhole that had ensnared him. When I left the parking lot, David had still not found his father's car.

I lay in my bed in the darkness wrestling with all that happened this day. My thoughts rambled and followed no logical direction: Jason in the hospital and lucky to be alive and Byrd lucky to be alive while living with an abusive father. I thought about my own dad in the other room, fighting cancer each day and not wanting to live. Nothing made sense to me anymore. There was too much change. Things moved too fast now. My head pounded when I thought about it, but I had to help Byrd survive. I had to help all of us survive. A prayer wouldn't do it.

I had prayed but there had been no results. God? Where are you when I need you? Thoughts kept coming like arrows being shot at a fleeing deer.

Life and death . . . death and life . . . these concepts had taken on new meanings for me. Tonight, I know they're fragile. Yet, people take them for granted. Why? I think I've thought more about living since I got that black and white photograph than all my other years put together. I'm not ready to die. I don't want to die. And the threats? . . . given so readily with one goal in mind, to frighten and to intimidate. Where is the honor in all of this? There is none. Is all of this part of the makeup of the adult world I'd hungered to enter? Why was I in such a hurry? Thoughts continued to bombard my mind, leaving my head throbbing.

How could things change so radically and so quickly? Each day of this summer is now a bad memory that I have to wrestle with for who knows how long. It all seems insane. And why did Mr. Byrd think I was such a bad person, such a bad influence on his son. Byrd and I, why we'd been friends since grammar school and I'd been in the Byrd's home so many times. I can remember a time when Mr. Byrd, this stranger to me now, said I was like a second son to him. These were ugly sounds that we were being forced to hear and keep to ourselves.

There would be no sleep for me this night. My body lay wet from sweat, compliments of another hot summer evening with no breeze. I tossed and turned surrounded by the chocolate walls of my bedroom. I remembered seeing three-thirty on the clock's dial. At four o'clock in the morning, I walked quietly onto the back porch and sat on the chaise lounge. I took a cigarette from the pack of Kools I had bought at Taps and lit it. I coughed a lungful of smoke. I laughed, knowing Jason would've said something about my faulty smoking. I inhaled again deeply, letting the smoke out slowly. I took another drag, exhaled the smoke, and put it out.

A dog barking in the distance carried me back to the time my daddy gave me my first dog. It was a shepherd collie mix and I named him Jojo. I missed my friend who'd sit faithfully by me when I was lonely and needed to spill my guts. I had many talks with him. He was the best listener I'd ever known. Jojo was content to let me stroke him and that was the only cost for hour upon hour of my talking and sharing all that went in and out of mind with him.

Thanks to Mr. Taylor I lost him. Jojo went mad one hot summer day after Mr. Taylor poisoned him. Mr. Taylor didn't like dogs and especially, dogs that came in his yard without his permission. I was twelve years old when all this began. Lily was standing on one of our kitchen chairs and Mother was on top of the kitchen table when I came home that afternoon. They yelled, telling me to hurry and to go for Mr. Ross; but instead, I came back to the kitchen area and saw Jojo foaming at the mouth, my collie growling and snarling when I spoke to him, my collie with a crazed look in his eye, wobbling from side to side, my collie—my Jojo who frightened me just the way Mr. Byrd initially did.

Dr. Bass had to put him to sleep because there was nothing he could do to help Jojo. After the poison invaded his body, Jojo went blind. I remember the last day I saw him standing in a cage with those whitish eyes that had once been brown. He was pitiful when I spoke to him. He couldn't see me but he could hear me and instinctively, he knew who I was. Jojo wobbled up to the wire that kept us apart and when I called his name, he whined and whimpered like a little baby wanting to be touched. He knew who I was and that bond we had together had not been severed by this unnecessary tragedy. I reached in and pulled his foot to me. He didn't resist and his tail wagged. I kissed his paw repeatedly to tell him goodbye. I told

Jojo how much I loved him and what a great friend he had been and how much I would miss him. I hope he understood. Finally, Dr. Bass said I had to leave. I cried the twelve-mile drive back from Bailey to Wilson. Mother and Daddy let me cry as loud as I wanted to. After that, I hated Mr. Taylor and when he died, I had no pity for him or his family. He had killed my only dog, the one thing on earth that loved me for who I was.

Now there is another Mr. Taylor in my life and in the lives of my four friends. I understand when Byrd says he wants his dad dead because he is trying to separate all of us from his son, to break another unconditional bond that exists. And that's unfair too—unfair because there is no honor in forcing a son to submit to immoral principles, regardless of the reason. We are encouraged to "honor our fathers" but I believe something needs to be added and that it should also read "honor thy sons."

These first weeks of June had become claustrophobic and there was no sign of a possible change. I had lived a lifetime since school had dismissed for the summer and the freedoms I normally enjoyed were now teasing me, close enough to enjoy but darting away whenever I reached out to enjoy one. My life had become one big headache. I returned to my room at the first signs of the morning light and crawled back into my bed. I wanted to get some sleep.

The doorbell rang at about eleven o'clock, awakening me from a deep sleep. I sat up in bed, thinking I was in the wrong place. My head felt like someone had hit it with a two-by-four and my mouth had the aftertaste of strong tobacco. It was unusual that someone would ring the doorbell since anyone who knew us always knocked out of respect for my father. Lily answered the door. She wasn't gone long before she came back to my room and knocked to see if I was awake.

"Braxton, you needs to get up cause you has a visitor at the front door."

"Who is it?" I didn't want to get out of bed for any visitor.

"It's the police. You best hurries," Lily said. "He's gots something for you."

"The police? What in the heck do they want?" My feet hit the floor.

"I don't knows but I do knows you best get dressed fast."

I stumbled through the living room while I pulled my shirt over my head. I could see the police officer standing on the porch through the screen door. My Mother was there and she stood silent, smoking a cigarette. I stepped onto the porch dressed but barefooted and to my surprise, I found myself, once again, looking into the beady-eyes of the plump police officer who tried to blame the broken street lights on my friends and me. He had one of those "don't mess around with me, kid" looks on his face. His left hand was on his hip and his right hand held his hat and some paper. His gun was in his holster and his sunglasses were hanging from his shirt pocket.

"Good morning, Sergeant Rankin," I said. "Did you want to see me?"

"Are you Louis Braxton Haywood, Jr.?" he asked with a grin on his face.

"That's correct," I said. He knew exactly who I was. I could tell by his look that he was enjoying this and would probably milk it for all it was worth.

"I'm serving you with a restraining order. Mr. Oscar Byrd made the complaint to Chief Mays first thing today. Judge Henry Ashworth signed the complaint no more than an hour ago." He handed the paper to me. "I suggest you read it now and if you have any questions, then you can ask me."

"Mr. Byrd? I don't understand." *That bastard!* I began to tremble.

"Braxton, read the order," said my mother. She was visibly upset at what was taking place.

"Okay," I said. By looking at officer Rankin, I knew any enjoyment received from this would be by him only. I read the paper carefully. It said I was not to go about or around his son, David Byrd, from this day forward. I was not to call him or speak to him or make any attempt to see him. If I did, I would be subject to arrest. "Why?"

"Mr. Byrd considers you a bad influence on his son," said Sergeant Rankin, touching his billy club with his right hand and smiling. "You can't stay out of trouble, can you, Braxton?"

Before I could respond, my mother spoke, "Officer Rankin, you have served your restraining order. I must ask you to leave now. You didn't come here to agitate my son, I hope."

"No, I didn't," the sergeant said. "But you know teenagers these days, you can't be too careful. It's hard to trust any of them." The officer stared at me.

"Sergeant Rankin, *leave now!*" Mother said. "You can dispense with the lecture."

"Yes, ma'am," he said, putting his hat back on. He took a minute to just stare at me. He crossed his arms over his chest and he didn't say anything; he just looked. He took his time walking down the steps. He stopped about ten feet from his car, turned, and shook his head as if in disgust. With his hand still resting on his billy club, he got into his car. He sat in front of the house for a few minutes watching us before he pulled off.

I turned to Mother and said, "Mother, we need to talk now. Can we go to the back porch?"

"That will be fine," she said.

I stopped by the bathroom to take a leak. I'd gotten so nervous on the porch that I was afraid I was going to embarrass myself. I went to my room and got the envelope with the black and white glossy in it and met Mother on the porch.

"I need to be in ear shot of your daddy. Let's move to the breakfast nook."

"Okay," I said. I dreaded the smoke but didn't think I had a choice.

"All right, tell me." Mother pulled out a cigarette from her wrinkled pack and lit it.

First, I pushed the picture across the table and showed it to her. She looked at it, studied it, nodded, turned it over and slid it back to me. "Do you know who sent it?"

"No ma'am. Possibly, Mr. Byrd or maybe someone who knows all that's gone on. All of us got a copy, even Byrd."

"What else?" She inhaled and blew the smoke away from me but it traveled right back and hung over my head.

"There have been other incidents, related and unrelated." I said, tapping softly on the white wooden tabletop. I told mother about Jason's stunt at Patsy Wentworth's party and I told her about my meeting last night with David Byrd. I explained to her what Mr.

Byrd did to David and me last night and what he said. When I had finished, I crossed my arms and rested them on the table.

"You have no choice but to obey that restraining order," said Mother. "I think Oscar Byrd has taken this whole situation and blown it out of proportion. He is not giving you a chance to prove you won't talk about what you saw. He has become fanatical. No one can control a fanatic until he makes a big mistake. And he will eventually. I can promise you that."

"In the meantime, what do we do?"

"You do exactly as you have been doing." Mother smiled. "Remember to obey the order."

Mother put her cigarette out. She got up and went into my daddy's room.

I called Thad and Matt after lunch. Neither of them had a visit from Sergeant Rankin. I called the hospital to ask about Jason. He was resting comfortably but was still on the respirator. Visitation was discouraged but the nurse said I could come by later if I wanted to. I went back to my room and closed the door. I wanted to be alone.

Chapter 37
MRS. PIDGEON AND THE RESPIRATOR

I DROVE DOWN West Nash Street towards downtown. Rain had begun to spit against my windshield, the kind of rain that came slowly and made just enough of a mess that the wipers had to be used. The swaying back and forth of the wiper's arms had an hypnotic effect on me as I drove across Raleigh Road and then several blocks later, past Byrd's Pharmacy and finally into the downtown area. I crossed Pine Street and then Tarboro Street and the courthouse, where the restraining order had been signed, stood on my left. Driving across Goldsboro Street, I saw the police station to my left and down a block. Slowing my speed, I turned left at the next corner onto Douglass Street. The hospital was one block down and on my right.

I had either walked or ridden my bike or driven down Nash Street practically every day of my life, but it had never looked like it did today. The darkening sky and misty rain gave an aura of gloom to this normally beautiful drive. Any other time, I, as a frivolous kid, would not have given much serious thought to the looks of Nash Street or anything for that matter. Today, on this steamy Saturday afternoon, I felt, for the first time in my life, estranged from this town I thought I loved and knew so well.

I had been in the Woodard-Herring Hospital so many times since I was a kid, I felt like I knew every nook and cranny. I parked in the staff parking lot and entered the red brick structure through the back entrance that is usually reserved for doctors, nurses, and their families only. I got in this habit when my uncle, Dr. Victor Thaxton, was still alive and a practicing physician at this hospital and adjoining clinic. I walked down the long, dingy gray corridor past the doctor's offices on either side and into the waiting room with its black and white checkerboard tile floor. The room greeted me with an antiseptic smell.

"Could you tell me what room Jason Parker is in?" I addressed the matronly woman with dyed black hair sitting behind the visitation desk. She was eating an apple and reading a magazine and didn't appear to hear me. "Excuse me, could you tell me . . ."

"I heard you the first time," she said with a sneer on her plump face. Peering over her thin, wire rimmed classes she continued, "You want to know what room the Parker boy is in?"

"That's correct." I answered, trying not to show my disgust.

"He's in room 212 but only family and close friends are allowed visitation privileges," she said with a smug grin wiped across her face. She picked a cigarette from her pack, took it out, lit it, and blew the smoke toward me. She set the cigarette down in the ashtray. There was a heavy red ring around the top where her lipstick had left its mark.

"I'm one of Jason's closest friends. Nurse Warren said I could visit." I turned my head and coughed.

"She did, did she?" She took another puff, this time blowing the smoke into the air.

"That's correct," I said. I couldn't help but wonder why this woman chose to make such a big deal over one visit. I watched her add another ring to the end of her cigarette.

"When?" she asked. She flipped a page in her magazine.

"When what?" I wanted to tell her I was not in the magazine but standing in front of her.

"Young man, are you trying to get smart with me?" She looked at me again over the top of the glasses that were far too small for her pudgy face. Just as I was about to answer, I saw Nurse Powell coming into the waiting room. Nurse Powell had been one of my uncle's nurses.

"Hester!" I waved and then walked over to where she stood and said hello.

"What brings you over here this afternoon, Braxton?" she asked, giving me a big hug.

"I came to see Jason Parker but the lady at the visitor's desk is giving me a hard time."

"She does that to just about every young person who comes in here. Come with me." I followed Nurse Hester Powell back to the visitor's desk.

"Mrs. Pidgeon, let Braxton have a pass to see Jason Parker," Nurse Powell said.

"Well, of all things, I didn't know whether he should be allowed up there or not." She picked up her cigarette, inhaled, and let it dangle from her lips while exhaling smoke through her nostrils and writing me a pass. She handed me a small, square piece of white paper saying "visitor's pass" with her initials on it.

"Braxton is Dr. Thaxton's nephew. Braxton, this is Mrs. Hazel Pidgeon."

"Hello, Mrs. Pidgeon. Thanks for the pass," I said, trying to avoid another head on collision with her smoke.

"Oh, I did luv your uncle to death. He was such a good-looking man and a mighty fine doctor, too," she said. Smiling at me, she continued, "Honey, anytime you want to visit someone here and I'm on duty, you'll get the green light."

"Why, thank you very much, Mrs. Pidgeon." Nurse Parker winked and I took the elevator to the second floor.

Mr. and Mrs. Samuel Parker were in the hall talking with Dr. Horne when I got to Jason's room. I stood aside under the bright fluorescent hallway lights until they had finished talking. "Hello, Mrs. Parker, Mr. Parker. I came to see Jason. How's he doing today?"

"Hello, Braxton, it's good to see you," said Mrs. Regina Parker. She walked over and put her arms around my shoulders and gave me a motherly hug. I could smell the alcohol on her breath. "We are very grateful to you for helping save Jason's life."

"I don't think I had much to do with that," I said. "Dr. Wentworth deserves that credit."

"Dr. Wentworth clued us in on much of what happened," said Mr. Parker. "Braxton, like my wife said, we are indeed thankful for all you did. Jason is fortunate to have you as a friend."

"Thank you," I said. "Is Jason okay?"

"Right now, he's resting, but the long term prognosis is still out," said Mr. Parker. The concerned look on his face told me that it was far more serious than I had realized. "Jason had a restless night and is still hooked up to the respirator."

"The fall he took was more serious than the doctors thought initially," Mrs. Parker continued. "Jason has a severe concussion. He took in a lot of water and lost a lot of blood. The nurses and doctors are carefully monitoring his condition."

"Wow! I'm surprised," I said. "He will be okay, won't he?"

"We hope so but we don't know yet," said Mr. Parker. "Braxton, I don't want you to tell anyone what I'm getting ready to tell you, but the doctors fear there may be brain damage. The extent of any damage is not known but Jason has had several petite mal seizures since he was admitted."

"Good *God!* I can't believe this!" I felt lightheaded. The sudden rush of news left me momentarily stunned.

"It's hard for all of us," Mrs. Parker said. "Jason is such a vibrant, unpredictable boy. You know how he is and probably know him, in some ways, better than we do."

"May I see him?" I asked.

"Yes, but for just a short time," Mrs. Parker said. "Millie is in with him."

"Thank you." I opened the door to 212 and walked in. The sterile colored room had been given life by several flower arrangements sitting on the dresser and windowsill. Jason's sister, Millie, a cute brunette with short hair and curls, sat by the window in front of Jason's hospital bed reading a magazine. "Knock, knock, Millie, I came to see Jason." Jason lay still on his side facing the window. Only the neck of his hospital gown could be seen under the white hospital sheet that was pulled tightly across his body. A respirator the size of a small basinet sat between the window and his bed. "Long time, no see, Millie."

"Braxton, it's good to see you." Millie got up, put her magazine on the table, and walked toward me. She wore a rose-colored cardigan sweater wrapped around her shoulders. "It has been a long time, almost a year," she said, giving me a hug around the neck and a peck on my right cheek. Little Millie all grown up—there was a time when she wore pig-tails and whenever I pulled them, the only thing she would give me was a slap across my face.

"How's Jason doing? I mean, really doing?" I walked around to the foot of the bed and saw a mask covering his tanned face. "What's the mask for?"

"To help him breath regularly. It's connected to the respirator," said Millie. "Hopefully, he'll come off of it tomorrow. At least, that's what Dr. Thorne hopes for."

"I still can't believe Jason hurt himself this bad!" I walked closer and bent over his back to get a good look at his face. I couldn't see much from where I stood. "Ouch! I know it hurts."

"It was a wicked blow to his head. He's lucky he didn't lose an eye." Millie winced.

"It must've been." I walked around the bed to get a better look at Jason. His entire head had been shaved and a bandage covered the left side area of his face where the doctors had taken the stitches. The rest of his face looked bruised and swollen. His eyes were closed.

"Braxton, what got into Jason last night?"

"Millie, Jason has a lot on him right now," I said. "You know how Jason is. He internalizes a lot of things and sometimes, he just can't handle them. Last night he chose to drink too much beer."

"Can you be more specific?" Millie turned and looked at her brother and then back at me.

"I can, but I shouldn't. Jason needs to talk with all of you," I said. "I will tell you that he's having problems with going to Fork Union."

"I know. He and I've talked about that but I told him he might like going away to school. I didn't want to go to Saint Mary's at first, but I love it now."

"Military school is a far cry from a private girl's school."

"I know, the discipline and all, but I told Jason he needed that. He doesn't disagree."

"Well, there's a whole lot more to it than that and some of it's pretty damn heavy," I said. "It's just that I can't talk about it. Please don't betray my trust!"

"Braxton, I wouldn't ever do that," Millie said. There was a low moan from Jason and we both turned back toward him. Jason had opened his eyes. "Jason, Braxton stopped by to see you."

"Well, old buddy, you picked a hell of a time to show us your back flip," I said in a humorous way. "I'm glad to see you doing this well."

"Grrrr," Jason attempted to growl. He turned over onto his back and stared at the ceiling.

"Thad and Matt send you their best. And so does Byrd!" Jason blinked his eyes as if he disbelieved me and then grunted again. "Oh yes he did. I was with him last night and I told him you had a nasty spill and were in the hospital. He said to tell that old fart . . . " I turned to Millie, "Excuse me, I apologize" and then back to Jason, "that you weren't to do any fancy tricks without him around to rescue you. Scouts honor, Jason!" Jason's eyes gleamed. I was glad to make him feel good for a moment even if the second part was not true.

"Time to go, Braxton," Mrs. Parker said, sticking her head in the room.

"Yes ma'am. Well, Jason, I got to go but I'll see you after church tomorrow. Promise."

"Thanks for coming, Braxton, and it's great seeing you again," said Millie. She walked with me out the door and down the hall where the evening meals sat on carts waiting to be delivered and to the elevator with the hospital green doors. She pushed the button marked one and stood with a worried look on her face among the shadows cast by the fluorescent lights.

"Please keep me informed, Millie. I don't want that butthole doing something stupid again." The elevator door opened and I got in. "Bye." The door closed and the rickety descent continued for one floor. I jumped when the elevator jarred and shook before the first floor door opened. I was glad to get back on solid flooring. I stepped out, waved to Mrs. Pidgeon, and walked back through the familiar hallway to the parking lot.

The rain had decided to hang over our dry town tonight and it shared with us a good, steady pour. Already little rain puddles like water spots left on the linoleum floor from a leaky ceiling formed in the parking lot. I ran to the Tank and got in and closed the door. I had hid a couple of Kool cigarettes under the driver's seat and now seemed like a good time to enjoy one. I put the cigarette to my lips and lit it. I blew the smoke toward the steering wheel and watched it drift, angling out my slightly opened window and disappear into the early evening. My smoking was about to become a nasty habit. I liked the taste and the surge of the smoke as it traveled through my lungs into my chest.

It was time to head home. I turned the key in the ignition and the motor roared. I shifted into reverse and backed out of R.N. Martha Olson's parking space then down shifted into first and drove out of the parking lot. I took an immediate right and hung it to the left, deciding to take an alternate route home. I passed the *Wilson Daily Time*'s building on my left reminding me of my paper route years, then by the First United Methodist Church on my right, and the old Victorian Buckner house on my left, famous for the four Buckner daughters, three of whom supposedly died mysterious deaths at the hands of a merciless father. The youngest, Daisy, is said to have disappeared but has reportedly been seen on occasions standing under the stone arch welcoming family and visitors alike as they entered Maplewood Cemetery. I hung a left onto Pine Street and then a right and I was back on Nash Street heading home.

There was little traffic as I drove under the tall oaks swaying with the hot, summer breeze. The overhead canopy allowed my windshield wipers to get a momentary respite and I rested my arm on the windowsill and enjoyed the wind blowing through my hair as if it was sent to console me. I couldn't help thinking about Jason and his future, whatever that might be. It was hard to imagine a different Jason, one inflicted with brain damage. What a waste of a great guy!

Kincaid Avenue was ahead on my right but rather than turning, I drove another block and pulled into Dick's for a quick bite of supper. I joined about six other cars in the paved parking lot that faced the front of the building. It was still too early for the usual, large supper crowd. I cut my motor off and ran to the door to avoid being pelted by the heavy rain. Wiping my feet on the outdoor mat, I pushed hard against the glass door handle and entered. The aroma of chili permeated the smoke-filled air circulating throughout the small restaurant.

"Hello, Braxton," Mr. Gliarmis said. "Please come over here and sit where we can talk."

"Thank you, Mr. Gliarmis." I took a seat on the swivel stool at the far end of the yellow Formica counter. "What's happening, Mr. Gliarmis?" I used my right foot to push myself around several times and then stopped.

"What would you like to eat, my friend?" Mr. Gliarmis asked. "Dinner is on me tonight!"

"Oh! No. I can't . . . no! You're far too generous."

"No, I insist. Please let me give my good neighbor dinner tonight."

"Well—okay, thank you, Mr. Gliarmis," I said. "I would like one dog all the way, a small order of fries, and a large Pepsi, but slow on the ice."

"Coming right up, my friend." I looked around the restaurant but saw no one I really knew. Several faces were vaguely familiar. Three young families sat in different booths at the far end of the room, two without fathers present. I got off the stool and went over to the jukebox. I put in a dime and hit R2 waiting to hear Guy Mitchell in "Singing The Blues." I returned to my seat at the counter.

"Tell me, Braxton, how is Jason faring?" Mr. Gliarmis asked. "I hear he's in the hospital."

"Yes sir. In fact, I just left his room," I said, trying to carefully weigh my thoughts before I continued. "Right now he is on a respirator. Jason got a nasty cut on his head when he fell on the diving board. The doctors want to observe him through the weekend."

"I'm so sorry to hear of this." Mr. Gliarmis was genuine in his expression of concern. "I trust that he will be coming home soon?"

"I didn't get when he's coming home. Hopefully, it won't be long."

"You and your friend come in as soon as he is well again and I will treat you to a real dinner." Mr. Gliarmis smiled and clasped his hands together. "You'll enjoy my specialty, I promise."

"We'll definitely take you up on it, Mr. Gliarmis," I said. "I'll let Jason know."

"Here is your tonight's dinner, Braxton. You are a good boy. Eat and enjoy."

"Thank you very much. You didn't have to do this, Mr. Gliarmis."

"Braxton, thank you. The pleasure is indeed mine." He saw the puzzled look on my face and anticipated my question. "I'm an old man but I'm wise and I know a man with a good heart. His eyes reveal his soul and your eyes have told me many times that you respect me and I appreciate that."

I ate too fast and I had a strong aftertaste of his onions. Oh well, I would deal with the indigestion when I got home. I thanked Mr. Gliarmis for his hospitality and ran to my car and got in. The rain continued to pound the surface of all that it struck and I heard the roar of approaching thunder. We needed this downpour and I knew the tobacco farmers, especially, were grateful. I started the car and drove around the block to Kincaid Avenue and turned into my driveway. Our front porch light was on, yet, it wasn't dark. The front door was open despite the approaching storm and there was a light coming from Anne's bedroom signaling she'd returned from the beach.

I found Mother sitting in our living room in the dark. She sat in her favorite chair, a rose embroidered Queen Anne, with a cigarette in one hand and a drink in the other—possibly a bourbon and water. She looked haggard and maybe she'd been crying. Her left hand shook and ice cubes tinkled against her glass.

"How did you find Jason?" She inhaled her cigarette and let the smoke out, sighing.

"He's on a respirator still. Doctors plan to monitor him the next few days."

"Is he hurt badly?" Mother sat forward in her chair and put her drink on the marble-top table beside her. Sweat ran down the outside of the glass. The house was comfortable for a change even though outside it was steamy and continued to rain.

"Pretty bad, I think. I'm going over after church tomorrow. He had a mask over his face so he couldn't talk. Just winked and grunted."

"I'm sorry to hear that," she said sadly. "Just one more thing you boys have to deal with this summer. Tell Jason I'm thinking of him."

"Mother, what's wrong now?" She wiped away a tear with the back of her hand and proceeded to give me an update on the afternoon. Dr. Hoke had just left. Daddy had taken another disastrous turn for the worse around four o'clock. No medicine had been delivered and Mother had no choice but to ask the doctor on-call to bring daddy his medication. This was one positive thing about Wilson—doctors still made house calls without resentment. Dennis Farmer, the weekend merchant's delivery driver, stopped voluntarily to tell Mother that Byrd's Pharmacy didn't have Daddy's medicine when he picked up their other orders. No reason was given and Mr. Farmer couldn't give Dr. Hoke, who was present at the time, a satisfactory explanation for the pharmacy's failure to have it ready. Dr. Hoke promised Mother it wouldn't happen again. He gave Daddy enough medication to sedate him for the night.

Jackson was off tonight and Mother and I, she said, would be on call to help Daddy if he needed anyone. She volunteered to stay with him first. I noticed that Mother's hands shook when she attempted to pick up her drink. I didn't know how many drinks preceded the one she now held in her hand. I'm not certain at the time it made any difference to me.

Anne was taking a bath and that meant a good hour that the bathroom would be out of commission. I told Mother about being treated for dinner by Mr. Gliarmis and then I retired to my room to read. I stretched across the bed but fell asleep after reading only five pages.

Chapter 38
A 2:00 A.M. WAKE-UP CALL

I AWOKE AT 2:00 A.M. Sunday morning. I awoke confused and disoriented. A noise made outside, perhaps. It was bizarre, almost like my awakening was intentional, that something or someone wanted me to remember this time. I still lay on top of my bed fully dressed with the exception of my shoes and socks. My bedside lamp was on and a little moth, also disoriented, banged itself against the interior of the lampshade. I vaguely remembered; a loud noise had aroused me from my sleep. Fully dressed, I got off the bed and tiptoed onto the back porch. I could smell as well as feel the humidity in the air. I opened the screen door and walked down the steps into the back-yard.

It was darker than dark outside, the kind of black night that even an owl would hide from. The black grass oozed between my toes and its moisture clung to the ball of my foot, reminding me of the earlier storm that had since moved on. A light wind still blew. The moon peeked once through the darkness and was, just as quickly, gone again. No stars, only stillness in their place, briefly interrupted by crickets calling to each other, joining in the dark night song.

I walked around the house careful in my steps to see if there might be an intruder. My hair stood up on the back of my neck when I passed the forsythia bush and turned the corner of the house and faced the porch. Both rockers swayed back and forth. A sudden chill grabbed me, for there was no one on the porch or in the chairs. It must be the wind making these rockers move. I walked around the other side of the house and jumped at the sound of movement from the playhouse next door. I stood rigid until a cat darted out from under the playhouse porch and ran across the yard into the street. I moved quietly to the back of the house again. Nothing unusual outside, but something had awakened me. I sat on the back steps and took the last cigarette from my shirt pocket. I lit it and enjoyed a quick smoke as I watched the darkness of the night.

Satisfied that what I heard did not come from outside, I walked quietly up the steps and into the kitchen. After lighting the candle that sat on top of our stove, I tiptoed across the speckled white linoleum floor and stopped in the breakfast room. The wooden floor creaked beneath my feet. I gently pushed on the swinging door that led into Daddy's room. A flickering light danced up and down on the television screen and a sound of static spoke from the TV box. No stations on air at this hour. My father was in his rocker slumped to one side with an IV needle still in his arm. There was no visual sign of his being awake. I stuck my head around the door. Mother was in the blue lounge chair with her feet on the ottoman. Her head bent sideways resting on her right shoulder. She would complain of a neck ache in the morning. Her breathing was heavy and an occasional snort shouted from her nostrils, indicative of her way of snoring. She would deny that she had fallen asleep. Her thin gown was pulled up over her knees and the ashtray beside her chair overflowed with cigarette butts. The room carried a ratty look and smelled equally offensive.

I backed out slowly, turned and walked silently to the door leading into my sister's room. It was slightly ajar. I could see Anne in her bed with only a sheet covering her small body. Her panda lay at the foot of her bed with some of her stuffed animals. The living room was clear of any distraction. En route to my bedroom, I made a quick pit stop and then returned to bed. A noise had awakened me. Of that, there was no doubt.

The phone rang at 7:30 A.M. I was awake but hadn't braved putting my feet on the floor. Mother was also up. After the second ring, I jumped from by bed, hit the floor running, and continued to the phone table and answered as Mother appeared. "Hello, Haywood's residence."

"Braxton, is that you?"

"Yes ma'am, it is."

"Braxton, this is Olivia . . . Olivia Pugh." Her voice had an urgency to it.

"Yes ma'am," I said. I stretched and wiped the sand from my right eye. "Good morning."

"Braxton, I hate to call you this early on Sunday morning, but I have some very bad news!"

"Ma'am?" I asked. Fearing the worst, "Please say it's not about Byrd."

"I'm afraid it is, Braxton," she said and then, hesitated. "I don't know how to say this other than to be forthcoming. Julian found David early this morning." She stopped and cleared her throat. "Braxton, David is . . . David's *dead!*" A prolonged silence followed and then . . .

"*My God, no! No!*" I banged my fist against the wall, bruising my knuckles on the hard plaster surface; the other side was my daddy's room. "*It's not true! It can't be true!*" Mother ran out, looking at me with shock in her eyes and stopped. She knew automatically what I had been told. Mother stepped back and put her right hand over her mouth.

"It's a terrible tragedy," Olivia continued. "I know how fond you and David were of each other and I wanted you to hear from me."

"When? When did it happen?"

"Around two o'clock this morning."

"*Wait!*" I needed time to think. "How did he die?"

"Braxton, he was shot. The coroner said it was self-inflicted, a gunshot wound to the head."

"*No, no! That's not true. David wouldn't ever kill himself! I know he wouldn't.*" I dropped the phone and stood transfixed in horror. Water ran down the inside of my right pant leg and onto the hall rug. I gasped and coughed, holding all my screams that were fighting to get out. I had to get back to my bedroom to deal with this. I ran as fast as I could and once inside, I closed both doors. Then I let go: I screamed and I cried and I screamed again. I grabbed my pillow to muffle my sobs. I kicked the stool that sat in front of my bed, knocking off the books that rested there. A knock at my door startled me, "*Go away! Go away!*" I yelled. I took my pillow and started beating the top of my bed. I hit it once, twice, three times, four times until a massive black hand grabbed mine and put a halt to my attempt to kill Mr. Byrd. Jackson threw the pillow on the bed and grabbed me, pulling me close to him. His strong, hairy black arms wrapped tightly around my back, held me firmly against his chest. I could barely breathe but Jackson wouldn't let go. I cried again, this time in continuous sobs, mourning the death of my best friend, David Byrd. My emotions raged inside me. A slice of me had been taken.

I began to rant, "My 'Tweetie Byrd' has left me. Why? It's not fair. He can't go now, not yet." I broke away from Jackson and walked around the room talking to the walls, talking to myself, and talking, talking, "We have things to work out together. *Byrd gone! It can't be possible! You just can't bail out on me like this. Why? Why, Byrd?*" I walked back to Jackson and as soon as my eye met his, I started choking back the tears. I wanted to cry but I didn't know how to let go and get rid of the pain that had penetrated my heart. It hurt so badly. It hurt so damn bad. I stood unable to think, to move.

"Let it out, you hear. Let it all out," his encouraging voice said. He grabbed me again and held me close until my sobs subsided. I became suddenly quiet.

"Braxton, may I come in?" asked my mother. She came over to where we were standing. "I spoke with Olivia and she plans to come over shortly and talk with you further. Get dressed and if you don't want to go to Sunday school, that's okay. I'll call your Aunt Eva to take Anne."

"Mother, it hurts so much. You know that, don't you?" I sat on my bed. "*No one will ever convince me that David Byrd shot himself. No one will!*"

"Jackson, let's let Braxton have some time alone," said my mother. "Louis needs you now." Before they closed my door, I saw Anne standing in the hall. She had no idea what was happening. I sat there for I don't know how many minutes, my head swimming. Nothing entered my mind coherently. My thoughts were seesawing in my brain. It hurt to think. I took a deep breath, got up, and went to my closet. I found a starched, long-sleeved white shirt with my initials monogrammed in red on it and pair of black slacks I recently got back from the cleaners. I found a madras tie that Byrd had given me for my birthday and a pair of dark socks. I would dress for him today. This would be my way of honoring my friend, David Byrd.

Mother answered the door shortly after eight-thirty. I could hear them greeting each other. Olivia Pugh, a spunky middle-aged woman, was a little on the chunky side but her tailored clothes hid that fact. She was forever effervescent and her voice was deep for a woman and carried like a baritone's when she spoke. Mrs. Pugh and Aunt Josephine sat in the living room while Mother came to get me. My door was opened and Mother spoke, "Braxton, Josephine and Olivia are here."

"I'll be right there." I was ready to hear what Olivia Pugh had to tell me. I walked into the living room and both women stood. An unusual gesture, I believe this was done out of respect for my grief. I greeted Aunt Josephine first with a kiss on the cheek and then gave Olivia a hug. She reached over and kissed me on the cheek and spoke, "Braxton, before this day gets any older, you need to hear some of the things I didn't think I could tell you on the phone." She pulled a handkerchief from the sleeve of her blue jacket and sat next to my aunt on the sofa. I sat in the Boston rocker and pulled it around so I could face them.

"I just can't believe this has happened," I said. "Byrd and I were together for a brief time on Friday night." I managed not to get emotional.

"After you called me the other night, I started doing some snooping," Olivia said. "I did find out as you suggested that David and his dad were not getting along well. Julian confirmed this to me and when I approached Oscar with the idea that maybe David could spend the summer with me, he went into a tirade. He made all kinds of accusations, one saying that you and I were in cahoots to take his son away. I knew then the problem was with my brother and not my nephew." She stopped a minute to catch her breath. "Anyway, I stopped by Friday night and he had just found out that David was not in the house and again, became maniacal making all kinds of threats about what he was going to do and not do. He brought your name up again and said that he had forbidden David from seeing you. I foolishly asked why and he immediately assumed that I knew all about why. I couldn't reason with him and I left. I saw David walking down Raleigh Road and stopped and picked him up. He told me he planned to meet you and I dropped him off." She stopped and asked for a glass of water. Mother got her some and after a sip, she continued. "When David got out of the car, he said something very peculiar to me. He thanked me for being a good aunt and told me that I might not see him for a long, long time."

"He told me that he might run away," I said, not meaning to interrupt her.

"Exactly! He called me yesterday morning and told me that Charles had told their father that he planned to run away and that his father beat him. Did you know that my brother beat David?"

"Yes ma'am," I said. "Byrd told me Friday night that his father had hit him a lot lately."

"In our conversation," Olivia continued, "David said his father threatened him."

"Yes, ma'am," I agreed. "Byrd told me that, too, and said his father told him if he ever tried anything that foolish again, he couldn't be held responsible for what might happen to him."

"Braxton, David wouldn't tell me anything specific about where he might go. He refused to come to my house. I didn't talk with him again," said Olivia.

I stood and took a deep breath. I didn't know what to say next. What I wanted was to be able to go to Byrd's home.

"Your Aunt Josephine told me about the restraining order, Braxton."

"Yes, ma'am," I said. "Your brother did everything he could to keep us apart."

"I told you all of this for a reason. You'll understand in a moment. No one found David's body until this morning around six o'clock. Julian went out to walk the dog and the dog actually found David first lying up on the side porch between the wicker furniture. The gun, a revolver, was on the porch floor somewhere beside him. The coroner was immediately summoned. It was he who determined that the death occurred around two in the morning and that David had lain there for over four hours."

"Didn't anyone hear the shot or shots?" I remembered at that instant my awakening at two in the morning hearing a loud noise. This was uncanny. Later, I decided it wasn't a coincidence.

"David's mother did and she actually got up and went outside. She acknowledges that she had been drinking and her head was not clear. She said that she thought maybe it was a car backfiring."

"Poor Byrd just lying there, all alone." I could feel my eyes getting moist. I stopped and wiped both with the back of my hand. "No one else heard anything?"

"No one said they did. Now this is very difficult for me to tell you, Braxton. Please listen carefully and this is why I asked your Aunt Josephine to come with me this morning. I know you'll want to go to the house and pay your respects but you can't. And I advise you now not to even consider going to the funeral. As of now, no decision has been made regarding David's burial."

"Excuse me, I don't understand," I said. "Why shouldn't I plan to be at my best friend's funeral?"

"Because . . ." Olivia took a deep breath. "Because when David's mother called to give me this terrible news, she said her husband was beside himself. And that he blamed you. Oscar Byrd is blaming you for David taking his own life."

"*What?*" I rose from my chair. "*That's absurd. If anyone killed David, it was Oscar Byrd. I can't believe this. It's a nightmare. Mother? Aunt Josephine? What am I to do?*"

Again, there was silence and then, "Braxton, the first thing you must do is calm down," Aunt Josephine said. "Sit down and quit screaming!"

"Sister, he's upset!" my mother said, coming to my defense.

"I realize that, Virginia, but yelling is not the answer," Aunt Josephine sat erect when she addressed my mother. "I know this has upset him; it has upset all of us, but Braxton needs to be calm. Please try, Braxton."

"Braxton, I don't know all the dynamics of what's going on here. One thing I do know is how much you cared for my nephew," Olivia said. "No one will believe my brother and hopefully, people will see him for the fool he has become. But your going over there will only add fuel to the fire. I'm asking you to please not go for David's sake. Let him be buried without anymore friction."

"It sounds like I'm to blame. I had nothing to do with it!" I stood again. I could feel my blood pressure rising and I was mad, damn mad. The kind of mad that liked to kick ass. I needed to think . . . to get alone and weigh this entire matter. I looked into Olivia's empathetic eyes. "Okay, I won't go to his house, but I'm not going to promise you that I won't go to his funeral."

"Fair enough," said Olivia. "I'll make you a promise, Braxton. I'll find a way for you to be at that funeral. Just give me some time to work it out."

"Thank you, Olivia," I said. "I don't mean to be rude but I'd like to be alone now. Would you please excuse me?"

"By all means," said Olivia.

"Of course," said Aunt Josephine.

I thanked both my aunt and Mrs. Olivia Pugh for coming this morning. Her presentation baffled me at first. However, the more I thought about what she'd said, the more I understood why Mr. Byrd thought he needed a scapegoat, and once again, it was going to be Louis Braxton Haywood. I closed my bedroom door shortly after nine o'clock.

My last memory of Byrd was his crouching before his father, his hands cupped over his face fearful of being hit. This was not the way I wanted to remember him. The fact I did nothing to help him will haunt me the rest of my life. The David Byrd I knew and will remember was unselfish, giving, and serious, but fun loving. He cared for all, like the day he took the wounded bird home to nurture. He nursed that bird to health and when the time came to give it back its freedom, he lifted the bird in his hands and extended his arms and gave it the needed boost to encourage it to fly again. This was how I will remember my friend, as an encourager, willing to help all.

Why did we go upstairs with Byrd that night? To protect him or was it out of selfish curiosity? We did have a choice. Did I make the right one? He asked us not to come with him.

He knew what was going on and he wanted to protect us, but he wanted us to know so we could protect him. He wanted us to share his pain, the internal struggle that was slowly killing him day by day. We did make the right decision. We needed to be there for him, to help him. This was the only way he could tell us.

His dad went wrong. I had forgotten but I remember now. It's been over three years, I think. His parents had gone to a party and would be returning late. I spent the night with Byrd that night and we went to bed around midnight, tired and exhausted. We were asleep in David's bed when his father came in. I remember now—he bumped against the table when he entered, knocking Byrd's basketball trophy to the floor. We were both awake when his father stumbled and fell in bed with us. He crawled on top of Byrd and Byrd screamed, alarming his father. Mr. Byrd saw us both lying there in our briefs and he mumbled something, got up, and staggered out. The next morning he apologized saying he'd had too much to drink and thought he was in his own room. I dismissed it at the time and buried it in the recesses of my mind but it wasn't forgotten. The right time to surface is now telling me the pattern of behavior has been there a long time. David protected himself and me that night from embarrassment and humiliation at the hands of his father. David, our protector, our encourager—the world will be a sad place without you. Dear friend, you have suffered far too long and you will be truly missed.

I arrived late to Sunday school that day. Class had started, Captain Chuck had been reinstated as our teacher, and I walked in on the middle of a lively discussion. When I entered, everything stopped. All eyes turned toward me. Matt and Thad sat together on the far side of the room. Both carried saddened faces. The room was packed with juniors and seniors. Captain Chuck took his chair and handed it to me. I placed it where I now stood and, immediately sat. There was not another available space in the room; that's how crowded it was. (We never had that many in attendance again. Our teacher later said, "Curiosity seekers emerge from the woodwork at strange times like when there is a death among them." I never forgot that and it's true.)

"Sorry to interrupt your class, Captain Chuck," I said. "I'm running late today."

"That's understandable, Braxton." Our teacher looked at me with a father's understanding. "We were talking about life and death."

"Please continue." I looked in the face of the boys I knew best sitting in our classroom on that Sunday morning in June. Some appeared sad, some angry, some seemed excited, and some seemed unaffected by the comments. I remembered what Mr. Gliarmis had recently said to me, "The eyes are the windows to the soul." I didn't know what David's death would do to me. It was too early to tell.

"A lot of your classmates have shared their thoughts about David Byrd and his death this morning," said a mellow Captain Chuck. "I don't mean to put you on the spot, but, I understand, you and David were very close. Would you like to share anything?"

"I . . . I don't . . . I'm still working through it. It's still very raw . . . David is . . . " I felt my emotions racing within me. I always get hot when this happens. "I felt a real need to be here this morning." I stared at the floor to avoid the pain of looking at my classmates. My ears burned.

"I'm glad you're here, Braxton," Captain Chuck said. "It's a sad time when anyone dies but especially a young person who is full of life and has so much potential, and it's doubly hard when it involves a suicide." That word, suicide, stung me. I hate that word. I gripped the edge of my chair and continued to stare at the floor.

"He didn't need to go to that extreme. Braxton, what got into him?" asked Zack Austin like I was supposed to have the answer. I had no insight into David's thoughts. If I did, maybe he would be alive this very moment. I didn't look up and I didn't respond.

"Maybe he didn't want to live anymore and thought it time to check out," said Richard Penny. "Sometimes life hands you a lot of . . . *you know* . . . and it's tough to deal with." Richard was right. He just didn't know he was right. Pretty smart for a jock repeating the eleventh grade. I just stared at the crack in the floor, but I smiled to myself.

"What a waste of humanity!" said Dwight Cummings. "My mother says anyone who turns to suicide is a coward and is going to hell."

"*Stop it!*" I stood. I couldn't seem to control myself. I guess it was Dwight's condemnation of Byrd that kicked me out of my chair. Before I knew it, I was up addressing the entire class, "What do any of you know? Most of you in here hardly know David Byrd. You see him in the halls at school or watch him play basketball for Coon or run into him at parties or the Creamery. But you don't know the real BYRD!" I stopped to take a breath and then continued,

"And you, Dwight Cummings, where do you get off calling him a coward. You just moved here and don't even know David Byrd. Well, let me tell *you* something now, *Mr. Trouble Maker, David Byrd is not and never was a coward. A coward is someone who hides behind his mother's skirt tail. David Byrd is one of the best friends a person could ever hope to have.* Your life has been blessed just by knowing who he is." I walked toward Dwight Cummings, bent over, got as close to his face as I could, and looked into his wimpy brown eyes and said, "*For your information, butthole, David Byrd did not, I repeat, did not kill himself! Go home and tell your mother that!*" I turned and walked rapidly out of the door in fear that I would deck the bastard for calling my friend a coward.

Out in the hall, I heard the applause from where I stood, trying to get a grip on myself and control my emotions. They were jumping up and down within me like a kid bouncing on a pogo stick. I figured I'd made an ass of myself but I didn't care; no one was going to say anything derogatory about David Byrd—*not today, not ever in my presence.* The bell rang signaling the end of the Sunday school hour. I ran down the two flights of stairs and toward my car parked across the street. The sun's brightness burned the pavement and made it difficult to see any oncoming cars. One lady zipping across the parking lot in her car blew her horn at me and I jumped. Disoriented for a second, I saw the Tank. I opened the door, slid in, and sat behind the steering wheel shaking and trying to catch my breath. "*Oh, shit! What did I do?*" I screamed out loud thinking no one could hear me. I realized I had a temper that needed to be bridled. I realized I had a passion, a burning flame inside of me, a righteousness that couldn't be stilled and it rose today to defend my friend, David Byrd.

"Braxton let me in!" I looked and saw Thad standing on the passenger side of my car. The window was up and the door locked. "Unlock the door!"

"Sorry, get in," I said, reaching over and pulling up on the door lock.

"Are you okay?"

"Yeah. Just a little embarrassed for showing my ass back there."

"Showing your ass?" Thad slapped me on the right leg. "Man, you were brilliant in there. You said what most of us wanted to say but didn't have the guts to say it. You put Dwight Cummings in his place, the little pipsqueak. He turned as red as a beet. And the applause! Did you hear everyone clapping for you? My man, you're a hero!"

"I don't want to be anybody's damn hero." I looked at Thad. "I want Byrd back and I want it to be the way it used to be with the five of us. I want to go back in time and start over." Tears ran down my cheeks. Thad gave me his handkerchief and I wiped my eyes.

"Those days are gone, Braxton! They'll never come back." Thad stopped and stared at me the longest time. "Damn! This has really hit you hard! Much harder than Matt and me. I don't know what to do or say. I hurt too, but not like you. Maybe time will take care of it . . . aw shit, I don't know. I miss him too, Braxton. I really do." I gave his handkerchief back. He wiped his eyes.

"We'll always miss him, Thad. Always!"

"Braxton, have you seen this?" He handed me a copy of the Metro section of our state's Sunday paper, *The News and Observer.*

"No, we don't take it. What am I looking for?" I said, confused.

"Look at the bottom of the page. Look who the paper picked to be "Tar Heel of the Week," none other than Oscar David Byrd, Sr.," said Thad.

"Oh, *shit!* You've got to be kidding me! I don't believe it? What timing—this will make him look like a fucking hero," I said, amazed and sickened by the headlines.

Taking the paper back, he read, "This week we recognize 'an upstanding citizen, father, and businessman whose contributions have enriched his family, community, and the state of North Carolina.' *Can you believe this crap?*" He gave the paper back to me.

I didn't even want to see it. This hurts . . . this is putting the knife in deep and turning it and turning it and twisting it until it can't hurt anymore. "The timing for Oscar is great! The timing for his son is *pathetic!*" I stopped, looked at Thad, and saw the disbelief on his face that I was internalizing at the moment. "Mr. Byrd will get a lot of sympathy votes with this. He'll use it! Watch him!"

"Braxton, are you going to be all right?"

"Yeah. Call me this afternoon. You, Matt, and I've got to talk about this."

"You've got it." Thad got out of the car and walked over to join a crowd of girls waiting for him. Thad amazes me. He has a solid grip on just about everything. I believe he's the strongest of all of us and doesn't even realize it.

The hospital stood three blocks down on my right, only one block this side of the railroad tracks. I needed to pound the pavement and think so I decided to foot it. I locked my car, put my sunglasses on, and walked the extra block to the train station. I passed two winos standing in front of the bus terminal asking for a handout. I shook my head no, crossed the street, bought a copy of *The News and Observer* at the terminal, tucked it under my arm, and walked the block back to the hospital.

I walked up the steps that led into the side street entrance of the hospital. The lobby was crowded with mainly Negroes and farmers who took advantage of the one day they had off to visit. The smoke from the pipes, cigars, and cigarettes was stifling and a low haze hung over the waiting room. I didn't see Mrs. Pidgeon. The lady at the visitor's desk smiled when she handed me a pass. Today it was pink. I took it, climbed the two flights of stairs, and walked the same long fluorescent-lit hallway to Room 212.

I tapped lightly on the door that stood partially open. I walked quietly over to Jason's bed. He was asleep on his side facing the window. A white mask covered his face and I could hear him breathing, almost in a light snore. He looked peaceful, contented, and free from worry but of course, I knew this wasn't true. I pulled the aluminum straight back chair up to his bed and sat with him. I watched him sleep, listened to the beeping of the monitor, and watched the occasional movement of his lips. His face had more color today and there wasn't as much facial swelling. A fly had gotten in the room. It would land on Jason's head, walk around, take off and come back, repeating the same ritual. I wanted to kill it. Jason smelled of antiseptic much like the hospital, itself. But that was okay because he was alive and there was great hope for a return to an almost normal life.

Jason knew nothing about what had happened to his friend, David Byrd. I wish he never had to know. I stood, moved closer to his bed, and touched his arm, saying as softly as I could, "Jason, I'm not going to let you leave us. You've got to make it. We need you. There are only four of us now."

Chapter 39
NO HONOR IN DYING

I DROVE DOWN Nash Street under the midday sun. Silhouettes of sunbeams floated through the overhead canopy casting shadows in the air. They reminded me of the rays of a rainbow stretching to touch the ground. By some, today would be defined as beautiful but it was hot again, the kind of hot that made going barefoot unpleasant. I was used to it now. The sweat that gathered under my shirt and clung to my chest and back didn't even bother me. The thought that if I lost ten pounds I wouldn't sweat as much ran through my mind but exited quickly. I passed the First Baptist Church, the doors were still closed, and a hundred or so cars sat in surrounding parking lots. A man in a blue suit and tie stood between the massive columns smoking a cigarette and looking at his watch. Must have been an usher counting the seconds he had left to sin. Those Baptists keep close tabs on their "do's" and "don'ts." I passed the Catholic Church and out on their massive lawn was a group of younger boys playing what appeared to be touch football. Any other week, it would be pretty much be a typical Sunday. Things looked the way they usually did on a hot Sabbath in Wilson, North Carolina, but today was anything but normal.

Another thought entered my brain, this one of more significance. I could use this time to ride by Byrd's house. I wonder where they've put his body. I wonder what he looks like now, in death. At least, he's at peace. I better not chance it, riding by Byrd's house. I'll go by later. No need for a restraining order anymore. The bastard blames me for his son's death. I think he killed Byrd. He hated his son; he said he was going bad.

David was a good son. Mr. Byrd said he was a problem child, that he was a troublemaker and disobedient. A troublemaker is like one of those students in the movie, *Rock Around the Clock*, with Glenn Ford playing the teacher. There's no way anyone could say Byrd was a problem.

Byrd was an average sixteen-year-old boy, coming into his own and having thoughts of his own. His father expected him to be obedient and do everything his way. He didn't want Byrd to be independent and have thoughts of his own. Byrd rejected some of his father's ideas but not his father, at least, not at first. It wasn't the fucking thing so much as not being able to choose his friends and stay here in school. It was the pressure, always the pressure—the pressure to please his dad and then there was the rejection. Mr. Byrd obviously didn't need his older boy for pleasure anymore. He had his younger brother now and Charles was fearful of not being submissive. Byrd's payment was rejection by his father in other ways.

Byrd had become a disappointment to his father. His grades weren't the best but he passed. He didn't like school but a lot of kids don't like school. I wondered if his parents liked school. His father probably did. He smoked some, but rarely took a drink. He played around with a few girls but to my knowledge, he'd never screwed one. He was a fairly good athlete and participated in sports, always had. Maybe he wasn't the most aggressive basketball player but he was a team player and believed in fair play. He didn't get into fights and didn't sass his mother or his father. He didn't like golf the way his father worshipped the sport, but he loved tennis. Byrd was a good son and a good human being. Why couldn't his father see that? Why did his father keep saying that Byrd was an embarrassment and that he would be no good? It wasn't because we were his friends. It was because his father couldn't manipulate him any more. Where is the honor in that?

Mr. Byrd was driving David crazy, always telling him he could do better in this or that. "David, remember you are a Byrd, and much is expected of you. You have to keep up the family heritage. You have as much potential as anyone of us and probably more! I don't expect you to let me down, boy. That's why I want you to go to Woodberry Forest. Son, it's a tradition with us and Byrds believe in tradition," his father would say. I heard him say it too many times. What a crock of shit! I never saw Byrd get disrespectful with his dad or throw things or get mad. Byrd didn't have a prayer of pleasing his dad, the "*Tar Heel of the Week*." David Byrd was a good boy and a good son who lacked honor in his own home and especially, in the eyes of his own father. His father pressured him and pressured him and this time Byrd wouldn't yield. And so, his father killed him.

I remember two summers ago when Jason, Byrd, Thad, Matt, Bruce Abbott, and I went camping in an undeveloped area of West Nash Street. Our way of camping wasn't at all fancy. We took a blanket, something to eat and drink, a pillow, a flashlight, and a couple of smokes. We would lay under the open night sky telling jokes, ghost stories, and talking about girls. It was Jason's idea. We'd brought a cooler of Mellow Yellow packed in ice. Jason and Thad had gone off looking for snakes. Bruce suggested that we empty the contents of one of the Mellow Yellow, piss in the bottle, put the cap back on, and return it to the cooler. We thought the idea was funnier than hell and we did it. The problem was only Bruce knew which bottle had the urine in it. Upon examination, each bottle looked as much like Mellow Yellow as any of the others. When it came time to have drinks with our dinner, Bruce passed them out. We didn't know it at the time but Byrd had gotten the "substitute" drink. Bruce had marked it so he knew. After we finished, we sat around laughing because we thought either Jason or Thad had drunk the piss. "Not necessarily," said Bruce. "It could've been any of you. One thing I do know is that I didn't drink it." He laughed and we chased him and we tackled him and made him swear to tell us who got it. He wouldn't and didn't until . . .

Last year in biology class, our teacher, Mrs. Hodge, passed out urine crystals for all of us to taste. She promised it wouldn't hurt us and the only student who put up a squawk was Byrd. He just had this thing about putting piss in his mouth. Everyone was chanting "Go on and taste it, David," and he kept saying no. Then Bruce stood up in front of the whole class and looked at Byrd and said, "I don't know what the big deal is. You drank a whole bottle of piss two years ago and you're still around!" Byrd got embarrassed but he did put the crystal in his mouth. I laughed so hard I cried. I thought I was the one who drank it. Byrd laughed too. He was a great guy and a fantastic sport. Everyone liked him. Everyone, but his father.

Olivia Pugh called me after lunch to tell me that the funeral was planned for Monday afternoon at one o'clock. There would be a graveside service only, family and close friends. I agreed to stand several plots over so I would be unnoticed. I wouldn't be able to hear anything; at least, I could watch what took place. This was the best Mrs. Pugh could come up with and I didn't have a better suggestion.

I thought, at the time, that was a mighty quick burial. It left little time for further investigation, if anyone should question Byrd's death. Right now, I was the only one I knew who stubbornly doubted the coroner's finding. After all, who would question the motive of the Tar Heel of the Week?

Matt, Thad, and I drove out to the Creamery on Sunday afternoon to sit and talk. We hadn't been together since Patsy's party and all hell broke loose there and the fires of hell have continued to spread. Thad didn't agree with me that Mr. Byrd would kill his son but Matt didn't have any trouble believing it. We went around and around on motives of why and why not the old man would or would not knock off his son. I told them about my last visit with Byrd and what Mr. Byrd had said. This didn't convince Thad at the time. Several months later, Thad, unwittingly found out from his uncle, an insurance agent, that Mr. Byrd had taken out a million dollar insurance policy on both boys sixteen months before Byrd died. Five months after Byrd's death, Mr. Byrd opened two more pharmacies in the county. Thad began to put things together and decided that we might have sufficient grounds for our conclusion.

"Where do we go from here?" asked Matt. He sipped on the Coke the colored boy brought him.

"We can't prove it without further proof. Mr. Byrd has a lot of money and there's no way we can go up against that."

"The threats should stop, don't you think?" asked Matt.

"I think they will," Thad said. "There is no reason to continue to harass us."

"I wouldn't be too sure about that, Thad." I took a swallow of Coca-Cola, then sighing, continued, "Remember it was Charles we saw Mr. Byrd with and that'll continue to bother him."

"Oh, yeah, you're right!" Thad turned to Matt in the back seat. "Do you have any ideas?"

"Nope, I'm with Braxton. Let's wait him out. The summer is young."

"Y'all are going to the graveside service tomorrow?" I asked. Both nodded yes. "Do me a favor, would you? Watch Mr. Byrd's eyes and see if you see any remorse."

"Good idea," said Matt. "Where will you be?'

"In the distance somewhere but I *will* be there."

"Jason doesn't know, does he?" asked Matt.

"No, I don't think so. I was there this morning after Sunday School," I said. "No one was in the room and he was asleep. As of last night, he didn't know."

"He'll be pissed off he wasn't there at the service," Thad said.

"Probably," said Matt. "Listen, I need to get back home. Let's go, Braxton."

I dropped Thad off at his house first and then took Matt home since he lived closest to me. We continued to talk about everything that had happened and wondered what long-term effect it would have on us. Matt hinted that a good God would not allow something like this to happen. I didn't have any answer to that; I'd been having enough trouble with understanding the same concept ever since my daddy tried to kill himself. I pulled up in front of Matt's house and as he got out of the car, I asked, "Matt, do you think we could've prevented Byrd's death if we had confronted Mr. Byrd?"

"I don't know." He closed the door and leaned into the window, "I've thought about it too."

"Is there anything we could've done?"

"Braxton, he was threatening us! Look what he did to your mother."

"I wish we had gone to the police."

"They would not have believed us. You know that."

"I just wanted confirmation," I said. "See you later."

I drove the three blocks to my house averaging about twenty miles per hour. The thought that God might be trying to get my attention again kept nagging at me. I wondered if He thought I was taking life too lightly. Did I think I was taking life for granted and reading God into this? I was confused. Somehow, I couldn't see God taking David away in order to teach me a lesson about life. Was God telling me to pay more attention to my own father? I didn't think my father loved me but he'd never treated me the way Byrd's father treated him. I knew my father didn't have a lot of time left. That should make a difference in the way I feel toward him but it does-n't. I know I love David Byrd more than I do my own father. I should feel guilty about saying that, but I don't.

Sunday night I called Rita again. Surprisingly, she answered. The first thing that came out of my mouth was an offer to baby-sit. She told me she had been out of town with some of her girlfriends from college. (That explains why I couldn't connect with her, but who was at her house?) Her boys were with her parents in Wilmington. Monday was her day to pick them up and she asked me to ride along with her. Unfortunately, I had to decline. I told her about Byrd's death and the memorial service. She seemed shocked and wanted to comfort me. Oh boy, I wanted her to but this time, it wasn't in the cards. I told her that I would call her sometime around mid-week.

My Aunt Josephine would be the only member of our family who would attend Byrd's funeral. She knew the Byrd family well. Her daughter, Ingrid, had worked at Byrd's Drugstore and at one time, she and her husband had been social acquaintances of the Byrds. And she knew David Byrd well because of my friendship with him. She had taken us to Morehead to her apartment a couple of times for long weekends.

On Monday when it was time to leave for Byrd's service, I drove the Tank the route I thought the hearse would take. I parked beside the Haywood plot, got out, and stood under the crepe myrtle, letting it shade me. I waited until after the service had begun and I walked up the knoll and stood behind the six-foot Thompson Memorial marker overlooking the Byrd plot. I had a good panoramic view of everything and I clearly saw the horde of people spread all over the area. There must have been two hundred and fifty to three hundred people in attendance. There were a lot of our high school friends and acquaintances in attendance. I could see Matt and Thad but they did-n't see me.

I could only see the backs of the Byrd family. Byrd's two grand-mothers, Olivia and the couple from Nash County sat with them and so did Julian. There were other family members but I didn't know them. Surprisingly, the service was short. The family took Holy Communion first. The minister said something. A boy from his church spoke. I watched everyone bow in prayer at the end and I saw his casket lowered into the ground. His sisters and brother and some of the basketball players threw flowers on top of his casket. Letting the Thompson marker shield me, I hid like a common criminal out of one of O. Henry's short stories until everyone had left and the last shovel of dirt had been thrown on top of Byrd's casket.

When I thought the coast was clear, I walked down to the gravesite of Oscar David Byrd, Jr. I stood in front of his headstone. It looked liked it had just been carved and unpacked. It was so clean and fresh. I knelt and touched it, running my finger around each let-ter in his name. The engraving was beautiful and etched with pre-ciseness. The letters felt good to my touch. There were no rough spots. It was very smooth and still hot from the sun beating down on it. I didn't exactly know what to say. I hadn't prepared anything. This was all so new to me. I felt a sudden urge to kiss his marker. I got down on my knees, bent over, and put my lips on the warm stone. I could feel my eyes moistening as I stood. Looking down on his marker, I said, "Byrd, you are the best friend a guy could ever want. Why did this have to happen? Why? We had a good friendship and no one can take that away from us. You'll always be my friend. Do you hear me? Don't forget the fun we had because I won't. These last weeks together have been hell, haven't they? You suffered more than I did and I won't forget that. I'm sorry I caused you pain. Thank you for standing by me. I'll never forget you and damn it, don't you forget me either. One last thing David Byrd, I don't believe you killed yourself and I hope one day to prove it." I stood for a while having some of my time with Byrd that his father took away from us. "I'll come by and visit you as often as I can . . . Keep you up with things and all. Good bye, good buddy." When I turned to walk back to my car, I found myself standing, face-to-face with Julian.

"You frightened me, Julian. I didn't know you were behind me."

"I just this minute walked up."

"Well, I'm on my way out."

"Please, don't go. Stand with me a minute."

"Okay." Julian moved up beside me and put his right arm around my shoulder. We stood in silence for a long time looking at Byrd's marker. It was almost as if we had rehearsed this scene. We both moved apart at exactly the same time and turned, facing each other. Julian spoke first.

"Braxton, David was a nice boy. I love him very much and I knows he love me. I'm gonna miss that sweet child. I surely am."

"You two went through a lot together, Julian."

"Braxton, Mr. David's told me more than one time that you was the best friend he had. He thought a lot of you."

"I know, Julian, and I cared for him a lot. I feel like I've lost a brother."

"I don't believe it was the Lord's time for this here boy to be leaving us. Strange things happen at that house on Saturday night. I can't tell you what, but I do believe Mr. David would want you to know that. He didn't have much of a chance."

I was silent for a moment. I wanted to put the question as delicately as possible. I didn't know how to ask it any other way. "Julian, do you think Byrd killed himself?"

"Braxton, I ain't ever known Mr. David to hurts anything. You knows how he always took care of them animals and birds. No sir, I don'ts believe he done this to himself." Julian knelt before the marker and cried like a baby. I knelt beside him and put my hand on his left shoulder.

"Julian, don't tell anyone else what you just said to me. I won't repeat it," I said. "I know you'll miss Byrd but you can help Charles. You know what I mean?"

"Yes, sir, I surely do." He stood up and wiped his eyes with the tips of his fingers. He pulled me to a standing position and shook hands with me. "You keep in touch with me, Mr. Braxton."

"I will, Julian. I will," I said. "I promise."

I watched Julian until he got back into his car and drove off. I turned again and spoke to Byrd, "That makes three of us who know the truth. I'm sorry I didn't do something. Please forgive me." Feeling a sense of shame, I backed away from his marker, turned, and ran back through the cemetery among the many, many gravestones until I got to my car. My eyes stung from the beads of sweat running from my forehead. I took my handkerchief and wiped them and then wiped my forehead. I opened the car door. Before getting in, I turned and walked back to our headstone. As I stood there gazing at the Haywood name, I wondered how long it would be before my father would be laid to rest.

Chapter 40
LOADING THE FILM RIGHT

I WAITED ON the front porch for the better part of an hour. I saw the red-headed paperboy madly pedaling on Nash Street and then turn the corner onto Kincaid Avenue. He was near the end of his route. I ran to the street and stood at the curb to meet him. I watched him take the *Wilson Daily Times* from his saddlebag and throw it from the middle of the street. It landed in the gutter below my feet. *A sorry shot,* I thought. When I had my paper route I always took time to stop and hand the paper to my customer no matter the age. I picked up the paper and took the rubber band off and opened it to the front page. Monday, June 17, 1957. The article I wanted to read was front-page center. The headline read "Wilson Boy Takes Own Life." A picture accompanied the news story.

Returning to the porch, I positioned myself on the hard cement stoop and began scanning the article about Byrd:

Oscar David Byrd, Jr., age 16, was found dead of a gunshot wound on the side porch of his family home at 1200 Raleigh Road Sunday morning. A single bullet struck him just below the left eye and ranged upward through the brain. The death is believed to be self-inflicted. A .45 automatic revolver was found next to the body.

Called David by his friends, he was a rising junior at Charles L. Coon High School in Wilson. David, a member of the Key Club, played center position on the Coon High School basketball team. David's coach, Bill Johnson, said, "David would be sadly missed. He had a lot of potential and was expected to fill a void on next year's squad. He was a super kid."

A servant, Julian W. Matthews, discovered young Byrd's body when he took the family dog for his morning walk around six o'clock. Young David was lying between a wicker chair and a wicker couch on the west side of the house. Matthews said the family dog, Chance, actually discovered the body.

David's mother, Helen Copeland Byrd, said David returned from a date around eleven-thirty but became restless and went out again. Mrs. Byrd stated she went to bed but got up again around two o'clock in the morning when she heard a noise she thought was a car backfiring. She reported that she went downstairs and looked around as well as went outside and walked around. Everything looked normal to her. The three family cars were in the garage. She acknowledges she did not see David and assumed he was out with some of his friends.

David is survived by his mother and father, one younger brother, Charles Reynolds Byrd, and twin older sisters, Emily Davis and Elizabeth Copeland Byrd. A graveside service was held today at one o'clock in the afternoon.

I put the paper down on the steps. I didn't know the woman who wrote this article and didn't care; however, the person she interviewed didn't give her the straight facts. David was not on a date and he didn't leave the house a second time. He'd been restricted to his room for the entire weekend. Julian could confirm this because he told me David came to his room around midnight upset over his father's decision to keep him at home his last weekend in Wilson. Lies, deceit, and cover up will keep the truth from being told.

I rolled the paper back up, put the rubber band around it, and laid it beside my father's door. He never liked anyone to touch the paper before he'd seen it except when I had my route and then he didn't have to pay for the paper. I paid for it then and usually had extras. My father didn't read now because his eyes couldn't adjust to the fine print, but Jackson would read to him. I'm not certain he even listened anymore but it helped Jackson pass the long hours when he sat with Daddy.

I walked to the kitchen and saw Lily bent over the sink washing vegetables. An eddy of smoke circulated above her head. As soon as

Lily heard my shoes on the linoleum floor, she dropped her cigarette in the sink and raised her right hand to brush away the smoke.

"That'll cost you a day's wages. You know how Mother feels about you smoking in here."

"Don't you dare tell her, Braxton. I means that." Lily frowned.

"How much you going to pay me to keep quiet?" I laughed.

"I ain't gonna pays you nothing. As many cigarettes as I've given you, you should be paying me to keep quiet. You knows what your mother would do if she knew you smoked around here?"

"What? Borrow some of mine?" I laughed.

"What's you up to carrying on like this?" Lily said, not sharing my humor.

"That's a darn good question. I think I'm trying not to lose my mind!"

"Braxton, you gonna hurt a long time, honey. It takes a long time to heal when a friend dies. You needs to face your fears and hurts and let them take you where they wants to." Lily stopped and turned around and came over to me. "You ain't never going to forgets David, honey. He wouldn't want you to neither but he don't want you walking around the rest of your life mourning for him neither." She leaned over, grabbed me, and gave me a strong hug.

"How can you be so sure, Lily?"

"I ain't never told no one in this here house this before. You must keep it to yourself."

"I promise." I watched the expression in her eyes turn to one of sadness.

"My only little boy died when he was five years old. He was one sweet, precious little boy. And I loved him. Jesus knows I loves that boy." She stopped.

"What happened?" I was baffled at her sudden confession.

"We was at his grannie's ones Sunday afternoon and little Zeb, that's what we called him, was running around her old porch having himself a good time. Well, Zeb's older cousins were in the backyard taking target practice with one of their granddaddie's rifles. They was supposed to be shooting at some old whiskey bottles. Well, little Zeb run around to the back and when his older cousin, Warren, gets ready to take his turn, little Zeb runs right into Warren's line of fire. The first shot out of that rifle kills my little boy."

"Oh, Lily, I'm sorry," I said, taking her right hand in mine. "I didn't know you had ever had any children."

"I never wants another child after that. I thought I would die, too." I watched her eyes fill with tears. The pain was still fresh. "It nearly kills me to think I won't watching my little boy that afternoon. His granny says I was an unfit mother. And I believes her for the longest time. If it hadn't been for little Zeb's father, I would have done lost my mind."

"How long ago was that?"

"Let me see." Lily hesitated, counting on her fingers. "That was in 1946. He'd be your age, Braxton. The very same age as you."

"Wow! You've made it though." I didn't know what to say.

"Yes, I made it . . . with the good Lord's help. He's been mighty good to me, mighty good."

Lily walked onto the back porch and stared into the yard. I followed. "I ain't told you to do anything that I hasn't done myself."

"Thank you for sharing that with me, Lily." I wanted to take her pain away but couldn't.

"Braxton, you probably don't knows this but I loves you about as good as I did my own boy." Her brown eyes mirrored a joy that I had never noticed. She pulled me to her again and hugged me tightly. I would cling to her strength in the days ahead, allowing it to cradle my anguish.

"Lily, let's go on the back porch and have a smoke together," I said.

"Thank you, Braxton, I will," she said with a hint of a smile in her eyes. "I don't suppose you has your own, do you?"

"Why, Lily, you surprise me! You know I rarely smoke," I said, winking. "I do have some matches though. I thought you might give me one of yours."

"I just bet you did." She took her pack of Kools out of her apron pocket and set it on the table. Taking one out for herself, she pushed the pack over to me. I took one and put it in my mouth. Lighting it, I took a deep drag, and reached toward Lily. She held my hand steady as she leaned in and put her cigarette tip to mine, inhaling heavy to get it started. We both took a drag and let the smoke out together. Neither of us said anything as we shared our smoke. I looked at Lily and realized for the first time she was old enough to be my mother and if it weren't for the skin color, I could just as easily be her son. In some ways, I already was and had been. I had just begun to realize it.

"Lords, I needs to get back to work." Lily stood. She put her cigarette out in the ashtray. "Your mother's gonna be mad with me if I don't have ya'lls supper on time."

"Don't worry about her," I said. "I'll handle that. What are we having tonight?"

"Fried chicken, mashed potatoes, garden peas, bread and okra if you want some."

"It all sounds good to me." Excited over the prospect of some of Lily's fried chicken, I opened the screened door and flicked my cigarette butt in the backyard. "I thought I might take a bath. How long do I have before we eat?"

"A good hour and maybe longer!" Lily went to the stove and opened the bottom drawer and took out her favorite cast iron skillet for frying chicken. The pan, weighing at least three pounds, had belonged to my grandmother and had to be at least fifty years old. Lily said the older a pan was, the better it cooked. I saw her getting her bacon grease down and the butter. She turned the back gas burner on with that "get out of my way cause I'm in a serious cooking mood" look. I smiled and went across the hall to my bedroom. My room was hot, a real scorcher. My window thermometer read ninety-four degrees. I took all my clothes off but my briefs and went into the bathroom. I dropped my briefs and knelt naked by the tub. When I had it three-fourths full of lukewarm water, I got in, sat down and leaned my head against the back of the tub. This was one of my favorite ways to relax, just letting the water gently roll over my stomach and legs. I closed my eyes thinking about Lily and her little boy, how life is full of tragedies, how some people cope better than others, how strong I had always thought she was and then someone knocked on the door. "I'm in the tub."

"Braxton, I need to bring your dad in," said Fletcher. "He needs to use the toilet."

"Oh, that's great!" I said. "Well, okay." I don't know why I felt ill at ease at the prospect of two grown men seeing me naked. I didn't remember the last time my daddy had seen me in my birthday suit. It must have been when I was around five or six years old. The door opened and I immediately cupped my hands and covered my genital area.

"Sorry to bother you," said Fletcher. The strong black man held the skeletal frame of my daddy, one hand on his chest and one on the base of his spine, to allow him to shuffle across the floor. Daddy was terribly thin and his flesh pulled across his bony arms and hollowed face. The pajamas that used to fit him nicely now hung from him like oversized clothes on a straw-filled scarecrow. He was alive but he didn't look like any recognizable life form, rather more like a cadaver being pushed across the room. Hanging from his mouth was a lighted cigarette, and in his right hand was the tube connected to his IV balanced by Fletcher's right arm. I didn't know whether to speak or remain silent. I decided to speak, thinking it would call more attention to both of us if I didn't. "Hello, Daddy."

He titled his head my way, squinted through the rising smoke, and when he spoke, ashes fell from his cigarette onto the speckled tiled floor, "Your thighs look like ham hocks, boy. You need to lose some weight." He turned just as quickly toward the commode and with Fletcher's help he pulled his shriveled penis from his pajama pants and proceeded to urinate. What didn't go into the commode went all over the floor and some rolled down his pants leg. He turned and looked at me again saying, "Don't you have a damn thing to do other than stare. Haven't you ever seen a grown man take a leak before?"

"Sorry." I immediately began to bathe myself rubbing soap over my face and body. I wasn't aware I had been staring at him. I was here first. I was thinking about how his words singed me with their acid thrust. I was thinking how mean he could be and how unnecessary his comment was. I was thinking why couldn't he either say something nice or nothing at all. I was thinking I'm sorry you're sick but that doesn't give you the right to treat me like shit. I was thinking how I wished you were dead.

After Fletcher helped daddy out of the bathroom, I sat in the tub just staring at the window with the forsythia bush on the other side. I felt humiliated. I rationalized that he saw me as a loser . . . that he was ashamed of me . . . that I was less than the son he wanted. This feeling began after a major operation when I was six years old. I had had my frontal skull removed not allowing me to do many of the things my friends could do. I tried to compensate for not being able to play contact sports so that he would be proud of me in other ways. I wanted him to love me the way he loved Anne. I succeeded in academics and in my artwork. I worked hard at being responsible and respectful and I tried to be the best son I knew how to be. He did not seem to care. Tonight with one comment he told me how despicable I was in his eyes. I knew that I would never forget those hateful words. I knew that I did not love him and I admitted to myself that night I hated him. That night I started praying that my father would die.

I got up and grabbed the towel off the back of the door. I dried myself quickly, wrapped my towel around my waist, and ran to my bedroom and dressed for dinner. There was a knock on my door. "Who is it?"

"It's me, Fletcher."

"What do you need?" I wanted to be alone.

"I need to speak to you a moment." His tone sounded more like an order than a request.

"Okay." I opened the door and Fletcher walked in and stood by my fireplace resting his muscular arm on the mantle. "Braxton, your daddy didn't mean what he said in there."

"The hell he didn't. He meant every damn word of it." No one would make me believe otherwise.

"Braxton, your daddy is a dying man and is in excruciating pain," Fletcher said, trying to appeal to my sympathy. "He's on fire inside and he's ashamed for you to see him that way. He doesn't want you to see him as a fourth of a man unable to care for himself."

"Is that supposed to excuse him? He can say anything because he's dying."

"No. It should help you understand him better."

"Fletcher, I'm tired of being his scapegoat. I'm tired of not being able to do anything because he's sick. I'm tired of not being able to have any friends over anymore because he's dying. I'm tired of having to tiptoe around this house all the time. I'm just tired of the whole damn situation."

"I didn't come here to argue, Braxton." Fletcher meant well. He seldom commented on any of our family disputes. He knew not to cross that sensitive line that existed in a man's home between a father and son's relationship, especially when harsh feelings were involved. Today, he wasn't out of place. He was my daddy's advocate. I didn't want to hear what he had to say.

"I know you didn't Fletcher," I said, moving toward him. "But you know, life is too short to have to keep taking crap from adults, especially men who are poor fathers."

"I know that you've been to hell and back this summer but you have got to look at things as they are." Fletcher said, his right hand gripping my bedpost.

"I thought that's what I've been doing," I sighed then became angry. "*In that bathroom tonight, my father rejected me. You know it and I know it. I didn't cause his cancer and he knows that. So he doesn't have to take it out on me. He doesn't treat Anne that way.*" I had yelled at the wrong man.

"You have a point and I don't deny that." He released his grip and moved toward the door. "Just try not to be so hard on your dad. I don't think he'll be here too much longer." Fletcher closed the door quietly and returned to sit with my father.

(It would take twenty-nine years for me to realize that Fletcher was right. I carefully packed all the anger, resentment, and hatred I had ever had for my father and tucked it away in my memory bank. I never forgot it and it did not become vague with time. Whenever I was told to open those memories by a thought, or a situation, or casual reminder from a movie or song, it did not take long to bring my bad feelings out. Everything I thought would be restored when my father was out of the picture never returned. The older I got, the more I needed him. The more I needed him, the fewer positive things I could remember. And then on the 18th of April in 1986, my birthday to be exact, I relinquished all those pent-up, angry feelings and all that hatred I had harbored and accepted him for the dying father he actually was. It was an unbelievable feeling of freedom to take all that excess garbage off my back and throw it away. I had been the selfish one, not him. It took twenty-nine years of growing up for me to accept my dad as he really was and to see the goodness in this dying man. *In my immaturity and desire to grow up, I had really misjudged my dad.*)

I heard Lily calling me from the kitchen. It was time for her to leave and catch her five forty-five bus. Dinner had been prepared and was ready to be served. Lily left it warming. Anne had a four-thirty appointment to get her annual physical. My Aunt Josephine had taken Anne and Mother. The fact they had not returned was a mystery but I was not alarmed, not yet at least.

I fixed myself a plate of fried chicken and mashed potatoes. Since Mother was not back, I piled the garden peas on top of the potatoes the way I had seen my daddy do so many times. The combination looked like a bunch of green bowling balls sitting on top of a snow mound. I poured myself a glass of sweet iced tea and took my dinner to the back porch.

Under normal circumstances, I would not hesitate to dig into the food sitting before me. I pushed my plate away. The words of my father conflicted with any appetite. Thanks to him, I had been dealt another dose of misery—something else to wrestle with—another weight of pressure and no way to express how I really felt at the moment.

I found myself staring into the backyard and thinking of nothing in particular or very important. Our yard was a view master when I wanted to see a scene from my younger days. It held a panoramic memory of my childhood. Everywhere I looked I saw a scene playing itself out for me. The three Catawba trees in different positions along the hedgerow caught my attention with their large green leaves. It would soon be time for the black and yellow worms that ate the tree's foliage to appear. I remembered the dozens of times I climbed these trees to collect the worms to sell them to the area firemen. Three for a dollar was a good price for a young boy but well deserved since one of the hazards of the job was being sprayed with a yellowish, foul smelling secretion these worms used as a defense. This could be hard if you were a prissy child.

In front of the Catawba trees was the four-foot cement wading pool my Uncle Jeff built for us. The pool, large enough for a small child to swim in, sat in the center of the backyard. It wasn't really funny but I couldn't help but laugh remembering Molly Vance's consequence for disobeying her mother. Mrs. Vance had repeatedly told Molly not to walk around on the ledge of the pool that summer afternoon. Molly was a stubborn child and had to have her way. She had her way and when she fell, she broke her nose. Molly still blamed me for her accident.

When I was younger, there were times I pretended to be Superman. I would tie a towel around my neck and jump off the garage. It was daring and I felt awfully brave. I loved those times. That is until Janice Bradley jumped with me and caught her left arm on the clothesline. I heard her arm pop when it was torn from its socket before large Janice hit the ground. My Superman days were over. I retired my towel.

The closest structure to me now was a one-room white playhouse that our uncle built for Anne. The little house had a large green front door, two windows with frilly curtains, electrical outlets, an overhead light, and crown molding around the ceiling. This is where I performed my first chemical experiment and started my first fire, trying to make a stink bomb.

It makes me feel good when I take time to remember the happier moments in my life. I wondered why I was so anxious to grow up when I was having so much fun. Life seemed uncomplicated and most of the time, others made my decisions for me. Lily says your future memories are built on past experiences so it behooves us to remember everything we possibly can.

Chapter 41
A CLOSED DOOR

IT WAS WEDNESDAY morning after Byrd's death, and I felt lost without him and Jason. Matt had his job to go to and Thad had his summer activities. I didn't feel sorry for myself but I felt lonely and somehow, cheated out of life. Three days of sticking close to home, doing chores, and watching Mother to see if she would pull anymore of her tricks had tired me and given me more than enough time to think. One thing I had learned this summer was that I was not ready to be a man. No matter how enticing wanting to grow up and be mature sounded a month ago, today, the whole idea seemed ridiculous to me.

I had always believed that once a door had been opened, it was pretty much a guarantee that it would stay opened unless a person chose to close it. This wasn't the case when I got the urge to visit Rita again. I kept telling myself that she needed me as much as I needed her. I kept asking myself if she was avoiding me or was it in my imagination. I felt like something wasn't right and I wanted to find out what. I needed her and I wanted her to need me. It was about ten-thirty when I opened the gate of the white picket fence that enclosed her backyard. Her back door was opened but her screened door was hooked from the inside. I knocked and kept my fingers crossed that my timing was right. I heard someone shuffling down the hall and then I saw Rita enter the kitchen. She had on one of those female nighties that dropped a little above the knees. It was a thin light green with short sleeves and a low cut v-neckline with frilly lace around the neckline and sleeves. She had matching cloth slippers on her feet. I thought that I could see the outline of her body underneath her nightie. The only thing holding it up was her larger-than-life boobs. They were beautiful and as usual, stood at attention.

"Rita," I said, using my best cheerful voice. It echoed through the kitchen. "It's Braxton. Is this a bad time?"

"Hey, sweetie," Rita said. As she got close to the door, I could see through the screen that she had been crying. Undoing the hook and opening the door, she reached for my hand and pulled me into the kitchen. My body responded before I could say anything. My dick got hard, my heart throbbed, and I felt a tingling sensation run up and down my entire anatomy. I hoped she wanted to hold me as much as I wanted to hold her. Leaning into me and pushing her breast against my chest, she planted her lips against mine. Oh God! I wanted more. "What brings you down here unannounced?"

When she backed away, I could see that she looked tired and her eye mascara had smeared from crying. I could detect alcohol on her body even though she had put on perfume to hide its smell. Her hair was a mess despite what appeared as an unsuccessful attempt to comb it. "Have you been waiting long?"

"What's going on?" I said, ignoring her question.

"I'd rather not tell you today."

"Where are the boys?"

"They are still with my parents."

"Why?" I was puzzled. "Didn't you go down Monday to get them?"

"Oh, yes, I went," she said. "I drove the four hours to get there but they didn't come back with me." Rita ran her left hand through her tousled hair attempting to straighten it. She walked over to the table and took a cigarette out of a nearly empty pack. This time she didn't ask me to light it. "It's probably not wise for you to be here today."

"Why?" I said. "Are you mad with me about something?"

"No, Braxton," she said, smiling and taking a long draw on her cigarette. Exhaling the smoke through her nostrils with as much grace as possible, Rita moved closer to me and put both of her hands on my shoulders. She still held the cigarette in her left hand. "Dear

Braxton, you are so sweet and kind. I could never get mad with you." Rita leaned over and kissed me on my cheek.

"Well, tell me what the matter is," I said. I wanted to be close to her. I wanted more than a peck on the cheek. I wanted to hold her and make her feel safe and take her worries away. I wanted to be her knight-in-shining-armor. Even now, despite her tousled appearance, she was gorgeous.

"Let me have a minute to put a blouse and shorts on," she said. "It will only take a sec. Make yourself at home." I watched her move across the floor, twitching her ass with precision.

"Can I have one of your cigarettes," I asked as she exited the kitchen. There was no answer. I sat down at the kitchen table, pulled a Kent from the package, and lit it with the match from the black matchbook. Blue Diamond Lounge of Myrtle Beach was etched in silver on the front of the cover. *Pretty classy looking,* I thought. When was Rita in Myrtle Beach?

Rita returned before I could finish my smoke. I put the cigarette out as she entered the kitchen. The Rita I recognized joined me at the table. The smeared mascara around her eyes was gone. She had taken time to put on some deep red lipstick and her hair had been combed and was tied with a multi-colored scarf, the way a lot of the girls at school do their hair. She had carefully left the top two buttons of her white blouse unbuttoned and she had not taken time to put on a bra. I began to get stiff again. I hated this teasing.

"Rita, it is good to see you again." I didn't want to get any more nervous than I was at this moment.

"I am glad to see you, too, Braxton." She reached over and grabbed my right hand, holding it with her right hand. Then she turned my hand over and started gently stroking my palm with her long, slender fingers.

"Tell me what is going on here?" It felt so good. I wanted to be natural and I didn't want to mess up. How could I be cool when she had me so excited I could hardly sit still? I was as fidgety as a little boy sitting on a nest of fire ants.

"Braxton, do you care for me at all?" Rita's eyes begged me to touch her but I didn't quite have the nerve yet.

"Rita, that's a foolish question," I said, reaching across the table to touch her. Her hand pushed mine aside.

"If you care for me, you will listen carefully," said Rita. "But first I am going to let you do something I hope I won't regret." Rita stood.

"I would never make you regret anything, Rita." I could imagine many things I wanted her to let me do. My mind began to swirl and I felt lightheaded.

"Stand up and come here," she said. "I know you have wanted to do this. Unbutton my blouse slowly."

"What?" My eyes widened. That was real cool, Braxton, you jerk. Just do it, you prick. My hand shook as I undid each of the remaining four buttons, slowly and carefully. My heart throbbed again and my mouth went dry on me. "They are so beautiful, Rita, so very beautiful!"

Rita took off her blouse and dropped it on the back of the chair. What she said next was unexpected. "Take your shirt off, Braxton."

"Yes, ma'am," I said. I wasted no time following her orders. After I had my shirt off and deposited on the floor, Rita pulled me against her, letting me feel her soft skin against my smooth, virgin chest. A flash of the night we played with Arlene's tits ran through my mind. Instinctively, I stepped back and putting my right index finger in my mouth, I licked it, and then ran it up and down and in between her bulging breasts whose movement begged me to give them a suck. "May I taste them?" I had waited days for this opportunity. This was a fantasy I never thought would become a reality. Rita smiled. I wasted no time running my tongue around each tit. I got carried away and started nibbling on her right tit when the damn phone rang. Rita jumped and pulled back. She reached over and grabbed her blouse and ran to catch the phone. "Shit! Shit! Shit! Shit!"

"That was my aunt," Rita said, retuning to the kitchen. "She's coming over."

"She has great timing," I said, putting on my shirt.

"This has to be our little secret, Braxton," Rita said.

"Don't worry, Rita. No one will ever hear about this from me," I said. "Besides, no one would believe me anyhow."

"Braxton, honey, look at me," Rita said.

"I don't like the tone of your voice, Rita," I said. "What gives?"

"Braxton, I can't ever see you like this again." Rita had tears in her eyes. "It would be better if you never came down here again."

"What? I don't understand?" I said. I felt flushed and confused and my stomach responded like it had been hit by a line drive. Why is she messing with my head? What is she trying to do to me? "Rita, no—it can't end this way."

"Braxton, you asked me what was wrong. Okay, I'm going to tell you, but please don't tell anyone—not even your mother."

"You have my word, Rita," I said. What could she tell me that would change things?

"Braxton, I'm pregnant."

"Pregnant?" I couldn't believe it. Well, it certainly wasn't my child. Oh God, that would be the last straw. Her announcement hit me like a two-by-four swung hard and fast against my butt. Her words stung and hurt and angered me. What in the hell was going on here?

"Yes, pregnant," reiterated Rita. "I found out yesterday after-noon. Now do you understand?"

"I guess so," I said. Boy, she knew how to knock the wind out of my sail. *What a fool I am. Who did I think I was kidding? I had plans for Rita and me—real plans—plans of ecstasy. Crap, Braxton, grow up. Get your head on straight. Put you mind in gear. That could have been your baby one day.* "I guess I need to go now."

"I'm afraid so," said Rita.

"Goodbye, my lady," I said, leaving through the back door.

"Goodbye, my lord," Rita said, blowing me a kiss and closing the door behind me.

I walked around the block thinking only of Rita'a body and her beautiful breasts and those magnificent tits—those exquisite tits that I rubbed and touched and tasted. A voice in my head told me I could cherish the moment but that it was time to move on. It would be my fantasy. I would never forget Rita. I wondered if she would for-get me. Sadly, I learned years later that the little girl she gave birth to was not her husband's but supposedly some guy she had been seeing on the sly. That had to be the reason she was crying that morning.

It was on Thursday that Mrs. Parker called and said that Jason would like to see me. He was still in the hospital. Her good news was that he was now sitting up and eating hospital food. The eating was a feat in itself. His visits were being regulated and I was told to try to be at his room around eleven o'clock. We could have thirty minutes together. I hadn't seen Jason since last Sunday; it was too disheartening to continue to visit and watch him lay there.

The morning was blustery, hot, and humid. The heat wave that had struck Wilson was now in its eighth straight day—we had not had a single day with less than ninety-six degrees. Today it would be hotter. The North Carolina coast stood watch for a possible visit from Hurricane Audrey. Black shank had taken over many of the tobacco fields and the problem had become serious. Ava Gardner, local girl turned Hollywood star, was in Wilson county visiting her sisters. Pictures of Ms. Gardner and former suitors, now bald and beer-bellied, were splashed across the front page of the *Wilson Daily Times* for several days. And Jason Parker awaited me with a surprise.

I was outside Jason's room at eleven o'clock on the nose. I knocked and a voice inside said, "*Enter.*" I pushed the metal door open and walked in. Jason, sitting in his pale green hospital gown tied around his chest, leaned casually against his pillows eating chocolate ice cream. He smiled and gave a thumb up when he saw me. No longer on the respirator, he looked more like his old self with the exception of his shaved head and head bandage. His coloring was returning.

"You were out for a right long time there," I said, reaching to shake his hand.

"That's what the doc tells me." He grabbed my hand and gave it a strong grip.

"How do you feel now?" A stupid question to ask, but I really wanted to know.

"I've still got a headache and my back's a little sore. Other than that, pretty good, I think."

"You gave us all a hell of a scare," I said. "I hope you've learned your lesson."

"Braxton, you need to know something." Jason sounded strange. He put his ice cream saucer down and stared out the window.

"What is it?" I asked without hesitation, anxious to know what he was about to say.

"I don't remember a thing about that night," Jason said sheepishly as he turned back and looked at me, begging my response.

"Not anything? Nothing at all?" Surprised and shocked were not strong enough adjectives to describe my reaction to the bombshell he had dropped.

"Not one damn thing. Dr. Wentworth had to tell me everything that happened. I don't even remember going to the club."

"How does he explain your forgetfulness?"

"You know that I had a concussion? The x-rays and other brain wave tests they've done indicate some bruising of the skull. They think I've lost some of my short term memory."

"Damn! Will you get it back?" That was a stupid and insensitive question to ask, jerko.

"There's a good chance but the doctors don't know when." Jason shrugged.

"Well, there can be a plus side to this." I tried to think of something positive to say. I didn't know how affected Jason was by what the doctor had told him. I had a sudden jerk of fear. "There are always some things we'd like to forget." I didn't do much to comfort him but he was unusually calm already. I don't know when I remember Jason being this laid back.

"Braxton, Mother told me about David Byrd."

"She did?" I wondered what he knew and didn't know. "What did she tell you?"

"That he died of a gunshot wound to the head."

"That's damn close," I said. "It's a real tragedy."

"He must've been under a lot of pressure to do that!" Jason wore a blank expression as if he didn't know anything that had transpired. "What got into him, Braxton? What made him do it?" I was surprised, completely taken aback. Jason didn't remember anything and he wasn't fishing around and he wasn't playing games with me. He, obviously, had forgotten everything that had occurred. His eyes showed no knowledge of anything concerning Byrd. *Eerie!* I had to ask.

"Jason, do you remember how mad Byrd's dad got with me?"

"No!"

"Do you remember the night we were locked out of Byrd's house?"

"Vaguely," said Jason.

"Do you remember how we got in the house?"

"Yes, we broke a downstairs window." He was wrong but seemed assured.

"Okay," I said, more to myself than Jason. He didn't have his facts straight, and it appeared his recollection of the events surrounding Byrd's death were either a blur or totally erased from his memory. "Can I ask you one more thing?"

"Yes."

"Give me your right hand." I took his hand and turned it over and showed him the scar on his palm. "Do you remember how you got this cut?" I pointed to where he'd made the slit.

He looked at me for a minute, scratched his head, and said, "I haven't got a clue."

"Remarkable!" I was blown away. I couldn't believe it. Jason's a prankster but he's not this good at disguising things. I was without words. I hesitated. I needed to get out of his room, to get some air. "I'm glad you're getting better, Jason. I really am."

"Braxton, do you think I'm crazy?"

"Absolutely not!" I didn't know what to believe anymore, but Jason crazy, no way. "Why?"

"What's wrong then? Something's bothering you." Now Jason is reading my mind.

"No, not really. Just a lot of shit happening and I've got a hundred things to do but I wanted to come down and see you first." I felt cold sweat grabbing my neck and face—the clammy kind that says you might be getting ready to throw up. I did feel a knot in my stomach and a little lightheaded. I never expected to hear this from Jason. It was like I'd walked into empty space. Maybe Jason was lucky. He had an out now, a legitimate excuse for no further involvement. Jason was certainly no threat to Mr. Byrd in his present condition. I was certain that Mr. Byrd would find out about Jason's memory loss at his next golf game with Mr. Parker. The way I fig-

ured it there were only three of us left who could still be in jeop-
ardy. Jason was lucky. "When will you be getting out?"

"They'll run more tests," said Jason. "Maybe, next week!"

"I'll be checking in with you in a day or two."

"Don't leave," he said. "You just got here."

"I have to, Jason. I've stayed longer than I was supposed to."

"Don't forget me, Braxton."

"Are you kidding? You know I won't." I walked down the hall
scratching my head in disbelief. I was happy for Jason, I think. But, I
almost felt like I had lost another friend. This wasn't the same Jason
I had taken to Patsy Wentworth's party.

I liked it better when Jason talked dirty, keeping me informed
about his latest conquests with the female sex. I liked it better when
Jason would make me laugh with his stupid, unpredictable pranks
and tricks. I liked it better when I could correct Jason when his
behavior got out of line.

I wanted the old Jason back—the Jason who saved my ass when
I got in over my head, the Jason who took me into his confidence,
the Jason who taught me how to smoke, the Jason who detested
fakes and snobs, the Jason who knew what was really going on, and
the Jason who reminded me of Holden Caulfield.

Chapter 42
GOD DEALS A BLOW!

MY MOTHER, THAD, and Matt were all caught off guard to hear the news of Jason's sudden loss of memory. Thad thought it was a blessing in disguise considering all the other garbage in Jason's life. Matt feared Jason would back into the truth and everything would hit the fan at once and then Jason might not remember the oath we had made together.

Two days after my visit, Jason awoke screaming in the middle of the night. I understand he scared the crap out of the night nurses and the orderly on duty. He got out of his bed, ran wildly up and down the hall knocking on doors, and yelling. He showed no signs of knowing who he was or where he was. When they were finally able to restrain him, his eyes had rolled back into his head and a white, creamy saliva drooled from his mouth. The doctors who examined him determined he had a reoccurrence of his petite mal seizures, maybe two in succession. He later lapsed into a coma. A day later, on Sunday, June 30th, Jason was transferred to the Medical College of Virginia in Richmond, Virginia, for further tests. The doctors at M.C.V. planned to keep him under observation for as long as necessary to run further tests.

Millie gave me this account based on Dr. Thorne's meeting with her parents. I didn't tell her about the afternoon of Jason's bizarre behavior and his shooting the cardinal. The thought crossed my mind again that maybe he had had a seizure that afternoon. Scary to think we didn't recognize his sickness then. And scary to think it would be God knows when—maybe as much as six to eight weeks—before we would see Jason again. Damn you, Jason! Why did you go and do this to yourself.

A stronger bond developed between Thad, Matt, and me. We agreed that one of us would write Jason at least once a week. Matt would be in charge of mailing our letters and he would hold us accountable. Thad and I agreed to form a committee when we returned to school to solicit money from students and businesses to fund a college scholarship in Byrd's honor. Thad would head the committee provided the school approved it. We did not foresee any problems with Coon's administration and this was not something Mr. Byrd would have the nerve to stop. I agreed to visit Byrd's grave at least once a week and keep him abreast of what we were doing. We would also keep fresh flowers on his grave throughout the summer months and we were still determined to prove that David Byrd did not kill himself.

The death of Byrd brought the three of us face to face with God in different ways. Matt was already on shaky grounds with God and this latest event turned him further away from God. He didn't think he could trust God, especially a God who let bad things happen to good people. His deity became Ayn Rand and her views of objectivism. Thad and I couldn't begin to understand what she was saying in *Atlas Shrugged* so Ayn Rand's philosophy of "the supremacy of reason" had no appeal to us.

I know Byrd's death affected Thad inside. He is too sensitive for it not to have, but outwardly, Thad became more stoical in his faith. He worked hard to teach himself to avoid showing any feelings and emotional responses and he transferred this practiced indifference to his approach to God. He didn't deny God but he showed no passion for God. He believed if Byrd's death was a part of God's plan, then he should accept this and show no outward and no inward signs of emotion. This response was contradictory to his whole personality and I wondered how long it would last.

If anything, I questioned God more. I had already had problems understanding God's ways regarding my father. Byrd's death complicated things further for me. The whole idea of trusting God became more confusing to me. It was hard to trust when I didn't know that much about the deity I was supposed to trust. My faith was like that of a ping pong ball being hit back and forth, then stopping, being hit back and forth, and then stopping again. It was situation-guided more than God-guided.

Regardless of our wrestling with God, we continued to go to Sunday school and church. At the time, I am not certain we saw any correlation between church attendance and what some churchgoers called an abiding faith. We went because our parents expected us to go. We went because our friends went. We went because we had fun. We went to hear Captain Chuck. We did not go to learn more about God or to deepen our faith. This came later for some of us.

Matt, Thad, and I were left to discover not only the doubt that comes when a young friend dies but also, we were faced with emptiness, not only in our own individual lives but also in our lives corporately. When someone dies suddenly, those who are left behind realize, in the days and months that follow, they didn't have the time to prepare to say goodbye. The "saying goodbye" we came to learn was an important step for the survivor. It was a closure we were denied. This definitely affected how we dealt with Byrd's death in those early months. We talked about him as if he was still alive, we talked with him at his grave about everything we thought he wanted to know, and we included him in everything we did. We were forever saying things like "What would Byrd think or say," if we needed another opinion. Then we would try to get into his mind and respond the way we thought he might. This was our way of keeping him alive, of not giving him up to death, of refusing to say goodbye. We never completely said goodbye but we tried to say goodbye a little at a time. It was never our intention to give David Byrd up totally but we had to learn to give him up one piece at a time. We taught each other to do this. If we had had that needed preparation time, maybe the act of giving him up would not have been so painful.

Five days after David Byrd's death, another event happened that would change my life dramatically in other ways for the next two years. It was a Friday morning, the twenty-eighth of June, and another hot, sticky day. Mosquitoes had invaded our town and they were everywhere. Our neighborhoods were being sprayed on a rotating basis with DDT between eight and nine o'clock nighttime. Ours was next, but this time I would get to escape the suffocating fumes.

I would not have to sleep with my windows closed, a precaution that had to be taken. I would not have to breathe the stale, humid air circulated by my yellow box fan. To stay would have been claustrophobic!

It was ideal weather at the coast and that was where Thad, Matt, and I were headed—away from death, away from disease, away from chemicals, away from pressure, just away to Atlantic Beach or Morehead depending on which side of the Bogue Sound you stayed. I got up early, packed, and was ready to exit Wilson by six o'clock. Thad's aunt and uncle would be taking the three of us for a week's stay at Thad's parent's cottage on the beach side of the sound. Mother, the brain behind this little vacation, knew we needed time away from Wilson. She convinced the others we needed a vacation from the confusion that had invaded our lives. Matt and Thad's parents were aware only of the pressure created by Byrd's death and Jason's accident. They suspected nothing more.

By staying at the Ruffin's cottage, the cost of the trip was negligible. Lily had cooked a turkey, made two lemon pound cakes, a container of chicken salad, and one of potato salad. The other families were supplying their share of the week's menu. I could not wait to leave. I just wanted to get away—to get out of this hellhole I found myself stuck in. Almost anywhere would do. Matt's mother was to pick me up at nine-thirty and take me to Thad's home.

Around seven o'clock Dr. Asbury and Dr. Woodard were called to our house. At or around eight-thirty, Dr. Tilghman and Dr. Hoke of the Woodard-Herring Clinic arrived. No one said a word to me. The house was still and hot. Mother and Fletcher remained in my father's room with the doctors. Sometime around nine o'clock, Aunt Eva, my grandmother, and Aunt Josephine were at the house. I held my breath, knowing the inevitable had or was about to happen—that Death had come knocking, making an expected house call. I knew instantly I'd be staying here.

I still remember the time. It was nine-twenty on a Friday morning. Aunt Josephine and Dr. Woodard entered my room and told me that my father had died shortly after nine o'clock. He was gone. The car horn beeped while I was being told of his death. Fletcher went out to break the news to Mrs. Beatty and Matt. The only thing I could think of was *damn him . . . damn him . . . damn him . . . he had rained on my parade again!*

I stayed in my room for over an hour. I did not get to see my father then or ever again. I was a son denied a last goodbye. Only my grandmother was sensitive to this fact. She walked into my room leaning against the doorframe for support, and pushing her silver tipped cane against the floor for balance. She used her cane only when her arthritis acted up. The summer's humidity was haunting her. Wearing a burgundy dress with white polka dots, she moved with an air of grace despite the difficulty of walking. My grandmother was my strength and my direction when I let her be. She knew when to make her presence known and when to leave. She knew that I might need her now.

She sat in my worn brown chair and said nothing, respecting my anguish. I was a mix master of conflicting emotions. I was angry and relieved. I was sad and happy. I was angry with my father for spoiling my trip. He'd had the whole summer to die. Why did he pick today? He knew I wanted to go. I was relieved that he no longer had to suffer. He had sat in that rocking chair far too long, almost seven years. I had watched him waste away to the ninety-eight pounds he weighed at his death. No man should have to endure that kind of suffering. I was relieved because I could have a normal life now, or so I thought. I could have my friends over and have parties again. I could laugh out loud. I could play the piano again.

I was sad because my father had died. I was supposed to be sad. I hated his dying more for my sister because she and my dad were close. He worshiped her. He tolerated me. I was happy because it was finally over. It was like a pressure release. It was like being able to breathe after holding your breath over the length of a one-mile bridge. Mother had given a big chunk of herself to waiting on my father and his sickness had drained all of us emotionally, physically, and financially. I got up off my bed and walked over to my grandmother and leaning, kissed her on the cheek.

"Braxton, your father doesn't have to suffer anymore." She stood with my help and pressed her cane against the hardwood floor.

"Yes, I know." I tried to sound mournful but I didn't feel it.

"His body has been taken to Thomas Yelverton funeral home." I winced. So soon, I thought.

"Your mother collapsed after your father died. Dr. Woodard gave her a sedative and she is resting in Anne's room."

"Has Anne returned from the Hinkle's?'

"No. She hasn't been told either. Mrs. Hinkle will keep her until your Aunt Josephine calls this afternoon." My grandmother spoke with calmness. She had a strong face, wrinkled but distinctive. Again, her rouge was too heavy and her lipstick had been put on in a hurry. Some of the red was over the top of her lip. I loved her. I loved everything about her. I depended on her.

"Fletcher and Lily are cleaning your dad's room now. That will take about two hours."

"What do you want me to do?"

"Nothing now. You can go to Josephine's house or you can stay here. There is a lot to be planned in a short amount of time."

"I'll stay here in my room." My grandmother hugged me, and returned to the living room. She left my door open and I could see a room full of faces, all sharing the same ruffled expression. I felt self-conscious when their mournful eyes met mine. I stood in the door-way for a minute to see who was in the room. Several neighbors and other family members had come. I closed the door and took the back porch exit to get out. I wandered aimlessly through the immediate neighborhood for the good part of an hour before I returned.

When I opened the back porch door, a whirl of smoke met me. A slender, nicotine stained finger holding a non-filtered cigarette welcomed me to sit down. My Aunt Mary, married to my mother's brother, was having a cup of coffee and enjoying the strong smoke she was inhaling from her Camel cigarette. Mary was a striking woman with chestnut colored hair now visited by some strands of gray. Her high cheekbones accentuated her oval face and her brown eyes sparkled when she spoke defying the struggles of her life. She had an appealing flirtatious personality that attracted men, some-times the wrong kind. The gossip mill of Wilson and my family, also said that in her younger days, Mary was considered to be a woman of questionable reputation. This was the socially polite way of brand-ing someone a "woman of the night." Despite the gossip mill, my

Uncle Jeff married her. My grandfather immediately disowned Jeff and my mother's extended family took up his clarion call and treated them like they were lepers. Mother seemed to get a long okay with her and Mary and Jeff came over a lot. They were great people in my book.

My Aunt Mary was fun to be around. She took me to my first movie at night when I was in junior high school. She had always treated me like I was important and I respected her. Uncle Jeff doted over Anne, primarily because they never had a little girl. A look in our backyard gave witness to how much he loved Anne.

"Mary, what're you doing sitting out here by yourself?" I asked, coming in from the backyard and realizing, at the same time, I could slam the screened door if I wanted.

"I just needed to get a breath of fresh air if you know what I mean."

"Unfortunately, I do. What's going on?" I peered into the hallway but saw nothing.

"They're planning your father's funeral. Eva, Grace, and Josephine are discussing the cost. Your mother's not in on this; she should be." She blew her smoke toward the screen. It dissipated before it got there.

"This soon? I guess they think they're helping her." I knew nothing about funeral costs but would soon learn.

"That's one way to put it but someone needs to watch the bottom line." Her cigarette dangled from her lips as she spoke. She cupped her other hand to catch any ashes that might fall.

"What do your mean?" I asked out of ignorance.

"The cost," Mary said. "Funerals can be expensive." She put her cigarette out in the ashtray. "Braxton, there's a high price to pay to be a member of your mother's family. They are high profile people and like to maintain a certain image. With the exception of your mother, your grandmother's children had the best—the best clothes, the best friends, the best schools, and the best colleges—then your granddaddy lost his money, and your mother was a victim of sorts. They're good people but they're trying to maintain an image and a standard of living that isn't affordable to all of them.

"What can I do?" I asked, knowing that I was like a baby in the deep end of a large pool.

"Alert your mother so she can be a part of it, but don't tell her I told you this. Your daddy's funeral doesn't have to match your Uncle Victor's funeral in cost. I know I sound like a nosey old bitch, but I know your aunts and I know your mother."

"I won't involve you," I promised. "Thanks a lot, Mary." Mary excused herself and went back into the living room with the others. I could tell she disliked being with them as much as they did with her. Interesting though, for a "supposed woman of the night" in her younger days, she showed more dignity than most of my other family members.

A Southern funeral puts people on show so to speak. If you're a friend of the family or a neighbor then it's time to do some cooking. By dinnertime, enough food had been brought to our house to feed our family for three weeks. Our kitchen and breakfast nook couldn't hold it all so some was taken to Aunt Josephine's home. A Southern funeral asks the servants to put out a little extra effort. Old Lizzie always said, "Some coloreds like it and some don't. It's a time when people you know only by name shake your hand and call you by your first name." This was one of those unfortunate times when Lily and Lulu got to wear their finest, starched white uniforms with lacy embroidery around the collar, sleeves and pockets. Most servants owned only one of these uniforms and after a day in their role of smiling and nodding and saying "Yes, ma'am and no, ma'am" and whatever else society demanded, it had to be washed out before bedtime and ironed over before the next morning. Lulu had the advantage here; Aunt Josephine had a washer and dryer. We only had a washer. Lulu was a whiz at maneuvering an iron, and she pressed hers when she got to work. Unfortunately, Lily did hers at home.

My daddy's death meant less cooking for Lily and Lulu; however, they had to keep up with who brought what, label each item, and clean the plates and platters. And if the food was brought on a silver platter, it required polishing until a person's reflection was recognizable, and then they had to make certain dishes got back to the right owner.

When I sat down to eat my dinner around seven o'clock, I dined alone. I had been alone most of the day so I was getting used to it. I didn't see Aunt Eva at first but I heard someone in the kitchen commenting on the food. I walked over to the door and she was pulling some skin off the turkey commenting on how good it was. It was from her that I found out about the events of the afternoon. Daddy's funeral arrangements were all but in concrete. Aunt Josephine and she had been to the funeral home and chosen several caskets for Mother to see. Aunt Grace, Aunt Eva's sister, had been through Mother's closet and had decided she had nothing appropriate to wear. She had called the Woman's Shop downtown and asked that several suits be selected for Mother's choosing. Mr. Bradshaw had been by and visited with my aunts regarding the type of service. Their decision was a private service at the home with an open casket and a graveside service to follow. Pallbearers had been called from a list left by my father. Two were uncles but the others were to be men from Exeter Tobacco Company. Daddy wanted to make certain that Mr. John Collins was asked but he was just as adamant that Dave Fuller and Jim Dibson were not asked. No flowers were requested. Donations could be made to the American Cancer Society, the United Methodist Church in my father's honor or to a charity of one's choice.

When I asked about Anne, Aunt Eva said that she had gone home to spend the night with my grandmother. When I asked about Mother, I was told that she had gone back to rest in Anne's room. Lily had left and Fletcher would leave no later than nine o'clock. Of course, I was expected to stay with Mother tonight. Aunt Eva fixed Aunt Grace and herself a dinner plate without asking and excused herself for the evening. I couldn't help glance at the quantity of food on her plate compared to her sister's. There was no doubt "whose eyes were too big for their stomach."

It was incomprehensible to me that I could have been through what I had since the school year had ended and yet, not one person consulted me about anything nor did anyone in my family with the exception of my grandmother care to check on me the entire afternoon. I realized they had been busy, but still . . .

I picked over my supper as I sat alone reviewing the events of the day. I wondered how my mother would manage without my father's illness to consume her and give her an outlet for her nervousness. He had been her whole life and she was not prepared to face the world with two children. Mother had no skills and her only real job experience had been working at her mother's tearoom. During my father's illness, Mr. Collins, a close friend of my parents, managed their finances for them. Mother would be on her own now like an orphan rendered helpless. Even I knew that my father had cashed in his insurance policies and used up any savings long ago. All assets that could be converted to cash had been used to finance Daddy's illness. Tomorrow, we would face the world as a family, almost penniless. Mother's only income would come from Daddy's retirement check and a monthly social security payment for each child.

When Mother did awake around seven o'clock, she refused to eat and she didn't want to talk, not with me, not about my father, not about herself, and not about Anne. What she wanted to do, she did, and that was drink herself back to sleep. This was the first of many nights to come that we had to watch over her and make certain that she was in bed safely and that all cigarettes had been extinguished.

Chapter 43
MESSAGES FROM AN ANGEL

THE NEXT MORNING, I awoke early. I'd had a night of wild and weird dreams, like running down a dark, slippery hallway dodging glass fragments being thrown by people who could not be seen. I had a terrible time breathing. My summer allergies had kicked in, coming in full force, all at once during the night. At times, I awoke thinking someone had attempted to choke me. My throat was dry, almost parched. I lost my daddy yesterday morning and I saw my mother losing touch with reality last night. I guess these are two good reasons for having nightmares.

Today Mother, Anne, and I will visit our Daddy one last time before he is buried. I have mixed feelings about our eleven o'clock appointment at the funeral home. I have only seen one dead person after he had been "fixed-up" by the mortician. I didn't even know Ted Applegate. I knew of him; he was the drum major of our high school band and two years older than I. The only reason I went was because Emily Andrews wanted to see his body. I am not even sure how well she knew him. One minute we were working on student council posters at her house and the next minute she was driving us to the funeral home. We walked in and told the man in charge we wanted to see Ted's body and he let us go in. The room was silent and dimly lit; his casket set in the middle of the room with large ferns on both sides, and he lay there as still as the silence. Dressed in his drum major uniform, he looked regal, like a prince who had fallen asleep. The uncanny thing about our visit was that it did not bother me to view Ted, but Emily ran out before she got close to the casket. I think that is the wrong reason to visit. I went to see Ted for the wrong reason but I'm glad I did because I learned the right reason for viewing a body. I hope no spectator comes to see my daddy.

"Braxton, I needs your help," Lily called from the hall. "I can't get your mother up."

"I'm not surprised." I walked to Anne's room where Mother lay sprawled across the bed. An empty scotch bottle lay on the floor. A partially filled glass set on the bedside table next to an ashtray of half-smoked cigarettes. I picked up the glass, put it to my nose, and took a deep sniff of its contents. "Whew! That's foul smelling."

"What happen here last night?" asked Lily. She picked up the bottle and set it on the table.

"It's call coping water." I reached over, took Mother's leg hanging off the bed, and laid it beside her other leg.

"Miss Virginia, you got to get up."

"Mother! Time to rise and shine. We have an appointment in less than three hours."

Mother moved on the bed. First, she turned over on her side and then she turned over on her back and opened her eyes and looked at the ceiling. She didn't move. She just lay there staring at the ceiling. She looked like she was asleep but with her eyes open.

"Miss Virginia, please get up."

"Mother, please get up!" I pushed her gently. Mother made no attempt to budge.

Her lips moved but nothing came out. Her lips moved again and a noise came out followed by some audible words, "Go away and leave me alone."

"We can't do that. You needs to gets up and gets dressed."

"Leave me alone. I'm going back to sleep. Move away, damn it."

I looked at Lily and she looked at me. We both acknowledged without speaking that she was not going to cooperate willingly. "You got any ideas, Lily?"

"Oh yes, lots of them. This here is a classic hangover! I know just the thing."

"What do you want to do?"

"Waits here. I'll be right back." Lily headed toward the kitchen.

"Mother, get up."

"Braxton," she said turning over on her left side. "Go away and *leave me alone!* I don't feel well. I have a headache."

"Mother, when you get up and move around, you'll feel better." I grabbed her arm like she did when we were children and imitated her pulling us out of the bed.

"What in the hell are you doing?" asked Mother, pulling away from me. "Let go of my arm. I told you to leave me alone and I mean it."

"And I told you that we have an eleven o'clock appointment at the funeral home. Now get up, *please!*"

"No! I'm not going," Mother said and she lay back down, this time on her back. "You and Anne go by yourself. I'm not going."

"She won't cooperate," I said to Lily who had returned with a spray bottle filled with water.

"Miss Virginia, forgives me for what I'm going to do to you." Lily began shooting water in Mother's face, one shot after another, not hard shots but light spray shots. I started to laugh. Mother put her hands up to her face, looked at Lily, and sat up. "Miss Virginia, I don't know what else to do to get you out of this bed."

"*Stop, Lily, right now!*" Mother said. "I'll get up. Just give me a minute." She pushed up against the back of the headboard, swung her legs off the bed, and grabbed the bedside table, trying to stand. A little shaky at first, she began to walk and stopped. "Help me to the bathroom, Lily."

"Yes ma'am. Braxton, strip the bed please," ordered Lily. "Come on Miss Virginia, we got lots to do in a short amount of time." Lily threw her right arm around Mother's back and guided her the short distance to the bathroom. I heard the water running in the tub. "Braxton, fix your mother a cup of black Maxwell House."

Lily worked for the next hour getting Mother ready to go to the funeral home. I drove to my grandmother's house to get Anne. My grandmother and Anne sat on the porch waiting for me. My grandmother leaned on her cane looking toward the elementary school next door like she was in deep thought. I pulled alongside the front of her house, went up the long paved walkway to her front steps, and up the dozen steps to her porch. My grandmother pushed on her cane into a standing position and moved toward me, kissing me on the cheek.

"Ready to go, Anne?"

"Anne, go inside and get those homemade cookies we baked," said my grandmother. As soon as Anne was inside the house, my grandmother spoke again, "Braxton, Anne is upset by this visit today. She doesn't want to go."

"Neither does Mother. What should I do with Anne?"

"I wouldn't force her." Anne returned with a plate of cookies.

"You carry the cookies and I'll carry your bag," I said.

"Thank you, Granny," Anne said. "Can I come back tonight? Please?"

"Let's see what your mother says," my grandmother said. She tapped Anne playfully on her fanny with the cane.

"Let's go, Anne. Thanks, Granny, I'll call you." We both ran down the steps like we were racing each other. "Don't drop the cookies."

Anne and I walked to the car. Pulling away from the curb, we waved another goodbye. Anne turned and said, "Braxton, I don't want to see Daddy dead. Don't make me go in there with him."

"I'm not going to make you do anything you don't want to do." I patted the top of her hand.

"I've never seen a dead person," said Anne. "I don't want to! Don't make me do it!"

"I won't, I promise." I put my hand around hers, feeling the sweat of her palm. I understood the emptiness and fear she faced. I could handle this but I was uncertain about Anne. She was so young and scared and overwhelmed. We both had reason to be uncertain about the future. We just did not know about it at the time.

I tried to change the subject to cheer her up. Anne didn't want to talk. We rode the rest of the way home in silence. I did not know how this would play out with my Aunt Josephine and my mother. But if I had anything to do with it, Anne would not have to view the body of our father.

Aunt Josephine stopped in front of our house around ten-thirty, and blew her horn one long blast. She was right on time. Anne and I got in the back of her eggshell blue Cadillac and Mother got in the front. Neither Mother nor Anne were in the best of spirits. My Aunt

Josephine picked up on their moodiness right away and began talking to me.

"Braxton, are Matt and Thad coming back from the beach for the funeral?"

"No ma'am," I said. "At least, I don't think so."

"Do you have anything to wear tomorrow?"

"Yes ma'am." I looked at my mother to see her reaction to my aunt's question. Mother called this meddling where you don't belong. Mother looked the same way she did when Lily sprayed her with water and that was angry. This became a permanent expression of my mother.

"Have you heard from Jason's parents?" My aunt wanted to be helpful but she should not try so hard. "I haven't heard anything yet." By now, Aunt Josephine just gave up and the four of us drove the rest of the way to the funeral home without talking to each other.

This was the very same place where I had viewed Ted Applegate's body. The same brick building with the four white columns out front, the same green carpet on the porch, and the same fake Oriental rug in the foyer. We stood quietly waiting for the man in charge to come out.

"This way, please, Mrs. Thaxton and Mrs. Haywood," said a tall, thin man of about forty with greasy black hair and an equally greased moustache. His dark blue suit looked shiny and worn and the right sleeve of his coat was missing two buttons. I'm not usually that observant but I was worried about what to wear after my aunt asked me about it in the car. We followed him down a long hallway. The floor was carpeted in red and there were pictures of men in dark suits hanging on the right side of the hall wall. He stopped and spoke again, "Mr. Haywood is in here." He pulled back a curtain and we saw a coffin in the far back of the room.

Immediately, Anne pulled back crying, "*No! No!* I don't want to go in there!"

"Anne, honey, you know you want to pay your final respects to your daddy," said Aunt Josephine.

"I don't want to." Anne pulled away. "Braxton said I didn't have to."

"I don't think that is a decision that Braxton should make for you," my aunt said.

"But he promised, he promised." Anne started to sniffle, grabbing my hand.

"Aunt Josephine, Anne's right. I did tell her she didn't have to go in there," I said, looking at the displeased expression of my aunt. "I stand by my decision. Anne doesn't have to go in. Subject closed." I spoke politely but with as much authority as I could muster.

"Virginia?" my aunt asked, turning to my mother.

"Braxton is right. Anne doesn't need to go if she doesn't want to."

"Anne has the right to change her mind." I said, turning to my sister. "If for some reason you change your mind, come on in or I'll come back and take you in."

"I won't change my mind," Anne said. "Braxton, come here a minute." She and I walked back to one of the metal chairs. She reached into her dress pocket and pulled out a small picture. It was one of her class pictures that she had gotten in the mail about a week ago. "Please put this in Daddy's hand and tell him that I will miss him and that I love him. I wrote him a message on the back."

"I'll make sure he has it," I said, taking it and putting it in my pocket. I took Mother by the arm and said, "Let's go in, Mother." Ahead of us at the far end of the room was a large, steel casket. I wondered why a small man needed something this big. Bright lights shined over the casket picking up reflections and then bounced them off the sides of the shiny surface. Tall green ferns in white urns sitting on pedestals surrounded the coffin, creating a shrine effect.

Mother and I took our time approaching the coffin. Every step Mother took was a step of hesitation. We stopped and I let go of Mother's arm. Mother reached over and touched the sleeve of my father's coat and tears began to mount in her eyes. She patted my father's hand and it moved under her touch. She took his wedding band out of her dress pocket and slid it on his bony finger. The ring could have easily fit around two of his fingers at once.

The gray suit my father had on fitted him when he was a man of one hundred and eighty-five pounds. On a man of ninety-eight pounds, it dwarfed him, calling more attention to his emaciated condition. There was so much excess material that his coat had been tucked under his back to make it appear form fitting. The collar of the white shirt was so large that it hung below his Adam's apple and the tie knot was too big. My father had too much make-up on. Someone had worked hard to cover up the blue veins that once streaked his cheekbones. His eyes had been painted with too much eye shadow in an attempt to take away his hollow look. His oval face was so small, so unreal looking, so thin that his flesh looked like that of a mannequin in a waxed museum. With the overhead lights, his skin took on a grayish hue. I did not like this makeover that had been done on my father. It wasn't him. It didn't look a thing like him. He looked worse now than when he was alive. I was glad Anne hadn't come in to say goodbye. I took her picture out of my pocket and on the back, she had written Daddy a note. It said, "Daddy, I love you one hundred times more than the last time I told you. Save me a seat beside you in heaven. I'll miss you. Your little earth angel, Anne." I took my handkerchief out and wiped the tear from my eye. I placed the picture in my father's hand exactly as Anne requested. I also responded, doing something so completely unrehearsed that it surprised even me. I took my right index finger, kissed it, and touched his lip. I turned and walked back and joined my sister.

Mother stayed talking to Daddy and wiping her eyes with her white handkerchief. At one time, she leaned over his body and laid her head on his chest and began sobbing. My Aunt Josephine told me that this was a time of parting, a goodbye if you will. I wanted to believe my parents had already said their goodbyes. They'd had enough time to do it. I couldn't be certain about that but I was very certain that my mother loved my father. I hoped he loved her as much and I hoped he died knowing how much she loved him.

Anne didn't return to the funeral home at seven o'clock to greet people who came to pay their last respects to Daddy. I don't remember the total number. Their names are in a register somewhere. We stood for over two hours and a half greeting people. Tobacco people and farmers and people who knew my father when he owned the Texaco station across the street from the Cherry Hotel in downtown Wilson came. I got tired of standing and shaking hands of people I didn't know. Just about every man who shook my hand said something nice about my father. I had never seen this side of him so in a way it was hard to believe they were talking about my father.

Anne got her wish and spent the night with our grandmother again. Mother repeated her habit of drinking herself to sleep. I stayed up until I was certain she had passed out and I put the bottle back in the pantry with the others. There were thirty bottles of liquor in our pantry this night. Lily said every one of them had been a gift to my father from someone related to the tobacco industry. There was scotch, Kentucky bourbon, blended whiskey, brandy and vodka. There were brand names too numerous to mention. I shuddered when I thought about my mother attempting to down all of this liquor. It never dawned on me that she would actually try.

Before I called it a night, I smoked one cigarette on the back steps. My thoughts retraced some of the day's events. Mother never did get a vote on the casket but she seemed to be satisfied with the one my father was in. And she refused to go to the Woman's Shop so Aunt Grace brought the outfits on approval to our house. She charged them to her own account. People continued to call, come and go, bringing food and even flowers that were not requested. There was a nice article in the paper about my father but there was no picture. We didn't own one picture of my father, not a single one. And I couldn't get the picture of my father in his coffin out of my mind. It haunted me. It wasn't him; at least, not the way I remembered him.

I awoke the next morning knowing I wouldn't go to Sunday school, not the day of my father's funeral. I got out of bed around seven-thirty. Mother was asleep in Anne's room. I dressed and walked onto the back porch. It rained overnight settling the dust that had hung around for better than a week. The porch was bone dry and I was thankful for that. I stood there like I had many times before, feeling no different from any other day. Wasn't I supposed to feel differently on the day of my father's funeral? I remember Ingrid told me when her father died a few years earlier that she didn't think she would get through the day, and then it was the week, and then it was the month. She told me that she thought she would never get used to her father being dead. I didn't feel that way. Did this make me a criminal? Did it make me a bad son? Did it mean I was uncaring? I didn't have the answer to those questions.

While I was standing, feeling guilty the darnedest thing happened. A blackish bird with a red marking across its breast flew up to the outside bottom screen ledge and sat there a minute. It looked all around and then flew to the birdbath flapping its wings in the water and then it flew to the clothesline and perched and then it flew back to the screen and perched. It tried hard to get my attention. The first thought I had was of David Byrd and that this was his way of telling me he was with me. This was a good feeling. I had never seen this kind of bird. I smiled, knowing that Byrd could identify it for me. I spoke to it and it left. I've never seen one like it again.

Lily came and repeated her routine of getting Mother up but today she didn't have to use water. Mother got up begrudgingly. Even after Mother had dressed for the morning, she had a haggard look. She cried over her toast and coffee and smoked one Kool after another. I don't know what Lily said to my mother but whatever she said got her attention. By late morning when out of town family members began arriving, she was dressed and making every attempt to be cordial.

Noontime was the gathering time for lunch. A buffet was set up on the back porch and people ate at intervals right up until shortly before the private ceremony was to begin at two-o'clock. Periodically, I saw Aunt Eva winding her way among the others, each time with a different food item. The temperature was the only factor that made eating outside unbearable. The back porch thermometer registered ninety-one degrees at one o'clock. People just stood around with their paper plate in hand, chatting and visiting, the way it should be.

The pre-burial service was for family and close friends. I developed a knot in my stomach when I saw Jeanette Eicher coming up the porch with Mrs. Thurston, finding a seat in the living room. She was definitely not a friend of our family. How could she have the nerve to step foot in our home on a day like today? I didn't hear a word Mr. Bradshaw, who had rushed to get here, said. I watched Mrs. Eicher the whole time. Twice she caught my eye and both times I tried my hardest to show her the disdain I felt toward her. I don't think it even fazed her. She came and did her neighborly duty. And that was all it was, a duty to assuage her conscience for all the times she had attacked my mother with her venomous tongue.

A black limousine and a black hearse waited in our driveway underneath a hot, red sun. It was the kind of afternoon a fair skinned person could get burnt. The harsh rays of light looking down on us would take no mercy and I squinted as our family walked to the waiting limo. A short, squatty driver with a crew cut dressed in a black suit opened the back door for us. Anne got in first, then Mother, and then I. My first cousin, Dr. Vic Thaxton, Jr., and his mother, Josephine, rode in the seats behind the driver. We waited in the hot car and watched the eight pallbearers bring the coffin holding my father out of the house. Mr. Weber missed the last porch step, stumbled, and the coffin tilted forward, then sideways, and the others stopped long enough to correct the imbalance. Mother took a deep breath and Anne made a guttural noise. The driver assured us that once inside the hearse, someone would check the inside of the casket. Finally, the driver cut the car on, turned on the air conditioner, and we pulled out of the driveway. I looked at the sea of faces milling around in the yard and walking to their cars. Everyone seemed to be staring at us—the widow and her two children. I felt a sense of importance for all the wrong reasons.

We turned left onto Kincaid Avenue and then right onto Gold Street. The hearse carrying my father was in front of us. Others in their freshly washed cars followed behind us. We were a motorcade of lights and passing motorists pulled to the side of the street out of respect for the deceased. The trip to the cemetery was a short one. The light hitting the hood of the limo blinded the driver causing him to swerve several times en route. This heightened Mother's anxiousness and her right hand already gripping the seat in front of her, dug into it harder.

Other than being intense, Mother sat quietly in her royal blue outfit that Aunt Grace had picked out for her. Mother liked nice clothes but she never shopped for any. Since she couldn't afford them, she normally bought at one of the mercantile stores on Tarboro Street. I thought Mother looked elegant in her white blouse and matching white collared suit. Her shoes matched her outfit and there was a small white clip on each shoe. She refused to wear a hat. A simple veil attached to a plain headband is what she chose, hiding her swollen, red eyes and some of her puffy face. Mother had cried continuously since the day my father died.

Our driver followed the hearse through the cemetery gates, around the Confederate monument, and past one white head marker after another. My father's was not the only funeral today. Several colorful tents from other funeral homes sat scattered over the sprawling plots of the cemetery. Our driver easily found our plot. A large red crepe myrtle guided us directly to the Haywood site. This magnificent tree distinguished ours from all the thousands of other plots. Royal red buds pushed from the crepe myrtle after the recent hard rain covered the freshly-cut grass like a well-worn blanket. Little annoying gnats hovered around the ground and among the chairs. Mother was the first to get out. Vic, Anne, and I followed her and joined Mr. Bradshaw who stood beside the Haywood headstone. He took Mother's hand and guided her to her seat.

This was a Southern graveside service entirely. Family sat in hard, folding metal chairs that rocked against the uneven ground. We sat beneath a hunter green canopy with the funeral home's name printed in big white letters on each of the four hanging flaps. Mother, Anne, and I were in the first three chairs on the first row. Aunt Josephine, my grandmother, and Vic, Jr., completed our row. My father's brother and his wife and our first cousins, and aunts and uncles filled in the hard metal bottoms. There were thirty-six family members squeezed together under the green tent on a blistering, hot June afternoon. There was no breeze; there were only gnats.

Mr. Bradshaw gave Lauren Anderson her cue and she stood and sang a cappella, "You'll Never Walk Alone." Lauren was a tall girl in her early thirties with long, flowing black hair that touched the top of her shoulders. She was fair of skin with a hint of peach in her cheeks and on her lips. A dark mole on her left cheek accentuated her good looks and her rich soprano voice enhanced her attractiveness even more. As she sang, I could hear the people behind me clearing their throats and blowing their noses, attempting to withhold their tears. Some standing around the tent had already given into their emotions and I could see Edna Fuller with her hand over her mouth, crying uncontrollably. Mr. Ralph Spencer provided her with his handkerchief. He resorted to using the back of his hand. Mother and Anne seemed to be in control emotionally at the moment. My eyes were moist. Lauren smiled, acknowledging her triumph when she'd finished and some one from the crowd shouted "*Amen,*" the way the Southern Baptists say amen. Aunt Eva later commented on the unsophisticated and out-of-place behavior of Charlie Daniels. Charlie, a black man, had a heart of gold and was one of the best auto mechanics in Wilson. That's what my father said when Charlie worked at the Texaco station. My father said, "Charlie on a sober day was worth any two white men."

Mr. Bradshaw stood and positioned himself in front of the casket. He had told Mother that at my father's request, he'd chosen the Twenty-third Psalm as his text. Standing erect, he cleared his throat, "We have come here this afternoon to celebrate the life of Louis Braxton Haywood, son of God, father of Anne and Louis Braxton, Jr., and husband of Virginia. As you all know Louis has suffered a long time, far too long. His battle with cancer attempted to deprive him of his dignity that is rightfully his. It prevented him from functioning the way he wanted to live and give to his family, church, and community. Louis and I have had many chats together over the last seven years and each time we sat together, he would always want to know how I was doing and how my family was, how our church was growing and how its members were. This was the kind of man he was, always thinking of others first. We shared laughs together, we prayed together, discussed sports and national events, and cried together. I knew personally that I was a better man after my visits with Louis."

I could see Mother out of the corner of my eye. She was becoming uncomfortable and edgy. I hoped this service wouldn't take long. It was hot as Hades under this tent and I couldn't predict what Mother would do. I held my breath, hoping that she would attempt to behave herself today, at the funeral of her husband. She hated crowds, disliked public functions, never went to funerals and weddings, and didn't like to think she was on display. I knew I could endure it but I was just as prepared to take her out if necessary. With that in mind, I undid the top button of my shirt and loosened my tie knot. I received a disapproving nudge from my mother. I just ignored her.

"Louis fought his battle with cancer with every ounce of energy he had. Through it all, he never complained about his illness and he never desired sympathy from others. Weak physically, he was strong in his spirit to endure and in his willpower to stay alive. At the end, the cancer took his spirit and squeezed this desire from him. It was at this time that he told me he was ready to die." I gave both Anne and Mother some Kleenex from my coat pocket. Mother dabbed at her eyes and Anne blew her nose. This solicited smiles from those standing around her.

"Those of you who knew Louis well know that he was a good man and a religious man. He was a man who had simple tastes. His desire was to live a productive life, provide for his family, and do well. Cancer robbed him of life but not his desires." The entire time Uncle Bobby talked, I realized I didn't know this man he talked about, at least not the way he described my father. My father had been sick so long that I couldn't remember a time since my childhood that he hadn't fought with cancer.

I believe I was in the fourth grade when a normal life began to evade him. He no longer followed the tobacco markets to Canada and the southern states. He only went to the factory twice a week, then it was once a week, then every other week, and finally, the checks were brought to him to sign so he could stay on the payroll.

We stopped taking vacations around the summer after my seventh grade year in school. I remember he stretched out on the back seat of the car and his brother drove us to the beach where we stayed a week. My father went outside two times the whole week. One time was to the dog races at night. The other time was to take me to see *Rock Around the Clock* with Glen Ford. That was the last movie I ever went to with him. What a powerful movie to end on.

He continued to take Anne to the movies in the summers but I quit going with them. He and Anne would go to one movie at the Wilson Theater and I would go to another at the Oasis. Maybe I was exerting my independence or maybe I didn't want to be with them. He would wait for me and the three of us would drive home together. Eventually, I decided Anne and he could have a better time without me tagging along. They would carry on about the movie they'd seen and I would pretend mine was equally as good. He always gave me that flexibility to do my own thing. That was a good thing but I saw it as rejection.

Mr. Bradshaw cleared his throat again and began leading us through the Twenty-third Psalm. "The Lord is my shepherd; I shall not want. He maketh me to lie down in green pastures, he leadeth me beside quiet waters, he restoreth my soul . . . " Uncle Bobby supported his text by talking about courage and prayer at times like this when we don't understand God's ways. He talked about death never being timely and that only God knows the exact moment we will leave this world. He reassured us that my father was at peace now.

Everyone stood. I thought I had missed something then I saw Uncle Bobby giving another signal. I needed to pay closer attention. It was just so muggy and hot, and people were getting restless, shuffling their feet, and there was drilling on the other side of the cemetery, and loud yells were coming from a nearby black church.

"In certain hope of the resurrection of our Lord Jesus Christ we commend to Almighty God our friend and servant Louis, and we commit his body to dust," spoke Uncle Bobby. He wiped his brow with his handkerchief.

The pallbearers stood around my father's coffin as it was lowered in the ground. Anne was as white as a sheet when she ran up to the casket screaming, "Daddy, don't go. Please don't go without me. I love you." Pete Foster, another good friend of my father, grabbed her and put his arms around her and pulled her close to him to muffle her screams. He picked her up cradling her in his arms and carried her to the other side of the road. I looked at Mother. She, too, was crying and swaying back and forth in her new shoes. Her face was constricted in anguish and she breathed irregularly. I motioned for Vic to stand next to her. He took one look and realized she was about to faint. He commented to Mr. Bradshaw to conclude the service.

Uncle Bobby immediately began the benediction. "The Lord bless him and keep him. The Lord makes his face to . . . " He motioned for me to come. I knelt and took some dirt and threw it on my father's coffin. My father's brother followed me and one by one the other mourners threw a handful of dirt on his coffin. I knew my father had once held the picture of Anne in his hand. I hoped it was still there and I hoped his suit was still in place.

Once back at the house, Mother was given a sedative to ease her headache. She went to Anne's room to take a short nap. Anne was taken to my grandmother's house. It was after five o'clock before the last person left. Lily fixed me a cold plate from the food that had been brought before she left.

"Is you gonna be all right?" she said in a motherly way.

"I'll be fine," I said, although I missed my friends, especially Matt, Thad, and Jason. I did see Cassie, Patsy, and some of my other friends at the gravesite. Some of my past teachers were there, too, as well as Chief Mays in uniform. Noticeably absent was Captain Chuck.

"You takes good care of your mother tonight," Lily said. "Make sure she doesn't get into this here pantry." Lily pointed to the door behind her.

"I don't know whether I can keep her out."

"I fear that woman is gonna develop herself a bad drinking habit."

"Lily, she already has." I said.

"You call your Aunt Josephine if you needs anything," Lily said. Before she left the back porch, she leaned over and gave me a big hug and a kiss on the forehead. "You is a good boy, you hear. You remember that."

"I will," I said. "See you tomorrow."

"I'll be here by eight o'clock." She lit a cigarette and walked down the back steps to the Red Bird cab waiting for her in the driveway.

I sat on the back porch playing with my food, wondering what life was going to be like now. The house was lonely and deafeningly quiet. Daddy was truly gone now. He had been absent from our life for a long time. This time his absence was final. I walked to the room that was used for his bedroom. His rocking chair sat next to the French doors. His bed was still under the windows, and the only other comfortable chair in the room was where it had always been.

I sat down in his rocking chair. I could still smell the Old Spice that he wore, now a part of the chair's fabric. This was countered by the stale smell of Chesterfields that fought for its rightful place in the fabric. I saw the worn carpet where his feet had shuffled back and forth as he sat day after day, and the fabric on the chair's right arm showed wear and little pieces of cotton were poking through from the days he had leaned on it. The upper back of the chair was a dingy black from the head moisture that had nowhere else to go on those nights when in pain he fought the toughest battles of his life. His marble ashtray sitting in its cherry stand still stood beside his chair as a reminder of the habit he turned to in order to past the minutes of each day. This was all I have left of my father. I decided to just sit in his chair and be with what he left of himself.

I remembered Lily saying, "Things happens in threes." Two people in my life had died. I only hoped there wouldn't be a third death. I closed my eyes and rocked where my father had rocked so many days of my life, days I had wished him gone. Tonight, I had my wish. The more I rocked, the louder the refrain, "Be careful what you wish for" rang out in my mind.

Chapter 44
A BOUT WITH JACK DANIELS

WITHIN DAYS AFTER my father's funeral, the food stopped coming, the people quit visiting, and fewer people telephoned. It is easy not to see things as they really are when the last thirty-six hours of your life has been a beehive of activity. It is easy to get caught up in the hoopla of things when someone else is doing everything for you, even your thinking. And then bang, just as quick as it starts, it ends. It seems that no one cares anymore. Everyone has moved on to more important things. At sixteen, I found this a difficult lesson to learn. Caring, I thought, was ongoing and not like stopping to fill a car up with gas.

A month ago, my life was full; today it is empty. I had only gone a week without my four good buddies and I hated it—I hated the prospect of loneliness and what my life in the future might be. Byrd was gone and Jason had departed and now my father. This translated into a life of hell. How did I ever end up in this mess? All I ever wanted to be was happy. All I ever wanted to do was grow up. All I wanted now was help.

The day after my father's funeral, my mother went back to spending her mornings in bed. Some days she didn't get up until after one o'clock. She never got up before ten-thirty. Lily, biting her lower lip the first two days, gave up on the water spraying and reluctantly adjusted to Mother's new schedule. Anne and I accepted it, although we didn't like it, but we had no other choice. It was embarrassing to see Mother fighting a hangover every morning of the week. I knew she missed my father but I guess I didn't understand how alcohol could become a substitute for him. I just didn't see the connection. Aunt Josephine's visits became at a minimum twice daily and sometimes, she stopped by three times. She was displeased at what she referred to as Mother's irresponsible and infantile behavior. Mother just ignored her. We watched as the bottles slowly disappeared from the pantry shelves. I realized my mother was losing her grip on life.

The last thing Mother needed was a drinking buddy but this was one of the first things she found after my father's death. His name was Jack Ross and he was the brother of Mr. Sam Ross, my friend who lived across the street. Mother had known Jack even before he married Effie, the sister of Aunt Grace, Aunt Eva and our grandmother. While Effie and Jack were married, there wasn't a need for excessive drinking, but after her death, this changed. Jack's reputation for around the clock drinking became as well known as his unfortunate inability to get rid of the hiccups, a sickness diagnosed as permanent. I didn't know whether he drank to cope with hiccupping or whether his drinking caused and/or increased his hiccupping.

After reconnecting with Jack who had been attentive to my father in his healthier years, Mother started visiting him at his house on Tuesday and Thursday nights. Her nights at Jack's home got longer and longer and too late for me to go and get her. Jack's son, Jack, Jr., started bringing her home either before he went to work the next morning or he would leave his store at mid-morning and bring Mother home.

Jack, Jr., was a few years younger than Mother, was married, and had four children, all still at home. He was an attractive man with olive skin, a mustache, and slightly balding head. Standing at about five-feet-ten-inches, he had a lean figure, wore expensive clothes and jewelry, and always drove a late model car. Because Jack, Jr., was Aunt Grace's favorite nephew and Mother was her favorite niece, there was some sort of a bond between them.

The first Tuesday in July, Jack came by to get Mother to go to his dad's for a cookout, steaks and baked potatoes. He didn't know I was at home at the time. Mother was getting dressed in the bathroom and I had just come in from the backyard. Jack and Anne were in Daddy's old room. When I entered the kitchen, I heard Anne say, "Don't, Jack!"

I quietly opened the swinging door from the breakfast nook. Jack had Anne in his lap facing him. His left hand rested on Anne's upper leg and his right hand was under her blouse, working its way up her back. She had been pulled too close to him and he was attempting to kiss her. "You're a pretty little girl, Anne. You look a lot like your mother."

"Please don't, Jack. Please don't!" said Anne, pleading.

"I'm not going to hurt you."

"*Get your hands off her you son of a bitch!*" I ran over to his chair and pulled Anne out of his lap. "*What do you think you're doing, pervert?*"

"It's not what you think," said Jack. Sweat broke out on his forehead. His lips were moist and quivering. He had a startled look in his eyes. I motioned for Anne to get out of the room. Wasting no time, she ran into the hall and waited. "I know exactly what I saw. Don't try to get out of it."

"Braxton, I can explain," he said. Jack had every reason to act nervous.

"*Explain?* What's there to explain? You were trying to kiss my sister."

"No . . . No . . . I wasn't," he said. "I was just going to hug her. I thought she might need a manly hug with your dad gone and all."

"*You're sick. Do you hear me? You're sick!*" I said, reaching over and pulling him with his left hand out of the rocking chair. "*Get out!* Wait for Mother outside."

"You won't say anything to her, will you?"

"Why not? You said you *were not doing* anything."

"I wasn't. I promise." Jack looked scared and horrified at getting caught. If there was one reaction I could recognize, it was *fear*.

"Leave! I'll decide later if I'm going to tell Mother." I watched Jack exit into the hall, walk past Anne, and walk through the living room and out onto the front porch. He lit a cigarette, threw his head back, exhaled, and walked down the steps to his car.

Coming back to where Anne stood trembling, I pulled her to me and held her tight, as tight as I could without crushing her or squeezing the breath out of her body. "Are you all right, Anne?" She clung to me and cried and cried. I held her, wiping her hair away from her face. I patted her on her back until her cries turned to jerky sobs, barely audible. Then she spoke.

"I'm not hurt." Anne said, stopping her crying. "He frightened me."

"He won't ever frighten you again. I promise." I hugged her again to reassure her.

"Promise," said Anne.

"I promise," I said. "If anyone ever tries to frighten you like this, you tell me immediately."

"I will, Braxton. I will." Anne attempted a smile.

We told Mother that Anne had fallen and that was why she had cried. Mother believed us and went on to her uncles for another night of drinking. I called Jack, Jr., the next day at work and told him that if he ever put his hands on my sister again or my mother, I'd make his life miserable. I also told him that on the nights that he acted as chauffeur for my mother, I would hold him directly responsible if anything happened to her. He understood and he gave me his word that he would act as a gentleman around my family from now on. He tried to apologize saying, "I don't know what came over me. I just don't know what I was thinking."

I surprised myself when I responded, "Jack, it is perverted lust. But with family members, it's sick." I know I scared the hell out of him. I hoped so because I meant every word I said to him. As far as I know, he kept his promise to me.

I couldn't help but wonder what it was with the adult world and their sexual obsession with kids. I had never heard of the term "sexual deviant" until after that night at Byrd's house. And my mother introduced us to that word. But if I had come across two of these in a matter of weeks, I questioned how many adults in this town were "doing it" with kids? It made me want to puke when I thought about it. If I had read about it in a magazine, I don't think it would have sickened me as much. When it involved a best friend and a sister, then it was a different matter. Is there a place these people can go and get well? Is there a hospital for people like this? Maybe Jason can tell me. Surely, M.C.V. has a program that can treat these men.

This town is full of jerks. I'm not joking, either. For a small town, we have our fair share of nut cases. What woodwork do they crawl out of? These are supposedly fine, upstanding citizens—what people call pillars of the community. I wondered what dark secret Jeanette Eichert had been hiding. What about Father Ray? I heard he was into men. And what about Alice Perry, Coon's only female P. E. teacher? I'd heard stinky things about her. Who was I supposed to believe? What I needed to do was turn my mind off these wanderings and get back on the scene at hand. I had enough to watch in my own household without walking into someone else's closet.

I got my first letter from Jason Parker during that first week of July. Anne came running to my room with it. She knew I would be excited to hear from him.

"Braxton, you've got some mail. It's a letter from the state of Virginia.

"*Virginia!*" I shouted. "Maybe it's from Jason."

"I hope so," said Anne. "I hope it'll make you happy."

"Why did you say that?"

"I don't know," said Anne. "You don't seem very happy, not like you usually are."

"You're observant, little sister." Anne stood and waited for me to open the letter. "Now go on and get out of here so I can read my letter."

"Will you tell me what he says?" said Anne with a hungry look of "I want to read it, too."

"Maybe, but I doubt it." I ripped open the envelope in my excitement to read what he had to say. That was a mistake because I tore through the return address in my attempt to get it open.

Braxton,

This is the first chance I've had to write you. Sorry to hear about your dad. That's a real bummer! I wish I could've been there for you. How's your mom doing? When you write, tell me how you're holding up. That means write me.

It's not too bad here. The doctors have done lots of tests on me. They got me seeing a psychiatrist; I guess they think I am crazy. His name is Lance Weir. He's called Dr. Weirdo around here. He's pretty damn cool though; he let's me smoke when I'm in his office. I smoke his. He smokes Lucky Strikes. I go to a neurologist twice a week. She's a knock out. Big boobs and curvy thighs and perfect ass. I call her Dr. Gold, short for Goldfinkle. She's a Jew and blonde. I still have those crazy sensations. They've got me on medicine I can't even pronounce. One begins with a D and the other begins with P. I can't tell you when I'm coming home because I don't know. I haven't had a drink since I got here. It's killing me. I understand I made a real ass of myself at Patsy's party. Sorry I embarrassed you.

Tell Matt and Thad hey for me. Please write because I do get lonely up here. Don't tell anyone I said that. Don't want to ruin my image. There's a cute number in my therapy group from Charleston, S.C. Her name is Chelsea Winthrop. She's as screwed up as I am. We have a lot in common. Right now I want to get in her pants but the security is tight and they are everywhere. Hell, we can't go outside without someone in a white uniform going with us. Tell you the truth, I'd leave here if I got the chance. It's dullsville at night. The weekends aren't worth shit. Lights out at ten o'clock. Got to go. Write me.
Your friend,
Jason Parker, Esq.

Jason's letter came at a perfect time. Anne was right when she said I wasn't myself. It's hard to manufacture happiness when you're not very happy. Jason gave me a good laugh. He sounded more like the old Jason I knew and liked so much. If I could make a bet, I'd say if given the chance, he'll have a hell of a time while he's there. Dr. Gold should watch herself because knowing Jason, there's a trick up his sleeve somewhere. I put his letter inside the book I'd been trying to finish. I thought he and Holden deserved to be together.

July Fourth came and most Americans across our country celebrated the nation's 181st birthday with hundreds of parades, picnics, and celebrations. I decided to stay at home. Anne was at our grandmother's spending the night and Mother was at her uncle's at a Fourth of July party. I fixed myself a grilled cheese sandwich, opened some potato chips, and poured myself a glass of sweet iced tea and headed for my father's bedroom, now our TV room, and his rocking chair. This was the first time since his death that I had turned the television on at night. For some bizarre reason, I found comfort sitting in his rocker and eating my dinner. I watched Grouch Marx and

You Bet Your Life at 8:00 and my favorite Thursday night show, *Dragnet,* at 8:30. A little after nine o'clock the phone rang. I walked out to the hall, picked up the receiver, and spoke, "Hello, Haywood residence."

"Braxton, this is Mrs. Parker, Jason's mother."

"Hello, Mrs. Parker," I said, thinking how strange it was for her to call me this late.

"Braxton, have you heard from Jason?" Mrs. Parker sounded flustered and anxious.

"Yes, ma'am," I said. "I got a letter from him in the mail yesterday."

"Have you heard from him today? I mean, has he called you?" Mrs. Parker's voice got higher as she spoke. Excitement was kicking in.

"No, ma'am," I said. "I didn't think he could call friends from the hospital."

"Yes, you are right. He's not supposed to," said Mrs. Parker, speaking faster now. "Braxton, apparently Jason has run away. I had hoped that you would have heard from him."

"No, he hasn't called me," I said, thinking if I should tell Mrs. Parker what he said in his letter to me.

"Will you call me the minute he contacts you?" said Mrs. Parker.

"Yes, ma'am, I surely will," I said. "Have you talked to Matt?"

"Not yet," said Mrs. Parker. "I really do not think he will call Matt or Thad but I know he will call you if he calls anyone."

"If he calls me, I will call you." I promised Mrs. Parker.

"Thank you, Braxton," said Mrs. Parker. "Goodnight."

"Mrs. Parker, wait," I said.

"Yes?"

"Will you let me know something if you hear anything?"

"I will do that, Braxton," said Mrs. Parker. "Goodnight, Braxton,"

"Good night," I said. But she had already hung up. I put the receiver of the phone back on its base and returned to the rocking chair. I sat there like my father had so many days and nights. I couldn't help but wonder why in hell Jason Parker would run away from an institution that was trying to help him. I stared at the TV screen. The picture was clear and the sound was audible. I couldn't see and hear what was pouring out of the television box because my brain, eyes, and senses refused to translate and transmit. My focus was completely on Jason Parker, wondering where Jason would go and how would he get there. I suspected that girl from Charleston might be with him. What was her name? I went and got the letter. Chelsea Winthrop from Charleston. Maybe I should call Mrs. Parker back. Something told me this wasn't a good idea, at least not tonight. I didn't even know if Chelsea was with Jason. I went back and sat in the rocker. This time I made a real attempt to watch and listen to the story being acted out on Lux Video Theatre. No use. Jason Parker had my full attention again. Where are you, Jason? Why haven't you called me? Jason, you can be an idiot sometimes.

At 11:20 P.M. I cut off the television and walked to the front door. I unlocked the screened door, opened it and walked out onto the front porch. Most of the neighbors had retired. I looked to my right toward Nash Street to see if Jack's car was in sight. Nothing headed this way. I stayed on the porch for another ten minutes looking at the stars and constellations. I could hear traffic in the distance, a far away firecracker popping, and the sound of a light breeze passing through the trees. My mind filled with all kinds of crazy images from this summer—none of them pleasant. I had too many questions invading my mind and no answers. No Byrd. No Jason. No Daddy. No Mother. Who else will I lose? What will happen next? Where did I go wrong this summer? I didn't have any answers.

I reached in my shirt pocket for the pack of Kool cigarettes I had pilfered from Mother a couple of days ago. Darn! The pack was empty. Forget it. I really didn't want a cigarette that badly anyway. Sighing, I walked back into the house and closed the front door, making certain I left it unlocked in case Mother returned. After cutting on the front porch light for Mother, I walked into Anne's room and cut on one of the bedside lamps and pulled back the bed covers. Knowing there was nothing else I could do, I went to my bedroom and closed the door and got in bed and lay there wide awake until the first ray of a Friday morning sun shot into my room.

It was six o'clock. I could hear Mother snoring when I cracked Anne's door. Mother was still in her slip and laying on her back in Anne's bed. Her skirt, blouse, purse, and shoes had been dropped into

a pile on the floor beside the bed. An unfamiliar glass sat on the bedside table. It smelled of tobacco and whiskey. The glass left a circular
water stain on the pine table. I knew once Mother was awake and
sober, she would get mad and blame Anne for ruining her antique
table.

As I turned to go back to my room, the phone rang. I walked
quickly but quietly to pick up the receiver before the ringing could
wake up Mother. "Hello," I said.

"Braxton, this is Jason." I could hear music in the background
and people talking. I looked at my watch. My God! It was only six-
fifteen in the morning.

"Jason, where in the hell are you?" I couldn't wait to hear his
answer.

"At the moment, I am standing in a telephone booth," he said.

"That's not what I mean," I shot back, trying not to be too loud.
"I mean where are you? What town?"

"I'm in Myrtle Beach, South Carolina, and it's hot as hell down
here. The bugs are driving me ape shit." Jason talked like everything
was normal.

"Bugs?" I said. "Jason, how did you get down there?"

"Hitchhiked. We had no problem. We got a trucker right out of
Richmond who brought us most of the way. Then some frat guys
delivered us here yesterday," Jason said.

"Jason, who's *we?*" I said. I kept thinking that Jason had gone off
the deep end and maybe he did need to be at M.C.V.

"Chelsea, the girl I wrote you about," he said like I was supposed
to know. "Did you get my letter?"

"Yeah, I got it," I said. "Where are you staying?"

"We slept on the beach last night but there is a motel not far
from here that we are going to check into," he said. "We need to
shower and get some sleep."

"What's the name of the motel?"

"I think it's called the Sandpiper, but I'm not really sure of the
name," said Jason.

"Jason, you are supposed to be in Richmond. Why are you calling me?" I said.

"Oh, yeah, I almost forgot," he said. "Can you come and get us?"

"You know I can't do that," I said, trying not to show my impatience with his plan. "Even if I could, the Tank would never make it and I don't have gas money."

"I can give you the money when you get here," he said.

"Jason, that's not the point—besides your mother called me last night," I said. "She's worried sick about you."

"Like shit she is, Braxton," said Jason. "Don't fall for her line. All she wants is to have me committed. That's why I ran away."

"I don't believe that!"

"Believe what you want to and don't tell her where I am, Braxton," said Jason.

"Jason, she can come and get you and take you back so you can get well," I said.

"Did you hear *anything* I just said?" Jason wanted his way again. I shook my head.

"Yes, I heard you, but I'm calling your mother." I said. "Give me your number."

"If you call her, Braxton, *I will never speak to you again,*" Jason said. I could hear the phone crack as he slammed the receiver back on its base.

"That's a chance I'll have to take, Jason," I said to myself. This time I knew I was doing the right thing. I called Mrs. Parker and gave her what little information I had. She and Mr. Parker planned to leave immediately for Myrtle Beach.

I was in the kitchen cleaning. Lily had the holiday weekend off. Shortly after nine o'clock, the phone rang again. I dried my hands and raced to phone.

"What is it this time, Jason?" I said into the receiver.

"Jason? This is Thad, Braxton," he said. "What gives calling me Jason?"

"I talked with him about two hours ago and I thought you were him calling back," I said.

"How is he?" said Thad. "Did you tell the old boy we missed him?"

"You wouldn't believe me if I told you," I said, debating whether to break the news.

"Try me and see," said Thad with his usual enthusiasm.

"I don't have time now," I said. "What going on?"

"I just wanted to know how you were holding up."

"Spectacularly," I lied. "Oh yeah, how was the beach?"

"Hot and hot and hotter," said Thad. "We missed you."

"I would like to have been with you guys," I said. "When did you get back?"

"About an hour ago," said Thad. "Say, I was sorry to hear about your dad."

"Thanks. It was a shocker at first . . . but, you know as . . . well, he's better off."

"I guess," said Thad. "I just wish you could've come with us. It was a blast!"

"I bet it was," I said, wishing I could have been on the beach for some of the last forty-eight hours. Only in a perfect world would that happen and I was definitely not there.

"Matt got stung by a jellyfish when we were floundering," said Thad.

"Did he survive?" I was losing my enthusiasm to continue this conversation.

"Yeah! Scared the hell out of him," said Thad.

"Look, Thad, I've really got to go," I said. "I'll call you back later."

"Hey Braxton, one thing—you want to get together tomorrow night? Thought you, Matt, and I might ride out to the Creamery and see what's cooking."

"It's a date," I said. "Call me and let me know what time."

"Talk to you tomorrow," he said.

"Thanks for calling," I said, hanging up the phone.

Looking at my watch and realizing I was supposed to pick up Anne thirty minutes ago, I grabbed the car keys off the living room table, locked the front door behind me, and ran to the car parked in the driveway. I ground the gears in my haste to put the car in reverse. Slow down and take your time, Tonto, and back out of the driveway like you were taught to do.

The time for Anne to go to camp had finally arrived. She had been on-again, off-again about the idea of going away. I thought it was a wonderful opportunity for her—it would be a lot of fun and it would get her out of the house for two weeks. Aunt Josephine,

Aunt Eva, and Aunt Grace had given her the two-week trip begin-ning today, Friday, July 5th through Friday, July 19th. When the trip was first mentioned, Anne immediately became defensive and said she wouldn't go. Not ever having been away from home by herself before, she was afraid. For the last three days, I had been telling her that fear was something she had to face and it was natural to be afraid. I also kept reminding her that four of her friends would be there with her and she wouldn't be alone. I promised to write three times a week and this made her happy. She reluctantly agreed to go.

I was in front of Grannie's house shortly before ten. Anne and Granny were waiting on the porch. I got out and waved and Anne ran down the cement steps and out to the street where I was parked. Upon our return home, we spent the remainder of the hour finish-ing her packing. We took the camp's checklist and did the best we could. If anything, we over packed. Mother never woke and I forged her signature on the health form Anne had to take with her. About eleven-fifteen, the Johnsons pulled up in front of the house. I walked out on the porch to signal that Anne was on her way. Anne was a combination of excitement and terror, anxiousness and fear, appre-hensiveness and dread. When I kissed her goodbye, I saw the fear in her little brown eyes. And her hand shook when I helped her carry her bags out to their car. I thanked Mr. Johnson, making some excuse for Mother not coming out, and I reminded Anne to keep her chin up. Mrs. Johnson smiled, assuring me she would be fine. As soon as Anne climbed into the back seat with her friend Janet, they began sharing a laugh. I stood in the front yard with tears in my eyes, watching the Johnsons and my sister turn onto Nash Street, heading toward the coast. Mother should have been out here with me.

I found out that this trip for Anne was a ploy to get her out of town until something could be decided about Mother. I believed it was a gift to help my little sister through a difficult period in her life. I was wrong. The real reason was revealed to me two hours after the Johnsons had left. I'm not certain it mattered. Anne didn't need to see Mother turning into an alcoholic. What Anne needed was a Mother who cared enough about her to put aside the bottle, at least long enough to help prepare for her first trip away from home. It was best this way, both for Anne and for my mother.

It had to be Aunt Eva who informed me of Aunt Josephine's idea. She stopped by shortly after lunch on her way home from some committee meeting at the church. I think Aunt Josephine should have told me herself. Aunt Eva has a great way of putting someone on the spot, so to speak, when she tells something and then she interrogates. I'm certain this became second nature to my aunt because of her many years as clerk of superior court.

Aunt Eva had no sooner stepped inside the living room of our house, when she started, "Braxton, are you here?" She didn't knock and she didn't ring the doorbell.

"Aunt Eva, lower your voice," I said, coming from the back of the house to meet her.

"Braxton, when was the last time you sat down and had a meal with your mother?"

"What?" I said. "I don't know, Aunt Eva. Why?"

"Well, stop and think for a minute." She stood with both arms folded over her buxom chest.

"What brought this on?" I said in confusion.

"Just answer my question, Braxton," she said. "When was the last time you . . . "

"I guess the day before Daddy died," I said, not allowing her to finish. "Why?"

"*Umph!*" She hesitated, cleared her throat, and leaned toward me with her index finger pointing at my nose. "Braxton, when was the last time you even spoke to your mother?"

"Aunt Eva, why are you asking me these questions?" I didn't like her insinuations. I knew exactly where she would go with this.

"It doesn't matter why *I am asking*. Just answer, *please*." Her stern look turned her double chin into three chins.

"I speak to Mother every day at some time."

"*You know exactly what I mean. Don't play your little games with me.*" Her patience with me had begun to wane.

"The last time I actually had a conversation with my mother was the afternoon of Daddy's burial," I said. "Now are you satisfied? *You know she's been under a lot of pressure. Why don't you mind your own business?*" With that show of disrespect, she pulled back her right hand and let me have it across the face using the back of her hand. Her ring pulled against my lip and cut it. Blood began to ooze from my mouth. This excited both of us. I started crying and Aunt Eva started apologizing. I ran to the bathroom with her right behind me.

"Where do you keep the iodine?" Her nervousness forced her words to run together.

"In the medicine cabinet." I reached for my bath cloth.

"Put cold water on that, Braxton, and don't rub it too hard!" she said, grabbing the cloth from my hand. "Just pat it! Pat it!" she said, demonstrating what I was to do and speaking like an Army drill sergeant giving one order after another. "Where are your cotton balls?"

"If we have any, they are in the linen closet."

"Just pat it," she said, handing me the cloth. "It'll absorb better." She spoke in rapid, short sentences. "My God! *Look at you!*"

I looked in the bathroom mirror. I didn't think I looked that bad. In fact, the bleeding had almost stopped. I turned toward my aunt and saw my mother standing at the entrance to the bathroom. Her hair needed combing. It looked wild, standing out in all different directions. Her gown was spotted on the front with numerous greenish, yellow stains. She held a burning cigarette in her left hand and the rest of her body with the help of her right hand braced itself against the doorframe. She looked smashed.

"What kind of an example of a mother are you setting for Braxton, Virginia?" said Aunt Eva in an accusatorial tone.

"What in the *hell* are you doing here this time of day?" Mother could barely get the words out, but I knew she was pissed.

"Virginia, you don't even know what day of the week it is!" Aunt Eva adopted a despicable expression and I feared she was ready to give Mother a smack. "You weren't even sober enough to tell your own daughter goodbye before she left."

"Aunt Eva, stop!" Mother didn't even seem to be focusing on what was taking place.

"I don't feel well," Mother said. "I need my aspirins."

"What you need, Virginia, I can't even say in front of your son. *You are disgusting.* You are a *drunk,* Virginia, *a damn drunk.*"

"*No, she's not! My mother is not a drunk. Quit calling her that!*"

"Look at *her,* Braxton! Everyone in this town is talking about your mother. Out every other night with Jack and his crowd drinking, leaving you here to take care of Anne and the house. She's a disgrace to our family. Do you hear? *She's a damn disgrace to our family!* I can't even go to church without someone saying something about her." Now I knew what put Aunt Eva on her soapbox.

"*Stop it! Stop it!*" Mother moved forward, turned, and fell against the porcelain tub, landing on the floor. I watched in disbelief at what had just happened. Mother lay there crying while holding her side. "*Now see what you've done!*" I shouted.

"Your mother is sick," said Aunt Eva. My aunt stood there, looking at Mother, not moving to help but just stood there condemning her. "She needs help and I mean professional help."

"What she needs is to go back to bed," I said, bending over to pick her up. "Would you please help me get her to Anne's bed?"

Aunt Eva left after we put Mother back in Anne's bed. I knew she would call my Aunt Josephine as soon as she got home. That meant I would get another visitor within the hour. I loved my mother. I didn't understand her obsession with alcohol, but I wasn't ready to condemn her. She had been through too damn much for everyone to turn against her. She did need help. I didn't know how to help her but I knew Aunt Eva didn't know how to help her either. She had just proven that. I had never seen my aunt this irrational. I thought only young kids and teenagers screamed and yelled at people. I guess I'm naïve.

The early afternoon seemed strange. It was unusually quiet. There was no one in the house but Mother and me, completely void of any activity. It was a sticky, hot outside but uncommonly comfortable inside. The absence of my father left an overpowering presence. The house begged for his return. The breathing of our home was too quiet. I couldn't even remember a time when our home was this silent. There had been plenty of quiet times for my father's sake and there were times when no activity was allowed. This silence demanded attention. I could hear every board creak, every window pop, and every unidentifiable noise that made itself known.

Mother remained in Anne's room sleeping off another hangover. This was a sad time in her life, a time she had chosen to remove herself from the core of life in our home. She must be terribly afraid to just give up. It was as if all her reason and willpower and steadfast-ness had been jerked out from under her, leaving her no foundation. I wondered how long Mother would continue to drink—one week, one month, six months, one year, indefinitely—something had to be done to help her. What?

Chapter 45
A WHITE JACKET

MOTHER WAS NOT in Anne's bed when I went to check on her. She wasn't in the bathroom or in the living room. I walked to the back porch thinking she might be there smoking. I heard a noise coming from inside the kitchen. I walked into the kitchen and saw Mother in the pantry.

Her left hand rested against the back shelf where the canned vegetables were kept. Her right arm was stretched out as far as she could extend it in an attempt to grab a bottle of whiskey from the top of the three shelves that held the liquor. She had changed into a pink nightgown with a white lacey hem that hung around her ankles. She was barefoot. I smelled smoke and could only guess the cigarette was in her mouth. I took one step into the pantry, the size of a small bathroom and spoke.

"Mother, please don't get any more." I took a step toward her.

"Braxton, I need a drink." Mother did not turn around.

"Mother, you don't need a drink." I walked over to her and took her hand that had just grabbed a bottle of Kentucky bourbon.

"Don't touch me!" She pulled back, slurring. An ugly scowl glared at me as she turned her body toward me. "I know what I need and I know when I need it."

"Mother, you need to eat," I backed away. "Let me fix you some lunch."

"I'm not hungry!" She lost her balance momentarily and fell against the back shelves. "Now leave me alone, damn it, so I can have a drink."

I moved forward and reached for the bottle in her hand. I don't know what I thought I would do with it. It slipped from her hand, hit the floor, shattering into about a dozen pieces. The bourbon splashed against the lower part of her gown, her lower legs and ankles, and her feet. She cursed as she looked down at the glass fragments that lay around her bare feet.

"Don't move, Mother!" I knelt, feeling my body under attack by my emotions. "I'll get it up."

"*You're just like Josephine, Braxton, always trying to interfere.*" Mother attempted to take a step around me; instead she slipped again, this time knocking me against the liquor side of the pantry shelving. "*Now see what you've done. You've wasted a perfectly good bottle of whiskey.*" She caught her balance and walked into the kitchen, sat down at the worktable and began to cry.

I looked up at the three shelves holding the liquor. There were plenty more where that bottle came from. Getting up, I reached behind the pantry door for a paper bag to put the pieces of glass in. I left the liquid on the floor and walked back into the kitchen. "Mother, please go get your bath. You know someone might stop by today."

"You mean your Aunt Josephine." Mother glared at me with hate in her eyes. I didn't want to know this woman.

"Mother, please leave and go get dressed."

"Braxton, don't you dare tell me what to do. Now go back in there and get me another bottle of whiskey." Mother arose from her seat, stumbled, and fell forward against the worktable.

"I will *not* get you another bottle!" I said.

"Braxton, get me a bottle now!" Mother staggered toward me but caught her balance by placing her right hand against the nearby stove.

"*No! No! No! I will not get you another drink of whiskey!*" I had no idea what she would do next. My continued refusal angered her even more.

"Get out of the damn way," Mother said, moving toward me. She did not take her eyes off the entrance to the pantry.

"No!" I said, moving in front of the pantry door and blocking her entrance.

"Move, now!" she said, falling up against me.

"I will not let you in this pantry!" I pushed her back slowly, walking her with my hands on her upper arms. She reeked of alcohol and cigarette smoke.

"*I wish you had never been born.*" She broke away from my hold. Lifting her right arm, she stung my cheek with a slap across the right side of my face. Then she stumbled into the pantry.

I stood paralyzed in shock. I felt a sudden rush of fear. I felt shamed by her comment. It was hard to believe my mother had hit me over a bottle of whiskey. It hurt.

"See what you made me do." Her hand moved along the shelf looking for the right bottle.

"I didn't make you hit me." I braced myself. "Mother, you're drunk and you need to stop!"

"*Why?*" She stumbled again, but managed to grab a bottle of Jack Daniels from the shelf.

"You're killing yourself and *me!*" I stood back, not knowing how to interpret her savage-like behavior. I stood aside as she tripped back into the kitchen.

"*I don't want to live! Did you hear that? I don't want to live anymore!*" Mother stared at me with wide frightened eyes like a sheep before its slaughter.

Her breathing was heavy and her nostrils flared.

"What abut Anne and me?"

"*What about you?*" Mother glared at me, her mouth contorted in a half sneer, half mocking grin. She took the top off the bottle of Jack Daniels, put her lips over the top of the bottle, threw her head back and took a large swig. She licked her lips and put the bottle on the worktable. "I need a cigarette." She took the last one out of the glass cigarette holder on the stove, struck the kitchen match against one of the front eyes of the stove, and lit it. She inhaled deeply, coughing when she returned the smoke through her nostrils. She was an unattractive picture. Nothing is uglier than seeing smoke exiting a drunken woman's nostrils. She turned, picked up the bottle, and took another big swallow of Jack Daniels. She followed with another deep draw on her cigarette, again exhaling the smoke through her nose. I wondered if this was her drunken attempt to taunt me.

"Let me help you, Mother."

"I don't need your help, Braxton." She fell against the table and slid to the floor. She looked like she was about to pass out. "I don't need your help, Anne's help, or Josephine's help."

"Braxton, are you home?" Aunt Josephine's voice came from the front of the house.

Oh *shit!* "Back here in the kitchen," I called. "We're in the kitchen." I couldn't hide Mother—might as well let my aunt see the real thing.

"Is Virginia okay?" Aunt Josephine walked in and saw Mother sprawled across the kitchen floor. "My God, Virginia, what have you done?"

"She accidentally fell," I said, hoping to help Mother's case.

"*I'm drunk, big sister—what in the hell are you going to do about it?*" Mother's slurred her speech, shouting loud enough for our immediate neighbors to hear.

"Braxton, help me get her to the bathroom," my aunt said bending.

"*Don't put your damn hands on me!*" Mother began to move her legs on the floor and thrash the air with her hands. Suddenly, this woman I call my mother was an alien to me. How could this have happened?

"Mother, we just want to help you. Stop it!"

"Virginia, we're going to get you up and into the bathroom. Now, cooperate!"

"I'm going to stay right here and there's not one *damn* thing you can do about it."

"Braxton, get behind her," said Aunt Josephine. "I'll tell you when to lift her."

"*Josephine the crusader . . . Josephine the do-gooder . . . Josephine the bitch!*" said Mother, spitting saliva and uttering more obscenities.

"Mother, don't talk to Aunt Josephine like that!" I was embarrassed.

"That's right. Take her side. She never does anything wrong."

"*Now!*" said my aunt. She pulled and I lifted. When we got

Mother on her feet, Mother swung her fist at Aunt Josephine but missed her. "Virginia, you need to see a doctor and quick."

"How dare you come into my house, you *bitch,* and proceed to tell me *what I need!*" Mother pulled away from my aunt but only slid a few feet. I was able to hold on and keep her balanced and on her feet.

"Mother, for crying out loud, please cooperate," I said.

"*Mother, please cooperate,*" she said, mocking me.

"All right Braxton, let's get her into the bathroom. If we have to drag her, we'll do it." Physically, my aunt was not up to this task. Already saddled with back problems and arthritis, she didn't waste a second using what strength she had.

"*Don't touch me you damn bitch! I warned you!*" Mother reached over and pulled hard on Aunt Josephine's hair. "*I'll teach you to mess with me!*" Mother kicked her sister in the shin.

"Virginia, you asked for this." Aunt Josephine took her right hand and slapped Mother hard against her right cheek branding her with the palm of her hand. "*Now, you cooperate!*"

"*You son of a bitch!* You son of a *bitch!*" Mother folded, falling in our arms, her head jarred against her chest, and she started sobbing uncontrollably.

"Let's put her in your bedroom. It's closer." We pulled, pushed, and dragged until we had Mother sitting in the old lazy chair in my room. Once in the chair, Mother threw her head, wet from perspiration, back letting it fall against the upper back of the overstuffed chair. Her gown was pulled between her legs. She just sat there. Her eyes closed and her arms fell lifelessly over the sides of the chair arms. Her hair was in her face and she was as white as a sheet. She looked as bad as the night we found her on the street. "I'll be right back. I'm calling a doctor."

In no time Dr. Asbury and three men in white uniforms were in my room trying to restrain my mother. As soon as Mother saw them, she pulled herself out of my chair and stumbled around to the opposite side of the room. I marveled at her physical strength. Where did it come from? Attempting to dodge the short, chunky dark skinned man who carried the straight jacket in his right hand, Mother managed to position herself between my bed and the window overlooking the back porch. A taller, more muscular white man moved from the hall and stood in front of my bed, ready to grab her. The third male, a strong looking, large bodied white male stood in the other doorway that led into the hall. Aunt Josephine stood with Dr. Asbury in the hall. I stood in front of my fireplace frozen in fear, tears running down my cheeks. I was scared to death. I howled in my head the way wolves would before attacking its prey. The scene taking place in my bedroom was horrific and one I knew I would never forget.

"*Braxton, please save me. Don't let them do this to me!*" Mother's words stung my ears like an unending echo. How could I ever forget them? There was nothing I could do.

"Mother, stand still and let them help you." At the time I said this, I didn't fully comprehend where they were going to take Mother.

"*Josephine, how could you do this to me? How could you?*" Mother jumped up on my bed. She wobbled, attempting to stand.

"Grab her left leg, Arnold," said the taller, muscular man. "Don't allow her to hit her head on anything hard."

"I've got her," said Arnold, moving forward and obeying the directive. Arnold grabbed my mother's leg and the tall, muscular man caught her around the waist and pulled her off the bed and stood her upright on the floor. Arnold walked from his position beside the bed and stood in front of my mother. He placed his hands on her shoulders to restrain her. Mother screamed and screamed like a jungle cat watching her cubs being shot one by one. The dark man moved forward and attempted to put the straight jacket on my mother.

"Please don't hurt my mother." I stood transfixed, regretting that I had to witness whatever was about to take place in my bedroom. Mother was frightened. Her head had dropped and she cried. Arnold took control. It frightened me to see the amount of force he used when pulling and tightening the straps of the jacket around Mother's back. Each time Mother tried to move her arms, Arnold pulled the straps tighter until there was no opportunity for any movement. It was a scene of horror. I had seen this done to crazy people in movies. This wasn't a scene from a movie and my mother wasn't crazy. I agree that Mother was sick, but not crazy.

"*Josephine, I will never forgive you for this!*" The men carried my mother kicking and screaming out the front door, down the steps, and to an ambulance waiting at the curb. There was a police car parked directly behind the ambulance. It sat with its engine idling. Captain Mays was behind the wheel. I stood on the porch watching. My aunt and Dr. Asbury stood at the front door. It was a little after six o'clock. Up and down the street, nosy neighbors signaled their curiosity by stepping onto their porches. And just as quickly, a murmur of voices could be heard passing tidbits of gossip from front porch to front porch. "*Braxton, don't let them take me away. I promise I'll be good.*" Mother kicked and cursed while the men in white jackets forced her into the back of the ambulance. The door of the ambulance closed. The siren blared as it pulled away from the curb. The police car followed.

"Where are they taking Mother?" I looked at my aunt for a long awkward moment.

"To the state hospital in Raleigh," she said.

"Why to Raleigh?" I was frozen in my own shock.

"I've had her committed. She is a very sick woman and needs help that cannot be provided here." With my aunt and the doctor beside me, we walked down the front steps and stood in silence on the parched grass until the siren became a muffled sound somewhere in the future.

"Josephine, I'll call you in the morning as soon as I know something definite about Virginia. Wait for my call before you drive to Raleigh." Dr. Asbury started walking toward his car parked in our driveway.

"Thank you, Dr. Asbury," my aunt called softly. "I think I did what was right."

"You did the right thing for Virginia," he said, stopping and turning toward my aunt. "She can get the help she needs there." Dr. Asbury wasted no time getting into his Lincoln. He started the engine and backed out onto Kincaid Avenue. As he drove off, my aunt and I raised our hands to wave goodbye.

"Braxton, go get your things and let's go to my house," said Aunt Josephine.

"Not tonight. I'm going to stay here." I said. "I want to be here."

"I have to leave now," said Aunt Josephine. "If you should need me, call."

"Thanks," I said, leaning over to give her a kiss and hug. "I think you did the right thing."

I watched my weary aunt get into her car and drive up to Nash Street where she turned right. The night was young. The wind blew gently and the sky was somewhere between sunset and twilight. If there were any stars out tonight, they would be cold in the heavens. I walked up the familiar front steps, locked the screened door behind me, and followed the empty route to the kitchen. The only sound in the house was the clicking of the taps on my heels when they hit the wooden floor.

Lily would not be pleased if she didn't find her kitchen the way she left it. I wiped up the spilled whiskey, washed and dried the pantry floor, and straightened the kitchen furniture. I picked up the cigarette butts marked with Mother's lipstick that had fallen out of her ashtray. Like Lily, I ran hot water in the ashtray and set it on the windowsill, allowing the stains sufficient time to break loose. I inspected the kitchen and decided it would meet Lily's approval.

I reached into the flour canister where Lily hid her cigarettes. I took one of her filter king Kools and put it in my mouth. I lit it and took a drag and methodically exhaled the smoke. I squinted through the smoke that had gotten in my way long enough to look out the window over the stove into the backyard. All was quiet. I inhaled again, no longer like a novice, and this time blew the smoke through the screen into the night.

I stood there like I had so many other nights this summer. I felt a cold chill run up my spine. I walked through the breakfast nook and into what was now the TV room. The room was dark, lacked warmth and was still. My father's old rocking chair sat where it had always sat. I walked over the worn rug and settled in the chair that had been my father's resting place for so many years. *This will always be his chair,* I thought. And much of what I remember about him, I associate with him sitting here.

As I sat in his chair, I felt abandoned for the fist time in my life. I knew I wasn't because I had too many relatives living too close for that to happen. But, in my own home, at this particular time in my life, I had been abandoned. I was a stranger to this feeling of being left completely alone—feeling isolated from those I have loved. I got up from the chair and walked through the empty house. Each room took on an unfamiliar look. Things I took for granted, things all too familiar, things I had never noticed—they all took on new meanings for me—it was bizarre.

I stopped when I got to my room. I tiptoed in and looked carefully at the chocolate colored walls and beige molding, at the handsome mahogany furniture, and the oval throw rugs—my mother's creation. I knew then it would be known to me as the room of involuntary surrender.

I entered this summer right out of the tenth grade, wanting to grow up. Have I been given the test? I had wanted to be mature. Is facing loneliness a part of being mature? I stood looking at my trophies, books, and the pictures I had painted since the fifth grade. It occurred to me that I had lived a lifetime since that last day of school in May. I was still the same sixteen-year-old boy, yet—I was alone in the world.

It was ninety plus degrees outside I said to myself and yet, I stood here shivering. I was cold. I had Bermuda shorts on and I stood trembling in the middle of my bedroom on a hot summer night. This was crazy but I knew I was afraid, afraid of the immediate future. Loneliness had disguised itself as fear and I had no one to guide me through it. I was sickened by the situation I found myself in. I was repulsed by the onset of this fear that could control me. I opened my closet and took out a windbreaker and put it on. I felt momentary warmth and then the same chill took residence again, this time, inside my coat.

I don't know what made me think of what Mr. Sam Ross had said to me on several occasions, but I remembered his advice tonight. "Braxton, when you are all alone and have a problem to solve, look inside your heart for your answer." It suddenly made sense to me. It was like someone had hit me in the head with a two-by-four. It was the guidance I needed, a revelation of sorts.

I understood at sixteen that this problem of loneliness was uniquely mine and it could be no one else's unless I gave it to them. I had to find the solution. I couldn't depend on someone else to solve it for me. And if I was going to find an answer, I needed to accept the loneliness that had invaded my life. I needed to accept my situation here in my home and move on from here. I then did something that I was totally unprepared to do. I took a deep breath and prayed. "Dear God, please don't let my mother continue to depend on alcohol. Please break off her desire to drink with Jack Ross or anyone else. Give me the strength to get through this and make me stronger. This house is empty; fill it with happiness again. Amen." When I finished, I knew for the first time, what my grandmother had been trying to tell me all these years about talking with God.

There must be thousands of towns like Wilson. And in each of these towns, there must be a home with a teenager like myself feeling the same sadness and dealing with the same types of fears. Towns where teenagers see darkness when it is light . . . homes where horrible things happen in the night, threatening the goodness at the core of the town and frightening those whose only wrongdoing was in seeing darkness for what it is.

I have looked into the darkness and seen what is there. It is ugly, hideous, and not fit for unseasoned eyes. It is frightening and demoralizing and stands ready to grab its prey. Evading the darkness becomes a game sucking the very energy out of its participants.

Chapter 46
ANOTHER SEPARATION

ONE BY ONE the porch lights in our neighborhood disappeared like candles being blown out on a birthday cake. I returned to the back porch and sat, watching the night sky, wondering what it would be like to visit another planet or walk on the moon. More than one time, my daddy said to me, "Braxton, one day man will go to the moon." And he was right; but at the time, I thought he had read too many *Sky King* comics.

I heard the eleven o'clock Norfolk-Southern wail as it passed through town signaling the end of another workday. I got up and went to my daddy's rocker and sat, watching the last program on TV bow at midnight and disappear in the mythical tube like a firefly losing its glow.

I couldn't sleep. I was as anxious and as restless as a raging storm. I rambled most of the night. In my ramblings, I smoked too many cigarettes, rehearsing what had happened since the first day of June. I paced back and forth inside the house, thinking about the freedom my mother had forfeited. I heard the clock on the living room mantle strike one o'clock, two o'clock, and three o'clock. I heard the milkman clink his bottles together as he placed them on the doormats of Mrs. Thurston, Mrs. Vickers, and Mr. Ross.

I walked outside and circled the house too many times to remember. I stopped and sat on the front porch for a while, rocking in the white ladder-back rocker my daddy loved so much. Whatever it did for him, it didn't do for me.

I finished reading *The Catcher in the Rye* by Salinger. I thought Jason was a lot like Holden Caulfield and in some ways, I still do.

Both had problems communicating and dealing with adult situations. Both looked for escapes but on a positive note, Jason, like Holden, began to show signs of maturing. What surprised me was the realization that Holden and I were similar. I understood perfectly Holden's reaction to the phoniness and the ugliness he saw in his world. Like him, I too experienced the feeling of loneliness that summer and sometimes, alienation. But unlike Holden, I stayed connected to what was going on around me and I did learn to deal with adult situations. Jason, like Holden, struggled here and they both ran away.

At first I didn't agree with Holden Caulfield's closing comments, "It's funny. Don't ever tell anybody anything. If you do, you start missing everybody." But, in a way, I agreed with him. Holden was a prisoner to the problems his world threw at him and unquestionably, I remained a prisoner too long to some of the problems that summer tossed my way. I understood what it was like to be afraid and scared but I dealt with my world. Holden could not.

I don't think I will ever miss some of the people I knew here, and I knew I could never value them. I was certain I wouldn't miss this provincial little town with its caste system and its "social do-gooders" who tried their hardest to bury my mother along with my daddy. I didn't see myself as bitter or as a cynic but rather a realist—I didn't see much future living here—residing where a person was expected to bow to social pressure. I didn't want to be a paper doll—cut out of the same pattern and colored the same way and expected to play the same game. It should be okay to be ourselves. If we can't, we become numb. Isn't that what Holden wanted for himself?

During the receding of the night, I made myself three promises: first, I am going to try to see people for whom they are and treat them equally; second, I will not let money determine a person's worth as I get to know him; and third, I will get to the bottom of David Byrd's death.

"Braxton, what's you doing out here?" a soft voice asked, opening the door to the back porch.

"Huh?" I must have fallen asleep. I lay in a horizontal position on the chaise lounge on the far end of the porch.

"Braxton, it's time to get up," said Lily. "Did you sleeps out here last night?"

"If you want to call it that, I did."

"How's Miss Virginia on this glorious morning?" asked Lily.

"She probably has a heck of a headache." I sat up and stretched. The early morning air felt good against my face and arms. I stretched again and yawned. "What time is it?"

"It's just a little after eight o'clock. My bus didn't come this morning," said Lily. "That's how comes I'm late. I had to take a taxi."

"Doesn't make any difference," I said. "There's no one here but me."

"Where's Miss Virginia?"

"Mother was taken to the state hospital in Raleigh."

"The mental hospital?" Lily acted like she had been knocked down by my answer.

"Yes, ma'am, the mental hospital," I said.

"Your mama's not mental, Braxton!" I could tell Lily was stunned.

"You know that and I know that," I said, not wanting to believe it myself. "Try and tell Aunt Josephine."

"Your aunt's done gone and fixed things up real fine this time," said Lily. "Yes she has; she sure has." Lily picked up the ashtray off the back porch table and carried it into the kitchen with her. She took off her light summer sweater and hung it on the back of the pantry door. "Where is all those whiskey bottles that was in this here closet?"

"I poured the whiskey out of each of those damn bottles down the kitchen sink some time early this morning around one-thirty. The bottles are in some bags inside the garage. I didn't know where to put them."

"My Lords! What went on in this house last night?"

"First, Aunt Josephine came over and found Mother drunk. I mean real drunk. They exchanged words and Mother hit Aunt Josephine and Aunt Josephine slapped her back. Mother was on the floor cursing and it got worse and worse. Finally, Aunt Josephine called the doctor. And after he came, he called the ambulance. And Lily, they . . . they put . . . put her in a straightjacket."

"Oh, my Lords! Poor Miss Virginia!" Lily's eyes widened and her face flushed. Her hand began to shake. "Let's me sit down a minute."

"It was unbelievable, Lily. I don't know how to describe it to you. Mother screamed and cursed and begged. I couldn't do anything. I didn't know what to do." I walked over and grabbed Lily's outstretched hands. She squeezed my hands tightly with hers. I thought she would break my knuckles. She got up from her chair, hugged me hard, and stood back looking at me, tears running down her face. "Please don't start crying, Lily," I said, biting my lip. "You'll have me crying with you." And I did. We clung to each other and cried and then we stopped. Lily smiled but it was a sad smile—like the smile of an innocent person responding to a guilty verdict.

"I knows just what you need, Braxton," said Lily. She cooked a big breakfast for both of us.

We sat together on the back porch and ate the sausage and scrambled eggs. I even tried to get a cup of black coffee down. I finished telling her about Mother.

"I guess Miss Josephine will tells me today I don't have a job anymore." Her brightened eyes turned sad and she started weeping again.

"Maybe not," I said. "Maybe you can work for her." I knew this wasn't possible when I said it.

"She's already got a maid," said Lily, adding a dejected look to her facial repertoire.

"I don't want you to go, Lily," I said. "I really don't know what I will do if you leave."

"I know, but I suspects it's time," Lily's calloused hands rubbed against my smooth skin. Lily liked to pat. "Maybe I can comes back when Miss Virginia gets better." I knew she didn't believe that any more than I did. All I had to do was look at her face.

"Lily, Mother's real sick. I don't think she will be coming home any time soon."

"Poor Miss Virginia," said Lily. She looked at me again and said. "Your sweet mother's life has been a hard one to bear but I knows the good Lord is gonna reward her one day . . . cause Miss Virginia is a good woman in her heart. You remember Lily told you that,

Braxton. You might not understands that now but you wills some-
day . . . you will."

I never saw Lily again after that day. My aunt didn't need her and
she couldn't afford to keep her on at our house. There was little for
her do anyhow. Aunt Josephine offered to help her get another job
and did. Lily worked for Olivia, Byrd's aunt, twice a week through
August. Lily called me a couple of times and she was happy working for Olivia and I was glad for her. After being with us, Lily needed some joy because she got very little in our home. Lily and her
husband moved to the Washington, D.C. area after the tobacco season was over and I lost touch with her.

I loved Lily about as much as I did my own mother during those
days. I will never forget those early years. It was summertime and I
was little and I would run to the bus stop up on Nash Street in my
pajamas to meet her. We would walk hand-in-hand back to my
house and I would sit in the kitchen with her while she made breakfast and she'd tell me her made-up stories.

The bond between us grew stronger and stronger. Lily was
always my advocate when I needed her to be whether I was right or
not. She didn't always defend me but she made certain that the punishment meted by my mother would be fair. Lily was my sounding
board when I had trouble loving my daddy. Lily kept me focused and
I would tell her things that would only hurt my mother. She would
let me vent my anger but she wouldn't let me blame anyone for my
feelings.

People certainly do misjudge black people. I asked Lily one time
why some whites didn't like black people. She thought a long time
before she gave me her answer. After thinking and scratching her
chin, she said to me, "Braxton, this is my opinion only but I just
don't thinks white people understands us. They are afraid of us only
because we are colored. They forgets we has the same colored blood
and bleed just like they do. We can nurse their children, fix their
foods, hugs and kiss them, and take care of them as long as 'we stay
in our place.' Many white peoples need that feeling of being able to
control; it gives them feelings of security and importance. We came
to this here country as slaves sold by our owns people and I guess
the whites wants to keep us that way."

I asked Lily if that bothered her. She responded, "No and yes. It bothers me only because there's so much hatred tied up with blacks and whites. It don't bother me cause I knows who I am. And when the good Lord takes me, I gonna be sitting with the white people anyways. I can waits!" I knew what Lily meant and I understood her wisdom.

When I was without my father and mother and needed a role model, Lily was my role model. When I think of a best friend, I think of Lily. Lily's voice was one of the ones I listened to when I was confused and lonely and anxious and needed sound guidance.

While Lily cleaned the breakfast dishes, I mentally prepared myself for my next big adjustment. I would have to move to my Aunt Josephine's home temporarily. She didn't think I should stay here by myself and Anne certainly couldn't stay here. I didn't mind the move—it's just that . . . well, I did think I had earned the right to stay here . . . then there is the trust issue which should not have been a problem. It was easier to give in. The trade-off was Vic Junior's room with its hidden stairwell and larger closet and private bath. I could come back every Saturday, straighten up the house, and stay the night. I kept my end of the bargain and she kept hers. I got along with my aunt. She seemed to respect me and she liked my friends and that was as good as I could ask for.

Around mid-morning it suddenly dawned on me that we were fast approaching the middle of summer and I had no money and if I didn't get the job at Exeter, there would be no money to buy school clothes. Actually I knew this; but today, the realization slapped me in the face. It hit me hard and I began to sweat and to get nervous. The only constant in my life now was the weather. I could depend on it to be hot, muggy, and hazy. Today the air had that tobacco smell again.

Thad called and said that he would pick me up around seven o'clock tonight to go the Creamery. I told him that I would be at my Aunt Josephine's house and that I would explain later. It took me less than an hour to pack up what I wanted to take with me to my aunt's. When Anne returned from camp, I would have to help her get her things to go where she would be staying. No decision had been made yet. I had about an hour left before I would take Lily home.

The phone rang again about eleven-thirty and it was Mrs. Parker. She would be back in Wilson late afternoon. Jason was found where he told me he was staying. Arrangements had been made for Jason and the little girl, her reference to Chelsea, to be returned to the hospital. She would leave a note from Jason to me under the side doormat, on the carport side of the house. It would be best to wait until early evening or tomorrow to pick it up. After my last conversation with Jason, I wasn't too sure I wanted to see what else he had to say to me.

I found Lily sitting on the back porch, calmly smoking one of her filter king Kools. I hated to think this was it—final—there would be no more times together. She turned when she heard me and spoke.

"Are you ready to take me home?"

"I'll never be ready for that. But yes, I guess we'd better head out."

"Just a moment," she said. I watched her walk to the kitchen sink and run water over the lit cigarette and drop the butt into the paper bag she was carrying. "Let's go." She headed for the back porch.

"Oh, no," I said, grabbing her arm. "We will go out the front door." I locked the screen door and both doors leading onto the back porch were locked. Lily and I walked through the empty house. It was empty now except for the good and bad memories that we would lock in when we walked out the front door together. I turned to Lily, saying, "It will never be the same again."

"That's true," she said. "But it may be better!"

"I liked that, Lily," I said, locking the front door. We walked down the concrete steps and crossed the brown, water-starved grass and got in the Tank. I made Lily sit in the front seat with me. We shared one last Kool together. It took less than twenty minutes to get to her home. Lily waved good-bye and disappeared into her house. Another foundation of my life had been taken away.

Thad pulled up to the Clyde Avenue side of my aunt's house as her grandfather clock on the landing chimed seven bells. When he blew his horn, I told my aunt I would be back by eleven o'clock. She had already told me where she hid the house key. It was on a nail hidden in the ivy that grew over the bricks alongside the back door. I was to let myself in. She said she'd be in bed. I opened the screened door leading from the kitchen, ran out, letting it slam against the doorframe and turned the corner of the house and headed for Thad's '56 maroon Buick. (Exiting from her home took longer than the short distance of exiting from mine to the nearest car.) Since there was no one else in the car, I didn't need to call shotgun. His car was spic-n-span clean and shined like the top of a bald man's head under a glaring, bright sun. I spoke before I got in. "Hey, man, what you up to?"

"Not much, Braxton. What's with you?"

"Lots of water over the dam but might as well wait until Matt is with us. I don't want to repeat it twice." I beat on the dashboard keeping time with "All Shook Up." "This should be my theme song for the summer." I sang along with Elvis. Matt turned left on South Kincaid off of Vance Street reminding me of Jason's letter. Jason's house sat on the corner. "Pull into Jason's carport, would you? I have to pick something up."

"You bet," he said, barely having time to swerve into the gravel driveway. Thad stopped inside the carport.

"This will only take a second," I said, exiting the car. I ran around the front of Thad's car, up the three brick steps, and walked over to the side door. A white envelope stuck out from under the mat. I picked it up, deposited it in my shirt pocket, and returned to the car. "Thanks, Thad."

"News from Jason?"

"I don't know," I said. "I'll open it later." Now was not the time to find out I had permanently lost another friend.

"Jerry Riceman is spending the night with Matt so he'll be coming along," said Thad, turning right onto Nash Street. "Hope you don't mind too much."

"What's there to mind?" I said. Thad knew I didn't particular like Jerry Riceman. I mean he was a nice enough guy and smart as a whip. He had a big mouth and didn't know when to cut it off. I figured I could tolerate anything for one night. Besides, Matt and he were close friends. "I might as well tell you that Mother's in the state hospital in Raleigh. She has been sent for her drinking and erratic behavior. I'll tell Matt another time."

"Damn, Braxton!" said Thad, turning left on Lucas Avenue. "You've had more than your fair share of shit this summer. Damn, how much more can one man take?" He looked over with a sorrowful smile, revealing his magazine-perfect teeth as he turned right onto Vance Street.

"Well, Thad, hopefully there will be no more surprises this summer."

"Amen to that!" Thad pulled over in front of Matt's house that sat on the left side of the street, scraping his left front tire against the curb, and blew his horn. "There goes one of the white walls that I just cleaned."

Matt and Jerry raced to the car. Matt let him win. Jerry got in first and took the seat behind mine and Matt got in and closed the door. Between them, they had on enough cologne to sink the *Titanic.*

"Braxton, good to see you," said Matt, slapping my arm that rested across the top of the front seat.

"Good to see you, Matt," I said. "Hello, Jerry, how've you been this summer?"

"Life is great, Braxton," said Jerry. "Life is great!"

"That's good!" I said. *You are a real bull-shitter,* I thought to myself.

"Glad you could join us, Jerry," said Thad. "We'll go directly to the Creamery."

"Good to be with you guys. It's hard to break into this little club," said Jerry. "Now that David Byrd is gone, maybe I can take his place."

"*You'll never take Byrd's place, Jerry.*" I couldn't help myself. I don't know what came over me but I didn't appreciate his comment to begin with much less his presumption that he was an equal to Byrd. Jerry really "lit my fire." "Besides, who said there's an opening?"

"Forget it, Braxton," said Matt. "Jerry, that was a lousy comment."

"Hey, I'm sorry!" Jerry said. "Damn, you guys are a touchy lot tonight." Jerry leaned back against the seat and took out a pack of cigarettes.

"Not in here, Jerry!" said Thad. "My dad would kill me. You understand?"

"Damn bunch of prima donnas you guys are, too!" Jerry rolled down his window allowing the forced summer wind to blow his black curly hair all over his head. Jerry was a handsome kid with chiseled good looks. Like Kirk Douglas, he had a cleft in his chin. Some say he will be voted best looking male in our class. "What *can I do?*"

"You might sit back and listen for a change," said Matt, hitting him on his left knee at the same time.

"Amen!" I said, but too low for him to hear me.

"Oh, Braxton, have you heard from Jason?" asked Thad. (*Hell, Thad, we just stopped by his house.*)

"As a matter of fact, I got a letter from him on Saturday," I said, pulling it out of my back pocket. "Let's see, he says to tell both of you hello and that he's met a girl from Charleston, South Carolina. They're in the same group therapy sessions."

"She must be as crazy as he is," said Jerry. He hit the back of my seat and laughed.

"What's that supposed to mean?" I asked. This guy was really pushing my buttons tonight.

"Nothing," said Jerry. "You guys know Jason has a screw loose. Hell! Everyone in our class knows he's fucked up."

"What gives you the right to get in this car and talk about Jason like that?" I countered, turning around and staring him squarely in the eyes.

"Let up for Christ's sake, Braxton," said Matt.

"*No, I'm not!*" I said. "*I want an answer.*"

"It's a free country, Braxton," said Jerry. "Haven't you ever heard that or is it too much to expect the son of an alcoholic to know that?"

"*What the fuck did you say?*" I came over the back of the seat landing headfirst in Jerry's lap. I threw an upper jab, hitting him on the lower part of his chin with my fist. He reached down and grabbed my right arm and threw it backwards. "Stop it! You're killing me. Let go!"

"*Stop it!* Both of you," said Matt. "What in the hell has gotten into you tonight, Jerry?"

Pulling the car over next to the curb and throwing it into park, Thad turned and said, "Look, guys, we are about a block from the Creamery." He spoke directly to Jerry and me. "Do you want to go or not? If you're going to act like assholes, I'm taking you home." At first, no one said anything. We were too embarrassed.

"Let's go to the Creamery," I said, getting out of the backseat and opening the front door. I got back in the front seat and turned to Jerry. "Look, I'll be straight with you. I'm a little sensitive tonight. If you're trying to see how far you can push me, then you already know. I'd appreciate it if you'd keep your nasty comments about my family and friends to yourself. Any problems with it?"

"None. That's cool!" said Jerry. "I apologize. It was hitting below the belt."

We actually had some fun once we got to the Creamery. And believe it or not, before we split up, I felt comfortable enough around Jerry to include him in the conversation when I told Matt about Mother. Jerry and I became better friends after that night. We were never best friends but we could be around each other without arguing. We could tolerate each other and mostly, we had good times when he joined us. He never took David Byrd's place. No one did and no one could.

My first night at Aunt Josephine's house, I was too restless to get much sleep. There was no radio in Vic's room and there were too many new things to get used to. Actually, I was afraid but I refused to yield to fear. My spirit had been punched and kicked and could be broken if the wrong thing or person came along. I couldn't even enjoy the fantasies that used to run through my mind. I didn't want to forget my mother or let what she had done for me become some vague memory. As I lay there trying to fall asleep, I realized I had forgotten the letter in my shirt pocket. I opened the envelope carefully not certain I wanted to read what Jason had to say.

There was a postcard inside with a picture of a crimson sunset over the Atlantic Ocean. Myrtle Beach, South Carolina, was written across the bottom of the ocean. I turned the card over. Jason's note was short: "Braxton, I asked Mother to give this to you. You were right all along. I need to get well and I want to say I'm sorry I hung up on you. Thanks for being a real friend. Jason." (Jason and I drifted apart and never hung around together very much after that summer. When he got out of the hospital, he rarely came back to Wilson. Maybe Mr. Parker adopted Mr. Byrd's philosophy concerning my influence on his son. Somehow I doubted that, but who knows.)

Reading the card had thrown my mind into a state of separation from all that I knew and loved and wanted and counted on and trusted. I felt a surge of thankfulness. I was still here and as far as I could tell, I was still sane. I felt a tinge of regret for what could have been with my four good buddies; but, for whatever reason, I would have to learn to be satisfied with what we had as a memory.

Chapter 47
OTHER UNEXPECTED VISITORS

THE FIRST WEEK of July came and went and I was still without a job. I called Exeter's tobacco processing plant again. This time I finagled an interview with the branch manager for Monday, July 15th. There was still no word concerning Jason's recovery. Thad and his family were on vacation at the beach for two weeks and Matt continued to work. He and Jerry had become like two peas in a pod and I had been left to my own devices. I visited the cemetery and pulled weeds around my father's headstone and stopped by Byrd's to say hello. I picked up pocket money by mowing a couple of lawns and babysitting for some of the neighbors. And I learned to play bridge. When my aunts needed a foursome, I was it. Unfortunately, I was always paired with Aunt Eva and I was the dummy most of those evenings. I heard more gossip than I learned about how to play the game of bridge. The one thing I remembered was Aunt Eva telling my other aunts that Ava Gardner divorced her third husband, Frank Sinatra. That kept Wilson County buzzing for a while.

The second week of July I followed much the same pattern. There was a lot of community talk about the black people stepping out of line. On Thursday, July 11th, two black men were arrested in Durham for playing tennis on the city's tennis courts reserved for whites only. That sent out a clarion call to all towns and cities in our part of the state to keep an eye on their public facilities to make certain that only white people used them. Ironically, on the same Thursday, New York City held a hometown ticker tape parade for Althea Gibson for winning the Wimbledon Tennis Championship.

On Saturday night, the 13th of July, I went back to my house to spend the night. Anne was back from camp and the plan was for her to stay with my grandmother. I felt more grown-up when I came home to stay by myself. I parked the Tank in the driveway, waved to Mr. Ross, and unlocked the door and entered. I made a quick check around the house to make certain everything was in order and it was. I changed into a tee shirt and tennis shorts and sat down in Daddy's rocker. The time was a little after eight o'clock. I remembered about the time because I wanted to watch Alfred Hitchcock's show that came on at eight-thirty. I think G.E. Theatre was running when I cut the TV on, but I was interrupted by the ringing of the front door bell. I got up from my rocker and walked through the French doors into the living room and over toward the front door. I could see through the white sheer curtains that a policeman was standing on the porch. I unlocked the door and there stood Sergeant Rankin looking at me through the screened door. When he saw who I was, he got this hideous grin on his face, the kind of grin you'd like to knock off.

"May I help you, Sergeant Rankin?" I was polite. That is the one thing my mother had always insisted upon us being when people came to our house. Liking them had nothing to do with it.

"We've had a complaint from one of your neighbors down the street. We would like to come inside."

"Okay." I let the sergeant in and a young rookie who didn't look too much older than I. He was about six-foot-three-inches tall, and had blonde hair and green eyes. His name was Ray Joyner and he stood as erect as a Master Sergeant in the Marines. Sergeant Rankin's posture paled in comparison. "What is the complaint, Sergeant Rankin?"

"Mrs. Bateman on the corner of Nash and Kincaid said that someone had been peeping in her windows about thirty minutes ago. She described the man as being about five- feet-nine-inches tall, chunky and balding."

"That leaves me out," I said. "I'm not balding."

"She accused a man by the name of Louis Haywood," the rookie said. "Isn't that your father's name?"

"It was my father's name," I said, looking at rookie Joyner first and then at Sergeant Rankin. "Sergeant Rankin, you know Daddy died recently. Is this some kind of a sick joke?"

"We don't play jokes when we make house calls," said the rookie. "I didn't know about your father's death. I'm sorry. Well, Sarge, I guess we might as well go." I could tell from Rankin's reaction that the rookie had royally pissed him off.

"Not so fast, Joyner," said Sergeant Rankin. Pulling his potbelly in as far as it would go and staring at me with his beady bloodshot eyes he continued, this time speaking to me. "Where were you thirty minutes ago?" His expression became grave and he crossed his arms, resting them on his stomach. It was hard to take him serious.

"I was here in the house cleaning up."

"I just *bet* you were!" Rankin said. His belligerent attitude became him. "Do you have anyone who can verify your story?"

"Not a single one unless you want to count the TV." *Here we go again,* I thought.

"You trying to be funny with me?" the sergeant said, taking a step toward me.

"No, I'm not, but this is ridiculous," I said. "You know as well as I do I didn't peep in anyone's window. You're just dying to hang something on me, aren't you?" I was loaded for bear. Be careful Braxton! Don't be stupid, I told myself.

"I think you're a trouble maker, Braxton," Rankin said. "No one has been able to prove it but I will."

"Wait a minute!" I said. "Who did you say made that accusation?"

"Mrs. Ophelia Bateman."

"The woman on the corner of South Kincaid and West Nash in the next block?" I asked, pointing toward the southwest.

"That would be the very one," said the grinning Sergeant.

"Come with me," I said, remembering a similar incident about four months ago. "Call Captain Mays. He'll answer your question."

"I'm not bothering the captain on his night off," said the sergeant.

"Then I will." I knew Captain Mays' number since he had given it to me in case something like this happened. I dialed the four-digit number and lucky for me, he answered on the third ring. "Captain

Mays, this is Braxton Haywood. I hate to bother you on your night off but Sergeant Rankin is standing with me in my house. He's made an accusation that I think you can handle and perhaps, clear things up for him." I handed Rankin the receiver.

"Captain Mays, Sergeant Rankin here. We had a lady to make an accusation about a male at this address . . . " Rankin stopped abruptly to listen to his captain.

"That's right. The lady that lives in the neighborhood." Rankin smiled, hesitated and listened.

This time I could hear Captain Mays' voice rise when he spoke. "Oh, her name? Ophelia Bateman."

Captain Mays spoke again, but more rapidly. Rankin's smile turned into a look of hesitation. "You already know about it?" Rankin seemed surprised and disappointed at the same time.

The captain continued to talk. Rankin held the receiver away from his ear because his captain was yelling now. "I see. It's happened before." Rankin's expression turned to embarrassment and his chubby cheeks turned red. "No, sir, I won't. Thank you. Goodbye." Sergeant Rankin handed the phone receiver back to me. I smiled, put the receiver back on its base, and stood looking at him.

"Well, do you want to arrest me?" I said, enjoying every minute of this.

"One day, Braxton. One day you will push me too far." His disappointment was evident in his voice.

"Hey, I haven't done anything wrong," I said. "I believe you know your way out. Nice to meet you, Officer Joyner." I extended my hand and he shook it.

"Sorry we bothered you, Braxton," Officer Joyner said. He shook his head in disbelief at the foolish sergeant he had been assigned to.

"Let's go," said Rankin.

"Gladly," said Joyner. "Would you like to tell me what this is all about?"

"It seems the old lady, Mrs. Bateman, has a history of making these complaints against men in this neighborhood, living or dead." I heard him tell Officer Joyner as they walked down the steps. I watched the officers drive off. I couldn't help but laugh, thinking how Officer Joyner, poor fellow, had the unpleasant duty of being yoked with an idiot.

Almost three weeks later, Mrs. Bateman called the police to report that a man was peering in her windows. This time Sergeant Rankin paid no attention to the call when he received it. This time Mrs. Batmen was accurate in her accusation. This time the Peeping Tom broke into her house and beat her. There was a second attack that same evening on an elderly widow living on Ripley Road who was also left beaten. Rumor around town said both widows were raped. The next day the adult son of a well-to-do attorney was arrested and charged by Officer Joyner for trespassing, breaking and entering, molestation, to name a few. Sergeant Rankin was fired from the Wilson Police Department for negligence of duty, behavior unbecoming a police officer and not upholding the police code of ethics. Officer Joyner was promoted to sergeant.

As I stood on the porch smoking a cigarette, a fine rain began to fall. The smell of tobacco was in the air. The front porch lights of most of the houses on Kincaid Avenue had been turned on, signaling the beginning of an end to another day. Children could be heard running back to their respective houses. Skippy was in his usual spot in the middle of the street. An occasional bat could be seen weaving its way back and forth under the street lamp that marked our meeting place. And lightening bugs were waltzing in our yards. For all appearances, Kincaid Avenue looked like a normal street in a normal town in North Carolina.

I finished my cigarette and flipped it into the front yard. Upon opening the screened door, I felt grown-up. I knew I wasn't any older, but I definitely felt more mature. Walking into the living room, I thought about all I had learned this summer. Experience is the real teacher and I had been a good student. I had gotten my wish. As I cut the front porch light on and closed the front door, a frightening thought ran through my mind—if I was going to continue to grow and learn, I would have to be a student for life.

WE ARE NOW talking of a late afternoon in February of 1993, on the day of my mother's graveside service. As I drove back to the cemetery to say one last goodbye, I was thankful in my heart that my family had given me the time to ride around some of the old haunts. Although things had changed dramatically since the summer of 1957, my memory hadn't. It was never my intent to go back down memory lane but seeing, again, where it had all happened brought many other things back to my mind. I'm glad I did and Holden Caulfield, you were right, young man. As I have told this story, I have started missing the people who were part of my life back then.

I pulled my car along side the Haywood plot. *What a beautiful time of day,* I thought. A golden sun setting, a warm breeze blowing through the cemetery and memories to launch me forward, and I was more determined than ever to put an end to this mystery behind David Byrd's death. I knelt down once more to brush the little pieces of bone fragments off the face of my mother's head marker brought by the wind. It was hard to fathom that she was no longer alive. I leaned down once again to kiss her marker and the shadow of some-one standing behind me began to pass over and cover my mother's name. I turned and there standing behind me was a Negro man dressed in a three-piece suit. He had a camel hair overcoat draped over his left arm. It was an older Julian.

"Julian, this is an unexpected surprise," I said, shaking his hand.

"Mr. Braxton, it's so good to see you, too," he said. "I'm sorry for your mother."

"Thank you, Julian," I said. "You are very kind."

"I've thought about you boys so many, many times, Mr. Braxton." There were traces of moisture in his eyes.

"Me, too, Julian," I said. "Me, too. In fact, I plan to ride by Byrd's gravesite before I leave the cemetery.

"Mr. Braxton, I knew I would find you here cause I called Miss Ingrid's." Julian reached into his coat pocket and pulled out an enve-lope. "I wished I'd had the nerve to give this to you a long time ago when it happened. I was too afraid." Julian's hand began to shake. "I always admired you for the way you stood up to Mr. Byrd. What you need is in this here envelope. No one knows I'm here so please leave it that way until you need me again. My telephone number is in there too." He turned to walk away.

"Julian, wait!" I walked over to him and put my arms around his massive shoulders and pulled him to me. "Thank you, Julian, for all you did for Byrd. You are a brave man and your timing is perfect." I released him and he walked away. I watched a graying Julian drive away and when I no longer could see his car, I opened the envelope. I read the contents not once but three times. Everything I had suspected was written clearly here but with one twist. Julian had carefully detailed how he had found Byrd's body, which was not reported correctly to the public. He gave specific details on the hour before and after Byrd's death as well as enough information to incriminate the murderer. "Bless you, Julian. Bless you!"

I turned to my mother's marker and renewed my promise to her. "Mother, before I leave this town today, I will be stopping by the Byrd's home. I'm putting a stop to this once and for all. I'm doing this for Byrd, for Jason, for Matt and Thad, and for me. But I'm also doing this for you, too, because you had to suffer more than most of us. I love you, Mother. Even though you don't think so, you've been a good Mother." I kissed her marker one last time.

Before I left the cemetery, I rode over to Byrd's grave and got out. His marker had aged as much as the rest of us. I took the time to pull the grass that had grown over on the sides, covering parts of his first and last name. I felt sadness inside knowing after all these many years, a young man had to die because of another's misguided passion. Life was not fair to my friend. I was going to try to right it. I guess it's that righteous indignation of mine that has led me to take this final step. Also, it was one of the promises I made the summer of '57.

"It is now that time, old friend. I love you as much today as I ever did." I ran my fingers once again around each letter in each of his three names. Even though it was cooler now, the warmth of the day's sun still lingered on his face marker. "I'll be paying your dad a visit momentarily."

I got back into my car and cut on the ignition. I let the car idle while I reread the letter that had been handed to me. Unbelievable, I thought. I cut the air on in the car and cracked my window as I pulled out of the cemetery. I needed to mentally review exactly what I wanted to say. The drive to the Byrd's home on Raleigh Road did not take long. I pulled into their driveway and drove up under the side portico. Not much of the exterior appeared to have changed.

I walked to the front of the house and rang the bell. Julian answered the door. He didn't seem too alarmed to see me. "Mr. Braxton?"

"Don't worry about a thing," I whispered. "I would like to see Mr. Byrd and Charles if they are at home."

"Come in, please." Julian went to the study and announced my visit. He came back quickly. Sweat had popped out on his forehead. "Mr. Byrd will see you now."

"Thank you, Julian," I said. "It's good to see you again." In a whisper I told him to act natural and that I would not break my promise to him. I followed him through the familiar hallway, passed the circular staircase we went up that night, and to the door of the study.

"Mr. Byrd, Mr. Braxton is here to see you," Julian said, and abruptly turned and walked to the kitchen area.

"Come in, Braxton," said a frail, baldheaded man sitting in a blue leather wing chair. Mr. Byrd had a blanket across his knees. Even though it was warm outside, there was a roaring fire in the marble fireplace. "Will you be staying for dinner, Braxton?"

"No, thank you, Mr. Byrd," I said. I surveyed the room. Nothing of the décor had changed; the room smelled musty and it had an old, dingy look. There were still shelves of unused books taking up two walls, the pool table we could never use sat at one end of the room gathering dust, and the same brown leather couch sat in front of the fireplace. The room was unchanged. Even the other chairs were in the same place as they were the last time I was in this room. A picture of each of his four children framed in silver that needed polishing set on his desk. Byrd's picture sat between his sister's.

"To what do I owe the pleasure of your visit?" Mr. Byrd said. Sadly, he actually sounded like he meant it. "Forgive me for not shaking your hand. I no longer have use of my right hand." His right hand was shriveled and lay lifeless on the lap of his blanket. He looked at the door behind me and spoke, "Charles, do you remember Braxton Haywood, a friend of your brother?"

"Of course I do. How could I forget?" Charles extended his hand and I shook it. *He had a fish shake. How a man could aspire to polit-*

ical office with a handshake like that is beyond me, I thought. "Would you join me in a glass of sherry?"

"No thank, you, Charles," I said. "I can't stay long."

"Charles, would you pour your feeble father another glass?" I assumed this was an attempt to get my vote of sympathy.

"Certainly, Father." Charles dutifully took his father's glass and walked back to the decanter and poured the sherry slowly, not spilling a drop. *Very subservient,* I thought.

"Forgive me, Braxton," Mr. Byrd said. "Please sit down."

"Thank you, I'll wait for Charles." I wanted to make certain I had eye contact with both of them. Charles handed his father the glass of sherry and took a seat to his father's right. Mr. Byrd's good hand shook.

"If you don't mind, I'll stand here at the edge of the fireplace." The fire felt warm but good, even after being in the heat much of the day. The setting was apt for what I was about to say.

"Suit yourself," said Mr. Byrd, readjusting his upper body against the back of the chair.

"Charles, I understand you are up for a possible judgeship," I said. "Am I correct?"

"We are hoping that will happen soon, very soon," his father interrupted. He turned and smiled at his son.

"That is correct, Braxton." Charles seemed unbothered by his father's butting in to my question to him. "I've practiced criminal law for a long time. I think I'm qualified to handle criminal cases."

"I bet you are," I said. "I bet you are."

"Now what can my father and I do for you this late afternoon?"

"First, I want to thank both of you for paying your respects to my mother today." I paused and waited for their reaction. They looked at each other and turned back, facing me.

"Your mother was a fine lady," said Mr. Byrd, clearing his throat.

"Secondly, I wanted to let you know I received the letter you sent to Ingrid's home," I paused again. This time both of their calm, casual expressions changed. Both men furrowed their brows, turned, and looked at each other. They were visibly shaken. "I got it today."

"Pardon?" said Charles, turning again to look at his father as if to ask for direction on what to say next.

"Let's not be coy, Charles," I said. "After watching your father and realizing his inability to use his writing hand, I can surmise with accuracy that it was you who sent me one of your father's threats. You have learned to write almost exactly as he and you have mastered the art of forging a shaking man's signature."

"I don't know what you're talking about, Braxton," said Charles. He got up and poured himself another glass of sherry. This time he spilled some and acting without any dignity, wiped it up with the sleeve of his shirt.

"Mr. Byrd, I don't plan to beat around the bush any further. You know as well as I that I suspected you of killing Byrd that summer of '57. My God, you did everything you could to intimidate my mother, my friends, and especially, me. It almost worked, but it didn't. Now I have learned that it was not only your intent to have Byrd killed, you were going to force Charles here to take the rap for you." I stopped and gave them an opportunity to respond.

"Of all the preposterous . . . why, I've never . . . I don' know where you got these foolish ideas," said Mr. Byrd, his voice shaking now. My accusation had had a visible affect on him. "Charles, love, another glass of sherry please."

"Charles refused to play any part in the death of Byrd so you made him do it."

"*What? That's ludicrous,*" said Mr. Byrd.

"Anything, but the contrary," I said. "That explains the two different bullets. I never quite got that clear at first. The paper's report was totally contradictory to the coroner's report. I checked that out years ago. So apparently, you held a gun on Charles until he shot Byrd. When Charles refused initially, you shot a bullet that grazed his ear. And then, and only then, did Charles kill his brother. That explained the sudden appearance of stitches on your ear, Charles, after Byrd's death and the lingering scar that is apparent now."

"Again, this is *preposterous!*" said Mr. Byrd.

"I think you need to leave," said Charles, standing and motioning me to the door.

"I agree," I said. "Just one last thing, if you please. *How in the hell have the two of you lived with yourselves all these years?* Both of you make me sick." I stood there looking at the two most pathetic men I had seen in years.

"*Get out of our house!*" Charles said in a high-pitched voice, moving closer to me.

"I'll be filing a report on my return to Raleigh. First, I'll talk to my lawyer. He's a Wilson man. You might remember him. He knew Byrd. Charles, do you remember Jerry Riceman. He's a Duke grad and Harvard law grad as well! I'd say he has quite impressive credentials." I smiled and moved toward the door. "I'll show myself the way out." I turned and walked into the hall. I stopped to look at the circular staircase one last time. For a moment, I thought I saw Byrd standing there. I blinked. It was my imagination. I shuddered and walked out onto the porch. As I pulled out of the driveway, I had the satisfaction of knowing my friend could now rest in peace.

It was finally over. I drove the rest of the way back to Raleigh, knowing that the noise upstairs would never haunt me again. I had been imprisoned for thirty-five years. Now I was free. *Freedom.* I never knew what it fully felt like until now . . . It was truly a magnificent feeling.

Epilogue

THE SUMMER OF 1957, especially the month of June, had a lasting impact on my life. I wanted to grow up when I was sixteen. I wanted to be grown up so badly that I would have done most anything to get the chance. My chances came one right after another in quick succession. I was not equipped to handle all of them but the ones I could handle strengthened me to weather the others.

The events of that June gave me a sense of indignation. Some call this righteous indignation but whatever it is called, I don't think I will ever stand aside and let an innocent person be accused of something he or she didn't do. It was hell—those times—but, in reflection, they were good times and I say again, you were right Holden Caulfield.

It was during these days that I developed a "serious" attitude that people have sometimes accused me of having. People would say "loosen up" and have more fun. I knew they were right but somehow, I had been robbed of the ability to do this. It took me thirty plus year to learn to relax and have fun.

I need to say a few things about some of the people in this book. First, my mother spent about sixteen months in the psychiatric ward at the state hospital. Adapting to being a patient in a mental ward was a trying season for Mother. She loved her doctors and they loved her. Mother came home for occasional visits but she seemed estranged when she visited. She didn't return home to stay for good until the middle of my senior year in high school. She continued to drink socially on rare occasions but she never yielded to the state of drunkenness again. She attended AA but never joined. A year after

Mother's return, my sister found her unconscious, laying on the living room rug, upon coming home from school. She was taken by ambulance to the UNC Hospital in Chapel Hill, North Carolina. A blood clot was found on her brain that had been there for some time. The operation was successful and once out of the hospital again, Mother became a different person. She attempted to find employment but didn't have the skills to maintain a job that paid enough to sustain us. She received social security payments from my father's years of employment but had to declare disability to get them. She received social security payments for us until we reached eighteen. There were times when we would go out on the highway and pick up bottles and then redeem them so we could buy groceries. Mother instilled a work ethic in us that neither my sister nor I could ever thank her enough for.

Mother's true avocation and joy became her work with the American Red Cross. After a year of volunteer work, she was hired on a part-time basis. She was eventually forced to move back to the home where she was born. Living with her mother was not a good mix but she had no other choice and my grandmother was gracious to take her in. Mother lived there until the late 1960s. At that time she lived with Anne in Silver Springs, Maryland, while her husband was in Vietnam.

My sister, Anne, was affected more than I by the death of our father and the sickness of our mother. Anne ran away from my aunt's several times while we lived with her. My aunt criticized her for running around with the wrong crowd; in other words, they weren't the money crowd. Anne moved in with my grandmother during her senior year in high school. She chose not to attend college. Seeking direction for her life, Anne joined the WACS and was stationed at Walter Reed Army Hospital in Silver Springs, Maryland. It was here that she found herself. After an unsuccessful attempt at marriage, she moved back to North Carolina and works for the state in the town where she presently lives.

Jason Parker's stay in the hospital lasted for six months. He was diagnosed with a mild form of manic depression but the idea that he might be schizophrenic was dispelled by his doctors.

He did graduate from Fork Union Military Academy. Jason, never a student, tried college for two years but dropped out and worked with his father until he was drafted by the army. Jason was sent to Vietnam where he was killed while on active duty.

There is not much more to tell about Thad, Matt, and me. That summer Matt worked with his father in his business. Thad was lifeguard at the municipal pool. He had an entourage of girls at his feet constantly. I did get a job with Exeter Tobacco Company weighing tobacco hogsheads before they were loaded on railroad cars for eventual export to Great Britain and Ireland for the manufacturing of cigarettes. I did this every summer until I graduated from college. The three of us still stay in contact with each other on those special occasions. We all agreed on what I'm getting ready to tell you in regards to Charles and Oscar Byrd.

We decided not to prosecute Mr. Byrd because of his age and debilitating health. We told him if he ever sent a threatening note to any of us again, we would move forward with prosecution. He has since died, being preceded in his death by his wife.

We forced Charles to withdraw his name from being considered for a judgeship then or anytime in the future. We also made him agree never to seek any political office. He signed a note to this effect and my lawyer, Jerry Riceman, and I witnessed it. Charles was told if he broke this agreement, we would move forward with prosecution. I truly believe Charles has been punished enough.

Charles loved his brother, David Byrd, and shortly before the accident, Charles told Byrd that he was through letting his father abuse him. Byrd supported Charles in this decision. When they addressed their father with their decision and told him they were united, Mr. Byrd worked himself into a drunken rage and took measures to kill Byrd. Charles interfered and confronted his father, bringing a gun outside with him. He and his father tussled and somehow, Mr. Byrd ended up with both guns. It was then that Mr. Byrd threatened to kill Charles if he didn't shoot his brother. When Charles refused, Mr. Byrd grazed Charles' ear with a bullet. Oscar Byrd gave Charles a choice: be disobedient and die or kill his brother and sexual activity between them would cease. At this point,

554 • The Noise Upstairs

Charles took the revolver from his father, closed his eyes and shot his brother, thinking by doing this his father would keep his word. Mr. Byrd's sexual abuse of Charles did not stop at that time and continued until Mr. Byrd was in his late sixties.

Charles, himself was a victim. There were a lot of victims in our town that summer and I am certain there continue to be. But that was the summer of 1957 and it is now the year 2005. Let us hope we can learn from our fathers not to repeat their sins.

About the Author

Lucien Stark grew up in Wilson, North Carolina, and graduated from Fike High School. He completed his undergraduate degree at the University of North Carolina at Chapel Hill and received his master's degree from The University of Virginia at Charlottesville.

Stark is in his twenty-fifth year of teaching and presently teaches eighth grade language arts at Holly Ridge Middle School in Wake County, North Carolina. He has been nominated three times to appear in *Who's Who Among American Teachers.*

He currently resides in Holly Springs with his golden retriever, Belle, and his two mini-dachshunds, Barney and Otis. *The Noise Upstairs* is his first novel.